CW00402730

UNDER A DARK ANGEL'S EYE

Books by Patricia Highsmith

Strangers on a Train

Carol *(originally published
as* The Price of Salt*)*

The Blunderer

The Talented Mr Ripley

Deep Water

A Game for the Living

This Sweet Sickness

The Cry of the Owl

The Two Faces of January

The Glass Cell

A Suspension of Mercy

Plotting and Writing
Suspense Fiction

Those Who Walk Away

The Tremor of Forgery

Ripley Under Ground

A Dog's Ransom

Ripley's Game

Edith's Diary

The Boy Who
Followed Ripley

People Who Knock
on the Door

Found in the Street

Ripley Under Water

Small g

STORY COLLECTIONS

Eleven

Little Tales of Misogyny

The Animal-Lover's Book
of Beastly Murder

Slowly, Slowly in the Wind

Mermaids on the Golf Course

Tales of Natural and
Unnatural Catastrophes

Nothing That Meets the Eye:
The Uncollected Stories

UNDER A DARK ANGEL'S EYE

The Selected Stories of

Patricia Highsmith

Introduced by Carmen Maria Machado

virago

VIRAGO

First published in Great Britain in 2021 by Virago Press

1 3 5 7 9 10 8 6 4 2

Typeset in Perpetua by M Rules
Printed and bound in Great Britain by Clays Ltd, Elcograf S.p.A.

Papers used by Virago are from well-managed forests
and other responsible sources.

Virago Press
An imprint of
Little, Brown Book Group
Carmelite House
50 Victoria Embankment
London EC4Y 0DZ

An Hachette UK Company
www.hachette.co.uk

www.virago.co.uk

CONTENTS

INTRODUCTION

There has always been something fundamentally difficult about Patricia Highsmith. And not *difficult* in the way that most people mean it: ironic, quirky, feminist. ('Well-behaved women rarely make history,' etc.) I mean truly, legitimately difficult; a well of darkness with no discernible bottom.

Which is not to say that she wasn't, in her own way, endearing. She was, after all, a genius, a bonafide eccentric, a lesbian. She loved animals, particularly snails, who she 'kept by the hundred as pets and took to parties in a handbag, where they clung to a head of lettuce,'[1] and once 'smuggled her cherished pet snails through French customs by hiding six or eight of them under each bosom.'[2] She was famous for her wit and wicked sense of humour, which is evident in this collection, and she wrote compellingly of loneliness and empathetically about disempowered housewives and children.

And yet she was a hateful person – shockingly so. Unrepentantly racist and anti-Semitic, even with respect to the era in which she lived. She believed gay people 'were essentially unfaithful and

---

1 Margaret Talbot, 'Patricia Highsmith's Forbidden Love' (*The New Yorker*)
2 Terry Castle, 'The Ick Factor' (*The New Republic*)

promiscuous' and incapable of true sexual passion[3]; she had a nasty habit of murdering her ex-lovers in her fiction; she believed menstruating women should not be permitted in libraries. This mix of misogyny and homophobia coming from a gay woman might seem surprising; the truth was, while she didn't like other people, she didn't much like herself, either.

In *The Price of Salt* (later reissued as *Carol*) – the lesbian love story Highsmith published under the pen name Claire Morgan in 1952 – these pessimisms are curiously absent. There are no violent crimes here, and no sociopathic protagonists. Even though her reasons for distancing herself via a pseudonym have nothing to do with this fact – she had a career to worry about, and she didn't want to be 'labelled a lesbian-book writer' – it feels correct that she might also not want herself associated with such a fundamentally optimistic book. Because it was the opposite – violence, torment, obsession, all bubbling beneath a cool veneer – that was the signature of her fiction.

Here, now, at the centenary of her birth – her canonization cemented, her complete collected diaries on the verge of publication – readers grapple with this darkness. What does it mean to love the work of Patricia Highsmith, 'doyenne of the psychological suspense novel, depressive homosexual, mean drunk, and one of the greatest, darkest American storytellers since Poe?'[4] Perhaps they recognize that you don't come to Patricia Highsmith for goodness or light or comfort. You come to her for uncanny observations about human depravity; you come to her because you've forgotten the sour taste of fear.

Highsmith is probably most famous for her novels *The Talented Mr Ripley* and *Strangers on a Train*. And yet short stories were her foundation, as well as her bread and butter. The oldest story in this book

---

3 Kate Hart, 'The Inner Life of Patricia Highsmith' (*This Recording*)
4 Terry Castle, ibid.

was written when Highsmith was just fifteen; they were partially how she was earning a living when *Strangers on a Train* was written. At the time of her death, she'd published no fewer than seven collections of them, and there was ample material for a volume of uncollected stories to be published posthumously. 'Short stories are absolutely essential to me, like poetry: I write a lot of both,' she once told a *Sunday Times* interviewer, 'Only a fraction of the stories I have written ever appeared in print.' (This prodigious output is at least partially a result of her surfeit of ideas, which occurred to her, she said, 'as frequently as rats have orgasms'.)

In his introduction to her collection *Eleven*, Graham Greene talks about the way in which Highsmith adapts to the short story: 'She is after the quick kill rather than the slow encirclement of the reader, and how admirably and with what field-craft she hunts us down.' Here, in these prickly, misanthropic stories, her obsession with obsession is on display, a *Wunderkammer* full of big feelings and bad habits redirected to gruesome ends.

Sometimes it plays out with her telltale violence, filtered through what one critic called the 'casually treacherous personality'. In 'The Terrapin', a boy befriends a turtle and is forced to watch his mother cook it; in 'The Button', a father's disappointment in his life boils over into murder; in 'The Snail-Watcher', her beloved pets become an instrument of body horror and monstrosity. And elsewhere – like the protagonists of 'Not This Life, Maybe the Next' and 'The Romantic' – her characters are besieged by a quiet misery and loneliness; they have to learn to accept, if not prefer, their own company. (Even Highsmith's love of the third person seems tinged by self-loathing. 'I have bogged down twice in first-person-singular books, so emphatically that I abandoned any idea of writing the books,' she wrote in her only craft book, *Plotting and Writing Suspense Fiction*. 'I don't know what was the matter, except that I got sick and tired of writing the pronoun "I", and I was plagued with an idiotic feeling that the person telling the story was sitting at a desk writing it. Fatal!')

Rereading Highsmith's work, I was struck by how much she reminded me of Shirley Jackson.[5] Both wrote in a clean and economical style that often gave way to breathtaking flourishes; both wrote in genres (suspense, horror) in which their gender was a liability. Both wrote imaginative characters liberated by the deaths of their difficult mothers[6]; both had cartoonishly challenging relationships with the same.[7] Loneliness was a shared theme; menace, claustrophobia.

But Jackson's protagonists were predominantly women; Highsmith, on the other hand, preferred the voices of men. With Jackson, you get the sense that she is twitching the curtain for you, the reader, allowing you to see something she can see. With Highsmith, there is a distinct feeling of being chased toward something near and terrible, and not being able to look anywhere but where she wants you to look.

In the last few years, the unbearable nearness of sex and death has blossomed into its own queer meme: 'I would let Rachel Weisz run me over with a car.' 'I want Sandra Oh to throw me off a building.' 'Please, Cate Blanchett, step on my throat.' (I myself have been known to idly wonder what it would feel like for certain celebrities to 'rip me in two'.) Jia Tolentino calls this 'desiring a sensation strong enough to silence itself,' and with Highsmith this challenge is more literal than most. To read her is to access her desires, her

---

5 They met once, in fact. 'In 1943, Highsmith accompanied her friend the writer Seymour Krim to coffee at the apartment of Stanley Edgar Hyman and Shirley Jackson,' Jon Michaud wrote in *The New Yorker* in 2010. 'The visit . . . prompted Highsmith to make an anti-Semitic remark about the chatty Hyman in her diary.'

6 Or, in the case of the senile, infirm antagonist in 'No End in Sight', a difficult mother who has lived for over two hundred years and has no intention of dying.

7 Having unsuccessfully attempted to abort Patricia by drinking turpentine, Mary Highsmith would joke that her daughter loved the smell of turpentine. She was 'demanding, seductive, [and] catastrophically unloving,' Terry Castle wrote in *The New Republic*. 'For seven decades (she lived into her nineties) she ruled over her daughter's psychic life like an unasked-for bride – a malign, indestructible Miss Havisham of the soul.'

darkness, her difficulties; her loneliness and self-loathing and terrible mother and love of snails.

It feels good to be hunted. If you read the genres of suspense – crime and mystery and horror in its many iterations – you know the sensation of allowing a master of her craft to pursue you through a maze; the tingly energy of the chase, the eroticism of encountering the end of the line. 'Murder,' Highsmith wrote in her diary in 1950, 'is a kind of making love, a kind of possessing.'

You do not have to accept the chase – the love, or the murder – but if you're reading this, you probably already have. By opening this book, you've given her permission to follow you, catch you, take you apart. Get ready to run.

Carmen Maria Machado
Philadelphia, PA
September 2020

PRIMROSES ARE PINK

The beaming Mr Theodore Fleming strode into the lobby of his apartment building, greeted the elevator boy, and stepped into the elevator. At the twelfth floor he got out and walked gaily into his apartment. His wife was in the living room.

'Look,' he exclaimed, as he removed a brown wrapper from a rolled sheet of paper and triumphantly displayed his prize. 'It's just what I've been looking for for months.'

His wife didn't seem very impressed. She saw a gray-looking picture of a jockey on a horse. The picture had scroll writing below it.

'What's it supposed to be?' she ventured.

'It's Sainfoin,' said her husband. 'He was one of the most famous racehorses in England.'

'Oh,' said Catherine, not trying very hard to show interest. 'It looks rather drab.'

'Of course, it's uncolored, but wait till I have it tinted and shellacked.'

Mr Fleming carried his purchase into his room, held it against the wall, and viewed it approvingly. The picture was large, about two feet by three feet.

'Where did you find it?' asked Catherine.

'In one of those print shops in Greenwich Village. It would have

cost at least ten dollars at Brentano's.' He began to read the printing.
'"The first year of the guaranteed stakes . . . "'

'What color is it going to be?'

Mr Fleming stopped. A worried look came over his nervous face.

'Why, I don't know. I suppose the shopkeeper would know. They
must be the authentic colors, of course.'

Catherine knew what was coming. During the five years of their
married life, she had had many opportunities to observe her husband's mania for detail.

Mr Fleming's face had a glazed expression. His moustache
twitched anxiously. He walked to the closet in a preoccupied
manner, took his hat, and abruptly bade his wife goodbye.

The proprietor of the little bookshop was fat and cheerful.
Hopefully, Mr Fleming approached him.

'I'd like to see a color copy – if you have one – of that print of
Sainfoin I bought this afternoon.'

The shopkeeper's lips pressed together more tightly, making his
smile spread a little farther across his pudgy face. Slowly, regretfully,
he shook his head.

'What do you mean? You have no copy in color?'

The head continued to shake very slowly.

'I never even seen it in color,' he said in a slow baritone. 'You're
just supposed to put your own colors in.'

Mr Fleming's delicate sensibilities were outraged. He left hastily
and again bent his steps toward the subway. At Forty-Second Street,
he came out and walked determinedly toward the Public Library.
After much explanation, he was admitted to a room with a large table
and a few chairs in the center. He was told this was the special department devoted to English horses and racing prints. For two hours he
remained here, examining nearly a score of books which a silent
clerk, like an inarticulate genie in a fairy tale, brought to his table
at intervals. At last, he had scanned through every book and print
collection they had to offer, and he knew everything about Sainfoin
except the colors under which he had won the Derby of June 4, 1890.

It was evening when he returned to his home. Catherine looked up from her magazine.

'Theodore, where have you been?'

'Everywhere,' said her husband. 'I can't find it.'

'What?'

'The colors,' said Mr Fleming, and slumped into a chair. He felt tired and defeated.

'Why bother about the real colors? No one will know the difference anyway. I was thinking blue and white—'

'Catherine,' Mr Fleming explained patiently. 'This isn't an ordinary picture. It's a particular race. It's a real portrait of the jockey and the horse.' He lapsed dejectedly into silence.

Catherine looked at her husband, relaxed in his chair, his eyes closed. 'You could write and ask the Jockey Club,' she suggested, with the air of one who talks to a child.

'I shouldn't think they'd have any information on English racing.'

Catherine said they might, but he made no answer.

Mr Fleming did write to the Jockey Club, however, as a last resort. A week later he avidly opened his answer.

'The chestnut horse Sainfoin, owned by Sir James Miller, whose colors were primrose and white . . . '

He was jubilant. He unrolled the print, tried to visualize it colored, and realized he wasn't quite sure what color primrose was. Rapidly he consulted his dictionary.

He read: 'A pale greenish-yellow; a flower of that color.'

Mr Fleming had expected something brighter. He looked at the print again and consoled himself with the thought that the silks would be accurate anyway.

Two weeks later, he brought it home from the framer's. Again he unwrapped the handsome picture before Catherine.

'Is that primrose?' she asked.

He knew more than to expect a delighted exclamation from her, but this chilly reception was annoying. Mr Fleming said of course it was primrose.

'Primroses are pink,' she said laconically.

Theodore Fleming was in no mood to wrangle with his wife.

'The dictionary said "greenish-yellow", and this is greenish-yellow, isn't it?' he persisted, and it was evident he didn't want to talk any more about it.

'Mother always had primroses in her garden,' said Catherine placidly. 'They were pink. I've never seen them *that* color.'

'Look in the dictionary,' said Mr Fleming, who was growing more testy every moment.'

'I don't have to look in a dictionary. I know what color primroses are. Greenish-yellow is too pale for racing colors anyway.'

For the first time, Mr Fleming paused to consider his wife's argument. He looked at the picture again and realized with a vague tremor that the primrose didn't stand out well, and the preservative sprayed over it had subdued the colors somewhat. He was plunged into an abyss of doubt. He, too, seemed to remember pink primroses from somewhere.

A whole week passed before he could find the courage to look up the word in a larger dictionary. When he did, he found the same reassuring definition: greenish-yellow. But Catherine still held stubbornly to her opinion, and even he was forced to admit the colors were not so striking as one would expect to find in a racing print.

That was almost two years ago. The picture still hangs in his room, but Mr Fleming isn't over eager to display it. Though he has never been challenged, he still has a few misgivings whenever one of his friends examines it. He usually says shyly, 'That's primrose. English primroses are yellow, you know.'

A MIGHTY NICE MAN

The child Charlotte sat on the narrow curbstone, her cheek against one knee, drawing idly in the dust with a stick. She sniffed at the flesh of her leg, smelt the dust and the sweat on it. Then she sighed and threw away the stick.

'Em'lie,' she said.

Emilie, age nine, was standing behind her, with her back against the sun-warm wooden post, her toes braced on the edge of the sidewalk.

'Huh?' Emilie breathed.

'Play like I've got a store. Play like I've got a grocer store an' you've gotta buy stuff . . . Huh, Em'lie?'

Emilie was so bored and sleepy she did not reply. Her gray sullen eyes looked out across the road and the whole scene was yellow to her, the dirt of the road, the squatting house just beyond, the dry fields: yellow pulsing heat and silence.

'Em'lie! You crazy? . . . Answer me!' Charlotte turned around on the curb and glowered at her.

'Wha'?' said Emilie, and pushed herself away from the post.

'I've gotta store an' you must buy stuff.' She reached for the tiny red truck that was their common property and began filling it with pebbles. 'An' then I must deliver it. You gotta go home first an' then you must telephone.' She clutched the truck in one dirty hand as she scowled at Emilie.

They heard footsteps in the grit of the road. Charlotte forgot her game and they both looked up the slope. Emilie brushed the mottled blonde hair out of her eyes and squinted. Her left eye was cast, and she twisted up that side of her face whenever she looked at anything.

'I betcha it's a boarder from Mrs Osterman's,' Charlotte said. 'I betcha he's from New York, too.'

He turned onto the sidewalk that began half a block from Charlotte's house. Emilie could see him now, a short figure in unpressed white trousers. He saw them, too, and began whistling a tune.

'Hello,' he said, taking in both of them.

'H'lo,' they replied in unison.

He stopped a minute, looked about him. 'Gonna be here when I get back?' He spoke quietly, smiling. 'I'll bring you some candy.'

Charlotte and Emilie surveyed him silently.

'I like . . . I like *any* kind of candy,' Charlotte told him.

He laughed, winked at them and walked on down the sidewalk. Once he turned and waved, but only Charlotte saw that. They were both motionless a long time, watching.

'Reckon he'll come back, Em'lie?'

'Huh?'

'Reckon he'll come back this way?'

'Huh?'

'I sed . . . reckon he'll come *back*?'

But Emilie moved off without a word toward her house and Charlotte sat on the curb, resting her face against one knee as she traced in the dust. Soon the screen door to Emilie's house screeched, closed with a double slap, and Emilie's bare heels thudded across the porch.

'Huh,' said Emilie, and handed Charlotte a small pale peach. Charlotte took it silently, bit into the fruit with darkish baby teeth.

'Betcha that man's got a car.'

'Huh?'

'I sed' – she took a deep breath – 'I betcha that man's got a *ca-ar*.'

'Wha' man?'

'That *ma-an* . . . what just passed.'

Emilie licked her peach-stained fingers. 'He ain't comin' back.' She sighed, looked across the hot road to the blurry yellowish fields. The bugs in the grass, in the trees, were singing rhythmically. Two clicks and a long buzz. Down the road where it met the street that led into town they heard Mr Wynecoop's station wagon. They knew it from all the other cars in the neighborhood. Charlotte and Emilie sat on the edge of the curb and looked.

As he passed, Mr Wynecoop waved a stiff-fingered hand at them, and they chanted, 'H'lo, ol' man Wynecoop.'

The car pulled up the hill, reached the top, sighed as it hit level ground. Charlotte kept watching for the man in white. She stood up once and looked toward town, but the view was mostly shut out by the trees along the sidewalk.

Emilie smirked and grunted contemptuously.

Charlotte held the empty truck in one hand and stared down the walk. '*You* cou'nt see him if he *was* comin'.' Suddenly she drew in her breath. 'He's comin', all right,' she whispered, and ran stooping over to Emilie by the curb. She began stabbing in the dust, her heart beating fast.

Then Emilie heard his footsteps and twisted around and peered into the yellowness. He was whistling again. The blur of white came closer.

'He's got candy!' Charlotte said.

The man took his cigarette out of his mouth and threw it down.

'Hello,' he said quietly, then glanced at the houses and back at the two little girls on the curb. He handed the bag to Charlotte. Two licorice sticks stuck out of the top, and she was disappointed to see that it was all penny candy, unwrapped caramels and sugar hearts that sell five for a cent. Once an old man from Mrs Osterman's had brought her five-cent candy bars.

Slowly she put one end of a licorice stick into her mouth. The man shuffled uneasily, leaned against a tree and lighted another cigarette. 'You didn't tell me your name,' he said finally.

She told him, and he said his name was Robbie.

'I've got a car . . . Want to go riding sometime?' He kept shifting and taking his hands in and out of his pockets. 'I bet you like riding, Charlotte.'

'I sure do,' she said, and a dark stream of licorice juice ran down her chin.

The man leaning against the tree sprang toward her, drew a wadded handkerchief out of his hip pocket. He put one hand back of her head and wiped her face hard. 'You're . . . pretty messy.' Then he stood up again and put the handkerchief back. Emilie was watching him steadily, curiously. He felt the hostility in her twisted mouth.

He drew viciously on his cigarette. 'How'd you like to go riding this evening?' he whispered. 'After dinner.'

'I'd like that,' Charlotte said.

Then he went off quietly, looking back at them, smiling and friendly.

Charlotte was proud of herself. She leaned back on her hands and the thin muscles in her thighs showed under the dirt-streaked skin.

'He didn't ask *you* to go.'

Emilie sighed. 'He ain't comin'. You wait an' see.'

So Charlotte waited. She finished the candy alone, picked at her noon meal, and brooded happily in the shade of the house, humming to herself. Then she lay in the patched-up hammock on her front porch and looked at the pictures in a frayed funny paper book. The afternoon was hot and long and silent.

After supper Charlotte went out to the road and stood by the tree. Her mother had given her a sponge bath, and she had a cotton dress on instead of the thin romper suit she wore all day. She had told her mother nothing about the man from Mrs Osterman's. The fast-setting sun sent hot horizontal rays into her face. She was sure he would come. She tried to picture the car, like the ones she had seen in the movies. That was the kind of car *he* would have. And she would step into the big front seat and they would drive away with hardly a sound. They would drive fast.

But after a while she got tired and came in to the front porch. The wood was hot to her bare feet. She leaned on one side of the hammock, pushed herself into it. Still she listened and there was no sound of a car. Then the screen door to Emilie's house shrieked, stopped and shrieked again. Emilie appeared, unwashed and tousled, eating the remains of a slice of bread and butter. She came deliberately onto Charlotte's porch, stood chewing reflectively as she stared at her in the hammock. Charlotte disdained to look at her.

'Oh . . . *he* ain't comin',' she said, and turned around and walked to the steps. She heard something down the walk. 'That your mother comin'? *She* don't know, I betcha.'

Charlotte bounced out of the hammock. 'Listen, Em'lie . . . ' She frowned furiously. 'If you . . . if you say to her . . . ' She clenched her fists at her sides and Emilie gazed at her solemnly.

'Huh!'

But Charlotte had won.

There was no more sun, but it was still light. Charlotte's mother came back from the store. None of them said a word. The woman went into the house and Charlotte could hear her drawing water for the baby. Finally Emilie went hop-skipping across the front yard, into her house.

Charlotte lay in the hammock and listened for him. Someone was walking, whistling. She ran down to the sidewalk and saw him coming. He was dressed in white again with his jacket unbuttoned. He stopped when he saw her, smiled and beckoned. And she glanced once at her house, then ran up the warm pavement to where he stood.

'Where's your car?'

He looked about him, grinned and jerked his head. 'Up the road . . . We don't want nobody to know. You didn't tell nobody, did you?'

'No.'

They walked together. She could hardly keep up with him, so he took her hand. The fields opened up on either side after the pavement stopped. Charlotte strained up to see the car, and then the road turned suddenly and they came upon it parked by the roadside. It was big, but not so bright as those in the movies. He opened the door and lifted her in, her feet dangling over the edge of the seat. Then he came in from the other side.

'All set?'

'Uh-huh.' Charlotte was looking at the car inside.

'Like it?' he asked, and wiped his nose on the back of his hand.

They didn't drive off immediately. Charlotte was examining the gaudily colored dashboard, its clock with green numbers and silver hands. The other circles she did not understand, but they were all beautiful, colored and shining. The man caught her hand suddenly and she felt his fingers warm and moist, felt her mouth twist up as though she were about to cry. Then she wished that she had not come, wished that she were back on the front porch with Emilie. But he was smiling, laughing, even, as he started the car.

'You like to go fast?'

Charlotte tried to answer, but her lips were stiff. He squeezed her hand again.

'I like a lot of speed.'

Then through the engine's noise she heard someone calling her name. The man heard it, too, and released her hand. But the car was moving on toward her house.

'Charlotte! Charlo-otte!'

'That's my mother,' Charlotte said quietly.

Charlotte noticed that he frowned and that his hands tightened on the steering wheel. She felt the cool breeze in her face and she wanted to go on riding, but they were not going fast and she wanted to go fast. As they came near the house, she pressed herself against the seat, hoping her mother would not see her.

The woman stood with one foot on the curb, her apron hanging almost to the ground. She waved at them and he slowed the car. She came nearer, hiding her hands under her apron.

'Charlotte.' She grinned, but she looked at the man almost flirtatiously. 'Em'lie said you were out ridin'. I just wanted to make sure where you was . . . an' I need you to help with the baby now.' She pushed some strands of hair behind her ear.

The man at the wheel smiled broadly and said, 'How d'you do?'

Charlotte's mother nodded to him. 'I allus have Charlotte help me with the baby 'bout this time after supper . . . It's awful nice o' you to take her out ridin', mister, but she didn't say nothin' to me about it.' She laughed nervously.

'Sure, I know,' he said. He stretched one arm across and opened the door gallantly. 'Maybe tomorrow, then. I'll be around for a few days.'

The woman looked in awe at the shiny dials and knobs, the upholstered seats. 'Why . . . I'd like you to take her ridin' . . . most anytime.'

Then Charlotte and her mother walked hand in hand down the sidewalk. Once the woman cast a timid glance back at the car. 'He's a mighty nice man for a city fellah, Charlotte. Where'd you meet up with him? . . . An' say, ain't that a pretty car?'

Charlotte watched the ground pass below her bare feet. Her free hand brushed along the coarse grass that grew high.

'Maybe he'll be around tomorrow,' her mother said.

One blade of grass Charlotte caught convulsively and the edges jerked through her fingers. As she looked at her thumb, two thin red lines came out of the flesh.

THE HEROINE

The girl was so sure she would get the job, she had unabashedly come out to Westchester with her suitcase. She sat in a comfortable chair in the living room of the Christiansens' house, looking in her navy-blue coat and beret even younger than twenty-one, and replied earnestly to their questions.

'Have you worked as a governess before?' Mr Christiansen asked. He sat beside his wife on the sofa, his elbows on the knees of his gray flannel trousers, and his hands clasped. 'Any references, I mean?'

'I was a maid in Mrs Dwight Howell's house in New York for the last seven months.' Lucille looked at him with suddenly wide gray eyes. 'I could get a reference from there if you like . . . But when I saw your advertisement this morning, I didn't want to wait. I've always wanted a place where there were children.'

Mrs Christiansen smiled, but mainly to herself, at the girl's enthusiasm. She took a silver box from the coffee table, stood up and offered it to the girl. 'Will you have one?'

'No, thank you. I don't smoke.'

'Well,' Mrs Christiansen said, lighting her own cigarette, 'we might call them, of course, but my husband and I set more store by appearances than references . . . What do you say, Ronald? You told me you wanted someone who really liked children.'

And fifteen minutes later, Lucille Smith was standing in her room in the servants' quarters back of the house, buttoning the belt of her new white uniform. She touched her mouth lightly with lipstick. 'You're starting all over again, Lucille,' she told herself in the mirror. 'You're going to have a happy, useful life from now on, and forget everything that was before.'

But there went her eyes too wide again, as if to deny her words. Her eyes looked much like her mother's when they opened like that, and her mother was part of what she must forget. She must overcome that habit of stretching her eyes. It made her look sur-prised and uncertain, too, which was not at all the way to look around children. Her hand trembled as she set the lipstick down. She recomposed her face in the mirror, smoothed the starched front of her uniform. There were only a few things like the eyes to remember, a few silly habits, really, like burning little bits of paper in ash trays, forgetting time sometimes – little things that many people did, but that she must remember not to do. With practice the remembering would come automatically. Because she was just like other people (had the psychiatrist not told her so?), and other people never thought of them at all.

She crossed the room, sank onto the windowseat under the blue curtains, and looked out on the garden and lawn that lay between the servants' house and the big house. The yard was longer than it was wide, with a round fountain in the center and two flagstone walks lying like a crooked cross in the grass. There were benches here and there, against a tree, under an arbor, that seemed to be made of white lace. A beautiful yard!

And the house was the house of her dreams! A white, two-story house with dark-red shutters, with oaken doors and brass knockers and latches that opened with a press of the thumb . . . and broad lawns and poplar trees so dense and high one could not see through, so that one did not have to admit or believe that there was another house somewhere beyond . . . The rain-streaked Howell house in New York, granite pillared and heavily ornamented, had looked,

Lucille thought, like a stale wedding cake in a row of other stale wedding cakes . . .

She rose suddenly from her seat. The Christiansen house was blooming, friendly, and alive! There were children in it. Thank God for the children! But she had not even met them yet.

She hurried downstairs, crossed the yard on the path that ran from the door, lingered a few seconds to watch the plump faun blowing water from his reeds into the rock pond . . . What was it the Christiansens had agreed to pay her? She did not remember and she did not care. She would have worked for nothing just to live in such a place.

Mrs Christiansen took her upstairs to the nursery. She opened the door of a room whose walls were decorated with bright peasant designs, dancing couples and dancing animals, and twisting trees in blossom. There were twin beds of buff-colored oak, and the floor was yellow linoleum, spotlessly clean.

The two children lay on the floor in one corner, amid scattered crayons and picture books.

'Children, this is your new nurse,' their mother said. 'Her name is Lucille.'

The little boy stood up and said, 'How do you do,' as he solemnly held out a crayon-stained hand.

Lucille took it, and with a slow nod of her head repeated his greeting.

'And Heloise,' Mrs Christiansen said, leading the second child, who was smaller, toward Lucille.

Heloise stared up at the figure in white and said, 'How do you do.'

'Nicky is nine and Heloise six,' Mrs Christiansen told her.

'Yes,' Lucille said. She noticed that both children had a touch of red in their blonde hair, like their father. Both wore blue overalls without shirts, and their backs and shoulders were sun-brown beneath the straps. Lucille could not take her eyes from them. They were the perfect children of her perfect house. They looked up at her frankly, with no mistrust, no hostility. Only love, and some childlike curiosity.

'. . . and most people do prefer living where there's more country,' Mrs Christiansen was saying.

'Oh, yes . . . yes, ma'am. It's ever so much nicer here than in the city.'

Mrs Christiansen was smoothing the little girl's hair with a tenderness that fascinated Lucille. 'It's just about time for their lunch,' she said. 'You'll have your meals up here, Lucille. And would you like tea or coffee or milk?'

'I'd like coffee, please.'

'All right, Lisabeth will be up with the lunch in a few minutes.' She paused at the door. 'You aren't nervous about anything, are you, Lucille?' she asked in a low voice.

'Oh, no, ma'am.'

'Well, you mustn't be.' She seemed about to say something else, but she only smiled and went out.

Lucille stared after her, wondering what that something else might have been.

'You're a lot prettier than Catherine,' Nicky told her.

She turned around. 'Who's Catherine?' Lucille seated herself on a hassock, and as she gave all her attention to the two children who still gazed at her, she felt her shoulders relax their tension.

'Catherine was our nurse before. She went back to Scotland . . . I'm glad you're here. We didn't like Catherine.'

Heloise stood with her hands behind her back, swaying from side to side as she regarded Lucille. 'No,' she said, 'we didn't like Catherine.'

Nicky stared at his sister. 'You shouldn't say that. That's what I said!'

Lucille laughed and hugged her knees. Then Nicky and Heloise laughed, too.

A colored maid entered with a steaming tray and set it on the blond wood table in the center of the room. She was slender and of indefinite age. 'I'm Lisabeth Jenkins, miss,' she said shyly as she laid some paper napkins at three places.

'My name's Lucille Smith,' the girl said.

'Well, I'll just leave you to do the rest, miss. If you need anything else, just holler.' She went out, her hips small and hard-looking under the blue uniform.

The three sat down to the table, and Lucille lifted the cover from the large dish, exposing three parsley-garnished omelettes, bright yellow in the bar of sunlight that crossed the table. But first there was tomato soup for her to ladle out, and triangles of buttered toast to pass. Her coffee was in a silver pot, and the children had two large glasses of milk. The table was low for Lucille, but she did not mind. It was so wonderful merely to be sitting here with these children, with the sun warm and cheerful on the yellow linoleum floor, on the table, on Heloise's ruddy face opposite her. How pleasant not to be in the Howell house! She had always been clumsy there. But here it would not matter if she dropped a pewter cover or let a gravy spoon fall in someone's lap. The children would only laugh.

Lucille sipped her coffee.

'Aren't you going to eat?' Heloise asked, with her mouth already full.

The cup slipped in Lucille's fingers, and she spilled half her coffee on the cloth. No, it was not cloth, thank goodness, but oilcloth. She could get it up with a paper towel, and Lisabeth would never know.

'Piggy!' laughed Heloise.

'Heloise!' Nicky admonished, and went to fetch some paper towels from the bathroom.

They mopped up together.

'Dad always gives us a little of his coffee,' Nicky remarked as he took his place again.

Lucille had been wondering whether the children would mention the accident to their mother. She sensed that Nicky was offering her a bribe. 'Does he?' she asked.

'He pours a little in our milk,' Nicky went on, 'just so you can see the color.'

'Like this?' And Lucille poured a bit from the graceful silver spout into each glass.

The children gasped with pleasure. 'Yes!'

'Mother doesn't like us to have coffee,' Nicky explained, 'but when she's not looking, Dad lets us have a little like you did. Dad says his day wouldn't be any good without his coffee, and I'm the same way . . . Gosh, Catherine wouldn't give us any coffee like that, would she, Heloise?'

'Not her!' Heloise took a long, delicious draught from her glass which she held with both hands.

Lucille felt a glow rise from deep inside her until it settled in her face and burned there. The children liked her, there was no doubt of that. She remembered how often she had gone to the public parks in the city, during the three years she had worked as maid in various houses (to be a maid was all she was fit for, she used to think), merely to sit on a bench and watch the children play. But the children there had usually been dirty or foul-mouthed, and she herself had always been an outsider. Once she had seen a mother slap her own child across the face. She remembered how she had fled in pain and horror . . .

'Why do you have such big eyes?' Heloise demanded.

Lucille started. 'My mother had big eyes, too,' she said deliberately, like a confession.

'Oh,' Heloise replied, satisfied.

Lucille cut slowly into the omelette she did not want. Her mother had been dead three weeks now. Only three weeks and it seemed much, much longer. That was because she was forgetting, she thought, forgetting all the hopeless hope of the last three years, that her mother might recover in the sanatorium. But recover to what? The illness was something separate, something which had killed her. It had been senseless to hope for a complete sanity which she knew her mother had never had. Even the doctors had told her that. And they had told her other things, too, about herself. Good, encouraging things they were, that she was as normal as her father had been. Looking at Heloise's friendly little face across from her, Lucille felt the comforting glow return. Yes, in this perfect house, closed from all the world, she could forget and start anew.

'Are we ready for some Jello?' she asked.

Nicky pointed to her plate. 'You're not finished eating.'

'I wasn't very hungry.' Lucille divided the extra dessert between them.

'We could go out to the sandbox now,' Nicky suggested. 'We always go just in the mornings, but I want you to see our castle.'

The sandbox was in the back of the house in a corner made by a projecting ell. Lucille seated herself on the wooden rim of the box while the children began piling and patting like gnomes.

'I must be the captured princess!' Heloise shouted.

'Yes, and I'll rescue her, Lucille. You'll see!'

The castle of moist sand rose rapidly. There were turrets with tin flags sticking from their tops, a moat, and a drawbridge made of the lid of a cigar box covered with sand. Lucille watched, fascinated. She remembered vividly the story of Brian de Bois-Guilbert and Rebecca. She had read *Ivanhoe* through at one long sitting, oblivious of time and place just as she was now.

When the castle was done, Nicky put half a dozen marbles inside it just behind the drawbridge. 'These are good soldiers imprisoned,' he told her. He held another cigar box lid in front of them until he had packed up a barrier of sand. Then he lifted the lid and the sand door stood like a porte-cochère.

Meanwhile Heloise gathered ammunition of small pebbles from the ground next to the house. 'We break the door down and the good soldiers come down the hill across the bridge. Then I'm saved!'

'Don't tell her! She'll see!'

Seriously Nicky thumped the pebbles from the rim of the sandbox opposite the castle door, while Heloise behind the castle thrust a hand forth to repair the destruction as much as she could between shots, for besides being the captured princess she was the defending army.

Suddenly Nicky stopped and looked at Lucille. 'Dad knows how to shoot with a stick. He puts the rock on one end and hits the other. That's a balliska.'

'Ballista,' Lucille said.

'Golly, how did you know?'

'I read about it in a book – about castles.'

'Golly!' Nicky went back to his thumping, embarrassed that he had pronounced the word wrong. 'We got to get the good soldiers out fast. They're captured, see? Then when they're released that means we can all fight together and *take the castle!*'

'And save the princess!' Heloise put in.

As she watched, Lucille found herself wishing for some real catastrophe, something dangerous and terrible to befall Heloise, so that she might throw herself between her and the attacker, and prove her great courage and devotion . . . She would be seriously wounded herself, perhaps with a bullet or a knife, but she would beat off the assailant. Then the Christiansens would love her and keep her with them always. If some madman were to come upon them suddenly now, someone with a loose mouth and bloodshot eyes, she would not be afraid for an instant.

She watched the sand wall crumble and the first good soldier marble struggled free and came wobbling down the hill. Nicky and Heloise whooped with joy. The wall gave way completely, and two, three, four soldiers followed the first, their stripes turning gaily over the sand. Lucille leaned forward. Now she understood! She was like the good soldiers imprisoned in the castle. The castle was the Howell house in the city, and Nicky and Heloise had set her free. She was free to do good deeds. And now if only something would happen . . .

'O-o-ow!'

It was Heloise. Nicky had mashed one of her fingers against the edge of the box as they struggled to get the same marble.

Lucille seized the child's hand, her heart thumping at the sight of the blood that rose from many little points in the scraped flesh. 'Heloise, does it hurt very much?'

'Oh, she wasn't supposed to touch the marbles in the first place!' Disgruntled, Nicky sat in the sand.

Lucille held her handkerchief over the finger and half carried her into the house, frantic lest Lisabeth or Mrs Christiansen see them. She took Heloise into the bathroom that adjoined the nursery, and in the medicine cabinet found mercurochrome and gauze. Gently she washed the finger. It was only a small scrape, and Heloise stopped her tears when she saw how slight it was.

'See, it's just a little scratch!' Lucille said, but that was only to calm the child. To her it was not a little scratch. It was a terrible thing to happen the first afternoon she was in charge, a catastrophe she had failed to prevent. She wished over and over that the hurt might be on her own hand, twice as severe.

Heloise smiled as she let the bandage be tied. 'Don't punish Nicky,' she said. 'He didn't mean to do it. He just plays rough.'

But Lucille had no idea of punishing Nicky. She wanted only to punish herself, to seize a stick and thrust it into her own palm.

'Why do you make your teeth like that?'

'I – I thought it might be hurting you.'

'It doesn't hurt any more.' And Heloise went skipping out of the bathroom. She leaped onto her bed and lay on the tan cover that fitted the corners and came all the way to the floor. Her bandaged finger showed startlingly white against the brown of her arm. We have to take a nap now,' she told Lucille, and closed her eyes. 'Good-bye.'

'Good-bye,' Lucille answered, and tried to smile.

She went down to get Nicky and when they came up the stairs Mrs Christiansen was at the nursery door.

Lucille blanched. 'I don't think it's bad, ma'am. It – It's a scratch from the sandbox.'

'Heloise's finger? Oh, no, don't worry, my dear. They're always getting little scratches. It does them good. Makes them more careful.'

Mrs Christiansen went in and sat on the edge of Nicky's bed.

'Nicky, dear, you must learn to be more gentle. Just see how you frightened Lucille!' She laughed and ruffled his hair.

Lucille watched from the doorway. Again she felt herself an outsider, but this time because of her incompetence. Yet how different this was from the scenes she had watched in the parks!

Mrs Christiansen patted Lucille's shoulder as she went out. 'They'll forget all about it by nightfall.'

'Nightfall,' Lucille whispered as she went back into the nursery. 'What a beautiful word!'

While the children slept, Lucille looked through an illustrated book of *Pinocchio*. She was avid for stories, any kind of stories, but most of all adventure stories and fairy tales. And at her elbow on the children's shelf there were scores of them. It would take her months to read them all. It did not matter that they were for children. In fact, she found that kind more to her liking, because such stories were illustrated with pictures of animals dressed up, and tables and houses and all sorts of things come to life.

Now she turned the pages of *Pinocchio* with a sense of contentment and happiness so strong that it intruded upon the story she was reading. The doctor at the sanatorium had encouraged her reading, she remembered, and had told her to go to movies, too. 'Be with normal people and forget all about your mother's difficulties . . . ' (Difficulties, he had called it then, but all other times he had said strain. Strain it was, like a thread, running through the generations. She had thought, through her.) Lucille could still see the psychiatrist's face, his head turned a little to one side, his glasses in his hand as he spoke, just as she had thought a psychiatrist should look. 'Just because your mother had a strain, there's no reason why you should not be as normal as your father was. I have every reason to believe you are. You are an intelligent girl, Lucille . . . Get yourself a job out of the city . . . relax . . . enjoy life . . . I want you to forget even the house your family lived in . . . After a year in the country . . . '

That, too, was three weeks ago, just after her mother had died in the ward. And what the doctor had said was true. In this house where there were peace and love, beauty and children, she could feel the moils of the city sloughing off her like a snake's outworn skin. Already, in this one half day! In a week she would forget for ever her mother's face.

With a little gasp of joy that was almost ecstasy she turned to the bookshelf and chose at random six or seven tall, slender, brightly colored books. One she laid open, face down, in her lap. Another she opened and leaned against her breast. Still holding the rest in one hand, she pressed her face into *Pinocchio*'s pages, her eyes half closed. Slowly she rocked back and forth in the chair, conscious of nothing but her own happiness and gratitude. The chimes downstairs struck three times, but she did not hear them.

'What are you doing?' Nicky asked, his voice politely curious.

Lucille brought the book down from her face. When the meaning of his question struck her, she flushed and smiled like a happy but guilty child. 'Reading!' she laughed.

Nicky laughed, too. 'You read awful close.'

'Ya-yuss,' said Heloise, who had also sat up.

Nicky came over and examined the books in her lap. 'We get up at three o'clock. Would you read to us now? Catherine always read to us until dinner.'

'Shall I read to you out of *Pinocchio*?' Lucille suggested, happy that she might possibly share with them the happiness she had gained from the first pages of its story. She sat down on the floor so they could see the pictures as she read.

Nicky and Heloise pushed their eager faces over the pictures, and sometimes Lucille could hardly see to read. She did not realize that she read with a tense interest that communicated itself to the two children, and that this was why they enjoyed it so much. For two hours she read, and the time slipped by almost like so many minutes.

Just after five Lisabeth brought in the tray with their dinner, and when the meal was over Nicky and Heloise demanded more reading until their bedtime at seven. Lucille gladly began another book, but when Lisabeth returned to remove the tray, she told Lucille that it was time for the children's bath, and that Mrs Christiansen would be up to say good night in a little while.

Mrs Christiansen was up at seven, but the two children by that time were in their robes, freshly bathed, and deep in another story with Lucille on the floor.

'You know,' Nicky said to his mother, 'we've read all these books before with Catherine, but when Lucille reads them they seem like new books!'

Lucille flushed with pleasure. When the children were in bed, she went downstairs with Mrs Christiansen.

'Is everything fine, Lucille? . . . I thought there might be something you'd like to ask me about the running of things.'

'No, ma'am, except . . . might I come up once in the night to see how the children are doing?'

'Oh, I wouldn't want you to break your sleep, Lucille. That's very thoughtful, but it's really unnecessary.'

Lucille was silent.

'And I'm afraid the evenings are going to seem long to you. If you'd ever like to go to a picture in town, Alfred, that's the chauffeur, he'll be glad to take you in the car.'

'Thank you, ma'am.'

'Then good night, Lucille.'

'Good night, ma'am.'

She went out the back way, across the garden where the fountain was still playing. And when she put her hand on the knob of her door, she wished that it were the nursery door, that it were eight o'clock in the morning and time to begin another day.

Still she was tired, pleasantly tired. How very pleasant it was, she thought, as she turned out the light, to feel properly tired in the evening (although it was only nine o'clock) instead of bursting with energy, instead of being unable to sleep for thinking of her mother or worrying about herself . . . She remembered one day not so long ago when for fifteen minutes she had been unable to think of her name. She had run in panic to the doctor . . .

That was past! She might even ask Alfred to buy her a pack of cigarettes in town — a luxury she had denied herself for months.

She took a last look at the house from her window. The curtains in the nursery billowed out now and then and were swept back again. The wind spoke in the nodding tops of the poplars like friendly voices, like the high-pitched, ever-rippling voices of children . . .

The second day was like the first, except that there was no mishap, no scraped hand — and the third and the fourth. Regular and identical like the row of Nicky's lead soldiers on the playtable in the nursery. The only thing that changed was Lucille's love for the family and the children — a blind and passionate devotion which seemed to redouble each morning. She noticed and loved many things: the way Heloise drank her milk in little gulps at the back of her throat, how the blonde down on their backs swirled up to meet the hair on the napes of their necks, and when she bathed them the painful vulnerability of their bodies.

Saturday evening she found an envelope addressed to herself in the mailbox at the door of the servants' house. Inside was a blank sheet of paper and inside that a couple of new twenty-dollar bills. Lucille held one of them by its crisp edges. Its value meant nothing to her. To use it she would have to go to stores where other people were. What use had she for money if she were never to leave the Christiansen home? It would simply pile up, forty dollars each week. In a year's time she would have two thousand and eighty dollars, and in two years' time twice that. Eventually she might have as much as the Christiansens themselves and that would not be right.

Would they think it very strange if she asked to work for nothing? Or for ten dollars perhaps?

She had to speak to Mrs Christiansen, and she went to her the next morning. It was an inopportune time. Mrs Christiansen was making up a menu for a dinner.

'It's about my salary, ma'am,' Lucille began.

'Yes?' Mrs Christiansen said in her pleasant voice.

Lucille watched the yellow pencil in her hand moving swiftly over the paper. 'It's too much for me, ma'am.'

The pencil stopped. Mrs Christiansen's lips parted slightly in surprise. 'You are such a funny girl, Lucille!'

'How do you mean – funny?' Lucille asked curiously.

'Well, first you want to be practically day and night with the children. You never even want your afternoon off. You're always talking about doing something "important" for us, though what that could be I can't imagine . . . And now your salary's too much! We've never had a girl like you, Lucille. I can assure you, you're different!' She laughed, and the laugh was full of ease and relaxation that contrasted with the tension of the girl who stood before her.

Lucille was rapt by the conversation. 'How do you mean different, ma'am?'

'Why, I've just told you, my dear. And I refuse to lower your salary because that would be sheer exploitation. In fact, if you ever change your mind and want a raise—'

'Oh, no, ma'am . . . but I just wish there was something more I could do for you . . . all of you . . . '

'Lucille! You're working for us, aren't you? Taking care of our children. What could be more important than that?'

'But I mean something bigger – I mean more—'

'Nonsense, Lucille,' Mrs Christiansen interrupted. 'Just because the people you were with before were not so – friendly as we are doesn't mean you have to work your fingers to the bone for us.' She waited for the girl to make some move to go, but she still stood by the desk, her face puzzled. 'Mr Christiansen and I are very well pleased with you, Lucille.'

'Thank you, ma'am.'

She went back to the nursery where the children were playing. She had not made Mrs Christiansen understand. If she could just go back and explain what she felt, tell her about her mother and her fear of herself for so many months, how she had never dared take a drink or even a cigarette . . . and how just being with the family in this beautiful house had made her well again . . . telling her all that might relieve her. She turned toward the door, but the thought of disturbing her or boring her with the story, a servant girl's story, made her stop. So during the rest of the day she carried her unexpressed gratitude like a great weight in her breast.

That night she sat in her room with the light on until after twelve o'clock. She had her cigarettes now, and she allowed herself three in the evening, but even those were sufficient to set her blood tingling, to relax her mind, to make her dream heroic dreams. And when the three cigarettes were smoked, and she would have liked another, she rose very light in the head and put the cigarette pack in her top drawer to close away temptation. Just as she slid the drawer she noticed on her handkerchief box the two twenty-dollar bills the Christiansens had given her. She took them now, and sat down again in her chair.

From the book of matches she took a match, struck it, and leaned it, burning end down, against the side of her ashtray. Slowly she struck matches one after another and laid them strategically to make a tiny, flickering, well-controlled fire. When the matches were gone, she . tore the pasteboard cover into little bits and dropped them in slowly. Finally she took the twenty-dollar bills and with some effort tore bits from them of the same size. These, too, she meted to the fire.

Mrs Christiansen did not understand, but if she saw *this*, she might. Still *this* was not enough. Mere faithful service was not enough either. Anyone would give that, for money. She was different. Had not Mrs Christiansen herself told her that? Then she remembered what else she had said: 'Mr Christiansen and I are very well pleased with you, Lucille.'

The memory of those words brought her up from her chair with an enchanted smile upon her lips. She felt wonderfully strong and secure in her own strength of mind and her position in the household. *Mr Christiansen and I are very well pleased with you, Lucille.* There was really only one thing lacking in her happiness. She had to prove herself in crisis.

If only a plague like those she had read of in the Bible . . . 'And it came to pass that there was a great plague over all the land.' That was how the Bible would say it. She imagined waters lapping higher against the big house, until they swept almost into the nursery. She would rescue the children and swim with them to safety, wherever that might be.

She moved restlessly about the room.

Or if there came an earthquake . . . She would rush in among falling walls and drag the children out. Perhaps she would go back for some trifle, like Nicky's lead soldiers or Heloise's paint set, and be crushed to death. Then the Christiansens would know her devotion.

Or if there might be a fire. Anyone might have a fire. Fires were common things and needed no wrathful visitations from the upper world. There might be a terrible fire just with the gasoline in the garage and a match.

She went downstairs, through the inside door that opened to the garage. The tank was three feet high and entirely full, so that unless she had been inspired with the necessity and importance of her deed, she would not have been able to lift the thing over the threshold of the garage and of the servants' house, too. She rolled the tank across the yard in the same manner as she had seen men roll beer barrels and ashcans. It made no noise on the grass and only a brief bump and rumble over one of the flagstone paths, lost in the night.

No lights shone at any of the windows, but if they had, Lucille would not have been deterred. She would not have been deterred had Mr Christiansen himself been standing there by the fountain, for probably she would not have seen him. And if she had, was she not about to do a noble thing? No, she would have seen only the house and the children's faces in the room upstairs.

She unscrewed the cap and poured some gasoline on a corner of the house, rolled the tank farther, poured more against the white shingles, and so on until she reached the far corner. Then she struck her match and walked back the way she had come, touching off the wet places. Without a backward glance she went to stand at the door of the servants' house and watch.

The flames were first pale and eager, then they became yellow with touches of red. As Lucille watched, all the tension that was left in her, in body or mind, flowed evenly upward and was lifted from her forever, leaving her muscles and brain free for the voluntary tension of an athlete before a starting gun. She would let the flames leap tall, even to the nursery window, before she rushed in, so that the danger might be at its highest. A smile like that of a saint settled on her mouth, and anyone seeing her there in the doorway, her face glowing in the lambent light, would certainly have thought her a beautiful young woman.

She had lit the fire at five places, and these now crept up the house like the fingers of a hand, warm and flickering, gentle and caressing. Lucille smiled and held herself in check. Then suddenly the gasoline tank, having grown too warm, exploded with a sound like a cannon and lighted the entire scene for an instant.

As though this had been the signal for which she waited, Lucille went confidently forward.

THE WORLD'S CHAMPION
BALL-BOUNCER

'Ellie, eat your breakfast,' Elspeth's mother said from behind her, in the kind of voice she used when she was thinking about something else. 'Just look how thick the cream is this morning.'

'Mm-*hmm*,' Elspeth murmured politely. She wrung her hands in her lap and looked down at her oatmeal that was still steaming though surrounded by cream like a gray castle in a lake.

It was no use for her mother to pretend that the cream just happened to be thick this morning. It was thick because they were in New York. Everything they had this morning was boughten and very expensive. The coffee smelled shiny black, she could taste the bacon in the air. Yet beneath the breakfast smell was the smell of the room itself, an unfriendly and mixed-up smell of sweetness like ladies' perfume and powder, the clothiness of carpets and upholstery and the hot paint smell from the radiator. Elspeth could tell that many other people had lived here before them. It was not a definite smell such as she had noticed in certain people's houses.

'Mother, is this house a church?' Elspeth asked anxiously.

'No, darling. It's an apartment building.'

Through her sleepiness last night when they arrived, Elspeth had remembered the colored glass in the windows of a door downstairs. 'Not even *part* of a church?'

'No, Ellie. Where'd you get that idea? It's just a big apartment house. There are lots of big buildings like this in New York.'

Elspeth turned back, quelled.

She remembered how the name of New York had excited her when she heard it at home. She had used to jump and yell, 'I want to go to New York *now*!' like a silly thing whenever her parents had talked about going north. She had even boasted to Francey Pat and Jordy, her two best friends, that she was going north, where she would have all sorts of adventures and would see things they couldn't begin to think of. Now she felt old and ashamed of herself. Last night she had gone to sleep thinking of the Empire State Building, the tallest building in the world, and the trips she would make up and down in it. But now she did not want to go.

She pushed her clasped hands deeper into her lap and lowered her eyes. 'Excuse me, New York. Excuse me.' She did not even whisper, but her lips moved.

'You must write to Mrs Sears and thank her for the pocketbook, Ellie. It was thoughtful of her to give you a going-away present.'

'Um-hmm.'

Her mother stood behind her, smoothing her limp yellow-tan hair that splayed over the round cotton collar of her dress. Fortified by her mother's hands, by the tuneless yet familiar tune her mother hummed as her hands slipped under her chin, Elspeth leaned back against her and surveyed the room in a slow worried manner.

The room had a strange public look. Her family's things just seemed to sit in it like bundles in a waiting-room. The walls were a cold gray-white and Elspeth was aware that their smudges and the worn spots in the carpet had been made by other people they did not know. There was a long tub with real legs in the bathroom and there were brown streaks below the faucets where the water kept running down with a spooky sound like people whispering excitedly. She had heard it last night from the cot in the corner where she slept. She could hear it now every once in a while when the coffeepot stopped chugging.

'Why did Daddy go out again?'

'He went out to look for a paper. He'll be back directly.'

Their own clock ticked softly on a big bureau, telling a time that did not matter at all. Ten-thirty, it said. At home, ten-thirty Sunday, she would be sitting up straight in the front porch swing so she wouldn't wrinkle her dress, while she waited for Uncle John and Aunt Lettie and her cousin Paully to drive up and take her to Sunday school. She would be reading the funny papers but with only half her eyes, thinking how much better they would be to read when Sunday school was all over.

'Don't they deliver papers up here?'

'Of course, when people have been here long enough. But we just came yesterday, Ellie. Do you suppose they know we want a paper?' Her mother bent down and laughed, trying to make her laugh too.

Elspeth's mouth was set in a short horizontal line. There was nothing funny to her in the fact that no one knew or cared whether they got the Sunday paper or not. Suddenly the scary feeling that had been crawling around in her sprang all over her at once.

'Mother, what is the matter with this house?' Her voice sounded as shrill as though she were crying.

'Nothing, darling! What do you mean?'

Abashedly Elspeth bowed her head, as though she had seen something she shouldn't have seen. In that instant she knew that her mother knew. There was something the matter with the house and with the whole morning. It was something they could feel, hear, taste, smell – everything but see. Something that made her sit small and hold her breath, unable to find words to tell her mother the feeling. If her mother did not talk about it, maybe it was not to be talked about. Would the feeling go away, Elspeth wondered, or would something happen?

*

The light from the two tall windows was thin and glaring at once, reaching the farthest corners of the room. Elspeth's mother was still so pale from long protection against an impossible sun that the strange light seemed to pass through her as through a new blade of grass. She was in her late twenties and looked even younger.

She turned finally from her contemplation of the windows and lowered the fire under the bacon, slipping the egg flipper beneath the five rashers and turning them neatly.

She felt again the sensation of solemn lonely commencement in what she did. She had thought, this was the first meal she cooked in New York, these were the first pieces of bacon. And now, absurdly, she thought, this was the first time she turned their first New York bacon. There was, in the simple things that each of the three of them had done that morning, a quality of drama and inauguration that would have made her laugh had it not borne also a sense of their aloneness. She would remember the feeling of this Sunday all her life. This room that was indifferent to their presence as the whole north was indifferent, the hum of outdoors raised to a climax now and then by a rumble that she knew must be the elevated train, the sound of a phonograph down the hall playing a popular song over and over.

Incredulously she realized that all her senses told her of this morning and this city was destined to become so much part of her that what she knew of other mornings and another city would become unfamiliar, perhaps also tinged with fear. She would remember always, and the start in her heart as she remembered would always recapture precisely her consciousness of this instant in this room.

She turned the flame off under the coffee for the third time, then slowly relighted the burner because A. J. liked it strong. This morning she had wanted to cook a real breakfast such as they would have had at home on Sunday. It had been so long since they had cooked for themselves, not since the big dinner at Mama's Thursday night before they caught the train. It seemed a long time ago that she had candied the carrots and carried them in to the table herself. And here they were in a New York apartment. They were lucky to have found it, dingy as it was, for they couldn't have afforded a hotel for long.

This morning the gas hadn't been connected and the superintendent had told her it couldn't be fixed until Monday. She had stood there, burning with shame at her own rude insistence, saying, 'But I'd like it so much – if you possibly could.' Until finally the superintendent, with an ungraciousness that was the last humiliation, had fetched the janitor and she had got the gas connected just before A. J. came back from the grocery store. She did not tell A. J., though. There would be enough little difficulties later that both would know about. She felt proud of herself for succeeding with the superintendent. Everybody had told her that in the north you had to be persistent and finally northerners liked you for it. That was the way A. J. would have to be tomorrow when he looked for a job. It was hard to imagine him being really persistent, but surely his samples would speak for themselves. If he was the best letterer in Birmingham, he was bound to be worth a job somewhere in New York. And all at once she realized her really limitless faith in him.

It was strange, but she had more faith now that they were in New York than she had known back home, when they had talked of coming up. So many times they had discussed it, whether to go, then when to go, frightened as birds about to take a first flight from the nest. 'Anyone with real ambition,' A. J. had often said at those times, 'wants to go to New York, Lei.' But each new discussion had been followed by seconds of silence in which each of them, and even Ellie, had looked into a particular dream of New York composed of skyscrapers, multitudes and somehow a happier life for all of them, yet a dream that was frozen by the fear that somehow they might not be good enough to stay in New York once they got there. Yet now we are here, Leila thought, and the first hardship is over. The superintendent that morning, for instance, had not been the stone wall he seemed at first. All it would take was courage and persever-ance, and she was sure all three of them had both.

She caught sight of the new sable fur piece that hung inside the closet door and a throb of another kind of remembrance went through her. Mama and Lettie and her brother Reeves had given it to her Thursday night. It was too fine for the rest of her wardrobe, as yet too new and too much itself to seem her own possession. They had given it to her as a kind of armor against the unknown north, an assertion to all strangers of her own and of her family's decency. The fur piece, unlike the room, would grow with her. She would never quite feel again, even the next time she looked at it, her own youth and vulnerability and pride as she did at this moment.

The elevator rattled shut in the hall and A. J.'s footsteps sounded on the stone floor. Leila moved smiling toward them, smoothing her hair, and opened the door before he touched it.

His thin rather serious face smiled suddenly. 'Hello, Lei!' he said across an armful of newspapers. The freshness of the outdoors was in his topcoat and in his short straight fair hair, the scent of fresh ink in the papers he carried. 'Breakfast smells good! Hi. Ellie. Waiting for us as usual, I see.'

Elspeth twisted her hands, but now with pleasure. 'I really am!' She was glad she had waited.

'Oh, you really are?' he mocked her.

Leila followed him with her eyes as he hung his topcoat in the closet and adjusted his cuffs in the neat shy way she had noticed the first time she met him. She would never forget the way he had smiled just now when she opened the door. I have made this room a home for him already, she thought, knowing she would never tell him of her fear while he was gone that something might have happened to him.

'Had to walk a good ways to find a *New York Times*. I wanted it for the want ads.' He smiled as he sat down at the bridge table, careful not to bump the fragile legs. 'And you know, Lei, the fellow in the grocery store didn't know what I meant by "sweet milk." He said, "Wha-at?"' A. J. stretched his neck toward Elspeth to make her laugh.

'Oh, really!' Leila laughed, half closing her eyes and turning her head, as she often did when she was amused, but now mainly because A. J. expected her to be amused.

'Finally he understood I wanted milk but he told me he didn't have any sweet. "Then give me some buttermilk," I said. "We got no buttermilk either," he said.' A. J. reached for a piece of toast, laughing, but with a shadow across his blue eyes. He remembered the three people who had come into the store after him, their impatient smiles to one another during his stumbling conversation with the counterman, his realization that he spoke quite a different language from theirs. 'Anyway,' he finished, blushing a little, for he had not made Leila and Ellie laugh so much as he had hoped, 'there isn't any sweet milk in New York. It's either milk or buttermilk.'

Elspeth forced a little laugh for the first time. 'How funny,' she remarked. And suddenly she sounded grown-up to herself, for she had said this just to be nice, knowing that in the store, her daddy had felt the very same scary feeling she and her mother had felt here in the room. Elspeth was embarrassed. She wanted to hang her head, to get up from the table and run outdoors. But here she could not go outdoors.

'Mother, may I have some coffee?' she asked recklessly.

'Of course you may, honey!' Her mother smiled and Elspeth watched the cup grow more than half full while her mother and daddy talked.

Elspeth poured cream into her coffee from a little bottle shaped like a milk bottle, and watched as it swirled richly, making her coffee brown, then light tan. Slowly and guardedly she put three teaspoonfuls of sugar into it, expecting at each second to be challenged. But no one noticed. Elspeth stirred and stirred, then started to sip, but suddenly her mouth twisted up so she could not fit it to the cup. She began to cry, spilling the coffee as she tried to set it down.

'Elspeth!'

'What's the matter, Ellie?'

Elspeth bent her head lower and lower. She did not know exactly what was the matter except everything. She did not want the coffee. At home she wouldn't have been allowed coffee. It was one more proof.

'She's tired,' her mother said.

'No, I'm not!' Elspeth protested, lifting her head as high as she had bent it low. She got up from the table with dignity and went slowly to the window, not making a sound, although she was crying. She wanted to say casually that she was simply not hungry, but she could not trust herself to talk.

'Come on back and let's finish up,' her daddy called from the table. 'Then we'll all look at the funny papers together. Bet you never saw such a lot of funny papers as they have up here. I've got *three* papers with funny papers.'

Elspeth found she had not the least desire to read the funny papers. She began to cry again, silently, with a twisted turned-away face. Something really awful was wrong if the funny papers didn't seem like anything. She heard her parents talking about her but she did not even care to listen.

She stood by the window gazing dully out at the dirty yellow-gray face of the building across the street. The sills of the windows were thick and made of a pinkish stone. There was a blue awning at the front door that came all the way down to the sidewalk on the sides. She could see a door cut in each side, besides the opening at the end. She watched a fat man in a black suit walk through one side door and out the other, like a marble that rolled through a box with holes cut out.

She began to look at the street with more interest. A little girl had come out of the apartment house and was bouncing a ball on the sidewalk near the awning. She threw one leg, then the other, over the ball at regular intervals. A man passed and jostled her, but she kept the ball bouncing without a miss. The little girl was just about her size, Elspeth thought, only plumper. She wore a green jumper dress and no hat, and her hair swung in beautiful dark braids. She began to bounce the ball against the house, making it hit the sidewalk on its return and land right in her hands as though it were on a rubber band.

Then she bounced the ball in front of her and threw *both* legs over! It occurred to Elspeth suddenly, with a feeling of awe, that the little girl might be the world's champion ball-bouncer. The champion would certainly live in New York.

'Ellie?' her mother said slowly from behind her.

Elspeth twisted all the way around without moving her feet. 'I'm watching out the window,' she said, not wanting to miss anything of the little girl. When her mother came over Elspeth said, 'Look.'

'Why, she's just about your own age. Maybe she's someone for you to play with.'

'Yes,' Elspeth said, smitten with shyness. How could she ever play with the world's champion ball-bouncer?

'Why don't you go down and say hello to her, Ellie? I bet she'd like someone to play with.'

'I don't feel like it,' Elspeth said quietly.

'Of course you do. Run down and get acquainted with her. She can tell you all about New York and you can tell her about home. Won't you like that?'

Before Elspeth could say anything, her mother was brushing her hair, getting her hat and her red bolero from the closet.

'You go down and look up and see if you can see us,' her mother said, patting her gently in the direction of the door. 'We're on the eighth floor. Be careful crossing the street.'

Elspeth walked somberly toward the elevator and rang the elevator bell without even waiting to gather her courage. The elevator stopped almost immediately.

'By-by, darling,' her mother called. Her voice sounded so sweet, echoing in the hall, that Elspeth did not want to leave.

In the elevator Elspeth's lowered eyes saw, besides the elevator man's uniformed trousers, the ankles and feet of a man and a woman. The woman had long thin feet in pointed black pumps. Elspeth thought she would never forget the look of those feet, the stiff staring faces above them that she could imagine and could not look at.

She walked straight through the lobby toward the colored glass doors, one of which opened as a man came in. Everything happened fast, as though the whole world intended to get her outside with the world's champion ball-bouncer. There was not even a passing car to delay her in crossing the street at the corner.

On the sidewalk, tossing one leg, then the other, then filling an interval with little dancing, mock leg-throwing steps that kept in perfect rhythm with the bouncing ball, the plump little girl continued her wonderful performance and might not have stopped in all the time it took for Elspeth to be brushed and hatted and sent down to the place where she stood on the same sidewalk with her.

'Hello,' Elspeth whispered, trying her voice.

Then she sneaked close to the building against which the little girl bounced the ball. Elspeth pressed herself back against the yellow-gray bricks and raised her eyes to the building where her parents were. The pattern of the rows upon rows of windows made her eyes swim and her heart began to beat violently. Somewhere up there her parents stood looking down at her. Then she brought her eyes down to the bottom, counted one, two, three, up to eight and swept her eyes across, almost losing the row.

There they were, at the window with the thin white curtains that looked gray. They were waving slowly, as though they-had been waving a long while, waiting for her to find them. Elspeth started to wave, then brought her arm down hard at her side, not wanting to call attention to herself. They were waiting for her to make a move toward the world's champion ball-bouncer. She *had* to.

Elspeth gathered herself and it was like a pain when she began to move. She thought as she approached the little girl, her head hanging, that there was probably some place in New York that awarded prizes for various things and that surely this little girl had competed and easily won in the contest for sidewalk ball-bouncing. Elspeth was only some ten feet away now and still the rubber ball bounced as though the little girl did not even notice her. Her throat was dry again and she wondered if she could speak.

'Bok – bok – bok!' went the little rubber ball after a tiny hissing sound at the beginning of each bounce.

Elspeth stood still. She was so close she could see fine hairs on the little girl's plump legs. She was so close, she had come so far, she felt it was the other girl's turn now. She should stop bouncing and look at her, but she did not. Elspeth stood there as long as she could, doing nothing, then heard her own voice say: 'Hello.'

The ball darted into the little girl's hand and disappeared, as though it were hiding itself away at the mere sight of Elspeth. The little girl stared at Elspeth without any expression at all. Her eyes were dark brown and rather large, her mouth unsmiling, and there was neither curiosity nor hostility nor even a simple not-seeing in her face.

'How're *you*?' Elspeth asked desperately.

Still the little girl stared at her, her eyes moving slowly from Elspeth's round-brimmed hat that sat on the back of her head down to her patent leather shoes with buttoned cross-straps, and up again to a point near her chin. She took a step back, then began to concentrate on her bouncing. The ball bounced down, down, as oblivious of Elspeth as before she had arrived.

'My name is Elspeth Levering,' Elspeth squeezed out. The name hung in the air like a delicate naked thing. Like *herself*.

The other little girl stopped, stared longer, then took another step back. Her arm moved as though she were about to throw the ball, then she looked at Elspeth once more. 'You sure talk funny,' she said.

Elspeth started at the sound of her voice, feeling the unfriendliness before she made out the words. For the little girl had spoken so quickly, it took a moment for Elspeth to understand. Then Elspeth crumpled as though she were making a deep bow and fled.

She did not remember how she crossed the street or entered the red apartment house. She did not realize anything until she stood again in the elevator. She dashed down the hall and tapped on her parents' door. She pushed her face into her mother, embracing her high around her waist.

'Ellie!'

'Back so soon, Ellie?'

Elspeth released her mother and swallowed. They expected her to have succeeded and she had failed. She had failed her parents.

'What's her name?' her daddy smiled from the bed where he sat reading the papers.

'Is she nice?' her mother asked.

Elspeth nodded. 'Her name's Helen,' she replied, looking around at the floor. Then she walked quickly to the closet, slipping the hat string from beneath her chin. 'She's awful nice. Only she said she had to go some place right away, so I didn't stay.'

'Well, that's nice,' her mother said, so pleased-sounding that Elspeth's fib hurt her deeply. 'Are you going to see her again?'

'Uh-huh. Tomorrow. After school.'

The last word made Elspeth's heart turn over and lie like a heavy thing. She stared straight ahead, wide-eyed. School tomorrow was a real something to be afraid of, an unknown school with unknown boys and girls. She would be really alone then, facing people like the world's champion ball-bouncer multiplied a thousand times!

'Oh, Ellie!'

She felt her mother's fingers in her hair, holding her head close against her. Elspeth could not press her face hard enough against her mother, for she could feel the tears running hopelessly out of her eyes now and she did not want her mother to see. She did not know why her mother held her so, but she knew she felt better because she had fibbed about the little girl across the street. Tomorrow, at the new school, she would make up for it by making friends with a lot of people, even if each one was twice as unfriendly as the world's champion ball-bouncer. She felt her father pat her back and knew he had stooped down behind her too.

It was funny, Elspeth thought – they were both as quiet as she during that long minute while she held her breath.

THE STILL POINT OF THE TURNING WORLD

There is a small park, hardly more than a square, far over on the West Side in the lower Twenties, that is almost always deserted. A low iron fence runs around it, setting it off from a used car lot, a big redstone public dispensary of some sort, and the plain gray backs of shabby apartment buildings that share the same block with it. Three or four benches stand in pleasant places along the two curving cement paths that one may enter by, and that meet in the center at a cement drinking fountain forever bubbling an inch or so of cool water.

From quite a distance up or down the avenue the little park shines like an emerald isle, a bright and inviting surprise in a sea of drab grayness. Mrs Robertson noticed it one day from a corner of the Castle Terrace Apartments three blocks away, where she lived. She took her small son Philip to play there that afternoon. It was a splendid place for him, because the low iron fence kept him within bounds even when her back was turned, and it was quiet and sunny, unlittered and untrodden. For a city park it was unusually pretty, too, as if the gardeners had been inspired by a special and personal pride when they made it. The fine close-cropped grass extended into the very corners of the four vaguely triangular lawns. If the grass was not to be walked on, there was no one about to tell her so. Of course, the neighborhood was an abruptly sordid contrast with nearby Castle Terrace, but so was the neighborhood in every direction around Castle Terrace. Its square block of apartments stood like a feudal castle in the center of vassal land in which even the dingiest shops and restaurants bore sycophantic names like the King George, the Crown Tavern, the Belvedere Bar and Grill, as if to curry patronage from the manor. The only people Mrs Robertson saw near the park, however, were the busy truck drivers who came and went around a diner a block away, and an occasional old man in a pinned-together overcoat who shuffled by too drunk or too tired even to glance at the park. Mrs Robertson read her book until she grew tired of it, then picked up some knitting she had brought, and after a while just sat and daydreamed in the tranquillity. She debated the item she always left until last in her dinner, the vegetable she would buy in a frozen package on the way home.

She had just decided on mixed carrots and peas when a young woman with a child about the age of Philip came into the park and sat down on one of the benches. The little boy was dark-haired and had a blue and white beach ball which interested Philip.

The dark-haired little boy climbed over the scalloped wire fence into the lawn where Philip played. 'Hello,' he said.

'Hello,' said Philip.

In a minute they were playing together, Philip with the beach ball and the dark-haired little boy with Philip's tricycle. Mrs Robertson did not like Philip's playing with just any child, but this had happened so quickly there was nothing to be done about it. She intended to leave in about fifteen minutes anyway. Idly, she studied the other woman, surmising immediately that she was rather poor and that she lived in one of the shabby apartment buildings close by. She had very light blonde hair that did not quite look bleached, though, and she was rather pretty. She sat with her hands in the pockets of her black polo coat, her knees close together, almost as if she were cold, and she paid little attention to her child, Mrs Robertson thought, if it was hers. She stared straight before her with a faint smile on her lips, as if she were miles away in thought.

Soon Mrs Robertson got up and went to get Philip. He and the dark-haired child had become such good friends, Philip cried a little when she loosened his hands from the beach ball and drew him and his tricycle toward the path. Mrs Robertson and the blonde woman exchanged a smile of understanding, but they did not speak to each other. Mrs Robertson was not given to speaking to strangers, and the other woman seemed still lost in her trance.

The next afternoon, the blonde young woman was in the park when Mrs Robertson arrived, on the same bench, in the same attitude in the black polo coat.

'Dickie!' Philip shrieked when he saw the little boy, and his baby voice cracked with joy.

It gave Mrs Robertson a tweak of surprise, somehow of unease, that Philip knew the other little boy's name. She watched Philip run totteringly along the path to meet Dickie, who stood with a wide smile, holding his beach ball toward Philip in two outstretched arms. Philip's rush of greeting knocked the other little boy down, and they both scrambled after the rolling ball. Mrs Robertson knew suddenly in that instant they were together, bound up as one being in play, what had made her uneasy: she was not sure the other little boy was clean. He might even have things in his hair. Mrs Robertson had lived until recently in a suburb of Philadelphia, but she had heard about the unsanitary conditions of New York's tenement apartments. The dark-haired little boy *looked* washed enough in his pink-and-white striped play overalls, but one never knew what kind of disease a child who lived in a tenement might carry, and Philip would not have the resistance of a child brought up in such an environment. She would have to watch to see he did not put things in his mouth.

Mrs Robertson gave the blonde woman a nod and a smile as she sat down on the bench where she had been the day before. The other woman responded with a nod that Mrs Robertson could just detect, and her eyes resumed their vacant gaze, quite above the figures of the two little boys playing on the grass. Her expression was so completely oblivious, it aroused Mrs Robertson's curiosity. Her smile suggested that she saw into some pleasant and fascinating spectacle in a definite place in space. She was quite young, she decided, probably about twenty-one or -two. What was she thinking of? she wondered. And what would her little boy have to do to make her pay him any notice?

On the bench across the path, nearer the fountain than Mrs Robertson, the blonde young woman was awaiting her lover. She was thinking what a beautiful sunny, quiet day it was, and wishing, almost, that these meetings in the little park in April afternoons were all that he and she would know, could know, or would want to know. She was thinking that a mood came upon her every afternoon as she and Dickie left the house, as she descended the brownstone steps, feeling the warmth of the spring sunlight and its calm clarity upon her before she could take her eyes from Dickie's feet to look around her. The street where she lived was especially free of traffic, and at two or three in the afternoons almost as tranquil as the park itself. It presented two smooth parallel walls of brownstone, and even the gray-blue band of street between them was sharp and clear. Here and there a window was dotted by a white bottle of milk on the sill, or a pair of arms at rest on a flattened pillow. Above the arms, resigned and mildly curious eyes gazed down, athirst for any movement on the street, and there was so little: a woman in a housedress airing a nondescript white dog along the curb, a solitary child bouncing a ball beside a stoop post, maybe a boy with a rattly laundry cart, a passing cat. Everyone except the aged and a few women were off at work. Like her husband, Charles, who drove a bus on Broadway, who was gone by eight in the morning and generally did not return until after five. To her, the street seemed empty even of people, because she did not think the woman with her white dog or the arms on the two or three windowsills were alive in the way she knew she was alive. She did not believe they were aware in the same way of the serenity of the street, an odd kind of serenity that clamored to be noticed, or even of its dazzling cleanliness at that hour of the afternoon in the month of April. The woman with the dog did not feel the same as she, coming down her own steps onto the sidewalk, did not sense that the afternoon there belonged to women, to the wives who were alone now with the chores they were complete mistresses of, whose schedule they could rearrange with the flexibility of a woman's day, to an hour earlier if they chose, an hour later, or perhaps not until tomorrow – a woman's world, the street and its two or three reedy trees in iron cages, their thin heads green once more, the street and its unutterable peace. She did not, however, consider herself an ordinary housewife. And there was not the stillness of the street or of the park inside her on the afternoons when he was to come to meet her, though her perception of its stillness and the park's were dependent upon him. On the afternoons she was to see him, she saw beyond the street and the park. She would look eastward where the street disappeared in a huddled jagged mass of buildings, and imagine noise and seething people. She would look west and something in her would leap at the sight of the pier on the river, at a ship's high short mast rising in a cross like a strong and mystic promise above the sooty front of the dock building, above the squared top where the pier's number was written. From this very pier, so close to where she slept every night, she might leave for any corner of the earth, she supposed. And she would wonder if she and Lance would ever really make voyages to foreign places. If she asked him, of course, he would answer such a firm 'Certainly we will. Why not?' she would believe and not wonder any longer. Did the woman with the dog ever lift her eyes to look at the pier? Or the woman who had come to the park again today, with the washed and combed little blond boy, who must live in Castle Terrace, did she ever get chills at the sight and smell and sound of the river? But she had probably been all over the world already, been to Europe so many times she knew how each thing would look, what was going to happen next. She would not care to look at the pier.

The blonde young woman looked at her now, sitting reading her book, glancing once in a while to see if her little boy was safe. What could happen to anyone in this park? The sweater she wore over her dress was beautiful in the sunlight, the color of a stick of grape ice held to light. Cashmere. She was young, too, she thought, but her manner was so formal she seemed older. She had not talked with her, she supposed, because she considered her an inferior, but she did not care at all. She was not in a mood for talking. She was not in a mood for reading, either. She could have sat all day happily, dreaming on the bench and gazing into space with the green of the park beneath her eyes and reflecting up into them. She was waiting for Lance. And in this park, wasn't she able to sit like this even on the days when he could not come? After the hours here, she could smile, very quietly, as if it amused her, when Charles came in very drunk and cheerful late at night, having drunk up all his pay. Strangely, she did not even blame him, if she had spent the afternoon in the park. His job had ruined his nerves – the pushing crowds, the making change, stopping and starting, the schedules to be met, the dodging of darting pedestrians that made him start up in his sleep at night – so he drank to deaden his nerves. He drank to find the stillness that she found in the park. Once, months ago, before she had met Lance, she had brought Charles to the park and he had not liked it, because he could not sit still anymore anywhere. Now the park belonged to her and Lance. After the hours in the park, she could not blame Charles or herself for what had happened. They simply had stopped loving each other, first Charles, then herself. It might have been the lack of quiet that had exhausted them, from the very first when they lived in the ground-floor apartment on the East Side, that had left Charles not enough energy to love her any longer. If he could be bathed in stillness, drink it and hear it, see it and breathe it, sleep for hours in it, she could imagine his forehead smooth again, his eyes opening to look at her again as if he loved her. But she did not even want this now, it was too late. She had found Lance and she loved him. And Lance would love her no matter where he or she were, together or apart, in silence or noise, movement or stillness. Lance had something within him that Charles had not and never had. She knew now. She was not eighteen any longer, as she had been when she married Charles.

'Philip!'

Philip stood up and looked guiltily at his mother, who was waiting for him to say, 'Yes, Mama,' which he did, with the accent on the last syllable.

'Don't get mud on your playsuit, darling! Be careful, now.'

'Yes, Mama.' And he turned back and squatted down by his friend and finished pouring the Dixie cup of water from the fountain into the little pit they had dug in the smooth grass. Dickie had found the discarded cup at the end of the path, and Philip had automatically kept it out of sight when he spoke to his mother. They did not know what they were going to do with the little pit that kept drinking the water, but they were happy and they found something to say to each other every second, so that both talked at once almost all the time. Neither of them in his life had ever found anyone he liked so much as the other.

Mrs Robertson looked up immediately when the man came into the park, so few people ever came into the park. He was bareheaded, in a dark suit, and he stopped and stood for a moment on the cement walk, looking at the woman on the bench. Mrs Robertson's first reaction was the least sensation of alarm: there was something sinister in his intensity, in his half-smiling observation of the blonde woman, in his hands rammed into the pockets of his jacket almost as if he were cold – and as she recognized this single similarity between them, she recognized also that they knew each other, though neither made a sign of greeting. Now he walked with a kind of rigid caution in his shortened step toward the woman and sat down easily beside her, not taking his hands from his pockets or his eyes from her face. And the woman's expression of bemused content that Mrs

Robertson had remarked both yesterday and today did not alter
even in the least. The man's lips moved, the woman looked at him
and smiled, and Mrs Robertson again felt subtly disturbed by what
she beheld. It was vaguely disturbing that a man had come in and
sat down on a bench at all. That he was a stranger making advances
had flitted into her mind and out, because of the aura of intimacy
that wrapped them both. Both looked before them now, leaned very
slightly toward each other, though between them was one of the
iron arms that divided the bench into four or five seats, and then the
man reached over and took the young woman's hand gently from her
pocket, drawing it by the wrist beneath the iron bar until he held
it in his own hand, resting it on his crossed leg. And suddenly Mrs
Robertson knew: they were lovers. Of course! Why had it taken
her so long to guess? Now she began to watch fascinatedly, covertly.
For a few moments she was captured by the obvious and attractive
happiness in both of them, by the pride in the lift of their heads as
they gazed, he, too, now in the sightless, half-smiling way she had
seen first in the woman, straight ahead of them as if at something far
beyond the park's iron fence. They were certainly unlike husband
and wife, she thought, with a strange rise of excitement, yet neither did they behave quite as intensely as she thought lovers should
behave, though she reminded herself she had probably never seen
a pair of clandestine lovers, only read about them. And these were
certainly clandestine lovers. She saw it all: a husband (with dark hair)
who worked during the day and came home at six o'clock, all unsus-
pecting that his wife had spent the afternoon with another man.
Mrs Robertson felt a pang of compassion for the deceived husband.
Yes, the blonde woman was clearly rather cheap – her high-heeled
pumps, her hair lightened with peroxide probably. Would she take
the lover home with her? Mrs Robertson hoped she would not have
to witness that. And in the next moment, she admitted to herself she
would like to see just that, see them go away together. She turned a
page she hadn't read, conscious of the sound of her thin gold bracelet
touching her watch. She looked over her reading glasses again. The

man was talking, but so low she could hear not even a murmur. His head was back, resting on the back of the bench, and the woman watched his face, more alert now than Mrs Robertson had yet seen her, though still with her soft unconscious-looking smile. The man spread his fingers and took firmer grip on her hand, and Mrs Robertson felt a small wave of pleasure break over her. What did he talk to her about? she wondered. Or could she possibly be wrong about the whole thing? Was the woman not the child's mother, only a paid sitter, or a nursemaid? But both the woman and the child did not look well enough dressed for such a relationship to be likely. And as if to asseverate her opinion, the child suddenly came running across the path, she watched the woman gather him in her arms, take a handkerchief from her bag, and wipe his nose with a twist, and she caught a quality, in both of them, beyond a shadow of doubt now, that was like a statement that they were mother and child. The man had brought his other hand from his pocket with a handkerchief, too, and having put the handkerchief back, he held now, as if he had just discovered it, a small blue automobile on his palm. The woman said something, and the little boy threw his arms about the man's neck, kissed his cheek, and darted away, so quickly Mrs Robertson could hardly believe she had seen it. Yet she had seen it, of course, and there had been in that, too, an unmistakable look of its having been done before. She stared at the two unabashedly as they leaned forward together, smilingly watching the children.

Philip! He was playing with the automobile, too. The little boy was sharing it with him. Mrs Robertson stood up involuntarily, then sat down again. She did not like his playing with the toy, felt somehow that the automobile was not quite right, not quite clean, either, like the little boy. Again she looked at the two on the bench – she could look at them openly for all they appeared aware of her – and again they were leaning back comfortably, more comfortably than seemed possible on the hard bench, and their arms were interlocked, their hands clasped more closely under the iron bar between them. The man talked, and the woman now and again said something in response. It was unusual that he should be so fond of the child. Or was he only pretending? What were they talking about? How they must hate the bench arm between them! And she felt a taut, righteous satisfaction that the iron bar *was* between them. What would the park be like without the iron arms? Men sleeping along the benches. Couples . . .

'He's half you, isn't he?' Lance was saying.

'One day we'll have a child that's all us.'

Then they said nothing for a while. A bird sang a few annunciatory notes in a nearby tree – there were only three or four trees in the whole park – then swooped past so that both saw it. Not far away, on the river, a boat sounded its steam toot, not deep enough to be a big liner, not high enough to be a tug: a middle-sized vessel whose toot still said proudly, however, that it could go everywhere on earth and furthermore had been there.

'We'll make a lot of trips,' he remarked.

'I want to go to Scotland,' the girl said, even more quietly, but her tone was as if she had bought a ticket from someone.

'Scotland must be terrific. We'll definitely go to Scotland . . . the Hebrides.'

'Hebrides?'

'"As we in dreams behold the Hebrides."'

'What are they? Mountains?'

'Mountains and islands. Mountains.' He said the words so slowly, so roundly, it was as if he built the islands and the mountains right there.

'Don't say "dreams,"' the girl chided. 'Or is that another poem?'

'It's a poem. But poems are true.'

'Sometimes, I guess.'

He did not argue. They were silent a longer while.

'Then will you build me a house – after we've finished traveling?'

'I will build you not one house but three . . . four,' he said distinctly. 'One for every season of the year. A white house for spring, a red house for winter. For autumn, a brown house—'

'I don't like brown.'

'For autumn, a *tan* house.'

'Lance, are you watching the time?' she barely whispered, like an aside.

'Yes, I am watching the time. The clock in the steeple says five of four.'

The clock in the steeple of the little church was only half a block down the avenue, but she had told him she would never look at it while he was with her in the park. The clock in the steeple was always six minutes slow. At 4:09, therefore, he would have to leave in order to report back at his job in a big bookstore on Nassau Street, far downtown. Tomorrow he would not be able to come, nor the next day. He delivered only on Tuesdays and Fridays, an unpopular duty he had asked for so he might manage, perhaps, half an hour or forty-five minutes with her. It was the only time he could see her. As long as she was married to Charles, she would never let him see her in the evening. He put his other hand over hers and smiled at her with sudden tenderness. Somehow, in her mind, his meeting her in the park partook of the accidental, he knew. The one time he had seen her in the evening was the evening they had met, over by the park in Gramercy Square, a park they could not enter because it was locked. In the darkness he had seen her standing before the tall spears of the fence, and with a sense sharpened by his own solitude and loneliness, he had known that whoever and whatever she was, there was something of himself in her, so he had said good evening. They had both been to the same movie on Twenty-third Street that evening, each alone. The one evening they had seen each other, yet in his mind he liked to call himself her lover. What did she call him? She would not call him that, he thought. He lifted his head higher, lolled it back on the edge of the bench back, and one would have thought he had not a care in the world, that he would stay relaxed there the rest of the afternoon.

'This park is the still point of the turning world,' he said, and his low voice was steadied with reverence.

'I feel that, too. Yes. And the street where I live. And these days.'

'These days.' But suddenly he felt guilty for his idleness, even for these half hours with her, because there was so much he had to do. Not guilty so much because he spent the time with her, but that he allowed himself and her to dream so foolishly. Or were the dreams foolish? One could never really tell. He felt guilty because the little park was so good for dreaming, too good, he knew, too quiet and too like an imaginary heaven. And he began to examine caressingly, as he did every afternoon he sat here, the delicate convexity of the little lawns, the sharp delineation of the scalloped fences against their bright green fields. His eyes moved casually over Dickie and the other little boy playing with the new automobile. Dickie was always a part of the park, the cherub of its heaven. Today he looked happier than usual because he had the other little boy to play with. He looked at the woman over on the bench, who was again glancing at them, and he smiled a little at her, but she looked down at once at her knitting.

The knitting had got into a small snarl, and Mrs Robertson was plucking at it anxiously. There was a sensation of clash and disorder within her, as of a distant battle, for which she blamed the knitting. She was dimly aware of an impulse to take Philip and leave the park, correct the knitting at home, as well as a desire to remain because Philip was having such a good time and because the park – perhaps, she admitted, the sight of the two on the other bench – gave her a pleasure akin to an enchantment. The two forces were not at all clear in her mind, but the sense of struggle was as she plucked at the knitting, and while the crystals of herself suffered disorganization, she sat perfectly still except for her fingers, which worked skillfully to rescue the hitherto flawless mitten for Philip. And when the snarl was smoothed out and her course resumed, when the mysterious armies fell silent within her, the outcome of the struggle was veiled, too, leaving her only a subtle sense of irritation, of impatience and somehow of disappointment. *I shall not come here again*, she thought suddenly, and in that decision alone, which seemed to come out of nowhere, she felt substantiality. She would, however, stay just a few minutes more. There was nothing she need run from.

The sunlight stirred all at once like a living thing, climbed over the scalloped fence and fell lightly, soundlessly, half across the walk. Now it lay over the feet of Lance and the girl beside him. A long point of it strove diagonally across the path toward the woman on the bench. He saw her look at it even as he did, but she did not glance up again.

'The still point of the world,' the girl whispered.

'The turning world.' And again he felt the guilt: the world turned all around them, here on this green island of asylum, machines turned, clocks turned, but he and she were motionless and there was so much to be done and to be fought for.

'Yes, the turning world is nicer. I can feel it – but I can never say it like you. I felt it this afternoon, leaving the house—' But she would not be able to describe it, she knew. 'And now.'

'Only I didn't say it. That's Eliot. There's another part of it, " . . . at the still point, there the dance is."' He stopped, knowing suddenly that beside one's beloved is no fixity, though the stillness surpass all other stillnesses and all other kinds of peace, knowing suddenly as if it had been an eternal truth he had just stumbled over and discovered first, that beside one's beloved the beauty of a daydream is never thin, never motionless and flat like a picture as it is in solitude, because beside her there is movement forward and electrical energy in the air and a roundness, a wholeness to things real or imagined. He turned toward her, and he saw her glance prudently at the woman on the bench. But he had not intended to kiss her now.

Bells tinkled. Distant sheep bells on rolling green hills half hidden in mist, he thought: the Hebrides.

'There's the ice-cream man,' she said.

The ice-cream wagon came into the path at the downtown end of the park, pushed by a slender young man in white trousers, shirt, and cap.

'Mother,' Dickie said, climbing over the path fence, 'can I have some ice cream?'

Lance reached into his pocket.

Mrs Robertson watched the man give the coin to the little boy, who skipped with it to the ice-cream man. Philip stood where he was, watching, knowing he would not be allowed ice cream so soon before his suppertime.

'Can he have one, too?' The man had stood up and was smiling at her, reaching into his pocket again.

'Oh, thank you very much,' Mrs Robertson replied. 'It's a bit too near his suppertime.'

Her heart was beating faster, she noticed. It had excited her, in a way neither pleasant nor unpleasant, the exchange of conversation with him. His manner, even his face, she decided, were nicer than she had thought, than his unpressed suit had led her to believe. The dark-haired little boy clambered back over the fence in the act of taking his first bite of the ice-cream stick, then ran straight to Philip. She stood up, impelled to stop Philip before he could put the ice cream into his mouth.

'Philip, I don't think—'

She was too late. Philip had the whole top of the ice cream in his mouth, and the other little boy was holding it for him. She did not mean to snatch Philip away, but her tension made it a snatch, and the ice cream suddenly held by no one fell to the grass between the two children.

'Oh!' said Mrs Robertson, with genuine regret. 'I'm terribly sorry!'

After the first stunned moment, the dark-haired little boy stooped to pick it up. But the ice cream fell off the stick, hopelessly broken now, too far gone even for a three-year-old to rescue. Its chocolate crust cracked again even as he watched, as if it were determined to lose itself in the thick smooth grass. He stood up and looked at her, and wiped his hands shyly behind him.

'Where'd the ice-cream man go?' Mrs Robertson looked around for him, but he was out of sight. She heard his bell up the avenue.

'Lose your ice cream, Dickie?' called the man sympathetically.

'Oh, that's okay,' said the little boy, half to him, half to her. He was not angry, but he did not smile, either.

'It's my fault, I'm afraid,' Mrs Robertson said. Then, feeling suddenly ridiculous, she took Philip's arm in one hand and his tricycle handlebar in the other and urged them toward the scalloped fence.

'You have to go now, Philip?' asked the dark-haired little boy.

'Yes,' sighed Philip, with resignation. But at the fence he looked back sadly past the arm his mother lifted straight up, as if he had just realized he was actually going.

'See you tomorrow, Philip,' said the other little boy, a precocity of phrase that surprised Mrs Robertson.

He would not see him tomorrow. She did not want Philip to play with him again. She could not say why precisely, but she did not want it. She had been foolish not to take him away as soon as she realized what sort of person his mother was. There was something, somehow she knew it, impure about the little boy no matter how well he might be scrubbed, because his mother was impure. Yet she found herself going past the woman and the man on the bench, though it was the long way out of the park for her, found herself glancing once more at them, quite involuntarily and much to her own annoyance, a furtive sidewise glance that did not even feel like her own. But the man and the woman seemed lost in themselves again, holding hands. She was relieved they hadn't seen her. When she reached the end of the path, she knew she had left the man and the woman, the little boy and the park forever.

The blonde girl had seen the glance, seen in it for all its fleetness the ancient and imperishable look that one woman gives another she knows is well loved, a look made up of desire, admiration, wistfulness, of envy and vicarious pleasure, unveiled for an instant and then veiled again. Seeing it, she had pressed Lance's hand more tightly in quick reflexive pride. Had Lance seen it, too? But probably only a woman would have seen. She would have liked to tell him, but the words for it would be far more difficult to find even than the words about her inner peace as she came down the brownstone steps every afternoon, so instead she said:

'I don't think she likes me. She was here yesterday, too.'

Lance only smiled and tucked her arm closer. He had seven minutes more. He drew her arm close until he could feel it all along his side, not feeling any longer the iron arm cutting tense muscles through his jacket sleeve. 'Now there's no one,' he said.

There was no one. The long point of the wedge of sunlight had reached the bench the woman had been sitting on, had captured one of the curved metal legs. The bird dipped again, crossing their vision, asserting its absolute freedom and security within the tiny park. Now there was no human being along the avenue, not even a blind and impersonal truck hurrying past beyond the boundary of the low iron fence. Yes, there was a nun coming down the steps of the church half a block away, black-clad and in black bonnet, an erect and archaic figure, black skirts rippling with her pace like the carved robes of a ship's figurehead. They turned to each other and their lips met above their clasped hands and entwined arms, above the iron arm, and the kiss became the center of the stillness. The kiss became the narrowed center of the still point of the turning world, so that even the park was turning in comparison to the still peace at their lips.

Then, because there were only three minutes until he had to go, he began to talk casually, but seriously and quickly, of their plans, his work, their money, as if to fortify himself in these last moments before they parted for two days and nights. In three more months they would have enough money to open the next campaign in their struggle, her divorce. It was impossible to talk to her husband now about a divorce so long as she had to live with him. Only three more months. Twenty-four more meetings like this afternoon, he reckoned for the first time, and knew he could not prevent himself from counting them off from now on. Twenty-four . . .

Mrs Robertson did not go the next day to the little park down the avenue. She took Philip to a court in the center of Castle Terrace where there was a big sandbox and many small children for him to play with.

Philip stood where his mother had turned him loose and looked up at the building that rose like a great tan hollowed-out mountain around him, and asked, 'Aren't we going to the park later?'

'Aren't we going to the park later, Mama?' he asked again, when his mother had settled herself in a comfortable metal chair. 'I want to see Dickie.'

'No, darling, we're not going to the park today.' She tried to make her voice gentle and casual, too, and it was difficult. And perhaps she had failed, she thought as she watched Philip pedal off very slowly on his tricycle, with an air of seeing nothing around him.

There were many other young mothers in the play court, and Mrs Robertson was soon occupied in conversation. She felt right, here in the court of her own apartment building. Why had she tried to be different and find a nicer place? The park was pretty and Philip would miss it, of course, for a few days, but she did not regret her decision not to go back. Here there was sun, too, things for Philip to play on, and an abundance of children for him to make friends with, children she could be sure were clean and being well brought up. And other women, like herself, with whom she could exchange ideas.

'I want Dickie,' said Philip, coming up slowly on his tricycle. He had cruised the playground and found it unsatisfactory.

'Darling, there's some little boys over by the sandbox. Don't you want to go play with them?' She turned back to the women she had been talking with, lest she seem as concerned as she felt to Philip.

'I want Dickie!' said Philip two minutes later. Now he had got off his tricycle and stood away from it, as if he would never mount it again unless it was to go see his friend. He had tears in his eyes. He looked at his mother with resentment, and with determined, uncomprehending accusation.

This was the moment to be firm, Mrs Robertson knew, to ignore it or to say something that would satisfy or silence forever. She hesitated, at a loss.

'Who's Dickie?' asked one of the women.

'He's a little boy he met down the street,' Mrs Robertson answered.

As if piqued at their mention of his friend, Philip about-faced and wandered off with his head up, and thus his mother was spared making the answer she could not find.

Philip asked for Dickie the next afternoon, and the next and the next. But the fifth afternoon he did not ask.

WHEN THE FLEET
WAS IN AT MOBILE

With the bottle of chloroform in her hand, Geraldine stared at the man asleep on the back porch. She could hear the deep in, short out breaths whistling through the moustache, the way he breathed when he wasn't going to wake up till high noon. He'd been asleep since he came in at dawn, and she'd never known anything to wake him up in mid-morning when he'd been drinking all night, had she? Now was certainly the time.

She ran in her silk-stockinged feet to the rag drawer below the kitchen cabinets, tore a big rag from a worn-out towel, and then a smaller one. She folded the big rag to a square lump and on second thought wet it at the sink, and after some trouble because her hands had started shaking, tied it in front of her nose and mouth with the cloth belt of the dress she'd just ironed and laid out to wear. Then she got the claw hammer from the tool drawer in case she would need it, and went out on the back porch. She drew the straight chair close to the bed, sat down, and unstoppered the bottle and soaked the smaller rag. She held the rag over his chest for a few moments, then brought it slowly up toward his nose. Clark didn't move. But it must be doing something to him, she thought, she could smell it herself, sweet and sick like funeral flowers, like death itself.

Behind her, she heard the whine Red Dog always gave at the crest of a yawn, and his groan as he turned around and lay down in a cooler spot by the side of the house, and she thought: everybody thinks the chloroform is for Red Dog, and there he is out there sleeping, as alive as he's been in fourteen years.

Clark moved his head up and down as if he were agreeing with her, and her hand, her rigid body, followed his nose like a part of him, and a voice inside her screamed: *I wouldn't have dreamed of doing this if there were any other way, but he won't even let me out of the house!*

And she thought of Mrs Trelawney's nod of approval when she told her she was going to put Red Dog to sleep, because it wasn't safe for strangers to come around anymore, Red Dog nipping at them with his one eyetooth.

She peered at the pulse in Clark's temple. It beat at the bottom of a wriggly green vein along his hairline that had always reminded her of a map of the Mississippi River. Then the rag bumped the end of Clark's nose, he turned his head aside, and still her hand followed the nose as if she couldn't have dragged it away if she'd wanted to, and perhaps she couldn't have. But the black eyelashes did not move at all, and she remembered how distinguished she'd once thought Clark looked with the hollows either side of his high thin forehead and the black hair like a wild bush above it, and the black moustache so big it was old-fashioned but suited Clark, like his old-fashioned tailor-made jackets and his square-toed boots.

She looked at the gray alarm clock that had been watching it all from the shelf – for about seven minutes now. How long did it take? She opened the bottle and poured more until it fell cool onto her palm, and held it back under the nose. The pulse still beat, but the breaths were shorter and fainter. Her arm ached so, she looked off through the porch screen and tried to think of something else. A rooster crowed out by the cow barn, like a new day a-dawning, she thought remembering a song; and she counted twenty ticks on the clock, one for each year old she was, and looked at it, and it was twelve minutes now, and when she looked again, the pulse was gone. But she mustn't be fooled by that, she thought, and looked harder at the hairs in his nostrils that didn't move and maybe wouldn't have anyway, but she couldn't hear anything. Then she stood up, and on second thought set the rag on the black moustache and left it there. She stared at the arm lying out on the sheet and the hand, a well-shaped hand, she'd always thought, for all its hairiness, with the gold band on the little finger that was his mother's wedding ring, he said, but the very left hand that had hit her many a time nevertheless, and she'd probably felt the ring, too. She stood there several seconds, not knowing why, then she hurried into the kitchen and whipped off her apron and her housedress.

She put on the flowery-printed summer dress she deliberately hadn't worn much with Clark, because it reminded her of the happiest days at Mobile, tossed the ruffled short sleeves into place with a familiar almost forgotten shake of her shoulders that made her feel practically her old self again, and with the dress still unfastened, ran on tiptoe out on the porch and saw the rag was still lying on his mouth. For good measure, she poured the rest of the bottle on the rag. And didn't the claw hammer look silly now? She took the hammer back to the drawer.

When she was all dressed except for make-up, she took the towel from her face, and propped the window of her room as wide as it would go. She stepped back from the dresser mirror, appraising herself anxiously, then stepped forward and put wide arcs of red on the bows of her upper lip, the way she liked it, dropped a cloud of powder on her nose and spread it quickly in all directions. Her cheeks were so curved now, she'd hardly have known herself, she thought, but she wasn't too plump, just right. She still had that combination everyone said was unique of come-hither plus the bloom of youth, and how many girls had that? How many girls could be proposed to by a minister's son, which is what had happened to her in Montgomery, and then have a life like she'd had in Mobile, the toast of the fleet? She laughed archly at herself in the mirror, though without making a sound – but who was there to hear her if she did laugh – and jogged her brown-blonde curls superfluously with her palms. She'd curled her hair with the iron this morning after Clark got in, and done as good a job as she'd ever done in her life, though all the while she'd known what she was going to do to Clark. And had she packed the curling iron?

She dragged her old black suitcase from behind the curtain under the sink, and found the curling iron right on top. She went back into the bedroom for her handbag. Her cigarettes. She ran to get the package of Lucky Strikes from beside the soap dish in the kitchen, and for a moment her spaced front teeth bit her underlip, the penciled eyebrows lifted with a deploring quiver, as she gazed for the last time at the red rickrack she'd tacked around the shelf to beautify it, which had been completely lost on Clark, then she turned and went across the back porch and out.

Red Dog whined at her, and she dropped the suitcase and ran back into the house with his empty pan, got a hunk of stale cornbread from the breadbox and crumbled it, scraped skillet grease over it and with reckless extravagance the rest of the beef stew, too. Wouldn't Red Dog be surprised at such food at eleven in the morning? Red Dog was so surprised, he got onto his legs for it, wagging his old red tail that was as thin and full of jagged points as a rooster feather.

Hopping and dodging the puddles of red water, she ran daintily in her high-heeled gray lizard pumps down the rut of a road across the west meadow. She felt happy as a lark this morning in her best shoes that weren't at all practical for travelling, she supposed, with their open toes and heels, but gave her such a lift! At the edge of the thicket, she turned and looked back at the farm. It wasn't the time of day she liked best. She liked just before sunset and just after sunrise, when the sun caught the tops of things and the level country was dotted with little bright green islands and the grazing cows had streaks of red along their straight backs. Red and green like a Christmas tree, she'd said fourteen months ago when she'd come here to live with Clark, the land always so cool and fresh as if a light shower had just stopped falling and the sun had come out. It'll be Christmas from now on, Clark, she had said, feeling like the end of a movie, and the teeth bit ruefully for another delicious moment of self-pity. Good-bye to the long brown house, the cow barn and the henhouse and the little privy!

The northbound bus wouldn't pass for nearly an hour, she knew, so she went on across the highway and into the other woods where there was a brook, and sat down and washed the red mud off her heels with a piece of Kleenex. The smoke from her cigarette was exactly the color of the Spanish moss. It drifted upward as slow and unbroken as if she sat in a nice room somewhere talking. She sprang to her feet at the sound of a motor, but it was only a big gasoline truck coming up from New Orleans, and then she did hear the bus purring around the curve and she should have known the gasoline truck wasn't it, because her heart jumped now as if all the happiness in the world lay in the bus, and she was out in the road waving her arm before she knew it. The many, many times she'd watched the bus go by without being able to catch it!

And now she was climbing aboard, the floor rattling and swaying under her feet, northward.

'Where're you going, ma'am?' the driver asked.

She almost said Mobile, but she laughed and said, 'Birmingham,' instead, which was where her sister lived. 'But I'd like to go to Alistaire first.' Alistaire was just a little town in northern Louisiana where she'd stayed overnight once with her parents when she was a child, and she'd planned on stopping there for a couple of hours on her way to Birmingham. She paid with the 10-dollar bill she'd taken from Clark's pocket that morning. Besides that, she had nine dollars saved out of grocery money when Clark had used to let her go with the Trelawneys to Etienne Station.

The bus was so crowded, there were three or four people standing, but when she walked up the aisle, a young man in blue overalls got right up and gave her his seat. 'Thank you, sir,' she said.

'You're welcome, ma'am,' the young man said, and stood in the aisle beside her.

The woman next to her had a little boy asleep in her lap. His head pressed roundly against Geraldine's thigh. In a moment, she thought, she would ask the woman a question about her child, she didn't know what as yet. Loosening the imitation sable furpiece around her neck — she'd just realized from the dark blue splotch under the arm of the young man that it was really quite hot today — Geraldine settled back to enjoy the ride. She smiled up at the young man and he smiled back, and she thought: how nice everybody is on the bus and they know by looking at her she's just as nice as they are. And what a relief it was, too, not to have Clark along, accusing her of wanting to sleep with the young man in blue overalls, just because she'd accepted his seat! She shook her head deploringly, felt a curl come undone over her ear, and casually tucked it back. And accusing her of flirting with Mr Trelawney, when everybody knew Mrs Trelawney was her best friend and always was along when they drove to town, which was the only time she ever saw him.

'Women that sleep with ten men at a time never get pregnant!' Clark's voice boomed out from the privy before he banged the door to, and fidgeting, Geraldine leaned toward the woman beside her and asked, 'Do you have many children?' and the woman gave her such a long, funny stare that Geraldine almost laughed out loud despite herself before the woman answered:

'Four. That's enough.'

Geraldine nodded, and glanced up at the young man standing beside her who shifted and smiled down at her, showing pink gums and big white teeth with one upper molar missing. Young and shy and lonely, Geraldine thought, almost as fine as the young sailors in Mobile, only not so handsome as most, but she edged away from him nevertheless, because the blue overalls seemed to be rubbing against her shoulder in a way she didn't like, or was she getting just as prudish as Clark? Oh yes, if they asked her any questions, she'd tell them what a prudish old maid Clark really was, not even fulfilling his marital duties, not that she cared, but she'd heard of a lot of women suing for divorce just for that. Then accusing *her* of not being able to have children! Everyone in Etienne Parish knew Clark was strange. He'd served a jail sentence for swindling a business partner when he was young, and not so long ago people couldn't remember had been clapped in jail for preaching religion, but preaching like a maniac and nearly killing a man who had disagreed with him. Geraldine crossed her legs and pulled her skirt down.

The bus made her feel safe and powerful, as if she were in the center of a mountain, or awake in the center of a rather heavy, pleasant dream that would just keep on and on. She might stay on until her money gave out, then stop off and take a job somewhere. She'd go back to her own name, Geraldine Ann Lewis, plain and simple, and rent a little furnished apartment and potter around every evening cooking things, going to a movie maybe once a week and to church Sunday mornings, and be very cautious about making friends, especially men friends.

The little boy's head pressed harder against her thigh, the bus turned, and she saw they were approaching a town. She didn't know it, she thought excitedly, but she did. It was Dalton.

And if anyone cared to question her as to why she had done what she did, she thought as she made her way down the aisle, taking her suitcase with her, she would tell them the whole story, how Clark had told her he loved her and asked her to marry him and live with him in his house near Etienne Station, north of New Orleans, and how she had cooked and cleaned and been the best wife she knew, and how as the months went on she saw that Clark really hated her and had only married her to be able to pick on her and – she saw it clearly now – had deliberately chosen a wife from a place like the Star Hotel so he could hold it over her and make himself feel superior. She poked her straws through the hole in the top of the milk container.

'Hey, cain't you say *nothin'*, girl?' It was the young man in the blue overalls grinning down at her, the sudden burr of his voice making her think first of a man who'd bent down to say something to her in a wheatfield once where she'd come with her father to watch the threshing, then of the sailors' voices in Mobile, and fear dropped like a needle through her before she could even wonder why she'd thought of that wheatfield she hadn't thought of since, and she turned away, leaving the 15 cents on the counter, not knowing if it was his or hers, replying, strangely breathless:

'I just can't talk just now!'

She'd been riding several minutes on the bus before she noticed the young man wasn't aboard. If he got himself a girl in Dalton, she hoped she'd be a nice girl. But maybe he was just going home to his folks, why should she even think he was going to a girl? She'd stop thinking things like that once she got far enough away from Clark. Clark wouldn't even let her ride to Etienne Station with the Trelawneys any more. She could let them know about the last time she'd gone with the Trelawneys, when Clark had been off somewhere for two days and there'd been no food in the house. He'd knocked the groceries out of her arms and slapped her face, back and forth, not saying a word, until she just collapsed on the groceries, crying as if her heart would break. And the scar from the belt buckle, she could show them that.

Without looking at it, she massaged the U-shaped scar on the back of her hand. Since she had got on the bus, her hands had never been still, the long backward-bending fingers clamping the soft palms symmetrically against the corners of her handbag, only to fly off to some other perch, as if she kept trying to pose them properly for a photograph. Her lizard pumps stood upright, side by side on the vibrating floor.

Alistaire was the next rest-stop. She didn't remember too much about the town except the name, or perhaps the town had changed a good deal in ten years, but the name was enough, and the fact she'd spent one of those happy, carefree nights in a tourist home with her family on one of their summer vacations. The sun was already down, so she decided to stay the night and get an early start tomorrow, as her father had used to say on their tours in the car. 'Where you reckon we'll sleep *tonight*, papa?' she or her sister Gladys would ask him from the back seat, where the khaki blankets and the picnic lunch and probably a watermelon would be tied up and stowed away in such apple-pie order it was a pleasure just to crawl in the little space beside her sister. Her father'd say, 'Lord knows, sugar,' or maybe, 'Guess we'll make Aunt Doris' by tonight, Gerrie. Remember your Aunt Doris?' which was almost as exciting as a new tourist home, because like as not, she'd have forgotten her aunt's house since the year before. Wouldn't she like to forget Clark's house in a year's time, too, but the memory didn't work like that once you were grown, she knew. She remembered the Star Hotel only too well after fourteen months, every six-sided tile in the brown-and-white floor of the lobby that always smelled of disinfectant like a clinic; and the view from her room window of the lighted glass star that hung over the entrance.

Not far from the bus stop, she found a house with a roomers sign on the front lawn, and though the woman seemed a little suspicious at first because she didn't have a car and then because she didn't have a man with her – but what could be suspicious about not having a man? – she was soon in a clean, very tastefully furnished front room all to herself. Geraldine bathed in the bathroom down the hall, lifting the washrag so the water ran caressingly down her arms and legs, thinking – 'How long it's been since you've been my very own!'

She put on her nightgown and went right to bed, because she wanted to lie in the dark and think. No one would likely find Clark for three days, she thought. His cheeses were due at Etienne Station tomorrow, but they were used to his being a day late when he was on a bender. And since this was Thursday, the Trelawneys weren't likely to stop by until Saturday when they went to town, if then.

'I married you to help you, but the truth's not in you. You are the first entirely evil human soul I ever saw and it's my everlasting curse that I'm married to you!'

She spread her legs restlessly under the sheet, and brought them together again like scissors. The crisp new sheet rattled about her with a sound like thunder. She pressed her fingertips harder into her thighs. Her mother in Montgomery would say, 'Well, you did finally fill out, didn't you, child?' Geraldine turned on her side and let a few tears roll out, over the bridge of her nose and into the pillowcase, because her mother had been dead almost a year now. The wind gave a sigh that blew the bottoms of the curtains out, held them reaching toward her for a moment, then twirled them like two capes. And she let a few more tears roll, thinking of her and Marianne's apartment in Mobile and of how young and happy they'd been together when the fleet was first in. Oh, she'd tell them all about Mobile, too, if they wanted to ask her, she hadn't a thing to be ashamed of. It was the country's lawmakers themselves and the police who made money out of it who ought to be ashamed.

She wouldn't tell them about Doug, though, because it hadn't been his fault. She'd say she came to the Star Hotel accidentally when she hadn't any other place to stay, which was true. She could see herself telling it to some solemn judge with gray hair, asking him to judge for himself what on earth else she could have done – right up to the moment she lay here now in a strange tourist home – and she could hear him assuring her she couldn't have done otherwise. She'd come to Mobile with her friend Marianne Hughes, from Montgomery, to take factory jobs after they'd finished high school, but they'd had to take jobs as waitresses until the factory jobs were open. She and Marianne had had a little apartment together, and she'd been able to send fifteen dollars a week home to her mother, and they hadn't been there any time before the fleet came in. Not even the fleet, just a couple of cruisers and a destroyer stopping for repairs, but the city was suddenly full of sailors and officers, every-thing going full tilt day and night, and Marianne used to wake her up every morning at a quarter to six yelling, *'Out of bed, honey child, the fleet's in at Mobile!'* which might sound silly now she was grown, but at eighteen and free as the wind, it had made her jump out of bed feeling like a million dollars, laughing and tingling with energy, no matter how tired she might be really.

She and Marianne would throw on their waitress uniforms and hurry down to the restaurant without even coffee, through the streets that would be even then full of sailors, some up early and some still out and maybe drunk, but by and large, she'd still say they were the finest, cleanest young men she'd ever met. There were always sailors in the restaurant for breakfast, and she and Marianne would tell them they were going to work in the marine supplies factory in five weeks, and the sailors would probably ask them for dates, and if they were especially nice looking, she and Marianne would accept.

Then Marianne married a chief petty officer, and she'd had to give up the apartment. She'd known Douglas Ellison, a pharmacist's mate from Connecticut, for about three weeks then, and they intended to marry, too, when they were absolutely sure they loved each other. She hadn't yet found an apartment, so Doug had got her a room at the Star Hotel and paid a week's rent for it. And he stayed with her a couple of nights – the first fellow she'd ever had anything to do with, despite what most girls in Mobile were doing, Marianne included. His ship had been leaving at the end of the week, but he was due back in a month, and then they were going to be married.

That was also the month the job was to have been open at the factory, but wasn't. And then – it never rains but it pours – she lost her job at the restaurant, because the girl who'd had it before came back, or so they said, from the marine supplies factory that was laying off instead of hiring. And suddenly there were so many people unemployed, one couldn't even get a job washing dishes in exchange for three meals.

She'd been ready to go back to Montgomery, when the Star Hotel told her they couldn't get her trunk out of the basement for several more days, and upped the bill twice what it should have been so she wouldn't be able to pay it, and when she threatened to call the police, told her if she did, they'd have her in jail. She'd gone out to tell the police anyway, and the doorman had stopped her. Didn't she know the Star Hotel was a house, he said. Oh, she'd known a lot was going on at the Star Hotel, what else could you expect with the fleet in and right on the waterfront, but she hadn't known it was a common brothel. And suddenly there were strangers standing all around her, pretending to take it for granted she was one of those women, too, laughing at her when she said Doug Ellison was her fiancé. They dared her to talk to a policeman, the police would have her in for ten years, they said, and she got terrified. Some of the other girls there said they'd been in the same boat, but didn't mind now, because what work was there to be found outside anyway, and it was easier than a lot of work, whereupon she lost the bit of dinner she'd just eaten. She couldn't eat and barely slept, and they started sending sailors into her room as if she'd have anything to do with them after Doug Ellison. But no letter ever came from Doug, she knew because Connie, one of the girls there, promised she would see she got it, if it came. They watched the girls' mail, especially the outgoing, and she had to keep writing to her mother that she was still working at Carter's Restaurant and very happy, hoping her mother would read between the lines, but her mother's cancer was getting worse then, and she never did. The sailors that came into the Star Hotel, even if they were fairly decent looking, made her sick that she'd ever felt gay hearing Marianne yell in the mornings, and sicker that she'd ever thought she'd tell her grandchildren of the most exciting period in her life, stories that began, 'When the fleet was in at Mobile, I was just eighteen . . . '

And if anyone chose to cast the first stone at her because she finally yielded, she would relate how they stopped putting enough food on her trays, and how all the girls, even Connie Stegman, advised her to co-operate and lay a little money by, because they didn't give a snap for her life itself. But when they found she was hoarding her money, they came and found it and took it, for the truth was they didn't trust their own doorman when it came to taking bribes. She threatened to kill herself, and she meant it, so they sent her to Chattanooga with two other girls in a car, to a hotel owned by a partner of the Star Hotel manager. If anybody didn't believe her, let them go to Chattanooga and see the Blackstone Hotel standing there for themselves. Let them go inside and look around. She got so run down at the Blackstone, they sent her back to the Star Hotel. It worked this way: there was a whole syndicate all over the South, and wherever business was heavy, they shipped girls, or if they thought a girl was about to make a break, they shipped her where she didn't know anyone.

Geraldine sat up at the knock on the door.

'Got everything you need?' called the frail, high voice of the landlady.

'Yes—' She swallowed air, and her heart beat wildly. 'Thank you.'

'There's ice water in the pitcher on the dresser. Hope you weren't asleep, didn't see no light.'

'No, I wasn't asleep,' said Geraldine, beginning to smile.

'Awful early,' said the woman pleasantly, sounding as if she were turning away.

'Yes, it is.' Geraldine wished she could think of something nicer to say. 'Good night,' she called, and lay down on her back, still smiling.

And then Clark. She'd tell them about those first four visits of Clark's to the Star Hotel and every word he said, and just let them judge for themselves. She could still see him exactly as he looked when he stepped into her room for the first time, a really impressive man with his straight back and heavy black brows and moustache. He'd had on his square-toed boots with his trouser cuffs tucked into them and his long, nearly black jacket, and she'd thought right away he looked like some kind of a statesman or maybe an actor around the time of the Civil War. He was still and formal and hardly said a word or even looked at her until just as he went out the door, and she remembered that look like no other, because it had scared her. If she had only obeyed her instinct then! He had turned with his hand on the knob of the open door and looked back at her over his shoulder, as if he might have forgotten something or as if he wanted to remember her because he hated her. She hadn't liked him at all, and when he came in a few days later, she'd been about to tell him to leave, when he just sat down and lighted a cigar and started talking. He wanted to know all about her, how old she was and how she happened to be there, and though his brown eyes were really quite kind, almost fatherly if it wasn't sacrilegious to say such a thing, she'd resented his idle curiosity and not answered much.

Then the third time, he had brought her candy, and the fourth time flowers, presenting them with a bow, and the fourth time she'd told him the whole story and cried on his shoulder when he sat down beside her, because she'd never told anyone, not even Connie Stegman, that much. 'What would you say if I asked you to be my wife?' he'd asked right out of the blue. 'You think it over till I come back. I'll be back in a week.' She hadn't believed him, but naturally she'd thought about it, about the farm he'd described in the flat country north of New Orleans, and the fancy cheeses he made for a living and the duck-callers he made out of wood and shipped to hunters everywhere – little wooden boxes with a cover that scraped and made a sound like a duck, he'd brought her one to show her – and she'd thought what a special kind of farmer he was, not just a dirt farmer but an educated gentleman. And the girls at the hotel told her how lucky she was, for Clark Reeder was a fine man even if he was over forty and a little old-fashioned, and Margaret the hotel director had told her how many girls had found themselves good husbands that way and how often the husbands came back and said what fine wives the girls made. So she'd thought about being mistress of a farmhouse that she would make neat as a pin and stock with good things to eat, but mainly of course she'd thought of being free and the next time he'd come, she'd said yes. And like a bird out of a cage, she'd almost died of happiness at first, not even wanting the honeymoon Clark had suggested, just wanting to get settled at home. She'd cooked and sewed and scrubbed every inch of the place and been delighted to do it. But why even tell them all that if they couldn't imagine it? Or how good it felt just to be treated like a human being again, the way Clark had said, 'Herbert,' speaking to Mr Trelawney, 'I'd like you to meet my wife,' presenting her on his hand as if she were a queen.

She was pumping water by the back steps and the pump was acting queer, making a boom-crash-boom whenever the water gushed out, spilling all over the bucket but not filling it, and even Red Dog was up looking at it. Then she opened her eyes and discovered the sound came from out the window – a military band! Either a parade or a circus, she thought, jumping out of bed as gaily as when Marianne used to awaken her. The music was coming from a park a couple of blocks down the street where she saw a lot of colored lights like a celebration. She whirled around and pulled her nightgown over her head.

Clark!

He'd still be lying on the back porch with the rag on his moustache, if the breeze hadn't blown it off. She shimmied into her girdle. Well, so be it. Some actions were a necessity, like killing animals for food, or sawing through the bars of a prison to get free. And Clark's house had been a prison as bad as the Star Hotel, except he never touched her, saying she was too dirty for him. Clark set himself up as her savior while telling her all the time she tortured him. Did it make any sense to torture her and torture himself, too? She made the two red arcs on her upper lip that Clark said made her look like a harlot but were simply better for her kind of mouth, and combed what was left of the curls into a loose short bob. She snatched up her handbag and went out into the hall, but on second thought came back and left her money, except for one dollar, in the pocket of her coat in the closet.

From the sidewalk she could see a striped tent top and something like a ferris wheel lighted up and spinning, and could hear a man yelling over a loud-speaker, and between the *boom-crash-booms* that were louder than anything, the band played a song she was pleased she could recognize as 'The Stars and Stripes For Ever.' She looked down and concentrated on getting across the dark road in her wobbly high heels. Her heart was going like sixty and she really must stop and get her breath before she went one step farther. And it was only a church benefit at that, she saw by the streamer over the entrance. FIRST METHODIST ANNUAL WELFARE NIGHT.

'*Admission only twenty-five cents!*' roared the voice on one note. '*And dig down in your pocket for a second quarter if you're really thinking of entering the Kingdom of Heaven!*'

Geraldine pushed her money through the high window. 'I'll pay my two quarters.'

'*One?*' a voice roared.

'One.'

The music stopped as soon as she went in, and there wasn't any band, she saw, it was all from the merry-go-round that had a drum and cymbal machine in the center that kept going. A final *boom-crash* shimmered into silence, and Geraldine stood staring at the still bounding horses on the platform that made a hollow sound like roller skates on a wooden rink and for some reason excited her terribly. The roof of the merry-go-round was like a king's crown with gilt scallops hanging around the edge, each set with a blue or red light like a jewel. Suddenly something made her gasp, something blurred her vision with tears: she had been on this very spot before, been on this merry-go-round as a child, the time she'd passed through this town with her family. They might have stopped at the same tourist home for that matter. There was the Ferris wheel way back under the trees and the parking lot with the curb around it where her father's big car had stood, and the separate booth that sold pink cotton candy, and the big ice-cream parlor with an open porch all around it like a summerhouse – all just as it had been one night so long ago she didn't really remember. And laughing at herself, she hurried to buy her merry-go-round ticket.

The glare of white lights made her feel positively naked as she stepped onto the platform, but there were so many other grown-up people getting on – maybe some like her, coming back after many years — she forgot her self-consciousness and weaved right through the maze of nickel-plated poles to the pink horse she wanted. The *boom-crash-boom* started with a terrible din right in her ears, then music so loud she couldn't recognize it and had to laugh, and the pink horse rose slowly up and down. She felt herself sink again, and closed her eyes, letting it catch her up in swifter and swifter rhythm, pulling her outward so she had to hold on with both hands. She felt so happy, she could have cried. What was it, she wondered, with the music pounding in your ears and your two hands holding the pole and the small rise, small fall, so wonderful beyond all . . . Her throat closed, and she opened her eyes, seeing a blur of black trees and sliding dots of lights and a few figures standing at the edge of darkness smiling up. Where were her parents? She wanted to wave to them. Then her shoulders crumpled as if she had been struck and the tears fairly leapt from her eyes, because she knew it was only to be a child, with her parents waving and shouting to her to hold on, only to be astride the horse in a short dress and to be put to bed in less than an hour and to be too small to reach the bottom of the bed with her toes, and to get up tomorrow to ride in the back of the car, asking, 'Where you reckon we'll sleep *tonight*, papa?' that was so wonderful, and it was all, all gone now forever. She felt her face twist with a tragedy too profound for tears, and deliberately she looked away from the people standing watching to the merry-go-round's center where the scenic pictures showed 'A Swiss Chalet,' 'Pike's Peak,' 'Venice,' thinking quickly how she would tell them, if they asked her anything, how Clark had accused her of ever more disgusting practices, the worst he could think of, and how he brought men into the house on pretexts, just so he could accuse her of something later.

'Are you all right?' the man on the horse next to her asked, and realizing she'd been staring in his direction with what was probably a pretty funny expression, Geraldine said with a quick smile:

'Oh, perfectly all right, thank you.'

She put her head up then, her eyes darting to look at this and that as if she'd never been so gay in her life. A young man in a gray suit was waving at her from the other side of the merry-go-round, and she almost waved back, thinking she must know him, but she didn't. Or maybe he wasn't even waving at her, but she saw now he was, and she did know him, too. He was a boy she'd known in high school in Montgomery! His name was Franky McSomething, she remembered.

Now he waved at her again, and she gave a little wave back, timid as if she were merely brushing something out of the air in front of her, and when he smiled wider, she saw the two creases down his lean cheeks and the bright brown eyes not slipping away shyly as they used to do, but looking right back at her. Hadn't Franky grown up! He clearly wanted to talk to her, and maybe they'd have a soda in the ice-cream parlor and get re-acquainted and maybe like a fairy tale Franky would fall in love with her again. He'd had a crush on her one term, but he'd been such a bashful, watching-from-a-distance sort of boy, nothing had happened. Well, she knew how to put men at their ease now.

She watched Franky dismount as the horses slowed, and noticed how tall he'd grown and how clean-cut he looked with his collar and tie. She slipped down from her own horse. The platform was making the hollow sound of the roller-skating rink, but slower and slower, and there was a strange moment when she felt suddenly as sad and melancholy as autumn, really as sad as she'd ever felt in her life, so she had to force herself to smile as she stepped down to meet Franky who was holding his hand out for hers.

'Is your name Ger – Geraldine?' he asked, making her laugh, because he was still as bashful as ever, after all.

'Yes, and you're – Franky?'

He nodded with a smile and led her gently away. 'Yes.'

'Well, how are things back in Montgomery?' she asked.

'Oh, they're all right. What've you been doing?'

'Well, I had a job in Mobile for a while. I was in Mobile the time the fleet was in, we always said, but it wasn't the fleet, just a couple of cruisers and a destroyer stopping for repairs, but it was mighty gay!' She tipped her head back and swung her hand that Franky was holding. Franky had a little scar now on the bridge of his nose, and she thought of the scar on the back of her hand and decided not to ask him about his. Life had left its marks on both of them, she supposed, though they were still so young.

'Cigarette?'

'Still as shy as ever, Franky?' she blurted, because she thought his hand shook as he lighted it for her, though her hand was shaking, too.

Franky smiled. 'How about a cold drink, Geraldine?'

'Why, I'd love one!'

They stepped up on the open porch of the ice-cream parlor and sat down at one of the tables. Franky stared shyly past her, and she thought he nodded to someone and looked behind her, but it was only the waiter coming. They ordered black and white sodas.

'Are you living here now?' Franky asked her.

'No-o, just passing through. But I like it so here,' she hurried to add, 'I just might live here. Do you know I realized after I'd come here tonight that I'd been to this park before when I was a little girl? Oh, long before I even knew you!' She laughed. 'Are you living here now?'

'Um-hm,' he replied, still looking so pained and stiff that Geraldine had to smile.

She said nothing, letting her eyes roll up at the honeysuckle that grew along the porch eaves.

'You were in—'

'What?' Geraldine prompted.

'You were in a little town above New Orleans, weren't you, Geraldine?'

He'd even taken the trouble to ask her mother about her! 'Why, yes,' she said. She glanced up at a man in a dark suit standing by her elbow. There was another man on her right, between her and the porch rail. She looked at Franky with a bewildered smile.

Franky said, 'These are my friends, Geraldine. You'll come with us, won't you?' He stood up.

'But I didn't finish my—' The man on her left took her arm. She looked at Franky and saw his mouth close in a straight line she didn't know at all. The other man took her other arm. Franky wasn't making a move to help her, wasn't even looking! 'You're not – you're not Franky!'

Franky pulled something from his inside coat pocket and held it toward her.

LOUISIANA STATE POLICE, Geraldine read on a card in the billfold. She wanted to scream, but her mouth only hung open, limp.

The man who looked like Franky stood there staring at her, pocketing his billfold. 'It's all right,' he said so softly she could hardly hear. 'Your husband isn't dead. He just asked us to find you.'

Then her scream came as if it had been waiting just for that. She heard it reach the farthest corners of the park, and though they yanked her with them around the table, she took another breath and let it go again, let it shatter all the leaves and shatter her body, while she stared at the man in the gray suit simply because he wasn't Franky. Then his face and the lights and the park went out, though she knew as well as she knew she still screamed that her eyes were open under her hands.

THE SNAIL-WATCHER

W hen Mr Peter Knoppert began to make a hobby of snail-watching, he had no idea that his handful of specimens would become hundreds in no time. Only two months after the original snails were carried up to the Knoppert study, some thirty glass tanks and bowls, all teeming with snails, lined the walls, rested on the desk and windowsills, and were beginning even to cover the floor. Mrs Knoppert disapproved strongly, and would no longer enter the room. It smelled, she said, and besides she had once stepped on a snail by accident, a horrible sensation she would never forget. But the more his wife and friends deplored his unusual and vaguely repellent pastime, the more pleasure Mr Knoppert seemed to find in it.

'I never cared for nature before in my life,' Mr Knoppert often remarked – he was a partner in a brokerage firm, a man who had devoted all his life to the science of finance – 'but snails have opened my eyes to the beauty of the animal world.'

If his friends commented that snails were not really animals, and their slimy habitats hardly the best example of the beauty of nature, Mr Knoppert would tell them with a superior smile that they simply didn't know all that he knew about snails.

And it was true. Mr Knoppert had witnessed an exhibition

that was not described, certainly not adequately described, in any encyclopedia or zoology book that he had been able to find. Mr Knoppert had wandered into the kitchen one evening for a bite of something before dinner, and had happened to notice that a couple of snails in the china bowl on the draining board were behaving very oddly. Standing more or less on their tails, they were weaving before each other for all the world like a pair of snakes hypnotized by a flute player. A moment later, their faces came together in a kiss of voluptuous intensity. Mr Knoppert bent closer and studied them from all angles. Something else was happening: a protuberance like an ear was appearing on the right side of the head of both snails. His instinct told him that he was watching a sexual activity of some sort.

The cook came in and said something to him, but Mr Knoppert silenced her with an impatient wave of his hand. He couldn't take his eyes from the enchanted little creatures in the bowl.

When the ear-like excrescences were precisely together rim to rim, a whitish rod like another small tentacle shot out from one ear and arched over toward the ear of the other snail. Mr Knoppert's first surmise was dashed when a tentacle sallied from the other snail, too. Most peculiar, he thought. The two tentacles withdrew, then came forth again, and as if they had found some invisible mark, remained fixed in either snail. Mr Knoppert peered intently closer. So did the cook.

'Did you ever see anything like this?' Mr Knoppert asked.

'No. They must be fighting,' the cook said indifferently and went away. That was a sample of the ignorance on the subject of snails that he was later to discover everywhere.

Mr Knoppert continued to observe the pair of snails off and on for more than an hour, until first the ears, then the rods, withdrew, and the snails themselves relaxed their attitudes and paid no further attention to each other. But by that time, a different pair of snails had begun a flirtation, and were slowly rearing themselves to get into a position for kissing. Mr Knoppert told the cook that the snails were not to be served that evening. He took the bowl of them up to his study. And snails were never again served in the Knoppert household.

That night, he searched his encyclopedias and a few general science books he happened to possess, but there was absolutely nothing on snails' breeding habits, though the oyster's dull reproductive cycle was described in detail. Perhaps it hadn't been a mating he had seen after all, Mr Knoppert decided after a day or two. His wife Edna told him either to eat the snails or get rid of them – it was at this time that she stepped upon a snail that had crawled out on to the floor – and Mr Knoppert might have, if he hadn't come across a sentence in Darwin's *Origin of Species* on a page given to gastropoda. The sentence was in French, a language Mr Knoppert did not know, but the word *sensualité* made him tense like a bloodhound that has suddenly found the scent. He was in the public library at the time, and laboriously he translated the sentence with the aid of a French-English dictionary. It was a statement of less than a hundred words, saying that snails manifested a sensuality in their mating that was not to be found elsewhere in the animal kingdom. That was all. It was from the notebooks of Henri Fabre. Obviously Darwin had decided not to translate it for the average reader, but to leave it in its original language for the scholarly few who really cared. Mr Knoppert considered himself one of the scholarly few now, and his round, pink face beamed with self-esteem.

He had learned that his snails were the freshwater type that laid their eggs in sand or earth, so he put moist earth and a little saucer of water into a big wash-bowl and transferred his snails into it. Then he waited for something to happen. Not even another mating happened. He picked up the snails one by one and looked at them, without seeing anything suggestive of pregnancy. But one snail he couldn't pick up. The shell might have been glued to the earth. Mr Knoppert suspected the snail had buried its head in the ground to die. Two more days went by, and on the morning of the third, Mr Knoppert found a spot of crumbly earth where the snail had been. Curious, he investigated the crumbles with a match stem, and to his delight discovered a pit full of shiny new eggs. Snail eggs! He hadn't been wrong. Mr Knoppert called his wife and the cook to look at them. The eggs looked very much like big caviar, only they were white instead of black or red.

'Well, naturally they have to breed some way,' was his wife's comment. Mr Knoppert couldn't understand her lack of interest. He had to go and look at the eggs every hour that he was at home. He looked at them every morning to see if any change had taken place, and the eggs were his last thought every night before he went to bed. Moreover, another snail was now digging a pit. And another pair of snails was mating! The first batch of eggs turned a grayish color, and minuscule spirals of shells became discernible on one side of each egg.

Mr Knoppert's anticipation rose to a higher pitch. At last a morning arrived – the eighteenth after laying, according to Mr Knoppert's careful count – when he looked down into the egg pit and saw the first tiny moving head, the first stubby little antennae uncertainly exploring the nest. Mr Knoppert was as happy as the father of a new child. Every one of the seventy or more eggs in the pit came miraculously to life. He had seen the entire reproductive cycle evolve to a successful conclusion. And the fact that no one, at least no one that he knew of, was acquainted with a fraction of what he knew, lent his knowledge a thrill of discovery, the piquancy of the esoteric. Mr Knoppert made notes on successive matings and egg hatchings. He narrated snail biology to fascinated, more often shocked, friends and guests, until his wife squirmed with embarrassment.

'But where is it going to stop, Peter? If they keep on reproducing at this rate, they'll take over the house!' his wife told him after fifteen or twenty pits had hatched.

'There's no stopping nature,' he replied good-humoredly. 'They've only taken over the study. There's plenty of room there.'

So more and more glass tanks and bowls were moved in. Mr Knoppert went to the market and chose several of the more lively-looking snails, and also a pair he found mating, unobserved by the rest of the world. More and more egg pits appeared in the dirt floors of the tanks, and out of each pit crept finally from seventy to ninety baby snails, transparent as dewdrops, gliding up rather than down the strips of fresh lettuce that Mr Knoppert was quick to give all the pits as edible ladders for the climb. Matings went on so often that he no longer bothered to watch them. A mating could last twenty-four hours. But the thrill of seeing the white caviar become shells and start to move – that never diminished however often he witnessed it.

His colleagues in the brokerage office noticed a new zest for life in Peter Knoppert. He became more daring in his moves, more brilliant in his calculations, became in fact a little vicious in his schemes, but he brought money in for his company. By unanimous vote, his basic salary was raised from forty to sixty thousand dollars per year. When anyone congratulated him on his achievements, Mr Knoppert gave all the credit to his snails and the beneficial relaxation he derived from watching them.

He spent all his evenings with his snails in the room that was no longer a study but a kind of aquarium. He loved to strew the tanks with fresh lettuce and pieces of boiled potato and beet, then turn on the sprinkler system that he had installed in the tanks to simulate natural rainfall. Then all the snails would liven up and begin eating, mating, or merely gliding through the shallow water with obvious pleasure. Mr Knoppert often let a snail crawl on to his forefinger – he fancied his snails enjoyed this human contact – and he would feed it a piece of lettuce by hand, would observe the snail from all sides, finding as much aesthetic satisfaction as another man might from contemplating a Japanese print.

By now, Mr Knoppert did not allow anyone to set foot in his study. Too many snails had the habit of crawling around on the floor, of going to sleep glued to chair bottoms, and to the backs of books on the shelves. Snails spent much of their time sleeping, especially the older snails. But there were enough less indolent snails who preferred love-making. Mr Knoppert estimated that about a dozen pairs of snails must be kissing all the time. And certainly there was a multitude of baby and adolescent snails. They were impossible to count. But Mr Knoppert did count the snails sleeping and creeping on the ceiling alone, and arrived at something between eleven and twelve hundred. The tanks, the bowls, the underside of his desk and the bookshelves must surely have held fifty times that number. Mr Knoppert meant to scrape the snails off the ceiling one day soon. Some of them had been up there for weeks, and he was afraid they were not taking in enough nourishment. But of late he had been a little too busy, and too much in need of the tranquillity that he got simply from sitting in the study in his favorite chair.

During the month of June he was so busy he often worked late into the evening at his office. Reports were piling in at the end of the fiscal year. He made calculations, spotted a half-dozen possibilities of gain, and reserved the most daring, the least obvious moves for his private operations. By this time next year, he thought, he should be three or four times as well off as now. He saw his bank account multiplying as easily and rapidly as his snails. He told his wife this, and she was overjoyed. She even forgave him the ruination of the study, and the stale, fishy smell that was spreading throughout the whole upstairs.

'Still, I do wish you'd take a look just to see if anything's happening, Peter,' she said to him rather anxiously one morning. 'A tank might have overturned or something, and I wouldn't want the rug to be spoilt. You haven't been in the study for nearly a week, have you?'

Mr Knoppert hadn't been in for nearly two weeks. He didn't tell his wife that the rug was pretty much gone already. 'I'll go up tonight,' he said.

But it was three more days before he found time. He went in one evening just before bedtime and was surprised to find the floor quite covered with snails, with three or four layers of snails. He had difficulty closing the door without mashing any. The dense clusters of snails in the corners made the room look positively round, as if he stood inside some huge, conglomerate stone. Mr Knoppert cracked his knuckles and gazed around him in astonishment. They had not only covered every surface, but thousands of snails hung down into the room from the chandelier in a grotesque clump.

Mr Knoppert felt for the back of a chair to steady himself. He felt only a lot of shells under his hand. He had to smile a little: there were snails in the chair seat, piled up on one another, like a lumpy cushion. He really must do something about the ceiling, and immediately. He took an umbrella from the corner, brushed some of the snails off it, and cleared a place on his desk to stand. The umbrella point tore the wallpaper, and then the weight of the snails pulled down a long strip that hung almost to the floor. Mr Knoppert felt suddenly frustrated and angry. The sprinklers would make them move. He pulled the lever.

The sprinklers came on in all the tanks, and the seething activity of the entire room increased at once. Mr Knoppert slid his feet along the floor, through tumbling snail shells that made a sound like pebbles on a beach, and directed a couple of the sprinklers at the ceiling. This was a mistake, he saw at once. The softened paper began to tear, and he dodged one slowly falling mass only to be hit by a swinging festoon of snails, really hit quite a stunning blow on the side of the head. He went down on one knee, dazed. He should open a window, he thought, the air was stifling. And there were snails crawling over his shoes and up his trouser legs. He shook his feet irritably. He was just going to the door, intending to call for one of the servants to help him, when the chandelier fell on him. Mr Knoppert sat down heavily on the floor. He saw now that he couldn't possibly get a window open, because the snails were fastened thick and deep over the windowsills. For a moment, he felt he couldn't get up, felt as if he were suffocating. It was not only the musty smell of the room, but everywhere he looked long wallpaper strips covered with snails blocked his vision as if he were in a prison.

'Edna!' he called, and was amazed at the muffled, ineffectual sound of his voice. The room might have been soundproof.

He crawled to the door, heedless of the sea of snails he crushed under hands and knees. He could not get the door open. There were so many snails on it, crossing and recrossing the crack of the door on all four sides, they actually resisted his strength.

'Edna!' A snail crawled into his mouth. He spat it out in disgust. Mr Knoppert tried to brush the snails off his arms. But for every hundred he dislodged, four hundred seemed to slide upon him and fasten to him again, as if they deliberately sought him out as the only comparatively snail-free surface in the room. There were snails crawling over his eyes. Then just as he staggered to his feet, something else hit him – Mr Knoppert couldn't even see what. He was fainting! At any rate, he was on the floor. His arms felt like leaden weights as he tried to reach his nostrils, his eyes, to free them from the sealing, murderous snail bodies.

'Help!' He swallowed a snail. Choking, he widened his mouth for air and felt a snail crawl over his lips on to his tongue. He was in hell! He could feel them gliding over his legs like a glutinous river, pinning his legs to the floor. 'Ugh!' Mr Knoppert's breath came in feeble gasps. His vision grew black, a horrible, undulating black. He could not breathe at all, because he could not reach his nostrils, could not move his hands. Then through the slit of one eye, he saw directly in front of him, only inches away, what had been, he knew, the rubber plant that stood in its pot near the door. A pair of snails were quietly making love in it. And right beside them, tiny snails as pure as dewdrops were emerging from a pit like an infinite army into their widening world.

THE GREAT CARDHOUSE

L ucien Montlehuc started a little when he saw the notice. He read it twice, slowly, and then, as if he finally believed it, put down his newspaper and removed his monocle. A habitual expression of amusement returned to his face, and his lids fluttered over his bright blue eyes. 'Imagine Gaston Potin taken in by it!' he said to himself. 'Of all people to be fooled!'

This thought made him even more gleeful. It would not be the first time that he had proven Gaston Potin wrong. This particular Giotto was a forgery, and Gaston was putting it up for sale as a genuine. Lucien meant to have it, and the sale was that very afternoon. How fortunate he had been to see the notice in time! The magnificent counterfeit might have slipped through his fingers again.

Lucien put his monocle back in the grip of his slightly protruding brow, summoned François and ordered him to pack their bags for an overnight stay in Aix-en-Provence. While he waited, he turned to *The Revelation to the Shepherds* in his book of Giotto reproductions and studied it. Again he thought how odd it was that poor Gaston Potin would not have suspected it to be a forgery. Perhaps it was the too-rigid faces of the kneeling shepherds that told him the painting was not from Giotto's hand. There was no real religious feeling there. The annunciatory angel's robe was a too-brilliant pink. The composition itself was not right, not Giotto – but it *was* magnificent, as a forgery. Lucien did not need a magnifying glass to detect a forgery. Something within him, some inner sensory apparatus, betrayed the spurious instantly and always. It never failed.

Besides, hadn't an Englishman, Sir Ronald Dunsenny, questioned the authenticity of this *Revelation* around the time of the Fruehlingen purchase? Indeed, Sir Ronald had ventured that the original had been destroyed in a fire in the middle of the eighteenth century! Evidently Gaston Potin didn't know that.

It was Lucien's passion to collect the most perfect imitations, and only the imitations, of the great artists. He did not want genuine paintings. And he prided himself that his sham masterpieces were such fine shams that any could, if presented as the original, fool the eyes of the most astute dealers and critics in the world.

Lucien had played many such tricks during the fifteen years he had been collecting forgeries. He might submit one of his forgeries as a loan from an individual who owned the original, for instance, then attend the exhibition and remark his suspicions publicly, to be proven right in the end, of course. Twice he had subjected Gaston Potin – with his great reputation as an art dealer – to such embarrassment. And once, Lucien had made Gaston uneasy about an original by presenting one of his forgeries that was so good it had taken six experts three days to decide which picture *was* the original. All in all, it had caused Gaston Potin to refer scathingly to Lucien's well-known collection and to his lamentable taste for the bogus. Lamentable to whom? Lucien wondered. And why? His pranks had cost him a few friendships, perhaps, but then he cared as little for friendship as he cared for the true Leonardos, the true Renis, the true anything: friendship and bona fide masterpieces were too natural, too easy, too boring. Not that he actually disliked people, and people liked Lucien well enough, but if friendship threatened, Lucien withdrew.

His six-million-franc Delahaye sped along the Route Napoléon from Paris toward Aix at a hundred kilometers an hour. Plane trees in full leaf, their smooth bark peeling in purplish, pink, and beige patches, flickered by at the edges of the road like picket fences. A landscape of dusky orange and green and tan, the occasional blue of a farmer's cart – a landscape as beautifully composed as a Gobelin tapestry – unfolded continuously on right and left, but Lucien had no eye for it. Nature's creations did not interest him compared to man's, and his stocky body sat deep in the seat of the car. Today there was the Fruehlingen Giotto to think about, and he looked forward to the auction with the keen, single-minded anticipation of a hunter or a lover. Merely for Lucien Montlehuc to bid for a painting meant that the painting was, or most likely was, a counterfeit, and would in this case immediately throw suspicion upon Gaston, who was sponsoring the auction. Some of the audience at Aix might think he was trying to play another trick on Gaston, of course, by bidding. So much the better when the experts confirmed the falsity after the picture was his.

'Excellent snails,' Lucien remarked with satisfaction, his pink cheeks glowing after his luncheon. He and François walked quickly to the car.

'Excellent, monsieur,' François replied agreeably. His good humor reflected that of his master. François was tall and lean and congenitally lazy, though he never failed to carry out an order from Lucien. He had not forgotten that he had once been earmarked for execution by the Spanish government for being in possession of a false passport. Because François had been amused and cool about the whole thing, he had won Lucien's admiration, and Lucien had managed to buy his freedom. Since then François, actually a Russian who had escaped to Czechoslovakia with a price on his head, had lived in France, safe and content to be alive and in Lucien's employ.

Lucien himself had once lived in Czechoslovakia. In 1926, most European papers had carried an account of a very young Captain Lucas Minchovik, a soldier of fortune who had been severely wounded in a skirmish on the Yugoslav border. Years ago, in

Czechoslovakia, people had sometimes asked him about the 1926 report, the young captain's heroism having made the story memorable, but Lucien had always disclaimed any knowledge of it. It had been another soldier of the same name, he said. Finally, he had changed his name and come to France.

In Aix, Lucien and François stopped first at the Hôtel des Étrangers to reserve a three-room suite, then drove on to the Musée de Tapisserie beside the Cathedral Saint-Sauveur. The auction was to be held in the open court of the *musée*, and was scheduled to begin in half an hour, but things in Aix were always late. Cars of all sizes and manufacture cluttered the narrow streets around the cathedral, and the courtyard was a bedlam of hurrying workmen and chattering agents and dealers and private buyers who had not yet begun to seat themselves.

'Do you see M. Potin?' Lucien asked François, who was a good deal taller than Lucien.

'No, monsieur.'

An acquaintance of Lucien's, a dealer from Strasbourg, told him that M. Potin was giving a luncheon at his villa just outside the town, and that he had not yet arrived.

Lucien decided to pay Gaston Potin a visit. He was eager to let Gaston know of his interest in the Giotto. As they drew up to Gaston's Villa Madeleine, Lucien heard the treble notes of a piano from within. Faint but bell-like, it was a Scarlatti sonata. He was shown into the hall by a servant. Through the open door of the salon, Lucien saw a slender woman seated at the piano, and a score of men and a few women standing or sitting motionless, listening to her. Lucien paused at the threshold, adjusted his monocle, and espied Gaston just behind the piano, concentrating on the music with an expression of rapt and sentimental enjoyment. Lucien's eyes swept the rest of the company. They were all here – Font-Martigue of the Dauberville Gallery in Paris, Fritz Heber of Vienna, Martin Palmer of London. Certainly the cream.

And they were all listening to the sonata – with the same

absorption as Gaston. Lucien's appearance in the doorway had not even been noticed. The fast movement the woman was playing was splendid indeed. The notes sparkled from her fingers like drops of pure springwater. But to Lucien's ear, which was as infallible as his eye, an ingredient was missing – a pleasure in the performance. It was audible to Lucien that she detested Scarlatti, if not music itself. Lucien smiled. Could she really be holding the company as spellbound as it looked? But of course she was. How obtuse people were, even those who professed a knowledge of the arts! There was a perfect crash of applause from the little audience when she finished.

Lucien saw Gaston coming toward him with the pianist on his arm. Gaston smiled at Lucien as if the music had made him forget that there had ever been unpleasantnesses between them.

'Very happy and surprised to see you, Lucien!' Gaston said. 'May I present the music teacher of my childhood – Mlle Claire Duhamel of Aix.'

'*Enchanté, mademoiselle,*' said Lucien. He observed with satisfaction the stir of interest his entry into the salon had caused.

'She plays superbly, doesn't she?' Gaston went on. 'She has just been asked to give a series of concerts in Paris, but she has refused, *n'est-ce pas*, Mlle Claire? Aix should not be deprived of your music for so long!'

Lucien smiled politely, then said, 'I learned of your sale only this morning, Gaston. Why didn't you send me an announcement?'

'Because I was sure there is nothing here that would interest you. These are all authentic pictures of my own choosing.'

'But *The Revelation to the Shepherds* interests me *enormously*!' Lucien told him with a smile. 'I don't suppose if it's here you might let me see it now.'

Behind Gaston's frank surprise, there was just the least alarm. 'But with the greatest pleasure, Lucien. Follow me.'

Mlle Duhamel, who had been gazing at Lucien all the while, checked him with the question, 'Are you an admirer of Giotto, too, M. Montlehuc?'

Lucien looked at her. She was a typical *vieille femme* — an old maid – of a Provençal town, drab and shy, yet with an air of tenacious purpose in her own narrow, cramped way of life, a look of wiry vigor that suggested a plant growing at the edge of a wind-whipped cliff. Gentle, sad gray eyes looked out of her small face with such depression of spirit that one wanted to turn away immediately, because of an inability to help her. A less attractive person Lucien could not have imagined. 'Yes, mademoiselle,' he said, and hurried after Gaston.

Lucien's first sight of the picture brought that leap of excitement and recognition that only the finest forgeries gave him. From the patina, he judged the picture to be more than two hundred years old. And today it would be his.

'You see?' Gaston smiled confidently.

Lucien sighed, in mock defeat. 'I see. A beautiful piece indeed. My congratulations, Gaston.'

Lucien attended the auction in the subdued manner of one who watches from the outside, a bystander. He waited with impatience while an indifferent Messina and a miserable 'Ignoto Veneziano' from the Fruehlingen collection were put up and sold. Apart from the false Giotto, Lucien thought mischievously, the Barons von Fruehlingen did have execrable taste!

Mlle Duhamel, on a bench against the side wall, was again staring at him, he noticed, with what thoughts behind her quiet gray eyes, he could not guess. Lucien found something disturbing, something arrogantly omniscient in her scrutiny. For an instant, he resented her fiercely and unreasonably. Lucien removed his monocle and passed his fingertips lightly across his lids. When he looked up again, the *Revelation* was on the dais.

A man whom Lucien could not see bid a million new francs.

'A million and a half,' said Lucien calmly. He was in the last row.

Heads turned to look at him. There was a murmur as the crowd recognized Lucien Montlehuc.

'Two million!' cried the same unseen bidder.

'Two million ten thousand,' replied Lucien, intending to provoke laughter, as he did, by the insultingly small raise. He heard the sibilant whisper of 'Lucien' among the crowd. Someone laughed, a sardonic laugh that made a corner of Lucien's mouth go up in response. Lucien knew from the rising hum that people had begun to ask one another if the Giotto were indisputably genuine.

The unseen bidder stood up. It was Font-Martigue of Paris. His bald head turned its eagle profile for a moment to glance at Lucien coldly. 'Three million.'

Lucien also stood up. 'Three million five hundred.'

'Three million seven,' replied Font-Martigue, more to Lucien than to the auctioneer.

Lucien raised it to three million eight hundred and Font-Martigue to four million.

'And a hundred thousand,' added Lucien.

At this rate, the figure might be driven beyond the price of a genuine Giotto, but Lucien did not care. The joke on Gaston would be worth it. And the audience was wavering already. Only Font-Martigue was bidding. Everyone knew that Gaston Potin had been wrong a few times, but Lucien never.

'Four million two hundred thousand,' said Font-Martigue.

'Four million three,' said Lucien.

The audience tittered. Lucien wished he could see Gaston at this moment, but he couldn't. Gaston was doubtless in the front row with his back to Lucien. A pity. It was no longer a contest of bidding. It had become a contest of faith versus nonfaith, of believer versus nonbeliever. Fifteen meters away on the dais the *Revelation* stood like a reliquary in its golden-leaf frame, a reliquary of the divine fire of art – as each of them saw it.

'Four million four,' said Font-Martigue in a tone of finality.

'Four million five,' Lucien promptly replied.

Font-Martigue folded his arms and sat down.

The auctioneer rapped. 'Four million five hundred thousand new francs?'

Lucien smiled. Who could afford to outbid him when he wanted something?

'Four million six,' said a voice on Lucien's left.

A man who looked like a young Charles de Gaulle leaned forward on his knees, focusing his attention on the auctioneer. Lucien knew the type, the de Gaulle type indeed, another believer, an idealist. He was in for five million francs at least.

Five minutes later, the auctioneer pronounced *The Revelation to the Shepherds* the property of Lucien Montlehuc for the sum of five million two hundred and fifty thousand new francs.

Lucien came forward immediately to write his check and to take possession.

'My congratulations, Lucien,' Gaston Potin said. His forehead was damp with perspiration, but he managed a bewildered smile. 'A genuine work of art at last. The only one in your collection, I'm sure.'

'What is genuine?' Lucien asked. 'Is art genuine? What is more sincere than imitation, Gaston?'

'Do you mean to say you think this painting is a forgery?'

'If it is not, I shall give it back to you. What would I want with it if it were genuine? You know, though, you should not have represented it as a genuine painting. It ran my price up.'

Gaston's face was growing pink. 'There are a dozen men here who could prove you wrong, Lucien.'

'I invite them to prove me wrong,' Lucien said courteously. 'Seriously, Gaston, ask them to come to my suite at the Hôtel des Étrangers for aperitifs this afternoon. Let them bring their magnifying glasses and their history books. At six o'clock: May I expect you?'

'You may,' said Gaston Potin.

Lucien walked out of the courtyard to his waiting car. François had already strapped the *Revelation* carefully between the seat back and the spare tire. Lucien happened to look behind him as he reached the car. He saw Mlle Duhamel walking slowly from the doorway of the courtyard toward him, and he felt a throb in his chest, a strange premonition. Sunlight, broken into droplets by the trees, played like silent music over her moving figure, light and quick as her own fingers had played in Gaston's salon. He remembered his feeling, as he listened to her Scarlatti sonata, that she loathed playing it. And yet to play so brilliantly! That took a kind of genius, Lucien thought. He was aware suddenly of a great respect for Mlle Duhamel, and of something else, something he could not identify, perhaps compassion. It pained him that anyone with Mlle Duhamel's ability should take so little joy in it, that she should look so crushed, so agonizingly self-effacing.

'Do you know that I am receiving some friends at six o'clock this afternoon, Mlle Duhamel?' Lucien said with an unwonted awkwardness as she came closer. 'I should be honored if you would join us.'

Mlle Duhamel accepted with pleasure.

'Come a little early, if you will.'

'Five million two hundred and fifty thousand francs for a counterfeit,' Mlle Duhamel whispered with awe. She sat on the edge of a chair in the salon of Lucien's suite, gazing at the picture Lucien had leaned against the divan.

Lucien strolled back and forth before her, smiling, smoking a Turkish cigarette. François had gone out a few moments before to fetch Cinzano and pâté and biscuits, and now they were alone. Mlle Duhamel had been surprised, but not overly surprised, when he told her the Giotto was a forgery. Her reaction had been exactly right. And now she regarded the picture with the respect that was due it.

'One usually pays more dearly for the false than for the true, mademoiselle,' Lucien said, feeling expansive in his hour of triumph. 'This hair I touch, for instance,' he said, patting the top of his light brown, gently waving hair, 'is a toupee, the finest that Paris can make. Grown by nature, it would have cost nothing. Strictly speaking, it would have been worthless. It *is* worthless, to a man with hair of his own. But when I must buy it to hide a deficiency of nature, I must pay a hundred and fifty thousand francs for it. And it is a just price, when one thinks of the skill and labor that went into its creation.' Lucien swept off his toupee and held it in his hand, lustrous side uppermost. His bald crown was a healthy pink-tan, like his face, and really detracted little from the liveliness of his appearance, which was extraordinary for his age. The bald head was a surprise, that was all.

'I had no idea you wore a toupee, M. Montlehuc.'

Lucien eyed her sharply. He thought he saw amusement in her tilted head. She had one element of charm, he conceded: she had humor. 'And applying this same principle to the false Giotto,' Lucien continued, inspired by Mlle Duhamel's attention, 'we might say Giotto's genius was a thing of nature, too, a gift of the gods, perhaps, but certainly a faculty which cost him nothing, and in a sense cost him no effort, since he created as every artist creates, out of necessity. But consider the poor mortal who created this almost perfect imitation. Think of his travail in reproducing every stroke of the master exactly! Consider *his* effort!'

Mlle Duhamel was absorbing every word. 'Yes,' she said.

'You understand then why I value the imitators so highly, or rather give them their proper value?'

'I understand,' she answered.

Lucien felt perhaps she did. 'And you, Mlle Duhamel, may I say that is why I find you so valuable? You have a superb talent for deceiving. Your performance of Scarlatti this afternoon was by no means inferior to the best – technically. It was inferior in only one respect.' He hesitated, wondering if he dared go on.

'Yes?' Mlle Duhamel prompted, a little fearfully.

'You hated it, didn't you?'

She looked down at her slim, tense hands in her lap, hands that were still as smooth and flexible as a young girl's. 'Yes. Yes, I hated it. I hate music. It's—' She stopped. Her eyes had grown shiny with tears, but she held her head up and the tears did not drop.

Lucien smiled nervously. He was not good at comforting people, but he wanted to comfort Mlle Duhamel and did not know how to begin. 'What a silly thing to cry about!' he burst out. 'Such a talent! You play exquisitely! Why, if you could endure the boredom – and I really admire you for not being able to endure it – you might play in concerts all over the world! I daresay not a music critic in a thousand would recognize your real feelings. And what would he do if he did? Make some trifling comment that's all. But your playing would enchant millions and millions of people. Just as my forgeries could enchant millions and millions of people.' He laughed and, before he realized what he did, put out his hand and pressed her thin shoulder affectionately.

She shuddered under his touch and relaxed in her chair. She seemed to shrink until she was nothing but that small, unhappy core of herself. 'You are the only one who has ever known,' she said. 'It was my father who made me study music as a child and as a young girl, study and study until I had no time to do anything else – even to make a friend. My father was organist of the church here in Aix. He wanted me to be a concert pianist, but I knew I never could be, because I hated music too much. And finally – I was thirty-eight when my father died – it was too late to think of marriage. So I stayed on in the village, earning my living in the only way I could, by teaching music. And how ashamed I am! To pretend to love what I hate! To teach others to love what I hate – the piano!'

Her voice trailed off on 'piano' like a plaintive sob itself.

'You fooled Gaston,' Lucien reminded her, smiling. An excitement, a joy of life was rising in him. He could not stand still. He wanted – he did not know exactly what he wanted to do, except to convince Mlle Duhamel that she was wrong to feel ashamed, wrong to torture herself inwardly. 'Don't you see it isn't at all logical,' he began, 'to take seriously something you were never serious about in the first place? – Look, mademoiselle!' With a graceful movement, Lucien removed his right hand. He held the detached and perfectly natural-looking right hand in his left. His right arm ended in an empty white cuff.

Mlle Duhamel gasped.

'You never suspected that, did you?' asked Lucien, grinning like a schoolboy who has brought off a practical joke with success.

'No.' Obviously, Mlle Duhamel hadn't suspected that.

'You see, it's exactly the mate of the left, and by certain movements which have now become automatic, I can give the impression that my useless hand co-operates with the other.' Lucien replaced his hand quickly.

'Why, it's like a miracle!' Mlle Duhamel said.

'A miracle of modern plastics, that's all. And my right foot, I might add, too.' Lucien pulled up his trouser leg a few inches, though there was nothing to be seen but a normal-looking black shoe and sock. 'I was wounded once, literally blown apart, but should I have crept about the world like a crab, disgusting everyone, an object of horror and pity? Life is to be enjoyed, is it not? Life is to give and take pleasure, is it not? You give pleasure, Mlle Duhamel. It remains only for you to take it!' Lucien gave a great laugh that was so truly out of his heart, that rolled so solidly from his broad chest, Mlle Duhamel began to smile, too.

Then she laughed. At first, her laugh was no more than a feeble crack, like the opening of a door that had been closed for an incalculable length of time. But the laugh grew, seemed to reach out in all directions, like a separate being taking form, taking courage.

'And my ear!' Lucien went on with delight. 'It wasn't necessary to have two ears to hear what I heard in your music, mademoiselle. An excellent match, is it not, of my left ear? But not too perfect, because ears are never exactly alike.' He could not remove his grafted right ear, but he pinched it and winked at her. 'And my right eye – I will spare you that, but suffice it to say that it's made of glass. People often speak of my "magic monocle" when they mention my uncanny judgments. I wear the monocle as a joke, by way of adding an insult to an injury, as the English would say. Can you tell the difference between my eyes, Mlle Duhamel?' Lucien bent forward and looked into her gray eyes that were beginning to glow behind the tears.

'Indeed, I cannot,' she told him.

Lucien beamed with satisfaction. 'Did I say my foot? My entire *leg* is of hollow plastic!' Lucien struck his thigh with a pencil he picked up from the table, and it gave a hollow report. 'But does it stop me from dancing? And did anyone ever suggest that I limp? I don't limp. Shall I go on?' His affirmative clap of laughter came again.

Mlle Duhamel looked at him, fascinated. 'I've never——'

'Needless to say, my teeth!' Lucien interrupted her. 'I had scarcely three whole teeth left after my injury. I was a young man then. But that doesn't matter, I saved my employer's life, and he rewarded me with a trust fund that enables me to spend my life in luxury. Anyway, my teeth are the product of an artist in deception, a Japanese whose ingenuity and powers of depiction certainly rank him with the great Leonardo. His name is Tao Mishugawa, but few on earth will ever hear of him. My teeth are full of faults, of course, like real ones. Every so often, just to deceive myself, I go to Tao and have some more fillings or an inlay put in. Tell me, mademoiselle, did you suspect?'

'I certainly did not,' she assured him sincerely.

'If I could remove every artificial part of myself including the silver shin of my other leg and my plastic ribs, there wouldn't be much left of me, would there? Except the spirit. There would be that even more than now, I think! Does it seem strange to you that I speak of the spirit, Mlle Duhamel?'

'Not at all. Of course it doesn't.'

'I knew it wouldn't. There was no need to ask. You, too, are among the great in spirit, who respond to challenge and make nature appear niggardly. Your hours of tortured practice at the piano are not lost, mademoiselle. Not because of these words I say to you, but because you gave pleasure to a score of people this afternoon. Because you are able to give pleasure!'

Mlle Duhamel looked down at her hands again, but now there was a flush of her own pleasure in her cheeks.

'The critics and the art dealers call me a dilettante, the idiots! That I am an artist escapes them, of course. Let it! They are the real dilettanti, the do-nothings. You understand me because you are like me, Mlle Duhamel, but all those who sneer, who stare, who laugh at me and envy and admire me at once because I am not ashamed to confess what I love — And here they are now!'

Someone had rapped on the door.

Lucien glanced at his watch. François was having trouble finding the right kind of pâté, perhaps. Lucien did not like to answer his door himself.

Mlle Duhamel stood up. 'May I open the door for your guests?'

Lucien stared at her. She looked taller than before, and almost — he could hardly believe it — happy. The glow he had seen in her gray eyes seemed to have spread through her entire body. Lucien, too, felt a happiness he had never known before. Perhaps the kind of happiness an artist feels after creating something, he thought, an artist whose talent is given by nature.

'I should be honored,' Lucien said.

Gaston had come, and with him four other dealers, one of whom carried a picture which Lucien recognized as Giotto's *Magi in Bethlehem* from a private collection. Lucien greeted them hospitably. Then more people arrived, and finally François with the refreshments. The man with the picture set it next to Lucien's against the divan, and all got out their magnifying glasses.

'I assure you, you possess an original,' Gaston said cheerfully to Lucien. 'Not that you didn't pay a fitting price for it.' All of Gaston's confidence had returned.

Lucien gestured with his false hand at the group beside the divan. 'The experts have not said so yet, have they? Let their magnifying glasses discover what I can see with my naked eyes.' He strolled off toward Mlle Duhamel and M. Palissy, who were talking in a corner of the room. How charming she looked, Lucien thought. A half hour ago, she would have been afraid to use her beautiful hands to gesture as she spoke.

Gaston intercepted Lucien before he reached Mlle Duhamel. 'You agree that this picture is genuine, Lucien?' he said, pointing to the picture the dealer had brought.

'Certainly,' said Lucien, 'That *Magi* — a careless piece of work, I've always thought, but certainly genuine.'

'Examine the brushstrokes, Lucien. Compare them with the brushstrokes on your picture. It's so obvious, a child could see it. There is a fault in the brush that he used to paint the backgrounds of both pictures, a couple of bristles that made a scratch here and there. Evidently these pictures were painted at about the same time. It's the general opinion that they were, you know.' Gaston stooped down beside the pictures. 'One doesn't even need a magnifying glass to see it. But I had some photographs made and enlarged, just to be sure. Here they are, Lucien.'

Lucien ignored the photographs on the divan. He could see it, with his good eye; a hair-line scratch here and there with an even finer scratch beside it, the scratches of a single brushstroke, made by the same brush. It was the same in both pictures, like a pattern, obvious enough when one looked for it, yet not obvious enough to be worthy of forging. Lucien's head grew swimmy. For an instant, he felt only a keen discomfort. He was aware that the eyes of everyone in the room were upon him as he bent over the two pictures. Most painfully of all, he was aware of Mlle Duhamel. He felt he had failed her. He had been proven fallible.

'Now you see,' said Gaston calmly, without malice, merely as if he were pointing out something that Lucien might have seen from the first.

Lucien felt as if a house of cards were tumbling down inside him, all that was himself, in fact. He could see now, looking at the picture he had believed to be false, that a misconception — a quick, initial misconception — was possible. Just as it would have been equally possible to judge the picture correctly, as he did now, and to sense that it was genuine. But he had made the misjudgment.

Lucien turned to the room. 'I admit my error,' he said, his tongue as dry as ashes.

He had expected laughter, but there was only a murmur, a kind of sigh in the room. He would rather they had laughed at him. No, at least there was one exchange of smiles, one nod of satisfaction from Font-Martigue that Lucien Montlehuc could be wrong. Lucien would have felt quite lost if he had not seen it. Yet no one seemed to realize the catastrophe that was taking place inside him. The great cardhouse was still falling. For the first time in his life, he felt near tears. He had a vision of himself without his artifices, without his arrogant faith in his infallibility – a piece of a man, unable even to stand upright, a miserable fragment. For a few moments, Lucien's spirit bore the full weight of reality, and almost broke beneath it.

'If you'd like to sell it back, of course, Lucien,' Gaston's voice said kindly, distantly, whispering into the false ear, 'I'll pay you the same price—'

'No. No, thank you, Gaston.' Now he was being unreasonable to boot! What did he want with a genuine painting? Lucien stumbled toward Mlle Duhamel. He stumbled on his artificial leg.

Mlle Duhamel's face was as calm as if nothing had happened. 'Why don't you tell them you were pretending?' she asked him, out of hearing of the others. 'Why don't you pretend the whole afternoon was a great joke?'

Her face was even victorious, Lucien thought. He looked at it for a long moment, trying to draw strength from it, and failing. 'But I wasn't joking,' he said.

Then the guests were gone. Only he and Mlle Duhamel remained. And the genuine Giotto. François, who had witnessed his master's defeat, standing in the background like a silent tragic chorus, had excused himself last of all and gone out.

Lucien sat down heavily on the divan.

'I shall keep the painting,' Lucien said slowly, and with quiet, profound bitterness. He did not recognize his own voice, though he recognized that it was his real voice. It was the voice of the fragment of a man. 'It will be the one original that will spoil the purity of my forgeries. Nothing in life is pure. Nothing is one thing and nothing more. Nothing is absolute. When I was a young man, I believed no bullet would ever touch me. And then one day I was struck by a grenade. I thought I could never misjudge a painting. And today a public misjudgment!'

'But didn't you know that nothing is absolute? Why, even my kitten knows that much!'

Lucien glanced at Mlle Duhamel with the fiercest impatience. He had scarcely been aware of her the past few moments. Now he resented her presence as much as he had when she had spoken to him first in Gaston's salon.

She was standing by the little three-legged console table where lay her green string gloves and her big square pocketbook that was as flat as her own body. She looked at him anxiously, as if she were puzzled for a moment as to what to do. Then she came toward him, sat down beside him on the divan, and took his hand in hers. It happened to be his false hand, but she betrayed no surprise, if she felt any. She held his hand affectionately, as if it were real.

Lucien started to take his hand away, but only sighed instead. What did it matter? But then, with the touch he could not feel, he realized another misjudgment, a much older one. He had thought he could never feel close to any human being, never allow himself to be close. But now he did feel close to Mlle Duhamel. He felt closer to her than François, the only other person who knew of the great cardhouse that was Lucien Montlehuc. François had not suffered as Mlle Duhamel had suffered, the idiot. It was a tenderness he felt for Mlle Duhamel, and admiration. She lived within a cardhouse, too. Yet, if nothing was absolute, a cardhouse was not absolute, either. He might rebuild it, but it would never be perfect, and had never been perfect. How stupid he had been! He who had always prided himself that he knew the imperfections of everything, even art. Lucien looked down in wonder at his and Mlle Duhamel's clasped hands. It had been so many years since he had had a friend.

His heart began to thump like a lover's. How pleasant it would be, Lucien thought suddenly, to have Mlle Duhamel in his home, to have her play for him and his guests, to give her luxuries that she had never been able to afford. Lucien smiled, for the thought had only flitted across his mind like the shadow of a bird across the grass. Marriage, indeed! Hadn't he just realized that nothing was ever perfect? Why should he try to better what couldn't be bettered — the happiness he felt with Mlle Duhamel at this instant?

'Mlle Duhamel, would you consider being my friend?' Lucien asked, more seriously, he realized abashedly, than most men ask women to be their wives. 'Would you consider friendship with a man who is sincere only at the core of his ambiguous heart and in the way he wishes to be a friend to you? A man whose very right hand is false?'

Mlle Duhamel murmured adoringly, 'I was just thinking that I held a hero's hand.'

Lucien sat up a little. The words had taken him completely by surprise. 'A hero's hand,' he said sarcastically, but not without contentment.

ONE FOR THE ISLANDS

The voyage wasn't to be much longer. Most people were bound for the mainland, which was not far at all now. Others were bound for the islands to the west, some of which were very far indeed.

Dan was bound for a certain island that he believed probably farther than any of the others the ship would touch at. He supposed that he would be about the last passenger to disembark.

On the sixth day of the smooth, uneventful voyage, he was in excellent spirits. He enjoyed the company of his fellow-passengers, had joined them a few times in the games that were always in progress on the top deck forward, but mostly he strolled the deck with his pipe in his mouth and a book under his arm, the pipe unlighted and the book forgotten, gazing serenely at the horizon and thinking of the island to which he was going. It would be the finest island of them all, Dan imagined. For some months now, he had devoted much of his time to imagining its terrain. There was no doubt, he decided finally, that he knew more about his island than any man alive, a fact which made him smile whenever he thought of it. No, no one would ever know a hundredth of what he knew about his island, though he had never seen it. But then, perhaps no one else had ever seen it, either.

Dan was happiest when strolling the deck, alone, letting his eyes drift from soft cloud to horizon, from sun to sea, thinking always that his island might come into view before the mainland. He would know its outline at once, he was sure of that. Strangely, it would be like a place he had always known, but secretly, telling no one. And there he would finally be alone.

It startled him sometimes, unpleasantly, too, suddenly to encounter, face to face, a passenger coming round a corner. He found it disturbing to bump into a hurrying steward in one of the twisting, turning corridors of D-deck, which being third class was more like a catacomb than the rest, and which was the deck where Dan had his cabin. Then there had been the time, the second day of the voyage, when for an instant he saw very close to his eyes the ridged floor of the corridor, with a cigarette butt between two ridges, a chewing-gum wrapper, and a few discarded matches. That had been unpleasant, too.

'Are you for the mainland?' asked Mrs Gibson-Leyden, one of the first-class passengers, as they stood at the rail one evening.

Dan smiled a little and shook his head. 'No, the islands,' he said pleasantly, rather surprised that Mrs Gibson-Leyden didn't know by now. But on the other hand, there had been little talk among the passengers as to where each was going. 'You're for the mainland, I take it?' He spoke to be friendly knowing quite well that Mrs Gibson-Leyden was for the mainland.

'Oh, yes,' Mrs Gibson-Leyden said. 'My husband had some idea of going to an island, but I said, not for me!'

She laughed with an air of satisfaction, and Dan nodded. He liked Mrs Gibson-Leyden because she was cheerful. It was more than could be said for most of the first-class passengers. Now he leaned his forearms on the rail and looked out at the wake of moonlight on the sea that shimmered like the back of a gigantic sea dragon with silver scales. Dan couldn't imagine that anyone would go to the mainland when there were islands in abundance, but then he had never been able to understand such things, and with a person like Mrs Gibson-Leyden, there was no use in trying to discuss them and to understand. Dan drew gently on his empty pipe. He could smell a fragrance of lavender cologne from Mrs Gibson-Leyden's direction. It reminded him of a girl he had once known, and he was amused now that he could feel drawn to Mrs Gibson-Leyden, certainly old enough to have been his mother, because she wore a familiar scent.

'Well, I'm supposed to meet my husband back in the game room,' Mrs Gibson-Leyden said, moving away. 'He went down to get a sweater.'

Dan nodded, awkwardly now. Her departure made him feel abandoned, absurdly lonely, and immediately he reproached himself for not having made more of an effort at communication with her. He smiled, straightened, and peered into the darkness over his left shoulder, where the mainland would appear before dawn, then his island, later.

Two people, a man and a woman, walked slowly down the deck, side by side, their figures quite black in the darkness. Dan was conscious of their separateness from each other. Another isolated figure, short and fat, moved into the light of the windows in the superstructure: Dr Eubanks, Dan recognized. Forward, Dan saw a group of people standing on deck and at the rails, all isolated, too. He had a vision of stewards and stewardesses below, eating their solitary meals at tiny tables in the corridors, hurrying about with towels, trays, menus. They were all alone, too. There was nobody who touched anybody, he thought, no man who held his wife's hand, no lovers whose lips met – at least he hadn't seen any so far on this voyage.

Dan straightened still taller. An overwhelming sense of aloneness, of his own isolation, had taken possession of him, and because his impulse was to shrink within himself, he unconsciously stood as tall as he could. But he could not look at the ship any longer, and turned back to the sea.

It seemed to him that only the moon spread its arms, laid its web protectively, lovingly, over the sea's body. He stared at the veils of moonlight as hard as he could, for as long as he could – which

was perhaps twenty-five seconds – then went below to his cabin
and to sleep.

He was awakened by the sound of running feet on the deck, and
a murmur of excited voices.

The mainland, he thought at once, and threw off his bedcovers.
He did want a good look at the mainland. Then as his head cleared of
sleep, he realized that the excitement on deck must be about something else. There was more running now, a woman's wondering
'Oh!' that was half a scream, half an exclamation of pleasure. Dan
hurried into his clothes and ran out of his cabin.

His view from the A-deck companionway made him stop and
draw in his breath. The ship was sailing *downward*, had been sailing
downward on a long, broad path in the sea itself. Dan had never
seen anything like it. No one else had either, apparently. No wonder
everyone was so excited.

'When?' asked a man who was running after the hurrying captain. 'Did you see it? What happened?'

The captain had no time to answer him.

'It's all right. This is right,' said a petty officer, whose calm,
serious face contrasted strangely with the wide-eyed alertness of
everyone else.

'One doesn't notice it below,' Dan said quickly to Mr Steyne
who was standing near him, and felt idiotic at once, because what
did it matter whether one felt it below or not? The ship was sailing
downward, the sea sloped downward at about a twenty degree angle
with the horizon, and such a thing had never been heard of before,
even in the Bible.

Dan ran to join the passengers who were crowding the forward
deck. 'When did it start? I mean, where?' Dan asked the person
nearest him.

The person shrugged, though his face was as excited, as anxious
as the rest.

Dan strained to see what the water looked like at the side of the
swath, for the slope did not seem more than two miles broad. But

whatever was happening, whether the swath ended in a sharp edge or sloped up to the main body of the sea, he could not make out, because a fine mist obscured the sea on either side. Now he noticed the golden light that lay on everything around them, the swath, the atmosphere, the horizon before them. The light was no stronger on one side than on the other, so it could not have been the sun. Dan couldn't find the sun, in fact. But the rest of the sky and the higher body of the sea behind them was bright as morning.

'Has anybody seen the mainland?' Dan asked, interrupting the babble around him.

'No,' said a man.

'There's no mainland,' said the same unruffled petty officer.

Dan had a sudden feeling of having been duped.

'This is right,' the petty officer added laconically. He was winding a thin line around and round his arm, bracing it on palm and elbow.

'Right?' asked Dan.

'This is it,' said the petty officer.

'That's right, this is it,' a man at the rail confirmed, speaking over his shoulder.

'No islands, either?' asked Dan, alarmed.

'No,' said the petty officer, not unkindly, but in an abrupt way that hurt Dan in his breast.

'Well – what's all this talk about the mainland?' Dan asked.

'Talk,' said the petty officer, with a twinkle now.

'Isn't it wonderful!' said a woman's voice behind him, and Dan turned to see Mrs Gibson-Leyden – Mrs Gibson-Leyden who had been so eager for the mainland – gazing rapturously at the empty white and gold mist.

'Do you know about this? How much farther does it go?' asked Dan, but the petty officer was gone. Dan wished he could be as calm as everyone else – generally he was calmer – but how could he be calm about his vanished island? How could the rest just stand there at the rails, for the most part taking it all quite calmly, he could tell by the voices now and their casual postures.

Dan saw the petty officer again and ran after him. 'What happens?' he asked. 'What happens next?' His questions struck him as foolish, but they were as good as any.

'This is *it*,' said the petty officer with a smile. 'Good God, boy!'

Dan bit his lips.

'This is *it*!' repeated the petty officer. 'What did you expect?'

Dan hesitated. 'Land,' he said in a voice that made it almost a question.

The petty officer laughed silently and shook his head. 'You can get off any time you like.'

Dan gave a startled look around him. It was true, people were getting off at the port rail, stepping over the side with their suitcases. 'Onto what?' Dan asked, aghast.

The petty officer laughed again, and disdaining to answer him, walked slowly away with his coiled line.

Dan caught his arm. 'Get off here? Why?'

'As good a place as any. Whatever spot strikes your fancy.' The petty officer chuckled. 'It's all alike.'

'All sea?'

'There's no sea,' said the petty officer. 'But there's certainly no land.'

And there went Mr and Mrs Gibson-Leyden now, off the starboard rail.

'Hey!' Dan called to them, but they didn't turn.

Dan watched them disappear quickly. He blinked his eyes. They had not been holding hands, but they had been near each other, they had been together.

Suddenly Dan realized that if he got off the boat as they had done, he could still be alone, if he wanted to be. It was strange, of course, to think of stepping out into space. But the instant he was able to conceive it, barely conceive it, it became right to do it. He could feel it filling him with a gradual but overpowering certainty, that he only reluctantly yielded to. This was right, as the petty officer had said. And this was as good a place as any.

Dan looked around him. The boat was really almost empty now. He might as well be last, he thought. He'd meant to be last. He'd go down and get his suitcase packed. What a nuisance! The mainland passengers, of course, had been packed since the afternoon before.

Dan turned impatiently on the companionway where he had once nearly fallen, and he climbed up again. He didn't want his suitcase after all. He didn't want anything with him.

He put a foot up on the starboard rail and stepped off. He walked several yards on an invisible ground that was softer than grass. It wasn't what he had thought it would be like, yet now that he was here, it wasn't strange, either. In fact there was even that sense of recognition that he had imagined he would feel when he set foot on his island. He turned for a last look at the ship that was still on its downward course. Then suddenly, he was impatient with himself. Why look at a ship, he asked himself, and abruptly turned and went on.

VARIATIONS ON A GAME

It was an impossible situation. Penn Knowlton had realized that as soon as he realized he was in love with Ginnie Ostrander – Mrs David Ostrander. Penn couldn't see himself in the role of a marriage-breaker, even though Ginnie said she had wanted to divorce David long before she met him. David wouldn't give her a divorce, that was the point. The only decent thing to do, Penn had decided, was to clear out, leave before David suspected anything. Not that he considered himself noble, but there were some situations . . .

Penn went to Ginnie's room on the second floor of the house and knocked.

Her rather high, cheerful voice called, 'You, Penn? Come in!'

She was lying on the sunlit chaise longue, wearing black, close-fitting slacks and a yellow blouse, and she was sewing a button on one of David's shirts.

'Don't I look domestic?' she asked, pushing her yellow hair back from her forehead. 'Need any buttons sewed on, darling?' Sometimes she called him darling when David was around, too.

'No,' he said, smiling, and sat down on a hassock.

She glanced at the door as if to make sure no one was about, then pursed her lips and kissed the empty air between them. 'I'll miss you this weekend. What time are you leaving tomorrow?'

'David wants to leave just after lunch. It's my last assignment, Ginnie. David's last book with me. I'm quitting.'

'Quitting?' She let her sewing fall into her lap. 'You've told David, too?'

'No. I'll tell him tomorrow. I don't know why you're surprised. You're the reason, Ginnie. I don't think I have to make any speeches.'

'I understand, Penn. You know I've asked for a divorce. But I'll keep on asking. I'll work something out and then—' She was on her knees suddenly in front of him, crying, her head down on her hands that gripped his hands.

He turned his eyes away and slowly stood up, drawing her up with him. 'I'll be around another two weeks, probably; long enough for David to finish this book, if he wants me around that long. And you needn't worry. I won't tell him why I'm quitting.' His voice had sunk to a whisper, though David was downstairs in his soundproofed study, and the maid, Penn thought, was in the basement.

'I wouldn't care if you told him,' she said with quiet defiance.

'It's a wonder he doesn't know.'

'Will you be around, say in three months, if I can get a divorce?' she asked.

He nodded; then, feeling his own eyes start to burn, he smiled. 'I'll be around an awful long time. I'm just not so sure you want a divorce.'

Her eyebrows drew down, stubborn and serious. 'You'll see. I don't want to make David angry. I'm afraid of his temper, I've told you that. But maybe I'll have to stop being afraid.' Her blue eyes looked straight into his. 'Remember that dream you told us, about the man you were walking with on the country road, who disappeared? And you kept calling him and you couldn't find him?'

'Yes,' he said, smiling.

'I wish it would happen to you – with David. I wish David would just disappear suddenly, this weekend, and be out of my life forever, so I could be with you.'

Her words did strange and terrible things to him. He released her arm. 'People don't just disappear. There're other ways.' He was going to add, 'Such as divorce,' but he didn't.

'Such as?'

'I'd better get back to my typewriter. I've got another half-hour tape to do.'

David and Penn left in the black convertible the next afternoon with a small suitcase apiece, one typewriter, the tape recorder, and an iced carton of steaks and beer and a few other items of food. David was in a good mood, talking about an idea that had come to him during the night for a new book. David Ostrander wrote science fiction so prolifically that he used half a dozen pen names. He seldom took longer than a month to write a book, and he worked every month of the year. More ideas came to him than he could use, and he was in the habit of passing them on to other writers at his Wednesday night Guild meetings.

David Ostrander was forty-three, lean and wiry, with a thin, dry-skinned face thatched with fine, intersecting wrinkles — the only part of him that showed his age at all and exaggerated it at that — wrinkles that looked as if he had spent all his forty-three years in the dry, sterile winds of the fantastic planets about which he wrote.

Ginnie was only twenty-four, Penn remembered, two years younger than himself. Her skin was pliant and smooth, her lips like a poppy's petals. He stopped thinking about her. It irked him to think of David's lips kissing hers. How could she have married him? Or why? Or was there something about David's intellect, his bitter humor, his energy, that a woman would find attractive? Of course David had money, a comfortable income plus the profits of his writing, but what did Ginnie do with it? Nice clothes, yes, but did David ever take her out? They hardly ever entertained. As far as Penn had been able to learn, they had never traveled anywhere.

'Eh? What do you think of that, Penn? The poison gas emanating from the blue vegetation and conquering the green until the whole earth perishes! Say, where are you today?'

'I got it,' Penn said without taking his eyes from the road. 'Shall I put it down in the notebook?'

'Yes. No. I'll think about it a little more today.' David lit another cigarette. 'Something's on your mind, Penn, my boy. What is it?'

Penn's hands tightened on the wheel. Well, no other moment was going to be any better, was it? A couple of scotches this evening wouldn't help, just be a little more cowardly, Penn decided. 'David, I think after this book is over, I'll be leaving you.'

'Oh,' said David, not manifesting any surprise. He puffed on his cigarette. 'Any particular reason?'

'Well, as I've told you, I have a book of my own to write. The Coast Guard thing.' Penn had spent the last four years in the Coast Guard, which was the main reason David had hired him as a secretary. David had advertised for a secretary 'preferably with a firsthand knowledge of Navy life.' The first book he had worked on with David had a Navy background – Navy life in 2800 AD, when the whole globe had been made radioactive. Penn's book would have to do with real life, and it had an orthodox plot, ending on a note of hope. It seemed at that moment a frail and hopeless thing compared to a book by the great David Ostrander.

'I'll miss you,' David said finally. 'So'll Ginnie. She's very fond of you, you know.'

From any other man it might have been a snide comment, but not from David, who positively encouraged him to spend time with Ginnie, to take walks in the woods around the estate with her, to play tennis on the clay court behind the summer house. 'I'll miss you both, too,' Penn said. 'And who wouldn't prefer the environment to an apartment in New York?'

'Don't make any speeches, Penn. We know each other too well.' David rubbed the side of his nose with a nicotine-stained forefinger. 'What if I put you on a part-time basis and gave you most of the day for your own work? You could have a whole wing of the house to yourself.'

Penn declined it politely. He wanted to get away by himself for a while.

'Ginnie's going to sulk,' David said, as if to himself.

They reached the lodge at sundown. It was a substantial one-story affair made of unhewn logs, with a stone chimney at one end. White birches and huge pine trees swayed in the autumn breeze. By the time they unpacked and got a fire going for the steak, it was seven o'clock. David said little, but he seemed cheerful, as if their conversation about Penn's quitting had never taken place. They had two drinks each before dinner, two being David's limit for himself on the nights he worked and also those on which he did not work, which were rare.

David looked at him across the wooden table. 'Did you tell Ginnie you were leaving?'

Penn nodded, and swallowed with an effort. 'I told her yesterday.' Then he wished he hadn't admitted it. Wasn't it more logical to tell one's employer first?

David's eyes seemed to be asking the same question. 'And how did she take it?'

'Said she'd be sorry to see me go,' Penn said casually, and cut another bite of steak.

'Oh. Like that. I'm sure she'll be devastated.'

Penn jumped as if a knife had been stuck into him.

'I'm not blind, you know, Penn. I know you two think you're in love with each other.'

'Now listen, David, just a minute. If you possibly imagine—'

'I know what I know, that's all. I know what's going on behind my back when I'm in my study or when I'm in town Wednesday nights at the Guild meeting!' David's eyes shone with blue fire, like the cold lights of his lunar landscapes.

'David, there's nothing going on behind your back,' Penn said evenly. 'If you doubt me, ask Ginnie.'

'Hah!'

'But I think you'll understand why it's better that I leave. I should think you'd approve of it, in fact.'

'I do.' David lit a cigarette.

'I'm sorry this happened,' Penn added. 'Ginnie's very young. I also think she's bored — with her life, not necessarily with you.'

'Thanks!' David said like a pistol shot.

Penn lit a cigarette, too. They were both on their feet now. The half-eaten meal was over. Penn watched David moving about as he might have watched an armed man who at any minute might pull a gun or a knife. He didn't trust David, couldn't predict him. The last thing he would have predicted was David's burst of temper tonight, the first Penn had seen. 'Okay, David. I'll say again that I'm sorry. But you've no reason to hold a grudge against me.'

'That's enough of your words! I know a heel when I see one!'

'If you were my weight, I'd break your jaw for that!' Penn yelled, advancing on him with his fists clenched. 'I've had enough of your words tonight, too. I suppose you'll go home and throw your bilge at Ginnie. Well, where do *you* get off, shoving a bored, good-looking girl at your male secretary, telling us to go off on picnic lunches together? Can you blame either of us?'

David muttered something unintelligible in the direction of the fireplace. Then he turned and said, 'I'm going for a walk.' He went out and slammed the thick door so hard that the floor shook.

Automatically, Penn began clearing the dishes away, the untouched salad. They had started the refrigerator, and Penn carefully put the butter away on a shelf. The thought of spending the night here with David was ghastly, yet where else could he go? They were six miles from the nearest town, and there was only one car.

The door suddenly opened, and Penn nearly dropped the coffeepot.

'Come out for a walk with me,' David said. 'Maybe it'll do us both good.' He was not smiling.

Penn set the coffeepot back on the stove. A walk with David was the last thing he wanted, but he was afraid to refuse. 'Have you got the flashlight?'

'No, but we don't need it. There's moonlight.'

They walked from the lodge door to the car, then turned left onto the dirt road that went on for two miles through the woods to the highway.

'This is a half moon,' David said. 'Mind if I try a little experiment? Walk on ahead of me, here where it's pretty clear, and let me see how much of you I can make out at thirty yards. Take big strides and count off thirty. You know, it's for that business about Faro.'

Penn nodded. He knew. They were back on the book again, and they'd probably work a couple of hours tonight when they went back to the lodge. Penn started counting, taking big strides.

'Fine, keep going!' David called.

Twenty-eight ... twenty-nine ... thirty. Penn stopped and stood still. He turned around. He couldn't see David. 'Hey! Where are you?'

No answer.

Penn smiled wryly, and stuffed his hands into his pockets. 'Can you see me, David?'

Silence. Penn started slowly back to where he had left David. A little joke, he supposed, a mildly insulting joke, but he resolved to take no offense.

He walked on toward the lodge, where he was sure he would find David thoughtfully pacing the floor as he pondered his work, perhaps dictating already into the tape recorder; but the main room was empty. There was no sound from the corner room where they worked, nor from the closed room where David slept. Penn lit a cigarette, picked up the newspaper and sat down in the single armchair. He read with deliberate concentration, finished his cigarette and lit another. The second cigarette was gone when he got up, and he felt angry and a little scared at the same time.

He went to the lodge door and called, 'David!' a couple of times, loudly. He walked toward the car, got close enough to see that there was no one sitting in it. Then he returned to the lodge and methodically searched it, looking even under the bunks.

What was David going to do, come back in the middle of the night and kill him in his sleep? No, that was crazy, as crazy as one of David's story ideas. Penn suddenly thought of his dream, remembered David's brief but intense interest in it the night he had told it at the dinner table. 'Who was the man with you?' David had asked. But in the dream, Penn hadn't been able to identify him. He was just a shadowy companion on a walk. 'Maybe it was me,' David had said, his blue eyes shining. 'Maybe you'd like *me* to disappear, Penn.' Neither Ginnie nor he had made a comment, Penn recalled, nor had they discussed David's remark when they were alone. It had been so long ago, over two months ago.

Penn put that out of his mind. David had probably wandered down to the lake to be alone for a while, and hadn't been courteous enough to tell him. Penn did the dishes, took a shower and crawled into his bunk. It was twelve-ten. He had thought he wouldn't be able to sleep, but he was asleep in less than two minutes.

The raucous cries of ducks on the wing awakened him at six-thirty. He put on his robe and went into the bathroom, noting that David's towel, which he had stuck hastily over the rack last night, had not been touched. Penn went to David's room and knocked. Then he opened the door a crack. The two bunks, one above the other, were still made up. Penn washed hurriedly, dressed, and went out.

He looked over the ground on both sides of the road where he had last seen David, looking for shoe prints in the moist pine needles. He walked to the lake and looked around its marshy edge; not a footprint, not a cigarette butt.

He yelled David's name, three times, and gave it up.

By seven-thirty a.m. Penn was in the town of Croydon. He saw a small rectangular sign between a barber's shop and a paint store that said POLICE. He parked the car, went into the station, and told his story. As Penn had thought, the police wanted to look over the lodge. Penn led them back in David's car.

The two policemen had heard of David Ostrander, not as a writer, apparently, but as one of the few people who had a lodge in the area. Penn showed them where he had last seen David, and told them that

Mr Ostrander had been experimenting to see how well he could see him at thirty yards.

'How long have you been working for Mr Ostrander?'

'Four months. Three months and three weeks to be exact.'

'Had he been drinking?'

'Two scotches. His usual amount. I had the same.'

Then they walked to the lake and looked around.

'Mr Ostrander have a wife?' one of the men asked.

'Yes. She's at the house in Stonebridge, New York.'

'We'd better notify her.'

There was no telephone at the lodge. Penn wanted to stay on in case David turned up, but the police asked him to come with them back to the station, and Penn did not argue. At least he would be there when they talked with Ginnie, and he'd be able to speak with her himself. Maybe David had decided to go back to Stonebridge and was already home. The highway was only two miles from the lodge, and David could have flagged a bus or picked up a ride from someone, but Penn couldn't really imagine David Ostrander doing anything that simple or obvious.

'Listen,' Penn said to the policemen before he got into David's convertible, 'I think I ought to tell you that Mr Ostrander is kind of an odd one. He writes science fiction. I don't know what his objective is, but I think he deliberately disappeared last night. I don't think he was kidnapped or attacked by a bear or anything like that.'

The policemen looked at him thoughtfully.

'Okay, Mr Knowlton,' one of them said. 'Now you drive on ahead of us, will you?'

Back at the station in Croydon, they called the number Penn gave them. Hanna, the maid, answered. Penn, six feet from the telephone, could hear her shrill, German-accented voice; then Ginnie came on. The officer reported that David Ostrander was missing since ten o'clock last night, and asked her if she'd had any word from him. Ginnie's voice, after the first exclamation which

Penn had heard, sounded alarmed. The officer watched Penn as he listened to her.

'Yes . . . What's that again? . . . No, no blood or anything. Not a clue so far. That's why we're calling you.' A long pause. The officer's pencil tapped but did not write. 'I see . . . I see . . . We'll call you, Mrs Ostrander.'

'May I speak to her?' Penn reached for the telephone.

The captain hesitated, then said, 'Good-bye, Mrs Ostrander,' and put the telephone down. 'Well, Mr Knowlton, are you prepared to swear that the story you told us is true?'

'Absolutely.'

'Because I've just heard a motive if I ever heard one. A motive for getting Mr Ostrander out of the way. Now, just what did you do to him – or maybe say to him?' The officer leaned forward, palms on his desk.

'What did she just tell you?'

'That you're in love with her and you might have wanted her husband out of the picture.'

Penn tried to keep calm. 'I was quitting my job to get away from the situation! I told Mr Ostrander yesterday that I was going to quit, and I told his wife the day before.'

'So you admit there was a situation.'

The police, four of them now, looked at him with frank disbelief.

'Mrs Ostrander's upset,' Penn said. 'She doesn't know what she's saying. Can I talk to her, please? Now?'

'You'll see her when she gets here.' The officer sat down and picked up a pen. 'Knowlton, we're booking you on suspicion. Sorry.'

They questioned him until one p.m., then gave him a hamburger and a paper container of weak coffee. They kept asking him if there hadn't been a gun at the lodge – there hadn't been – and if he hadn't weighted David's body and thrown it in the lake along with the gun.

'We walked half around the lake this morning,' Penn said. 'Did you notice any footprints anywhere?'

By that time, he had told them about his dream and suggested that David Ostrander was trying to enact it, an idea that brought incredulous smiles, and he had laid bare his heart in regard to Ginnie, and also his intentions with her, which were nil. Penn didn't say that Ginnie had said she was in love with him, too. He couldn't bear to tell them that, in view of what she had said about him.

They went into his past. No police record. Born in Raleigh, Virginia, graduated from the state university, a major in journalism, worked on a Baltimore paper for a year, then four years in the Coast Guard. A clean slate everywhere, and this the police seemed to believe. It was, specifically, the cleanliness of his slate with the Ostranders that they doubted. He was in love with Mrs Ostrander and yet he was really going to quit his job and leave? Hadn't he any plans about her?

'Ask her,' Penn said tiredly.

'We'll do that,' replied the officer who was called Mac.

'She knows about the dream I had, too, and the questions her husband asked me about it,' Penn said. 'Ask her in privacy, if you doubt me.'

'Get this, Knowlton,' Mac said. 'We don't fool around with dreams. We want facts.'

Ginnie arrived a little after three p.m. Catching a glimpse of her through the bars of the cell they had put him in, Penn sighed with relief. She looked calm, perfectly in command of herself. The police took her to another room for ten minutes or so, and then they came and unlocked Penn's cell door. As he approached Ginnie, she looked at him with a hostility or fear that was like a kick in the pit of his stomach. It checked the 'Hello, Ginnie' that he wanted to say.

'Will you repeat to him what he said to you day before yesterday, Mrs Ostrander?' asked Mac.

'Yes. He said, "I wish David would disappear the way he did in my dream. I wish he were out of your life so I could be alone with you."'

Penn stared at her. 'Ginnie, *you* said that!'

'I think what we want to know from you, Knowlton, is what you did with her husband,' said Mac.

'Ginnie,' Penn said desperately, 'I don't know why you're saying that. I can repeat every word of the conversation we had that afternoon, beginning with me saying I wanted to quit. That much you'll agree with, won't you?'

'Why, my husband had *fired* him — because of his attentions to me!' Ginnie glared at Penn and at the men around her.

Penn felt a panic, a nausea rising. Ginnie looked insane — or like a woman who was positive she was looking at her husband's murderer. There flashed to his mind her amazing coolness the moment after the one time he had kissed her, when David, by an unhappy stroke of luck, had tapped on her door and walked in. Ginnie hadn't turned a hair. She was an actress by nature, apparently, and she was acting now. 'That's a lie and you know it,' Penn said.

'And it's a lie what you said to her about wanting to get rid of her husband?' Mac asked.

'Mrs Ostrander said that, I didn't,' Penn replied, feeling suddenly weak in the knees. 'That's why I was quitting. I didn't want to interfere with a marriage that—'

The listening policeman smiled.

'My husband and I were devoted.'

Then Ginnie bent her head and gave in, it appeared, to the most genuine tears in the world.

Penn turned to the desk. 'All right, lock me up. I'll be glad to stay here till David Ostrander turns up — because I'll bet my life he's not dead.'

Penn pressed his palms against the cool wall of the cell. He was aware that Ginnie had left the station, but that was the only external circumstance of which he was aware.

A funny girl, Ginnie. She was mad about David, after all. She must worship David for his talent, for his discipline, and for his liking her. What was she, after all? A good-looking girl who hadn't succeeded as an actress (until now), who hadn't enough inner resources to amuse herself while her husband worked twelve hours a day, so she had started flirting with her husband's secretary. Penn remembered that Ginnie had said their chauffeur had quit five months ago. They hadn't hired another. Penn wondered if the chauffeur had quit for the same reason he had been going to leave. Or had David fired him? Penn didn't dare believe anything, now, that Ginnie had ever said to him.

A more nightmarish thought crossed his mind: suppose Ginnie really didn't love David, and had stopped on her way to Croydon and found David in the lodge and had shot him? Or if she had found him on the grounds, in the woods, had she shot him and left him to be discovered later, so that he would get the blame? So that she would be free of David and free of him, too? Or was there even a gun in Stonebridge that Ginnie could have taken?

Did Ginnie hate David or love him? On that incredible question his own future might hang, because if Ginnie had killed him herself . . . But how did it explain David's voluntarily disappearing last night?

Penn heard footsteps and stood up.

Mac stopped in front of his cell. 'You're telling the truth, Knowlton?' he asked a little dubiously.

'Yes.'

'So, the worst that can happen is, you'll sit a couple of days till Ostrander turns up.'

'I hope you're looking for him.'

'That we are, all over the state and farther if we have to.' He started to go, then turned back.

'Thought I'd bring you a stronger light bulb and something to read, if you're in any mood for reading.'

There was no news the next morning.

Then, around four p.m., a policeman came and unlocked Penn's cell.

'What's up?' Penn asked.

'Ostrander turned up at his house in Stonebridge,' the man said with a trace of a smile.

Penn smiled, too, slightly. He followed him out to the front desk.

Mac gave Penn a nod of greeting. 'We just called Mr Ostrander's house. He came home half an hour ago. Said he'd taken a walk to do some thinking, and he can't understand what all the fuss is about.'

Penn's hand shook as he signed his own release paper. He was dreading the return to the lodge to get his possessions, the inevitable few minutes at the Stonebridge house while he packed up the rest of his things.

David's convertible was at the curb where Penn had left it yesterday. He got in and headed for the lodge. There, he packed first his own things and closed his suitcase, then started to carry it and the tape recorder to the car, but on second thought decided to leave the tape recorder. How was he supposed to know what David wanted done with his stuff?

As he drove south toward Stonebridge, Penn realized that he didn't know what he felt or how he ought to behave. Ginnie: it wasn't worthwhile to say anything to her, either in anger or by way of asking her why. David: it was going to be hard to resist saying, 'I hope you enjoyed your little joke. Are you trying to get a plot out of it?' Penn's foot pressed the accelerator, but he checked his speed abruptly. *Don't lose your temper*, he told himself. *Just get your stuff quietly and get out.*

Lights were on in the living room, and also in Ginnie's room upstairs. It was around nine o'clock. They'd have dined, and sometimes they sat awhile in the living room over coffee, but usually David went into his study to work. Penn couldn't see David's study window. He rang the bell.

Hanna opened the door. 'Mister Knowlton!' she exclaimed. 'They told me you'd gone away for good!'

'I have,' Penn said. 'Just came by to pick up my things.'

'Come right in, sir! Mister and Missus are in the living room. I'll tell them you're here.' She went trotting off before he could stop her.

Penn followed her across the broad foyer. He wanted a look at David, just a look. Penn stopped a little short of the door. David and Ginnie were sitting close together on the sofa, facing him, David's arm on the back of the sofa, and as Hanna told them he was here, David dropped his arm so that it circled Ginnie's waist. Ginnie did not show any reaction, only took a puff on her cigarette.

'Come on in, Penn!' David called, smiling. 'What're you so shy about?'

'Nothing at all.' Penn stopped at the threshold now. 'I came to get my things, if I may.'

'If you may!' David mocked. 'Why, of course, Penn!' He stood up, holding Ginnie's hand now, as if he wanted to flaunt before Penn how affectionate they had become.

'Tell him to get his things and go,' Ginnie said, smashing her cigarette in the ashtray. Her tone wasn't angry, in fact it was gentle, but she'd had a few drinks.

David came toward Penn, his lean, wrinkled face smiling. 'I'll come with you. Maybe I can help.'

Penn turned stiffly and walked to his room, which was down the hall. He went in, dragged a large suitcase out of the bottom of a closet, and began with a bureau drawer, lifting out socks and pajamas. He was conscious of David watching him with an amused smile. The smile was like an animal's claws in Penn's back. 'Where'd you hide that night, David?'

'Hide? Nowhere!' David chuckled. 'Just took a little walk and didn't answer you. I was interested to see what would happen. Rather, I knew what would happen. Everything was just as I'd predicted.'

'What do you mean?' Penn's hands trembled as he slid open his top drawer.

'With Ginnie,' David said. 'I knew she'd turn against you and turn to me. It's happened before, you see. You were a fool to think if you waited for her she'd divorce me and come to you. An absolute fool!'

Penn whirled around, his hands full of folded shirts. 'Listen, David, I wasn't waiting for Ginnie. I was clearing out of this—'

'Don't give me that, you sneak! Carrying on behind your employer's back!'

Penn flung the shirts into his suitcase. 'What do you mean, it's happened before?'

'With our last chauffeur. And my last secretary, too. I'd get a girl secretary, you see, but Ginnie likes these little dramas. They serve to draw us together and they keep her from getting bored. Your dream gave me a splendid idea for this one. You see how affectionate Ginnie is with me now? And she thinks you're a prizewinning sucker.' David laughed and lifted his cigarette to his lips.

A second later, Penn landed the hardest blow he had ever struck, on David's jaw. David's feet flew up in the wake of his body, and his head hit a wall six feet away.

Penn threw the rest of his things into his suitcase and crushed the lid down as furiously as if he were still fighting David. He pulled the suitcase off the bed and turned to the door.

Ginnie blocked his way. 'What've you *done* to him?'

'Not as much as I'd like to do.'

Ginnie rushed past him to David, and Penn went out the door.

Hanna was hurrying down the hall. 'Something the matter, Mr Knowlton?'

'Nothing serious. Good-bye, Hanna,' Penn said, trying to control his hoarse voice. 'And thanks,' he added, and went on toward the front door.

'He's *dead*!' Ginnie cried wailingly.

Hanna was running to the room. Penn hesitated, then went on toward the door. The little liar! Anything for a dramatic kick!

'*Stop him!*' Ginnie yelled. 'Hanna, he's trying to get away!'

Penn set his suitcase down and went back. He'd yank David up and douse his head in water. 'He's not dead,' Penn said as he strode into the room.

Hanna was standing beside David with a twisted face, ready for tears. 'Yes – he is, Mr Knowlton.'

Penn bent to pull David up, but his hand stopped before it

touched him. Something shiny was sticking out of David's throat, and Penn recognized it – the haft of his own paper knife that he'd neglected to pack.

A long, crazy laugh – or maybe it was a wailing sob – came from Ginnie behind him. 'You *monster*! I suppose you wiped your finger-prints off it! But it won't do you any good, Penn! Hanna, call the police at once. Tell them we've got a murderer here!'

Hanna looked at her with horror. 'I'll call them, ma'am. But it was you that wiped the handle. You were wiping it with your skirt when I came in the door.'

Penn stared at Ginnie. He and she were not finished with each other yet.

A DANGEROUS HOBBY

Andrew Forster, thirty-seven, married, the father of a fourteen-year-old girl and a topnotch salesman of the Marvel Vacuum Company, had developed a curious hobby. He would call up women, give them a long, slow, subtly flattering line, make a date with them (sometimes it took two dates, if the woman did not permit him on the first date to call for her at her house), and then he would rob them of some possession small enough to be put in his pocket.

Sometimes it was no more than a silver cigarette lighter or a ring of middling value that he picked up from a dressing table; but it satisfied him, and after his petty thievery, he dropped the women. He was never, so far as he knew, suspected. His courteous, serious, intelligent manner put him above reproach. After all, his job was selling, and the first thing a salesman had to do in order to get into a living room to demonstrate a vacuum was to sell himself. This Andy Forster could do superbly well.

And of course he picked his victims with care. They were all women with careers or professions, and all were single, though this last did not matter too much. One had been an actress, one a fairly well-known journalist, another a dress designer. He had boned up on their careers and current activities so that he could sing their praises in his very first telephone conversation.

To the dress designer he had spoken about his fourteen-year-old daughter who, he said, was determined to be a dress designer herself, and though he realized it was an unusual request from a total stranger, could he possibly meet her and talk with her for fifteen minutes or so somewhere? He had made sure he had seen the actress's last play and could therefore talk about it with conviction. He had especially admired the journalist's piece on such and such, and had some flattering questions to ask her. He had never been refused an appointment.

His appearance, when he arrived at their doors or when he stood up with a quizzical expression, not quite sure they were the right women, to greet them in a tearoom or a cocktail lounge, was even more reassuring than his voice on the telephone. He was about five-ten, a trifle overweight though not soft, conservatively dressed, and his cheeks were pink and firm, suggestive of clean living. His manner was quiet and soft-spoken, but not unpleasantly so. He gave an impression of being somewhat in awe of the particular woman he was with, or at least of being extremely respectful of her. His conversation was always intelligent, since Andy kept himself well informed on many subjects.

He always had his car with him, a big impressive company car but with no insignia of the company on it, and at the end of the tea or the two-drink-apiece cocktail date (that was all women dared to have with a strange man, it seemed) he had so won the women's confidence that they invariably accepted his offer to drive them back to their apartments or to wherever they were going. His robberies were usually committed during the second meeting. In two instances he had made third dates, after the robberies, as a kind of challenge to fate. But the missing articles had not even been mentioned.

'How do you know so much?' they would ask him, fascinated by his explanation of the failure of the Gallipoli campaign in the First World War.

Then Andy would tell them that he had been going to be a professor of history, or of physics, or of geography, or of oceanography, but had his mind changed for him by his wife, who had said (when he was twenty-two and just about to get his degree) that she would never be happy as the wife of a college professor, because their salaries were so low.

This pitiful story, told with manly understatement and absence of resentment, made women feel extremely sympathetic, and they loudly decried the selfishness and pettiness of their own sex. They were different, of course. Just see how they could talk on an equal footing with a man, how this man listened when they spoke, and seemed to value them as a person, not just a female to jump into bed with. The furthest Andy went in familiarity was to touch their elbows as they crossed a street or got into or out of his car.

As a matter of fact, an injury Andy had received in the Korean War had made him impotent, and psychologically also he had given women up now, beginning with his wife, who had in a sense given Andy up a decade ago. His wife, Juliette, was home to cook his dinner every evening, but as likely as not she went out after dinner to work at some hospital – volunteer work or paid work, it didn't matter to Juliette. She was a registered nurse, slender, quietly efficient, with the energy of two men in her short, compact body. Juliette never talked about her work. It was simply her whole world and she could not wait to get back to it after her minimal attentions to her husband and daughter.

Andy was bright enough to realize that he hated women, though he had not realized it until after the Korean injury. That incident had made him realize that he had hated Juliette and very likely all other women for nearly the past ten years. He had once loved Juliette, but she had let him down – stupidly and without mercy let him down. And yet she was the mother of his daughter Martha, whom he adored.

In the evenings, every evening, Andy read, and he read until nearly three a.m. He was a poor sleeper. Sometimes even between three and seven a.m. when he got up, it seemed he did not sleep at all, merely rested his eyes beneath closed lids. Twelve years ago he had bought an *Encyclopedia Britannica*, and he was eighty percent through it now. Usually he read this in the evenings, propping the heavy volumes against the wall as he lay on his stomach in bed. When Juliette finally crawled into the bed on the opposite side, he simply tried to ignore her.

The loot from his encounters with women he put into a leather briefcase stamped with the Marvel Vacuum Company's trademark, which he kept at the back of his bottom drawer. Nothing was more certain than that Juliette would never look into that drawer: his bottom drawers for as long as he could remember had amassed, as if by their own power of attraction, unmended socks, shirts with missing buttons, shorts too worn out to wear but not worn out enough to be discarded, pajama tops with no pants, and vice versa. Andy did his own button-sewing and sock-mending, when he troubled to do it.

The briefcase now contained the actress's wristwatch, a sculptress's ring, the dress designer's silver twelve-inch ruler, the journalist's Javanese cigarette box studded with garnets, a thin gold necklace from a violinist of the New York Philharmonic, a pretty little silver pencil whose owner he had forgotten, a perfume bottle of blue glass enclosed in filigreed silver, a topaz ring he had picked up from the top of a toilet tank in the bathroom of a slightly tipsy nightclub singer who hadn't minded drinking a good deal in her own apartment, a Tanagra figurine that he kept wrapped in a handkerchief, and an antique silver flask of pocket size.

Andy had in mind giving many of these things to Martha when she would be twenty-one or so and out of college, and perhaps even out of the house, if she were married by then. He would bestow the presents slowly over the years, in a way that would excite no suspicion in Juliette, he hoped. She paid so little attention to what he did that it was hard to imagine her being suspicious of anything.

After six weeks of selling vacuums all day and coming home to a more or less silent wife, Andy would begin to feel restless and start planning a new adventure. One afternoon in mid-May he entered a telephone booth in the Bronx to call a woman anthropologist named

Rebecca Wooster, whom he had seen one Sunday afternoon on a television program. She had just returned from the West Indies and Central America, where she had been making studies. Andy had found her number in the telephone book, but the number had been changed, the operator said, and she gave him the new one, which he made a note of, and dialed. A woman's voice answered, and when Andy ascertained that she was Miss Wooster, he continued in his usual style.

'My name is Robert Garrett.' (He never gave his real name.) 'I hope you'll forgive me for calling you out of the blue like this, but I saw you on television a few Sundays ago, and I've been — well, I've been thinking ever since about some of the things you said. I'm something of an amateur anthropologist myself, and I'm working on a theory just now using psychological rather than racial grouping. I'd like very much to ask you a few questions, that is, if you've got half an hour to spare — and I'd be very grateful to you if you could possibly spare the time to look over the outline I've made. It's just a matter of three pages.'

He went on for another few minutes in a slow, earnest way, giving her time to respond now and then with a word or two that showed she was following him, in fact listening with interest. He had seen in the television show that she was a warm and friendly woman, patient with the questions that had been asked her at the end of the program, some of which had not been very pertinent. Finally, he apologized for taking so much of her time with the telephone call, and put in a modest plea that she would grant him a personal interview, however brief.

'Why, I think I can manage that,' she said in her slow, pleasant voice. 'How would tomorrow be? Say around five-thirty?'

'That would be fine,' Andy replied. 'Really I'm very honored, Miss Wooster.' He asked for her address, she gave it to him, and they said good-bye cordially.

Andy was punctual the following afternoon, bringing with him a folded map of the world on which he had drawn various circles, some overlapping, to indicate his 'psychologically similar groups.' Most of it had no validity at all, he knew, but he had made the circles as best he could after consulting a few sociology books. He also had an 'outline' of three typed pages.

Miss Wooster lived on the fourteenth floor – actually the thirteenth of a rather formal building on Park Avenue. She received him in a foyer as soon as he stepped out of the elevator. Andy introduced himself with a little bow, and they went into a large room that looked like a living room except for a massive desk near the window.

'You say you're not an anthropologist by profession,' Miss Wooster began after they had seated themselves on the sofa.

'No. I work for a company that compiles reference books for the public library, not a very interesting job, I'm afraid, but it gives me a chance to read a lot.' He got up with a murmured apology and walked in an awestruck way toward her bookshelves, on which stood, among the books, a dozen or more small sculptures and jeweled pieces of primitive art. 'I hope you don't mind,' he apologized. 'These fascinate me, and I've never seen anything like these except in a glass case in a museum.'

She got up, smiling with pleasure at his interest, and they talked and examined the pieces for fifteen minutes. What interested Andy most was a Mayan ornament of hammered gold, all a-tinkle with small gold pendants, each weighted with a tiny green stone. It was small enough to fit into his jacket pocket, and he had only to wait for the proper time to whisk it there, perhaps when Miss Wooster would turn to answer the telephone on the desk. Andy hated to resort to asking for a glass of water, though sometimes he had done so. At any rate, if he did have to ask for water, there did not seem to be any servant about who might get it for him.

'Well, let me see the outline you were talking about,' Miss Wooster said, seating herself in a chair near the bookshelves. 'I have an appointment at six, I'm sorry to say, but I couldn't arrange it any later.'

Andy glanced at his watch, saw that it was 5:47, and said, 'I'll make it as brief as I can.' He crossed the room for his briefcase, and from among pamphlets concerning Marvel vacuums removed his map of the world and his three-page outline. Then he took a deep breath and began, slowly, but in a way that did not permit Miss Wooster to interrupt him.

A smile of incredulity, perhaps of amusement, was growing on her lips.

'You may think – I suppose I am incompetent to make such a study,' he finished.

'No. It's quite interesting. I admire your enthusiasm.' She had looked over his outline. 'But I think you're wrong about the Adonis and the Chinese. I mean, the similarity you spoke of . . . '

Andy listened carefully as she talked and as the minutes ticked away. He wondered if he could get the Mayan piece on his first visit and if not, could he persuade her to let him see her again. Immediately, he forced the doubt from his mind. To doubt was fatal. At any rate, she was not telling him that his idea was *absolutely* off the beam, or unworthy of being written about.

A bell rang in the hall.

'Oh, dear, that must be my appointment,' Miss Wooster said, getting up. 'It's a bit early. Excuse me, Mr Garrett.'

Andy stood up, smiling. He couldn't have planned it better. Miss Wooster went into the foyer to speak over the telephone to the caller downstairs, and Andy quickly pocketed the Mayan piece, making sure that the gap it left would not be noticed until he was out of the house.

When Miss Wooster came in again, he was slowly putting his papers back into his briefcase.

'I've overstayed,' he said sadly.

'Oh, no. But I do have to see this person now, because she's coming to interview me.' She smiled and held out her hand. 'It's been such a pleasure meeting you. I hope you'll go on with your book. You say you've written a hundred pages?'

'Yes.' Andy was now moving toward the foyer.

'If you hit any snags, don't hesitate to call me. I'm always glad to talk about my favorite subject.'

'Thank you—'

The elevator door had slid open. A tall woman of about thirty-five came slowly out and looked at Andy in a puzzled way. He looked at her in the same way, and then realized with horror that she was the journalist from whom he had stolen – what was it?

'Well! Mr – O'Neill, isn't it?' she asked.

'No,' said Miss Wooster. 'This is Mr Garrett. Mr Garrett, Miss Holquist. Or – have you met before?'

'*Yes,*' said Miss Holquist.

Andy knew he couldn't get away with it. Even though his face was more or less ordinary, Myra Holquist had seen him on two occasions not more than six months ago. 'Sorry,' he said. 'My name is Garrett. I don't know why I told you it was O'Neill. Just to be adventurous, I guess. Or I think I was trying out my pen name. There are enough writers named Garrett.'

Myra Holquist nodded, as if she were thinking of something else. 'How's the journalism going? Weren't you interested in writing something about the passing of the vacant lot in the lives of New York children? Something like that?'

Now Miss Wooster was looking at him oddly.

'Something like that,' Andy admitted weakly. 'Well, I must be going.'

He felt utterly defeated, shamed, humiliated. All his style was gone. He rang for the elevator, which unfortunately had closed and disappeared.

'Just a minute – Mr Garrett. Excuse me, Miss Wooster. I wondered why you disappeared so suddenly,' Miss Holquist continued to Andy. 'It didn't by any chance have anything to do with a Javanese cigarette box?'

'I don't know what you mean,' Andy said, frowning with feigned perplexity.

She gave him a bitter smile. 'But you look as if you do. Miss Wooster, have you known this man very long?'

'Why, no,' Miss Wooster replied. 'Just this afternoon. He—'

'Then before he leaves, I think you'd be wise to look around your house and see if anything's missing.'

Miss Wooster gasped, and Andy gritted his teeth and prayed for the elevator door to slide open. But he couldn't even hear the thing coming.

'I mean it, Miss Wooster,' said Miss Holquist in a tone of command.

Some remnant of pride, perhaps even the beginning of a plan, inspired Andy to motion the elevator away as its door slid open. 'Thanks, not just yet,' he said to the elevator man, and turned like one about to be executed and followed Miss Wooster back into the living room.

Myra Holquist also came in from the foyer.

'Why – my gold Mayan piece!' Miss Wooster exclaimed. 'It's gone!' And she looked at Andy with wide, frightened eyes. 'D-did you see it?' she stammered.

'Give it to her, Mr O'Neill, or Mr Garrett,' said Miss Holquist coolly.

Then Andy struck her in the side of the head with all the force of his muscular right arm, and she fell to the floor. He knelt and throttled her, bumping her head again and again on the floor, oblivious of Miss Wooster's screams, of her ineffectual efforts to pull him away. Nothing that could be described as a thought was in Andy's mind during those few violent seconds, only a feeling, a consciousness that the woman he was attacking had betrayed him, stripped him of decency, had filled him with an intolerable shame. Her overly made-up face symbolized to him all that he despised in the female sex – its coldness, mercilessness, indifference.

'Shut up!' Andy blazed at Miss Wooster as he got to his feet. But when he saw her retreating from him, he became frightened himself. She had become silent now, but he was afraid someone might appear at any moment in response to her screams. She kept retreating and he kept walking toward her. He wanted a rope, a gag – anything to tie her up until he could get away.

'Where's the bedroom? Go in the bedroom,' he ordered. He saw the bedroom behind her and there was a key in its ornate door. 'Get in there.'

She went in obediently.

'And here. You can have this,' he said, pulling the Mayan piece from his jacket pocket. He laid it on the top of a chest just inside the bedroom door. 'I'm sorry, really sorry.' Inarticulate, he jerked his head to one side in shamed apology, pulled the door to, and locked it, leaving the key in it.

Then he dashed back to the living room for his briefcase – Miss Holquist was motionless – and not daring to leave by the elevator he looked for the kitchen. Just as he had hoped, it had a delivery entrance, and outside this door he found a service elevator and some stairs.

He took the stairs. Down and down, thirteen unlucky floors. It put him out in a cellar, unlighted except for a little daylight that showed through an open door. He went out this door, up some iron steps, and he was on Seventy-eighth Street, between Park and Lexington, only fifteen feet from his car. Slowly he walked to the car, feeling in his pocket for his keys.

He lived on one of those peculiarly gloomy streets of apartment houses near the Manhattan approach of the George Washington Bridge. The bars of that neighborhood were gloomy, too, but Andy went into one and had two quick shots of rye to steady himself before he went home. For once he was grateful that Juliette scarcely spoke to him and never looked him fully in the face. And Martha, he remembered, was having supper with a school friend tonight, and was going to spend the evening with the friend doing homework.

That night Andy did not sleep at all. He was haunted by Miss Wooster's muffled cries through her bedroom door. Had there been a telephone in the room? How soon had she been able to get out? *Mr Garrett, Mr O'Neill*, she had called and called.

Andy turned in his bed with shame and thought of the cache of treasures in his bottom drawer. It was as if he had never seen his revolting pastime objectively before – he who had always considered himself a fairly intelligent man!

The next morning Andy bought a paper at the newsstand near his office, where he checked in every morning at eight forty-five. He found nothing in it about the nightmare of the last evening, but he was not sure if the morning papers could have picked up the story in time. He sold one vacuum cleaner to an elderly lady who had an apartment full of singing canaries.

Then he bought an afternoon paper, which said that Myra Holquist, the well-known journalist, had been throttled to death in the apartment of Rebecca Wooster, the eminent anthropologist, whom she had come to interview. Like the encounter itself yesterday, it seemed fantastic and unreal, until he went on to read the doctor's statement and also the description of 'Robert Garrett or O'Neill' given by Miss Wooster. It was him to a T, a portrait of himself in words.

But a *murderer!* Murder was something Andy had not bargained for.

He knew what the police would do first: look for a Robert Garrett or an O'Neill answering his description, not find any (Andy hoped they would not find any), then a man of his description connected with any company that compiled reference books for the public library. Then they would start looking for a man of his description in the streets, anywhere. And maybe one day——

It crossed Andy's mind to turn himself in, and yet the murder, to him, seemed such an accident, such a piece of bad luck, that he felt he deserved better than to give himself into the merciless custody of the law. So he steeled himself to live with the awful fact that another person, a woman, had witnessed his crime and could, if she ever spotted him, put an end to his present way of life. The briefcase of stolen articles in the bottom of his drawer he could not even touch now. Merely the thought of it was enough to paralyze any action he might have taken to get rid of it.

Six months went by. Andy lost a little weight, but it was so gradual that neither Juliette nor anyone at his office made a remark about it. He could not look a policeman in the face on the street and he could not get over the habit of glancing quickly at all the faces that came flooding out from any opened elevator. The one time he and Juliette had gone to the theater (Juliette's request on her birthday), the intermissions in the lobby had been hell for him.

And then Andy read in the newspaper that Rebecca Wooster, forty-nine, had succumbed to a heart attack while at work in Ceylon. His reaction to this was very slow, covering a period of three days, at the end of which he took the briefcase from his bottom drawer and dropped it from the George Washington Bridge.

After this he felt better, and he expected that he would feel better and better as time went on. He did sleep better for a while, and then his sleep began to grow worse again. He developed circles under his eyes, permanent circles of purple.

Tossing in his bed one night, sleepless, he knew what was the matter. He had no specific enemy now, no one who shared the knowledge of his guilt. He had only himself.

For weeks now he had fought against a compulsion to confess, realizing what it would mean to his daughter and even to Juliette. But he could not convince himself that he was not behaving more heinously by keeping his secret, his unpunished crime, to himself. After all, he was a member of society, and so were his daughter and his wife.

So one cold afternoon in February, Andy went into a police station in the east fifties and gave himself up. He said that he was the Robert Garrett, alias O'Neill, who last May had throttled Myra Holquist to death in the apartment of the late Rebecca Wooster.

His eyelids twitched, as they did habitually now, and he realized that he did not sound very convincing. But he was not prepared for the stone wall of disbelief that confronted him in that police station. A high-ranking officer questioned him in detail for several minutes, called another station for a check on the description of Garrett-O'Neill, and even then expressed his doubt.

'Have you ever been in a mental institution?' the officer asked.

'No,' Andy answered.

Another officer of rank arrived and Andy repeated his story, adding now the details of his petty larcenies. But somehow his memory had deserted him. He could not remember more than one name of all the women he had pilfered from – Irene Cassidy, the dress designer. But what had be taken from her? He could describe several of the articles he had stolen, but he could not produce them, he explained, because he had dropped them off the George Washington Bridge two weeks ago.

'Call Irene Cassidy,' the new officer said.

Miss Cassidy worked in her own studio, and she was in. The officer explained the situation laboriously – as if he were trying deliberately to muddle the woman, Andy thought. He could tell from the officer's words that he was getting negative replies to everything, so Andy asked if he could speak with her. The telephone was passed over to him.

'Hello, Miss Cassidy,' Andy said. 'I can't remember the name I used when I saw you, but I asked to talk to you because I had a fourteen-year-old daughter who wanted to be a dress designer. Remember that? It must have been – I suppose over a year ago.' Maybe it had been two years ago.

'Well – I might remember if I saw you,' Miss Cassidy replied, 'but I see a lot of people who want to talk to me because they or somebody they know wanted to be dress designers.'

'You didn't notice that something was missing – after I saw you that time?'

'Missing? What?'

'Some small thing from your studio – or your desk – I don't remember exactly.'

'The guy's nuts,' murmured a voice behind him.

'Can you come down to this station? Please?' Andy pleaded.

Miss Cassidy did not want to be bothered. Andy asked her to wait a moment, then passed the telephone to an officer and told him to do what he could to persuade her to come to the station. The officer was more successful.

There was a painful wait of forty-five minutes, during which time they let Andy sit on a bench from which he could easily have slipped out the door and into the street. At last Miss Cassidy arrived, small and chic, in a short fur wrap, a hat of bird feathers. The police led her to Andy and asked her if she had ever seen him before. Miss Cassidy looked blank.

'I've lost a little weight,' Andy said to her. 'Not much, but it might make a difference. We talked about Yves St Laurent, remember? The talent of youth and all that?'

It was hopeless. There was a run-down, somewhat shabby look about him now. He was no longer the robust, self-confident man she had talked with a year ago, or perhaps two years ago.

Miss Cassidy shook her head, and looked at the officers. 'I hope I'm not standing in the way of justice or anything like that, but to the best of my recollection I never saw this man before. Is he trying to save himself from something?'

'No, he's trying to confess to a murder,' the officer said with a smile. 'A sensation seeker. We get a lot of 'em like this. He's throwing in a lot of other things about robberies all over town.'

Now Miss Cassidy looked positively frightened of him. Women, Andy thought. Why should she have forgotten? It was not even deliberate, he thought, only an unconscious blow she had struck in the eternal battle of the sexes.

'We checked with the company he works for,' the officer continued. 'He hasn't missed a day's work in the nine years he's been there. Hey, is there a psychiatrist or something your company uses?' he asked Andy. 'I think you better have a checkup, Forster. Maybe you've been working too hard lately.'

A few minutes later Andy was released and out on the street again.

He went into a subway and threw himself on the tracks in front of an onrushing train.

THE TERRAPIN

V ictor heard the elevator door open, his mother's quick footsteps
in the hall, and he flipped his book shut. He shoved it under the
sofa pillow out of sight, and winced as he heard it slip between sofa
and wall and fall to the floor with a thud. Her key was in the lock.

'Hello, Vee-ector-r!' she cried, raising one arm in the air. Her
other arm circled a big brown paper bag, her hand held a cluster of
little bags. 'I have been to my publisher and to the market and also
to the fish market,' she told him. 'Why aren't you out playing? It's
a lovely, lovely day!'

'I was out,' he said. 'For a little while. I got cold.'

'Ugh!' She was unloading the grocery bag in the tiny kitchen off
the foyer. 'You are seeck, you know that? In the month of October,
you are cold? I see all kinds of children playing on the sidewalk.
Even, I think, that boy you like. What's his name?'

'I don't know,' Victor said. His mother wasn't really listening,
anyway. He pushed his hands into the pockets of his short, too small
shorts, making them tighter than ever, and walked aimlessly around
the living room, looking down at his heavy, scuffed shoes. At least
his mother had to buy him shoes that fit him, and he rather liked
these shoes, because they had the thickest soles of any he had ever
owned, and they had heavy toes that rose up a little, like mountain

climbers' shoes. Victor paused at the window and looked straight out at a toast-colored apartment building across Third Avenue. He and his mother lived on the eighteenth floor, next to the top floor where the penthouses were. The building across the street was even taller than this one. Victor had liked their Riverside Drive apartment better. He had liked the school he had gone to there better. Here they laughed at his clothes. In the other school, they had finally got tired of laughing at them.

'You don't want to go out?' asked his mother, coming into the living room, wiping her hands briskly on a paper bag. She sniffed her palms. 'Ugh! That stee-enk!'

'No, Mama,' Victor said patiently.

'Today is Saturday.'

'I know.'

'Can you say the days of the week?'

'Of course.'

'Say them.'

'I don't want to say them. I know them.' His eyes began to sting around the edges with tears. 'I've known them for years. Years and years. Kids five years old can say the days of the week.'

But his mother was not listening. She was bending over the drawing-table in the corner of the room. She had worked late on something last night. On his sofa bed in the opposite corner of the room, Victor had not been able to sleep until two in the morning, when his mother had gone to bed on the studio couch.

'Come here, Veector. Did you see this?'

Victor came on dragging feet, hands still in his pockets. No, he hadn't even glanced at her drawing-board this morning, hadn't wanted to.

'This is Pedro, the little donkey. I invented him last night. What do you think? And this is Miguel, the little Mexican boy who rides him. They ride and ride all over Mexico, and Miguel thinks they are lost, but Pedro knows the way home all the time, and . . . '

Victor did not listen. He deliberately shut his ears in a way he had learned to do from many years of practice, but boredom, frustration – he knew the word frustration, had read all about it – clamped his shoulders, weighed like a stone in his body, pressed hatred and tears up to his eyes, as if a volcano were churning in him. He had hoped his mother might take a hint from his saying that he was cold in his silly short shorts. He had hoped his mother might remember what he had told her, that the fellow he had wanted to get acquainted with downstairs, a fellow who looked about his own age, eleven, had laughed at his short pants on Monday afternoon. *They make you wear your kid brother's pants or something?* Victor had drifted away, mortified. What if the fellow knew he didn't even own any longer pants, not even a pair of knickers, much less *long* pants, even blue jeans! His mother, for some cock-eyed reason, wanted him to look 'French,' and made him wear short shorts and stockings that came to just below his knees, and dopey shirts with round collars. His mother wanted him to stay about six years old, for ever, all his life. She liked to test out her drawings on him. *Veector is my sounding board*, she sometimes said to her friends. *I show my drawings to Veector and I know if children will like them.* Often Victor said he liked stories that he did not like, or drawings that he was indifferent to, because he felt sorry for his mother and because it put her in a better mood if he said he liked them. He was quite tired now of children's book illustrations, if he had ever in his life liked them – he really couldn't remember – and now he had two favorites: Howard Pyle's illustrations in some of Robert Louis Stevenson's books and Cruikshank's in Dickens. It was too bad, Victor thought, that he was absolutely the last person of whom his mother should have asked an opinion, because he simply *hated* children's illustrations. And it was a wonder his mother didn't see this, because she hadn't sold any illustrations for books for years and years, not since *Wimple-Dimple*, a book whose jacket was all torn and turning yellow now from age, which sat in the center of the bookshelf in a little cleared spot, propped up against the back of the bookcase so everyone could see it. Victor had been seven years old when that book was printed. His mother liked to tell people and remind him, too, that he had told her what he wanted to see her draw, had watched her make every drawing, had shown his opinion by laughing or not, and that she had been absolutely guided by him. Victor doubted this very much, because first of all the story was somebody else's and had been written before his mother did the drawings, and her drawings had had to follow the story, naturally. Since then, his mother had done only a few illustrations now and then for magazines for children, how to make paper pumpkins and black paper cats for Hallowe'en and things like that, though she took her portfolio around to publishers all the time. Their income came from his father, who was a wealthy businessman in France, an exporter of perfumes. His mother said he was very wealthy and very handsome. But he had married again, he never wrote, and Victor had no interest in him, didn't even care if he never saw a picture of him, and he never had. His father was French with some Polish, and his mother was Hungarian with some French. The word Hungarian made Victor think of gypsies, but when he had asked his mother once, she had said emphatically that she hadn't any gypsy blood, and she had been annoyed that Victor brought the question up.

And now she was sounding him out again, poking him in the ribs to make him wake up, as she repeated:

'Listen to me! Which do you like better, Veector? "In all Mexico there was no bur-r-ro as wise as Miguel's Pedro," or "Miguel's Pedro was the wisest bur-r-ro in all Mexico."?'

'I think – I like it the first way better.'

'Which way is that?' demanded his mother, thumping her palm down on the illustration.

Victor tried to remember the wording, but realized he was only staring at the pencil smudges, the thumbprints on the edges of his mother's illustration board. The colored drawing in the center did not interest him at all. He was not-thinking. This was a frequent, familiar sensation to him now, there was something exciting and important about not-thinking, Victor felt, and he thought one day he would find something about it – perhaps under another name – in the Public Library or in the psychology books around the house that he browsed in when his mother was out.

'Veec-tor! What are you doing?'

'Nothing, Mama!'

'That is exactly it! Nothing! Can you not even *think*?'

A warm shame spread through him. It was as if his mother read his thoughts about not-thinking. 'I am thinking,' he protested. 'I'm thinking about *not*-thinking.' His tone was defiant. What could she do about it, after all?

'About what?' Her black, curly head tilted, her mascaraed eyes narrowed at him.

'Not-thinking.'

His mother put her jewelled bands on her hips. 'Do you know, Veec-tor, you are a little bit strange in the head?' She nodded. 'You are seeck. Psychologically seeck. And retarded, do you know that? You have the behavior of a leetle boy five years old,' she said slowly and weightily. 'It is just as well you spend your Saturdays indoors. Who knows if you would not walk in front of a car, eh? But that is why I love you, little Veector.' She put her arm around his shoulders, pulled him against her and for an instant Victor's nose pressed into her large, soft bosom. She was wearing her flesh-colored dress, the one you could see through a little where her breast stretched it out.

Victor jerked his head away in a confusion of emotions. He did not know if he wanted to laugh or cry.

His mother was laughing gaily, her head back. 'Seeck you are! Look at you! My lee-tle boy still, lee-tle short pants — Ha! Ha!'

Now the tears showed in his eyes, he supposed, and his mother acted as if she were enjoying it! Victor turned his head away so she would not see his eyes. Then suddenly he faced her. 'Do you think I like these pants? *You* like them, not me, so why do you have to make fun of them?'

'A lee-tle boy who's crying!' she went on, laughing.

Victor made a dash for the bathroom, then swerved away and dived onto the sofa, his face toward the pillows. He shut his eyes tight and opened his mouth, crying but not-crying in a way he had learned through practice also. With his mouth open, his throat tight, not breathing for nearly a minute, he could somehow get the satisfaction of crying, screaming even, without anybody knowing it. He pushed his nose, his open mouth, his teeth, against the tomato-red sofa pillow, and though his mother's voice went on in a lazily mocking tone, and her laughter went on, he imagined that it was getting fainter and more distant from him. He imagined, rigid in every muscle, that he was suffering the absolute worst that any human being could suffer. He imagined that he was dying. But he did not think of death as an escape, only as a concentrated and painful incident. This was the climax of his not-crying. Then he breathed again, and his mother's voice intruded:

'Did you hear me? – *Did you hear me?* Mrs Badzerkian is coming for tea. I want you to wash your face and put on a clean shirt. I want you to recite something for her. Now what are you going to recite?'

'In winter when I go to bed,' said Victor. She was making him memorize every poem in *A Child's Garden of Verses*. He had said the first one that came into his head, and now there was an argument, because he had recited that one the last time. 'I said it, because I couldn't think of any other one right off the bat!' Victor shouted.

'Don't yell at me!' his mother cried, storming across the room at him.

She slapped his face before he knew what was happening.

He was up on one elbow on the sofa, on his back, his long, knobby-kneed legs splayed out in front of him. All right, he thought, if that's the way it is, that's the way it is. He looked at her with loathing. He would not show the slap had hurt, that it still stung. No more tears for today, he swore, no more even not-crying. He would finish the day, go through the tea, like a stone, like a soldier, not wincing. His mother paced around the room, turning one of her rings round and round, glancing at him from time to time, looking quickly away from him. But his eyes were steady on her. He was not afraid. She could even slap him again and he wouldn't care.

At last, she announced that she was going to wash her hair, and she went into the bathroom.

Victor got up from the sofa and wandered across the room. He wished he had a room of his own to go to. In the apartment on Riverside Drive, there had been three rooms, a living room and his and his mother's rooms. When she was in the living room, he had been able to go into his bedroom and vice versa, but here . . . They were going to tear down the old building they had lived in on Riverside Drive. It was not a pleasant thing for Victor to think about. Suddenly remembering the book that had fallen, he pulled out the sofa and reached for it. It was Menninger's *The Human Mind*, full of fascinating case histories of people. Victor put it back on the bookshelf between an astrology book and *How to Draw*. His mother did not like him to read psychology books, but Victor loved them, especially ones with case histories in them. The people in the case histories did what they wanted to do. They were natural. Nobody bossed them. At the local branch library, he spent hours browsing through the psychology shelves. They were in the adults' section, but the librarian did not mind his sitting at the tables there, because he was quiet.

Victor went into the kitchen and got a glass of water. As he was standing there drinking it, he heard a scratching noise coming from one of the paper bags on the counter. A mouse, he thought, but when he moved a couple of the bags, he didn't see any mouse. The scratching was coming from inside one of the bags. Gingerly, he opened the bag with his fingers, and waited for something to jump out. Looking in, he saw a white paper carton. He pulled it out slowly. Its bottom was damp. It opened like a pastry box. Victor jumped in surprise. It was a turtle on its back, a live turtle. It was wriggling its legs in the air, trying to turn over. Victor moistened his lips, and frowning with concentration, took the turtle by its sides with both hands, turned him over and let him down gently into the box again. The turtle drew in its feet then, and its head stretched up a little and it looked straight at him. Victor smiled. Why hadn't his mother told him she'd brought him a present? A live turtle. Victor's eyes glazed with anticipation as he thought of taking the turtle down, maybe with a leash around its neck, to show the fellow who'd laughed at his short pants. He might change his mind about being friends with him, if he found he owned a turtle.

'Hey, Mama! Mama!' Victor yelled at the bathroom door. 'You brought me a tur-rtle?'

'A what?' The water shut off.

'A turtle! In the kitchen!' Victor had been jumping up and down in the hall. He stopped.

His mother had hesitated, too. The water came on again, and she said in a shrill tone, 'C'est une terrapène! Pour un ragoût!'

Victor understood, and a small chill went over him because his mother had spoken in French. His mother addressed him in French when she was giving an order that had to be obeyed, or when she anticipated resistance from him. So the terrapin was for a stew. Victor nodded to himself with a stunned resignation, and went back to the kitchen. For a stew. Well, the terrapin was not long for this world, as they say. What did a terrapin like to eat? Lettuce? Raw bacon? Boiled potato? Victor peered into the refrigerator.

He held a piece of lettuce near the terrapin's horny mouth. The terrapin did not open its mouth, but it looked at him. Victor held the lettuce near the two little dots of its nostrils, but if the terrapin smelled it, it showed no interest. Victor looked under the sink and pulled out a large wash pan. He put two inches of water into it. Then he gently dumped the terrapin into the pan. The terrapin paddled for a few seconds, as if it had to swim, then finding that its stomach sat on the bottom of the pan, it stopped, and drew its feet in. Victor got down on his knees and studied the terrapin's face. Its upper lip overhung the lower, giving it a rather stubborn and unfriendly expression, but its eyes – they were bright and shining. Victor smiled when he looked hard at them.

'Okay, monsieur terrapène,' he said, 'just tell me what you'd like to eat and we'll get it for you! – Maybe some tuna?'

They had had tuna fish salad yesterday for dinner, and there was a small bowl of it left over. Victor got a little chunk of it in his fingers and presented it to the terrapin. The terrapin was not interested. Victor looked around the kitchen, wondering, then seeing the sunlight on the floor of the living room, he picked up the pan and carried it to the living room and set it down so the sunlight would fall on the terrapin's back. All turtles liked sunlight, Victor thought. He lay down on the floor on his side, propped up on an elbow. The terrapin stared at him for a moment, then very slowly and with an air of forethought and caution, put out its legs and advanced, found the circular boundary of the pan, and moved to the right, half its body out of the shallow water. It wanted out, and Victor took it in one hand, by the sides, and said:

'You can come out and have a little walk.'

He smiled as the terrapin started to disappear under the sofa. He caught it easily, because it moved so slowly. When he put it down on the carpet, it was quite still, as if it had withdrawn a little to think what it should do next, where it should go. It was a brownish green. Looking at it, Victor thought of river bottoms, of river water flowing. Or maybe oceans. Where did terrapins come from? He jumped up and went to the dictionary on the bookshelf. The dictionary had a picture of a terrapin, but it was a dull, black and white drawing, not so pretty as the live one. He learned nothing except that the name was of Algonquian origin, that the terrapin lived in fresh or brackish water, and that it was edible. Edible. Well, that was bad luck, Victor thought. But he was not going to eat any terrapène tonight. It would be all for his mother, that ragoût, and even if she slapped him and made him learn an extra two or three poems, he would not eat any terrapin tonight.

His mother came out of the bathroom. 'What are you doing there? – Veector?'

Victor put the dictionary back on the shelf. His mother had seen the pan. 'I'm looking at the terrapin,' he said, then realized the terrapin had disappeared. He got down on hands and knees and looked under the sofa.

'Don't put him on the furniture. He makes spots,' said his mother. She was standing in the foyer, rubbing her hair vigorously with a towel.

Victor found the terrapin between the wastebasket and the wall. He put him back in the pan.

'Have you changed your shirt?' asked his mother.

Victor changed his shirt, and then at his mother's order sat down on the sofa with *A Child's Garden of Verses* and tackled another poem, a brand new one for Mrs Badzerkian. He learned two lines at a time, reading it aloud in a soft voice to himself, then repeating it, then putting two, four and six lines together, until he had the whole thing. He recited it to the terrapin. Then Victor asked his mother if he could play with the terrapin in the bathtub.

'No! And get your shirt all splashed?'

'I can put on my other shirt.'

'No! It's nearly four o'clock now. Get that pan out of the living room!'

Victor carried the pan back to the kitchen. His mother took the terrapin quite fearlessly out of the pan, put it back into the white paper box, closed its lid, and stuck the box in the refrigerator. Victor jumped a little as the refrigerator door slammed. It would be awfully cold in there for the terrapin. But then, he supposed, fresh or brackish water was cold now and then, too.

'Veector, cut the lemon,' said his mother. She was preparing the big round tray with cups and saucers. The water was boiling in the kettle.

Mrs Badzerkian was prompt as usual, and his mother poured the tea as soon as she had deposited her coat and pocketbook on the foyer chair and sat down. Mrs Badzerkian smelled of cloves. She had a small, straight mouth and a thin moustache on her upper lip which fascinated Victor, as he had never seen one on a woman before, not one at such short range, anyway. He never had mentioned Mrs Badzerkian's moustache to his mother, knowing it was considered ugly, but in a strange way, her moustache was the thing he liked best about her. The rest of her was dull, uninteresting, and vaguely unfriendly. She always pretended to listen carefully to his poetry recitals, but he felt that she fidgeted, thought of other things while he spoke, and was glad when it was over. Today, Victor recited very well and without any hesitation, standing in the middle of the living-room floor and facing the two women, who were then having their second cups of tea.

'Très bien,' said his mother. 'Now you may have a cookie.'

Victor chose from the plate a small round cookie with a drop of orange goo in its center. He kept his knees close together when he sat down. He always felt Mrs Badzerkian looked at his knees and with distaste. He often wished she would make some remark to his mother about his being old enough for long pants, but she never had, at least not within his hearing. Victor learned from his mother's conversation with Mrs Badzerkian that the Lorentzes were coming for dinner tomorrow evening. It was probably for them that the terrapin stew was going to be made. Victor was glad that he would have the terrapin one more day to play with. Tomorrow morning, he thought, he would ask his mother if he could take the terrapin down on the sidewalk for a while, either on a leash or in the paper box, if his mother insisted.

'—like a chi-ild!' his mother was saying, laughing, with a glance at him, and Mrs Badzerkian smiled shrewdly at him with her small, tight mouth.

Victor had been excused, and was sitting across the room with a book on the studio couch. His mother was telling Mrs Badzerkian how he had played with the terrapin. Victor frowned down at his book, pretending not to hear. His mother did not like him to open his mouth to her or her guests once he had been excused. But now she was calling him her 'lee-tle ba-aby Veec-tor . . . '

He stood up with his finger in the place in his book. 'I don't see why it's childish to look at a terrapin!' he said, flushing with sudden anger. 'They are very interesting animals, they—'

His mother interrupted him with a laugh, but at once the laugh disappeared and she said sternly, 'Veector, I thought I had excused you. Isn't that correct?'

He hesitated, seeing in a flash the scene that was going to take place when Mrs Badzerkian had left. 'Yes, Mama. I'm sorry,' he said. Then he sat down and bent over his book again.

Twenty minutes later, Mrs Badzerkian left. His mother scolded him for being rude, but it was not a five- or ten-minute scolding of the kind he had expected. It lasted hardly two minutes. She had forgotten to buy heavy cream, and she wanted Victor to go downstairs and get some. Victor put on his gray woolen jacket and went out. He always felt embarrassed and conspicuous in the jacket, because it came just a little bit below his short pants, and he looked as if he had nothing on underneath the coat.

Victor looked around for Frank on the sidewalk, but he didn't see him. He crossed Third Avenue and went to a delicatessen in the big building that he could see from the living room window. On his way back, he saw Frank walking along the sidewalk, bouncing a ball. Now Victor went right up to him.

'Hey,' Victor said. 'I've got a terrapin upstairs.'

'A what?' Frank caught the ball and stopped.

'A terrapin. You know, like a turtle. I'll bring him down tomorrow morning and show you, if you're around. He's pretty big.'

'Yeah? — Why don't you bring him down now?'

'Because we're gonna eat now,' said Victor. 'See you.' He went into his building. He felt he had achieved something. Frank had looked really interested. Victor wished he could bring the terrapin down now, but his mother never liked him to go out after dark, and it was practically dark now.

When Victor got upstairs, his mother was still in the kitchen. Eggs were boiling and she had put a big pot of water on a back burner. 'You took him out again!' Victor said, seeing the terrapin's box on the counter.

'Yes, I prepare the stew tonight,' said his mother. 'That is why I need the cream.'

Victor looked at her. 'You're going to – You have to kill it tonight?'

'Yes, my little one. Tonight.' She jiggled the pot of eggs.

'Mama, can I take him downstairs to show Frank?' Victor asked quickly. 'Just for five minutes, Mama. Frank's down there now.'

'Who is Frank?'

'He's that fellow you asked me about today. The blond fellow we always see. Please, Mama.'

His mother's black eyebrows frowned. 'Take the terrapène downstairs? Certainly not. Don't be absurd, my baby! The terrapène is not a toy!'

Victor tried to think of some other lever of persuasion. He had not removed his coat. 'You wanted me to get acquainted with Frank—'

'Yes. What has that got to do with a terrapin?'

The water on the back burner began to boil.

'You see, I promised him I'd—' Victor watched his mother lift the terrapin from the box, and as she dropped it into the boiling water, his mouth fell open. *'Mama!'*

'What is this? What is this noise?'

Victor, open-mouthed, stared at the terrapin whose legs were now racing against the steep sides of the pot. The terrapin's mouth opened, its eyes looked directly at Victor for an instant, its head arched back in torture, the open mouth sank beneath the seething water – and that was the end. Victor blinked. It was dead. He came closer, saw the four legs and the tail stretched out in the water, its head. He looked at his mother.

She was drying her hands on a towel. She glanced at him, then said, 'Ugh!' She smelled of her hands, then hung the towel back.

'Did you have to kill him like that?'

'How else? The same way you kill a lobster. Don't you know that? It doesn't hurt them.'

He stared at her. When she started to touch him, he stepped back. He thought of the terrapin's wide open mouth, and his eyes suddenly flooded with tears. Maybe the terrapin had been screaming and it hadn't been heard over the bubbling of the water. The terrapin had looked at him, wanting him to pull him out, and he hadn't moved to help him. His mother had tricked him, done it so fast, he couldn't save him. He stepped back again. 'No, don't touch me!'

His mother slapped his face, hard and quickly.

Victor set his jaw. Then he about-faced and went to the closet and threw his jacket onto a hanger and hung it up. He went into the living-room and fell down on the sofa. He was not crying now, but his mouth opened against the sofa pillow. Then he remembered the terrapin's mouth and he closed his lips. The terrapin had suffered, otherwise it would not have moved its legs so terribly fast to get out. Then he wept, soundlessly as the terrapin, his mouth open. He put both hands over his face, so as not to wet the sofa. After a long while, he got up. In the kitchen, his mother was humming, and every few minutes he heard her quick, firm steps as she went about her work. Victor had set his teeth again. He walked slowly to the kitchen doorway.

The terrapin was out on the wooden chopping board, and his mother, after a glance at him, still humming, took a knife and bore down on its blade, cutting off the terrapin's little nails. Victor half closed his eyes, but he watched steadily. The nails, with bits of skin attached to them, his mother scooped off the board into her palm and dumped into the garbage bag. Then she turned the terrapin onto its back and with the same sharp, pointed knife, she began to cut away the pale bottom shell. The terrapin's neck was bent sideways. Victor wanted to look away, but still he stared. Now the terrapin's insides were all exposed, red and white and greenish. Victor did not listen to what his mother was saying, about cooking terrapins in Europe, before he was born. Her voice was gentle and soothing, not at all like what she was doing.

'All right, don't look at me like that!' she suddenly threw at him, stomping her foot. 'What's the matter with you? Are you crazy? Yes, I think so! You are seeck, you know that?'

Victor could not touch any of his supper, and his mother could not force him to, even though she shook him by the shoulders and threatened to slap him. They had creamed chipped beef on toast.

Victor did not say a word. He felt very remote from his mother, even when she screamed right into his face. He felt very odd, the way he did sometimes when he was sick at his stomach, but he was not sick at his stomach. When they went to bed, he felt afraid of the dark. He saw the terrapin's face very large, its mouth open, its eyes wide and full of pain. Victor wished he could walk out the window and float, go anywhere he wanted to, disappear, yet be everywhere. He imagined his mother's hands on his shoulders, jerking him back, if he tried to step out the window. He hated his mother.

He got up and went quietly into the kitchen. The kitchen was absolutely dark, as there was no window, but he put his hand accurately on the knife rack and felt gently for the knife he wanted. He thought of the terrapin, in little pieces now, all mixed up in the sauce of cream and egg yolks and sherry in the pot in the refrigerator.

His mother's cry was not silent; it seemed to tear his ears off. His second blow was in her body, and then he stabbed her throat again. Only tiredness made him stop, and by then people were trying to bump the door in. Victor at last walked to the door, pulled the chain bolt back, and opened it for them.

He was taken to a large, old building full of nurses and doctors. Victor was very quiet and did everything he was asked to do, and answered the questions they put to him, but only those questions, and since they didn't ask him anything about a terrapin, he did not bring it up.

ANOTHER BRIDGE TO CROSS

The top of the car was down, and Merrick saw the man on the bridge from a good mile away. The car in which Merrick rode was speeding toward him, and Merrick thought: 'It's like something in a Bergman film. The man has a gun in his hand now, and when the car gets so near the bridge he can't miss, he'll fire it at me, I'll be hit through the chest, and that's probably just as well.' Merrick kept looking at the hunched figure on the bridge – the man was leaning on his forearms on the rail – both because he expected catastrophe, and because the man on the bridge was the only human figure in the landscape to look at. They were in Italy on the southern Riviera. The Mediterranean's serene blueness lay on their left, and on the right powdery green olive fields, that looked in need of water, straggled up the hills until stopped by the rocky feet of mountains. The bridge spanned the road, carried a crossroad, and was at least three stories high.

But the man did not move as Merrick's car reached the bridge. Merrick saw a breeze stir his dark hair. The danger was over.

Then above the roar of an oncoming truck, Merrick heard a faint thud, as if a sandbag had fallen off the back of the car. He turned around, raising himself slightly. 'Stop!' he shouted to his driver.

A dark blob lay on the road under the bridge, and Merrick looked around just in time to see the truck pass over it with the left pairs of its enormous double tires. The truck then screeched to a halt. The driver was getting out. Merrick pulled his hand down his forehead, over his eyes.

'What happened?' asked Merrick's driver, yanking his sunglasses off, squinting behind him to see. He backed the car.

'A man was killed,' Merrick said.

The driver backed the car neatly to the extreme right-hand side of the road, pulled the handbrake, and jumped out.

For a few moments, the driver and the truck driver had an animated conversation which Merrick could not hear. Merrick did not get out of the car. The truck driver had pulled the body onto the grass at the side of the road. No doubt he was explaining to Merrick's driver that he could not possibly have stopped, because the man jumped right in front of him.

'Dio mio,' Merrick's driver said, coming back, getting into the car. 'A suicide. Not an old man, either.' The driver shook his head.

Merrick said nothing.

They drove on.

After ten minutes, the driver said, 'A pity you don't like Amalfi, sir.'

'Yes. Well—' Merrick was in no mood for talking. His Italian was limited to a basic vocabulary, which however he knew thoroughly and pronounced correctly. Amalfi was where he had had his honeymoon twenty-five years ago. No use mentioning that to an Italian from Messina who was only about thirty himself.

They stopped at a village Merrick had seen on the map in Palermo and inquired about. The tourist agent had said, 'Very pretty, very quiet,' so Merrick intended to try it. He had telephoned from Messina and booked a room and bath. The driver took him to the hotel, and Merrick paid him off, tipping him so well the driver broke into a big smile.

'Many thanks, sir. May you enjoy your holiday here!' Then he was gone, back to Messina.

The Hotel Paradiso was very pretty, but not what Merrick wanted. He knew this after two minutes' inspection of its main hall with its inner court of little fruit trees and a sixteenth-century well, open to the sky. The tiles of the floors were lovely, the view from his window of the Mediterranean as commanding as that from the bridge of a ship, but it was not what he wanted. Nevertheless, Merrick stayed the night, and the next morning hired a car to go on. While he waited in the hotel for the car to arrive, he looked in the small local newspaper for anything about the man who had jumped from the bridge.

It was a short one-column item on the second page. His name was Dino Bartucci, 32, unemployed mason, with a wife and five children (their names and ages were given, all were under ten); his wife was in poor health, and Bartucci had been extremely depressed and anxious for many months. He had twice said to friends, 'If I were dead, the State would at least give my wife and children a small pension.'

Merrick knew how small that pension must be. There was the extreme, Merrick thought, of human anxiety: poverty, a sick wife, hungry children, and no work. And he found it mysterious that he had correctly anticipated death as soon as he saw the man, but that he had imagined it turned against himself.

Merrick got into the car with the new driver. At one, they reached Amalfi, and stopped for lunch. The driver went off by himself with the thousand lire Merrick gave him for his meal, and Merrick lunched at a hotel whose dining terrace overlooked the sea. He had been here for lunch or dinner a couple of times with Helena, but he did not dwell on that as he slowly ate the good meal. He found that being in Amalfi did not trouble him. Why should it? The very hotel where he and she had stayed had been destroyed one winter in a landslide caused by heavy rains. They had built it back, of course, and in the former style, Merrick had heard, but he was sure this was not quite true. There would have been a few changes, probably in the direction of enlargement, and they could not have recovered every rock and stone and tree. But if the hotel had remained exactly the same, Merrick would not have gone to it now. He knew that his own memory in twenty-five years must have undergone slow changes, and that reality would be a shock, useless and depressing.

Merrick lingered over his lunch, then had a leisurely coffee and brandy down on the main plaza. It was nearly five before they went on.

The next town of any size was Positano. It was the end of the day, and a huge orange sun was just dropping into the sea beyond the purple hump of Capri. Merrick imagined that he heard the sun hiss as it touched the water, but the hiss was the lappings of waves against the rocky cliffs below. Positano, though objectively beautiful set in its curve of mountains – like the banked benches of an amphitheater whose stage was the flat sea in front – looked no more inviting to Merrick than a half dozen other villages he had seen. Still, he told the driver that he would stay here for the night. The driver was quite surprised, because Merrick had told him they might drive to Naples and even to Rome. Merrick said he would pay him what he would have paid him to go to Rome, and this pleased the driver.

'I know the best hotel here, sir. Shall I take you there?'

Merrick did not want to come to a decision so soon. 'No. Drive through the town first. Please.'

The road took them above the town, round the semicircle of the amphitheater. There were no roads in the town proper, only steps and slanting footpaths.

'What about this?' Merrick said, indicating a hotel on their left. Its wrought-iron sign said Hotel Orlando, flat and black against its white front.

'Very well.' The driver pulled into the parking area in front of the hotel.

A bellboy came out.

It was probably a very ordinary hotel, Merrick thought, but it looked rather expensive, so he supposed it would be clean and the service good. Merrick paid the driver and tipped him.

Merrick undressed in his room and had a slow, hot bath. Then he put on his dressing-gown and ordered a half bottle of Champagne to be sent to his room. With the cheer of the Champagne, he forced himself to write a postcard to his sister in New York and to his daughter-in-law, both of whom were worried about him. To both he wrote the same thing:

Having a very enjoyable time, resting as prescribed. Joining the Denises in Munich soon. Hope you are well. Don't worry. Much love,

Charles

His doctors had told him to rest for two hours in bed in the afternoons. Merrick had done this until Palermo, but not since, not for three days. Four months ago his wife Helena and their only son, their only child, Adam, had been killed in a collision on a New Jersey parkway in a car driven by Adam. Merrick had not reacted badly at first, but he had three months later. He had had to stop going to his office at Merrick Weaves, Inc. in White Plains, not really because he felt as bad as the doctors thought he did, but because his going seemed to have no purpose. The textile factory continued to produce just as well without him as with him. His sister Wynne had come to stay in his White Plains house with him for two weeks, but since she had a household of her own, that couldn't last forever. Her presence in the empty house, wonderful as Wynne was, had really not touched Merrick's melancholia, anyway, though he had pretended to her that he felt better. He lost weight even though it seemed to him, perhaps because of the effort it took, that he was poking the same amount of food down himself as he always had. He had not realized that he loved Helena so much, that he so needed her simply to exist. The loss of her, plus his son just out of college, just finished his military service, just married, just ready to start living – had been enough to shake his faith in every-thing he had lived by until then. The virtues of hard work, honesty, respect for one's fellow man, belief in God, had seemed suddenly

thin and abstract. His convictions had become ghostlike, whereas
the bodies of his wife and son in the funeral chapel had been as tangible as stone. The emptiness of his home had been real, but not the
abstract ideal of manly fortitude. At the same time, Merrick knew
that millions of men had been here before, since the beginning of
time. There was nothing unusual or original about his feelings. It
was what people called 'life' – the two deaths in his life, and their
aftermath. Finally his doctors had recommended a leisurely trip
to Europe, but before endorsing this prescription had made sure
that Merrick planned to see friends in London, Paris, Rome and
Munich, and that the friends were the kind who would have time
to spend with him. Though his boat went to Genoa, Merrick had
abandoned it in Lisbon, its first port, and had taken another boat
to Palermo. The Martins in Rome wanted him to stay with them
for a week in their large house on the Via Appia Antica. Merrick
hoped to make that an overnight stay, on the excuse that the Denises
were expecting him in Munich earlier than he had thought. The
Denises lived in Zurich and were coming to Munich especially to
join him. From Munich, they were to drive down to Venice, then
into Yugoslavia and down its coast.

Dinner was served at eight, Merrick had been told. At seven-
thirty, he wandered into the garden behind the terrace where all
the tables were set for dinner. The garden was dimly lighted by a
few candles in glasses set along the low stone wall and on nearly
buried stones in the grass. It was a wild garden, if one could call it a
garden at all, but as soon as Merrick saw it, he was entranced. There
was a swing chair on the left, half hidden by a low tree, where two
people sat, a small table in front of them with drinks on it. There
was no one else in the garden. Far behind, black now since the sun
had gone down, rose the forms of huge mountains that seemed very
close, walling the garden in. The candlelight lit up the faces of the
couple in the swing chair like the faces of children around a lighted
Hallowe'en pumpkin. Perhaps they were newlyweds, Merrick
thought. Something about them suggested it, not their physical

closeness because they were not even touching each other, but their quiet happiness and familiarity, their youth.

A guitar began to play. It seemed to come from below, where the ground fell in dark clumps of bush and tree — though there was nothing down there, no light. The guitar was unaccompanied, yet it had the richness of three instruments playing together. The song glided in an easy, self-confident manner. Its melody line was long and intricate, down to a bass note that seemed to vibrate in Merrick's blood when the player came to it now and again. He realized it was probably only a popular slow foxtrot, yet now it seemed far better, almost like an aria destined to be famous, from an opera by a great composer. Merrick took a deep breath. There had been such a song in Amalfi when he and Helena had been there. He had never heard the song since, and he and Helena had never taken the trouble to find out its name or to buy a record of it to take back to the States. It had simply been played, on a guitar also, now and then in the evening at their hotel. They had known it would turn up, like a certain bird at sunset, sometimes, and it would not have been fitting to ask its name, to ask a musician to play it for them, because it had its own times of turning up.

At dinner, Merrick had a table, which might have seated four, to himself, set against a decorative rail of the terrace. Bougainvillea grew up from below and climbed the rail, so close that a pale purple clump of it could lie on the white tablecloth beside his right hand.

Merrick looked around at his fellow diners. There were more young people than old. He saw the newlyweds, still engrossed in each other and talking, at a table in the center of the terrace. In the far corner sat a middle-aged woman with light-brown hair, a very well-dressed woman who looked American, eating by herself. Merrick blinked and stared at her, then at the corner — less than a right angle — made by the terrace and the rail behind her. It was exactly like a certain corner of the terrace in the hotel in Amalfi. There had been bougainvillaea there, too. But the rest of the hotel was not like the hotel in Amalfi, not like it, and yet just enough like it. There had been, for instance, a garden left rather in a state of nature in the Amalfi hotel, like this one. Then Merrick realized he had at last come to the right place.

'Finished, *signor?*'

Merrick's antipasto plate was taken away, and the smiling Italian waiter, who looked no more than sixteen, held a large tray of *fettucine* for him to help himself. This was followed by roast veal, a green salad, then a large basket of fruit, from which Merrick chose a pear, then a sweet. Merrick ordered coffee served to him in the garden, and he drank it standing at the garden rail, though there was no one now in the swing seat or in the two deck chairs near it.

The woman with the light-brown hair and small pendant earrings came into the garden, and bent her head to light her cigarette. Her lighter only sparked.

'Allow me?' said Merrick, coming toward her, pulling his lighter out of his jacket pocket with his free hand.

'Oh! – I didn't see anybody there. Thank you.'

She was not in the least like Helena, though when he had seen her sitting in the corner of the terrace, he had thought she was – like Helena as she might have looked today, if she had sat in the corner of the Amalfi hotel terrace.

'You've just arrived, haven't you?' said the woman pleasantly. Her blue eyes had little crinkles of lines around them. Her face was suntanned.

'Yes. You've been here a long while?'

'Five weeks. I come here every year. I paint at the art school. Mostly as a hobby, you know. You must come and see our school. Come before twelve-thirty, because it closes then, then we all go down to have lunch on the beach.'

Merrick made a little bow. 'Thank you. I would like to.' He hesitated, then drifted away.

The next morning, he passed the art school, which was in an old palace with huge doors that stood open to an inner loggia and court, but he did not go in. He went down and stared at the water and the bathers for a while, bought the New York and the London *Times* at the newspaper store, and while he was sitting on the low cement parapet above the beach reading them, a small boy came up and asked him if he would like a shine.

Merrick looked at him and smiled with amusement. 'A shine? For these shoes?' Merrick was wearing dark-blue espadrilles.

The boy was grinning, too. His pale-blue trousers were dirty and had a patch on one knee. 'I can ask, can't I?'

'And you haven't any equipment,' Merrick said. 'Where's your polish?'

'Here,' the boy said, slapping a pocket that obviously contained nothing. 'Fifty lire. Cheap.'

Merrick laughed. 'I'll buy you an ice-cream cone. Here—' He pulled his change out of his pocket. 'Here's fifty lire.' Merrick got up as if motivated by some force not his own. 'Let's get an ice-cream cone.'

They went to the *gelateria* on the beach front, the boy skipping in circles about Merrick as if Merrick were some captive he was throwing invisible ropes around. Merrick bought him a double chocolate cone. It put a wide border of sticky brown around the boy's mouth.

'Where are you from in America? . . . Why are you here? . . . How long are you staying? . . . Have you got a car? . . . Have you got a boat? . . . Have you got a wife? . . . Have you got a big house in America? . . . How old are you?'

Merrick answered all his questions honestly, without restraint, smiling, even to the 'No' that he said when the boy asked if he had a wife.

The boy accompanied him to the post office, where he had to post an airmail letter to Merrick Weaves, then walked on up the road with him toward his hotel. Merrick was charmed by his naturalness, his utter lack of inhibition – the boy paused by the roadside to urinate, not even stepping behind a tree – and he almost invited the boy into the hotel. He could have ordered iced lemonade and cake as a treat. But Merrick thought it was probably not the thing to do.

He wished he could be as free as the child. The boy made Merrick think of a small puppy with the miraculous ability to talk.

That evening Merrick was more than ever delighted with the Hotel Orlando. The guitar played the wonderful song again. Merrick was so lost in his dreams of Helena, he scarcely heard the few remarks of the waiter, and only replied by gestures. He had coffee at the table.

'Good evening! We're playing bridge in the lounge tonight, and I wonder if you'd like to join us? Just myself and Mr and Mrs Gifford. Have you met them?' It was the woman with the light-brown hair again.

Merrick looked at her as though she were a thousand miles away instead of right by his table. Her voice had even sounded faint, and now, suddenly, he could not even remember what she had said. At last, he got to his feet. 'Good evening, I—'

'You're not sick?'

'No.'

'Good. So many people do get sick here at first.' She smiled.

'I did go by the art school, but I didn't go in,' Merrick said, thinking she had said something about the school.

'Oh. Well, any time for that. What about bridge?'

Merrick suddenly saw the suicide on the bridge, all over again, and again pulled his hand down his face. 'No, thank you. I don't like it,' he said gently.

The woman's face looked surprised. 'All right. Never mind. Sorry.' With a faint smile she was gone.

The next day, Merrick did not leave the hotel until afternoon. The small boy was on the beach front again, standing and chatting with a young couple who looked English, but when he saw Merrick, he detached himself with a wave of his hand to the couple, and came running.

'Hello! How are you today? . . . What have you been doing? . . . Why weren't you here this morning? . . . How much did your shirt cost? . . . Were you *born* in America?'

They walked along the beach, picking up interesting pebbles and fragments of colored tiles, worn smooth by the water. The boy chatted with some fishermen who were sitting on the sand mending long, rust-colored nets. The fishermen called him Seppe or Giuseppe, and laughed and winked at Merrick as they talked with him. Merrick could understand little of what they said, because it was all in dialect. Seppe was barefoot and thin, but in his eyes and his laughing mouth, Merrick saw the vitality of a people that poverty could never crush. Merrick thought of the suicide Bartucci's children, knew the same vitality would be in them, though perhaps not now the laughter. He decided to send the widow some money. He remembered the name of the town to the south where she lived. He could send a money order, anonymously. This thought made him feel happy.

'Seppe,' he said as they walked on past the net-menders. 'Would you like to have dinner with me in my hotel tonight?'

'Ah-h-h!' Seppe stopped, crouched with his hands in an attitude of prayer, and beamed up at Merrick. *'Momma mia, si!'*

'But you've got to be quiet at dinner. And maybe you have some cleaner pants?'

'Ah, *si*! I've got a real suit at home!'

'Wear it. Dinner is at eight. Not too late for you?'

'*Late?*' Seppe said, insulted, laughing.

That evening, Merrick was by the steps of the hotel at seven-thirty, fearing that Seppe would be early. He was. He was wearing his suit, new and brown and too big for him, but his shoes were worn and needed a shine. His wetted black hair showed the marks of a comb.

'Hello!' the boy called loudly to Merrick, but his eyes darted everywhere else, taking in the splendor.

'Hello,' Merrick said. 'We have time for a lemonade or something. Let's go in the garden.'

They went into the garden. Merrick found a waiter and ordered one lemonade and one Cinzano. In the garden, the boy continued to

chatter and peer at everything, but for once Merrick did not listen
to him. Merrick lifted his head a little and listened to the guitar
music, gazed at the tree-sheltered swing chair in which the newlyweds again sat, and he dreamed. The boy did not seem to mind. He
drank his lemonade thirstily between his sentences.

At dinner, the boy ate heartily of everything, and had a glass of
Merrick's wine. Seppe declared that he was going to be a hotel-
keeper when he grew up. He accepted Merrick's offer of a second
helping of dessert. Afterward, the boy put one hand over his stomach, closed his eyes and said, 'Oooooh,' but he was feeling very well.
Merrick smoked over his coffee. They had taken long over dinner,
and the terrace was almost deserted.

'Can I go to the toilet?' asked the boy.

'Certainly. It's inside that door—' Merrick pointed, got it wrong,
shook his head, and pointed to the right door. 'You'll see a door
saying *signori*. *Not* the *signore*.'

Seppe smiled and dashed away.

He was gone quite a while, Merrick thought, though he was not
sure, and automatically looked at his watch, as if that could tell him
anything, for he hadn't the slightest idea what time it had been when
the boy left. Then just as Merrick turned around, the boy appeared,
on his way back.

'Can I have a cigarette?' It was the second time Seppe had
asked him.

'I'm afraid not,' Merrick said, refusing for the second time,
though he felt himself relenting. Alone, he would have given the boy
a cigarette. 'Why don't we take a little walk?'

They walked up road that went past the hotel. Seppe was
quieter, as if the darkness had muted him.

'Where do you live?' Merrick asked.

'Down there.' Seppe pointed behind him.

'We should walk that way then. It's late.' Merrick turned.

When they came to the Hotel Orlando again, Seppe waved a hand
and said, 'I'll see you tomorrow on the beach. Good-bye!'

'Good-bye,' Merrick said.

'*Grazie!*'

'*Prego!*'

Merrick went into his hotel. As he crossed the lobby, the manager, a man of about forty with a moustache, came toward him.

'*Signor* Merrick – ah—' He beckoned Merrick into a corner of the lobby. Before he could speak, a large-breasted blonde Italian woman came up and joined them, saying to Merrick:

'*Signor*, excuse me, but we cannot take street boys into our hotel. Never!'

'*Signor* – Just a minute, Eleanora, *piano piano*, I will talk to him. First of all, we are not sure.'

'Ah-h, sure enough!' said Eleanora.

'*Signor*,' continued the manager, 'there has been a small robbery.'

Now the American woman with the light-brown hair was walking toward them. 'Hello. Look – I'm not trying to make any accusations, but my gold compact, my cigarette lighter—'

'And fifty thousand lire,' Eleanora put in.

'All I had in this bag,' said the American woman, holding out a tapestry bag to show Merrick. 'I didn't miss anything till two minutes ago. The only time it was out of my sight was when I had it on the table in the ladies' room for two minutes.'

'A clever thief. He put rocks in it to weight it,' said Eleanora. 'Show them.'

'Yes,' said the American woman, smiling a little. 'Stones from the beach.'

Merrick looked into her open pocketbook and saw some broken tiles of the sort he and Seppe had gathered that afternoon.

'Did that street boy leave you this evening to go to the toilet?' asked Eleanora. 'He did. I saw him leave the table. That boy, I know him, I know his face. He is not a good boy. They call him Seppe. What is his last name?' She frowned as if the name would come to her, and looked at the manager. Then to Merrick, 'Where does he live?'

'I don't know,' Merrick said, in a daze. 'I am sure he *didn't*,' he said earnestly.

But despite his conviction, Merrick was completely overridden. The manager went to the desk to call the police. The blonde Italian woman continued to rant about street boys in decent hotels, the American woman was downcast over her gold compact, but not angry at Merrick.

'I will certainly do what I can,' Merrick said. 'Certainly.' But he hadn't the least idea what to do.

Somehow, Merrick and the American woman found themselves out in the garden. Each was having a brandy. Merrick was jolted by its sharpness in his mouth. He tried to listen to what the woman was saying. But it seemed of no importance whatever. It seemed they were waiting for something. When Merrick finally looked at his watch, it was after midnight.

The hotel manager came out to tell them that the police had gone to the boy's house, but that the boy had not come home. 'His name is Dell' Isola. He lives up in Città Morta.' He waved an arm at another section of the town, which Merrick knew sat halfway up a mountain. '*Signora*, I am sorry. The morning should shed some light.' The manager smiled, and left.

The next thing Merrick was really conscious of was the hot water in his bath. He could not believe it. No, it was too absurd. The stones – they could have been put there by anybody. Certainly it was a clever action, the action of an old, experienced thief.

The next morning at nine, when Merrick came out of his room, the manager greeted him in the hall and said, 'Well, the boy is home this morning. He came in very late last night, his mother said. But of course they deny everything. No money, no compact, nothing. They are together, the whole family.' He waggled his hand, palm downward. 'The police searched the house, of course.'

'Well – you see?' Merrick replied calmly. 'I'm sorry it happened, but you see it wasn't Seppe.'

The manager's lips parted, but he did not say anything.

Merrick walked on. In the lobby, the desk clerk handed him a telegram that he said had just come in. It was from the Denises.

DON'T WORRY. YOU ARE AHEAD SCHEDULE.
STILL IN ZURICH. MUNICH SENT US TELEGRAM.
SEE YOU SOON MUNICH. LOVE. BETTY-ALEX

He must have wired them that he would be late for Munich, Merrick realized. But when had he sent the wire? He didn't remember sending it. He only remembered feeling intensely a couple of days ago that he must stay on and on at the Orlando, and that he didn't want any engagements to pry him away.

Merrick stopped at the small bank of the town and cashed two thousand dollars in Travelers Checks into lire. Then he took the lire to the post office and made out four money orders for lire to the equivalent of five hundred dollars each, and sent them to Mrs Dino Bartucci in the little town.

Seppe was not down at the beach that morning. Merrick lunched at a beach front restaurant, and around two, he saw Seppe hopping down the plaza steps on one bare foot, his hands in his pockets. Then he whirled in circles, his eyes shut, like a blind dancer. From these antics, Merrick knew that Seppe had seen him, no doubt before Merrick saw him. At last Seppe drifted over, hands still in his pockets, and with a timid smile.

'Well, good afternoon,' said Merrick.

'Hi.'

'I hear the police called on you last night. This morning, too.'

'Yes, but they didn't find anything. Why should they?' His hands flew out. 'I didn't have anything.' Seppe's eyes were earnest and intense.

Merrick smiled and relaxed. 'No, I didn't think you did.'

'*Gesu Maria!* Police in my house!' He glanced around to see if anyone were listening, though he had not spoken loudly, and the man at the nearest table was buried behind the Paris *Herald-Tribune*.

'I never had police in *my* house before. What did you tell them?'

'Well – I certainly didn't tell them to go looking for you. It was the hotel manager's idea. Sit down, Seppe. – They thought you robbed a woman's pocketbook. I couldn't stop them from going to you.'

Seppe said something under his breath that Merrick could not understand, and shook his head.

'I've just had lunch. Would you like something?'

They spent the afternoon together, taking a carozza ride around the town, and shooting rifles at a booth in a corner of the plaza. But Seppe did not walk all the way back to the hotel with Merrick. He stopped at the last curve in the road before the hotel, and said with an air of contempt (for the hotel) that he didn't care to walk any farther.

'Okay,' Merrick said agreeably. 'Well – take it easy, Seppe. See you tomorrow maybe.' He went on.

The woman who had been robbed did not speak to Merrick that evening, or even nod to him. Merrick didn't care. She associated him with her loss, mistakenly, and there was nothing he could do about it. Merrick sat long in the swing chair after dinner, alone and dreaming.

Seppe seemed much happier the next day, and also the day after that, when he announced that his father was going to buy a television set.

Merrick looked at Seppe and thought, *could* it be that he had stolen all those lire, the compact? Merrick frowned. No. His whole mind and his heart rejected the idea. 'Seppe, you did not take the money from the lady's pocketbook – did you?'

They were leaning against an inverted fishing boat on the beach.

'No,' Seppe said, but less positively than three days before.

Merrick frowned harder, and forced himself to say, 'I'll give you – ten thousand lire if you tell me the truth.'

Seppe grinned mischievously. 'Let's see the ten thousand.'

'Tell me the truth first.'

'All right. I stole it,' he said softly.

Merrick began to breathe shallowly, as if a weight sat on his chest. *I don't believe you*, he thought. And he made no move to reach for the lire.

'Where is the ten thousand?'

'I don't believe you. Prove that you stole it.'

'Prove it?' The mischievous grin grew wider. Seppe pulled a hand slowly from his pocket, and looked around him as the hand came out in a fist. The fist opened, and in his palm lay a lipstick which looked like gold, but wasn't, Merrick knew, though it was obviously expensive. It was set with small red stones that sparkled like cut rubies. The lipstick case seemed to scream that it was American, and the possession of the rich woman with the light-brown hair.

Merrick believed. He saw in a rush, Seppe spilling out his loot in his house, the fifty thousand lire being hidden somewhere, the gold compact and the lighter whisked off by someone, maybe by an older brother, to be sold in Rome. Merrick ground his teeth and set them together. Then he walked away. He walked slowly. The boy came tagging after him, asking him questions in an anxious tone, pleading with him, hanging finally to Merrick's wrist, but Merrick paid no attention to him. Merrick walked on past the place where people turned to go into the town. He walked on along the beach, and finally Seppe unstuck himself and hung back and Merrick was alone.

That night, Merrick sat so long in the garden that a busboy, come to collect the glasses of the candles that had burned out, told him that they were about to close the gates. Merrick detested walking into the hotel hall, into his room. It was like living the naked, painful moment all over again, when he had learned that Seppe had stolen.

Merrick received in the morning post his four money orders with their envelopes unopened. On each one was stamped *defunto*, the Italian word for deceased. They had mistaken *Signora* for *Signor*, Merrick thought, though on each envelope, *Signora* was clearly spelled out. Merrick went straight to the post office with the envelopes.

'Ah, *si*,' said the woman behind the money order window. 'We noticed these this morning . . . No, it is not a mistake, the wife is dead also.' She turned around. 'Franco! Come here a moment.'

A dark-haired young man in shirtsleeves came over, glanced at the envelopes and said, 'Ah, *si!*' then looked at Merrick. '*Si, signor,* I happen to know, because I have a cousin who lives in that town. The mother killed herself and her five children with gas from the oven. Just two or three days ago.'

Merrick was stunned. 'You're sure?'

'Sure, *signor. Sicuro.* The *defunto* was stamped in the village. Besides, my cousin wrote me.'

'Thank you.' Merrick gathered his envelopes together. One, two, three, four. Each seemed to be a slap in his face.

'*Signor!* — You must cash them,' said the woman at the window, and Merrick turned back. 'What can you do with them?' she asked rhetorically, with a smile and a shrug. 'You knew the woman, too?'

Merrick shook his head. 'No.'

Five minutes later, he walked out of the post office with a piece of paper that would enable him to get the money from the town bank. He went back to the hotel and sat in the garden. He missed lunch, and only reluctantly left the garden around eight to bathe and then to have dinner. That night, he told the busboy that he wished to spend the night in the garden, whether they locked the gate or not.

'It becomes cold, sir,' said the boy.

'Not very cold.'

It became cold toward dawn, but Merrick did not mind it. He changed his clothes early in the morning for slacks and a sport-shirt, then returned to the garden with a book, which he did not read. Only in the garden did he feel secure, as if he had a grasp of any kind on life or his own existence. Though he was quite aware that Helena was not with him, in the flesh, she was with him every other way in the garden. He did not have illusions of hearing her voice, it was not so physical, what he felt, but he felt her presence in every particle of the air, in every blade of grass, every flower, bush and tree. She loved the garden as much as he. His thoughts were also unphysical, never of Helena's smile, but of her good nature, of her wonderful health that had let her ride horseback, play tennis and swim right up to the time of her death, of her love and her care for their home, whatever and wherever it had been – a simple home at first, yet even when they had acquired a staff of servants, Helena had never stopped doing some of the cooking: every dinner had to have some item in it that she had prepared with her own hands.

The blonde Italian woman whose name Merrick had forgotten came out to speak to him.

'I'm quite comfortable here,' Merrick said. 'If I'm not bothering anyone else,' he added somewhat challengingly. He did not monopolize the swing chair, certainly, but frequently walked about or sat on a rock.

She said something about his health, catching a cold, and about his room being unsatisfactory.

'There's nothing wrong with my room, I prefer the garden,' Merrick said.

Some time later, it rained. Merrick sat in the swing chair, which had a short roof, but his feet and the lower part of his legs got soaked. He was oblivious of it, or rather he didn't mind. A garden could not for ever be a garden without rain. Two or three people ran out to speak to him during the rain, and ran back again, but when the rain stopped, five people came out, three who spoke to him and two who just stood and watched curiously.

'I don't see that I'm bothering anyone,' Merrick said. This was all he said, but even this seemed to bother them.

Finally, a single new man came out, and said he was a doctor. He sat on a chair and talked calmly to Merrick, but Merrick was not interested in anything he had to say.

'I prefer the garden,' Merrick said.

The man went away.

Merrick knew what would happen if he enjoyed the garden much longer, however, so after smoking a cigarette he got up, went into the lobby and asked for his bill. Then he sent a telegram of confirmation to the Denises about Munich. The next leg of the journey.

THE TROUBLE WITH
MRS BLYNN, THE TROUBLE
WITH THE WORLD

M rs Palmer was dying, there was no doubt of that to her or to anyone else in the household. The household had grown from two, Mrs Palmer and Elsie the housemaid, to four in the past ten days. Elsie's daughter Liza, age fourteen, had come to help her mother, and had brought their shaggy sheepdog Princy — who to Mrs Palmer made a fourth presence in the house. Liza spent most of her time doing things in the kitchen, and slept in the little low-ceilinged room with double-deck bunks down the steps from Mrs Palmer's room. The cottage was small — a sitting room and dining alcove and kitchen downstairs, and upstairs Mrs Palmer's bedroom, the room with the two bunks, and a tiny back room where Elsie slept. All the ceilings were low and the doorways and the ceiling above the stairway even lower, so that one had to duck one's head constantly.

Mrs Palmer reflected that she would have to duck her head very few times more, as she rose only a couple of times a day, making her way, her lavender dressing gown clutched about her against the chill, to the bathroom. She had leukemia. She was not in any pain, but she was terribly weak. She was sixty-one. Her son Gregory, an officer in the RAF, was stationed in the Middle East, and perhaps would come in time and perhaps wouldn't. Mrs Palmer had purposely not made her telegram urgent, not wanting to upset or inconvenience him, and his telegraphed reply had simply said that he would do his best to get leave to fly to her, and would let her know when. A cowardly telegram hers had been, Mrs Palmer thought. Why hadn't she had the courage to say outright, 'Am going to die in about a week. Can you come to see me?'

'Missus Palmer?' Elsie stuck her head in the door, one floury hand resting against the doorjamb. 'Did Missus Blynn say four-thirty or five-thirty today?'

Mrs Palmer did not know, and it did not seem in the least important. 'I think five-thirty.'

Elsie gave a preoccupied nod, her mind on what she would serve for five-thirty tea as opposed to four-thirty tea. The five-thirty tea could be less substantial, as Mrs Blynn would already have had tea somewhere. 'Anything I can get you, Missus Palmer?' she asked in a sweet voice, with a genuine concern.

'No, thank you, Elsie, I'm quite comfortable.' Mrs Palmer sighed as Elsie closed the door again. Elsie was willing, but unintelligent. Mrs Palmer could not *talk* to her, not that she would have wanted to talk intimately to her, but it would have been nice to have the feeling that she could talk to someone in the house if she wished to.

Mrs Palmer had no close friends in the town, because she had been here only a month. She had been en route to Scotland when the weakness came on her again and she had collapsed on a train platform in Ipswich. A long journey to Scotland by train or even airplane had been out of the question, so on a strange doctor's recommendation, Mrs Palmer had hired a taxi and driven to a town on the east coast called Eamington, where the doctor knew there was a visiting nurse, and where the air was splendid and bracing. The doctor had evidently thought she needed only a few weeks' rest and she would be on her feet again, but Mrs Palmer had had a premonition that this wasn't true. She had felt better the first few days in the quiet little town, she had found the cottage called Sea Maiden and rented it at once, but the spurt of energy had been brief. In Sea Maiden she had collapsed again, and Mrs Palmer had the feeling that Elsie and even a few other acquaintances she had made, like Mr Frowley the real estate agent, resented her faiblesse. She was not only a stranger come to trouble them, to make demands on them, but her relapse belied the salubrious powers of Eamington air – just now mostly gale-force winds which swept from the northeast day and night, tearing the buttons from one's coat, plastering a sticky, opaque film of salt and spray on the windows of all the houses on the seafront. Mrs Palmer was sorry to be a burden herself, but at least she could pay for it, she thought.

She had rented a rather shabby cottage that would otherwise have stayed empty all winter, since it was early February now, she was employing Elsie at slightly better than average Eamington wages, she paid Mrs Blynn a guinea per half-hour visit (and most of that half hour was taken up with her tea), and she soon would bring business to the undertaker, the sexton, and perhaps the shopkeeper who sold flowers. She had also paid her rent through March.

Hearing a quick tread on the pavement, in a lull in the wind's roar, Mrs Palmer sat up a little in bed. Mrs Blynn was arriving. An anxious frown touched Mrs Palmer's thin-skinned forehead, but she smiled faintly, too, with beforehand politeness. She reached for the long-handled mirror that lay on her bedtable. Her gray face had ceased to shock her or to make her feel shame. Age was age, death was death, and not pretty, but she still had the impulse to do what she could to look nicer for the world. She tucked some hair back into place, moistened her lips, tried a little smile, pulled a shoulder of her nightdress even with the other and her pink cardigan closer about her. Her pallor made the blue of her eyes much bluer. That was a pleasant thought.

Elsie knocked and opened the door at the same time. 'Missus Blynn, ma'am.'

'Good afternoon, Mrs Palmer,' said Mrs Blynn, coming down the two steps from the threshold into Mrs Palmer's room. She was a full-bodied, dark blonde woman of middle height, about forty-five, and she wore her usual bulky, two-piece black suit with a rose-colored floral pin on her left breast. She also wore a pale pink lipstick and rather high heels. Like many women in Eamington, she was a sea widow, and had taken up nursing after she was forty. She was highly thought of in the town as an energetic woman who did useful work. 'And how are you this afternoon?'

'Good afternoon. Well as can be expected, I think you'd say,' said Mrs Palmer with an effort at cheerfulness. Already she was loosening the covers, preparatory to pushing them back entirely for her daily injection.

But Mrs Blynn was standing with an absent smile in the center of the room, hands folded backward on her hips, surveying the walls, gazing out the window. Mrs Blynn had once lived in this house with her husband, for six months when they were first married, and every day Mrs Blynn said something about it. Mrs Blynn's husband had been the captain of a merchant ship, and had gone down with it ten years ago in a collision with a Swedish ship only fifty nautical miles from Eamington. Mrs Blynn had never married again. Elsie said her house was filled with photographs of the captain in uniform and of his ship.

'Yes-s, it's a wonderful little house,' said Mrs Blynn, 'even if the wind does come in a bit.' She looked at Mrs Palmer with brighter eyes, as if she were about to say, 'Well, now, a few more of these injections and you'll be as fit as can be, won't you?'

But in the next seconds, Mrs Blynn's expression changed. She groped in her black bag for the needle and the bottle of clear fluid that would do no good. Her mouth lost its smile and drooped, and deeper lines came at its corners. By the time she plunged the needle into Mrs Palmer's fleshless body, her bulging green-gray eyes were glassy, as if she saw nothing and did not need to see anything: this was her business, and she knew how to do it. Mrs Palmer was an object, which paid a guinea a visit. The object was going to die. Mrs Blynn became apathetic, as if even the cutting off of the guinea in three days or eight days mattered nothing to her, either.

Guineas as such mattered nothing to Mrs Palmer, but in view of the fact she was soon quitting this world, she wished that Mrs Blynn could show something so human as a desire to prolong the guineas. Mrs Blynn's eyes remained glassy, even when she glanced at the door to see if Elsie was coming in with her tea. Occasionally the floorboards in the hall cracked from the heat or the lack of it, and so they did when someone walked just outside the door.

The injection hurt today, but Mrs Palmer did not flinch. It was really such a small thing, she smiled at the slightness of it. 'A little sunshine today, wasn't there?' Mrs Palmer said.

'Was there?' Mrs Blynn jerked the needle out.

'Around eleven this morning. I noticed it.' Weakly she gestured toward the window behind her.

'We can certainly use it,' Mrs Blynn said, putting her equipment back in her bag. 'Goodness, we can use that fire, too.' She had fastened her bag, and now she chafed her palms, huddling toward the grate.

Princy was stretched full length before the fire, looking like a rolled-up shag rug.

Mrs Palmer tried to think of something pleasant to say about Mrs Blynn's husband, their time in this house, the town, anything. She could only think of how lonely Mrs Blynn's life must be since her husband died. They had had no children. According to Elsie, Mrs Blynn had worshiped her husband, and took a pride in never having remarried. 'Have you many patients this time of year?' Mrs Palmer asked.

'Oh, yes. Like always,' Mrs Blynn said, still facing the fire and rubbing her hands.

Who? Mrs Palmer wondered. *Tell me about them.* She waited, breathing softly.

Elsie knocked once, by bumping a corner of the tray against the door.

'Come in, Elsie,' they both said, Mrs Blynn a bit louder.

'Here we are,' said Elsie, setting the tray down on a hassock made by two massive olive-green pillows, one atop the other. Butter slid down the side of a scone, spread onto the plate, and began to congeal while Elsie poured the tea.

Elsie handed Mrs Palmer a cup of tea with three lumps of sugar, but no scone, because Mrs Blynn said they were too indigestible for her. Mrs Palmer did not mind. She appreciated the sight of well-buttered scones, anyway, and of healthy people like Mrs Blynn eating them. She was offered a ginger biscuit and declined it. Mrs Blynn talked briefly to Elsie about her water pipes, about the reduced price of something at the butcher's this week, while Elsie stood with folded arms, leaning against the edge of the door, letting in a frigid draft on Mrs Palmer. Elsie was taking in all Mrs Blynn's information about prices. Now it was catsup at the health store. On sale this week.

'Call me if you'd like something,' Elsie said as usual, ducking out the door.

Mrs Blynn was sunk in her scones, leaning over so the dripping butter would fall on the stone floor and not her skirt.

Mrs Palmer shivered, and drew the covers up.

'Is your son coming?' Mrs Blynn asked in a loud, clear voice, looking straight at Mrs Palmer.

Mrs Palmer did not know what Elsie had told Mrs Blynn. She had told Elsie that he might come, that was all. 'I haven't heard yet. He's probably waiting to tell me the exact time he'll come – or to find out if he can or not. You know how it is in the Air Force.'

'Um-m,' said Mrs Blynn through a scone, as if of course she knew, having had a husband who had been in service. 'He's your only son and heir, I take it.'

'My only one,' said Mrs Palmer.

'Married?'

'Yes.' Then, anticipating the next question, 'He has one child, a daughter, but she's still very small.'

Mrs Blynn's eyes kept drifting to Mrs Palmer's bedtable, and suddenly Mrs Palmer realized what she was looking at – her amethyst pin. Mrs Palmer had worn it for a few days on her cardigan sweater, until she had felt so bad, the pin ceased to lift her spirits and became almost tawdry, and she had removed it.

'That's a beautiful pin,' said Mrs Blynn.

'Yes. My husband gave it to me years ago.'

Mrs Blynn came over to look at it, but she did not touch it. The rectangular amethyst was set in small diamonds. She stood up, looking down at it with alert, bulging eyes. 'I suppose you'll pass it on to your son – or his wife.'

Mrs Palmer flushed with embarrassment, or anger. She hadn't thought to whom she would pass it on, particularly. 'I suppose my son will get everything, as my heir.'

'I hope his wife appreciates it,' Mrs Blynn said, turning on her heel with a smile, setting her cup down in its saucer.

Then Mrs Palmer realized that for the last few days it was the pin Mrs Blynn had been looking at when her eyes drifted over to the bedtable. When Mrs Blynn had gone, Mrs Palmer picked up the pin and held it in her palm protectively. Her jewel box was across the room. Elsie came in, and Mrs Palmer said, 'Elsie, would you mind handing me that blue box over there?'

'Certainly, ma'am,' Elsie said, swerving from the tea tray to the box on the top of the bookshelf. 'This the one?'

'Yes, thank you.' Mrs Palmer took it, opened the lid, and dropped the pin on her pearls. She had not much jewelry, perhaps ten or eleven pieces, but each piece meant a special occasion in her life, or a special period, and she loved them all. She looked at Elsie's blunt, homely profile as she bent over the tray, arranging everything so that it could be carried out at once.

'That Missus Blynn,' said Elsie, shaking her head, not looking at Mrs Palmer. 'Asked me if I thought your son was coming. How was I to know? I said yes, *I* thought so.' Now she stood with the tray, looking at Mrs Palmer, and she smiled awkwardly, as if she had said perhaps too much. 'The trouble with Missus Blynn is she's always nosing – if you'll pardon me saying so. Asking questions, you know?'

Mrs Palmer nodded, feeling too low just at that moment to make a comment. She had no comment anyway. Elsie, she thought, had passed back and forth by the amethyst pin for days and never mentioned it, never touched it, maybe never even noticed it. Mrs Palmer suddenly realized how much more she liked Elsie than she liked Mrs Blynn.

'The trouble with Missus Blynn – she means well, but . . . ' Elsie floundered and jiggled the tray in her effort to shrug. 'It's too bad. Everyone's always saying it about her,' she finished, as if this summed it up, and started out the door. But she turned with the door open. 'At tea, for instance. It's always get this and get that for her, as if she were a grand lady or something. A day ahead she tells me. I don't see why she don't bring what she wants from the bakery now and then herself. If you know what I mean.'

Mrs Palmer nodded. She supposed she knew. She knew. Mrs Blynn was like a nursemaid she had for a time for Gregory. Like a divorcée she and her husband had known in London. She was like a lot of people.

Mrs Palmer died two days later. It was a day when Mrs Blynn came in and out, perhaps six times, perhaps eight. A telegram had arrived that morning from Gregory, saying he had at last wangled leave and would take off in a matter of hours, landing at a military field near Eamington. Mrs Palmer did not know if she would see him again or not, she could not judge her strength that far. Mrs Blynn took her temperature and felt her pulse frequently, then pivoted on one foot in the room, looking about as if she were alone and thinking her own thoughts. Her expression was blankly pleasant, her peaches-and-cream cheeks aglow with health.

'Your son's due today,' Mrs Blynn half said, half asked, on one of her visits.

'Yes,' said Mrs Palmer.

It was then dusk, though it was only four in the afternoon.

That was the last clear exchange she had with anyone, for she sank into a kind of dream. She saw Mrs Blynn staring at the blue box on the top of the bookshelf, staring at it even as she shook the thermometer down. Mrs Palmer called for Elsie and had her bring the box to her. Mrs Blynn was not in the room then.

'This is to go to my son when he comes,' Mrs Palmer said. 'All of it. Everything. You understand? It's all written . . . ' But even though it was all itemized, a single piece like the amethyst pin might be missing and Gregory would never do anything about it, maybe not even notice, maybe think she'd lost it somewhere in the last weeks and not reported it. Gregory was like that. Then Mrs Palmer smiled at herself, and also reproached herself. *You can't take it with you.* That was very true, and people who tried to were despicable and rather absurd. 'Elsie, this is yours,' Mrs Palmer said, and handed Elsie the amethyst pin.

'Oh, Missus Palmer! Oh, no, I couldn't take *that*!' Elsie said, not taking it, and in fact retreating a step.

'You've been very good to me,' Mrs Palmer said. She was very tired, and her arm dropped to the bed. 'Very well,' she murmured, seeing it was really of no use.

Her son came at six that evening, sat with her on the edge of her bed, held her hand and kissed her forehead. But when she died, Mrs Blynn was closest, bending over her with her great round, peaches-and-cream face and her green-gray eyes as expressionless as some fantastic reptile's. Mrs Blynn to the last continued to say crisp, efficient things to her like, 'Breathe easily. That's it,' and 'Not chilly, are you? Good.' Somebody had mentioned a priest earlier, but this had been overruled by both Gregory and Mrs Palmer. So it was Mrs Blynn's eyes she looked into as her life left her. Mrs Blynn so authoritative, strong, efficient, one might have taken her for God Himself. Especially since when Mrs Palmer looked toward her son, she couldn't really see him, only a vague pale blue figure in the corner, tall and erect, with a dark spot at the top that was his hair. He was looking at her, but now she was too weak to call him. Anyway, Mrs Blynn had shooed them all back. Elsie was also standing against the closed door, ready to run out for something, ready to take any order. Near her was the smaller figure of Liza, who occasionally whispered something and was shushed by her mother. In an instant, Mrs Palmer saw her entire life – her carefree childhood and youth, her happy marriage, the blight of the death of her other son at the age of ten, the shock of her husband's death eight years ago – but all in all a happy life, she supposed, though she could wish her own character had been better, purer, that she had never shown temper or selfishness, for instance. All that was past now, but what remained was a feeling that she had been imperfect, wrong, like Mrs Blynn's presence now, like Mrs Blynn's faint smile, wrong, wrong for the time and the occasion. Mrs Blynn did not understand her. Mrs Blynn did not know her. Mrs Blynn, somehow, could not comprehend goodwill. Therein lay the flaw, and the flaw of life itself. Life is a long failure of understanding, Mrs Palmer thought, a long, mistaken shutting of the heart.

Mrs Palmer had the amethyst pin in her closed left hand. Hours ago, sometime in the afternoon, she had taken it with an idea of safekeeping, but now she realized the absurdity of that. She had also wanted to give it to Gregory directly, and had forgotten. Her closed hand lifted an inch or so, her lips moved, but no sound came. She wanted to give it to Mrs Blynn: one positive and generous gesture she could still make to this essence of nonunderstanding, she thought, but now she had not the strength to make her want known – and that was like life, too, everything a little too late. Mrs Palmer's lids shut on the vision of Mrs Blynn's glassy, attentive eyes.

THE CRIES OF LOVE

Hattie pulled the little chain of the reading-lamp, drew the covers over her shoulders and lay tense, waiting for Alice's sniffs and coughs to subside. 'Alice?' she said. No response. Yes, she was sleeping already, though she said she never closed an eye before the bedroom clock struck eleven.

Hattie eased herself to the edge of the bed and slowly put out a white-stockinged foot. She twisted round to look at Alice, of whom nothing was visible except a thin nose projecting between the ruffle of her nightcap and the sheet pulled over her mouth. She was still.

Hattie rose gently from the bed, her breath coming short with excitement. In the semi-darkness she could see the two sets of false teeth in their glasses of water on the table. She giggled nervously.

Like a white ghost she made her way across the room, past the Victorian settle. She stopped at the sewing-table, lifted the folding top and groped among the spools and pattern papers until she found the scissors. Then, holding them tightly, she crossed the room again. She had left the wardrobe door slightly ajar earlier in the evening, and it swung open noiselessly. Hattie reached a trembling hand into the blackness, felt the two woolen coats, a few dresses. Finally, she touched a fuzzy thing, and lifted the hanger down. The scissors slipped out of her hand. There was a clatter, followed by half-suppressed laughter.

She peeked round the wardrobe door at Alice, motionless on the bed. Alice was rather hard of hearing.

With her white toes turned up stiffly, Hattie clumped to the easy chair by the window where a bar of moonlight slanted, and sat down with the scissors and the angora cardigan in her lap. In the moonlight her face gleamed, toothless and demoniacal. She examined the cardigan in the manner of a person who toys with a piece of steak before deciding where to put his knife.

It was really a lovely cardigan. Alice had received it the week before from her niece as a birthday present. Alice would never have indulged herself in such a luxury. She was happy as a child with the cardigan and had worn it every day over her dresses.

The scissors cut purringly up the soft wool sleeves, between the wristbands and the shoulders. She considered. There should be one more cut. The back, of course. But only about a foot long, so that it wouldn't immediately be visible.

A few seconds later, she had put the scissors back into the table, hung the cardigan in the wardrobe, and was lying under the covers. She heaved a tremendous sigh. She thought of the gaping sleeves, of Alice's face in the morning. The cardigan was quite beyond repair, and she was immensely pleased with herself.

They were awakened at eight-thirty by the hotel maid. It was a ritual that never failed: three bony raps on the door and a bawling voice with a hint of insolence, 'Eight-thirty. You can get breakfast now!' Then Hattie, who always woke first, would poke Alice's shoulder.

Mechanically they sat up on their respective sides of the bed and pulled their nightgowns over their heads, revealing clean white undergarments. They said nothing. Seven years of co-existence had pared their conversation to an economical core.

This morning, however, Hattie's mind was on the cardigan. She felt self-conscious, but she could think of nothing to say or do to relieve the tension, so she spent more time than usual with her hair. She had a braid nearly two feet long that she wound around her head, and every morning she undid it for its hundred strokes. Her hair was her only vanity. Finally, she stood shifting uneasily, pretending to be fastening the snaps on her dress.

Alice seemed to take an age at the washbasin, gargling with her solution of tepid water and salt. She held stubbornly to water and salt in the mornings, despite Hattie's tempting bottle of red mouthwash sitting on the shelf.

'What are you giggling at now?' Alice turned from the basin, her face wet and smiling a little.

Hattie could say nothing, looked at the teeth in the glass on the bedtable and giggled again. 'Here's your teeth.' She reached the glass awkwardly to Alice. 'I thought you were going down to breakfast without them.'

'Now when did I *ever* go off without my teeth, Hattie?'

Alice smiled to herself. It was going to be a good day, she thought. Mrs Crumm and her sister were back from a weekend, and they could all play gin rummy together in the afternoon. She walked to the wardrobe in her stockinged feet.

Hattie watched as she took down the powder-blue dress, the one that went best with the beige angora cardigan. She unfastened all the little buttons in front. Then she took the cardigan from the hanger and put one arm into a sleeve.

'Oh!' she breathed painfully. Then like a hurt child her eyes almost closed and her face twisted petulantly. Tears came quickly down her cheeks. 'H-Hattie.'

Hattie smirked, uncomfortable yet enjoying herself thoroughly. 'Well, I do know!' she exclaimed. 'I wonder who could have done a trick like that!' She went to the bed and sat down, doubled up with laughter.

'Hattie, you did this,' Alice declared in an unsteady voice. She clutched the cardigan to her. 'Hattie, you're just wicked!'

Lying across the bed, Hattie was almost hysterical. 'You know I didn't now, Alice . . . haw-haw! . . . Why do you think I'd—' Her voice was choked off by uncontrollable laughter. Hattie lay there for several minutes before she was calm enough to go down to breakfast. And when she left the room, Alice was sitting in the big chair by the window, sobbing, her face buried in the angora cardigan.

Alice did not come down until she was called for lunch. She chatted at the table with Mrs Crumm and her sister and took no notice of Hattie. Hattie sat opposite her, silent and restless, but not at all sorry for what she had done. She could have endured days of indifference on Alice's part without feeling the slightest remorse.

It was a beautiful day. After lunch they went with Mrs Crumm, her sister and the hotel hostess, Mrs Holland, and sat in Gramercy Park.

Alice pretended to be absorbed in her book. It was a detective story by her favorite author, borrowed from the hotel's circulating library. Mrs Crumm and her sister did most of the talking. A weekend trip provided conversation for several afternoons, and Mrs Crumm was able to remember every item of food she had eaten for days running.

The monotonous tones of the voices, the warmth of the sunshine, lulled Alice into half-sleep. The page was blurred to her eyes.

Earlier in the day, she had planned to adopt an attitude toward Hattie. She should be cool and aloof. It was not the first time Hattie had committed an outrage. There had been the ink spilt on her lace tablecloth months ago, the day before she was going to give it to her niece . . . And her missing volume of Tennyson that was bound in morocco. She was sure Hattie had it, somewhere. She decided that that evening, she should calmly pack her bag, write Hattie a note, short but well-worded, and leave the hotel. She would go to another hotel in the neighborhood, let it be known through Mrs Crumm where she was, and have the satisfaction of Hattie's coming to her and apologizing. But the fact was, she was not at all sure Hattie would come to her, and this embarrassing possibility prevented her taking such a dangerous course. What if she had to spend the rest of her life alone? It was much easier to stay where she was, to have a pleasant game of gin rummy in the afternoons, and to take out her revenge in little ways. It was also more lady-like, she consoled herself. She did not think beyond this, of the particular times she would say or do things calculated to hurt Hattie. The opportunities would just come of themselves.

Mrs Holland nudged her. 'We're going to get some ice cream now. Then we're going back to play some gin rummy.'

'I was just at the most exciting part of the book.' But Alice rose with the others and was almost cheerful as they walked to the drug store.

Alice won at gin rummy, and felt pleased with herself. Hattie, watching her uneasily all day, was much relieved when she decreed speaking terms again.

Nevertheless, the thought of the ruined cardigan rankled in Alice's mind, and prodded her with a sense of injustice. Indeed, she was ashamed of herself for being able to take it as lightly as she did. It was letting Hattie walk over her. She wished she could muster a really strong hatred.

They were in their room reading at nine o'clock. Every vestige of Hattie's shyness or pretended contrition had vanished. 'Wasn't it a nice day?' Hattie ventured.

'Um-hm.' Alice did not raise her head.

'Well,' Hattie made the inevitable remark through the inevitable yawn, 'I think I'll be going off to bed.'

And a few minutes later they were both in bed, propped up by four pillows. Hattie with the newspaper and Alice with her detective story. They were silent for a while, then Hattie adjusted her pillows and lay down. 'Good night, Alice.'

'Good night.'

Soon Alice pulled out the light, and there was absolute silence in the room except for the soft ticking of the clock and the occasional purr of an automobile. The clock on the mantel whirred and began to strike ten.

Alice lay open-eyed. All day her tears had been restrained, and now she began to cry. But they were not the childish tears of the morning, she felt. She wiped her nose on the top of the sheet.

She raised herself on one elbow. The darkish braid of hair outlined Hattie's neck and shoulder against the white bedclothes. She felt very strong, strong enough to murder Hattie with her own hands. But the idea of murder passed from her mind as swiftly as it had entered. Her revenge had to be something that would last, that would hurt, something that Hattie must endure and that she herself could enjoy.

Then it came to her, and she was out of bed, walking boldly to the sewing-table, as Hattie had done twenty-four hours before . . . and she was standing by the bed, bending over Hattie, peering at her placid, sleeping face through her tears and her short-sighted eyes. Two quick strokes of the scissors would cut through the braid, right near the head. But Alice lowered the scissors just a little, to where the braid was tighter. She squeezed the scissors with both hands, made them chew on the braid, as Hattie slowly awakened with the touch of cold metal on her neck. *Whack*, and it was done.

'What is it? . . . What——?' Hattie said.

The braid was off, lying like a dark gray snake on the bedcover.

'Alice!' Hattie said, and groped at her neck, felt the stiff ends of the braid's stump. 'Alice!'

Alice stood a few feet away, staring at Hattie who was sitting up in bed, and suddenly Alice was overcome with mirth. She tittered, and at the same time tears started in her eyes. 'You did it to me!' she said. 'You cut my cardigan!'

Alice's instant of self-defense was unnecessary, because Hattie was absolutely crumpled and stunned. She started to get out of bed, as if to go to the mirror, but sat back again, moaning and weeping, feeling of the horrid thing at the end of her hair. Then she lay down again, still moaning into her pillow. Alice stayed up, and sat finally in the easy chair. She was full of energy, not sleepy at all. But toward dawn, when Hattie slept, Alice crept between the covers.

Hattie did not speak to her in the morning, and did not look at her. Hattie put the braid away in a drawer. Then she tied a scarf around her head to go down to breakfast, and in the dining-room, Hattie took another table from the one at which Alice and she usually sat. Alice saw Hattie speaking to Mrs Holland after breakfast.

A few minutes later, Mrs Holland came over to Alice, who was reading in a corner of the lounge.

'I think,' Mrs Holland said gently, 'that you and your friend might be happier if you had separate rooms for a while, don't you?'

This took Alice by surprise, though at the same time she had been expecting something worse. Her prepared statement about the spilt ink, the missing Tennyson and the ruined angora subsided in her, and she said quite briskly, 'I do indeed, Mrs Holland. I'm agreeable to anything Hattie wishes.'

Alice offered to move out, but it was Hattie who did. She moved to a smaller room three doors down on the same floor.

That night, Alice could not sleep. It was not that she thought about Hattie particularly, or that she felt in the least sorry for what she had done – she decidedly didn't – but that things, the room, the darkness, even the clock's ticking, were so different because she was alone. A couple of times during the night, she heard a footstep outside the door, and thought it might be Hattie coming back, but it was only people visiting the w.c. at the end of the hail. It occurred to Alice that she could knock on Hattie's door and apologize but, she asked herself, why should she?

In the morning, Alice could tell from Hattie's appearance that she hadn't slept either. Again, they did not speak or look at each other all day, and during the gin rummy and tea at four-thirty, they managed to take different tables. Alice slept very badly that night also, and blamed it on the lamb stew at dinner, which she was having trouble digesting. Hattie would have the same trouble, perhaps, as Hattie's digestion was if anything worse.

Three more days and nights passed, and the ravages of Hattie's and Alice's sleepless nights became apparent on their faces. Mrs Holland noticed, and offered Alice some sedatives, which Alice politely declined. She had her pride, she wasn't going to show anyone she was disturbed by Hattie's absence, and besides, she thought it was weak and self-indulgent to yield to sleeping-pills – though perhaps Hattie would.

On the fifth day, at three in the afternoon, Hattie knocked on Alice's door. Her head was still swathed in a scarf, one of three that Hattie possessed, and this was one Alice had given her last Christmas. 'Alice, I want to say I'm sorry, if *you're* sorry,' Hattie said, her lips twisting and pursing as she fought to keep back the tears.

This was or should have been a moment of triumph for Alice. It was, mainly, she felt, though something – she was not sure what – tarnished it a little, made it not quite pure victory. 'I am sorry about your braid, if you're sorry about my cardigan,' Alice replied.

'I am,' said Hattie.

'And about the ink stain on my tablecloth and – where is my volume of Alfred Lord Tennyson's poems?'

'I have not got it,' Hattie said, still tremulous with tears.

'You haven't *got* it?'

'No,' Hattie declared positively.

And in a flash, Alice knew what had really happened: Hattie had at some point, in some place, destroyed it, so it was in a way true now that she hadn't 'got' it. Alice knew, too, that she must not stick over this, that she ought to forgive and forget it, though neither emotionally nor intellectually did she come to this decision: she simply knew and behaved accordingly, saying, 'Very well, Hattie. You may move back, if you wish.'

Hattie then moved back, though at the card game at four-thirty, they still sat at separate tables.

Hattie, having swallowed the biggest lump of pride she had ever swallowed in knocking on Alice's door and saying she was sorry, slept very much better back in the old arrangement, but suffered a lurking sense of unfairness. After all, a book of poems and a cardigan could be replaced, but could her hair? Alice had got back at her all right, and then some. The score was not quite even.

After a few days, Hattie and Alice were back to normal, saying little to each other, but outwardly being congenial, taking meals and playing cards at the same table. Mrs Holland seemed pleased.

It crossed Alice's mind to buy Hattie some expensive hair tonic she saw in a Madison Avenue window one day while on an outing with Mrs Holland and the group. But Alice didn't. Neither did she buy a 'special treatment' for hair which she saw advertised in the back of a magazine, guaranteed to make hair grow thicker and faster, but Alice read every word of the advertisement.

Meanwhile, Hattie struggled in silence with her stump of braid, brushed her hair faithfully as usual, but only when Alice was having her bath or was out of the room, so Alice would not see it. Nothing in Alice's possession now seemed important enough for Hattie's vengeance. But Christmas was coming soon. Hattie determined to wait patiently and see what Alice got then.

NOT IN THIS LIFE, MAYBE THE NEXT

Eleanor had been sewing nearly all day, sewing after dinner, too, and it was getting on for eleven o'clock. She looked away from her machine, sideways towards the hall door, and saw something about two feet high, something grayish black, which after a second or two moved and was lost from view in the hall. Eleanor rubbed her eyes. Her eyes smarted, and it was delicious to rub them. But since she was sure she had not really seen something, she did not get up from her chair to go and investigate. She forgot about it.

She stood up after five minutes or so, after tidying her sewing table, putting away her scissors, and folding the yellow dress whose side seams she had just let out. The dress was ready for Mrs Burns tomorrow. Always letting out, Eleanor thought, never taking in. People seemed to grow sideways, not upward any more, and she smiled at this fuzzy little thought. She was tired, but she had had a good day. She gave her cat Bessie a saucer of milk – rather creamy milk, because Bessie liked the best of everything – heated some milk for herself and took it in a mug up to bed.

The second time she saw it, however, she was not tired, and the sun was shining brightly. This time, she was sitting in the armchair, putting a zipper in a skirt, and as she knotted her thread, she happened to glance at the door that went into what she called the side room, a room off the living room at the front of the house. She saw a squarish figure about two feet high, an ugly little thing that at first suggested an upended sandbag. It took a moment before she recognized a large square head, thick feet in heavy shoes, incredibly short arms with big hands that dangled.

Eleanor was half out of her chair, her slender body rigid.

The thing didn't move. But it was looking at her.

Get it out of the house, she thought at once. Shoo it out the door. What *was* it? The face was vaguely human. Eyes looked at her from under hair that was combed forward over the forehead. Had the children put some horrid toy in the house to frighten her? The Reynoldses next door had four children, the oldest eight. Children's toys these days – You never knew what to expect!

Then the thing moved, advanced slowly into the living room, and Eleanor stepped quickly behind the armchair.

'Get out! Get away!' she said in a voice shrill with panic.

'Um-m,' came the reply, soft and deep.

Had she really heard anything? Now it looked from the floor – where it had stared while entering the room – to her face. The look at her seemed direct, yet was somehow vague and unfocused. The creature went on, towards the electric bar heater, where it stopped and held out its hands casually to the warmth. It was masculine, Eleanor thought, its legs – if those stumpy things could be called legs – were in trousers. Again the creature took a sidelong look at her, a little shyly, yet as if defying her to get it out of the room.

The cat, curled on a pillow in a chair, lifted her head and yawned, and the movement caught Eleanor's eye. She waited for Bessie to see the thing, straight before her and only four feet away, but Bessie put her head down again in a position for sleeping. That was curious!

Eleanor retreated quickly to the kitchen, opened the back door and went out, leaving the door open. She went round to the front door and opened that wide, too. Give the thing a chance to get out!

Eleanor stayed on her front path, ready to run to the road if the creature emerged.

The thing came to the front door and said in a deep voice, the words more a rumble than articulated, 'I'm not going to harm you, so why don't you come back in? It's your house.' And there was the hint of a shrug in the chunky shoulders.

'I'd like you to get out, please!' Eleanor said.

'Um-m.' He turned away, back into the living room.

Eleanor thought of going for Mr Reynolds next door, a practical man who probably had a gun in the house, as he was a captain in the Air Force. Then she remembered the Reynoldses had gone off before lunch and that their house was empty. Eleanor gathered her courage and advanced towards the front door.

Now she didn't see him in the living room. She even looked behind the armchair. She went cautiously towards the side room. He was not in there, either. She looked quite thoroughly.

She stood in the hall and called up the stairs, really called to all the house, 'If you're still in this house, I wish you would leave!'

Behind her a voice said, 'I'm still here.'

Eleanor turned and saw him standing in the living room.

'I won't do you any harm. But I can disappear if you prefer. Like this.'

She thought she saw a set of bared teeth, as if he were making an effort. As she stared, the creature became paler gray, more fuzzy at the edges. And after ten seconds, there was nothing. *Nothing!* Was she losing her mind? She must tell Dr Campbell, she thought. First thing tomorrow morning, go to his office at 9 a.m. and tell him honestly.

The rest of the day, and the evening, passed without incident. Mrs Burns came for her dress, and brought a coat to be shortened. Eleanor watched a television program, and went to bed at half past ten. She had thought she would be frightened, going to bed and turning all the lights out, but she wasn't. And before she had time to worry about whether she could get to sleep or not, she had fallen asleep.

But when she woke up, he was the second thing she saw, the first thing being her cat, who had slept on the foot of the bed for warmth. Bessie stretched, yawned and meowed simultaneously, demanding breakfast. And hardly two yards away, he stood, staring at her. Eleanor's promise of immediate breakfast to Bessie was cut short by her seeing him.

'I could use some breakfast myself.' Was there a faint smile on that square face? 'Nothing much. A piece of bread.'

Now Eleanor found her teeth tight together, found herself wordless. She got out of bed on the other side from him, quickly pulled on her old flannel robe, and went down the stairs. In the kitchen, she comforted herself with the usual routine: put the kettle on, feed Bessie while the kettle was heating, cut some bread. But she was waiting for the thing to appear in the kitchen doorway, and as she was slicing the bread, he did. Trembling, Eleanor held the piece of bread towards him.

'If I give you this, would you go away?' she asked.

The monstrous hand reached out and up, and took the bread. 'Not necessarily,' rumbled the bass voice. 'I don't need to eat, you know. I thought I'd keep you company, that's all.'

Eleanor was not sure, really not sure now if she had heard it. She was imagining telling Dr Campbell all this, imagining the point at which Dr Campbell would cut her short (politely, of course, because he was a nice man) and prescribe some kind of sedative.

Bessie, her breakfast finished, walked so close by the creature, her fur must have brushed his leg, but the cat showed no sign of seeing anything. That was proof enough that he didn't exist, Eleanor thought.

A strange rumbling, 'Um-hm-hm,' came from him. He was laughing! 'Not everyone – or everything – can see me,' he said to Eleanor. 'Very few people can see me, in fact.' He had eaten the bread, apparently.

Eleanor steeled herself to carry on with her breakfast. She cut another piece of bread, got out the butter and jam, scalded the teapot. It was ten to eight. By nine she'd be at Dr Campbell's.

'Maybe there's something I can do for you today,' he said. He had not moved from where he stood. 'Odd jobs. I'm strong.' The last word was like a nasal burr, like the horn of a large and distant ship.

At once, Eleanor thought of the rusty old lawn roller in her barn. She'd rung up Field's, the secondhand dealers, to come and take it away, but they were late as usual, two weeks late. 'I have a roller out in the barn. After breakfast, you can take it to the edge of the road, if you will.' That would be further proof, Eleanor thought, proof he wasn't real. The roller must weigh two or three hundred pounds.

He walked, in a slow, rolling gait, out of the kitchen and into the sitting room. He made no sound.

Eleanor ate her breakfast at the scrubbed wooden table in the kitchen, where she often preferred to eat instead of in the dining room. She propped a booklet on sewing tips before her, and after a few moments, she was able to concentrate on it.

At 8:30, dressed now, Eleanor went out to the barn behind her house. She had not looked for him in the house, didn't know where he was now, in fact, but somehow it did not surprise her to find him beside her when she reached the barn door.

'It's in the back corner. I'll show you.' She removed the padlock which had not been fully closed.

He understood at once, rubbed his big yellowish hands together, and took a grip on the wooden stick of the roller. He pulled the thing towards him with apparently the greatest ease, then began to push it from behind, rolling it. But the stick was easier, so he took the stick again, and in less than five minutes, the roller was at the edge of the road, where Eleanor pointed.

Jane, the girl who delivered morning papers, was cycling along the road just then.

Eleanor tensed, thinking Jane would cry out at the sight of him, but Jane only said shyly (she was a very shy girl), 'Morning, Mrs Heathcote,' and pedaled on.

'Good morning to you, Jane,' Eleanor answered.

'Anything else?' he asked.

'I can't think of anything, thank you,' Eleanor replied rather breathlessly.

'It won't do you any good to speak to your doctor about me,' he said.

They were both walking back towards the house, up the carelessly flagged path that divided Eleanor's front garden.

'He won't be able to see me, and he'll just give you useless pills,' he continued.

What made you think I was going to a doctor? Eleanor wanted to ask. But she knew. He could read her mind. *Is he some part of myself?* she asked herself, with a flash of intuition which went no further than the question. If no one *else* can see him—

'I am myself,' he said, smiling at her over one shoulder. He was leading the way into the house. 'Just me.' And he laughed.

Eleanor did not go to Dr Campbell. She decided to try to ignore him, and to go about her usual affairs. Her affairs that morning consisted of walking a quarter of a mile to the butcher's for some liver for Bessie and a half-chicken for herself, and of buying several things at Mr White's, the grocer. But Eleanor was thinking of telling all this to Vance – Mrs Florence Vansittart – who was her best friend in the town. Vance and she had tea together, at one or the other's house, at least once a week, usually once every five days, in fact, and Eleanor rang up Vance as soon as she got home.

The creature was not in sight at that time.

Vance agreed to come over at four o'clock. 'How *are* you, dear?' Vance asked as she always did.

'All right, thanks!' Eleanor replied, more heartily than usual. 'And you? . . . I'll make some blueberry muffins if I get my work done in time . . . '

That afternoon, though he had kept out of sight since the morning, he lumbered silently into the room just as Eleanor and Vance were starting on their second cups of tea, and just as Eleanor was drawing breath for the first statement, the first introductory statement, of her strange story. She had been thinking, the roller at the edge of the road (she must ring Field's again first thing in the morning) would be proof that what she said was not a dream.

'What's the matter, Eleanor?' asked Vance, sitting up a little. She was a woman of Eleanor's age, about fifty-five, one of the many widows in the town, though unlike Eleanor, Vance had never worked at anything, and had been left a little more money. And Vance looked to her right, at the side room's door, where Eleanor had been looking. Now Eleanor took her eyes away from the creature who stood four feet within the room.

'Nothing,' Eleanor said. Vance didn't see him, she thought. Vance can't see him.

'She can't see me,' the creature rumbled to Eleanor.

'Swallow something the wrong way?' Vance asked, chuckling, helping herself to another blueberry muffin.

The creature was staring at the muffins, but came no closer.

'You know, Eleanor—' Vance chewed, '—if you're still charging only a dollar for putting a hem up, I think you need your head examined. People around here, all of them could afford to give you two dollars. It's criminal the way you cheat yourself.'

Vance meant, Eleanor thought, that it was high time she had her house painted, or re-covered the armchair, which she could do herself if she had the time. 'It's not easy to mention raising prices, and the people who come to me are used to mine by now.'

'Other people manage to mention price-raising pretty easily,' Vance said as Eleanor had known she would. 'I hear of a new one every day!'

The creature took a muffin. For a few seconds, the muffin must have been visible in midair to Vance, even if she didn't see him. But suddenly the muffin was gone, being chewed by the massive, wooden-looking jaw.

'You look a bit absent today, my dear,' Vance said. 'Something worrying you?' Vance looked at her attentively, waiting for a confidence – such as another tooth extraction that Eleanor felt doomed to, or news that her brother George in Canada, who had never made a go of anything, was once more failing in business. Eleanor braced herself and said, 'I've had a visitor for the last two days. He's standing right here by the table.' She nodded her head in his direction.

The creature was looking at Eleanor.

Vance looked where Eleanor had nodded. 'What do you mean?'

'You can't see him? – He's quite friendly,' Eleanor added. 'It's a creature two feet high. He's right there. He just took a muffin! I know you don't believe me,' she rushed on, 'but he moved the roller this morning from the barn to the edge of the road. You saw it at the edge of the road, didn't you? You *said* something about it.'

Vance tipped her head to one side, and looked in a puzzled way at Eleanor. 'You mean a handyman. Old Gufford?'

'No, he's—' But at this moment, he was walking out of the room, so Vance couldn't possibly have seen him, and before he disappeared into the side room, he gave Eleanor a look and pushed his great hands flat downward in the air, as if to say, 'Give it up,' or 'Don't talk.' 'I mean what I said,' Eleanor pursued, determined to share her experience, determined also to get some sympathy, even protection. 'I am not joking, Vance. It's a little – creature two feet high, and he talks to me.' Her voice had sunk to a whisper. She glanced at the side room doorway, which was empty. 'You think I'm seeing things, but I'm not, I swear it.'

Vance still looked puzzled, but quite in control of herself, and she even assumed a superior attitude. 'How long have you – been seeing him, my dear?' she asked, and chuckled again.

'I saw him first two nights ago,' Eleanor said, still in a whisper. 'Then yesterday quite plainly, in broad daylight. He has a deep voice.'

'If he just took a muffin, where is he now?' Vance asked, getting up. 'Why can't I see him?'

'He went into the side room. All right, come along.' Eleanor was suddenly aware that she didn't know his name, didn't know how to address him. She and Vance looked into an apparently empty room, empty of anything alive except some plants on the windowsill.

Eleanor looked behind the sofa end. 'Well – he has the faculty of disappearing.'

Vance smiled, again superiorly. 'Eleanor, your eyes are getting worse. Are you using your glasses? That sewing—'

'I don't need them for sewing. Only for distances. Matter of fact I did put them on when I looked at him yesterday across the room.' She was wearing her glasses now. She was nearsighted.

Vance frowned slightly. 'My dear, are you afraid of him? – It looks like it. Stay with me tonight. Come home with me now, if you like. I can come back with Hester and look the house over thoroughly.' Hester was her cleaning woman.

'Oh, I'm sure you wouldn't see him. And I'm not afraid. He's rather friendly. But I *did* want you to believe me.'

'How can I believe you, if I don't see him?'

'I don't know.' Eleanor thought of describing him more accurately. But would this convince Vance, or anybody? 'I think I could take a photograph of him. I don't think he'd mind,' Eleanor said.

'A good idea! You've got a camera?'

'No. Well, I have, an old one of John's, but—'

'I'll bring mine. This afternoon. – I'm going to finish my tea.'

Vance brought the camera just before six. 'Good luck, Eleanor. This should be interesting!' Vance said as she departed.

Eleanor could tell that Vance had not believed a word of what she had told her. The camera said '4' on its indicator. There were eight more pictures on the roll, Vance had said. Eleanor thought two would be enough.

'I don't photograph, I'm sure,' his deep voice said on her left, and Eleanor saw him standing in the doorway of the side room. 'But I'll pose for you. Um-hm-hm.' It was the deep laugh.

Eleanor felt only a mild start of surprise, or of fear. The sun was still shining. 'Would you sit in a chair in the garden?'

'Certainly,' the creature said, and he was clearly amused.

Eleanor picked up the straight chair which she usually sat on when she worked, but he took it from her and went out the front door with it. He set the chair in the garden, careful not to tread on flowers. Then with a little boost, he got himself on to the seat and folded his short arms.

The sunlight fell full on his face. Vance had showed Eleanor how to work the camera. It was a simple one compared to John's. She took the picture at the prescribed six-foot distance. Then she saw old Gufford, the town handyman, going by in his little truck, staring at her. They did not usually greet each other, and they did not now, but Eleanor could imagine how odd he must think she was to be taking a picture of an ordinary chair in the garden. But she had seen him clearly in the finder. There was no doubt at all about that.

'Could I take one more of you standing by the chair?' she asked.

'Um-m.' That was not a laugh, but a sound of assent. He slid off the chair and stood beside it, one hand resting on the chair's back.

This was splendid, Eleanor thought, because it showed his height in proportion to the chair.

Click!

'Thank you.'

'They won't turn out, as they say,' he replied, and took the chair back into the house.

'If you'd like another muffin,' Eleanor said, wanting to be polite and thinking also he might have resented her asking him to be pho-tographed, 'they're in the kitchen.'

'I know. I don't need to eat. I just took one to see if your friend would notice. She didn't. She's not very observant.'

Eleanor thought again of the muffin in midair for a few seconds – it must have been – but she said nothing. 'I – I don't know what to call you. Have you got a name?'

A fuzzy, rather general expression of amusement came over his square face. 'Lots of names. No one particular name. No one speaks to me, so there's no need of a name.'

'I speak to you,' Eleanor said.

He was standing by the stove now, not as high, not nearly as high as the gas burners. His skin looked dry, yellowish, and his face somehow sad. She felt sorry for him.

'Where have you been living?'

He laughed. 'Um-hm-hm. I live anywhere, everywhere. It doesn't matter.'

She wanted to ask some questions, such as, 'Do you feel the cold?' but she did not want to be personal, or prying. 'It occurred to me you might like a bed,' she said more brightly. 'You could sleep on the sofa in the side room. I mean, with a blanket.'

Again a laugh. 'I don't need to sleep. But it's a kind thought. You're very kind.' His eyes moved to the door, as Bessie walked in, making for her tablecloth of newspaper, on which stood her bowl of water and her unfinished bowl of creamy milk. His eyes followed the cat.

Eleanor felt a sudden apprehension. It was probably because Bessie had not seen him. That was certainly disturbing, when she could see him so well that even the wrinkles in his face were quite visible. He was clothed in strange material, gray-black, neither shiny nor dull.

'You must be lonely since your husband died,' he said. 'But I admit you do well. Considering he didn't leave you much.'

Eleanor blushed. She could feel it. John hadn't been a big earner, certainly. But a decent man, a good husband, yes, he had been that. And their only child, a daughter, had been killed in a snow avalanche in Austria when she was twenty. Eleanor never thought of Penny. She had set herself never to think of Penny. She was disturbed, and felt awkward, because she thought of her now. And she hoped the creature would not mention Penny. Her death was one of life's tragedies. But other families had similar tragedies, only sons killed in useless wars.

'Now you have your cat,' he said, as if he read her thoughts.

'Yes,' Eleanor said, glad to change the subject. 'Bessie is ten. She's had fifty-seven kittens. But three — no four years ago, I finally had her doctored. She's a dear companion.'

Eleanor slipped away and got a big gray blanket, an army surplus blanket, from a closet and folded it in half on the sofa in the side room. He stood watching her. She put a pillow under the top part of the blanket. 'That's a little cozier,' she said.

'Thank you,' came the deep voice.

In the next days, he cut the high grass around the barn with a scythe, and moved a huge rock that had always annoyed Eleanor, embedded as it was in the middle of a grassy square in front of the barn. It was August, but quite cool. They cleared out the attic, and he carried the heaviest things downstairs and to the edge of the road to be picked up by Field's. Some of these things were sold a few days later at auction, and fetched about thirty dollars. Eleanor still felt a slight tenseness when he was present, a fear that she might annoy him in some way, and yet in another way she was growing used to him. He certainly liked to be helpful. At night, he obligingly got on to his sofa bed, and she wanted to tuck him in, to bring him a cup of milk, but in fact he ate next to nothing, and then, as he said, only to keep her company. Eleanor could not understand where all his strength came from.

Vance rang up one day and said she had the pictures. Before Eleanor could ask about them, Vance had hung up. Vance was coming over at once.

'You took a picture of a chair, dear! Does he look like a chair?' Vance asked, laughing. She handed Eleanor the photographs.

There were twelve photographs in the batch, but Eleanor looked only at the top two, which showed him seated in the straight chair and standing by it. 'Why, there he *is*!' she said triumphantly.

Vance hastily, but with a frown, looked at the pictures again, then smiled broadly. 'Are you implying there's something wrong with *my* eyes? It's a chair, darling!'

Eleanor knew Vance was right, speaking for herself. Vance couldn't see him. For a moment, Eleanor couldn't say anything.

'I told you what would happen. Um-hm-hm.'

He was behind her, in the doorway of the side room, Eleanor knew, though she did not turn to look at him.

'All right. Perhaps it's my eyes,' Eleanor said. 'But I *see* him there!' She couldn't give up. Should she tell Vance about his Herculean feats in the attic? Could she have got a big chest of drawers down the stairs by herself?

Vance stayed for a cup of tea. They talked of other things – everything to Eleanor was now 'other' and a bit uninteresting and unimportant compared to *him* – and then Vance left, saying, 'Promise me you'll go to Dr Nimms next week. I'll drive you, if you don't want to drive. Maybe you shouldn't drive if your eyes are acting funny.'

Eleanor had a car, but she seldom used it. She didn't care for driving. 'Thanks, Vance, I'll go on my own.' She meant it at that moment, but when Vance had gone, Eleanor knew she would not go to the eye doctor.

He sat with her while she ate her dinner. She now felt defensive and protective about him. She didn't want to share him with anyone.

'You shouldn't have bothered with those photographs,' he said. 'You see, what I told you is true. Whatever I say is true.'

And yet he didn't look brilliant or even especially intelligent, Eleanor reflected.

He tore a piece of bread rather savagely in half, and stuffed a half into his mouth. 'You're one of the very few people who can see me. Maybe only a dozen people in the world can see me. Maybe less than that. – Why should the others see me?' he continued, and shrugged his chunky shoulders. 'They're just like me.'

'What do you mean?' she asked.

He sighed. 'Ugly.' Then he laughed softly and deeply. 'I am not nice. Not nice at all.'

She was too confused to answer for a moment. A polite answer seemed absurd. She was trying to think what he really meant.

'You enjoyed taking care of your mother, didn't you? You didn't mind it,' he said, as if being polite himself and filling in an awkward silence.

'No, of course not. I loved her,' Eleanor said readily. How could he know? Her father had died when she was eighteen, and she hadn't been able to finish college because of a shortage of money. Then her mother had become ill with leukemia, but she had lived on for ten years. Her treatment had taken all the money Eleanor had been able to earn as a secretary, and a little more besides, so that everything of value they had possessed had finally been sold. Eleanor had married at twenty-nine, and gone with John to live in Boston. Oh, the gone and lovely days! John had been so kind, so understanding of the fact that she had been exhausted, in need of human company – or rather, the company of people her own age. Penny had been born when she was thirty.

'Yes, John was a good man, but not so good as you,' he said, and sighed. 'Hm-mm.'

Now Eleanor laughed spontaneously. It was a relief from the thoughts she had been thinking. 'How can one be good – or bad? Aren't we all a mixture? You're certainly not all bad.'

This seemed to annoy him. 'Don't tell me what I am.'

Rebuffed, Eleanor said nothing more. She cleared the table.

She put him to bed, thanked him for his work in the garden that day – gouging up dandelions, no easy task. She was glad of his company in the house, even glad that no one else could see him. He was a funny doll that belonged to her. He made her feel odd, different, yet somehow special and privileged. She tried to put these thoughts from her mind, lest he disapprove of them, because he was looking, vaguely as usual, at her, with a resentment or a reproach, she felt. 'Can I get you anything?' she asked.

'No,' he answered shortly.

The next morning, she found Bessie in the middle of the kitchen floor with her neck wrung. Her head sat in the strangest way on her neck, facing backwards. Eleanor seized up the corpse impulsively and pressed the cat to her breast. The head lolled. She knew he had done it. But why?

'Yes, I did it,' his deep voice said.

She looked at the doorway, but did not see him. 'How could you?

Why did you do it?' Eleanor began to weep. The cat was not warm any longer, but she was not stiff.

'It's my nature.' He did not laugh, but there was a smile in his voice. 'You hate me now. You wonder if I'll be going. Yes, I'll be going.' His voice was fading as he walked through the living room, but still she could not see him. 'To prove it, I'll slam the door, but I don't need to use the door to get out.' The door slammed.

She was looking at the front door. The door had not moved.

Eleanor buried Bessie in the back lawn by the barn, and the pitch-fork was heavy in her hands, the earth heavier on her spade. She had waited until late afternoon, as if hoping that by some miracle the cat might come alive again. But Bessie's body had grown rigid. Eleanor wept again.

She declined Vance's next invitation to tea, and finally Vance came to see her, unexpectedly. Eleanor was sewing. She had quite a bit of work to do, but she was depressed and lonely, not knowing what she wanted, there being no person she especially wanted to see. She realized that she missed him, the strange creature. And she knew he would never come back.

Vance was disappointed because she had not been to see Dr Nimms. She told Eleanor that she was neglecting herself. Eleanor did not enjoy seeing her old friend Vance. Vance also remarked that she had lost weight.

'That – little monster isn't annoying you still, is he? Or is he?' Vance asked.

'He's gone,' Eleanor said, and managed a smile, though what the smile meant, she didn't know.

'How's Bessie?'

'Bessie – was hit by a car a couple of weeks ago.'

'Oh, Eleanor! I'm sorry. – Why didn't you – You should've told me! What bad luck! You'd better get another kitty. That's always the best thing to do. You're so fond of cats.'

Eleanor shook her head a little.

'I'm going to find out where there's some nice kittens. The

Carters' Siamese might've had another illegitimate batch.' Vance smiled. 'They're always nice, half-Siamese. Really!'

That evening, Eleanor ate no supper. She wandered through the empty-feeling rooms of her house, thinking not only of him, but of her lonely years here, and of the happier first three years here when John had been alive. He had tried to work in Millersville, ten miles away, but the job hadn't lasted. Or rather, the company hadn't lasted. That had been poor John's luck. No use thinking about it now, about what might have been if John had had a business of his own. Yes, once or twice, certainly, he had failed at that, too. But she thought more clearly of when *he* had been here, the funny little fellow who had turned against her. She wished he were back. She felt he would not do such a horrid thing again, if she spoke to him the right way. He had grown annoyed when she had said he was not entirely bad. But she knew he would not come back, not ever. She worked until ten o'clock. More letting out. More hems taken up. People were becoming square, she thought, but the thought did not make her smile that night. She tried to add three times eighty cents plus one dollar and twenty-five cents, and gave it up, perhaps because she was not interested. She looked at his photographs again, half expecting not to see him – like Vance – but he was still there, just as clear as ever, looking at her. That was some comfort to her, but pictures were so flat and lifeless.

The house had never seemed so silent. Her plants were doing beautifully. She had not long ago repotted most of them. Yet Eleanor sensed a negativity when she looked at them. It was very curious, a happy sight like blossoming plants causing sadness. She longed for something, and did not know what it was. That was strange also, the unidentifiable hunger, this loneliness that was worse and more profound than after John had died.

Tom Reynolds rang up one evening at 9 p.m. His wife was ill and he had to go at once to an 'alert' at the Air Base. Could she come over and sit with his wife? He hoped to be home before midnight. Eleanor went over with a bowl of fresh strawberries sprinkled with powdered sugar. Mary Reynolds was not seriously ill, it was a daylong virus attack of some kind, but she was grateful for the strawberries. The bowl was put on the bedtable. It was a pretty color to look at, though Mary could not eat anything just then. Eleanor felt herself, heard herself smiling and chatting as she always did, though in an odd way she felt she was not really present with Mary, not really even in the Reynoldses' house. It wasn't a 'miles away' feeling, but a feeling that it was all not taking place. It was not even as real as a dream.

Eleanor went home at midnight, after Tom returned. Somehow she knew she was going to die that night. It was a calm and destined sensation. She might have died, she thought, if she had merely gone to bed and fallen asleep. But she wished to make sure of it, so she took a single-edged razor blade from her shelf of paints in the kitchen closet – the blade was rusty and dull, but no matter – and cut her two wrists at the bathroom basin. The blood ran and ran, and she washed it down with running cold water, still mindful, she thought with slight amusement, of conserving the hot water in the tank. Finally, she could see that the streams were lessening. She took her bath towel and wrapped it around both her wrists, winding her hands as if she were coiling wool. She was feeling weak, and she wanted to lie down and not soil the mattress, if possible. The blood did not come through the towel before she lay down on her bed. Then she closed her eyes and did not know if it came through or not. It really did not matter, she supposed. Nor did the finished and unfinished skirts and dresses downstairs. People would come and claim them.

Eleanor thought of him, small and strong, strange and yet so plain and simple. He had never told her his name. She realized that she loved him.

WOODROW
WILSON'S NECKTIE

The façade of Madame Thibault's Waxwork Horrors glittered and throbbed with red and yellow lights, even in the daytime. Golden balls like knobs – the yellow lights – pulsated amid the red lights, attracting the eye, holding it.

Clive Wilkes loved the place, the inside and outside equally. Since he was a delivery boy for a grocery store, it was easy for him to say a certain delivery had taken him longer than might be expected – he'd had to wait for Mrs So-and-so to get home, because the doorman had told him she was due any minute, or he'd had to go five blocks to find some change, because Mrs Zilch had had only a fifty-dollar bill. At these spare moments, and Clive found one or two a week, he visited Madame Thibault's Waxwork Horrors.

Inside the establishment, you went through a dark passage to get in the mood, and then you were confronted by a bloody murder scene: a girl with long blonde hair was sticking a knife into the neck of an old man who sat at a kitchen table eating his dinner. His dinner was a couple of wax frankfurters and wax sauerkraut. Then came the Lindbergh kidnapping, with Hauptmann climbing down a ladder outside a nursery window. You could see the top of the ladder outside the window, and the top half of Hauptmann's figure, clutching the little boy. Also there was Marat in his bath with Charlotte nearby. And Christie with his stocking throttlings of women. Clive loved every tableau, and they never became stale. But he didn't look at them with the solemn, vaguely startled expression of the other people who looked at them. Clive was inclined to smile, even to laugh. They were amusing. Why not laugh? Farther on in the museum were the torture chambers – one old, one modern, purporting to show twentieth-century torture methods in Nazi Germany and in French Algeria. Madame Thibault – who Clive strongly suspected did not exist – kept up to date. There were the Kennedy assassinations, of course, the Tate massacre, and as like as not a murder that had happened just a month ago somewhere.

Clive's first definite ambition in regard to Madame Thibault's Waxwork Horrors was to spend a night there. This he did one night, providently taking along a cheese sandwich in his pocket. It was fairly easy to accomplish. Clive knew that three people worked in the museum proper, down in the bowels as he thought of it, though the museum was on street level, while another man, a plumpish middle-aged fellow in a nautical cap, sold tickets out in front at a booth. There were two men and a woman who worked in the bowels. The woman, also plump with curly brown hair and glasses and about forty, took the tickets at the end of the dark corridor, where the museum began. One of the men lectured constantly, though not more than half the people ever bothered to listen. 'Here we see the fanatical expression of the true murderer, captured by the wax artistry of Madame Thibault . . . blah-blah-blah . . . ' The other man had black hair and black-rimmed glasses, and he just drifted around, shooing away kids who wanted to climb into the tableaux, maybe watching for pickpockets, or maybe protecting women from unpleasant assaults in the semi-darkness of the place, Clive didn't know.

He only knew it was quite easy to slip into one of the dark corners or into a nook next to one of the Iron Molls – maybe even into one of the Iron Molls, but slender as he was, the spikes might poke him, Clive thought, so he ruled out this idea. He had observed that people were gently urged out around 9:15 p.m. as the museum closed at 9:30 p.m. And lingering as late as possible one evening, Clive had learned that there was a sort of cloakroom for the staff behind a door in one back corner, from which he had also heard the sound of a toilet flushing.

So one night in November, Clive concealed himself in the shadows, which were abundant, and listened to the three people as they got ready to leave. The woman – whose name seemed to be Mildred – was lingering to take the money box from Fred, the ticket-seller, and to count it and deposit it somewhere in the cloakroom. Clive was not interested in the money, at least not very interested. He was interested in spending a night in the place, to be able to say that he had.

'Night, Mildred! See you tomorrow!' called one of the men.

'Anything else to do? I'm leaving now,' said Mildred. 'Boy, am I tired! But I'm still going to watch Dragon Man tonight.'

'Dragon Man,' the other man repeated, uninterested.

Evidently the ticket-seller Fred left from the front of the building after handing in the money box, and in fact Clive recalled seeing him close up the front once, cutting the lights from inside the entrance door, locking it.

Clive stood in a nook by an Iron Moll. When he heard the back door shut, and the key turn in the lock, he waited for a moment in delicious silence, aloneness, and suspense, then ventured out. He went first on tiptoe to the room where they kept their coats, because he had never seen it. He had brought matches (also cigarettes, though smoking was not allowed, according to several signs), and with the aid of a match, he found the light switch. The room contained an old desk, four or five metal lockers, a tin wastebasket, an umbrella stand, and some books in a bookcase against a rather grimy wall that had once been white. Clive slid open a drawer or two, and found the well-worn wooden box which he had once seen the ticket-seller carrying in through the front door. The box was locked. He could walk out with the box, he thought, but in fact he didn't care to, and he considered this rather decent of himself. He gave the box a wipe with the side of his hand, not forgetting the bottom where his fingertips had touched. That was funny, he thought, wiping something he hadn't stolen.

Clive set about enjoying the night. He found the lights, and put them on, so that the booths with the gory tableaux were all illuminated. He was hungry, and took one bite of his sandwich and put it back in the paper napkin in his pocket. He sauntered slowly past the John F. Kennedy assassination – Robert, Jackie, doctors bending anxiously over the white table on which JFK lay, leaking an ocean of blood which covered the floor. This time Hauptmann's descent of the ladder made Clive giggle. Charles Lindbergh Jr.'s face looked so untroubled, one might have thought he was sitting on the floor of his nursery playing with blocks. Clive swung a leg over a metal bar and climbed into the Judd-Snyder fracas. It gave him a thrill to be standing right *with* them, inches from the throttling-from-behind which the lover was administering to the husband. Clive put a hand out and touched the red-paint blood that was beginning to come from the man's throat where the wire pressed. Clive also touched the cool cheekbones of the victim. The popping eyes were of glass, vaguely disgusting, and Clive did not touch those.

Two hours later, he was singing a church hymn, 'Nearer My God to Thee' and 'Jesus Wants Me for a Sunbeam.' Clive didn't know all the words. He smoked.

By 2 a.m. he was bored, and tried to get out by both front door and back, but couldn't. No spare keys anywhere that he could find. He'd thought of having a hamburger at an all-night place between here and home. His incarceration didn't bother him, however, so he finished the now dry cheese sandwich, made use of the toilet, and slept for a bit on three straight chairs which he arranged in a row. It was so uncomfortable, he knew he would wake up in a while, which he did at 5 a.m. He washed his face, and went for another look at the wax exhibits. This time he took a souvenir – Woodrow Wilson's necktie.

As the hour of nine approached – Madame Thibault's Waxwork Horrors opened at 9:30 a.m. – Clive hid himself in an excellent spot, behind one of the tableaux whose backdrop was a black and gold Chinese screen. In front of the screen was a bed and in the bed lay a wax man with a handlebar moustache, who was supposed to be dead from poisoning by his wife.

The public began trickling in shortly after 9:30 a.m., and the taller, solemn man began mumbling his boring lecture. Clive had to wait till a few minutes past ten before he felt safe enough to mingle with the crowd and make his exit, with Woodrow Wilson's necktie rolled up in his pocket. He was a bit tired, but happy. Though on second thought, who would he tell about it? Joey Vrasky, that blond idiot who worked behind the counter at Simmons's Grocery? Hah! Why bother? Joey didn't deserve a good story. Clive was half an hour late for work.

'I'm sorry, Mr Simmons, I overslept,' Clive said hastily, but he thought quite politely, as he came into the store. There was a delivery job awaiting him. Clive took his bicycle and put the box in front of the handlebars on a platform which had a curb, so a box would not fall off.

Clive lived with his mother, a thin, highly strung woman who was a saleswoman in a shop that sold stockings, girdles and underwear. Her husband had left her when Clive was five. She had no other children but Clive. Clive had quit high school a year before graduating, to his mother's regret, and for a year he had done nothing but lie around the house or stand on street corners with his chums. But Clive had never been very chummy with any of his friends, for which his mother was thankful, as she considered them a worthless lot. Clive had had the delivery job at Simmons's for nearly a year now, and his mother felt that he was settling down.

When Clive came home that evening at 6:30 p.m., he had a story ready for his mother. Last night he had run into his old friend Richie, who was in the army and home on leave, and they had sat up at Richie's talking so late, that Richie's parents had invited him to stay, and Clive had slept on the couch. His mother accepted this explanation. She made a supper of beans, bacon and eggs.

There was really no one to whom Clive felt like telling his exploit of the night. He couldn't have borne someone looking at him and saying, 'Yeah? Well, so what?' because what he had done had taken a bit of planning, even a little daring. He put Woodrow Wilson's tie among his others that hung over a string on the inside of his closet door. It was a gray silk tie, conservative and expensive. Several times that day, Clive imagined the two men in the place, or maybe the woman named Mildred, glancing at Woodrow Wilson and exclaiming:

'Hey! What happened to Woodrow Wilson's tie, I wonder?'

Each time Clive thought of this, he had to duck his head to hide his smile.

After twenty-four hours, however, the exploit had begun to lose its charm and excitement. Clive's excitement arose only again – and it could arise every day and two or three times a day – when he cycled past the twinkling façade of Madame Thibault's Waxwork Horrors. His heart would give a leap, his blood would run a little faster, and he would think of all the motionless murders going on in there, and all the stupid faces of Mr and Mrs Johnny Q. Public gaping at them. But Clive didn't even buy another ticket – price sixty-five cents – to go in and look at Woodrow Wilson and see that his tie was missing and his collar button showing – his work.

Clive did get another idea one afternoon, a hilarious idea that would make the public sit up and take notice. Clive's ribs trembled with suppressed laughter as he pedaled towards Simmons's, having just delivered a carton of groceries.

When should he do it? Tonight? No, best to take a day or so to plan it. It would take brains. And silence. And sure movements – all the things Clive admired. He spent two days thinking about it. He went to his local snack bar and drank Coca-Cola and beer, and played the pinball machines with his pals. The pinball machines had pulsating lights, too – MORE THAN ONE CAN PLAY and IT'S MORE FUN TO COMPETE – but Clive thought only of Madame Thibault's as he stared at the rolling, bouncing balls that mounted a score he cared nothing about. It was the same when he looked at the rainbow-colored jukebox whose blues, reds and yellows undulated, and when he went over to drop a few coins in it. He was thinking of what he was going to do in Madame Thibault's Waxwork Horrors.

On the second night, after a supper with his mother, Clive went to Madame Thibault's and bought a ticket. The old guy who sold tickets barely looked at people, he was so busy making change and tearing off tickets, which was just as well. Clive went in at 9 p.m.

He looked at the tableaux, though they were not so fascinating to him tonight as usual. Woodrow Wilson's tie was still missing, as if no one had noticed it, and Clive had a good chuckle over this, which he concealed behind his hand. Clive remembered that the solemn-faced pickpocket-watcher – the drifting snoop – had been the last to leave the night Clive had stayed, so Clive assumed he had the keys, and therefore he ought to be the last to be killed.

The woman was the first. Clive hid himself beside one of the Iron Molls again, while the crowd oozed out, and as Mildred walked past him, in her hat and coat, to leave via the back door, Clive stepped out and wrapped an arm around her throat from behind.

She made only a small 'U-rk' sound.

Clive squeezed her throat with his hands, stopping her voice. At last she slumped, and Clive dragged her into a dark, recessed corner to the left of the cloakroom as one faced that room, and he knocked an empty cardboard box of some kind over, but it didn't make enough noise to attract the attention of the other two men.

'Mildred's gone?' one of the men said.

'She might be still in the office.'

'No, she's not.' This voice had already gone into the corridor where Clive crouched over Mildred, and had looked into the empty cloakroom where the light was still on. 'She's left. Well, I'm calling it a day, too.'

Clive stepped out then, and encircled this man's neck in the same manner. The job was more difficult, because the man struggled, but Clive's arm was thin and strong, he acted with swiftness, and he knocked the man's head against the nearest wall.

'What's going on?' The thump had brought the second man.

This time, Clive tried a punch to the man's jaw, but missed and hit his neck. However, this so stunned the man – the solemn fellow, the snoop – that a second blow was easy, and then Clive was able to take him by the shirtfront and bash his head against the wall which was harder than the wooden floor. Then Clive made sure all three were dead. The two men's heads were bleeding. The woman was bleeding slightly from the mouth. Clive reached for the keys in the second man's pockets. They were in his left trousers pocket and with them was a penknife. Clive took the knife also.

Then the taller man moved slightly. Alarmed, Clive opened the pearl-handled penknife and went to work with it. He plunged it into the man's throat three or four times.

Close call! Clive thought, and he checked again to make sure they were all dead now. They most certainly were, and that was most certainly real blood coming out, not the red paint of Madame Thibault's Waxwork Horrors. Clive switched on the lights for the tableaux, and went into the exhibition hall for the interesting task of choosing the right places for the corpses.

The woman belonged in Marat's bath, not much doubt about that, and Clive debated removing her clothing, but decided against it, simply because she would look much funnier sitting in a bath with a fur-trimmed coat and hat on than naked. The figure of Marat sent him off in laughter. He'd expected sticks for legs, and nothing between the legs, because you couldn't see any more of Marat than from the middle of his torso up, but Marat had no legs at all, and his wax body ended just below the waist in a fat stump which was planted on a wooden platform so it would not topple. This crazy item Clive carried into the cloakroom and set squarely in the middle of the desk, like a Buddha. He then carried Mildred – who weighed a good bit – onto the Marat scene and stuck her in the bath. Her hat fell off and he pushed it on again, a bit over one eye. Her bleeding mouth hung open.

God, it *was* funny!

Now for the men. Obviously, the one whose throat he had cut would look good in the place of the old man who was eating franks and sauerkraut, because the girl behind him was supposed to be stabbing him in the throat. This work took Clive some fifteen minutes. Since the wax figure of the old man was in a seated position, Clive stuck him on the toilet off the cloakroom. It was amusing to see the old man on the toilet, throat bleeding, a knife in one hand and a fork in the other, apparently waiting for something to eat. Clive lurched against the doorjamb laughing loudly, not even caring if someone heard him, because it was so ludicrous, it was worth getting caught for.

Next, the little snoop. Clive looked around him, and his eye fell on the Woodrow Wilson scene, which depicted the signing of the armistice in 1918. A wax figure – Woodrow Wilson – sat at a huge desk signing a paper, and that was the logical place for a man whose head was split open and bleeding. With some difficulty Clive got the pen out of Woodrow Wilson's fingers, laid it to one side on the desk, and carried the figure – they did not weigh very much – into the cloakroom where Clive seated him at the desk, rigid arms in attitude of writing, and Clive stuck a ballpoint pen into his right hand. Now for the last heave. Clive saw that his jacket was now quite spotted with blood, and he would have to get rid of it, but so far no blood was on his trousers.

Clive dragged the second man to the Woodrow Wilson tableau, heaved him up onto the platform, and rolled him towards the desk. His head was still leaking blood. Clive got him up onto the chair, but the head toppled forward onto the green-blottered desk, onto the phony blank pages, and the pen barely stood upright in the limp hand.

But it was done. Clive stood back and smiled. Then he listened.

Clive sat down on a straight chair somewhere and rested for a few minutes, because his heart was beating fast, and he suddenly realized that every muscle in his body was tired. Ah, well, now he had the keys. He could get out, go home, have a good night's rest, because he wanted to be ready to enjoy tomorrow. Clive took a sweater from one of the male figures in a log cabin tableau. He had to pull the sweater down over the feet to get it off, because the arms would not bend, and it stretched the neck of the sweater but that couldn't be helped. Now the wax figure had a bib of a shirtfront, and naked arms and chest.

Clive wadded up his jacket and went everywhere with it, erasing fingerprints wherever he thought he had touched. He turned the lights off, and made his way carefully to the back door, which was not locked. Clive locked it behind him, and would have left the keys in a mailbox, if there had been one, but there was none, so he dropped the keys on the doorstep. In a wire rubbish basket, he found some newspapers, and he wrapped his jacket in them, and walked on with it until he found another wire rubbish basket, where he forced the bundle down among candy wrappers and beer cans.

'A new sweater?' his mother asked that night.

'Richie gave it to me – for luck.'

Clive slept like the dead, too tired even to laugh again at the memory of the old man sitting on the toilet.

The next morning, Clive was standing across the street when the ticket-seller arrived just before 9:30 a.m. By 9:35 a.m., only three people had gone in (evidently Fred had a key to the front door, in case his colleagues were late), but Clive could not wait any longer, so he crossed the street and bought a ticket. Now the ticket-seller was doubling as ticket-taker, or telling people, 'Just go on in. Everybody's late this morning.' The ticket man stepped inside the door to put on some lights, then walked all the way into the place to put on the display lights, which worked from switches in the hall that led to the cloakroom. And the funny thing to Clive, who was walking behind him, was that the ticket man didn't notice anything odd, didn't notice Mildred in hat and coat sitting in Marat's bathtub.

The customers so far were a man and woman, a boy of fourteen or so in sneakers, and a single man. They looked expressionlessly at Mildred in the tub, as if they thought it quite 'normal,' which could have sent Clive into paroxysms of mirth, except that his heart was thumping madly, and he was hardly breathing for suspense. Also, the man with his face in franks and sauerkraut brought no surprise either. Clive was a bit disappointed.

Two more people came in, a man and a woman.

Then at last by the Woodrow Wilson tableau, there was a reaction. One of the women clinging to a man's arm, asked:

'Was there someone shot when the armistice was signed?'

'I don't know. I don't *think* so,' the man replied vaguely. 'Yes-s — Let me think.'

Clive's laughter pressed like an explosion in his chest, he spun on his heel to control himself, and he had the feeling he knew all about history, and that no one else did. By now, of course, the real blood had turned dark red. The green blotter was now dark red, and blood had run down the side of the desk.

A woman on the other side of the hall, where Mildred was, let out a scream.

A man laughed, but only briefly.

Suddenly everything happened. A woman shrieked, and at the same time, a man yelled, 'My God, it's *real*!'

Clive saw a man climbing up to investigate the corpse with its face in the frankfurters.

'The blood's *real*! It's a dead *man*!'

Another man — one of the public — slumped to the floor. He had fainted!

The ticket-seller came bustling in. 'What's the trouble?'

'Coupla corpses here! *Real* ones!'

Now the ticket-seller looked at Marat's bathtub and fairly jumped into the air with surprise. 'Holy Christmas! Holy *cripes*! — *Mildred*!'

'And this one!'

'And the one here!'

'My God, got to – got to call the police!' said the ticket-seller Fred. 'Could you all, please – just leave?'

One man and woman went out hurriedly. But the rest lingered, shocked, fascinated.

Fred had trotted into the cloakroom, where the telephone was, and Clive heard him yell something. He'd seen the man at the desk, of course, Woodrow Wilson, and Marat on the desk.

Clive thought it was time to drift out, so he did, sidling his way through four or five people who were peering in the door, coming in maybe because there was no ticket-seller.

That was good, Clive thought. That was all right. Not bad.

He had not intended to go to work that day, but suddenly he thought it wiser to check in and ask for the day off. Mr Simmons was of course as sour as ever when Clive said he was not feeling well, but as Clive held his stomach and appeared weak, there was little old Simmons could do. Clive left the store. He had brought with him all his ready cash, about twenty-three dollars.

Clive wanted to take a long bus ride somewhere. He realized that suspicion was likely to fall on him, if the ticket-seller remembered his coming to Madame Thibault's very often, or especially if he remembered his being there last night, but this had little to do with his desire to take a bus ride. His longing for a bus ride was simply, somehow, irresistible and purposeless. He bought a ticket westward for something over seven dollars, one way. This brought him, by about 7 p.m., to a good-sized town in Indiana, whose name Clive paid no attention to.

The bus spilled a few passengers, Clive included, at a terminal where there was a cafeteria and a bar. Clive by now was curious about the newspapers, and went at once to the newsstand near the street door of the cafeteria. And there it was:

TRIPLE MURDER IN WAXWORKS

MASS MURDER IN WAXWORKS MUSEUM

MYSTERY KILLER: THREE DEAD IN WAXWORKS MUSEUM

Clive liked the last headline best. He bought the three newspapers, and stood at the bar with a beer.

This morning at 9:30 a.m., ticket man Fred J. Keating and several of the public who had come to see Madame Thibault's Waxworks Horrors, a noted attraction of this city, were confronted by three genuine corpses among the displays. They were the bodies of Mrs Mildred Veery, 41; George P. Hartley, 43; and Richard K. MacFadden, 37, all employed at the waxworks museum. The two men were killed by concussions to the head, and in the case of one also by stabbing, and the woman by strangulation. Police are searching for clues on the premises. The murders are believed to have taken place shortly before 10 p.m. last evening, when the three employees were about to leave the museum. The murderer or murderers may have been among the last patrons of the museum before closing time at 9:30 p.m. It is thought that he or they may have concealed themselves somewhere in the museum until the rest of the patrons had left . . .

Clive was pleased. He smiled as he sipped his beer. He hunched over the papers, as if he did not wish the rest of the world to share his pleasure, but this was not true. After a few minutes, Clive looked to right and left to see if anyone else among the men and a few women at the bar were reading the story also. Two men were reading newspapers, but Clive could not tell if they were reading about him necessarily, because their newspapers were folded. Clive lit a cigarette and went through all three newspapers to see if there was any clue about him. He found none at all. One paper said specifically that Fred J. Keating had not noticed any person or persons entering the museum last evening who looked suspicious.

. . . Because of the bizarre arrangement of the victims and of the displaced wax figures in the exhibitions, in whose places the victims were put, police are looking for a psychopathic killer.

Residents of the area have been warned by radio and television to take special precautions on the street and to keep their homes locked . . .

Clive chuckled over that one. Psychopathic killer. He was sorry about the lack of detail, the lack of humor in the three write-ups. They might have said something about the old guy sitting on the toilet. Or the fellow signing the armistice with the back of his head bashed in. Those were strokes of genius. Why didn't they appreciate them?

When he had finished his beer, Clive walked out onto the sidewalk. It was now dark and the streetlights were on. He enjoyed looking around in the new town, looking into shop windows. But he was aiming for a hamburger place, and he went into the first one he came to. It was a diner made up to look like a crack train made of chromium. Clive ordered two hamburgers and a cup of coffee. Next to him were two Western-looking men in cowboy boots and rather soiled broad-brimmed hats. Was one a sheriff, Clive wondered? But they were talking, in a drawl, about acreage somewhere. Land. Money. They were hunched over hamburgers and coffee, one so close his elbow kept brushing Clive's. Clive was reading his newspapers all over again, and he had propped one against the napkin container in front of him.

One of the men asked for a napkin and disturbed Clive, but Clive smiled, and said in a friendly way:

'Did you read about the murders in the waxworks?'

The man looked blank, then said, 'Saw the headlines.'

'Someone killed the three people who worked in the place. Look.' There was a photograph in one of the papers, but Clive didn't much like it, because it showed the corpses lined up on the floor. He would have preferred Mildred in the bathtub.

'Yeah,' said the Westerner, edging away from Clive as if he didn't like him.

'The bodies were put into a few of the exhibitions. Like the wax figures. They say that, but they don't show a picture of it,' said Clive.

'Yeah,' said the Westerner, and went on with his hamburger.

Clive felt let down and somehow insulted. His face grew a little warm as he stared back at his newspapers. In fact, anger was growing very quickly inside him, making his heart go faster, as it did when he passed Madame Thibault's Waxwork Horrors, though now the sensation was not at all pleasant. Clive put on a smile, however, and turned again to the man on his left. 'I mention it, because I did it. That's my work there.' He pointed at the picture of the corpses.

'Listen, boy,' said the Westerner, chewing, 'you just keep to yourself tonight. Okay? We ain't botherin' you, and don't you go botherin' us.' He laughed a little, and glanced at his companion.

His friend was staring at Clive, but looked away at once when Clive looked at him.

This was a double rebuff, and quite enough for Clive. Clive got his money out and paid for his unfinished food with a dollar bill and a fifty-cent piece. He left the change and walked to the sliding door exit.

'But y'know, maybe that kid ain't kiddin',' Clive heard one of the men say.

Clive turned and said, '*I* ain't kiddin'!' Then he went out into the night.

Clive slept at a YMCA. The next day, he half expected he would be picked up by any passing cop on the beat, but he wasn't, and he passed a few. He got a lift to another town, nearer his home town. The day's newspapers brought no mention of his name, and no clues. In another café that evening almost the identical conversation took place between Clive and a couple of fellows around his own age. They didn't believe him. It was stupid of them, Clive thought, and he wondered if they were pretending? Or lying?

Clive hitched his way to his hometown, and headed for the police station. He was curious to see what *they* would say. He imagined what his mother would say after he confessed. Probably the same thing she had said to her friends sometimes, or that she'd said to a policeman when he was sixteen and had stolen a car:

'Clive hasn't been the same boy since his father went away. I know he needs a man around the house, a man to look up to, imitate, y'know. That's what people tell me. Since fourteen, Clive's been asking me questions like, "Who am I, anyway?" and "Am I a person, mom?"' Clive could see and hear her already in the police station.

'I have an important confession to make,' Clive said to a guard, or somebody, sitting at a desk at the front of the station.

The guard's attitude was rude and suspicious, Clive thought, but he was told to walk to an office, where he spoke with a police officer who had gray hair and a fat face. Clive told his story.

'Where do you go to school, Clive?'

'I don't. I'm eighteen.' Clive told him about his job at Simmons's Grocery.

'Clive, you've got troubles, but they're not the ones you're talking about,' said the officer.

Clive had to wait in a room, and nearly an hour later a psychiatrist was brought in. Then his mother. Clive became more and more impatient. They didn't believe him. They were saying he was a typical case of false confessing in order to attract attention to himself. His mother's repeated statements about his asking questions like 'Am I a person?' only seemed to corroborate the psychiatrist and the police in their opinion.

Clive was to report somewhere twice a week for psychiatric therapy.

He fumed. He refused to go back to Simmons's Grocery, but found another delivery job, because he liked having a little money in his pocket, and he was fast on his bicycle and honest with the change.

'You haven't *found* the murderer, have you?' Clive said to the psychiatrist, associating him, Clive realized, with the police. 'You're all the biggest bunch of jackasses I've ever seen in my life!'

The psychiatrist lost his temper, which was at least human.

'You'll never get anywhere talking to people like that, boy.'

Clive said, 'Some perfectly ordinary strangers in Indiana said, "Maybe that kid ain't kiddin'".' They seem to have had more sense than you!'

The psychiatrist laughed.

Clive smoldered. One thing might have helped to prove his story, Woodrow Wilson's necktie, which still hung in his closet. But these bastards damned well didn't deserve to see that tie. Even as he ate his suppers with his mother, went to movies with her, and delivered groceries, he was planning. He'd do something more important next time: start a fire in the depths of a big building, plant a bomb some-where, take a machine gun up to some penthouse and let 'em have it down on the street. Kill a hundred people at least. They'd have to come up in the building to get him. They'd know then. They'd treat him like somebody who existed.

A CURIOUS SUICIDE

D r Stephen McCullough had a first-class compartment to himself on the express from Paris to Geneva. He sat browsing in one of the medical quarterlies he had brought from America, but he was not concentrating. He was toying with the idea of murder. That was why he had taken the train instead of flying, to give himself time to think or perhaps merely dream.

He was a serious man of forty-five, a little overweight, with a prominent and spreading nose, a brown moustache, brown-rimmed glasses, a receding hairline. His eyebrows were tense with an inward anxiety, which his patients often thought a concern with their problems. Actually, he was unhappily married, and though he refused to quarrel with Lillian – that meant answer her back – there was discord between them. In Paris yesterday he had answered Lillian back, and on a ridiculous matter about whether he or she would take back to a shop on the Rue Royale an evening bag that Lillian had decided she did not want. He had been angry not because he had had to return the bag, but because he had agreed, in a weak moment fifteen minutes before, to visit Roger Fane in Geneva.

'Go and see him, Steve,' Lillian had said yesterday morning. 'You're so close to Geneva now, why not? Think of the pleasure it'd give Roger.'

What pleasure? Why? But Dr McCullough had rung Roger at the American Embassy in Geneva, and Roger had been very friendly, much too friendly, of course, and had said that he must come and stay a few days and that he had plenty of room to put him up. Dr McCullough had agreed to spend one night. Then he was going to fly to Rome to join Lillian.

Dr McCullough detested Roger Fane. It was the kind of hatred that time does nothing to diminish. Roger Fane, seventeen years ago, had married the woman Dr McCullough loved. Margaret. Margaret had died a year ago in an automobile accident on an Alpine road. Roger Fane was smug, cautious, mightily pleased with himself and not very intelligent. Seventeen years ago, Roger Fane had told Margaret that he, Stephen McCullough, was having a secret affair with another girl. Nothing was further from the truth, but before Stephen could prove anything, Margaret had married Roger. Dr McCullough had not expected the marriage to last, but it had, and finally Dr McCullough had married Lillian whose face resembled Margaret's a little, but that was the only similarity. In the past seventeen years, Dr McCullough had seen Roger and Margaret perhaps three times when they had come to New York on short trips. He had not seen Roger since Margaret's death.

Now as the train shot through the French countryside, Dr McCullough reflected on the satisfaction that murdering Roger Fane might give him. He had never before thought of murdering anybody, but yesterday evening while he was taking a bath in the Paris hotel, after the telephone conversation with Roger, a thought had come to him in regard to murder: most murderers were caught because they left some clue, despite their efforts to erase all the clues. Many murderers wanted to be caught, the doctor realized, and unconsciously planted a clue that led the police straight to them. In the Leopold and Loeb case, one of them had dropped his glasses at the scene, for instance. But suppose a murderer deliberately left a dozen clues, practically down to his calling card? It seemed to Dr McCullough that the very obviousness of it would throw suspicion off. Especially if the person were a man like himself, well thought of, a nonviolent type. Also, there'd be no motive that anyone could see, because Dr McCullough had never even told Lillian that he had loved the woman Roger Fane had married. Of course, a few of his old friends knew it, but Dr McCullough hadn't mentioned Margaret or Roger Fane in a decade.

He imagined Roger's apartment formal and gloomy, perhaps with a servant prowling about full time, a servant who slept in. A servant would complicate things. Let's say there wasn't a servant who slept in, that he and Roger would be having a nightcap in the living room or in Roger's study, and then just before saying good night, Dr McCullough would pick up a heavy paperweight or a big vase and— Then he would calmly take his leave. Of course, the bed should be slept in, since he was supposed to stay the night, so perhaps the morning would be better for the crime than the evening. The essential thing was to leave quietly and at the time he was supposed to leave. But the doctor found himself unable to plot in much detail after all.

Roger Fane's street in Geneva looked just as Dr McCullough had imagined it – a narrow, curving street that combined business establishments with old private dwellings – and it was not too well lighted when Dr McCullough's taxi entered it at 9 p.m., yet in law-abiding Switzerland, the doctor supposed, dark streets held few dangers for anyone. The front door buzzed in response to his ring, and Dr McCullough opened it. The door was heavy as a bank vault's door.

'Hullo!' Roger's voice called cheerily down the stairwell. 'Come up! I'm on the third floor. Fourth to you, I suppose.'

'Be right there!' Dr McCullough said, shy about raising his voice in the presence of the closed doors on either side of the hall. He had telephoned Roger a few moments ago from the railway station, because Roger had said he would meet him. Roger had apologized and said he had been held up at a meeting at his office, and would Steve mind hopping into a taxi and coming right over? Dr McCullough suspected that Roger had not been held up at all, but simply hadn't wanted to show him the courtesy of being at the station.

'Well, well, Steve!' said Roger, pumping Dr McCullough's hand. 'It's great to see you again. Come in, come in. Is that thing heavy?' Roger made a pass at the doctor's suitcase, but the doctor caught it up first.

'Not at all. Good to see you again, Roger.' He went into the apartment.

There were oriental rugs, ornate lamps that gave off dim light. It was even stuffier than Dr McCullough had anticipated. Roger looked a trifle thinner. He was shorter than the doctor, and had sparse blond hair. His weak face perpetually smiled. Both had eaten dinner, so they drank scotch in the living room.

'So you're joining Lillian in Rome tomorrow,' said Roger. 'Sorry you won't be staying longer. I'd intended to drive you out to the country tomorrow evening to meet a friend of mine. A woman,' Roger added with a smile.

'Oh? Too bad. Yes, I'll be off on the one o'clock plane tomorrow afternoon. I made the reservation from Paris.' Dr McCullough found himself speaking automatically. Strangely, he felt a little drunk, though he'd taken only a couple of sips of his scotch. It was because of the falsity of the situation, he thought, the falsity of his being here at all, of his pretending friendship or at least friendliness. Roger's smile irked him, so merry and yet so forced. Roger hadn't referred to Margaret, though Dr McCullough had not seen him since she died. But then, neither had the doctor referred to her, even to give a word of condolence. And already, it seemed, Roger had another female interest. Roger was just over forty, still trim of figure and bright of eye. And Margaret, that jewel among women, was just something that had come his way, stayed a while, and departed, Dr McCullough supposed. Roger looked not at all bereaved.

The doctor detested Roger fully as much as he had on the train, but the reality of Roger Fane was somewhat dismaying. If he killed him, he would have to touch him, feel the resistance of his flesh at any rate with the object he hit him with. And what was the servant situation? As if Roger read his mind, he said:

'I've a girl who comes in to clean every morning at ten and leaves at twelve. If you want her to do anything for you, wash and iron a shirt or something like that, don't hesitate. She's very fast, or can be if you ask her. Her name's Yvonne.'

Then the telephone rang. Roger spoke in French. His face fell slightly as he agreed to do something that the other person was asking him to do. Roger said to the doctor:

'Of all irritating things. I've got to catch the seven o'clock plane to Zurich tomorrow. Some visiting fireman's being welcomed at a breakfast. So, old man, I suppose I'll be gone before you're out of bed.'

'Oh!' Dr McCullough found himself chuckling. 'You think doctors aren't used to early calls? Of course I'll get up to tell you good-bye – see you off.'

Roger's smile widened slightly. 'Well, we'll see. I certainly won't wake you for it. Make yourself at home and I'll leave a note for Yvonne to prepare coffee and rolls. Or would you like a more substantial brunch around eleven?'

Dr McCullough was not thinking about what Roger was saying. He had just noticed a rectangular marble pen and pencil holder on the desk where the telephone stood. He was looking at Roger's high and faintly pink forehead. 'Oh, brunch,' said the doctor vaguely. 'No, no, for goodness' sake. They feed you enough on the plane.' And then his thoughts leapt to Lillian and the quarrel yesterday in Paris. Hostility smoldered in him. Had Roger ever quarreled with Margaret? Dr McCullough could not imagine Margaret being unfair, being mean. It was no wonder Roger's face looked relaxed and untroubled.

'A penny for your thoughts,' said Roger, getting up to replenish his glass.

The doctor's glass was still half full.

'I suppose I'm a bit tired,' said Dr McCullough, and passed his

hand across his forehead. When he lifted his head again, he saw a
photograph of Margaret which he had not noticed before on the
top of the highboy on his right. Margaret in her twenties, as she
had looked when Roger married her, as she had looked when the
doctor had so loved her. Dr McCullough looked suddenly at Roger.
His hatred returned in a wave that left him physically weak. 'I
suppose I'd better turn in,' he said, setting his glass carefully on
the little table in front of him, standing up. Roger had showed him
his bedroom.

'Sure you wouldn't like a spot of brandy?' asked Roger. 'You look
all in.' Roger smiled cockily, standing very straight.

The tide of the doctor's anger flowed back. He picked up the
marble slab with one hand, and before Roger could step back,
smashed him in the forehead with its base. It was a blow that would
kill, the doctor knew. Roger fell and without even a last twitch lay
still and limp. The doctor set the marble back where it had been,
picked up the pen and pencil which had fallen, and replaced them in
their holders, then wiped the marble with his handkerchief where
his fingers had touched it and also the pen and pencil. Roger's forehead was bleeding slightly. He felt Roger's still-warm wrist and
found no pulse. Then he went out the door and down the hall to
his own room.

He awakened the next morning at 8:15, after a not very sound
night's sleep. He showered in the bathroom between his room and
Roger's bedroom, shaved, dressed and left the house at a quarter past
nine. A hall went from his room past the kitchen to the flat's door; it
had not been necessary to cross the living room, and even if he had
glanced into the living room through the door he had not closed,
Roger's body would have been out of sight to him. Dr McCullough
had not glanced in.

At 5:30 p.m. he was in Rome, riding in a taxi from the airport
to the Hotel Majestic where Lillian awaited him. Lillian was out,
however. The doctor had some coffee sent up, and it was then that he
noticed his briefcase was missing. He had wanted to lie on the bed and

drink coffee and read his medical quarterlies. Now he remembered distinctly: he had for some reason carried his briefcase into the living room last evening. This did not disturb him at all. It was exactly what he should have done on purpose if he had thought of it. His name and his New York address were written in the slot of the briefcase. And Dr McCullough supposed that Roger had written his name in full in some engagement book along with the time of his arrival.

He found Lillian in good humor. She had bought a lot of things in the Via Condotti. They had dinner and then took a carozza ride through the Villa Borghese, to the Piazza di Spagna and the Piazza del Populo. If there were anything in the papers about Roger, Dr McCullough was ignorant of it. He bought only the Paris *Herald-Tribune*, which was a morning paper.

The news came the next morning as he and Lillian were breakfasting at Donay's in the Via Veneto. It was in the Paris *Herald-Tribune*, and there was a picture of Roger Fane on the front page, a serious official picture of him in a wing collar.

'Good Lord!' said Lillian. 'Why – it happened the night you were there!'

Looking over her shoulder, Dr McCullough pretended surprise. '"—died some time between eight p.m. and three a.m.,"' the doctor read. 'I said good night to him about eleven, I think. Went into my room.'

'You didn't *hear* anything?'

'No. My room was down a hall. I closed my door.'

'And the next morning. You didn't—'

'I told you, Roger had to catch a seven o'clock plane. I assumed he was gone. I left the house around nine.'

'And all the time he was in the living room!' Lillian said with a gasp. 'Steve! Why, this is terrible!'

Was it, Dr McCullough wondered. Was it so terrible for her? Her voice did not sound really concerned. He looked into her wide eyes. 'It's certainly terrible – but I'm not responsible, God knows. Don't worry, Lillian.'

The police were at the Hotel Majestic when they returned, waiting for Dr McCullough in the lobby. They were both plain-clothes Swiss police, and they spoke English. They interviewed Dr McCullough at a table in a corner of the lobby. Lillian had, at Dr McCullough's insistence, gone up to their room. Dr McCullough had wondered why the police had not come for him hours earlier than this – it was so simple to check the passenger list of planes leaving Geneva – but he soon found out why. The maid Yvonne had not come to clean yesterday morning, so Roger Fane's body had not been discovered until 6 p.m. yesterday, when his office had become alarmed by his absence and sent someone around to his apartment to investigate.

'This is your briefcase, I think,' said the slender blond officer with a smile, opening a large manila envelope he had been carrying under his arm.

'Yes, thank you very much. I realized today that I'd left it.' The doctor took it and laid it on his lap.

The two Swiss watched him quietly.

'This is very shocking,' Dr McCullough said. 'It's hard for me to realize.' He was impatient for them to make their charge – if they were going to – and ask him to return to Geneva with them. They both seemed almost in awe of him.

'How well did you know Mr Fane?' asked the other officer.

'Not too well. I've known him many years, but we were never close friends. I hadn't seen him in five years, I think.' Dr McCullough spoke steadily and in his usual tone.

'Mr Fane was still fully dressed, so he had not gone to bed. You are sure you heard no disturbance that night?'

'I did not,' the doctor answered for the second time. A silence. 'Have you any clues as to who might have done it?'

'Oh, yes, yes,' the blond man said matter of factly. 'We suspect the brother of the maid Yvonne. He was drunk that night and hasn't an alibi for the time of the crime. He and his sister live together and that night he went off with his sister's batch of keys – among which were the keys to Mr Fane's apartment. He didn't come back until nearly noon yesterday. Yvonne was worried about him, which is why she didn't go to Mr Fane's apartment yesterday – that plus the fact she couldn't have got in. She tried to telephone at eight-thirty yesterday morning to say she wouldn't be coming, but she got no answer. We've questioned the brother Anton. He's a ne'er-do-well.' The man shrugged.

Dr McCullough remembered hearing the telephone ring at eight-thirty. 'But – what was the motive?'

'Oh – resentment. Robbery maybe if he'd been sober enough to find anything to take. He's a case for a psychiatrist or an alcoholic ward. Mr Fane knew him, so he might have let him into the apartment, or he could have walked in, since he had the keys. Yvonne said that Mr Fane had been trying for months to get her to live apart from her brother. Her brother beats her and takes her money. Mr Fane had spoken to the brother a couple of times, and it's on our record that Mr Fane once had to call the police to get Anton out of the apartment when he came there looking for his sister. That incident happened at nine in the evening, an hour when his sister is never there. You see how off his head he is.'

Dr McCullough cleared his throat and asked, 'Has Anton confessed to it?'

'Oh, the same as. Poor chap, I really don't think he knows what he's doing half the time. But at least in Switzerland there's no capital punishment. He'll have enough time to dry out in jail, all right.' He glanced at his colleague and they both stood up. 'Thank you very much, Dr McCullough.'

'You're very welcome,' said the doctor. 'Thank you for the briefcase.'

Dr McCullough went upstairs with his briefcase to his room.

'What did they say?' Lillian asked as he came in.

'They think the brother of the maid did it,' said Dr McCullough. 'Fellow who's an alcoholic and who seems to have had it in for Roger. Some ne'er-do-well.' Frowning, he went into the bathroom to wash his hands. He suddenly detested himself, detested Lillian's long sigh, an 'Ah-h' of relief and joy.

'Thank God, thank God!' Lillian said. 'Do you know what this would have meant if they'd – if they'd have accused *you*?' she asked in a softer voice, as if the walls had ears, and she came closer to the bathroom door.

'Certainly,' Dr McCullough said, and felt a burst of anger in his blood. 'I'd have had a hell of a time proving I was innocent, since I was right there at the time.'

'Exactly. You couldn't have proved you were innocent. Thank God for this Anton, whoever he is.' Her small face glowed, her eyes twinkled. 'A ne'er-do-well. Ha! He did us some good!' She laughed shrilly and turned on one heel.

'I don't see why you have to gloat,' he said, drying his hands carefully. 'It's a sad story.'

'Sadder than if they'd blamed you? Don't be so – so altruistic, dear. Or rather, think of us. Husband kills old rival-in-love after – let's see – seventeen years, isn't it? And after eleven years of marriage to another woman. The torch still burns high. Do you think I'd like that?'

'Lillian, what're you talking about?' He came out of the bathroom scowling.

'You know exactly. You think I don't know you were in love with Margaret? *Still* are? You think I don't know you killed Roger?' Her gray eyes looked at him with a wild challenge. Her head was tipped to one side, her hands on her hips.

He felt tongue-tied, paralyzed. They stared at each other for perhaps fifteen seconds, while his mind moved tentatively over the abyss her words had just spread before him. He hadn't known that she still thought of Margaret. Of course she'd known about Margaret. But who had kept the story alive in her mind? Perhaps himself by his silence, the doctor realized. But the future was what mattered. Now she had something to hold over his head, something by which she could control him forever. 'My dear, you are mistaken.'

But Lillian with a toss of her head turned and walked away, and the doctor knew he had not won.

Absolutely nothing was said about the matter for the rest of the day. They lunched, spent a leisurely hour in the Vatican museum, but Dr McCullough's mind was on other things than Michelangelo's paintings. He was going to go to Geneva and confess the thing, not for decency's sake or because his conscience bothered him, but because Lillian's attitude was insupportable. It was less supportable than a stretch in prison. He managed to get away long enough to make a telephone call at five p.m. There was a plane to Geneva at 7:20 p.m. At 6:15 p.m., he left their hotel room empty-handed and took a taxi to Ciampino airport. He had his passport and traveler's checks.

He arrived in Geneva before eleven that evening, and called the police. At first, they were not willing to tell him the whereabouts of the man accused of murdering Roger Fane, but Dr McCullough gave his name and said he had some important information, and then the Swiss police told him where Anton Carpeau was being held. Dr McCullough took a taxi to what seemed the outskirts of Geneva. It was a new white building, not at all like a prison.

Here he was greeted by one of the plainclothes officers who had come to see him, the blond one. 'Dr McCullough,' he said with a faint smile. 'You have some information, you say? I am afraid it is a little late.'

'Oh? – Why?'

'Anton Carpeau has just killed himself – by bashing his head against the wall of his cell. Just twenty minutes ago.' The man gave a hopeless shrug.

'Good God,' Dr McCullough said softly.

'But what was your information?'

The doctor hesitated. The words wouldn't come. And then he realized that it was cowardice and shame that kept him silent. He had never felt so worthless in his life, and he felt infinitely lower than the drunken ne'er-do-well who had killed himself. 'I'd rather not. In this case – I mean – it's so all over, isn't it? It was something else against Anton, I thought – and what's the use now? It's bad enough—' The words stopped.

'Yes, I suppose so,' said the Swiss.

'So – I'll say good night.'

'Good night, Dr McCullough.'

Then the doctor walked on into the night, aimlessly. He felt a curious emptiness, a nothingness in himself that was not like any mood he had ever known. His plan for murder had succeeded, but it had dragged worse tragedies in its wake. Anton Carpeau. And *Lillian*. In a strange way, he had killed himself just as much as he had killed Roger Fane. He was now a dead man, a walking dead man.

Half an hour later, he stood on a formal bridge looking down at the black water of Lake Leman. He stared down a long while, and imagined his body toppling over and over, striking the water with not much of a splash, sinking. He stared hard at the blackness that looked so solid but would be so yielding, so willing to swallow him into death. But he hadn't even the courage or the despair as yet for suicide. One day, however, he would, he knew. One day when the planes of cowardice and courage met at the proper angle. And that day would be a surprise to him and to everyone else who knew him. Then his hands that gripped the stone parapet pushed him back, and the doctor walked on heavily. He would see about a hotel for tonight, and then tomorrow arrange to get back to Rome.

THE MAN WHO WROTE
BOOKS IN HIS HEAD

E Taylor Cheever wrote books in his head, never on paper. By the
time he died aged sixty-two, he had written fourteen novels and
created one hundred and twenty-seven characters, all of whom he,
at least, remembered distinctly.

It came about like this: Cheever wrote a novel when he was
twenty-three called *The Eternal Challenge* which was rejected by
four London publishers. Cheever, then a sub-editor on a Brighton
newspaper, showed his manuscript to three or four journalist and
critic friends, all of whom said, in quite as brusque a tone it seemed
to Cheever as the London publishers' letters, 'Characters don't come
through . . . dialogue artificial . . . theme is unclear . . . Since you ask
me to be frank, may I say I don't think this has a hope of being published even if you work it over . . . Better forget this one and write
another . . . ' Cheever had spent all his spare time for two years on
the novel, and had come near losing the girl he intended to marry,
Louise Welldon, because he gave her so little attention. However
he did marry Louise just a few weeks after the deluge of negative
reports on his novel. It was a far cry from the note of triumph on
which he had intended to claim his bride and embark upon marriage.

Cheever had a small private income, and Louise had more. Cheever didn't need a job. He had imagined quitting his newspaper job (on the strength of having his first novel published), writing more novels and book reviews and maybe a column on books for the Brighton newspaper, climbing up from there to the *Times* and *Guardian*. He tried to get in as book critic on the Brighton *Beacon*, but they wouldn't take him on any permanent basis. Besides, Louise wanted to live in London.

They bought a town house in Cheyne Walk and decorated it with furniture and rugs given them by their families. Meanwhile Cheever was thinking about another novel, which he intended to get exactly right before he put a word on paper. So secretive was he, that he did not tell Louise the title or theme or discuss any of the characters with her, though Cheever did get his characters clearly in mind – their backgrounds, motivations, tastes, and appearance down to the color of their eyes. His next book would be definite as to theme, his characters fleshed out, his dialogue spare and telling.

He sat for hours in his study in the Cheyne Walk house, indeed went up after breakfast and stayed until lunchtime, then went back until tea or dinnertime like any other working writer, but at his desk he made hardly a note except an occasional '1877 + 53' and '1939–83,' things like that to determine the age or birth year of certain characters. He liked to hum softly to himself while he pondered. His book, which he called *The Spoiler of the Game* (no one else in the world knew the title), took him fourteen months to think out and write in his mind. By that time, Everett Junior had been born. Cheever knew so well where he was going with the book that the whole first page was etched in his mind as if he saw it printed. He knew there would be twelve chapters, and he knew what was in them. He committed whole sequences of dialogue to memory, and could recall them at will. Cheever thought he could type the book out in less than a month. He had a new typewriter, a present from Louise on his last birthday.

'I *am* ready – finally,' Cheever said one morning with an unaccustomed air of cheer.

'Oh, splendid, darling!' said Louise. Tactfully she never asked him how his work was going, because she sensed that he didn't like that.

While Cheever was looking over the *Times* and filling his first pipe before going up to work, Louise went out in the garden and cut three yellow roses, which she put into a vase and took up to his room. Then she silently withdrew.

Cheever's study was attractive and comfortable with a generous desk, good lighting, books of reference and dictionaries to hand, a green leather sofa he could take catnaps on if he chose, and a view of the garden. Cheever noticed the roses on the small roller table beside his desk and smiled appreciatively. *Page One, Chapter One*, Cheever thought. The book was to be dedicated to Louise. *To my wife Louise.* Simple and clear. *It was on a gray morning in December that Leonard . . .*

He procrastinated, and lit another pipe. He had put a sheet of paper in the typewriter, but this was the title page, and as yet he had written nothing. Suddenly, at 10:15 a.m., he was aware of boredom – oppressive, paralyzing boredom. He knew the book, it was in his mind entirely, and in fact why write it?

The thought of hammering away at the keys for the next many weeks, putting words he already knew onto two hundred and ninety-two pages (so Cheever estimated) dismayed him. He fell onto the green sofa and slept until eleven. He awakened refreshed and with a changed outlook: the book was done, after all, not only done but polished. Why not go on to something else?

An idea for a novel about an orphan in quest of his parents had been in Cheever's mind for nearly four months. He began to think about a novel around it. He sat all day at his desk, humming, staring at the slips of paper, almost all blank, while he rapped the eraser end of a yellow pencil. He was creating.

By the time he had thought out and finished the orphan novel, a long one, his son was five years old.

'I can *write* my books later,' Cheever said to Louise. 'The important thing is to think them out.'

Louise was disappointed, but hid her feelings. 'Your father is a writer,' she said to Everett Junior. 'A novelist. Novelists don't have to go to work like other people. They can work at home.'

Little Everett was in a day nursery school, and the children had asked him what his father did. By the time Everett was twelve, he understood the situation and found it highly risible, especially when his mother told him his father had written six books. Invisible books. This was when Louise began to change her attitude to Cheever from one of tolerance and laissez-faire to one of respect and admiration. Mainly, consciously, she did this to set an example for Everett. She was conventional enough to believe that if a son lost respect for his father, the son's character and even the household would fall apart.

When Everett was fifteen, he was not amused by his father's work any longer, but ashamed and embarrassed by it when his friends came to visit.

'Novels? . . . Any good? . . . Can I see one?' asked Ronnie Phelps, another fifteen-year-old and a hero of Everett's. That Everett had been able to bring Ronnie home for the Christmas hols was a stupendous coup, and Everett was anxious that everything should go right.

'He's very shy about them,' Everett replied. 'Keeps 'em in his room, you know.'

'Seven novels. Funny I never heard of him. Who's his publisher?'

Everett found himself under such a strain, Ronnie became ill at ease too, and after only three days went down to his family in Kent. Everett refused to eat, almost, and kept to his room where his mother twice found him weeping.

Cheever knew nothing of this. Louise shielded him from every domestic upset, every interruption. But since the holidays stretched ahead nearly a month and Everett was in such a bad state, she gently suggested to Cheever that they take a cruise somewhere, maybe to the Canaries.

At first, Cheever was startled by the idea. He didn't like vacations, didn't need them, he often said. But after twenty-four hours, he decided that a cruise was a good idea. 'I can still work,' he said.

On the boat, Cheever sat for hours in his deck chair, sometimes with pencil, sometimes not, working on his eighth novel. He never made a note in twelve days, however. Louise, next to him in her chair, could tell when he sighed and closed his eyes that he was taking a breather. Towards the end of the day, he often appeared to be holding a book in his hands and to be thumbing through it, and she knew he was browsing in his past work which he knew by heart.

'Ha-ha,' Cheever would laugh softly, when a passage amused him. He would turn to another place, appear to be reading, then murmur, 'Um-m. Not bad, not bad.'

Everett, whose chair was on the other side of his mother's, would tear himself up grimly and stalk away when his father gave these contented grunts. The cruise was not an entire success for Everett, there being no people his own age except one girl, and Everett announced to his parents and the friendly deck steward that he had no desire whatever to meet her.

But things went better when Everett got to Oxford. At least his attitude towards his father became once more one of amusement. His father had made him quite popular at Oxford, Everett declared. 'It's not everyone who's got a living limerick for a father!' he said to his mother. 'Shall I recite one I—'

'Please, Everett,' said his mother with a coldness that took the grin at once from Everett's face.

In his late fifties, Cheever showed signs of the heart disease which was to kill him. He wrote on as steadily as ever in his head, but his doctor counseled him to cut down on his hours of work, and to nap twice in the day. Louise had explained to the doctor (a new doctor to them, a heart specialist) what kind of work Cheever did.

'He is thinking out a novel,' Louise said. 'That can be just as tiring as writing one, of course.'

'Of course,' the doctor agreed.

When the end came for Cheever, Everett was thirty-eight and had two teenaged children of his own. Everett had become a zoologist. Everett and his mother and five or six relatives assembled in the hospital room where Cheever lay under an oxygen tent. Cheever was murmuring something, and Louise bent close to hear.

'. . . ashes unto ashes,' Cheever was saying. 'Stand back! . . . No photographs allowed . . . "Next to Tennyson?"' This last in a soft high voice. '. . . monument to human imagination . . .'

Everett was also listening. Now his father seemed to be delivering a prepared speech of some kind. A *eulogy*, Everett thought.

'. . . tiny corner revered by a grateful people . . . Clunk! . . . Careful!'

Everett suddenly bent forward in a spasm of laughter. 'He's burying himself in *Westminster Abbey*!'

'Everett!' said his mother. 'Silence!'

'*Ha-ha-ha!*' Everett's tension exploded in guffaws, and he staggered out of the room and collapsed on a bench in the hall, pressing his lips together in a hopeless effort to control himself. What made it funnier was that the others in the room, except for his mother, didn't understand the situation. They knew his father wrote books in his head, but they didn't appreciate the Poets' Corner bit at all!

After a few moments, Everett sobered himself and walked back into the room. His father was humming, as he had often done while he worked. Was he still working? Everett watched his mother lean low to listen. Was he mistaken, or was it a ghost of *Land of Hope and Glory* that Everett heard coming from the oxygen tent?

It was over. It seemed to Everett, as they filed out of the room, that they should go now to his parents' house for the funeral meats, but no – the funeral had not really taken place yet. His father's powers were truly extraordinary.

Some eight years later, Louise lay dying of pneumonia which had followed flu. Everett was with her in the bedroom of the Cheyne Walk house. His mother was talking about his father, about his never having received the fame and respect due him.

'—until the last,' said Louise. 'He is buried in Poets' Corner, Everett – mustn't forget that . . .'

'Yes,' said Everett, somehow impressed, almost believing it.

'Never room for the wives there, of course — otherwise I could join him,' she whispered.

And Everett forbore to tell her she *was* going to join him in the family plot outside Brighton. Or was that true? Could they not find another niche in Poets' Corner? *Brighton*, Everett said to himself as reality started to crumble. *Brighton*, Everett recovered himself. 'I'm not so sure,' he said. 'Maybe it can be arranged, Mummy. We'll see.'

She closed her eyes, and a soft smile settled on her lips, the same smile of contentment that Everett had seen on his father's face when he had lain under the oxygen tent.

THE BREEDER

To Elaine, marriage meant children. Marriage meant a lot of other things too, of course, such as creating a home, being a morale-booster to her husband, jolly companion, all that. But most of all children – that was what marriage was for, what it was all about.

Elaine, when she married Douglas, set about becoming the creature of her imagination, and within four months she had succeeded quite well. Their home sparkled with cleanliness and charm, their parties were successes, and Douglas received a small promotion in his firm, Athens Insurance Inc. Only one thing was missing, Elaine was not yet pregnant. A consultation with her doctor soon set this problem to rights, something having been askew, but after another three months, she still had not conceived. Could it be Douglas's fault? Reluctantly, somewhat shyly, Douglas visited the doctor and was pronounced fit. What could be wrong? Closer tests were made, and it was discovered that the fertilized egg (indeed at least one egg had been fertilized) had traveled upward instead of downward, in apparent defiance of gravity, and instead of developing somewhere had simply vanished.

'She should get out of bed and stand on her head!' said a wag of Douglas's office, after a couple of drinks one lunchtime.

Douglas chuckled politely. But maybe there was something to it. Hadn't the doctor said something along these lines? Douglas suggested the headstand to Elaine that evening.

Around midnight, Elaine jumped out of bed and stood on her head, feet against the wall. Her face became bright pink. Douglas was alarmed, but Elaine stuck it out like a Spartan, collapsing finally after nearly ten minutes in a rosy heap on the floor.

Their first child, Edward, was thus born. Edward started the ball rolling, and slightly less than a year later came twins, two girls. The parents of Elaine and Douglas were delighted. To become grandparents was as great a joy for them as it had been to become parents, and both sets of grandparents threw parties. Douglas and Elaine were only children, so the grandparents rejoiced that their lines would be continued. Elaine no longer had to stand on her head. And ten months later, a second son was born, Peter. Then came Philip, then Madeleine.

This made six small children in the household, and Elaine and Douglas had to move to a slightly larger apartment with one more room in it. They moved hastily, not realizing that their landlord was rather against children (they'd lied and told him they had four), especially little ones who howled in the night. Within six months, they were asked to leave – it being obvious then that Elaine was due to have another child soon. By now, Douglas was feeling the pinch, but his parents gave him $2,000 and Elaine's parents came up with $3,000, and Douglas made a down payment on a house fifteen minutes' drive from his office.

'I'm glad we've got a house, darling,' he said to Elaine. 'But I'm afraid we've got to watch our pennies if we keep up the mortgage payments. I think – at least for a while – we ought not to have any more children. Seven, after all——' Little Thomas had arrived.

Elaine had said before that it would be up to her, not him, to do the family planning. 'I understand, Douglas. You're perfectly right.'

Alas, Elaine disclosed one overcast winter day that she was pregnant again. 'I can't account for it. I'm on the pill, you know that.'

Douglas had certainly assumed that. He was speechless for a few moments. How were they going to manage? He could already see that Elaine was pregnant, though he'd been trying to convince himself for days that he was only imagining it, because of his anxiety. Already their parents were handing out fifty- and one-hundred-dollar presents on birthdays – with nine birthdays in the family, birthdays came along pretty frequently – and he knew they couldn't contribute a bit more. It was amazing how much shoes alone could cost for seven little ones.

Still, when Douglas saw the beatific, contented smile on Elaine's face as she lay against her pillows in the hospital, a baby boy in one arm and a baby girl in the other, Douglas could not find it in himself to regret these births, which made nine.

But they'd been married just a little more than seven years. If this kept up—

One woman in their social circle remarked at a party, 'Oh, Elaine gets pregnant every time Doug looks at her!'

Douglas was not amused by the implied tribute to his virility.

'Then they ought to make love with the lights out!' replied the office wag. 'Ha-ha-ha! Easy to see the only reason is, Douglas is *looking* at her!'

'Don't even glance at Elaine tonight, Doug!' someone else yelled, and there were gales of laughter.

Elaine smiled prettily. She imagined, nay, she was sure, that women envied her. Women with only one child, or no children, were just dried up beanbags in Elaine's opinion. Green beanbags.

Things went from bad to worse, from Douglas's point of view. There was an interval of a whole six months when Elaine was on the pill and did not become pregnant, but then suddenly she was.

'I can't understand it,' she said to Douglas and to her doctor too. Elaine really couldn't understand it, because she had forgotten that she had forgotten to remember the pill – a phenomenon that her doctor had encountered before.

The doctor made no comment. His lips were ethically sealed.

As if in revenge for Elaine's absenting herself from fecundity for a while, for her trying to put a lid on nature's cornucopia, nature hurled quintuplets at her. Douglas could not even face the hospital, and took to his bed for forty-eight hours. Then he had an idea: he would ring up some newspapers, ask them a fee for interviews and also for any photographs they might take of the quints. He made painful efforts in this direction, such exploitation being against his grain. But the newspapers didn't bite. Lots of people had quintuplets these days, they said. Sextuplets might interest them, but quints no. They'd take a photograph, but they wouldn't pay anything. The photograph only brought literature from family planning organizations and unpleasant or downright insulting letters from individual citizens telling Douglas and Elaine how much they were contributing to pollution. The newspapers had mentioned that their children now numbered fourteen after about eight years of marriage.

Since it seemed the pill was not working, Douglas proposed that he do something about himself. Elaine was dead against it.

'Why, things just wouldn't be the same!' she cried.

'Darling, everything would be the same. Only—'

Elaine interrupted. They got nowhere.

They had to move again. The house was big enough for two adults and fourteen children, but the added expense of the quints made the mortgage payments impossible. So Douglas and Elaine and Edward, Susan and Sarah, Peter, Thomas, Philip and Madeleine, the twins Ursula and Paul, and the quints Louise, Pamela, Helen, Samantha and Brigid moved to a tenement in the city – tenement being a legal term for any structure housing more than two families, but in common parlance a tenement was a slum, which this was. Now they were surrounded by families with nearly as many children as they had. Douglas, who sometimes took papers home from the office, stuffed his ears with cotton wool and thought he would go mad. 'No danger of going mad, if I *think* I'm going mad,' he told himself, and tried to cheer up. Elaine, after all, was on the pill again.

But she became pregnant again. By now, the grandparents were no longer so delighted. It was plain that the number of offspring had lowered Douglas's and Elaine's standard of living – the last thing the grandparents wished. Douglas lived in a smoldering resentment against fate, and with a desperate hope that something – something unknown and perhaps impossible might happen, as he watched Elaine growing stouter day by day. Might this be quints again? Even sextuplets? Dreadful thought. What was the matter with the pill? Was Elaine some exception to the laws of chemistry? Douglas turned over in his mind their doctor's ambiguous reply to his question on this point. The doctor had been so vague, Douglas had forgotten not only the doctor's words, but even the sense of what he'd said. Who could think in all the noise, anyway? Diaper-clad midgets played tiny xylophones and tootled on a variety of horns and whistles. Edward and Peter squabbled over who was going to mount the rocking horse. All the girls burst into tears over nothing, hoping to gain their mother's attention and allegiance to their causes. Philip was prone to colic. All the quints were teething simultaneously.

This time it was triplets. Unbelievable! Three rooms of their flat now had nothing but cribs in them, plus a single bed in each, in which at least two children slept. If their ages only varied more, Douglas thought, it would somehow be more tolerable, but most of them were still crawling around on the floor, and to open the apartment door was to believe that one had come upon a day nursery by mistake. But no. All these seventeen were his own doing. The new triplets swung in an ingenious suspended playpen, there being absolutely no room on the floor for them. They were fed, and their nappies changed, through bars of the pen, which made Douglas think of a zoo.

Weekends were hell. Their friends simply did not accept invitations any longer. Who could blame them? Elaine had to ask guests to be very quiet, and even so, something always woke one of the little ones by 9 p.m. and then the whole lot started yowling, even the seven- and eight-year-olds who wanted to join the party. So their social life became nil, which was just as well, because they hadn't the money for entertaining.

'But I do feel fulfilled, dear,' Elaine said, laying a soothing hand upon Douglas's brow, as he sat poring over office papers one Sunday afternoon.

Douglas, perspiring from nerves, was working in a tiny corner of what they called their living room. Elaine was half-dressed, her usual state, because in the act of dressing, some child always interrupted her, demanding something, and also Elaine was still nursing the last arrivals. Suddenly something snapped in Douglas, and he got up and walked out to the nearest telephone. He and Elaine had no telephone, and they had had to sell their car also.

Douglas rang a clinic and inquired about vasectomy. He was told there was a waiting list of four months, if he wanted the operation free of charge. Douglas said yes, and gave his name. Meanwhile, chastity was the order of the day. No hardship. Good God! Seventeen now! Douglas hung his head in the office. Even the jokes had worn thin. He felt that people pitied him, and that they avoided the subject of children. Only Elaine was happy. She seemed to be in another world. She'd even begun to talk like the kids. Douglas counted the days till the operation. He was not going to say anything to Elaine about it, just have it. He rang up a week before the date to confirm it, and was told he would have to wait another three months, because the person who had fixed his appointment must have made a mistake.

Douglas banged the telephone down. It wasn't abstinence that was the problem, just goddamned fate, just the nuisance of waiting another three months. He had an insane fear that Elaine would become pregnant again on her own.

It happened that the first thing he saw when he entered the apartment that afternoon was little Ursula waddling around in her rubber panties, diligently pushing a miniature pram in which sat a tiny replica of herself.

'*Look at it!*' Douglas yelled at no one. 'Motherhood already and she can hardly *walk*!' He snatched the doll out of the toy pram and hurled it through a window.

'Doug! What's come over you?' Elaine rushed towards him with one breast bared, baby Charles clamped to it like a lamprey.

Douglas pushed a foot through the side of a crib, then seized the rocking horse and smashed it against a wall. He kicked a doll's house into the air and when it fell, demolished it with a stomp.

'*Maa-aa* – maa-aa!'

'Daa-aaddy!'

'Ooooo-ooo!'

'*Boo-hooo-oo-oo-hoo-oo!*' from a half dozen throats.

Now the household was in an uproar with at least fifteen kids screaming, plus Elaine. Toys were Douglas's targets. Balls of all sizes went through the windowpanes, followed by plastic horns and little pianos, cars and telephones, then teddy bears, rattles, guns, rubber swords and peashooters, teething rings and jigsaw puzzles. He squeezed two formula bottles and laughed with lunatic glee as the milk spurted from the rubber teats. Elaine's expression changed from surprise to horror. She leaned out of a broken window and screamed.

Douglas had to be dragged away from an Erector set construction which he was smashing with the heavy base of a roly-poly clown. An intern gave him a punch in the neck which knocked him out. The next thing Douglas knew, he was in a padded cell somewhere. He demanded a vasectomy. They gave him a needle instead. When he woke up, he again yelled for a vasectomy. His wish was granted the same day.

He felt better then, calmer. He was just sane enough, however, to realize that his mind, so to speak, was 'gone.' He was aware that he didn't want to go back to work, didn't want to do anything. He didn't want to see any of his old friends, all of whom he felt he had lost, anyway. He didn't particularly want to go on living. Dimly, he remembered that he was a laughing stock for having begotten seventeen children in not nearly so many years. Or was it nineteen? Or twenty-eight? He'd lost count.

Elaine came to see him. Was she pregnant again? No. Impossible.

It was just that he was so used to seeing her pregnant. She seemed remote. She was fulfilled, Douglas remembered.

'Stand on your head again. Reverse things,' Douglas said with a foolish smile.

'He's mad,' Elaine said hopelessly to the intern, and calmly turned away.

OONA, THE JOLLY CAVE WOMAN

She was a bit hairy, one front tooth missing, but her sex appeal was apparent at a distance of two hundred yards or more, like an odor, which perhaps it was. She was round, round-bellied, round-shouldered, round-hipped, and always smiling, always jolly. That was why men liked her. She had always something cooking in a pot on a fire. She was simple-minded and never lost her temper. She had been clubbed over the head so many times, her brain was addled. It was not necessary to club Oona to have her, but that was the custom, and Oona barely troubled to dodge to protect herself.

Oona was constantly pregnant and had never experienced the onset of puberty, her father having had at her since she was five, and after him, her brothers. Her first child was born when she was seven. Even in late pregnancy she was interfered with, and men waited impatiently the half hour or so it took her to give birth before they fell on her again.

Oddly, she kept the birthrate of the tribe more or less steady, and if anything tended to decrease the population, since men neglected their own wives because of thinking of her, or occasionally were killed in fighting over her.

Oona was at last killed by a jealous woman whose husband had not touched her in many months. This man was the first to fall in love. His name was Vipo. His men-friends had laughed at him for not taking some other woman, or his own wife, in the times when Oona was not available. Vipo had lost an eye in fighting his rivals. He was only a middle-sized man. He had always brought Oona the choicest things he had killed. He worked long and hard to make an ornament out of flint, so he became the first artist of his tribe. All the others used flint only for arrowheads or knives. He had given the ornament to Oona to hang around her neck by a string of leather.

When Vipo's wife slew Oona out of jealousy, Vipo slew his wife in hatred and wrath. Then he sang a loud and tragic song. He continued to sing like a madman, as tears ran down his hairy cheeks. The tribe considered killing him, because he was mad and different from everyone else, and they were afraid. Vipo drew images of Oona in the wet sand by the sea, then pictures of her on the flat stones on the mountains near by, pictures that could be seen from a distance. He made a statue of Oona out of wood, then one of stone. Sometimes he slept with these. Out of the clumsy syllables of his language, he made a sentence which evoked Oona whenever he uttered it. He was not the only one who learned and uttered this sentence, or who had known Oona.

Vipo was slain by a jealous woman whose man had not touched her for months. Her man had purchased one of Vipo's statues of Oona for a great price – a vast piece of leather made of several bison hides. Vipo made a beautiful watertight house of it, and had enough left over for clothing for himself. He created more sentences about Oona. Some men had admired him, others had hated him, and all the women had hated him because he had looked at them as if he did not see them. Many men were sad when Vipo was dead.

But in general people were relieved when Vipo was gone. He had been a strange one, disturbing some people's sleep at night.

THE ARTIST

At the time Jane got married, one would have thought there was nothing unusual about her. She was plump, pretty and practical: she could give artificial respiration at the drop of a hat or pull someone out of a faint or a nosebleed. She was a dentist's assistant, and as cool as they come in the face of crisis or pain. But she had enthusiasm for the arts. What arts? All of them. She began, in the first year of her married life, with painting. This occupied all her Saturdays, or enough of Saturdays to prevent adequate shopping for the weekend, but her husband Bob did the shopping. He also paid for the framing of muddy, run-together oil portraits of their friends, and the sittings of the friends took up time on the weekends too. Jane at last faced the fact she could not stop her colors from running together, and decided to abandon painting for the dance.

The dance, in a black leotard, did not much improve her robust figure, only her appetite. Special shoes followed. She was studying ballet. She had discovered an institution called The School of Arts. In this five-story edifice they taught the piano, violin and other instruments, music composition, novel writing, poetry, sculpture, the dance and painting.

'You see, Bob, life can and should be made more beautiful,' Jane said with her big smile. 'And everyone wants to contribute, if he or she can, just a little bit to the beauty and poetry of the world.'

Meanwhile, Bob emptied the garbage and made sure they were not out of potatoes. Jane's ballet did not progress beyond a certain point, and she dropped it and took up singing.

'I really think life is beautiful enough as it is,' Bob said. 'Anyway I'm pretty happy.' That was during Jane's singing period, which had caused them to crowd the already small living room with an upright piano.

For some reason, Jane stopped her singing lessons and began to study sculpture and wood carving. This made the living room a mess of dropped bits of clay and wood chips which the vacuum could not always pick up. Jane was too tired for anything after her day's work in the dentist's office, and standing on her feet over wood or clay until midnight.

Bob came to hate The School of Arts. He had seen it a few times, when he had gone to fetch Jane at 11 p.m. or so. (The neighborhood was dangerous to walk in.) It seemed to Bob that the students were all a lot of misguided hopefuls, and the teachers a lot of mediocrities. It seemed a madhouse of misplaced effort. And how many homes, children and husbands were being troubled now, because the women of the households – the students were mainly women – were not at home performing a few essential tasks? It seemed to Bob that there was no inspiration in The School of Arts, only a desire to imitate people who had been inspired, like Chopin, Beethoven and Bach, whose works he could hear being mangled as he sat on a bench in the lobby, awaiting his wife. People called artists mad, but these students seemed incapable of the same kind of madness. The students did appear insane, in a certain sense of the word, but not in the right way, somehow. Considering the time The School of Arts deprived him of his wife, Bob was ready to blow the whole building to bits.

He had not long to wait, but he did not blow the building up himself. Someone – it was later proven to have been an instructor – put a bomb under The School of Arts, set to go off at 4 p.m.

It was New Year's Eve, and despite the fact it was a semi-holiday, the students of all the arts were practising diligently. The police and some newspapers had been forewarned of the bomb. The trouble was, nobody found it, and also most people did not believe that any bomb would go off. Because of the seediness of the neighborhood, the school had been subjected to scares and threats before. But the bomb went off, evidently from the depths of the basement, and a pretty good-sized one it was.

Bob happened to be there, because he was to have fetched Jane at 5 p.m. He had heard about the bomb rumor, but did not know whether to believe it or not. With some caution, however, or a premonition, he was waiting across the street instead of in the lobby.

One piano went through the roof, a bit separated from the student who was still seated on the stool, fingering nothing. A dancer at last made a few complete revolutions without her feet touching the ground, because she was a quarter of a mile high, and her toes were even pointing skyward. An art student was flung through a wall, his brush poised, ready to make the master stroke as he floated horizontally towards a true oblivion. One instructor, who had taken refuge as often as possible in the toilets of The School of Arts, was blown up in proximity to some of the plumbing.

Then came Jane, flying through the air with a mallet in one hand, a chisel in the other, and her expression was rapt. Was she stunned, still concentrating on her work, or even dead? Bob could not tell about Jane. The flying particles subsided with a gentle, diminishing clatter, and a rise of gray dust. There were a few seconds of silence, during which Bob stood still. Then he turned and walked homeward. Other schools of art, he knew, would arise. Oddly, this thought crossed his mind before he realized that his wife was gone forever.

THE FULLY LICENSED
WHORE, OR, THE WIFE

S arah had always played the field as an amateur, and at twenty she
got married, which made her licensed. To top it, the marriage
was in a church in full view of family, friends and neighbors, maybe
even God as witness, for certainly He was invited. She was all in
white, though hardly a virgin, being two months pregnant and not
by the man she was marrying, whose name was Sylvester. Now she
could become a professional, with protection of the law, approval
of society, blessing of the clergy, and financial support guaranteed
by her husband.

Sarah lost no time. It was first the gas meter reader, to limber
herself up, then the window cleaner, whose job took a varying
number of hours, depending on how dirty she told Sylvester the
windows had been. Sylvester sometimes had to pay for eight hours'
work plus a bit of overtime. Sometimes the window cleaner was
there when Sylvester left for work, and still there when he came
home in the evening. But these were small fry, and Sarah progressed
to their lawyer, which had the advantage of 'no fee' for any services
performed for the Sylvester Dillon family, now three.

Sylvester was proud of baby son Edmund, and flushed with

pleasure at what friends said about Edmund's resemblance to him-self. The friends were not lying, only saying what they thought they should say, and what they would have said to any father. After Edmund's birth, Sarah ceased sexual relations with Sylvester (not that they'd ever had much) saying, 'One's enough, don't you think?' She could also say, 'I'm tired,' or 'It's too hot.' In plain fact, poor Sylvester was good only for his money – he wasn't wealthy but quite comfortably off – and because he was reasonably intelligent and presentable, not aggressive enough to be a nuisance and – Well, that was about all it took to satisfy Sarah. She had a vague idea that she needed a protector and escort. It somehow carried more weight to write 'Mrs' at the foot of letters.

She enjoyed three or four years of twiddling about with the lawyer, then their doctor, then a couple of maverick husbands in their social circle, plus a few two-week sprees with the father of Edmund. These men visited the house mainly during the afternoons Monday to Friday. Sarah was most cautious and insisted – her house front being visible to several neighbors – that her lovers ring her when they were already in the vicinity, so she could tell them if the coast was clear enough for them to nip in. One-thirty p.m. was the safest time, when most people were eating lunch. After all, Sarah's bed and board was at stake, and Sylvester was becoming restless, though as yet not at all suspicious.

Sylvester in the fourth year of marriage made a slight fuss. His own advances to his secretary and also to the girl who worked behind the counter in his office supplies shop had been gently but firmly rejected, and his ego was at a low ebb.

'Can't we try again?' was Sylvester's theme.

Sarah counterattacked like a dozen battalions whose guns had been primed for years to fire. One would have thought she was the one to whom injustice had been done. 'Haven't I created a lovely home for you? Aren't I a good hostess – the *best* according to all our friends, isn't that true? Have I ever neglected Edmund? Have I ever failed to have a hot meal waiting for you when you come home?'

I wish you would forget the hot meal now and then and think of something else, Sylvester wanted to say, but was too well brought up to get the words out.

'Furthermore I have taste,' Sarah added as a final volley. 'Our furniture is not only good, it's well cared for. I don't know what more you can expect from me.'

The furniture was so well polished, the house looked like a museum. Sylvester was often shy about dirtying ashtrays. He would have liked more disorder and a little more warmth. How could he say this?

'Now come and eat something,' Sarah said more sweetly, extending a hand in a burst of contact unprecedented for Sylvester in the past many years. A thought had just crossed her mind, a plan.

Sylvester took her hand gladly, and smiled. He ate second helpings of everything that she pressed upon him. The dinner was as usual good, because Sarah was an excellent and meticulous cook. Sylvester was hoping for a happy end to the evening also, but in this he was disappointed.

Sarah's idea was to kill Sylvester with good food, with kindness in a sense, with wifely *duty*. She was going to cook more and more elaborately. Sylvester already had a paunch, the doctor had cautioned him about overeating, not enough exercise and all that rot, but Sarah knew enough about weight control to know that it was what you ate that counted, not how much exercise you took. And Sylvester loved to eat. The stage was set, she felt, and what had she to lose?

She began to use richer fats, goose fat, olive oil, and to make macaroni cheese, to butter sandwiches more thickly, to push milk-drinking as a splendid source of calcium for Sylvester's falling hair. He put on twenty pounds in three months. His tailor had to alter all his suits, then make new suits for him.

'Tennis, darling,' Sarah said with concern. 'What you need is a bit of exercise.' She was hoping he'd have a heart attack. He now weighed nearly 225 pounds, and he was not a tall man. He was already breathing hard at the slightest exertion.

Tennis didn't do it. Sylvester was wise enough, or heavy enough, just to stand there on the court and let the ball come to him, and if the ball didn't come to him, he wasn't going to run after it to hit it. So one warm Saturday, when Sarah had accompanied him to the courts as usual, she pretended to faint. She mumbled that she wanted to be taken to the car to go home. Sylvester struggled, panting, as Sarah was no lightweight herself. Unfortunately for Sarah's plans, two chaps came running from the club bar to give assistance, and Sarah was loaded easily into the Jag.

Once at home, with the front door closed, Sarah swooned again, and mumbled in a frantic but waning voice that she had to be taken upstairs to bed. It was their bed, a big double one, and two flights up. Sylvester heaved her into his arms, thinking that he did not present a romantic picture trudging up step by step, gasping and stumbling as he carried his beloved towards bed. At last he had to maneuver her on to one shoulder, and even then he fell on his own face upon reaching the landing on the second floor. Wheezing mightily, he rolled out from under her limp figure, and tried again, this time simply dragging her along the carpeted hall and into the bedroom. He was tempted to let her lie there until he got his own breath back (she wasn't stirring), but he could anticipate her recrimination if she woke up in the next seconds and found he had left her flat on the floor.

Sylvester bent to the task again, put all his will power into it, for certainly he had no physical strength left. His legs ached, his back was killing him, and it amazed him that he could get this burden (over 150 pounds) on to the double bed. 'Whoosh-sh!' Sylvester said, and went reeling back, intending to collapse in an armchair, but the armchair had rollers and retreated several inches, causing him to land on the floor with a house-shaking thump. A terrible pain had struck his chest. He pressed a fist against his breast and bared his teeth in agony.

Sarah watched. She lay on the bed. She did nothing. She waited and waited. She almost fell asleep. Sylvester was moaning, calling for help. How lucky, Sarah thought, that Edmund was parked out with a baby-sitter this afternoon, instead of a baby-sitter being in the house. After some fifteen minutes, Sylvester was still. Sarah did fall asleep finally. When she got up, she found that Sylvester was quite dead and becoming cool. Then she telephoned the family doctor.

All went well for Sarah. People said that just weeks before, they'd been amazed at how *well* Sylvester looked, rosy cheeks and all that. Sarah got a tidy sum from the insurance company, her widow's pension, and gushes of sympathy from people who assured her she had given Sylvester the best of herself, had made a lovely home for him, had given him a son, had in short devoted herself utterly to him and made his somewhat short life as happy as a man's life could possibly have been. No one said, 'What a perfect murder!' which was Sarah's private opinion, and now she could chuckle over it. Now she could become the Merry Widow. By exacting small favors from her lovers — casually of course — it was going to be easy to live in even better style than when Sylvester had been alive. And she could still write 'Mrs' at the foot of letters.

THE PERFECT LITTLE LADY

Theadora, or Thea as she was called, was the perfect little lady born. Everyone said that who had seen her from her first months of life, when she was being wheeled about in her white satin-lined pram. She slept when she should have slept. Then she woke and smiled at strangers. She almost never wet her diapers. She was the easiest child in the world to toilet train, and she learned to speak remarkably early. Next came reading when she was hardly two. And always she showed good manners. At three, she began to curtsy on being introduced to people. Her mother taught her this, of course, but Thea took to etiquette like a duck to water.

'Thank you, I had a lovely time,' she was saying glibly at four, dropping a farewell curtsy, on departing from children's parties. She would return home with her little starched dress as neat and clean as when she had put it on. She took great care of her hair and nails. She was never dirty, and she watched other children running and playing, making mud pies, falling and skinning their knees, and she thought them utterly silly. Thea was an only child. Other mothers, more harassed than Thea's mother, with two or three offspring to look after, praised Thea's obedience and neatness, and Thea loved this. Thea basked also in the praise she got from her own mother. Thea and her mother adored each other.

Among Thea's contemporaries, the gang age began at eight or nine or ten, if the word gang could be used for the informal group that roved the neighborhood on roller skates and bicycles. It was a proper middle-class neighborhood. But if a child didn't join in the 'crazy poker' game in the garage of one of their parents, or go on aimless follow-my-leader bicycle rides through the residential streets, that child was nowhere. Thea was nowhere, as far as this gang went. 'I couldn't care less, because I don't want to be one of *them*, anyway,' Thea said to her mother and father.

'Thea cheats at games. That's why we don't want her,' said a ten-year-old boy in one of Thea's father's history classes.

Thea's father Ted taught in a local grade school. He had long suspected the truth, but had kept his mouth shut and hoped for the best. Thea was a mystery to Ted. How could he, such an ordinary, plodding fellow, have begotten a full-blown woman?

'Little girls are born women,' said Thea's mother Margot. 'But little boys are not born men. They have to learn to be men. Little girls have already a woman's character.'

'But this isn't character,' Ted said. 'It's scheming. Character takes time to be formed. Like a tree.'

Margot smiled tolerantly, and Ted had the feeling he was talking like someone from the Stone Age, while his wife and daughter lived in the jet age.

Thea's main objective in life seemed to be to make her contemporaries feel awful. She'd told a lie about another little girl, in regard to a little boy, and the little girl had wept and nearly had a nervous breakdown. Ted couldn't remember the details, though he'd been able to follow the story when he had heard it first, summarized by Margot. Thea had managed to blame the other little girl for the whole thing. Machiavelli couldn't have done better.

'She's simply not a ruffian,' said Margot. 'Anyway, she's got Craig to play with, so she's not alone.'

Craig was ten and lived three houses away. What Ted did not realize for a while was that Craig was ostracized too, and for the same reason. One afternoon, Ted observed one of the boys of the neighborhood make a rude gesture, in ominous silence, as he passed Craig on the pavement.

'Scum!' Craig replied promptly. Then he trotted, in case the other boy gave chase, but the other boy simply turned and said:

'And you're a *shit*, like Thea!'

It was not the first time that Ted had heard such language from the local kids, but he certainly didn't hear it often, and he was impressed. 'But what do they do – all alone, Thea and Craig?' Ted asked his wife.

'Oh, they take walks. I dunno,' said Margot. 'I suppose Craig has a slight crush on her.'

Ted had thought of that. Thea had a candy-box prettiness that would assure her of boyfriends by the time she reached her early teens, and of course Thea was starting earlier than that. Ted had no fear of misbehavior on Thea's part, because she was the teasing type, and basically prim.

What Thea and Craig were then engaged in was observing the construction of a dugout, tunnel and two fireplaces in a vacant lot about a mile away. Thea and Craig would go there on their bicycles, conceal themselves in the bushes nearby, and spy and giggle. A dozen or so of the gang were working like navvies, hauling out buckets of earth, gathering firewood, preparing roasted potatoes with salt and butter, which was the high point of all this slavery, around 6 p.m. Thea and Craig intended to wait until the excavation and embellishments were completed, and then they meant to smash the whole thing.

Meanwhile, Thea and Craig came up with what they called 'a new ballgame,' this being their code word for a nasty scheme. They sent a typewritten announcement to the biggest blabble-mouth of the school, Veronica, saying that a girl called Jennifer was having a surprise birthday party on a certain date, and please tell everyone, but don't tell Jennifer. The letter was presumably from Jennifer's mother. Then Thea and Craig hid in the hedges and watched their schoolmates turn up at Jennifer's, some dressed in their best, nearly all bearing gifts, as Jennifer grew more and more embarrassed on the doorstep, saying she didn't know anything about a party. Since Jennifer's family was well-to-do, all the kids had expected a big evening.

When the tunnel and dugout, fireplaces and candle niches were all completed, Thea and Craig in their respective homes pretended bellyaches one day, and did not go to school. By prearrangement, they sneaked out and met at 11 a.m. with their bicycles. They went to the dugout and jumped in unison on the tunnel top until it caved in. Then they broke the chimney tops, and scattered the carefully gathered firewood. They even found the potatoes and salt reserve, and flung that into the woods. Then they cycled home.

Two days later, on Thursday which was a school day, Craig was found at 5 p.m. behind some elm trees on the lawn of the Knobel house, stabbed to death through the throat and heart. He had ugly wounds also about the head, as if he had been hit repeatedly by rough stones. Measurements of the knife wounds showed that at least seven different knives had been used.

Ted was profoundly shocked. By then he had heard of the destroyed tunnel and fireplaces. Everyone knew that Thea and Craig had been absent from school on the Tuesday that the tunnel had been ruined. Everyone knew that Thea and Craig were constantly together. Ted feared for his daughter's life. The police could not lay the blame for Craig's death on any member of the gang, neither could they charge an entire group with murder or manslaughter. The inquiry was concluded with a warning to all parents of the children in the school.

'Just because Craig and I were absent from school on the same day doesn't mean that we went together to break up a stupid old tunnel,' said Thea to a friend of her mother's, a mother of one of the gang members. Thea could lie like an accomplished crook. It was difficult for an adult to challenge her.

So Thea's gang age, such as it was, ended with Craig's death.

Then came boyfriends and teasing, opportunities for intrigues and betrayals, and a constant stream, ever changing, of young men aged sixteen to twenty, some of whom lasted only five days with Thea.

We take leave of Thea as she sits primping, aged fifteen, in front of her looking-glass. She is especially happy this evening, because her nearest rival, a girl named Elizabeth, has just been in a car accident and had her nose and jaw broken, plus an eye damaged, so she will never look quite the same again. The summer is coming up, with all those dinner dances on terraces and swimming pool parties. There is even a rumor that Elizabeth may have to acquire a lower denture, so many of her teeth got broken, but the eye damage must be the most telling. Thea, however, will escape every catastrophe. There is a divinity that protects perfect little ladies like Thea.

THE DAY OF RECKONING

John took a taxi from the station, as his uncle had told him to do in case they weren't there to meet him. It was less than two miles to Hanshaw Chickens, Inc., as his Uncle Ernie Hanshaw now called his farm. John knew the white two-story house well, but the long gray barn was new to him. It was huge, covering the whole area where the cow barn and the pigpens had been.

'Plenty of wishbones in that place!' the taxi driver said cheerfully as John paid him.

John smiled. 'Yes, and I was just thinking – not a chicken in sight!'

John carried his suitcase towards the house. 'Anybody home?' he called, thinking Helen would probably be in the kitchen now, getting lunch.

Then he saw the flattened cat. No, it was a kitten. Was it real or made of paper? John set his suitcase down and bent closer. It was real. It lay on its side, flat and level with the damp reddish earth, in the wide track of a tire. Its skull had been crushed and there was blood there, but not on the rest of the body which had been enlarged by pressure, so that the tail looked absurdly short. The kitten was white with patches of orange, brindle and black.

John heard a hum of machinery from the barn. He put his suitcase on the front porch, and hearing nothing from the house, set off at a trot for the new barn. He found the big front doors locked, and went round to the back, again at a trot, because the barn seemed to be a quarter of a mile long. Besides the machine hum, John heard a high-pitched sound, a din of cries and peeps from inside.

'Ernie?' John yelled. Then he saw Helen. '*Hello*, Helen!'

'John! Welcome! You took a taxi? We didn't hear any car!' She gave him a kiss on the cheek. 'You've grown another three inches!'

His uncle climbed down from a ladder and shook John's hand. 'How're you, boy?'

'Okay, Ernie. What's going on here?' John looked up at moving belts which disappeared somewhere inside the barn. A rectangular metal container, nearly as big as a boxcar, rested on the ground.

Ernie pulled John closer and shouted that the grain, a special mixture, had just been delivered and was being stored in the factory, as he called the barn. This afternoon a man would come to collect the container.

'Lights shouldn't go on now, according to schedule, but we'll make an exception so you can see. Look!' Ernie pulled a switch inside the barn door, and the semi-darkness changed to glaring light, bright as full sun.

The cackles and screams of the chickens augmented like a siren, like a thousand sirens, and John instinctively covered his ears. Ernie's lips moved, but John could not hear him. John swung around to see Helen. She was standing farther back, and waved a hand, shook her head and smiled, as if to say she couldn't bear the racket. Ernie drew John farther into the barn, but he had given up talking and merely pointed.

The chickens were smallish and mostly white, and they all shuffled constantly. John saw that this was because the platforms on which they stood slanted forward, inclining them towards the slowly moving feed troughs. But not all of them were eating. Some were trying to peck the chickens next to them. Each chicken had its own little wire coop. There must have been forty rows of chickens on the ground floor, and eight or ten tiers of chickens went up to the ceiling. Between the double rows of back-to-back chickens were aisles wide enough for a man to pass and sweep the floor, John supposed, and just as he thought this, Ernie turned a wheel, and water began to shoot over the floor. The floor slanted towards various drain holes.

'*All automatic! Somethin', eh?*'

John recognized the words from Ernie's lips, and nodded appreciatively. 'Terrific!' But he was ready to get away from the noise.

Ernie shut off the water.

John noticed that the chickens had worn their beaks down to blunt stubs, and their white breasts dripped blood where the horizontal bar supported their weight. What else could they do but eat? John had read a little about battery chicken farming. These hens of Ernie's, like the hens he had read about, couldn't turn around in their coops. Much of the general flurry in the barn was caused by chickens trying to fly upward. Ernie cut the lights. The doors closed after them, apparently also automatically.

'Machine farming has really got me over the hump,' Ernie said, still talking loudly. 'I'm making good money now. And just imagine, one man – me – can run the whole show!'

John grinned. 'You mean you won't have anything for me to do?'

'Oh, there's plenty to do. You'll see. How about some lunch first? Tell Helen I'll be in in about fifteen minutes.'

John walked towards Helen. 'Fabulous.'

'Yes. Ernie's in love with it.'

They went on towards the house, Helen looking down at her feet, because the ground was muddy in spots. She wore old tennis shoes, black corduroy pants, and a rust-colored sweater. John purposely walked between her and where the kitten lay, not wanting to mention it now.

He carried his suitcase up to the square, sunny corner room which he had slept in since he was a boy of ten, when Helen and Ernie had bought the farm. He changed into blue jeans, and went down to join Helen in the kitchen.

'Would you like an old-fashioned? We've got to celebrate your arrival,' Helen said. She was making two drinks at the wooden table.

'Fine. – Where's Susan?' Susan was their eight-year-old daughter.

'She's at a – Well, sort of summer school. They'll bring her back around four-thirty. Helps fill in the summer holidays. They make awful clay ashtrays and fringed money-purses – you know. Then you've got to praise them.'

John laughed. He gazed at his aunt-by-marriage, thinking she was still very attractive at – what was it? Thirty-one, he thought. She was about five feet four, slender, with reddish blonde curly hair and eyes that sometimes looked green, sometimes blue. And she had a very pleasant voice. 'Oh, thank you.' John accepted his drink. There were pineapple chunks in it, topped with a cherry.

'Awfully good to see you, John. How's college? And how're your folks?'

Both those items were all right. John would graduate from Ohio State next year when he would be twenty, then he was going to take a post-graduate course in government. He was an only child, and his parents lived in Dayton, a hundred and twenty miles away.

Then John mentioned the kitten. 'I hope it's not yours,' he said, and realized at once that it must be, because Helen put her glass down and stood up. Who else could the kitten have belonged to, John thought, since there was no other house around?

'Oh, Lord! Susan's going to be—' Helen rushed out of the back door.

John ran after her, straight for the kitten which Helen had seen from a distance.

'It was that big truck this morning,' Helen said. 'The driver sits so high up he can't see what's—'

'I'll help you,' John said, looking around for a spade or a trowel. He found a shovel and returned, and prised the flattened body up gently, as if it were still alive. He held it in both his hands. 'We ought to bury it.'

'Of course. Susan mustn't see it, but I've got to tell her. – There's a fork in back of the house.'

John dug where Helen suggested, a spot near an apple tree behind the house. He covered the grave over, and put some tufts of grass back so it would not catch the eye.

'The times I've brought that kitten in the house when the damned trucks came!' Helen said. 'She was barely four months, wasn't afraid of anything, just went trotting up to cars as if they were something to play with, you know?' She gave a nervous laugh. 'And this morning the truck came at eleven, and I was watching a pie in the oven, just about to take it out.'

John didn't know what to say. 'Maybe you should get another kitten for Susan as soon as you can.'

'What're you two doing?' Ernie walked towards them from the back door of the house.

'We just buried Beansy,' Helen said. 'The truck got her this morning.'

'Oh.' Ernie's smile disappeared. 'That's too bad. That's really too bad, Helen.'

But at lunch Ernie was cheerful enough, talking of vitamins and antibiotics in his chicken feed, and his produce of one and a quarter eggs per day per hen. Though it was July, Ernie was lengthening the chicken's 'day' by artificial light.

'All birds are geared to spring,' Ernie said. 'They lay more when they think spring is coming. The ones I've got are at peak. In October they'll be under a year old, and I'll sell them and take on a new batch.'

John listened attentively. He was to be here a month. He wanted to be helpful. 'They really do eat, don't they? A lot of them have worn off their beaks, I noticed.'

Ernie laughed. 'They're de-beaked. They'd peck each other through the wire, if they weren't. Two of 'em got loose in my first batch and nearly killed each other. Well, one did kill the other. Believe me, I de-beak 'em now, according to instructions.'

'And one chicken went on eating the other,' Helen said. 'Cannibalism.' She laughed uneasily. 'Ever hear of cannibalism among chickens, John?'

'No.'

'Our chickens are insane,' Helen said.

Insane. John smiled a little. Maybe Helen was right. Their noises had sounded pretty crazy.

'Helen doesn't much like battery farming,' Ernie said apologetically to John. 'She's always thinking about the old days. But we weren't doing so well then.'

That afternoon, John helped his uncle draw the conveyor belts back into the barn. He began learning the levers and switches that worked things. Belts removed eggs and deposited them gently into plastic containers. It was nearly 5 p.m. before John could get away. He wanted to say hello to his cousin Susan, a lively little girl with hair like her mother's.

As John crossed the front porch, he heard a child's weeping, and he remembered the kitten. He decided to go ahead anyway and speak to Susan.

Susan and her mother were in the living room – a front room with flowered print curtains and cherrywood furniture. Some additions, such as a bigger television set, had been made since John had seen the room last. Helen was on her knees beside the sofa on which Susan lay, her face buried in one arm.

'Hello, Susan,' John said. 'I'm sorry about your kitten.'

Susan lifted a round, wet face. A bubble started at her lips and broke. 'Beansy—'

John embraced her impulsively. 'We'll find another kitten. I promise. Maybe tomorrow. Yes?' He looked at Helen.

Helen nodded and smiled a little. 'Yes, we will.'

The next afternoon, as soon as the lunch dishes had been washed, John and Helen set out in the station wagon for a farm eight miles away belonging to some people called Ferguson. The Fergusons had two female cats that frequently had kittens, Helen said. And they were in luck this time. One of the cats had a litter of five – one black, one white, three mixed – and the other cat was pregnant.

'White?' John suggested. The Fergusons had given them a choice.

'Mixed,' Helen said. 'White is all good and black is – maybe unlucky.'

They chose a black and white female with white feet.

'I can see this one being called Bootsy,' Helen said, laughing.

The Fergusons were simple people, getting on in years, and very hospitable. Mrs Ferguson insisted they partake of a freshly baked coconut cake along with some rather powerful homemade wine. The kitten romped around the kitchen, playing with gray rolls of dust that she dragged out from under a big cupboard.

'That ain't no battery kitten!' Frank Ferguson remarked, and drank deep.

'Can we see your chickens, Frank?' Helen asked. She slapped John's knee suddenly. 'Frank has the most *wonderful* chickens, almost a hundred!'

'What's wonderful about 'em?' Frank said, getting up on a stiff leg. He opened the back screen door. 'You know where they are, Helen.'

John's head was buzzing pleasantly from the wine as he walked with Helen out to the chicken yard. Here were Rhode Island Reds, big white Leghorns, roosters strutting and tossing their combs, half-grown speckled chickens, and lots of little chicks about six inches high. The ground was covered with claw-scored watermelon rinds, tin bowls of grain and mush, and there was much chicken dung. A wheelless wreck of a car seemed to be a favorite laying spot: three hens sat on the back of the front seat with their eyes half closed, ready to drop eggs which would surely break on the floor behind them.

'It's such a wonderful *mess!*' John shouted, laughing.

Helen hung by her fingers in the wire fence, rapt. 'Like the chickens I knew when I was a kid. Well, Ernie and I had them too, till about—' She smiled at John. 'You know – a year ago. Let's go in!'

John found the gate, a limp thing made of wire that fastened with a wooden bar. They went in and closed it behind them.

Several hens drew back and regarded them with curiosity, making throaty, skeptical noises.

'They're such stupid darlings!' Helen watched a hen fly up and perch herself in a peach tree. 'They can see the sun! They can fly!'

'And scratch for worms – and eat watermelon!' John said.

'When I was little, I used to dig worms for them at my grand-mother's farm. With a hoe. And sometimes I'd step on their droppings, you know – well, on purpose – and it'd go between my toes. I loved it. Grandma always made me wash my feet under the garden hydrant before I came in the house.' She laughed. A chicken evaded her outstretched hand with an '*Urrr-rrk!*' 'Grandma's chick-ens were so tame, I could touch them. All bony and warm with the sun, their feathers. Sometimes I want to open all the coops in the barn and open the doors and let ours loose, just to see them walking on the grass for a few minutes.'

'Say, Helen, want to buy one of these chickens to take home? Just for fun? A couple of 'em?'

'No.'

'How much did the kitten cost? Anything?'

'No, nothing.'

Susan took the kitten into her arms, and John could see that the tragedy of Beansy would soon be forgotten. To John's disappoint-ment, Helen lost her gaiety during dinner. Maybe it was because Ernie was droning on about his profit and loss – not loss really, but outlay. Ernie was obsessed, John realized. That was why Helen was bored. Ernie worked hard now, regardless of what he said about machinery doing everything. There were creases on either side of his mouth, and they were not from laughing. He was starting to get a paunch. Helen had told John that last year Ernie had dismissed their handyman, Sam, who'd been with them seven years.

'Say,' Ernie said, demanding John's attention. 'What d'you think of the idea? Start a battery chicken farm when you finish school, and hire one man to run it. You could take another job in Chicago or Washington or wherever, and you'd have a steady *separate* income for life.'

John was silent. He couldn't imagine owning a battery chicken farm.

'Any bank would finance you – with a word from Clive, of course.'

Clive was John's father.

Helen was looking down at her plate, perhaps thinking of something else.

'Not really my lifestyle, I think,' John answered finally. 'I know it's profitable.'

After dinner, Ernie went into the living room to do his reckoning, as he called it. He did some reckoning almost every night. John helped Helen with the dishes. She put a Mozart symphony on the record player. The music was nice, but John would have liked to talk with Helen. On the other hand, what would he have said, exactly? *I understand why you're bored. I think you'd prefer pouring slop for pigs and tossing grain to real chickens, the way you used to do.* John had a desire to put his arms around Helen as she bent over the sink, to turn her face to his and kiss her. What would Helen think if he did?

That night, lying in bed, John dutifully read the brochures on battery chicken farming which Ernie had given him.

. . . The chickens are bred small so that they do not eat so much, and they rarely reach more than 3½ pounds . . . Young chickens are subjected to a light routine which tricks them into thinking that a day is 6 hours long. The objective of the factory farmer is to increase the original 6-hour day by leaving the lights on for a longer period each week. Artificial Spring Period is maintained for the hen's whole lifetime of 10 months . . . There is no real falling off of egg-laying in the natural sense, though the hen won't lay quite so many eggs towards the end . . . [Why, John wondered.

And wasn't 'not quite so many' the same as 'falling off'?] At 10 months the hen is sold for about 30¢ a pound, depending on the market . . .

And below:

Richard K. Schultz of Poon's Cross, Pa., writes: 'I am more than pleased and so is my wife with the modernization of my farm into a battery chicken farm operated with Muskeego-Ryan Electric equipment. Profits have quadrupled in a year and a half and we have even bigger hopes for the future . . . '

Writes Henry Vliess of Farnham, Kentucky: 'My old farm was barely breaking even. I had chickens, pigs, cows, the usual. My friends used to laugh at my hard work combined with all my tough luck. Then I . . . '

John had a dream. He was flying like Superman in Ernie's chicken barn, and the lights were all blazing brightly. Many of the imprisoned chickens looked up at him, their eyes flashed silver, and they were struck blind. The noise they made was fantastic. They wanted to escape, but could no longer see, and the whole barn heaved with their efforts to fly upward. John flew about frantically, trying to find the lever to open the coops, the doors, anything, but he couldn't. Then he woke up, startled to find himself in bed, propped on one elbow. His forehead and chest were damp with sweat. Moonlight came strong through the window. In the night's silence, he could hear the steady high-pitched din of the hundreds of chickens in the barn, though Ernie had said the barn was absolutely soundproofed. Maybe it was 'daytime' for the chickens now. Ernie said they had three more months to live.

John became more adept with the barn's machinery and the fast artificial clocks, but since his dream he no longer looked at the chickens as he had the first day. He did not look at them at all if he could help it. Once Ernie pointed out a dead one, and John removed it. Its breast, bloody from the coop's barrier, was so distended, it might have eaten itself to death.

Susan had named her kitten 'Bibsy,' because it had a white oval on its chest like a bib.

'Beansy and now Bibsy,' Helen said to John. 'You'd think all Susan thinks about is food!'

Helen and John drove to town one Saturday morning. It was alternately sunny and showery, and they walked close together under an umbrella when the showers came. They bought meat, potatoes, washing powder, white paint for a kitchen shelf, and Helen bought a pink-and-white striped blouse for herself. At a pet shop, John acquired a basket with a pillow to give Susan for Bibsy.

When they got home, there was a long dark gray car in front of the house.

'Why, that's the doctor's car!' Helen said.

'Does he come by just to visit?' John asked, and at once felt stupid, because something might have happened to Ernie. A grain delivery had been due that morning, and Ernie was always climbing about to see that everything was going all right.

There was another car, dark green, which Helen didn't recognize beside the chicken factory. Helen and John went into the house.

It was Susan. She lay on the living-room floor under a plaid blanket, only one sandaled foot and yellow sock visible under the fringed edge. Dr Geller was there, and a man Helen didn't know. Ernie stood rigid and panicked beside his daughter.

Dr Geller came towards Helen and said, 'I'm sorry, Helen. Susan was dead by the time the ambulance got here. I sent for the coroner.'

'What *happened*?' Helen started to touch Susan, and instinctively John caught her.

'Honey, I didn't see her in time,' Ernie said. 'She was chasing under that damned container after the kitten just as it was lowering.'

'Yeah, it bumped her on the head,' said a husky man in tan work-clothes, one of the delivery men. 'She was running out from under it, Ernie said. My *gosh*, I'm sorry, Mrs Hanshaw!'

Helen gasped, then she covered her face.

'You'll need a sedative, Helen,' Dr Geller said.

The doctor gave Helen a needle in her arm. Helen said nothing. Her mouth was slightly open, and her eyes stared straight ahead. Another car came and took the body away on a stretcher. The coroner took his leave then too.

With a shaky hand, Ernie poured whiskeys.

Bibsy leapt about the room, and sniffed at the red splotch on the carpet. John went to the kitchen to get a sponge. It was best to try to get it up, John thought, while the others were in the kitchen. He went back to the kitchen for a saucepan of water, and scrubbed again at the abundant red. His head was ringing, and he had difficulty keeping his balance. In the kitchen, he drank off his whiskey at a gulp and it at once burnt his ears.

'Ernie, I think I'd better take off,' the delivery man said solemnly. 'You know where to find me.'

Helen went up to the bedroom she shared with Ernie, and did not come down when it was time for dinner. From his room, John heard floorboards creaking faintly, and knew that Helen was walking about in the room. He wanted to go in and speak to her, but he was afraid he would not be capable of saying the right thing. Ernie should be with her, John thought.

John and Ernie gloomily scrambled some eggs, and John went to ask Helen if she would come down or would prefer him to bring her something. He knocked on the door.

'Come in,' Helen said.

He loved her voice, and was somehow surprised to find that it wasn't any different since her child had died. She was lying on the double bed, still in the same clothes, smoking a cigarette.

'I don't care to eat, thanks, but I'd like a whiskey.'

John rushed down, eager to get something that she wanted. He brought ice, a glass, and the bottle on a tray. 'Do you just want to go to sleep?' John asked.

'Yes.'

She had not turned on a light. John kissed her cheek, and for an instant she slipped her arm around his neck and kissed his cheek also. Then he left the room.

Downstairs the eggs tasted dry, and John could hardly swallow even with sips of milk.

'My God, what a day,' Ernie said. 'My God.' He was evidently trying to say more, looked at John with an effort at politeness, or closeness.

And John, like Helen, found himself looking down at his plate, wordless. Finally, miserable in the silence, John got up with his plate and patted Ernie awkwardly on the shoulder. 'I am sorry, Ernie.'

They opened another bottle of whiskey, one of the two bottles left in the living-room cabinet.

'If I'd known this would happen, I'd never have started this damned chicken farm. You know that. I meant to earn something for my family – not go limping along year after year.'

John saw that the kitten had found the new basket and gone to sleep in it on the living-room floor. 'Ernie, you probably want to talk to Helen. I'll be up at the usual time to give you a hand.' That meant 7 a.m.

'Okay. I'm in a daze tonight. Forgive me, John.'

John lay for nearly an hour in his bed without sleeping. He heard Ernie go quietly into the bedroom across the hall, but he heard no voices or even a murmur after that. Ernie was not much like Clive, John thought. John's father might have given way to tears for a minute, might have cursed. Then with his father it would have been all over, except for comforting his wife.

A raucous noise, rising and falling, woke John up. The chickens, of course. What the hell was it now? They were louder than he'd ever heard them. He looked out of the front window. In the pre-dawn light, he could see that the barn's front doors were open. Then the lights in the barn came on, blazing out on to the grass. John pulled on his tennis shoes without tying them, and rushed into the hall.

'Ernie! – Helen!' he yelled at their closed door.

John ran out of the house. A white tide of chickens was now oozing through the wide front doors of the barn. What on earth had happened? 'Get *back*!' he yelled at the chickens, flailing his arms.

The little hens might have been blind or might not have heard him at all through their own squawks. They kept on flowing from the barn, some fluttering over the others, and sinking again in the white sea.

John cupped his hands to his mouth. 'Ernie! The *doors*!' He was shouting into the barn, because Ernie must be there.

John plunged into the hens and made another effort to shoo them back. It was hopeless. Unused to walking, the chickens teetered like drunks, lurched against each other, stumbled forward, fell back on their tails, but they kept pouring out, many borne on the backs of those who walked. They were pecking at John's ankles. John kicked some aside and moved towards the barn doors again, but the pain of the blunt beaks on his ankles and lower legs made him stop. Some chickens tried to fly up to attack him, but had no strength in their wings. They are insane, John remembered. Suddenly frightened, John ran towards the clearer area at the side of the barn, then on towards the back door. He knew how to open the back door. It had a combination lock.

Helen was standing at the corner of the barn in her bathrobe, where John had first seen her when he arrived. The back door was closed.

'What's *happening*?' John shouted.

'I opened the coops,' Helen said.

'Opened them – why? – Where's Ernie?'

'He's in there.' Helen was oddly calm, as if she were standing and talking in her sleep.

'Well, what's he *doing*? Why doesn't he close the place?' John was shaking Helen by the shoulders, trying to wake her up. He released her and ran to the back door.

'I've locked it again,' Helen said.

John worked the combination as fast as he could, but he could hardly see it.

'Don't open it! Do you want them coming this way?' Helen was suddenly alert, dragging John's hands from the lock.

Then John understood. Ernie was being killed in there, being pecked to death. Helen wanted it. Even if Ernie was screaming, they couldn't have heard him.

A smile came over Helen's face. 'Yes, he's in there. I think they will finish him.'

John, not quite hearing over the noise of chickens, had read her lips. His heart was beating fast.

Then Helen slumped, and John caught her. John knew it was too late to save Ernie. He also thought that Ernie was no longer screaming.

Helen straightened up. 'Come with me. Let's watch them,' she said, and drew John feebly, yet with determination, along the side of the barn towards the front doors.

Their slow walk seemed four times as long as it should have been. He gripped Helen's arm. 'Ernie in there?' John asked, feeling as if he were dreaming, or perhaps about to faint.

'In there.' Helen smiled at him again, with her eyes half closed. 'I came down and opened the back door, you see – and I went up and woke Ernie. I said, "Ernie, something's wrong in the factory, you'd better come down."' He came down and went in the back door – and I opened the coops with the lever. And then – I pulled the lever that opens the front door. He was – in the middle of the barn then, because I started a fire on the floor.'

'A fire?' Then John noticed a pale curl of smoke rising over the front door.

'Not much to burn in there – just the grain,' Helen said. 'And there's enough for them to eat outdoors, don't you think?' She gave a laugh.

John pulled her faster towards the front of the barn.. There seemed to be not much smoke. Now the whole lawn was covered with chickens, and they were spreading through the white rail fence on to the road, pecking, cackling, screaming, a slow army without direction. It looked as if snow had fallen on the land.

'Head for the house!' John said, kicking at some chickens that were attacking Helen's ankles.

They went up to John's room. Helen knelt at the front window, watching. The sun was rising on their left, and now it touched the reddish roof of the metal barn. Gray smoke was curling upward from the horizontal lintel of the front doors. Chickens paused, stood stupidly in the doorway until they were bumped by others from behind. The chickens seemed not so much dazzled by the rising sun – the light was brighter in the barn – as by the openness around them and above them. John had never before seen chickens stretch their necks just to look up at the sky. He knelt beside Helen, his arm around her waist.

'They're all going to – go away,' John said. He felt curiously paralyzed.

'Let them.'

The fire would not spread to the house. There was no wind, and the barn was a good thirty yards away. John felt quite mad, like Helen, or the chickens, and was astonished by the reasonableness of his thought about the fire's not spreading.

'It's all over,' Helen said, as the last, not quite the last chickens wobbled out of the barn. She drew John closer by the front of his pajama jacket.

John kissed her gently, then more firmly on the lips. It was strange, stronger than any kiss he had ever known with a girl, yet curiously without further desire. The kiss seemed only an affirmation that they were both alive. They knelt facing each other, tightly embracing. The cries of the hens ceased to sound ugly, and sounded only excited and puzzled. It was like an orchestra playing, some members stopping, others resuming instruments, making a continuous chord without a tempo. John did not know how long they knelt like that, but at last his knees hurt, and he stood up, pulling Helen up, too. He looked out of the window and said:

'They must be all out. And the fire isn't any bigger. Shouldn't we—' But the obligation to look for Ernie seemed far away, not at all pressing on him. It was as if he dreamed this night or this dawn, and Helen's kiss, the way he had dreamed about flying like Superman in the barn. Were they really Helen's hands in his now?

She slumped again, and plainly she wanted to sit on the carpet, so he left her and pulled on his blue jeans over his pajama pants. He went down and entered the barn cautiously by the front door. The smoke made the interior hazy, but when he bent low, he could see fifty or more chickens pecking at what he knew must be Ernie on the floor. Bodies of chickens overcome by smoke lay on the floor, like little white puffs of smoke themselves, and some live chickens were pecking at these, going for the eyes. John moved towards Ernie. He thought he had braced himself, but he hadn't braced himself enough for what he saw: a fallen column of blood and bone to which a few tatters of pajama cloth still clung. John ran out again, very fast, because he had breathed once, and the smoke had nearly got him.

In his room, Helen was humming and drumming on the window-sill, gazing out at the chickens left on the lawn. The hens were trying to scratch in the grass, and were staggering, falling on their sides, but mostly falling backwards, because they were used to shuffling to prevent themselves from falling forward.

'Look!' Helen said, laughing so, there were tears in her eyes. 'They don't know what grass is! But they like it!'

John cleared his throat and said, 'What're you going to say? – What'll we say?'

'Oh – say.' Helen seemed not at all disturbed by the question. 'Well – that Ernie heard something and went down and – he wasn't completely sober, you know. And – maybe he pulled a couple of wrong levers. – Don't you think so?'

NOTES FROM A
RESPECTABLE COCKROACH

I have moved. I used to live at the Hotel Duke on a corner of Washington Square. My family has lived there for generations, and I mean at least two or three hundred generations. But no more for me. The place has degenerated. I've heard my great-great-great – go back as far as you like, she was still alive when I spoke to her – talk about the good old days when people arrived in horse-drawn carriages with suitcases that smelled of leather, people who had breakfast in bed and dropped a few crumbs for us on the carpet. Not purposely, of course, because we knew our place then, too, and our place was in the bathroom corners or down in the kitchen. Now we can walk all over the carpets with comparative impunity, because the clients of the Hotel Duke are too stoned blind to see us, or they haven't the energy to step on us if they did see us – or they just laugh.

The Hotel Duke has now a tattered green awning extending to the curb, so full of holes it wouldn't protect anyone from the rain. You go up four cement steps into a dingy lobby that smells of pot smoke, stale whiskey, and is insufficiently lighted. After all, the clientele now doesn't necessarily want to see who else is staying here. People reel into each other in the lobby, and might thereby strike up an acquaintance, but more often it's an unpleasant exchange of words that results. To the left in the lobby is an even darker hole called Dr Toomuch's Dance Floor. They charge two dollars admission, payable at the inside-the-lobby door. Jukebox music. Puke box customers. Egad!

The hotel has six floors, and I usually take the elevator, or the lift as people say lately, imitating the English. Why climb those grimy cement air shafts, or creep up staircase after staircase, when I can leap the mere half-inch gap between floor and lift and whisk myself safely into the corner beside the operator at the controls? I can tell each floor by its smell. Fifth floor, that's a disinfectant smell since more than a year, because a shoot-up occurred and there was lots of blood-and-guts spilt smack in front of the lift. Second floor boasts a worn-out carpet, so the odor is dusty, faintly mingled with urine. Third floor stinks of sauerkraut (somebody must have dropped a glass jar of it, the floor is tile here) and so it goes. If I want out on the third, for instance, and the elevator doesn't stop there, I just wait for the next trip, and sooner or later I make it.

I was at the Hotel Duke when the U.S. Census forms came in in 1970. What a laugh. Everybody got a form, and everybody was laughing. Most of the people here probably haven't any homes to begin with, and the census was asking, 'How many rooms in your house?' and 'How many bathrooms have you?' and 'How many children?' and so forth. And what is your wife's age? People think that roaches can't understand English, or whatever is the going lingo in their vicinity. People think roaches understand only a suddenly turned-on light, which means 'Scram!' When you've been around as long as we have, which is long before the *Mayflower* got here, you dig the going yak. So I was able to appreciate many a comment on the U.S. Census, which none of the cruds at the Duke bothered filling out. It was amusing to think of myself filling it out – and why not? I was more of a resident by hereditary seat than any of the human beasts in the hotel. I am (though I am not Franz Kafka in disguise) a cockroach, and I do not know my wife's age or for that matter how many wives I have. Last week I had seven, in a manner of speaking, but how many of these have been stepped on? As for children, they're beyond count, a boast I've heard my two-legged neighbors make also, but when it comes to the count, if the count is what they want (the more the merrier, I assume), I will bet on myself. Only last week I recall two egg capsules about to be delivered from two of my wives, both on the third (sauerkraut) floor. Good God, I was in a hurry myself, off in pursuit – I blush to mention it – of food which I had smelled and which I estimated to be at a distance of one hundred yards. Cheese-flavored potato chips, I thought. I did not like to say 'Hello' and 'Good-bye' so quickly to my wives, but my need was perhaps as great as theirs, and where would they be, or rather our race be, if I could not keep my strength up? A moment later I saw a third wife crunched under a cowboy boot (the hippies here affect Western gear even if they are from Brooklyn), though at least she wasn't laying an egg at that time, only hurrying along like me, in an opposite direction. Hail and farewell! – though, alas, I am sure she did not even see me. I may never again see my parturient wives, those two, though perhaps I saw some of our offspring before I left the Duke. Who knows?

When I see some of the people here, I count myself lucky to be a cockroach. I'm at least healthier, and in a small way I clean up garbage. Which brings me to the point. There used to be garbage in the form of breadcrumbs, an occasional leftover canapé from a champagne party in a room. The present clientele of the Hotel Duke doesn't eat. They either take dope or drink booze. I've only heard about the good old days from my great-great-great-great-grandmothers and -fathers. But I believe them. They said you could jump into a shoe, for instance, outside the door, and be taken into a room along with the tray by a servant at eight in the morning, and thus breakfast on croissant crumbs. Even the shoe-polishing days are gone, because if anybody put shoes outside his room these days, they'd not only not be polished, they'd be stolen. Nowadays it's all you can hope for that these hairy, buckskin-fringed monsters and their see-through girls will take a bath once in a while and leave a few drops of water in the tub for me to drink. It's dangerous drinking out of a toilet, and at my age I won't do it.

However, I wish to speak of my newfound fortune. I'd just about had enough last week, what with another young wife squashed before my eyes by a lurching step (she had been keeping out of the *normal* path, I remember), and a moronic roomful of junkies licking up – I mean this – food from the floor as a kind of game. Young men and women, naked, pretending to be handless for some insane reason, trying to eat their sandwiches like dogs, strewing them all over the floor, then writhing about together amid salami, pickles and mayonnaise. Plenty of food this time, but unsafe to dart among those rolling bodies. Worse than feet. But to see sandwiches at all was exceptional. There's no restaurant anymore, but half the rooms in the Hotel Duke are 'apartments,' meaning that they have refrigerators and small stoves. But the main thing people have in the way of food is tinned tomato juice for vodka Bloody Marys. Nobody even fries an egg. For one thing, the hotel does not furnish skillets, pans, can openers or even a single knife or fork: they'd be pinched. And none of these charmers is going to go out and buy so much as a pot to heat soup in. So the pickings is slim, as they say. And that isn't the worst of the 'service' department here. Most of the windows don't shut tightly, the beds look like lumpy hammocks, straight chairs are falling apart at the joints, and the so-called armchairs, maybe one to a room, can inflict injury by releasing a spring in a tender place. Basins are often clogged, and toilets either don't flush or keep flushing maniacally. And robberies! I've witnessed a few. A maid gives the passkey and someone's in, absconding with suitcase contents under an arm, in pockets, or in a pillowcase disguised as dirty laundry.

Anyway, about a week ago I was in a temporarily vacant room at the Duke, scrounging about for a crumb or a bit of water, when in walked a black bellhop with a suitcase that smelled of *leather*. He was followed by a gentleman who smelled of aftershave lotion, plus of course tobacco, that's normal. He unpacked, put some papers out on the writing table, tried the hot water and muttered something to himself, jiggled the running toilet, tested the shower which shot all over the bathroom floor, and then he rang up the desk. I could understand most of what he was saying. He was essentially saying that at the price he was paying per day, this and that might be improved, and could he change his room, perhaps?

I lurked in my corner, thirsty, hungry, but interested, knowing also that I would be stepped on by this same gentleman if I made an appearance on the carpet. I well knew that I would be on his list of complaints if he saw me. The old French window blew open (it was a gusty day) and his papers went in all the four corners. He had to close the window by propping the back of a straight chair against it, and then he gathered his papers, cursing.

'*Washington Square! — Henry James would turn in his grave!*'

I remember those words, uttered at the same time as he slapped his forehead as if to hit a mosquito.

A bellhop in the threadbare maroon livery of the establishment arrived stoned and fiddled with the window to no avail. The window leaked cold air, made a terrible rattle, and everything, even a cigarette pack, had to be anchored down or it would have blown off a table or whatever. The bellhop in looking at the shower managed to drench himself, and then he said he would send for 'the engineer.' The engineer at the Hotel Duke is a joke on his own, which I won't go into. He didn't turn up that day, I think because the bellhop made the final bad impression, and the gentleman picked up the telephone and said:

'Can you send someone sober, if possible, to carry my suitcases down? . . . Oh, keep the money, I'm checking out. And get me a taxi, please.'

That was when I made up my mind. As the gentleman was packing, I mentally kissed good-bye to all my wives, brothers, sisters, cousins, children and grandchildren and great-grandchildren and then climbed aboard the beautiful suitcase that smelled of leather. I crawled into a pocket in the lid, and made myself snug in the folds of a plastic bag, fragrant of shaving soap and the aftershave lotion, where I would not be squashed even when the lid was closed.

Half an hour later, I found myself in a warmer room where the carpet was thick and not dusty-smelling. The gentleman has breakfast in bed in the mornings at 7:30. In the corridor, I can get all sorts of things from trays left on the floor outside the doors – even remnants of scrambled eggs, and certainly plenty of marmalade and butter on rolls. Had a narrow squeak yesterday when a white-jacketed waiter chased me thirty yards down the hall, stomping with both feet but missing me every time. I'm nimble yet, and life at the Hotel Duke taught me plenty!

I've already cased the kitchen, going and coming by lift, of course. Lots of pickings in the kitchen, but unfortunately they fumigate once a week. I met four possible wives, all a bit sickly from the fumes, but determined to stick it out in the kitchen. For me, it's upstairs. No competition, and plenty of breakfast trays and sometimes midnight snacks. Maybe I'm an old bachelor now, but there's life in me yet if a possible wife comes along. Meanwhile I consider myself a lot better than those bipeds in the Hotel Duke, whom I've seen eating stuff I wouldn't touch – or mention. They do it on bets. Bets! All life is a gamble, isn't it? So why bet?

CHORUS GIRL'S ABSOLUTELY FINAL PERFORMANCE

They call me Chorus Girl – shouts of 'Chorus Girl' go up when I stand and swing my left leg, then my right, and so on. Before that, however, maybe ten, twenty years ago, I was 'Jumbo Junior,' mostly 'Jumbo.' Now it's Chorus Girl entirely. My name must be written on the wooden board at the front of my cage, along with 'Africa.' People stare at the board, sometimes say 'Africa,' then start calling me 'Chorus Girl! – Hey, Chorus Girl!' If I swing my legs, a small cheer goes up.

I live alone. I never saw another creature like myself, in this place at any rate. I remember when I was small, though, following my mother everywhere, and I remember many creatures like myself, much bigger, a few even smaller. I remember following my mother up a sloping wooden board on to a boat, the boat a bit unsteady. My mother was led and prodded away, back the same board, and I was on the boat. My mother, wanting me to join her, lifted her trunk and bellowed. I saw ropes flung about her, ten or twenty men tugging to hold her back. Someone fired a gun at her. Was it a deadly gun or a dope gun? I will never know that. The smell is different, but the wind was not blowing towards me that day. I only know my mother collapsed after a little while. I was on the deck, screaming shrilly like a baby. Then I was shot with a dope gun. The boat finally moved, and after a very long time during which I mainly slept and ate in semidarkness in a box, we arrived in another land where there were no forests, no grass. Into another box I went, more movement, another place with cement underfoot, hard stone everywhere, bars, and foul-smelling people. Worst of all, I was alone. No little creatures my own age. No mother, no friendly grandfather, no father. No play. No baths in a muddy river. Alone with bars and cement.

But the food was all right, and there was plenty of it. Also a nice man took care of me, a man named Steve. He carried a pipe in his mouth, but almost never did he light it, just held it between his teeth. Even so he could talk and I could soon understand what he said, or at least what he meant.

'Kneel, Jumbo!' and a tap on my knees meant to get down on my knees. If I held my trunk up, Steve would clap his hands once in appreciation, and toss some peanuts or a small apple into my mouth.

I liked it when he got astride my back and I would get up, and we would walk around the cage. People seeing this would clap their hands, especially little children would clap.

Steve kept the flies off my eyes in summer by means of a string fringe which he fixed around my head. He would hose the cement floor, the shady part, so I could lie down and keep cool. He would hose me. When I became bigger, Steve would sit on my trunk and I would lift him into the air, being careful not to tip him, because he had nothing to hold on to except the end of my trunk. Steve took special care of me in winter also, making sure I had enough straw, even sometimes blankets if it was very cold. One particularly bad winter, Steve brought me a little box with a cord attached which blew warm air on to me. Steve nursed me through an illness caused by the cold.

The people here wear large hats. Some of the men carry short guns on their belts. Once in a while one pulls a gun and fires it into the air to try to scare me or the gazelles who live next door to me and whom I can see through the bars. The gazelles react violently, leap into the air, then huddle together in a far corner of their cage. A pitiable sight. By the time Steve or one of the caretakers arrives, the man who fired the shot has put his gun back in his belt, and looks like all the other men – who are laughing and won't point out the man who did it.

This reminds me of one of my pleasanter moments. There was a red-faced fat fellow about five years ago who on two or three Sundays fired his loud gun into the air. It annoyed me, though I would never have dreamt of showing my annoyance. But the third or fourth Sunday when this particular fellow fired his gun, I quietly took a snoutful of water from my trough and let him have it full force through the bars. I hit him in the chest and he went over backwards with his boots in the air. Most of the crowd laughed. A few of the people were surprised or angry. Some threw a few stones at me – which didn't hurt, or missed entirely, or hit the bars and bounced in another direction. Then Steve came trotting up, and I could see that Steve (having heard the shot) knew exactly what had happened. Steve laughed, but he patted the shoulder of the wet man, trying to calm him down. The man was probably denying having fired the shot. But I saw Steve give me a nod which I took for approval. The gazelles came forth timidly, staring through the bars at the crowd and also at me. I fancied they were pleased with my action, and I felt proud of myself that day. I dreamt even of seizing the wet man, or a man like him, of squeezing his soft body until he died, then of trampling him under my feet.

During Steve's time with me, which must have been thirty years, we would occasionally take a walk in the park and children, sometimes three at a time, would ride on my back. This was at least amusing, a nice change. But the park is anything but a forest. It is just a few trees growing from rather hard, dry soil. It is almost never wet. The grass is close cut, and I was not allowed to pull any grass up, not that I much wanted to. Steve managed everything, managed me, and carried a stick made of woven leather with which he prodded me to make me turn in a certain direction, kneel, stand up, and at the end of the outing stand on my hind legs. (More cheering.) Steve did not need the stick, but it was part of the show, like my turning in a couple of stupid circles before standing on my hind legs at the end. I could also stand on my front legs, if Steve asked me to. I remember my temper was better in those days, and I would avoid without Steve's telling me the low branches of some of the trees so the children on my back would not be knocked off. Given a chance, I am not sure I would be that careful any more. What have people, except Steve, ever given me? Not even grass under my feet. Not even companionship of another creature like myself.

Now that I am older, my legs heavier, my temper shorter, there are no more rides for children, though the band still plays on summer Sunday afternoons – 'Take Me Out to the Ball Game' and lately 'Hello, Dolly!' Sometimes I wish I could take a walk again, with Steve again, wish I could be young again. And yet, what for? For more years in this place? Now I spend more time lying down than standing up. I lie in the sun, which doesn't seem as hot as it used to. The people's clothing has changed a little, not so many guns and boots, but still the same broad-brimmed hats on the men and some of the women. Still the same tossed peanuts, not always shelled, that I used to stick my trunk through the bars for so eagerly when I was younger and had better appetite. Still the same popcorn and sweet Cracker Jack. I don't always bother getting on my feet Saturday and Sunday. This infuriates Cliff, the new young keeper. He wants me to do my stuff, as in the old days. It is not that I am so old and tired, but I don't like Cliff.

Cliff is tall and young, with red hair. He likes to show off, cracking a long whip at me. He thinks he can make me do things according to certain jabs and commands. There is a sharp point of metal on his stick, which is annoying, although it doesn't break my skin by any means. Steve approached me as one creature to another, making acquaintance with me and not assuming I was going to be what he expected. That is why we got along. Cliff doesn't really care about me, and does nothing to help me against the flies in summer, for instance.

Of course when Steve retired, I continued to go through the Saturday and Sunday rounds with the children, once in a while with adults on my back. One man (another trying to show off) dug his spurs into me one Sunday, whereupon I put on a very little speed of my own accord and did not duck under a low branch but deliberately trotted under it. It was too low for the man to duck, and he was swept neatly off my back, landed on his knees and howled with pain. This caused a lot of disturbance, the man groaned for a while, and what was worse Cliff took the man's side, or tried to placate the man, by yelling and prodding at me with the pointed stick. I snorted with rage myself – and was gratified to see the crowd fall back in terror of me. I was nowhere near charging them, which I'd have liked to do, but responded to Cliff's prods and headed back to my cage. Cliff was muttering at me. I took a snoutful of water, and Cliff saw it. Cliff retreated. But he came back after nightfall when the park gates were closed, and gave me a whipping and a lecture. The whipping did not hurt at all, but must have exhausted Cliff who was staggering when he finished.

The following day Steve turned up in a wheelchair. His hair had become white. I had not seen him in four or five years, perhaps, but he was really the same, with his pipe in his mouth, the same kind voice, the same smile. I swung my legs with joy in my cage, and Steve laughed and said something pleasant to me. He had brought some small red apples to give me. He came in his wheelchair into the cage. This was pretty early one morning, so there was hardly any of the public in the park as yet. Steve said something to Cliff and gestured towards Cliff's pointed stick, so that I knew Steve meant that Cliff should get rid of it.

Then Steve made a sign to me. 'Up! Lift me up, Chorus Girl!'

I knew what he meant. I knelt, and stuck my trunk under the seat of Steve's wheelchair, sideways, so he could grab the end of my trunk with his right hand and with his other hand press against my head for balance. I did not get to my feet for fear of toppling Steve's chair, but I lifted him off the cement by quite a distance. Steve laughed. I set the chair down gently.

But that was years ago, Steve's visit. It was not his last visit. He came two or three times in his wheelchair, but never on the two days of the week when there were the most people. Now I have not seen Steve in about three years. Is he dead? This possibility makes me sad whenever I think of it. But then it is equally sad to expect, to hope for Steve to appear some morning of the quiet days, when just a few people straggle in, and Steve is not among them. Sometimes I raise my trunk and bellow my chagrin and disappointment because Steve doesn't come. It seems to amuse people, my bellowing – just as my mother bellowed on the dock when she couldn't reach me. Cliff pays no attention, only sometimes puts his hands over his ears, if he happens to be near.

This brings me close to the present time. Just yesterday, Sunday, there was the usual crowd, even more than usual. There was a man in a red suit with a white beard ringing a bell in his hand, walking about talking to everyone, especially to children. This man appears every now and then. People had peanuts and popcorn to give me through the bars. As usual, I held my snout through the bars, and my mouth was open also, in case someone aimed a peanut correctly. Someone threw a round object into my mouth, and I thought it was a red apple until I crunched on it, whereupon it started stinging my mouth horribly. I immediately took some water into my trunk, rinsed my mouth and spat. I had not swallowed any of the stuff, but the whole inside of my mouth was burning. I took more water, but it did little good. The pain made me shift from foot to foot, and at last I trotted around my cage in agony. The people laughed and pointed. I became angry, furious. I took as big a snoutful of water as I could manage and walked rather casually to the front of my cage. Standing a little way back from the bars so I could hit them all, I forced the water through my snout with all my power.

No one quite fell, but more than twenty people staggered, fell back against each other, choking and blinded for a few seconds. I went to my trough and took on more water, and not a moment too soon, because the crowd had armed itself also. Rocks and sticks came flying at me, empty Cracker Jack boxes, anything. I aimed at the biggest man, knocked him down, and used the rest of the water to spray the whole assembly again. A woman was screaming for help. Others retreated. A man pulled his gun, shot at me and missed. Another gun was being drawn, although the first man who had shot was at once jumped on by another man. A bullet hit me in the shoulder, not going through but rather skimming the surface. A second bullet knocked off the end of my right tusk. With the last of my trough water in my snout, I attacked one of the gunmen squarely in the chest. It should have been enough to break his bones. At any rate he flew backward and knocked a woman down as he fell. Feeling I had won that set-to, in spite of my burning mouth, I withdrew prudently to my sleeping quarters (also of cement) where no bullets could hit me. Three more shots rang out, echoing in empty space. I don't know what they hit, but they did not hit me.

I could smell blood from my shoulder. I was still so angry, I was snorting instead of breathing, and almost to my own surprise, I found myself barricading the entrance to my sleeping quarters with the bales of hay which lined the place. I pulled the bales down from their stacks against the walls, shoved and kicked them, and with my trunk managed to boost one up on to the top of the heap of eight or nine, thereby closing the doorway except at the very top. This was bulletproof, anyway. But the bullets had ceased. Now I could hear Cliff outside, shouting to the crowd.

'Take it easy there, Chorus Girl!' Cliff's voice said.

I was familiar with the phrase. But I had never heard the fear, like a shaking, in Cliff's voice before. The crowd was watching him, of course. Cliff had to show himself powerful, able to control me. This thought plus my dislike of Cliff set me off again, and I butted my head against the barricade I'd made. Cliff had been pulling at the top bale, but now the whole heap fell on him.

The crowd gave a cry, a scream of shock.

I saw Cliff's legs, his black boots kicking underneath the bales.

A shot sounded, and this time I was hit in the left side. Cliff had a gun in his hand, but it was not his gun that had gone off. Cliff was not moving now. Neither was I. I expected another shot from the crowd, from someone in the crowd.

The crowd only stared back at me. I glared at them, with my mouth slightly open: the inside of my mouth was still burning.

Two uniformed men of the place arrived via the side door of my cage. They carried long guns. I stood still and did nothing, barely looked at them. Crazy and excited as they were, they might have shot me at once out of fear, if I had shown any sign of anger. My self-possession was returning. And I thought Cliff might be dead, which gave me pleasure.

But no, he wasn't. One man bent over him, pulled a bale of hay off him, and I saw Cliff's red-haired head move. The other man prodded me rudely with the point of his gun towards my sleeping quarters. He was yelling something at me. I turned and strolled, not hurrying, into my cement room which was now bestrewn with hay and bales in disorder. Suddenly I was not feeling well, and my mouth still hurt. A man stood in the doorway with his gun pointed at me. I regarded him calmly. I could see Cliff getting up. The other man was talking with Cliff in an angry tone. Cliff was talking and waving his hands, though he didn't look like himself at all. He looked unsteady on his feet, and he kept feeling his head.

Then a man with grayish hair, not as gray as Steve's, came to the gate with another man who carried a bag. They were let into the cage. Both of them came quite close to me and looked at me. Blood was dripping from my left side on to the cement. Then the gray-haired man spoke to Cliff angrily, kept on talking when Cliff interrupted – a string of words from both of them. The gray-haired man pointed to the cage door, a sign for Cliff to leave. The next moments are vague to me, because the man with the bag put a cloth over my snout and tied it firmly. He also gave me a prod with a needle. By now, during the loud talk, I had lain down. The cloth smelt cool but awful, and I went into a frightening sleep in which I saw animals like huge cats leaping about, attacking me, my mother, my family. I saw green trees again, high grass. But I felt that I was dying.

When I awakened, it was dark, and there was some kind of grease in my mouth. My mouth no longer hurt, and my side hurt only a little. Was this death? But I could smell the hay in my room. I got to my legs and felt sick. I threw up a little.

Then I heard the side gate clang as someone closed it. I recognized the step of Cliff, though he was walking softly in his boots. I considered going out of the small sleeping-room, which was like a trap with no other exit but the door, but I was too sleepy still to move. I could barely see Cliff kneeling with a bag like the one the man had carried. Then I smelt the same sweet, thin smell that the man had put over my nose. Even Cliff snorted, and turned his head away, then he came at me with a rush, tossing the cloth around my nose and pulling it tight at once with a rope. I flicked my snout and knocked Cliff down with a blow against his hip. I beat my trunk against his fallen form, trying more to get the cloth off than to hurt Cliff, who was writhing and groaning. The rope loosened, and with a toss I managed to shake off the cloth. It fell on Cliff's chest and part of his legs – stinking, evil, dangerous. I went out into the purer air of my cage.

Cliff was getting to his feet, gasping. He too came out for air, then rushed back, muttering, seized the cloth and came at me again. I rose a little on my hind legs and pivoted away from him. Cliff nearly fell. I gave Cliff the merest bump with my trunk and it lifted him off his feet. He fell his whole length on to the cement. Now I was angry. It was a fight between the two of us, Cliff with the evil-smelling cloth still in his hand. Cliff was getting to his knees.

I gave Cliff a kick, hardly more than a prod, with my left foot. I caught him in the side, and I heard a cracking sound like the breaking of tree branches. After that Cliff did not move again. Now there was the awful smell of blood mixed with the sweet and deadly smell. I went to the front corner of my cage, as far from the cloth as possible and lay down, trying to recover in the fresher air. I was cold, but that was of little importance. Slowly I began to feel calmer. I could breathe again. I had one brief desire to go and stomp a foot on Cliff, but I hadn't the energy. What I felt was rage. And little by little even the rage went away. But I was still too upset to sleep. I waited in my cement corner for the dawn.

And this is where I am now, lying in a corner of the cement and steel cage where I have spent so many years. The light comes slowly. First there is the familiar figure of the old man who feeds the two musk oxen. He pushes a cart, opens another cage where there are more horned animals. At last he passes my cage, glances twice at me, and says something with 'Chorus Girl' in it, surprised to see me lying where I am. Then he sees Cliff's form.

'Cliff? — Hey, Cliff! What's the matter?'

The cage isn't locked, it seems, and the old man comes right in, bends over Cliff, says something, holds his nose and drags the big white cloth out of the cage. Then he runs off, yelling. I get to my feet. The cage door is slightly open. I walk past Cliff's body, nudge the gate wider and walk out.

There is no one in the park. It is pleasant to walk on the ground again, as I haven't done since they stopped the weekend rides so long ago. The dry ground even feels soft. I pause to raise my trunk, pull some green leaves off a branch, and eat them. The leaves are tough and prickly, but at least they are fresh. Here is the round fountain, that I was never allowed to pause at, or drink from, on the weekend outings. Now I take a long cool draft.

Behind me there are excited voices. The voices are no doubt back at my cage, but I don't even bother looking. I enjoy my freedom. Above me is the great blue sky, a whole world of emptiness overhead. I go into a thicket of trees growing so close that they scrape both my sides. But there are so few trees, I am immediately out again, and on a cement path where apes and monkeys in cages stare goggle-eyed and chatter in amazement as I stroll by. A couple of them huddle at the back of their cage, little hairy fellows. Gray monkeys yell shrilly at me, then turn their blue behinds at me and scamper to the far corner of their cage. But perhaps some of them would like to ride on my back? From somewhere I remember that. I pull some flowers and eat them, just for amusement. The black monkeys with long arms are grinning and laughing, holding on to their bars, jerking the bars up and down and making a clatter.

I stroll over, and they are only a little afraid, much more curious than afraid, as I stick my trunk around two of the bars and pull the bars towards me. Then a third bar, and there is room for the black monkeys to scramble out.

They scream and titter, leaping along the ground, using their hands to boost them. One grabs my tail mischievously. Two of them take to a tree with delight.

But now there are footsteps from somewhere, sounds of running feet, shouts.

'There she is! By the monkeys!'

I turn to face them. A monkey scrambles on to my back, using my tail to get up. He slaps my shoulders, wanting a ride. He seems to weigh nothing at all. Two men, the same as yesterday, with the long guns, come running towards me, then halt, skidding, and raise their guns. Before I can lift my trunk in a gesture that might indicate friendliness, before I can kneel even, three shots go off.

'Don't hit the monkey!'

But they hit me.

Bang!

Now the sun is coming up and the tops of the trees are green-ish, not all the trees being bare. My eyes go up and up. My body sinks. I am aware of the monkey leaping nimbly from my back to the ground, loping off, terrified by the gunshots. I feel very heavy suddenly, as if falling asleep. I mean to kneel and lie down, but my body sways sideways and I strike the cement. Another shot jolts my head. That was between the eyes, but my eyes are still open.

Men scamper round me as the monkeys did, kicking me, shouting to one another. Again I see the huge cats leaping in the forest, leaping on me now. Then through the blur of the men's figures I see Steve very clearly, but Steve as he was when he was young – smiling, talking to me, with his pipe in his teeth. Steve moves slowly and gracefully. So I know I am dying, because I know Steve is dead. He is more real than the others. There is a forest around him. Steve is my friend, as always. There are no cats, only Steve, my friend.

MING'S BIGGEST PREY

Ming was resting comfortably on the foot of his mistress's bunk, when the man picked him up by the back of the neck, stuck him out on the deck and closed the cabin door. Ming's blue eyes widened in shock and brief anger, then nearly closed again because of the brilliant sunlight. It was not the first time Ming had been thrust out of the cabin rudely, and Ming realized that the man did it when his mistress, Elaine, was not looking.

The sailboat now offered no shelter from the sun, but Ming was not yet too warm. He leapt easily to the cabin roof and stepped on to the coil of rope just behind the mast. Ming liked the rope coil as a couch, because he could see everything from the height, the cup shape of the rope protected him from strong breezes, and also minimized the swaying and sudden changes of angle of the *White Lark*, since it was more or less the center point. But just now the sail had been taken down, because Elaine and the man had eaten lunch, and often they had a siesta afterward, during which time, Ming knew that the man didn't like him in the cabin. Lunchtime was all right. In fact, Ming had just lunched on delicious grilled fish and a bit of lobster. Now, lying in a relaxed curve on the coil of rope, Ming opened his mouth in a great yawn, then with his slant eyes almost closed against the strong sunlight, gazed at the beige hills and the white and pink houses and hotels that circled the bay of Acapulco. Between the *White Lark* and the shore where people plashed inaudibly, the sun twinkled on the water's surface like thousands of tiny electric lights going on and off. A water-skier went by, skimming up white spray behind him. Such activity! Ming half dozed, feeling the heat of the sun sink into his fur. Ming was from New York, and he considered Acapulco a great improvement over his environment in the first weeks of his life. He remembered a sunless box with straw on the bottom, three or four other kittens in with him, and a window behind which giant forms paused for a few moments, tried to catch his attention by tapping, then passed on. He did not remember his mother at all. One day a young woman who smelled of something pleasant came into the place and took him away – away from the ugly, frightening smell of dogs, of medicine and parrot dung. Then they went on what Ming now knew was an airplane. He was quite used to airplanes now and rather liked them. On airplanes he sat on Elaine's lap, or slept on her lap, and there were always tidbits to eat if he was hungry.

Elaine spent much of the day in a shop in Acapulco, where dresses and slacks and bathing suits hung on all the walls. This place smelled clean and fresh, there were flowers in pots and in boxes out front, and the floor was of cool blue and white tile. Ming had perfect freedom to wander out into the patio behind the shop, or to sleep in his basket in a corner. There was more sunlight in front of the shop, but mischievous boys often tried to grab him if he sat in front, and Ming could never relax there.

Ming liked best lying in the sun with his mistress on one of the long canvas chairs on their terrace at home. What Ming did not like were the people she sometimes invited to their house, people who spent the night, people by the score who stayed up very late eating and drinking, playing the gramophone or the piano – people who separated him from Elaine. People who stepped on his toes, people who sometimes picked him up from behind before he could do anything about it, so that he had to squirm and fight to get free, people who stroked him roughly, people who closed a door somewhere, locking him in. *People!* Ming detested people. In all the world, he liked only Elaine. Elaine loved him and understood him.

Especially this man called Teddie Ming detested now. Teddie was around all the time lately. Ming did not like the way Teddie looked at him, when Elaine was not watching. And sometimes Teddie, when Elaine was not near, muttered something which Ming knew was a threat. Or a command to leave the room. Ming took it calmly. Dignity was to be preserved. Besides, wasn't his mistress on his side? The man was the intruder. When Elaine was watching, the man sometimes pretended a fondness for him, but Ming always moved gracefully but unmistakably in another direction.

Ming's nap was interrupted by the sound of the cabin door opening. He heard Elaine and the man laughing and talking. The big red-orange sun was near the horizon.

'Ming!' Elaine came over to him. 'Aren't you getting *cooked*, darling? I thought you were *in*!'

'So did I!' said Teddie.

Ming purred as he always did when he awakened. She picked him up gently, cradled him in her arms, and took him below into the suddenly cool shade of the cabin. She was talking to the man, and not in a gentle tone. She set Ming down in front of his dish of water, and though he was not thirsty, he drank a little to please her. Ming did feel addled by the heat, and he staggered a little.

Elaine took a wet towel and wiped Ming's face, his ears and his four paws. Then she laid him gently on the bunk that smelled of Elaine's perfume but also of the man whom Ming detested.

Now his mistress and the man were quarrelling, Ming could tell from the tone. Elaine was staying with Ming, sitting on the edge of the bunk. Ming at last heard the splash that meant Teddie had dived into the water. Ming hoped he stayed there, hoped he drowned, hoped he never came back. Elaine wet a bathtowel in the aluminum sink, wrung it out, spread it on the bunk, and lifted Ming on to it. She brought water, and now Ming was thirsty, and drank. She left him to sleep again while she washed and put away the dishes. These were comfortable sounds that Ming liked to hear.

But soon there was another *plash* and *plop*, Teddie's wet feet on the deck, and Ming was awake again.

The tone of quarreling recommenced. Elaine went up the few steps on to the deck. Ming, tense but with his chin still resting on the moist bath-towel, kept his eyes on the cabin door. It was Teddie's feet that he heard descending. Ming lifted his head slightly, aware that there was no exit behind him, that he was trapped in the cabin. The man paused with a towel in his hands, staring at Ming.

Ming relaxed completely, as he might do preparatory to a yawn, and this caused his eyes to cross. Ming then let his tongue slide a little way out of his mouth. The man started to say something, looked as if he wanted to hurl the wadded towel at Ming, but he wavered, whatever he had been going to say never got out of his mouth, and he threw the towel in the sink, then bent to wash his face. It was not the first time Ming had let his tongue slide out at Teddie. Lots of people laughed when Ming did this, if they were people at a party, for instance, and Ming rather enjoyed that. But Ming sensed that Teddie took it as a hostile gesture of some kind, which was why Ming did it deliberately to Teddie, whereas among other people, it was often an accident when Ming's tongue slid out.

The quarreling continued. Elaine made coffee. Ming began to feel better, and went on deck again, because the sun had now set. Elaine had started the motor, and they were gliding slowly towards the shore. Ming caught the song of birds, the odd screams, like shrill phrases, of certain birds that cried only at sunset. Ming looked forward to the adobe house on the cliff that was his and his mistress's home. He knew that the reason she did not leave him at home (where he would have been more comfortable) when she went on the boat, was because she was afraid that people might trap him, even kill him. Ming understood. People had tried to grab him from almost under Elaine's eyes. Once he had been suddenly hauled away in a cloth bag, and though fighting as hard as he could, he was not sure he would have been able to get out, if Elaine had not hit the boy herself and grabbed the bag from him.

Ming had intended to jump up on the cabin roof again, but after glancing at it, he decided to save his strength, so he crouched on the warm, gently sloping deck with his feet tucked in, and gazed at the approaching shore. Now he could hear guitar music from the beach. The voices of his mistress and the man had come to a halt. For a few moments, the loudest sound was the *chug-chug-chug* of the boat's motor. Then Ming heard the man's bare feet climbing the cabin steps. Ming did not turn his head to look at him, but his ears twitched back a little, involuntarily. Ming looked at the water just the distance of a short leap in front of him and below him. Strangely, there was no sound from the man behind him. The hair on Ming's neck prickled, and Ming glanced over his right shoulder.

At that instant, the man bent forward and rushed at Ming with his arms outspread.

Ming was on his feet at once, darting straight towards the man, which was the only direction of safety on the railless deck, and the man swung his left arm and cuffed Ming in the chest. Ming went flying backwards, claws scraping the deck, but his hind legs went over the edge. Ming clung with his front feet to the sleek wood which gave him little hold, while his hind legs worked to heave him up, worked at the side of the boat which sloped to Ming's disadvantage.

The man advanced to shove a foot against Ming's paws, but Elaine came up the cabin steps just then.

'What's happening? *Ming*!'

Ming's strong hind legs were getting him on to the deck little by little. The man had knelt as if to lend a hand. Elaine had fallen on to her knees also, and had Ming by the back of the neck now.

Ming relaxed, hunched on the deck. His tail was wet.

'He fell overboard!' Teddie said. 'It's true, he's groggy. Just lurched over and fell when the boat gave a dip.'

'It's the sun. Poor *Ming*!' Elaine held the cat against her breast, and carried him into the cabin. 'Teddie – could you steer?'

The man came down into the cabin. Elaine had Ming on the bunk and was talking softly to him. Ming's heart was still beating fast. He was alert against the man at the wheel, even though Elaine was with him. Ming was aware that they had entered the little cove where they always went before getting off the boat.

Here were the friends and allies of Teddie, whom Ming detested by association, although these were merely Mexican boys. Two or three boys in shorts called 'Señor Teddie!' and offered a hand to Elaine to climb on to the dock, took the rope attached to the front of the boat, offered to carry *'Ming! – Ming!'* Ming leapt on to the dock himself and crouched, waiting for Elaine, ready to dart away from any other hand that might reach for him. And there were several brown hands making a rush for him, so that Ming had to keep jumping aside. There were laughs, yelps, stomps of bare feet on wooden boards. But there was also the reassuring voice of Elaine warning them off. Ming knew she was busy carrying off the plastic satchels, locking the cabin door. Teddie with the aid of one of the Mexican boys was stretching the canvas over the cabin now. And Elaine's sandaled feet were beside Ming. Ming followed her as she walked away. A boy took the things Elaine was carrying, then she picked Ming up.

They got into the big car without a roof that belonged to Teddie, and drove up the winding road towards Elaine's and Ming's house. One of the boys was driving. Now the tone in which Elaine and Teddie were speaking was calmer, softer. The man laughed. Ming sat tensely on his mistress's lap. He could feel her concern for him in the way she stroked him and touched the back of his neck. The man reached out to put his fingers on Ming's back, and Ming gave a low growl that rose and fell and rumbled deep in his throat.

'Well, well,' said the man, pretending to be amused, and took his hand away.

Elaine's voice had stopped in the middle of something she was saying. Ming was tired, and wanted nothing more than to take a nap on the big bed at home. The bed was covered with a red and white striped blanket of thin wool.

Hardly had Ming thought of this, when he found himself in the cool, fragrant atmosphere of his own home, being lowered gently on to the bed with the soft woolen cover. His mistress kissed his cheek, and said something with the word hungry in it. Ming understood, at any rate. He was to tell her when he was hungry.

Ming dozed, and awakened at the sound of voices on the terrace a couple of yards away, past the open glass doors. Now it was dark. Ming could see one end of the table, and could tell from the quality of the light that there were candles on the table. Concha, the servant who slept in the house, was clearing the table. Ming heard her voice, then the voices of Elaine and the man. Ming smelled cigar smoke. Ming jumped to the floor and sat for a moment looking out of the door towards the terrace. He yawned, then arched his back and stretched, and limbered up his muscles by digging his claws into the thick straw carpet. Then he slipped out to the right on the terrace and glided silently down the long stairway of broad stones to the garden below. The garden was like a jungle or a forest. Avocado trees and mango trees grew as high as the terrace itself, there were bougainvillea against the wall, orchids in the trees, and magnolias and several camellias which Elaine had planted. Ming could hear birds twittering and stirring in their nests. Sometimes he climbed trees to get at their nests, but tonight he was not in the mood, though he was no longer tired. The voices of his mistress and the man disturbed him. His mistress was not a friend of the man's tonight, that was plain.

Concha was probably still in the kitchen, and Ming decided to go in and ask her for something to eat. Concha liked him. One maid who had not liked him had been dismissed by Elaine. Ming thought he fancied barbecued pork. That was what his mistress and the man had eaten tonight. The breeze blew fresh from the ocean, ruffling

Ming's fur slightly. Ming felt completely recovered from the awful experience of nearly falling into the sea.

Now the terrace was empty of people. Ming went left, back into the bedroom, and was at once aware of the man's presence, though there was no light on and Ming could not see him. The man was standing by the dressing table, opening a box. Again involuntarily Ming gave a low growl which rose and fell, and Ming remained frozen in the position he had been in when he first became aware of the man, his right front paw extended for the next step. Now his ears were back, he was prepared to spring in any direction, although the man had not seen him.

'Ssss-st! Damn you!' the man said in a whisper. He stamped his foot, not very hard, to make the cat go away.

Ming did not move at all. Ming heard the soft rattle of the white necklace which belonged to his mistress. The man put it into his pocket, then moved to Ming's right, out of the door that went into the big living room. Ming now heard the clink of a bottle against glass, heard liquid being poured. Ming went through the same door and turned left towards the kitchen.

Here he meowed, and was greeted by Elaine and Concha. Concha had her radio turned on to music.

'Fish? – Pork. He likes pork,' Elaine said, speaking the odd form of words which she used with Concha.

Ming, without much difficulty, conveyed his preference for pork, and got it. He fell to with a good appetite. Concha was exclaiming 'Ah-eee-ee!' as his mistress spoke with her, spoke at length. Then Concha bent to stroke him, and Ming put up with it, still looking down at his plate, until she left off and he could finish his meal. Then Elaine left the kitchen. Concha gave him some of the tinned milk, which he loved, in his now empty saucer, and Ming lapped this up. Then he rubbed himself against her bare leg by way of thanks, and went out of the kitchen, made his way cautiously into the living room en route to the bedroom. But now Elaine and the man were out on the terrace. Ming had just entered the bedroom, when he heard Elaine call:

'Ming? Where are you?'

Ming went to the terrace door and stopped, and sat on the threshold.

Elaine was sitting sideways at the end of the table, and the candle-light was bright on her long fair hair, on the white of her trousers. She slapped her thigh, and Ming jumped on to her lap.

The man said something in a low tone, something not nice.

Elaine replied something in the same tone. But she laughed a little.

Then the telephone rang.

Elaine put Ming down, and went into the living room towards the telephone.

The man finished what was in his glass, muttered something at Ming, then set the glass on the table. He got up and tried to circle Ming, or to get him towards the edge of the terrace, Ming realized, and Ming also realized that the man was drunk – therefore moving slowly and a little clumsily. The terrace had a parapet about as high as the man's hips, but it was broken by grills in three places, grills with bars wide enough for Ming to pass through, though Ming never did, merely looked through the grills sometimes. It was plain to Ming that the man wanted to drive him through one of the grills, or grab him and toss him over the terrace parapet. There was nothing easier for Ming than to elude him. Then the man picked up a chair and swung it suddenly, catching Ming on the hip. That had been quick, and it hurt. Ming took the nearest exit, which was down the outside steps that led to the garden.

The man started down the steps after him. Without reflecting, Ming dashed back up the few steps he had come, keeping close to the wall which was in shadow. The man hadn't seen him, Ming knew. Ming leapt to the terrace parapet, sat down and licked a paw once to recover and collect himself. His heart beat fast as if he were in the middle of a fight. And hatred ran in his veins. Hatred burned his eyes as he crouched and listened to the man uncer-tainly climbing the steps below him. The man came into view.

Ming tensed himself for a jump, then jumped as hard as he could, landing with all four feet on the man's right arm near the shoulder. Ming clung to the cloth of the man's white jacket, but they were both falling. The man groaned. Ming hung on. Branches crackled. Ming could not tell up from down. Ming jumped off the man, became aware of direction and of the earth too late, and landed on his side. Almost at the same time, he heard the thud of the man hitting the ground, then of his body rolling a little way, then there was silence. Ming had to breathe fast with his mouth open until his chest stopped hurting. From the direction of the man, he could smell drink, cigar, and the sharp odor that meant fear. But the man was not moving.

Ming could now see quite well. There was even a bit of moonlight. Ming headed for the steps again, had to go a long way through the bush, over stones and sand, to where the steps began. Then he glided up and arrived once more upon the terrace.

Elaine was just coming on to the terrace.

'Teddie?' she called. Then she went back into the bedroom where she turned on a lamp. She went into the kitchen. Ming followed her. Concha had left the light on, but Concha was now in her own room, where the radio played.

Elaine opened the front door.

The man's car was still in the driveway, Ming saw. Now Ming's hip had begun to hurt, or now he had begun to notice it. It caused him to limp a little. Elaine noticed this, touched his back, and asked him what was the matter. Ming only purred.

'Teddie? – Where are you?' Elaine called.

She took a torch and shone it down into the garden, down among the great trunks of the avocado trees, among the orchids and the lavender and pink blossoms of the bougainvilleas. Ming, safe beside her on the terrace parapet, followed the beam of the torch with his eyes and purred with content. The man was not below here, but below and to the right. Elaine went to the terrace steps and carefully, because there was no rail here, only broad steps, pointed the beam of the light downward. Ming did not bother looking. He sat on the terrace where the steps began.

'Teddie!' she said. '*Teddie!*' Then she ran down the steps.

Ming still did not follow her. He heard her draw in her breath. Then she cried:

'*Concha!*'

Elaine ran back up the steps.

Concha had come out of her room. Elaine spoke to Concha. Then Concha became excited. Elaine went to the telephone, and spoke for a short while, then she and Concha went down the steps together. Ming settled himself with his paws tucked under him on the terrace, which was still faintly warm from the day's sun. A car arrived. Elaine came up the steps, and went and opened the front door. Ming kept out of the way on the terrace, in a shadowy corner, as three or four strange men came out on the terrace and tramped down the steps. There was a great deal of talk below, noises of feet, breaking of bushes, and then the smell of all of them mounted the steps, the smell of tobacco, sweat, and the familiar smell of blood. The man's blood. Ming was pleased, as he was pleased when he killed a bird and created this smell of blood under his own teeth. This was big prey. Ming, unnoticed by any of the others, stood up to his full height as the group passed with the corpse, and inhaled the aroma of his victory with a lifted nose.

Then suddenly the house was empty. Everyone had gone, even Concha. Ming drank a little water from his bowl in the kitchen, then went to his mistress's bed, curled against the slope of the pillows, and fell fast asleep. He was awakened by the *rr-rr-r* of an unfamiliar car. Then the front door opened, and he recognized the step of Elaine and then Concha. Ming stayed where he was. Elaine and Concha talked softly for a few minutes. Then Elaine came into the bedroom. The lamp was still on. Ming watched her slowly open the box on her dressing table, and into it she let fall the white necklace that made a little clatter. Then she closed the box. She began to unbutton her shirt, but before she had finished, she flung herself on the bed and stroked Ming's head, lifted his left paw and pressed it gently so that the claws came forth.

'Oh, Ming – Ming,' she said.

Ming recognized the tones of love.

IN THE DEAD OF
TRUFFLE SEASON

S amson, a large white pig in the prime of life, lived on a rambling
old farm in the Lot region, not far from the grand old town of
Cahors. Among the fifteen or so other pigs on the farm was Samson's
mother Georgia (so named because of a song the farmer Emile had
heard once on the television) but not Samson's grandmother, who
had been hauled away, kicking and squealing, about a year ago, and
not Samson's father, who lived many kilometers away and arrived
on a pick-up car a few times a year for brief visits. There were also
countless piglets, some from Samson's mother, some not, through
whom Samson disdainfully waded, if they were between him and a
feed trough. Samson never bothered shoving even the adult pigs, in
fact, because he was so big himself, he had merely to advance and
his way was clear.

His white coat, somewhat thin and bristly on his sides, grew fine
and silky on the back of his neck. Emile often squeezed Samson's
neck with his rough fingers when boasting about Samson to another
farmer, then he would kick Samson gently in his larded ribs. Usually
Samson's back and sides bore a gray crust of sun-dried mud, because
he loved to roll in the mud of the unpaved farmyard court and in the

thicker mud of the pig pen by the barn. Cool mud was pleasant in the southern summer, when the sun came boiling down for weeks on end, making the pig pen and the courtyard steam. Samson had seen two summers.

The greatest season of the year for Samson was the dead of winter, when he came into his own as truffle-hunter. Emile and often his friend René, another farmer who sometimes took a pig, sometimes a dog with him, would stroll out with Samson on a rope lead of a Sunday morning, and walk for nearly two kilometers to where some oak trees grew in a small forest.

'*Vas-y!*' Emile would say as they entered the forest's edge, speaking however in the dialect of the region.

Samson, perhaps a bit fatigued or annoyed by the long promenade, would take his time, even if he did happen to smell truffles at once at the base of a tree. An old belt of Emile's served as his collar, very little of its end hanging, so big was Samson's neck, and Samson could easily tug Emile in any direction he chose.

Emile would laugh in anticipation, and say something cheery to René, or to himself if he were alone, then pull from a pocket of his jacket the bottle of Armagnac he took along to keep the cold out.

The main reason Samson took his time about disclosing any truffles was that he never got to eat any. He did get a morsel of cheese as a reward, if he indicated a truffle spot, but cheese was not truffles, and Samson vaguely resented this.

'Huh-*wan-nk!*' said Samson, meaning absolutely nothing by it, wasting time as he sniffed at the foot of a tree which was not an appropriate tree in the first place.

Emile knew this, and gave Samson a kick, then blew on his free hand: his woolen gloves were full of holes, and it was a damned freezing day. He threw down his Gauloise, and pulled the collar of his turtleneck sweater up over his mouth and nose.

Then Samson's nostrils filled with the delicate, rare aroma of black truffles, and he paused, snorting. The hairs on his back rose a little with excitement. His feet of their own accord stomped, braced themselves, and his flat nose began to root at the ground. He drooled.

Emile was already tugging at the pig. He looped the rope a few times around a tree some distance away, then attacked the spot cautiously with the fork he had been carrying.

'Ah! A-hah!' There they were, a cluster of crinkly black fungus as wide as his hand. Emile put the truffles gently into the cloth knapsack that was swung over his shoulder. Such truffles were worth a hundred and thirty new francs the *livre* in Cahors on the big market days, which were every other Saturday, and Emile got just a trifle less where he usually sold them, at a Cahors delicacy shop which in turn sold the truffles to a pâté manufacturer called Compagnie de la Reine d'Aquitaine. Emile could have got a bit more by selling direct to La Reine d'Aquitaine, but their plant was the other side of Cahors, making the trip more expensive because of the cost of petrol. Cahors, where Emile went every fortnight to buy animal feed and perhaps a tool replacement, was only ten kilometers from his home.

Emile found with his fingers a bit of gruyère in his knapsack, and approached Samson with it. He tossed it on the ground in front of Samson, remembering Samson's teeth.

'*Us-ssh!*' Samson inhaled the cheese like a vacuum cleaner. He was ready for the next tree. The smell of truffles in the knapsack inspired him.

They found two more good spots that morning, before Emile decided to call it a day. They were hardly a kilometer from the Café de la Chasse, on the edge of Emile's home town Cassouac, and the bar-café was on the way home. Emile stomped his feet a few times as he walked, and tugged at Samson impatiently.

'Hey, fatso! Samson! – Get a move on! Of course you're not in a hurry with all that lard on you!' Emile kicked Samson on a back leg.

Samson pretended indifference, but condescended to trot for a few steps before he lapsed into his oddly dainty, I'll-take-my-time gait. Why should he hurry, why should he do everything to suit Emile? Also Samson knew where they were heading, knew he'd have a long wait outside in the cold while Emile drank and talked with his friends. There was the café in view now, with a few dogs tied up outside it. Samson's blood began to course a little faster. He could hold his own with a dog, and enjoyed doing so. Dogs thought they were so clever, so superior, but one lunge from Samson and they flinched and drew back as far as their leads permitted.

'Bonjour, Pierre! . . . Ha-ha-ha!' Emile had encountered the first of his cronies outside the café.

Pierre was tying up his dog, and had made some risible remark about Emile's *chien de race*.

'Never mind, I've got nearly a *livre* of truffles today!' Emile countered, exaggerating.

The barks of more dogs sounded as Emile and Pierre went into the small café. Dogs were allowed in, but some dogs who might snarl at the others were always tied outside.

One dog nipped playfully at Samson's tail, and Samson turned and charged in a leisurely way, not going far enough to make his rope taut, but the dog rolled over in his effort to escape. All three dogs barked, and to Samson it sounded derogatory – towards him. Samson regarded the dogs with a sullen and calm antipathy. Only his pinkish little eyes were quick, taking in all the dogs, daring them or any one of them to advance. The dogs smiled uneasily. At last Samson collapsed by leaning back and letting his legs fold under him. He was in the sun and comfortable enough despite the cold air. But he was hungry again, therefore a bit annoyed.

Emile had found René in the café, drinking pastis at the bar. Emile meant to linger until there was just time to walk home and not annoy his wife Ursule, who liked Sunday dinner to start not later than a quarter past noon.

René wore high rubber boots. He'd been cleaning a drain of his cow-barn, he said. He talked about the truffle-hunting contest that was to take place in two weeks. Emile had not heard of it.

'Look!' said René, pointing to a printed notice at the right of the door. La Compagnie de la Reine d'Aquitaine offered a first prize of a cuckoo clock plus a hundred francs, a second prize of a transistor radio (one couldn't tell the size from the picture), a third prize of fifty francs to the finders of the most truffles on Sunday, January 27. Judges' decisions to be final. Local newspaper and television coverage was promised, and the town of Cassouac was to be the judges' base.

'I'm giving Lunache a rest this Sunday, maybe next too,' René said. 'That way she'll have time to work up a truffle appetite.'

Lunache was René's best truffling pig, a black and white female. Emile smiled a little slyly at his friend, as if to say, 'You know very well Samson's better than Lunache!' Emile said, 'That should be amusing. Let's hope it's not raining.'

'Or snowing! Another pastis? I invite you.' René put some money on the counter.

Emile glanced at the clock on the wall and accepted.

When he went out ten minutes later, he saw that Samson had chased the three tied-up dogs to the extremity of their leads, and was pretending to strain at his rope – a sturdy rope, but Samson might have been able to break it with a good tug. Emile felt rather proud of Samson.

'This monster! He needs a muzzle!' said a youngish man in muddy riding boots, a man Emile didn't recognize. He was patting one of the dogs in a reassuring way.

Emile was ready to return a spate of argument: hadn't the dog been annoying the pig first? But it crossed his mind that the young man might be a representative of La Reine d'Aquitaine come to look the scene over. Silence and a polite nod was best, Emile thought. Was one of the dogs bleeding a little on the hind leg? Emile didn't tarry to look more closely. He untied Samson and ambled off. After all, Emile was thinking, he'd had Samson's lower tusks sawed off three or four months ago. The tusks had started to grow higher than his snout. His upper tusks were still with him, but they were less dangerous because they curved inward.

Samson, in a vaguer though angrier way, was also thinking about his teeth at that moment. If he hadn't been mysteriously deprived of his rightful lower tusks long ago, he could have torn that dog up. One upward sweep of his nose under the dog's belly, which in fact Samson had given . . . Samson's breath steamed in the air. His four-toed feet, only the two middle toes on each foot touching the ground, bore him along as if his great bulk were light as a white balloon. Now Samson was leading like a thoroughbred dog straining at the leash.

Emile, knowing Samson was angry, gave him serious and firm tugs. Emile's hand hurt, his arms were growing tired, and as soon as they neared the open gate of the farm's court, Emile gladly released the rope. Samson went trotting directly towards the pig pen where the food was. Emile opened the low gate for him, followed Samson's galloping figure, and unbuckled the belt collar while Samson guzzled potato peelings.

'*Oink!* – Oink-oink!'

'Whuff-f!'

'*Hwon-nk!*'

The other pigs and piglets fell back from Samson.

Emile went into the kitchen. His wife was just setting a big platter of cold diced beets and carrots, sliced tomatoes and onions in the center of the table. Emile gave a greeting which included Ursule, their son Henri and his wife Yvonne and their little one Jean-Paul. Henri helped a bit on the farm, though he was a full-time worker in a Cahors factory that made Formica sheets. Henri was not fond of farm work. But it was cheaper for him and his family to live here than to take an apartment or buy a house just now.

'Good truffling?' asked Henri, with a glance at the sack.

Emile was just emptying the contents of the sack into a pan of cold water in the sink. 'Not bad,' said Emile.

'Eat, Emile,' said Ursule. 'I'll wash them later.'

Emile sat down and began eating. He started to tell them about the truffle-hunting contest, then decided it might be bad luck to mention it. There were still two weeks in which to mention it,

if he felt like it. Emile was imagining the cuckoo clock fixed on
the wall in front of him, striking about now the quarter hour past
twelve. And he would say a few words on the television (if it was
true that there'd be television), and he'd have his picture in the local
newspaper.

The main reason Emile did not take Samson truffling the following weekend was that he did not want to diminish the amount
of truffles in that particular forest. This forest was known as 'the-
little-forest-down-the-slope' and was owned by an old man who
didn't even live on his land any more but in a nearby town. The old
man had never objected to truffle-hunting on his land, nor had the
current caretakers who lived in the farmhouse nearly a kilometer
away from the forest.

So Samson had a leisurely fortnight of eating and of sleeping in
the scoop of hard-packed hay in the pig shed, which was a lean-to
against the main barn.

On the big day, January 27, Emile shaved. Then he made his
way to the Café de la Chasse in his village, the meeting point. Here
were René and eight or ten other men, all of whom Emile knew and
nodded a greeting to. There were also a few boys and girls of the
village come to watch. They were all laughing, smoking, pretending it was a silly game, but Emile knew that inside each man with a
truffle-dog or truffle-pig was a determination to win first prize, and
if not first then second. Samson showed a desire to attack Georges's
dog Gaspar, and Emile had to tug at him and kick him. Just as Emile
had suspected, the young man of two weeks ago, again in the riding
boots, was master of ceremonies. He put on a smile, and spoke to
the group from the front steps of the café.

'Gentlemen of Cassouac!' he began, then proceeded to announce
the terms of the contest sponsored by La Reine d'Aquitaine, manu-
facturers of the best *pâté aux truffes* in all France.

'Where's the television?' a man asked, more to raise a laugh from
his chums than to get an answer.

The young man laughed too. 'It'll be here when we all come

back – a special crew from Toulouse – around eleven-thirty. I know all of you want to get home soon after noon so as not to annoy your wives!'

More good-natured 'Ha-ha's!' It was a frosty day, sharpening everyone's edge.

'Just for formality,' said the young man in riding boots, 'I'll take a look in your sacks to see that all's correct.' He stepped down and did so, and every man showed a clean bag or sack except for apples and bits of cheese or meat which were to be rewards for their animals.

One of the onlookers made a side bet: dogs against pigs. He had manged to find a pig man.

Final *petits rouges* were downed, then they were off, straggling with dogs and pigs down the unpaved road, fanning off into favorite fields, towards cherished trees. Emile and Samson, who was full of honks and oinks this morning, made for the-little-forest-down-the-slope. He was not the only man to do so: François with his black pig was going there too.

'Plenty of room for both of us, I think,' said François pleasantly.

That was true, and Emile agreed. He gave Samson a kick as they entered the forest, letting the cleats of his boot land solidly on Samson's backside, trying to convey that there was a greater urgency about the truffle-hunting today. Samson turned irritably and made a feint at Emile's legs, but bent to his work and snuffled at the foot of a tree. Then he abandoned the tree.

François, quite a distance away among the trees, was already digging with his fork, Emile saw. Emile gave Samson his head and the pig lumbered on, nose to the ground.

'Hwun-nf! – *Ha-wun-nf! Umpf!*' Samson had found a good cache and he knew it.

So did Emile. Emile tied Samson up, and dug as fast as he could. The ground was harder than a fortnight ago.

The aroma of truffles came stronger to Samson as Emile unearthed them. He strained at his rope, recoiled and charged forward again. There was a dull snap – and he was free! His leather

collar had broken. Samson plunged his snout into the hollowed earth
and began to eat with snorts of contentment.

'*Son of a bitch! — Merde!*' Emile gave Samson a mighty kick in his
right ham. Goddamn the old belt! Emile had no choice but to waste
precious minutes untying the rope from the tree and tying it again
around the neck of Samson, who made every effort to evade him.
That was to say, Samson rotated in a circle around the truffle hoard,
keeping his muzzle on the same spot, eating. Emile got the rope tied,
and at once tugged and cursed with all his might.

François's distant but loud laughter did not make Emile feel any
more kindly towards Samson. Damn the beast, he'd eaten at least
half the find here! Emile kicked Samson where his testicles would
have been, if Emile had not had them removed at the same time as
Samson's lower tusks.

Samson retaliated by charging Emile at knee level. Emile fell
forward over the rushing pig, and barely had time to protect his
face from the ground. The pain in his knees was agonizing. He was
afraid for a few seconds that his legs had been broken. Then he heard
François yelling with indignation. Samson was loose again and was
invading François's place.

'Hey, Emile! You're going to be disqualified! Get this goddamn
pig away from me! Get him — or I'll *shoot* him!'

Emile knew that François had no gun. Emile got to his feet
carefully. His legs were not broken, but his eyes felt awful from the
shock, and he knew he'd have a pair of prize shiners by tomorrow.
'*Damn* you, Samson, get the hell away!' Emile yelled, trudging
towards François and the two pigs. François was now whacking
at Samson with a tree branch he had found, and Emile couldn't
blame François.

'A hell of a way to . . . ' François's words were lost.

Emile had never been very chummy with François Malbert, and
he knew François would try to disqualify him, if he possibly could,
mainly because Samson was an excellent truffler and presented a
threat. This thought, however, concentrated Emile's anger more on

Samson for the moment than on François. Emile pulled at Samson's rope, yanked it hard, and François came down at the same time with the branch on Samson's head, and the branch broke.

Samson charged again, and Emile, suddenly nimble in desperation, looped the end of the rope a couple of times around a tree. Samson was jerked off his feet.

'No use digging any more here! That's not fair!' François said, indicating his half-eaten truffle bed.

'Ah, oui? It's an *accident!*' Emile retorted.

But François was trudging away, in the direction of the Café de la Chasse.

Emile now had the little forest to himself. He set about gathering what was left of François's truffle find. But he was afraid he was going to be disqualified. All because of Samson.

'Now get to work, you bastard!' Emile said to Samson, and hit him on the rump with a short piece of the branch that had broken.

Samson only stared at Emile, facing him, in case another blow was coming.

Emile groped for a piece of cheese in his sack, and tossed it on the ground as an act of appeasement, also to whet Samson's appetite, perhaps. Samson did look as angry as a pig could look.

Samson snuffed up the cheese.

'Let's go, boy!' Emile said.

Samson got moving, but very slowly. He simply walked. He wasn't even sniffing the ground. Emile fancied that Samson's shoulders were hunched in anger, that he was ready to charge again. But that was absurd, he told himself. Emile pulled Samson towards a promising birch tree.

Samson smelled the truffles in Emile's sack. His saliva was still running from the truffles he had gobbled up from the hole in the ground. Samson turned with agility and pressed his nose against the sack at Emile's side. Samson had stood up a little on his hind legs, and his weight knocked Emile down. Samson poked his nose into the sack. What a blissful smell! He began to eat. There was cheese too.

Emile, on his feet now, jabbed at Samson with his fork, hard enough to break the skin in three places where the tines sank. '*Get away, you bastard!*'

Samson did leave the sack, but only to rush at Emile. *Crack!* He hit Emile's knees again. The man lay on the ground, trying to bring his fork into position for striking, and in a flash Samson charged.

Somehow the pig's belly hit Emile in the face, or the point of his chin, and Emile was knocked half unconscious. He shook his head, and made sure he still had a good grip on his fork. He had suddenly realized that Samson could and might kill him, if he didn't protect himself.

'*Au secours!*' Emile yelled. '*Help!*'

Emile brandished the fork at Samson, intending to scare the pig off while he got to his feet.

Samson had no intention, except to protect himself. He saw the fork as an enemy, a very clear challenge, and he blindly attacked it. The fork went askew and dropped as if limp. Samson's front hooves stood triumphant on Emile's abdomen. Samson snorted. And Emile gasped, but only a few times.

The awful pink and damp nose of the pig was almost in Emile's face, and he recalled from childhood many pigs he had known, pigs who had seemed to him as gigantic as this Samson now crushing the breath out of him. Pigs, sows, piglets of all patterns and coloring seemed to combine and become this one monstrous Samson who most certainly – Emile now knew it – was going to kill him, just by standing on him. The fork was out of reach. Emile flailed his arms with his last strength, but the pig wouldn't budge. And Emile could not gasp one breath of air. Not even an animal any longer, Emile thought, this pig, but an awful, evil force in a most hideous form. Those tiny, stupid eyes in the grotesque flesh! Emile tried to call out and found that he couldn't make as much noise as a small bird.

When the man became quiet, Samson stepped off his body and nuzzled him in the side to get at the truffle sack again. Samson was calming down a bit. He no longer held his breath, or panted, as he had done alternately for the last minutes, but began to breathe normally. The heavenly scent of truffles further soothed him. He snuffled, sighed, inhaled, ate, his snout and tongue seeking out the last morsels from the corners of the khaki sack. And all his own gleanings! But this thought came not at all clearly to Samson. In fact, he had a vague feeling that he was going to be shooed away from his banquet, yet who was there to shoo him away now?

This very special sack, into which he had seen so many black truffles vanishing, out of which had come measly, contemptible crumbs of yellow cheese – all that was finished, and now the sack was his. Samson even ate some of the cloth.

Then, still chewing, he urinated. He listened, and looked around, and felt quite secure and in command of things – at least of himself. He could walk anywhere he chose, and he chose to walk away from the village of Cassouac. He trotted for a bit, then walked, and was sidetracked by the scent of still more truffles. It took Samson some time to dig them up, but it was glorious work, and his reward was his own, every gritty, superb crinkle. Samson came to a stream, a little crusty at the edges with ice, and drank. He went on, dragging his rope, not caring where he went. He was hungry again.

Hunger impelled him towards a group of low buildings, whence he smelled chicken dung and the manure of horses or cows. Samson strolled a little diffidently into the cobbled courtyard where some pigeons and chickens walked about. They made way for Samson. Samson was used to that. He was looking for a feed trough. He found a trough with some wet bread in it, a low trough. He ate. Then he collapsed against a stack of hay, half sheltered by a roof. It was now dark.

From the two lighted windows in the lower part of the house near by came music and voices, sounds of an ordinary household.

As dawn broke, the wandering, pecking chickens in the courtyard and near Samson did not really awaken him. He dozed on, and only opened one eye sleepily when he heard the gritty tread of a man.

'Ho-ha! What have we got here?' murmured the farmer, peering at the enormous pale pig lying in his hay. A rope dangled from the pig's neck, a good sturdy rope, he saw, and the pig was an even more splendid specimen of his kind. Whom did he belong to? The farmer knew all the pigs in the district, knew their types, anyway. This one must have come from a long way. The end of the rope was frayed.

The farmer Alphonse decided to keep his mouth shut. After more or less hiding Samson for a few days in a back field which was enclosed, Alphonse brought him forward once more and let him join the pigs he had, all black ones. He wasn't concealing the white pig, he reasoned, and if anyone came looking for such a pig, he could say the pig had simply wandered on to his land, which was true. Then he would give the pig back, of course, after being sure the inquirer knew that the pig's lower tusks had been sawn off, that he'd been castrated and so forth. Meanwhile Alphonse debated selling him on the market or trying him out at truffle-hunting before the winter was over. He'd try the truffling first.

Samson grew a little fatter, and dominated the other pigs, two sows and their piglets. The food was slightly different and more abundant than at the other farm. Then came the day – an ordinary working day, it seemed to Samson from the look of the farm – when he was taken on a lead to go to the woods for truffles. Samson trotted along in good spirits. He intended to eat a few truffles today, besides finding them for the man. Somewhere in his brain, Samson was already thinking that he must from the start show this man that he was not to be bossed.

SLOWLY, SLOWLY
IN THE WIND

Edward (Skip) Skipperton spent most of his life in a thunder-ous rage. It was his nature. He had been full of temper as a boy, and as a man impatient with people's slowness or stupidity or inefficiency. Now Skipperton was fifty-two. His wife had left him two years ago, unable to stand his tantrums any longer. She had met a most tranquil university professor from Boston, had divorced Skipperton on the grounds of incompatibility, and married the professor. Skipperton had been determined to get custody of their daughter, Margaret, then fifteen, and with clever lawyers and on the grounds that his wife had deserted him for another man, Skipperton had succeeded. A few months after the divorce, Skipperton had a heart attack, a real stroke with hemi-paralysis from which he mirac-ulously recovered in six months, but his doctors gave him warning.

'Skip, it's life or death. You quit smoking and drinking and right now, or you're a dead man before your next birthday.' That was from his heart specialist.

'You owe it to Margaret,' said his GP. 'You ought to retire, Skip. You've plenty of money. You're in the wrong profession for your nature – granted you've made a success of it. But what's left of your life is more important, isn't it? Why not become a gentleman farmer, something like that?'

Skipperton was a management adviser. Behind the scenes of big business, Skipperton was well known. He worked freelance. Companies on the brink sent for him to reorganize, reform, throw out – anything Skip advised went. 'I go in and kick the ass off 'em!' was the inelegant way Skip described his work when he was interviewed, which was not often, because he preferred a ghostly role.

Skipperton bought Coldstream Heights in Maine, a seven-acre farm with a modernized farmhouse, and hired a local man called Andy Humbert to live and work on the place. Skipperton also bought some of the machinery the former owner had to sell, but not all of it, because he didn't want to turn himself into a full-time farmer. The doctors had recommended a little exercise and no strain of any kind. They had known that Skip wouldn't and couldn't at once cut all his connections with the businesses he had helped in the past. He might have to make an occasional trip to Chicago or Dallas, but he was officially retired.

Margaret was transferred from her private school in New York to a Swiss boarding school. Skipperton knew and liked Switzerland, and had bank accounts there.

Skipperton did stop drinking and smoking. His doctors were amazed at his willpower – and yet it was just like Skip to stop overnight, like a soldier. Now Skip chewed his pipes, and went through a stem in a week. He went through two lower teeth, but got them capped in steel in Bangor. Skipperton and Andy kept a couple of goats to crop the grass, and one sow who was pregnant when Skip bought her, and who now had twelve piglets. Margaret wrote filial letters saying she liked Switzerland and that her French was improving no end. Skipperton now wore flannel shirts with no tie, low boots that laced, and woodsmen's jackets. His appetite had improved, and he had to admit he felt better.

The only thorn in his side – and Skipperton had to have one to feel normal – was the man who owned some adjacent land, one

Peter Frosby, who wouldn't sell a stretch Skipperton offered to buy at three times the normal price. This land sloped down to a little river called the Coldstream, which in fact separated part of Skipperton's property from Frosby's to the north, and Skipperton didn't mind that. He was interested in the part of the river nearest him and in view from Coldstream Heights. Skipperton wanted to be able to fish a little, to be able to say he owned that part of the landscape and had riparian rights. But old Frosby didn't want anybody fishing in his stream, Skipperton had been told by the agents, even though Frosby's house was upstream and out of sight of Skipperton's.

The week after Peter Frosby's rejection, Skipperton invited Frosby to his house. 'Just to get acquainted – as neighbors,' Skipperton said on the telephone to Frosby. By now Skipperton had been living at Coldstream Heights for four months.

Skipperton had his best whiskey and brandy, cigars and cigarettes – all the things he couldn't enjoy himself – on hand when Frosby arrived in a dusty but new Cadillac, driven by a young man whom Frosby introduced as his son, Peter.

'The Frosbys don't sell their land,' Frosby told Skipperton.'We've had the same land for nearly three hundred years, and the river's always been ours.' Frosby, a skinny but strong-looking man with cold gray eyes puffed his cigar daintily and after ten minutes hadn't finished his first whiskey. 'Can't see why you want it.'

'A little fishing,' Skipperton said, putting on a pleasant smile. 'It's in view of my house. Just to be able to wade, maybe, in the summer.' Skipperton looked at Peter Junior, who sat with folded arms beside and behind his father. Skipperton was backed only by shambly Andy, a good enough handyman, but not part of his dynasty. Skipperton would have given anything (except his life) to have been holding a straight whiskey in one hand and a good cigar in the other. 'Well, I'm sorry,' Skipperton said finally. 'But I think you'll agree the price I offer isn't bad – twenty thousand cash for about two hundred yards of riparian rights. Doubt if you'll get it again – in your lifetime.'

'Not interested in my lifetime,' Frosby said with a faint smile. 'I've got a son here.'

The son was a handsome boy with dark hair and sturdy shoulders, taller than his father. His arms were still folded across his chest, as if to illustrate his father's negative attitude. He had unbent only briefly to light a cigarette which he had soon put out. Still, Peter Junior smiled as he and his father were leaving, and said:

'Nice job you've done with the Heights, Mr Skipperton. Looks better than it did before.'

'Thank you,' Skip said, pleased. He had installed good leather-upholstered furniture, heavy floor-length curtains, and brass firedogs and tongs for the fireplace.

'Nice old-fashioned touches,' Frosby commented in what seemed to Skipperton a balance between compliment and sneer. 'We haven't seen a scarecrow around here in maybe – almost before my time, I think.'

'I like old-fashioned things – like fishing,' Skipperton said. 'I'm trying to grow corn out there. Somebody told me the land was all right for corn. That's where a scarecrow belongs, isn't it? In a cornfield?' He put on as friendly a manner as he could, but his blood was boiling. A mule-stubborn Maine man, Frosby, sitting on several hundred acres that his more forceful ancestors had acquired for him.

Frosby Junior was peering at a photograph of Maggie, which stood in a silver frame on the hall table. She had been only thirteen or fourteen when the picture had been taken, but her slender face framed in long dark hair showed the clean-cut nose and brows, the subtle smile that would turn her into a beauty one day. Maggie was nearly eighteen now, and Skip's expectations were being confirmed.

'Pretty girl,' said Frosby Junior, turning towards Skipperton, then glancing at his father, because they were all lingering in the hall.

Skipperton said nothing. The meeting had been a failure. Skipperton wasn't used to failures. He looked into Frosby's greenish-gray eyes and said, 'I've one more idea. Suppose we make an arrangement that I rent the land for the duration of my life, and then it goes to you – or your son. I'll give you five thousand a year. Want to think it over?'

Frosby put on another frosty smile. 'I think not, Mr Skipperton. Thanks anyway.'

'You might talk to your lawyer about it. No rush on my part.'

Frosby now chuckled. 'We know as much about law as the lawyers here. We know our boundaries anyway. Nice to meet you, Mr Skipperton. Thank you for the whiskey and – good-bye.'

No one shook hands. The Cadillac moved off.

'Damn the bastard,' Skipperton muttered to Andy, but he smiled. Life was a game, after all. You won sometimes, you lost sometimes.

It was early May. The corn was in, and Skipperton had spotted three or four strong green shoots coming through the beige, well-turned earth. That pleased him, made him think of American Indians, the ancient Mayans. Corn! And he had a classic scarecrow that he and Andy had knocked together a couple of weeks ago. They had dressed the crossbars in an old jacket, and the two sticks – nailed to the upright – in brown trousers. Skip had found the old clothes in the attic. A straw hat jammed onto the top and secured with a nail completed the picture.

Skip went off to San Francisco for a five-day operation on an aeronautics firm which was crippled by a lawsuit, scared to death by unions and contract pull-outs. Skip left them with more redundancies, three vice-presidents fired, but he left them in better shape, and collected fifty thousand for his work.

By way of celebrating his achievement and the oncoming summer that would bring Maggie, Skip shot one of Frosby's hunting dogs which had swum the stream onto his property to retrieve a bird. Skipperton had been waiting patiently at his bedroom window upstairs, knowing a shoot was on from the sound of guns. Skip had his binoculars and a rifle of goodly range. Let Frosby complain! Trespassing was trespassing.

Skip was almost pleased when Frosby took him to court over

the dog. Andy had buried the dog, on Skipperton's orders, but Skipperton readily admitted the shooting. And the judge ruled in Skipperton's favor.

Frosby went pale with anger. 'It may be the law but it's not human. It's not fair.'

And a lot of good it did Frosby to say that!

Skipperton's corn grew high as the scarecrow's hips, and higher. Skip spent a lot of time up in his bedroom, binoculars and loaded rifle at hand, in case anything else belonging to Frosby showed itself on his land.

'Don't hit me,' Andy said with an uneasy laugh. 'You're shooting on the edge of the cornfield there, and now and then I weed it, y'know.'

'You think there's something wrong with my eyesight?' Skip replied.

A few days later Skip proved there was nothing wrong with his eyesight, when he plugged a gray cat stalking a bird or a mouse in the high grass this side of the stream. Skip did it with one shot. He wasn't even sure the cat belonged to Frosby.

This shot produced a call in person from Frosby Junior the following day.

'It's just to ask a question, Mr Skipperton. My father and I heard a shot yesterday, and last night one of our cats didn't come back at night to eat, and not this morning either. Do you know anything about that?' Frosby Junior had declined to take a seat.

'I shot the cat. It was on my property,' Skipperton said calmly.

'But the cat – What harm was the cat doing?' The young man looked steadily at Skipperton.

'The law is the law. Property is property.'

Frosby Junior shook his head. 'You're a hard man, Mr Skipperton.' Then he departed.

Peter Frosby served a summons again, and the same judge ruled that in accordance with old English law and also American law, a cat was a rover by nature, not subject to constraint as was a dog. He gave Skipperton the maximum fine of one hundred dollars, and a warning not to use his rifle so freely in future.

That annoyed Skipperton, though of course he could and did laugh at the smallness of the fine. If he could think of something else annoying, something really *telling*, old Frosby might relent and at least lease some of the stream, Skip thought.

But he forgot the feud when Margaret came. Skip fetched her at the airport in New York, and they drove up to Maine. She looked taller to Skip, more filled out, and there were roses in her cheeks. She was a beauty, all right!

'Got a surprise for you at home,' Skip said.

'Um-m – a horse maybe? I told you I learned to jump this year, didn't I?'

Had she? Skip said, 'Yes. Not a horse, no.'

Skip's surprise was a red Toyota convertible. He had remembered at least that Maggie's school had taught her to drive. She was thrilled, and flung her arms around Skip's neck.

'You're a darling, Daddy! And you know, you're looking *very* well!'

Margaret had been to Coldstream Heights for two weeks at Easter, but now the place looked more cared for. She and Skip had arrived around midnight, but Andy was still up watching television in his own little house on the grounds, and Maggie insisted on going over to greet him. Skip was gratified to see Andy's eyes widen at the sight of her.

Skip and Maggie tried the new car out the next day. They drove to a town some twenty miles away and had lunch. That afternoon, back at the house, Maggie asked if her father had a fishing rod, just a simple one, so she could try the stream. Skip of course had all kinds of rods, but he had to tell her she couldn't, and he explained why, and explained that he had even tried to rent part of the stream.

'Frosby's a real s.o.b., 'Skip said. 'Won't give an inch.'

'Well, never mind, Daddy. There's lots else to do.'

Maggie was the kind of girl who enjoyed taking walks, reading or fussing around in the house rearranging little things so that they looked prettier. She did these things while Skip was on the telephone sometimes for an hour or so with Dallas or Detroit.

Skipperton was a bit surprised one day when Maggie arrived in her Toyota around 7 p.m. with a catch of three trout on a string. She was barefoot, and the cuffs of her blue dungarees were damp. 'Where'd you get those?' Skip asked, his first thought being that she'd taken one of his rods and fished the stream against his instructions.

'I met the boy who lives there,' Maggie said. 'We were both buying gas, and he introduced himself – said he'd seen my photograph in your house. Then we had a coffee in the diner there by the gas station—'

'The Frosby boy?'

'Yes. He's awfully nice, Daddy. Maybe it's only the father who's not nice. Anyway Pete said, "Come on and fish with me this afternoon," so I did. He said his father stocks the river farther up.'

'I don't – Frankly, Maggie, I *don't* want you associating with the Frosbys!'

'There's only two.' Maggie was puzzled. 'I barely met his father. They've got quite a nice house, Daddy.'

'I've had unpleasant dealings with old Frosby, I told you, Maggie. It just isn't fitting if you get chummy with the son. Do me this one favor this summer, Maggie doll.' That was his name for her in the moments he wanted to feel close to her, wanted her to feel close to him.

The very next day, Maggie was gone from the house for nearly three hours, and Skip noticed it. She had said she wanted to go to the village to buy sneakers, and she was wearing the sneakers when she came home, but Skip wondered why it had taken her three hours to make a five-mile trip. With enormous effort, Skip refrained from asking a question. Then Saturday morning, Maggie said there was a dance in Keensport, and she was going.

'And I have a suspicion who you're going with,' Skip said, his heart beginning to thump with adrenaline.

'I'm going alone, I swear it, Daddy. Girls don't have to be escorted any more. I could go in blue jeans, but I'm not. I've got some white slacks.'

Skipperton realized that he could hardly forbid her to go to a dance. But he damn well knew the Frosby boy would be there, and would probably meet Maggie at the entrance. 'I'll be glad when you go back to Switzerland.'

Skip knew what was going to happen. He could see it a mile away. His daughter was 'infatuated,' and he could only hope that she got over it, that nothing happened before she had to go back to school (another whole month), because he didn't want to keep her prisoner in the house. He didn't want to look absurd in his own eyes, even in simpleminded Andy's eyes, by laying down the law to her.

Maggie got home evidently very late that night, and so quietly Skip hadn't wakened, though he had stayed up till 2 a.m. and meant to listen for her. At breakfast, Maggie looked fresh and radiant, rather to Skip's surprise.

'I suppose the Frosby boy was at the dance last night?'

Maggie, diving into bacon and eggs, said, 'I don't know what you've got against him, Daddy – just because his father didn't want to sell land that's been in their family for ages!'

'I don't want you to fall in love with a country bumpkin! I've sent you to a good school. You've got background – or at least I intend to give you some!'

'Did you know Pete had three years at Harvard – and he's taking a correspondence course in electronic engineering?'

'Oh! I suppose he's learning computer programming? Easier than shorthand!'

Maggie stood up. 'I'll be eighteen in another month, Daddy. I don't want to be told whom I can see and can't see.'

Skip got up too and roared at her. *'They're not my kind of people or yours!'*

Maggie left the room.

In the next days, Skipperton fumed and went through two or

three pipe stems. Andy noticed his unease, Skipperton knew, but Andy made no comment. Andy spent his nonworking hours alone, watching drivel on his television. Skip was rehearsing a speech to Maggie as he paced his land, glancing at the sow and piglets, at Andy's neat kitchen-garden, not seeing anything. Skip was groping for a lever, the kind of weapon he had always been able to find in business affairs that would force things his way. He couldn't send Maggie back to Switzerland, even though her school stayed open in summer for girls whose home was too far away to go back to. If he threatened not to send her back to school, he was afraid Maggie wouldn't mind. Skipperton maintained an apartment in New York, and had two servants who slept in, but he knew Maggie wouldn't agree to go there, and Skip didn't want to go to New York either. He was too interested in the immediate scene in which he sensed a battle coming.

Skipperton had arrived at nothing by the following Saturday, a week after the Keensport dance, and he was exhausted. That Saturday evening, Maggie said she was going to a party at the house of someone called Wilmers, whom she had met at the dance. Skip asked her for the address, and Maggie scribbled it on the hall telephone pad. Skip had reason to have asked for it, because by Sunday morning Maggie hadn't come home. Skip was up at seven, nervous as a cat and in a rage still at 9 a.m., which he thought a polite enough hour to telephone on Sunday morning, though it had cost him much to wait that long.

An adolescent boy's voice said that Maggie had been there, yes, but she had left pretty early.

'Was she alone?'

'No, she was with Pete Frosby.'

'That's all I wanted to know,' said Skip, feeling the blood rush to his face as if he were hemorrhaging. '*Oh!* Wait! Do you know where they went?'

'Sure don't.'

'My daughter went in her car?'

'No, Pete's. Maggie's car's still here.'

Skip thanked the boy and put the phone down shakily, but he was shaking only from energy that was surging through every nerve and muscle. He picked up the telephone and dialed the Frosby home.

Old Frosby answered.

Skipperton identified himself, and asked if his daughter was possibly there?

'No, she's not, Mr Skipperton.'

'Is your son there? I'd like—'

'No, he doesn't happen to be in just now.'

'What do you mean? He was there and went out?'

'Mr Skipperton, my son has his own ways, his own room, his own key – his own life. I'm not about—'

Skipperton put the telephone down suddenly. He had a bad nose-bleed, and it was dripping onto the table edge. He ran to get a wet towel.

Maggie was not home by Sunday evening or Monday morning, and Skipperton was reluctant to notify the police, appalled by the thought that her name might be linked with the Frosbys', if the police found her with the son somewhere. Tuesday morning, Skip was enlightened. He had a letter from Maggie, written from Boston. It said that she and Pete had run away to be married, and to avoid 'unpleasant scenes.'

> . . . Though you may think this is sudden, we do love each other and are sure of it. I did not really want to go back to school, Daddy. I will be in touch in about a week. Please don't try to find me. I have seen Mommie, but we are not staying with her. I was sorry to leave my nice new car, but the car is all right.
>
> Love always,
> Maggie

For two days Skipperton didn't go out of the house, and hardly ate. He felt three-quarters dead. Andy was very worried about him, and finally persuaded Skipperton to ride to the village with him, because they needed to buy a few things. Skipperton went, sitting like an upright corpse in the passenger seat.

While Andy went to the drugstore and the butcher's, Skipperton sat in the car, his eyes glazed with his own thoughts. Then an approaching figure on the sidewalk made Skipperton's eyes focus. Old Frosby! Frosby walked with a springy tread for his age, Skip thought. He wore a new tweed suit, black felt hat, and he had a cigar in his hand. Skipperton hoped Frosby wouldn't see him in the car, but Frosby did.

Frosby didn't pause in his stride, just smiled his obnoxious, thin-lipped little smile and nodded briefly, as if to say—

Well, Skip *knew* what Frosby might have wanted to say, what he had said with that filthy smile. Skip's blood seethed, and Skip began to feel like his old self again. He was standing on the sidewalk, hands in his pockets and feet apart, when Andy reappeared.

'What's for dinner tonight, Andy? I've got an appetite!'

That evening, Skipperton persuaded Andy to take not only Saturday night off, but to stay overnight somewhere, if he wished. 'Give you a couple of hundred bucks for a little spree, boy. You've earned it.' Skip forced three hundred-dollar bills into Andy's hand. 'Take off Monday too, if you feel like it. I'll manage.'

Andy left Saturday evening in the pick-up for Bangor.

Skip then telephoned old Frosby. Frosby answered, and Skipperton said, 'Mr Frosby, it's time we made a truce, under the circumstances. Don't you think so?'

Frosby sounded surprised, but he agreed to come Sunday morning around eleven for a talk. Frosby arrived in the same Cadillac, alone.

And Skipperton wasted no time. He let Frosby knock, opened the door for him, and as soon as Frosby was inside, Skip came down on his head with a rifle butt. He dragged Frosby to the hall to make sure the job was finished: the hall was uncarpeted, and Skip wanted no blood on the rugs. Vengeance was sweet to Skip, and he almost smiled. He removed Frosby's clothes, and wrapped his body in three or four burlap sacks which he had ready. Then he burnt Frosby's clothing in the fireplace, where he had a small fire already crackling. Frosby's wristwatch and wallet and two rings Skip put aside in a drawer to deal with later.

He had decided that broad daylight was the best time to carry out his idea, better than night when an oddly playing flashlight that he would have had to use might have caught someone's eye. So Skip put one arm around Frosby's body and dragged him up the field towards his scarecrow. It was a haul of more than half a mile. Skip had some rope and a knife in his back pockets. He cut down the old scarecrow, cut the strings that held the clothing to the cross, dressed Frosby in the old trousers and jacket, tied a burlap bag around his head and face, and jammed the hat on him. The hat wouldn't stay without being tied on, so Skip did this after punching holes in the brim of the hat with his knife point. Then Skip picked up his burlap bags and made his way back towards his house down the slope with many a backward look to admire his work, and many a smile. The scarecrow looked almost the same as before. He had solved a problem a lot of people thought difficult: what to do with the body. Furthermore, he could enjoy looking at it through his binoculars from his upstairs window.

Skip burnt the burlap bags in his fireplace, made sure that even the shoe soles had burnt to soft ash. When the ashes were cooler, he'd look for buttons and the belt buckle and remove them. He took a fork, went out beyond the pig run and buried the wallet (whose papers he had already burnt), the wristwatch and the rings about three feet deep. It was in a patch of stringy grass, unused for anything except the goats, not a place in which anyone would ever likely do any gardening.

Then Skip washed his face and hands, ate a thick slice of roast beef, and put his mind to the car. It was by now half past twelve. Skip didn't know if Frosby had a servant, someone expecting him for lunch or not, but it was safer to assume he had. Skip's aversion to Frosby had kept him from asking Maggie any questions about his household. Skip got into Frosby's car, now with a kitchen towel in his back pocket to wipe off fingerprints, and drove to some woods he knew from having driven past them many times. An unpaved lane went off the main road into these woods, and into this Skip turned. Thank God, nobody in sight, not a woodsman, not a picnicker. Skip stopped the car and got out, wiped the steering wheel, even the keys, the door, then walked back towards the road.

He was more than an hour getting home. He had found a long stick, the kind called a stave by the wayfarers of old, Skip thought, and he trudged along with the air of a nature-lover, a bird-watcher, for the benefit of the people in the few cars that passed him. He didn't glance at any of the cars. It was still Sunday dinnertime.

The local police telephoned that evening around seven, and asked if they could come by. Skipperton said of course.

He had removed the buttons and buckle from the fireplace ashes. A woman had telephoned around 1:30, saying she was calling from the Frosby residence (Skip assumed she was a servant) to ask if Mr Frosby was there. Skipperton told her that Mr Frosby had left his house a little after noon.

'Mr Frosby intended to go straight home, do you think?' the plump policeman asked Skipperton. The policeman had some rank like sergeant, Skipperton supposed, and he was accompanied by a younger policeman.

'He didn't say anything about where he was going,' Skipperton replied. 'And I didn't notice which way his car went.'

The policeman nodded, and Skip could see he was on the brink of saying something like, 'I understand from Mr Frosby's housekeeper that you and he weren't on the best of terms,' but the cop didn't say anything, just looked around Skip's living room, glanced around his front and back yards in a puzzled way, then both policemen took their leave.

Skip was awakened around midnight by the ring of the telephone at his bedside. It was Maggie calling from Boston. She and Pete had heard about the disappearance of Pete's father.

'Daddy, they said he'd just been to see you this morning. What happened?'

'Nothing happened. I invited him for a friendly talk – and it was friendly. After all we're fathers-in-law now . . . Honey, how do I know where he went?'

Skipperton found it surprisingly easy to lie about Frosby. In a primitive way his emotions had judged, weighed the situation, and told Skip that he was right, that he had exacted a just revenge. Old Frosby might have exerted some control over his son, and he hadn't. It had cost Skip his daughter – because that was the way Skip saw it, Maggie was lost to him. He saw her as a provincial-to-be, mother-to-be of children whose narrow-mindedness, inherited from the Frosby clan, would surely out.

Andy arrived next morning, Monday. He had already heard the story in the village, and also the police had found Mr Frosby's car not far away in the woods, Andy said. Skip feigned mild surprise on hearing of the car. Andy didn't ask any questions. And suppose he discovered the scarecrow? Skip thought a little money would keep Andy quiet. The corn was all picked up there, only a few inferior ears remained, destined for the pigs. Skipperton picked them himself Monday afternoon, while Andy tended the pigs and goats.

Skipperton's pleasure now was to survey the cornfield from his upstairs bedroom with his 10x binoculars. He loved to see the wind tossing the cornstalk tops around old Frosby's corpse, loved to think of him, shrinking, drying up like a mummy in the wind. Twisting slowly, slowly in the wind, as a Nixon aide used to put it about the president's enemies. Frosby wasn't twisting, but he was hanging, in plain view. No buzzards came. Skip had been a little afraid of buzzards. The only thing that bothered him, once, was seeing one afternoon some schoolboys walking along a road far to the right (under which road the Coldstream flowed), and pointing to the scare-crow. Bracing himself against the window jamb, arms held tightly at his sides so the binoculars would be as steady as possible, Skip saw a couple of the small boys laughing. And had one held his nose? Surely not! They were nearly a mile away from the scarecrow! Still, they had paused, one boy stamped his foot, another shook his head and laughed.

How Skip wished he could hear what they were saying! Ten days had passed since Frosby's death. Rumors were rife, that old Frosby had been murdered for his money by someone he'd picked up to give a lift to, that he had been kidnapped and that a ransom note might still arrive. But suppose one of the schoolkids said to his father — or anyone — that maybe the dead body of Frosby was inside the scarecrow? This was just the kind of thing Skip might have thought of when he had been a small boy. Skip was consequently more afraid of the schoolkids than of the police.

And the police did come back, with a plainclothes detective. They looked over Skipperton's house and land — maybe looking for a recently dug patch, Skip thought. If so, they found none. They looked at Skip's two rifles and took their caliber and serial numbers.

'Just routine, Mr Skipperton,' said the detective.

'I understand,' said Skip.

That same evening Maggie telephoned and said she was at the Frosby house, and could she come over to see him?

'Why not? This is your house!' Skip replied.

'I never know what kind of mood you'll be in — or temper,' Maggie said when she arrived.

'I'm in a pretty *good* mood, I think,' Skipperton said. 'And I hope you're happy, Maggie — since what's done is done.'

Maggie was in her blue dungarees, sneakers, a familiar sweater. It was hard for Skip to realize that she was married. She sat with hands folded, looking down at the floor. Then she raised her eyes to him and said:

'Pete's very upset. We never would have stayed a week in Boston unless he'd been sure the police were doing all they could here. Was Mr Frosby — depressed? Pete didn't think so.'

Skip laughed. 'No! Best of spirits. Pleased with the marriage and all that.' Skip waited, but Maggie was silent. 'You're going to live at the Frosby place?'

'Yes.' Maggie stood up. 'I'd like to collect a few things, Daddy. I brought a suitcase.'

His daughter's coolness, her sadness, pained Skip. She had said something about visiting him often, not about his coming to see them – not that Skip would have gone.

'I know what's in that scarecrow,' said Andy one day, and Skip turned, binoculars in hand, to see Andy standing in the doorway of his bedroom.

'Do you? – And what're you going to do about it?' Skip asked, braced for anything. He had squared his shoulders.

'Nothin'. Nothin',' Andy replied with a smile.

Skip didn't know how to take that. 'I suppose you'd like some money, Andy? A little present – for keeping quiet?'

'No, sir,' Andy said quietly, shaking his head. His wind-wrinkled face bore a faint smile. 'I ain't that kind.'

What was Skip to make of it? He was used to men who liked money, more and more of it. Andy was different, that was true. Well, so much the better, if he didn't want money, Skip thought. It was cheaper. He also felt he could trust Andy. It was strange.

The leaves began to fall in earnest. Halloween was coming, and Andy removed the driveway gate in advance, just lifted it off its hinges, telling Skip that the kids would steal it if they didn't. Andy knew the district. The kids didn't do much harm, but it was trick or treat at every house. Skip and Andy made sure they had lots of nickels and quarters on hand, corn candy, licorice sticks, even a couple of pumpkins in the window, faces cut in them by Andy, to show any comers that they were in the right spirit. Then on Halloween night, nobody knocked on Skip's door. There was a party at Coldstream, at the Frosbys', Skip knew because the wind was blowing his way and he could hear the music. He thought of his daughter dancing, having a good time. Maybe people were wearing masks, crazy costumes. There'd be pumpkin pie with whipped cream, guessing games, maybe a treasure hunt. Skip was lonely, for the first time in his life.

Lonely. He badly wanted a scotch, but decided to keep his oath to himself, and having decided this, asked himself why? He put his hands flat down on his dresser top and gazed at his own face in the mirror. He saw creases running from the flanges of his nose down beside his mouth, wrinkles under his eyes. He tried to smile, and the smile looked phony. He turned away from the mirror.

At that instant, a spot of light caught his eyes. It was out the window, in the upward sloping field. A procession – so it seemed, maybe eight or ten figures – was walking up his field with flashlights or torches or both. Skip opened the window slightly. He was rigid with rage, and fear. They were on his land! They had no right! And they were kids, he realized. Even in the darkness, he could see by the procession's own torches that the figures were a lot shorter than adults' figures would be.

Skip whirled around, about to shout for Andy, and at once decided that he had better not. He ran downstairs and grabbed his own powerful flashlight. He didn't bother grabbing his jacket from a hook, though the night was crisp.

'*Hey!*' Skip yelled, when he had run several yards into the field. 'Get off my property! What're you doing walking up there!'

The kids were singing some crazy, high-pitched song, nobody singing on key. It was just a wild treble chant. Skip recognized the word 'scarecrow.'

'*We're going to burn the scarecrow . . .*' something like that.

'Hey, there! Off my land!' Skip fell, banged a knee, and scrambled up again. The kids had heard him, Skip was pretty sure, but they weren't stopping. Never before had anyone disobeyed Skip – except of course Maggie. '*Off my land!*'

The kids moved on like a black caterpillar with an orange headlight and a couple of other lights in its body. Certainly the last couple of kids had heard Skip, because he had seen them turn, then run to catch up with the others. Skip stopped running. The caterpillar was closer to the scarecrow than he was, and he was not going to be able to get there first.

Even as he thought this, a whoop went up. A scream! Another scream of mingled terror and delight shattered their chant. Hysteria broke out. What surely was a little girl's throat gave a cry as shrill as a dog whistle. Their hands must have touched the corpse, maybe touched bone, Skip thought.

Skip made his way back towards his own house, his flashlight pointed at the ground. It was worse than the police, somehow. Every kid was going to tell his parents what he had found. Skip knew he had come to the end. He had seen businessmen, seen a lot of men come to the end. He had known men who had jumped out of windows, who had taken overdoses.

Skip went at once to his rifle. It was in the living room downstairs. He put the muzzle in his mouth and pulled the trigger.

When the kids streaked down the field, heading for the road a few seconds later, Skip was dead. The kids had heard the shot, and thought someone was trying to shoot at them.

Andy heard the shot. He had also seen the procession marching up the field and heard Skipperton shouting. He understood what had happened. He turned his television set off, and made his way rather slowly towards the main house. He would have to call the police. That was the right thing to do. Andy made up his mind to say to the police that he didn't know a thing about the corpse in the scarecrow's clothes. He had been away some of that weekend after all.

SOMETHING YOU HAVE
TO LIVE WITH

'Don't forget to lock all the doors,' Stan said. 'Someone might think because the car's gone, nobody's home.'

'All the doors? You mean two. You haven't asked me anything – aesthetic, such as how the place looks now.'

Stan laughed. 'I suppose the pictures are all hung and the books are in the shelves.'

'Well, not quite, but your shirts and sweaters – and the kitchen. It looks – I'm happy, Stan. So is Cassie. She's walking around the place purring. See you tomorrow morning then. Around eleven, you said?'

'Around eleven. I'll bring stuff for lunch, don't worry.'

'Love to your mom. I'm glad she's better.'

'Thanks, darling.' Stan hung up.

Cassie, their ginger and white cat aged four, sat looking at Ginnie as if she had never seen a telephone before. Purring again. Dazed by all the space, Ginnie thought. Cassie began kneading the rug in an ecstasy of contentment, and Ginnie laughed.

Ginnie and Stan Brixton had bought a house in Connecticut after six years of New York apartments. Their furniture had been here for a week while they wound things up in New York, and yesterday had been the final move of smaller things like silverware, some dishes, a few pictures, suitcases, kitchen items and the cat. Stan had taken their son Freddie this morning to spend the night in New Hope, Pennsylvania, where Stan's mother lived. His mother had had a second heart attack and was recuperating at home. 'Every time I see her, I think it may be the last. You don't mind if I go, do you, Ginnie? It'll keep Freddie out of the way while you're fiddling around.' Ginnie hadn't minded.

Fiddling around was Stan's term for organizing and even cleaning. Ginnie thought she had done a good job since Stan and Freddie had taken off this morning. The lovely French blue and white vase which reminded Ginnie of Monet's paintings stood on the living-room bookcase now, even bearing red roses from the garden. Ginnie had made headway in the kitchen, installing things the way she wanted them, the way they would remain. Cassie had her litter pan ('What a euphemism, litter ought to mean a bed,' Stan said) in the downstairs john corner. They now had an upstairs bathroom also. The house was on a hill with no other houses around it for nearly a mile, not that they owned all the land around, but the land around was farmland. When she and Stan had seen the place in June, sheep and goats had been grazing not far away. They had both fallen in love with the house.

Stanley Brixton was a novelist and fiction critic, and Ginnie wrote articles and was now half through her second novel. Her first had been published but had had only modest success. You couldn't expect a smash hit with a first novel, Stan said, unless the publicity was extraordinary. Water under the bridge. Ginnie was more interested in her novel-in-progress. They had a mortgage on the house, and with her and Stan's freelance work they thought they could be independent of New York, at least independent of nine-to-five jobs. Stan had already published three books, adventure stories with a political slant. He was thirty-two and for three years had been overseas correspondent for a newspaper syndicate.

Ginnie picked up a piece of heavy twine from the living-room rug, and realized that her back hurt a little from the day's exertions. She had thought of switching on the TV, but the news was just over, she saw from her watch, and it might be better to go straight to bed and get up earlyish in the morning.

'Cassie?'

Cassie replied with a courteous, sustained, 'M-wah-h?'

'Hungry?' Cassie knew the word. 'No, you've had enough. Do you know you're getting middle-aged spread? Come on. Going up to bed with me?' Ginnie went to the front door, which was already locked by its automatic lock, but she put the chain on also. Yawning, she turned out the downstairs lights and climbed the stairs. Cassie followed her.

Ginnie had a quick bath, second of the day, pulled on a night-gown, brushed her teeth and got into bed. She at once realized she was too tired to pick up one of the English weeklies, political and Stan's favorites, which she had dropped by the bed to look at. She put out the lamp. *Home.* She and Stan had spent one night here last weekend during the big move. This was the first night she had been alone in the house, which still had no name. *Something like White Elephant maybe*, Stan had said. *You think of something.* Ginnie tried to think, an activity which made her instantly sleepier.

She was awakened by a crunching sound, like that of car tires on gravel. She raised up a little in bed. Had she heard it? Their driveway hadn't any gravel to speak of, just unpaved earth. But—

Wasn't that a *click*? From somewhere. Front, back? Or had it been a twig falling on the roof?

She had locked the doors, hadn't she?

Ginnie suddenly realized that she had not locked the back door. For another minute, as Ginnie listened, everything was silent. What a bore to go downstairs again! But she thought she had better do it, so she could honestly tell Stan that she had. Ginnie found the lamp switch and got out of bed.

By now she was thinking that any noise she had heard had been imaginary, something out of a dream. But Cassie followed her in a brisk, anxious way, Ginnie noticed.

The glow from the staircase light enabled Ginnie to find her way to the kitchen, where she switched on the strong ceiling light. She went at once to the back door and turned the Yale bolt. Then she listened. All was silent. The big kitchen looked exactly the same with its half modern, half old-fashioned furnishings – electric stove, big white wooden cupboard with drawers below, shelves above, double sink, a huge new fridge.

Ginnie went back upstairs, Cassie still following. Cassie was short for Cassandra, a name Stan had given her when she had been a kitten, because she had looked gloomy, unshakably pessimistic. Ginnie was drifting off to sleep again, when she heard a bump downstairs, as if someone had staggered slightly. She switched on the bedside lamp again, and a thrust of fear went through her when she saw Cassie rigidly crouched on the bed with her eyes fixed on the open bedroom door.

Now there was another bump from downstairs, and the unmistakable rustle of a drawer being slid out, and it could be only the dining room drawer where the silver was.

She had locked someone in with her!

Her first thought was to reach for the telephone and get the police, but the telephone was downstairs in the living room.

Go down and face it and threaten him with something – or them, she told herself. Maybe it was an adolescent kid, just a local kid who'd be glad to get off unreported, if she scared him a little. Ginnie jumped out of bed, put on Stan's bathrobe, a sturdy blue flannel thing, and tied the belt firmly. She descended the stairs. By now she heard more noises.

'Who's *there*?' she shouted boldly.

'Hum-hum. Just me, lady,' said a rather deep voice.

The living-room lights, the dining-room lights were full on.

In the dining room Ginnie was confronted by a stocking-hooded figure in what she thought of as motorcycle gear: black trousers, black boots, black plastic jacket. The stocking had slits cut in it for eyes. And the figure carried a dirty canvas bag like a railway mail-bag, and plainly into this the silverware had already gone, because the dining-room drawer gaped, empty. He must have been hiding in a corner of the dining room, Ginnie thought, when she had come down to lock the back door. The hooded figure shoved the drawer in carelessly, and it didn't quite close.

'Keep your mouth shut, and you won't get hurt. All right?' The voice sounded like that of a man of at least twenty-five.

Ginnie didn't see any gun or knife. 'Just what do you think you're doing?'

'What does it look like I'm doing?' And the man got on with his business. The two candlesticks from the dining-room table went into the bag. So did the silver table lighter.

Was there anyone else with him? Ginnie glanced towards the kitchen, but didn't see anyone, and no sound came from there. 'I'm going to call the police,' she said, and started for the living-room telephone.

'Phone's cut, lady. You better keep quiet, because no one can hear you around here, even if you scream.'

Was that true? Unfortunately it was true. Ginnie for a few seconds concentrated on memorizing the man's appearance: about five feet eight, medium build, maybe a bit slender, broad hands – but since the hands were in blue rubber gloves, were they broad? – rather big feet. Blond or brunette she couldn't tell, because of the stocking mask. Robbers like this usually bound and gagged people. Ginnie wanted to avoid that, if she could.

'If you're looking for money, there's not much in the house just now,' Ginnie said, 'except what's in my handbag upstairs, about thirty dollars. Go ahead and take it.'

'I'll get around to it,' he said laughing, prowling the living room now. He took the letter-opener from the coffee table, then Freddie's photograph from the piano, because the photograph was in a silver frame.

Ginnie thought of banging him on the head with – with what? She saw nothing heavy enough, portable, except one of the dining-room chairs. And if she failed to knock him out with the first swat? Was the telephone really cut? She moved towards the telephone in the corner.

'Don't go near the door. Stay in sight!'

'Ma-wow-wow-*wow*!' This from Cassie, a high-pitched wail that to Ginnie meant Cassie was on the brink of throwing up, but now the situation was different. Cassie looked ready to attack the man.

'Go back, Cassie, take it easy,' Ginnie said.

'I don't like cats,' the hooded man said over his shoulder.

There was not much else he could take from the living room, Ginnie thought. The pictures on the walls were too big. And what burglar was interested in pictures, at least pictures like these which were a few oils done by their painter friends, two or three water-colors – Was this really happening? Was a stranger picking up her mother's old sewing basket, looking inside, banging it down again? Taking the French vase, tossing the water and roses towards the fireplace? The vase went into the sack.

'What's upstairs?' The ugly head turned towards her. 'Let's go upstairs.'

'There's *nothing* upstairs!' Ginnie shrieked. She darted towards the telephone, knowing it would be cut, but wanting to see it with her own eyes – cut – though her hand was outstretched to use it. She saw the abruptly stopped wire on the floor, cut some four feet from the telephone.

The hood chuckled. 'Told you.'

A red flashlight stuck out of the back pocket of his trousers. He was going into the hall now, ready to take the stairs. The staircase light was on, but he pulled the flashlight from his pocket.

'Nothing *up* there, I tell you!' Ginnie found herself following him like a ninnie, holding up the hem of Stan's dressing gown so she wouldn't trip on the stairs.

'Cosy little nook!' said the hood, entering the bedroom. 'And what have we here? Anything of interest?'

The silver-backed brush and comb on the dresser were of interest, also the hand mirror, and these went into the bag, which was now dragging the floor.

'Aha! I like that thing!' He had spotted the heavy wooden box with brass corners which Stan used for cufflinks and handkerchiefs and a few white ties, but its size was apparently daunting the man in the hood, because he swayed in front of it and said, 'Be back for that.' He looked around for lighter objects, and in went Ginnie's black leather jewelry box, her Dunhill lighter from the bedside table. 'Ought to be glad I'm not raping you. Haven't the time.' The tone was jocular.

My God, Ginnie thought, you'd think Stan and I were rich! She had never considered herself and Stan rich, or thought that they had anything worth invading a house for. No doubt in New York they'd been lucky for six years – no robberies at all – because even a typewriter was valuable to a drug addict. No, they weren't rich, but he was taking all they had, all the *nice* things they'd tried over the years to accumulate. Ginnie watched him open her handbag, lift the dollar bills from her billfold. That was the least of it.

'If you think for one minute you're going to get away with this,' Ginnie said. 'In a small community like *this*? You haven't a prayer. If you don't leave those things here tonight, I'll report you so quick—'

'Oh, shut up, lady. Where's the other rooms here?'

Cassie snarled. She had followed them both up the stairs.

A black boot struck out sideways and caught the cat sharply in the ribs.

'*Don't touch that cat!*' Ginnie cried out.

Cassie sprang growling onto the man's boot top, at his knee.

Ginnie was astounded – and proud of Cassie – for a second.

'Pain in the ass!' said the hood, and with a gloved hand caught the cat by the loose skin on her back and flung her against a wall with a backhand swing. The cat dropped, panting, and the man stomped on her side and kicked her on the head.

'You *bastard*!' Ginnie screamed.

'So much for your stinking – yowlers!' said the beige hood, and kicked the cat once again. His voice had been husky with rage, and now he stalked with his flashlight into the hall, in quest of other rooms.

Dazed, stiff, Ginnie followed him.

The guest room had only a chest of drawers in it, empty, but the man slid out a couple of drawers anyway to have a look. Freddie's room had nothing but a bed and table. The hood wasted no time there.

From the hall, Ginnie looked into the bedroom at her cat. The cat twitched and was still. One foot had twitched. Ginnie stood rigid as a column of stone. She had just seen Cassie die, she realized.

'Back in a flash,' said the hooded man, briskly descending the stairs with his sack which was now so heavy he had to carry it on one shoulder.

Ginnie moved at last, in jerks, like someone awakening from an anesthetic. Her body and mind seemed not to be connected. Her hand reached for the stair rail and missed it. She was no longer afraid at all, though she did not consciously realize this. She simply kept following the hooded figure, her enemy, and would have kept on, even if he had pointed a gun at her. By the time she reached the kitchen, he was out of sight. The kitchen door was open, and a cool breeze blew in. Ginnie continued across the kitchen, looked left into the driveway, and saw a flashlight's beam swing as the man heaved the bag into a car. She heard the hum of two male voices. So he had a pal waiting for him!

And here he came back.

With sudden swiftness, Ginnie picked up a kitchen stool which had a square formica top and chromium legs. As soon as the hooded figure stepped onto the threshold of the kitchen, Ginnie swung the stool and hit him full on the forehead with the edge of the stool's seat.

Momentum carried the man forward, but he stooped, staggering, and Ginnie cracked him again on the top of the head with all her strength. She held two legs of the stool in her hands. He fell with a great thump and clatter onto the linoleum floor. Another whack for good measure on the back of the stockinged head. She felt pleased and relieved to see blood coming through the beige material.

'Frankie? — You okay? — *Frankie!*'

The voice came from the car outside.

Poised now, not at all afraid, Ginnie stood braced for the next arrival. She held a leg of the stool in her right hand, and her left supported the seat. She awaited, barely two feet from the open door, the sound of boots in the driveway, another figure in the doorway.

Instead, she heard a car motor start, saw a glow of its lights through the door. The car was backing down the drive.

Finally Ginnie set the stool down. The house was silent again. The man on the floor was not moving. Was he dead?

I don't care. I simply don't give a damn, Ginnie said inside herself.

But she did care. What if he woke up? What if he needed a doctor, a hospital right away? And there was no telephone. The nearest house was nearly a mile away, the village a good mile. Ginnie would have to walk it with a flashlight. Of course if she encountered a car, a car might stop and ask what was the matter, and then she could tell someone to fetch a doctor or an ambulance. These thoughts went through Ginnie's head in seconds, and then she returned to the facts. The fact was, he *might* be dead. Killed by her.

So was Cassie dead. Ginnie turned towards the living room. Cassie's death was more real, more important than the body at her feet which only might be dead. Ginnie drew a glass of water for herself at the kitchen sink.

Everything was silent outside. Now Ginnie was calm enough to realize that the robber's chum had thought it best to make a getaway. He probably wasn't coming back, not even with reinforcements. After all, he had the loot in his car — silverware, her jewelry box, all the nice things.

Ginnie stared at the long black figure on her kitchen floor. He hadn't moved at all. The right hand lay under him, the left arm was outstretched, upward. The stockinged head was turned slightly towards her, one slit showing. She couldn't see what was going on behind that crazy slit.

'Are you *awake?*' Ginnie said, rather loudly.

She waited.

She knew she would have to face it. Best to feel the pulse in the wrist, she thought, and at once forced herself to do this. She pulled the rubber glove down a bit, and gripped a blondish-haired wrist which seemed to her of astonishing breadth, much wider than Stan's wrist, anyway. She couldn't feel any pulse. She altered the place where she had put her thumb, and tried again. There was no pulse.

So she had murdered someone. The fact did not sink in.

Two thoughts danced in her mind: she would have to remove Cassie, put a towel or something around her, and she was not going to be able to sleep or even remain in this house with a corpse lying on the kitchen floor.

Ginnie got a dishtowel, a folded clean one from a stack on a shelf, took a second one, went to the hall and climbed the stairs. Cassie was now bleeding. Rather, she had bled. The blood on the carpet looked dark. One of Cassie's eyes projected from the socket. Ginnie gathered her as gently as if she were still alive and only injured, gathered up some intestines which had been pushed out, and enfolded her in a towel, opened the second towel and put that around her too. Then she carried Cassie to the living room, hesitated, then laid the cat's body to one side of the fireplace on the floor. By accident, a red rose lay beside Cassie.

Tackle the blood now, she told herself. She got a plastic bowl from the kitchen, drew some cold water and took a sponge. Upstairs, she went to work on hands and knees, changing the water in the bathroom. The task was soothing, as she had known it would be.

Next job: clothes on and find the nearest telephone. Ginnie kept moving, barely aware of what she was doing, and suddenly she was standing in the kitchen in blue jeans, sneakers, sweater and jacket with her billfold in a pocket. Empty billfold, she remembered. She had her house keys in her left hand. For no good reason, she decided to leave the kitchen light on. The front door was still locked, she realized. She found she had the flashlight in a jacket pocket too, and supposed she had taken it from the front hall table when she came down the stairs.

She went out, locked the kitchen door from the outside with a key, and made her way to the road.

No moon at all. She walked with the aid of the flashlight along the left side of the road towards the village, shone the torch once on her watch and saw that it was twenty past one. By starlight, by a bit of flashlight, she saw one house far to the left in a field, quite dark and so far away, Ginnie thought she might do better to keep on.

She kept on. Dark road. Trudging. Did *everybody* go to bed early around here?

In the distance she saw two or three white streetlights, the lights of the village. Surely there'd be a car before the village.

There wasn't a car. Ginnie was still trudging as she entered the village proper, whose boundary was marked by a neat white sign on either side of the road saying EAST KINDALE.

My God, Ginnie thought. *Is this true? Is this what I'm doing, what I'm going to say?*

Not a light showed in any of the neat, mostly white houses. There was not even a light at the Connecticut Yankee Inn, the only functioning hostelry and bar in town, Stan had remarked once. Nevertheless, Ginnie marched up the steps and knocked on the door. Then with her flashlight, she saw a brass knocker on the white door, and availed herself of that.

Rap-rap-rap!

Minutes passed. *Be patient*, Ginnie told herself. *You're overwrought.* But she felt compelled to rap again.

'Who's there?' a man's voice called.

'A neighbor! There's been an accident!'

Ginnie fairly collapsed against the figure who opened the door. It was a man in a plaid woolen bathrobe and pajamas. She might have collapsed also against a woman or a child.

Then she was sitting on a straight chair in a sort of living room. She had blurted out the story.

'We'll – we'll get the police right away, ma'am. Or an ambulance, as you say. But from what you say—' The man talking was in his sixties, and sleepy.

His wife, more efficient looking, had joined him to listen. She wore a dressing gown and pink slippers. 'Police, Jake. Man sounds dead from what the lady says. Even if he isn't, the police'll know what to do.'

'Hello, Ethel! That you?' the man said into the telephone. 'Listen, we need the police right away. You know the old Hardwick place? . . . Tell 'em to go there . . . No, *not* on fire. Can't explain now. But somebody'll be there to open the door in – in about five minutes.'

The woman pushed a glass of something into Ginnie's hand. Ginnie realized that her teeth were chattering. She was cold, though it wasn't cold outside. It was early September, she remembered.

'They're going to want to speak with you.' The man who had been in the plaid robe was now in trousers and a belted sports jacket. 'You'll have to tell them the time it happened and all that.'

Ginnie realized. She thanked the woman and went with the man to his car. It was an ordinary four-door, and Ginnie noticed a discarded Cracker Jack box on the floor of the passenger's seat as she got in.

A police car was in the drive. Someone was knocking on the back door, and Ginnie saw that she'd left the kitchen light on.

'Hya, Jake! What's up?' called a second policeman, getting out of the black car in the driveway.

'Lady had a house robbery,' the man with Ginnie explained. 'She thinks – Well, you've got the keys, haven't you, Mrs Brixton?'

'Oh yes, yes.' Ginnie fumbled for them. She was gasping again, and reminded herself that it was a time to keep calm, to answer questions accurately. She opened the kitchen door.

A policeman stooped beside the prone figure. 'Dead,' he said.

'The – Mrs Brixton said she hit him with the kitchen stool. That one, ma'am?' The man called Jake pointed to the yellow formica stool.

'Yes. He was coming *back*, you see. You see—' Ginnie choked and gave up, for the moment.

Jake cleared his throat and said, 'Mrs Brixton and her husband just moved in. Husband isn't here tonight. She'd left the kitchen door unlocked and two – well, one fellow came in, this one. He went out with a bag of stuff he'd taken, put it in a waiting car, then came back to get more, and that's when Mrs Brixton hit him.'

'Um-*hum*,' said the policeman, still stooped on his heels. 'Can't touch the body till the detective gets here. Can I use your phone, Mrs Brixton?'

'They cut the phone,' Jake said. 'That's why she had to walk to my place.'

The other policeman went out to telephone from his car. The policeman who remained put on water for coffee (or had he said tea?), and chatted with Jake about tourists, about someone they both knew who had just got married – as if they had known each other for years. Ginnie was sitting on one of the dining-room chairs. The policeman asked where the instant coffee was, if she had any, and Ginnie got up to show him the coffee jar which she had put on a cabinet shelf beside the stove.

'Terrible introduction to a new house,' the policeman remarked, holding his steaming cup. 'But we all sure hope—' Suddenly his words seemed to dry up. His eyes flickered and looked away from Ginnie's face.

A couple of men in plainclothes arrived. Photographs were taken of the dead man. Ginnie went over the house with one of the men, who made notes of the items Ginnie said were stolen. No, she hadn't seen the color of the car, much less the license plate. The body on the floor was wrapped and carried out on a stretcher. Ginnie had only a glimpse of that, from which the detective even tried to shield her. Ginnie was in the dining room then, reckoning up the missing silver.

'I didn't mean to kill him!' Ginnie cried out suddenly, interrupting the detective. 'Not *kill* him, honestly!'

Stan arrived very early, about 8 a.m., with Freddie, and went to the Inn to fetch Ginnie. Ginnie had spent the night there, and someone had telephoned Stan at the number Ginnie had given.

'She's had a shock,' Jake said to Stan.

Stan looked bewildered. But at least he had heard what happened, and Ginnie didn't have to go over it.

'All the nice things we had,' Ginnie said. 'And the cat—'

'The police might get our stuff back, Ginnie. If not, we'll buy more. We're all safe, at least.' Stan set his firm jaw, but he smiled. He glanced at Freddie who stood in the doorway, looking a little pale from lack of sleep. 'Come on. We're going home.'

He took Ginnie's hand. His hand felt warm, and she realized her own hands were cold again.

They tried to keep the identity of the dead man from her, Ginnie knew, but on the second day she happened to see it printed – on a folded newspaper which lay on the counter in the grocery store. There was a photograph of him too, a blondish fellow with curly hair and a rather defiant expression. *Frank Collins, 24, of Hartford* . . .

Stan felt that they ought to go on living in the house, gradually buy the 'nice things' again that Ginnie kept talking about. Stan said she ought to get back to work on her novel.

'I don't want any nice things any more. Not again.' That was true, but that was only part of it. The worst was that she had killed someone, stopped a life. She couldn't fully realize it, therefore couldn't believe it somehow, or understand it.

'At least we could get another cat.'

'Not yet,' she said.

People said to her (like Mrs Durham, Gladys, who lived a mile or so out of East Kindale on the opposite side from the Brixtons), 'You mustn't reproach yourself. You did it in defense of your house. Don't you think a lot of us wish we had the courage, if someone comes barging in intending to rob you . . . '

'I wouldn't hesitate – to do what you did!' That was from perky Georgia Hamilton, a young married woman with black curly hair, active in local politics, who lived in East Kindale proper. She came especially to call on Ginnie and to make acquaintance with her and Stan. 'These hoodlums from miles away – Hartford! – they come to rob us, just because they think we still have some family silver and a few *nice* things . . . '

There was the phrase again, the *nice* things.

Stan came home one day with a pair of silver candlesticks for the dining-room table. 'Less than a hundred dollars, and we can afford them,' Stan said.

To Ginnie they looked like bait for another robbery. They were pretty, yes. Georgian. Modern copy, but still beautiful. She could not take any aesthetic pleasure from them.

'Did you take a swat at your book this afternoon?' Stan asked cheerfully. He had been out of the house nearly three hours that afternoon. He had made sure the doors were locked, for Ginnie's sake, before he left. He had also bought a metal wheelbarrow for use in the garden, and it was still strapped to the roof of the car.

'No,' Ginnie said. 'But I suppose I'm making progress. I have to get back to a state of concentration, you know.'

'Of course I know,' Stan said. 'I'm a writer too.'

The police had never recovered the silverware, or Ginnie's leather box which had held her engagement ring (it had become too small and she hadn't got around to having it enlarged), and her grandmother's gold necklace and so forth. Stan told Ginnie they had checked all the known pals of the man who had invaded the house, but hadn't come up with anything. The police thought the dead man might have struck up acquaintance with his chum very recently, possibly the same night as the robbery.

'Darling,' Stan said, 'do you think we should *move* from this house? I'm willing – if it'd make you feel – less—'

Ginnie shook her head. It wasn't the house. She didn't any longer (after two months) even think of the corpse on the floor when she went into the kitchen. It was something inside her. 'No,' Ginnie said.

'Well – I think you ought to talk to a psychiatrist. Just one visit even,' Stan added, interrupting a protest from Ginnie. 'It isn't enough for neighbors to say you did the natural thing. Maybe you need a professional to tell you.' Stan chuckled. He was in tennis shoes and old clothes, and had had a good day at the typewriter.

Ginnie agreed, to please Stan.

The psychiatrist was in Hartford, a man recommended to Stan by a local medical doctor. Stan drove Ginnie there, and waited for her in the car. It was to be an hour's session, but Ginnie reappeared after about forty minutes.

'He gave me some pills to take,' Ginnie said.

'Is *that* all? – But what did he say?'

'Oh.' Ginnie shrugged. 'The same as they all say, that – nobody blames me, the police didn't make a fuss, so what—' She shrugged again, glanced at Stan and saw the terrible disappointment in his face as he looked from her into the distance through the windshield.

Ginnie knew he was thinking again about 'guilt' and abandoning it, abandoning the word again. She had said no, she didn't feel guilty, that wasn't the trouble, that would have been too simple. She felt disturbed, she had said many times, and she couldn't do anything about it.

'You really ought to write a book about it, a novel,' Stan said – this for at least the fourth time.

'And how can I, if I can't come to terms with it myself, if I can't even analyze it first?' This Ginnie said for at least the third time and possibly the fourth. It was as if she had an unsolvable mystery within her. 'You can't write a book just stammering around on paper.'

Stan then started the car.

The pills were mild sedatives combined with some kind of mild picker-uppers. They didn't make change in Ginnie.

Two more months passed. Ginnie resisted buying any 'nice things,' so they had nothing but the nice candlesticks. They ate with stainless steel. Freddie pulled out of his period of tension and suppressed excitement (he knew quite well what had happened in the kitchen), and in Ginnie's eyes became quite normal again, whatever normal was. Ginnie got back to work on the book she had started before moving to the house. She didn't ever dream about the murder, or manslaughter, in fact she often thought it might be better if she did dream about it.

But among people – and it was a surprisingly friendly region, they had all the social life they could wish – she felt compelled to say sometimes, when there was a lull in the conversation:

'Did you know, by the way, I once killed a man?'

Everyone would look at her, except of course those who had heard her say this before, maybe three times before.

Stan would grow tense and blank-minded, having failed once more to spring in in time before Ginnie got launched. He was jittery at social gatherings, trying like a fencer to dart in with something, anything to say, before Ginnie made her big thrust. *It's just something they, he and Ginnie, had to live with*, Stan told himself.

And it probably would go on and on, even maybe when Freddie was twelve and even twenty. It had, in fact, half-ruined their marriage. But it was emphatically not worth divorcing for. He still loved Ginnie. She was still Ginnie after all. She was just somehow different. Even Ginnie had said that about herself.

'It's something I just have to live with,' Stan murmured to himself.

'What?' It was Georgia Hamilton on his left, asking him what he had said. 'Oh, I know, I know.' She smiled understandingly. 'But maybe it does her good.'

Ginnie was in the middle of her story. At least she always made it short, and even managed to laugh in a couple of places.

A GIRL LIKE PHYL

J eff Cormack stood looking through a thick glass window onto a
field of Kennedy Airport, drawing on a cigarette that he hoped
would be his last before he boarded. Twice they had announced
delays that had caused the passengers to disperse, humping hand
luggage back to the departure lounge or to one of the bars for a
drink. It was a foggy day in November.

Here it came again, the droning female voice, 'Passengers on
TWA Flight eight-oh-seven to Paris are kindly requested . . . '

A collective groan, mumbles of impatience drowned out the
voice, so that people asked others, 'Did she say half an hour?' The
answer was yes.

Jeff picked up his attaché case, and was turning toward the doorway when he saw a face some five yards away that made him stop and
stay motionless for a few seconds. *Phyl.* No, it couldn't be. This girl
looked hardly twenty. But the resemblance! The light brown eyes
with the sharp upward slant at the outer corners, the fresh pink at
the cheekbones, the soft abundant hair of the same dark brown as
Phyl's. And the lips! The girl was like Phyl at the time Jeff had met
her. Jeff tore his eyes away and reached for his black case, which was
somehow on the floor again.

He felt shattered, and noticed that his hands trembled a little.

He mustn't look at the girl again, he thought, not try to find her again. She was evidently on the same flight. He walked slowly toward the bar, not caring where he walked, because he had no purpose in doing anything except to kill the next half hour. He'd be quite late getting to Paris at this rate, after midnight certainly before he got to his hotel. He would still try to reach Kyrogin by telephone tonight, and he envisaged staying up all night, because he didn't know and his office scouts hadn't been able to find out exactly when Kyrogin was arriving in Paris and where he was staying. At least it wouldn't be at the Russian Embassy, Jeff thought. Kyrogin was an engineer, an important man but not a Communist deputy. Jeff knew that Kyrogin's mission was semi-secret, that he was in search of a bargain, and Jeff wanted to get to him first, meaning before any other American firm, or maybe an English firm, got to him. Jeff had to convince Kyrogin that his company, Ander-Mack, was the best possible one for setting up oil rigs.

Thinking of the job he had to do in the next twenty-four hours gave Jeff a sense of solidity, of definite time and place.

The girl's face had whisked him back eighteen — no, twenty — years, to the year he had met Phyl. Not that he had stopped thinking about Phyl during all that time. They had been together for a little over a year. Then, after they had parted, he had thought about her a lot for the next two years, the Awful Years, as he called them. Then had come a three- or four-year break, in a manner of speaking, when he had not thought about her (not with the same intensity), when he had worked even harder at his own work in order to keep Phyl out of his mind, not to mention that during that period he had met someone else and got married. His son Bernard was now fifteen, going to Groton and not doing too well. Bernard had no idea of what he wanted to be as yet. Maybe an actor. And Betty, his wife, lived in Manhattan. He'd said good-bye to her this morning, and said he would be back in three days, maybe sooner. Just three hours ago. Was it possible?

Jeff found himself stirring his usual one lump of sugar into his coffee. He didn't remember ordering coffee. He stood with one leg over the seat of a stool, his topcoat folded over his arm. And his black case was at his feet, he saw. In it was the informal contract that he wanted Kyrogin to sign, or agree to. He'd make it. Jeff downed the last of his coffee and, feeling more sure of himself, surveyed the people at the little tables along the glass wall. He was looking deliberately now for the girl who resembled Phyl.

There she was, seated at a table with a young man in blue jeans and denim jacket, and Jeff judged from their attitudes that they were not together. The girl was neatly dressed (as Phyl would have been) in a well-cut navy blue coat, an expensive-looking scarf at her neck. Suddenly it crossed Jeff's mind that she could be Phyl's daughter. How else could there be such a resemblance? Phyl had married — nineteen years ago, Jeff remembered with painful accuracy — a man called Guy. Guy what? Fraser or Frazier, something like that. Jeff had deliberately tried to forget how to spell it, and had succeeded.

The girl looked at him, happened to lift her eyes straight toward him, and Jeff felt as if he had been shot.

Jeff dropped his own eyes, closed them, heard his heart catching up, and he slowly reached for his wallet and put a dollar bill on the counter. That had been like the first time he had seen Phyl, in that room full of other people. Worse now, because he knew Phyl. He knew also that he still loved her. He had come to terms with that years ago, he reminded himself. A man didn't commit suicide, didn't ruin his career, just because he was in love with a girl he couldn't have. There was such a thing as trying to forget, which really meant trying not to dwell upon it, or let it become an obsession. His love for Phyl was now something he had to live with, he had decided. But he had to admit that not a month, not a week went by, even now, when he didn't think of Phyl, didn't imagine being with her — in bed, out of bed, just existing, with her. And now he was married, the outer trappings were there, solid, tangible as his son Bernard, real as the ugly brown formica bar under his fingers now, or as a bullet that might penetrate his forehead and kill him.

He hoped he would not be seated next to the girl on the seven-hour flight to Paris. If that happened, he'd ask for his seat to be changed on some pretext. But with two hundred or so passengers, it wasn't likely.

Twenty minutes later, Jeff was being borne at increasing speed across the airfield, and then came the lift, the wonderful lightness as the air took over and the ground dropped below and the roar of the motors became fainter. On Jeff's left was a window looking out on a gray wing, and on his right a plump woman with a midwestern accent, and next to her a man who was probably her husband. From where he sat, Jeff couldn't see the girl, and he had avoided looking for her when the scores of passengers had been boarding.

Jeff unfastened his seat belt and lit a cigarette. A stewardess made slow progress up the aisle, and when she arrived, Jeff ordered a scotch on the rocks. Then came lunch. Then the sky began to darken as they raced in the same direction as the earth turned. A film made its appearance at the end of the plane's aisle. Jeff had declined the use of earphones. He wanted to snooze if he could. He lowered the back of his seat, closed his eyes and loosened his tie.

Kyrogin, Jeff was thinking, might not be difficult. Kyrogin had showed a sense of humor on the telephone last week. 'Our seas are not made of vodka,' Kyrogin had said, his accent heavy in a baritone voice. Meaning it was not pleasant to fall into the White Sea in winter or any other time. That was a crack against Ander-Mack's safety laws. Jeff's company avoided unions. They hired roustabouts for dangerous work at high wages. The Russians were not famous for unions or for respect for life and limb, so Jeff wasn't worried. If he could only show Kyrogin the contract, then the deal was clinched, Jeff thought. Jeff envisaged Russian labor plus some Scots and English dropouts from the British North Sea oil operations. The boys were tough, they got injured, or killed, they became bored, a lot quit. But no one could deny that the pay was good. That was what counted for them, and what counted for the Russians was speed.

As a matter of fact, Jeff thought as he looked down the dimly lit aisle of the plane, there might be a representative of a rival firm on this flight. If so, Jeff didn't know what man, even what type of man to look for. Young or old, conservative or – the opposite, he'd be carrying the same kind of papers as Jeff, carrying the same kind of hope. Jeff slumped in his seat, and tried to relax and doze off.

You haven't any time for me *anymore* . . .

Jeff sat up again. Through the gentle hum of the jets, Phyl's voice had come, straight into his ears. Jeff rubbed his eyes, deliberately yawned, and lay back again. He locked his fingers across his waist, and was about to close his eyes when the girl who looked like Phyl, coatless now and in a light-colored blouse, dark skirt, walked toward him in the aisle. She was going to stop and say something to him, he thought. Absurd! He was half asleep. But he sat up just as the girl passed his seat row, as if to brace himself, as if there weren't two people between him and the girl.

Down the aisle, a pair of horses galloped noiselessly, in color, straight toward the audience. Wide awake now, Jeff suffered a long minute of depression, as if his mind, somewhere unknown even to him, had taken a toboggan ride into a dark valley. He knew why he had gone over his current assignment, why he had reaffirmed his confidence in himself: his work was all he had. And yet he knew that because of his work he had lost Phyl. Phyl had been engaged to Guy. And Guy – or rather his family – had money. Jeff had wanted to compete, to prove himself, in the way he thought would count with Phyl, by making money, solid, big money. Oddly and ironically, Jeff thought, Phyl might have stayed with him if he hadn't made a lot of money, just a bit, and if he'd spent more time with her. Ironically, Phyl had drifted away, because she had thought he was drifting away. They'd had just thirteen months together, composed of a week snatched here and there, a few days in hotels in Chicago, San Francisco, Dallas, happy moments when Jeff had clasped Phyl in his arms (in motels, hotels, in a certain apartment in Evanston rented in Phyl's name), when he had said to her, 'Everything went great today! We're ten thousand dollars richer. Maybe more, I haven't figured it out yet.' But what had counted, it seemed, and against him, was the time he had spent away from Phyl, too many days, perhaps just three days at a time, but too many. That was how Jeff saw it, anyway. But the loss! When he had thought he had 'succeeded' to find it a 'failure'! For Phyl, he had summoned all his drive. He didn't regret that.

Wasn't the girl going to return down the aisle? Jeff slumped again and put his hand over his eyes, so he couldn't possibly know when she passed again.

At Roissy Airport, the passengers from Flight 807 trickled toward the passport control desks and became three solid lines. The girl, Jeff saw, was the second person in front of him. Then the man between them hailed someone behind Jeff and quit the line, and Jeff was right behind the girl. She had a white plastic carryall at her feet, and out of the top of it, beside an open carton of Camels from which one pack had been removed, poked the furry head of a toy panda. Jeff let the distance between him and the girl widen by a few inches. The passport stamps thumped, the lines crept. When the girl reached for the carryall, the panda fell out, and the girl didn't notice.

Jeff retrieved the panda. 'Excuse me,' he said. 'You dropped this.'

Phyl's eyes glanced at him, then the panda. 'Oh, thank you! My good luck piece!' She smiled.

Even her teeth were like Phyl's, the eyeteeth slightly pointed. Jeff acknowledged her thanks with a slight nod. The line moved.

'I'd've missed that. If I'd lost it, I mean. Thanks very much,' the girl said over her shoulder.

'Not at all.' Was her voice like Phyl's? Not really, Jeff thought.

The girl, then Jeff, passed the control desk and walked into the freedom of Paris. Jeff's pulse slowed to normal. He did not look to see if the girl was being met by any of the people waiting, some of them waving to faces that they recognized.

Jeff was able to claim his suitcase quickly, and then he headed for the taxi rank. He asked the driver to go to the Hôtel Lutetia. It was just after one a.m. and raining slightly.

'*Bon soir*,' Jeff said to the clerk at the hotel desk, and continued in French, 'I have a reservation since yesterday. Cormack.'

The clerk smiled as he greeted Jeff. Jeff didn't know this clerk, but the clerk evidently knew Jeff's name. 'Monsieur Cormack! Yes, sir. You have an *appartement*, as your cable requested. That is number twenty-four, sir.'

The bar was still functioning, Jeff saw. He intended to send for a bottle of cold mineral water, maybe coffee also. In his room – a nice, spacious room adjoining a salon – Jeff hung up a dark blue suit and tossed folded white silk pajamas on the turned-down bed, washed his face and hands at the bathroom basin, then picked up the telephone. He had a sudden hunch, for no reason at all, that Kyrogin was at the George V, and he was going to try it.

There was a soft knock at the door. Jeff put the telephone down.

A bellhop stood outside the door with a message on a tray. 'A cable for you, sir. We regret we forgot to give it to you downstairs.'

'Thank you,' Jeff said, and took the cable. He closed the door and tore the envelope open. The cable said:

EITHER INTER-CONTINENTALE OR GEORGE V.

Jeff smiled a little. He'd been right about the George V. That was a good omen. The cable was unsigned. Jeff knew it was from Ed Simmons. Ed had been pulling every string in New York and Moscow to find out where Kyrogin would be staying in Paris, in order to save Jeff some time.

Jeff picked up the telephone again. 'I would like to ring the George V, please.' After a few seconds, he had the George V switchboard. 'May I speak with Monsieur Kyrogin, please? That's K-y-r-o-g-i-n.'

'One moment, sir.'

If the clerk demurred about ringing Kyrogin, Jeff was prepared to say that Monsieur Kyrogin was expecting his call, regardless of the hour.

'I am sorry, sir, there is no Monsieur Kyrogin here.'

'May I ask what time you are expecting him?' Jeff asked in a tone of confidence.

'We are not expecting him, sir. I have the reservations here before me. No one by the name of Kyrogin is expected.'

'I see. Thank you.' Jeff put the telephone down. That was a disappointment. Was the operator correct?

There was still the Inter-Continentale, and Jeff took up the phone again, and glanced at his watch. Exactly two AM Jeff asked the Lutetia operator to ring the Inter-Continentale for him and, when Jeff's telephone rang, went through the same procedure.

'One moment, sir,' said the Inter-Continentale operator. And then, after a moment, 'He has not yet arrived, sir.'

Jeff smiled, relieved. 'But you are expecting him – when?'

'Any moment, sir. The note here says he will be arriving tonight but possibly quite late.'

'May I leave a message? I would like him to ring Monsieur Cormack' – Jeff spelled this – 'at the Hôtel Lutetia.' He gave his hotel's number, which was on a card by the telephone. 'It is most important, tell him, and he may ring me when he comes in, at any hour tonight. Is this understood?'

'Yes, sir. Very good, sir.'

Jeff was not at all sure Kyrogin would ring at any hour, not if he came in tired at three a.m., not if he was in Paris this very minute, still with his suitcase, talking to the representative of some other firm, and maybe concluding a deal. Kyrogin would know what Jeff's message meant, and he would know the name Cormack from Ander-Mack. So what Jeff had to do tonight was ring every fifteen minutes or so, and hope to catch Kyrogin at the Inter-Continentale when he arrived and before he went to bed and refused to take any calls.

Jeff unpacked the rest of his things, put his attaché case on the writing table in his bedroom and his memo book on the oval table in the salon by the telephone. There was also a telephone by his bedside. Then he lifted the telephone again and ordered a large bottle of Vichy. 'Just put it in my room, would you? I'm going down to the bar for a coffee.' Jeff suddenly wanted to get out of his room, to move around a little.

He took the stairs down. The first thing he saw, the first thing his eyes focused on, when he reached the lobby, was the girl. The *girl* again. Yes. With the long brown hair, and in the navy blue coat. She stood talking to the man behind the desk. Jeff wanted to speak with the clerk before he went into the bar, and he walked toward the desk with a deliberate casualness.

The clerk looked at him, and Jeff said:

'I'm expecting a telephone call at any moment. I'll be in the bar – at least for the next fifteen minutes.'

'*Oui, monsieur,*' said the clerk.

The girl recognized Jeff. 'Well – hello again!' She looked a little tired, and worried.

Jeff smiled. 'Hello again.' He went into the nearly empty bar, and took a stool at the counter. When the barman had finished polishing a glass, Jeff ordered a coffee.

'We are closing soon, sir, but there is just time for a coffee.'

The girl – Jeff could see half her figure, the back of her head and coat – stood with an indefinite air in front of the desk. Then she walked slowly with her suitcase and the carryall into the bar. She gave him barely a glance, and took one of the stools three distant from Jeff, occupied it by putting her handbag on it.

'Have you any fresh orange juice?' she asked the barman in English.

'I am sorry, mademoiselle, the bar is close,' said the barman in English also. He was again polishing glasses.

'A glass of water?' the girl asked.

'Certainly, miss.' The barman poured it and set it in front of her.

She was waiting for someone, Jeff supposed. Maybe the room reserved wasn't in her name. If so, the hotel perhaps couldn't let her take the room. Jeff concentrated on finishing his coffee, which was very hot.

Suddenly – Jeff felt it – the girl turned her eyes toward him.

'Can you imagine, I've had a room reserved here for at least two weeks, and because I'm a day early, maybe a typographical error on somebody's part, not mine——' She gave a sigh. 'Well, I'm supposed to wait till noon tomorrow and take a seat in the lobby, unless some other hotel comes up with a room tonight, and it doesn't look like it, because they've already called three.'

This burst made Jeff dismount from his stool. His mind was dazzled by the memory of Phyl losing her temper in the same manner, talking in the same way. Jeff was also trying to think of a solution. Some fleabag hotel would have a room at this hour, but he didn't think the girl would want such a hotel. 'That's tough. – There's not even a small room free here?'

'No! I've really asked.' She sipped her water with an air of disgust.

Jeff put a five-franc piece on the counter. 'I'll speak with the desk, see what I can do,' he said to the girl, and went into the lobby.

The desk clerk, courteous as ever, said, 'I know, Monsieur Cormack, it is a mistake with the date. By one day. But we simply have no room, not even a little one. There is only a cot in a servants' corridor – absurd! And the less good hotels – they are not even answering the telephone at this hour!' He shrugged.

'I see.' Jeff went back into the bar.

The girl looked at him with a faint hope in her face.

'No luck there. If it's just a matter of waiting . . . ' He struggled with his words, reassured himself that his objective was to be helpful, and plunged ahead. 'You could sit down more comfortably in my suite. I've got two rooms. In what's left of the night . . . '

The girl was hesitating, too tired to decide at once.

'We can speak to the desk, tell them you're in my suite, if you're expecting someone.'

'Yes, but I'm expecting someone tomorrow. – Frankly, I'd give anything just to wash my face,' the girl said in a whisper. She looked near tears.

Jeff smiled. 'Come on, we'll tell the desk,' he said, and picked up her suitcase. He noticed that the panda was still in the carryall.

At the desk, he said, 'Mademoiselle has decided to wait in my apartment.'

The clerk looked a little surprised, then relieved that the problem had been solved. '*Très bien, monsieur.*' He nodded a good night to them.

They went up in the elevator, which was self-operating, and Jeff pulled out his key and opened the door.

He had left the lights on. He followed the girl into the salon with her suitcase, and closed the door. 'Please make yourself at home.' He put her suitcase by the sofa. 'The bathroom's beyond the bedroom. I think I've got to stay up all night for a business call, so it won't bother me at all if you walk through.'

'Thanks *very* much,' the girl said.

Then she was in the bathroom, her coat lay on the sofa, her suitcase was opened on the floor, and Jeff stood listening to the water running. He felt curiously stunned. Frightened, even. He didn't want to know if the girl was Phyl's daughter, he realized. He wasn't going to ask her anything that might lead to information about her mother.

Jeff picked up the telephone and asked for the Inter-Continentale again. Now it was 2:37 a.m.

'No, Monsieur Kyrogin has not arrived, sir,' said the male voice at the other end.

'Thank you.' Jeff felt suddenly discouraged. He imagined Kyrogin having been met at the airport by some enterprising fellow who had found out his arrival time, imagined them talking now in a bar or in the hotel room of the other man, and Kyrogin agreeing to the other man's proposal. They'd maybe toast it in vodka.

The girl came back. Jeff was still standing by the telephone.

She smiled, fresh-faced. 'That was wonderful!'

Jeff nodded absently. He had been calculating flying time from Moscow. And could Kyrogin be at another hotel, not the Inter-Continentale, even though he'd made a reservation there? Of course he could be. 'I'll go into the bedroom. So make yourself comfortable here. You probably want to sleep. I think that sofa's just about long enough.'

She had sat down on the sofa, slipped off her shoes. 'Why do you have to stay up all night?' she asked with a childlike curiosity.

'Because – I'm trying to reach a man who's due in from Moscow. And he hasn't arrived at his hotel yet.'

'Moscow – you're a government official?'

'No, just an engineer.' Jeff smiled. 'Would you like some mineral water? It's all I have to offer.' The Vichy stood in an ice bucket on the oval table.

The girl said she would, and Jeff poured it. He went to get a glass for himself from the bathroom. The girl had left her wash cloth spread on the basin rim, out of habit, probably. He took off his tie, opened his shirt collar, then took off his jacket. He went back to the anteroom and poured himself a glass of Vichy. He was thirsty.

'I'm going to have a shower,' he said. 'If the telephone rings, give me a shout, would you? I'm not sure I'll be able to hear it.'

'Sure.'

Jeff showered, put on pajamas and because of the girl's presence put on also a seersucker dressing gown. He had closed the door to the salon, and now he knocked gently, in case she was asleep.

'Yes?'

He opened the door. The girl was half reclined on the sofa, still dressed, reading a magazine.

'It just occurred to me you might want a shower or a bath. Why not? Anyway you're not going to sit up all night, I hope.'

'I don't know. I suddenly don't feel sleepy. Second wind, maybe. It's so strange being here.'

Jeff gave a laugh. 'It's a strange night. Or morning. I've got to try my quarry again in a minute and after that I'll be reading, too, so it won't bother me in the least if you walk through to the bathroom.'

'Thanks. Maybe I will.'

Jeff went into his room, this time did not quite close his door, and tried the Inter-Continentale again. The answer was the same. Now it was after three. What other hotel should he try? The Hilton? Should he ring Roissy and ask about incoming flights from Moscow? Abruptly Jeff remembered that he had a bottle of scotch in a plastic bag by his suitcase. He opened the bottle, and poured some into his glass.

Then he tapped on the half-open door again. 'Hey . . . ' The girl was still reading. 'I don't even know your name.'

'Eileen.'

Eileen what? he wondered, then remembered that he didn't want to know. 'Eileen – would you possibly like a nightcap? Scotch.'

'Yes! I think that would be nice.'

He added scotch to her Vichy water, then brought the bucket and offered it to her. 'Ice down there.'

'Any luck with your phone calls?' She fished ice cubes out.

'No. No.' Jeff took a cigarette.

'What's it all about? – Or is it a secret?'

'Not unless you're a competitor. It's about setting up oil rigs in the White Sea. My firm does that – that kind of thing. We want the job. – And I have a good offer to make,' he added, as if thinking out loud or justifying himself, and he began walking slowly around the room. He remembered talking to Phyl about his work, just like this, but in those days he would have been smiling, would have gone to Phyl and kissed her, and then—

'You're a very serious man, aren't you?'

You haven't any time for me *anymore,* Jeff heard in his ears again. The girl's voice was like Phyl's, or her accent was, and there was a ringing quality in the higher tones, a resonance like that of a stringed instrument, that was also like Phyl's.

'I hope you make it,' the girl said. 'The White Sea – I only know where the Baltic is.'

Jeff smiled. 'The White Sea's north of that. The big port there's Archangel.' The girl was looking at him in awe, Jeff could see.

She took a swallow of her drink. 'I wish I were here for something as sensible as that – as important as that.'

Jeff looked at his watch, wishing the time would pass faster, that it would be eight or nine a.m., hours when people could do business. Maybe. 'You're here on vacation?'

'I'm here to get married.'

'Really?'

'Yeah. It's funny, isn't it? I mean, since I'm alone now. But my mother's due tomorrow and my – my fiancé's coming in a couple of days. We're going to Venice – for the wedding. Well, I'm not sure Mom's coming to Venice. She's funny.' The girl looked suddenly uncomfortable and glanced at Jeff with a nervous smile.

Mom was coming to this hotel, Jeff was thinking. He put out his cigarette, started to sit down and didn't. 'She's funny?'

'Oh, she thinks *I'm* funny. Maybe it's true. But I'm not sure I want to get married. You see?'

Jeff supposed the young man was a 'nice' young man, approved by her family. Jeff wasn't interested in asking anything about him. 'If you're not sure, then why do you even consider marrying?'

'That's just it! That's the way *I* feel. – Do you think I could have just a little more scotch?'

'All you want,' Jeff said, and set the bottle on the table in front of the sofa. 'You pour it.'

She poured an inch, the bottle slipped and more went in. Jeff brought the Vichy bottle.

'I wish I were someone else. I wish I weren't *here*. He's—' She stopped, frowning into space. 'It's not so much him as the fact I don't want to get tied down. After all, I'm only eighteen.'

'Well . . . can't you postpone it?'

'Yes-s. Indefinitely. That's what I'd like to do.' She drank off all her glass. 'You really wouldn't mind if I took a shower? That's what I need.' She stood up.

'All yours,' Jeff said, nodding toward the bathroom. 'You can even borrow my dressing gown.'

In the doorway the girl hesitated, as if it were a big decision, then said, 'I'd like to borrow it, if I may, even though I've got one.' She held out her hand.

Smiling, Jeff untied his belt, and handed the dressing gown to her. Ah, youth! Troubles! Rebellion! Eileen didn't know yet what troubles were! Apparently she wasn't even in love with the young man. Or was she? Jeff looked into the long mirror between the windows, reassured himself that he was presentable in his pajamas, then something occurred to him that had to do with the word *rebellion*. Phyl had rebelled against her fiancé Guy. Almost for the sake of rebelling, it seemed to Jeff in retrospect – and it was a horrible thought for him. She'd fairly jilted Guy and run off with him, Jeff, for more than a year. Then convention or 'sanity' had returned to Phyl, according to her lights. And at what pain to him! He still had the pain, and it was still sharp – after nineteen years. The girl Eileen needed a lecture, Jeff thought, from someone. He wasn't going to give it to her.

He looked at his watch again, as if to drag himself back to his job, his search for the elusive Kyrogin. Before long, they'd be serving breakfast in the hotel. That was what he and the girl needed, a seven a.m. breakfast with strong coffee.

Jeff laughed out loud. Here he was, a forty-four-year-old man in a Paris hotel suite with a good-looking girl he hadn't made the slightest pass at, longing for breakfast at seven a.m., or even earlier if possible. Jeff stared into his own smiling eyes in the long mirror, then the smile left his eyes as it had left his lips. He thought his dark hair had a bit more gray in it than the last time he had taken a look. He touched his cheek. He could use a shave.

The girl was coming in, barefoot, carrying her clothes over her arm. Now she looked even lovelier with her hair slightly dampened. 'What were you laughing at?'

Jeff shook his head. 'Can't tell you.'

'You were laughing at me,' she said.

'No! – What does your father say about your marriage?'

'Oh – Dad.' She collapsed on the sofa again, dumped her clothes beside her, then took a cigarette and lit it. 'Well, basically he takes an "I'll keep out" attitude, but he definitely wants me to get married. Now, I mean. After all, I quit college because I fell in love, I thought – and because I thought I preferred to get married rather than spend another nearly three years in college. You see?'

Jeff was sitting in an upholstered chair. 'I suppose I see. In other words, your mother and father are in agreement – that you ought to get married.'

'Yes. But Phyl – that's my mother, and half the time I call her Phyl – she's more insistent about it. I mean, she tries to exert more control over me than Dad. – What's the matter?'

Jeff felt weak, a little dizzy. He sat up and leaned forward, like a man trying to pull out of a faint. 'Nothing. Suddenly tired. I think I'll have another snort. I need it.' He got up and poured some scotch, straight, into his empty glass. He sipped it, letting it burn his tongue and his throat back to life.

'You look pale. I bet you've been working like mad lately . . . '

Now she was just like Phyl, comforting in a crisis, ready to minister – providing it was a minor crisis like this one. Jeff slowly felt stronger. The sips of scotch did him good, and quickly.

' . . . tell you how much I admire you. You're doing something important. You're a man of the world. You've achieved something.'

Jeff exploded in a laugh.

'Don't laugh,' the girl said, frowning. 'How many men – and you're not even old. My dad's important, maybe, but he just inherited his job and I bet *you* didn't. And I frankly can't imagine Malc getting very far in life. He's had it too easy.'

Malc, Malcolm was doubtless the fiancé. Had Phyl ever mentioned his own name? Jeff wondered. Maybe once or twice? But if only once or twice, the girl wouldn't remember, probably. He hoped she didn't know, or hadn't heard his name. Suddenly the girl stood close in front of him, her hands on his shoulders. She put her arms around his neck.

'Do you mind,' she whispered, 'if I put my arms around you?'

Jeff's hands lifted also, he pulled the girl toward him, for seconds closed his eyes and felt her hair against his forehead. She was the same height as Phyl. How well he remembered! Then he released her and stepped back.

'You're annoyed?' she asked. 'I'll tell you something – straight – if I may. I'd like to go to bed with you.' The last words were so soft, he barely heard them.

But he had heard them.

'Are you afraid of me? I'm not going to tell anybody. And I'm not feeling my drinks, if I may say so. I'm quite sober.' Her eyes, Phyl's eyes, looked straight at him, steady, and with a smile in them.

'It's not that.'

'Not what?'

Why not? Jeff was thinking then. As the girl said, who would know? And what would it matter even if Phyl found out? If Jeff wanted to be vindictive – it would serve Phyl right if she found out. But Jeff really didn't feel vindictive.

'And another thing,' the girl continued in the same soft voice, 'I'd like to see you again. Maybe again and again. Do you travel a lot? So could I. I'm in the mood for traveling a lot.' She still held to Jeff's right hand, and her fingers tightened on his.

His desire was there, and so was a thought, and the thought was that he'd be taking advantage of the girl when she was in an upset state (as nearly every man would, he realized, too), and he was also thinking that he didn't want to lose his memory of Phyl, Phyl as she had been with him, not as this girl would be, a nearly identical copy of Phyl, but not *quite* identical. Even her face wasn't quite identical. Jeff smiled, and tugged his hand from hers. 'Take it easy. You're upset.'

She wasn't hurt. She looked at him mischievously. 'You're an odd one.'

He didn't rise to the bait. He lit another cigarette. 'You know you're going to marry your Mister Right, so why do you fool around with other people?'

'Do you think I'm in the habit of—'

'Oh, stop the crap!'

This time it sank in. 'Now you sound like an American.'

'I said I was an American.' He was angry, and now he knew why, exactly why. This girl would lead him on, might lead other younger men on, exactly as Phyl had, lead them into misery if they were dumb enough to fall in love. The very harshness of his thoughts made him feel a sudden pity for the girl, as if he had said out loud what he was thinking, and had wounded her. 'It doesn't mean . . . I'm your enemy,' he said. But of course it did. 'Why not leave things the way they are? Simple.'

Now she looked puzzled.

The telephone rang, and Jeff for a second relaxed, as if he had been a boxer, saved, and in the next second thought, who could it be except Kyrogin, then thought that was too good to be true. He lifted the telephone.

'Allo?' said a deep voice.

'Hello. Cormack here.'

'Ha-ha. Kyrogin here. What time is it?'

Kyrogin sounded a bit drunk. 'I dunno. Four, maybe. Mr Kyrogin, I'd like very much to see you. And thank you for ringing me. You're at the Inter-Continentale?'

'Yes, and I am very sleepy. But I know – I know – you are an American engineer.'

'Yes. Look, can I see you early tomorrow morning? I mean this morning? After you've had some sleep?'

Silence. Deep breathing. Was Kyrogin lighting a cigarette or passing out?

'Mr Kyrogin – Semyon,' Jeff said.

'Semyon here,' said Kyrogin.

'It's about the White Sea thing, you know,' Jeff persisted, thinking if anyone were listening at this hour, they deserved a medal. 'Have you – have you done anything about the deal, or can we still discuss it?' Long pause. 'Have you spoken with anybody else about it tonight?'

'I was with my French girlfriend tonight,' said Kyrogin.

Jeff smiled. 'I see.' He sat down in the chair behind him. 'In that case, after you've slept – can I phone you around ten? I'll phone you around ten. Your first appointment is with *me*, understand, Mr Kyrogin? Jeff Cormack.'

'Right you are,' said Kyrogin, as if remembering some of his English lessons. 'I have done no work at all tonight,' he added sadly.

It was the sweetest confession Jeff had ever heard. 'That's all right, Semyon. Sleep well. Good night.' Jeff hung up and turned to the girl, beaming.

Eileen smiled back at him, with a look of triumph, as if the victory was hers, too. 'You're going to be the first to see him.'

'Yes, so it seems.' Jeff slapped his hands together, then stood up. 'And I'm going to have another scotch.'

'Good. May I join you?'

Jeff made them both fresh drinks. The Vichy bottle was empty. He filled the third glass in the bathroom and brought it, in case they wanted more water. He could feel the girl's zest and pleasure in his success (the first step to success, anyway) as he had felt Phyl's in the old days. It was the same. The girl had brought him luck, as Phyl had done. It was Phyl who had given Jeff the courage to break away from his boss, and start a company on his own. Phyl who had launched him like a rocket, Phyl who had given him all the confidence in the world and all the happiness. And Jeff knew he could go to bed with the girl now, as he had so often with Phyl, under the same circumstances, in the same mood. Jeff felt the same desire, and he looked at the girl differently now, as if seeing her for the first time.

She understood. She put her glass down and embraced him, pressed herself against him. 'Yes?' she said.

It was still no. And this time Jeff couldn't explain, didn't want to try to find words to explain to himself or to her. 'No,' he said, and extricated himself.

He went into the bedroom, got his battery razor and went to work on his beard. He brushed his teeth. Then he went in to see the girl.

'I'm going to get some sleep till nine-thirty. Don't you want to do the same? – Maybe you'd prefer my bed and I'll take the sofa?'

'No,' she said sleepily, tired at last.

Jeff wasn't going to argue. He was also tired. 'Can I ask you one favor?'

'Sure.'

'Don't mention my name to your mother – ever. All right?'

'Why should I? You haven't done anything.'

He smiled. Maybe she wouldn't remember his name, anyway. 'Okay, Eileen. Good night.' He closed his door, then rang the desk downstairs and asked to be called at nine-thirty a.m. He got into bed, and after one long sigh fell sound asleep.

When the telephone rang the next morning and awakened him, he found the girl already up and dressed, putting on makeup in the salon mirror. Jeff had ordered breakfast for two.

'What time is your mother due?' he asked.

'Oh – her plane comes in at ten, I think.'

Jeff was relieved. He would pack his suitcase, check out this morning and spend – he hoped – most of the morning with Kyrogin. Anyway, Phyl was not due now, or even in the next hour, at the hotel. With his first cup of coffee, Jeff rang up Kyrogin. To Jeff's surprise, Kyrogin answered promptly and sounded wide awake.

'Fine, Mr Cormack! Come over anytime!'

Jeff packed his suitcase quickly, and when he had closed it, he said to the girl, 'You're welcome to stay here till noon, if you like. I'm checking out now, because—'

'Good luck with the Russian,' she interrupted him. She was having her breakfast at the oval table in the salon.

Jeff grinned. 'Thanks, Eileen. I've got an optimistic feeling. You brought me luck, I think. I'm due there now, so I'll say good-bye.'

She had lit a cigarette, and now she stood up. 'Bye-bye. Thank you – thank you for putting me up.'

'No thanks necessary. Be happy! Bye-bye, Eileen.' Jeff went out with his suitcase and attaché case.

He left his suitcase downstairs with the desk clerk, asked for his bill, and said he would settle it later when he came to pick up the suitcase. He was in a hurry to get to Kyrogin. He took a taxi. The ride was not long.

Kyrogin asked Jeff to come up to his room. Kyrogin was in a silk dressing gown, and there was a demolished breakfast tray and a bottle of vodka, half empty, on his table. They ordered more coffee. Kyrogin added vodka to his. The telephone rang, and Kyrogin spoke in English, telling someone he was sorry, he was busy just now. In less than half an hour, Jeff had Kyrogin's verbal agreement. Jeff used his usual method of persuasion, talking first about the difficulties and expense, then estimating the expense and time that another company might take in comparison with Ander-Mack, leaving Kyrogin to make the decision – a verbal one at that, so Kyrogin would not feel bound. Jeff had six copies of his estimate with him, and he gave Kyrogin what he wanted, four, to show his colleagues.

'Now you'll have a vodka maybe,' said Kyrogin.

'Now maybe I will. With pleasure! I've got good news to take back to New York.'

'Phone them now. Tell them!' said Kyrogin with a wave of his hand toward the telephone.

'I'd like to. You really don't mind?' Jeff was moving toward the telephone. Plainly Kyrogin wouldn't mind. Jeff asked the operator to dial a New York number which was Ed Simmons's home number. It would be around five a.m. in New York, but Ed wouldn't mind being awakened with the news Jeff had. The operator said she would ring Jeff back, and then said the call was going through at once, and Jeff could hear Ed's telephone ringing.

Ed answered sleepily, and came awake at the sound of Jeff's voice.

'It's okay at this end!' Jeff said.

'We've got the deal?'

'We've got it. See you soon as pos, old pal.' Jeff hung up.

Kyrogin gave Jeff an excellent cigar. It was like the old days, Jeff thought, when he'd been twenty-three and had concluded a fabulous deal (or so he'd thought then) and would be going home to – to Phyl, Phyl somewhere. It was because of the girl Eileen that Phyl seemed so close now, Phyl with the twinkle in her eyes, her pride in his victory that was like a whole football stadium cheering. And each victory had meant he was closer to her . . .

'What are you thinking about?' Kyrogin asked through a cloud of cigar smoke, smiling.

'I was daydreaming. It's your good vodka,' Jeff said, and stood up and took his leave. They shook hands warmly. The Russian had a powerful grip.

It was already two minutes to noon. Jeff took a taxi at the door of Kyrogin's hotel and rode to the Lutetia.

When he walked into the lobby, he saw the girl again. And with her was Phyl. Now he really stopped dead, a couple of paces within the lobby. Phyl wore a hat. She was standing at a little distance from the desk, and she was plainly angry, furious even. Her cheeks were a bright pink as she delivered a tirade, apparently, to her daughter. Phyl looked shorter than the girl, than he remembered her, but it was because she had gained weight, Jeff realized. Phyl raised a fist and brandished it. The girl barely turned her head, didn't retreat. What was Phyl scolding her about? Phyl might have heard that the girl had spent the night in a man's suite, either from the girl herself or from the desk, Jeff supposed.

Suddenly his dream fell away. Something fell away, something died. Everything died. Phyl turned toward him, but in her anger didn't see him, and Jeff saw that her face had grown pudgy, that her shorter hair under the hat was some odd reddish color. But it wasn't that that upset him, it was the wrath in her face, the ugliness of spirit – her scolding of the girl. And he was positive Phyl was scolding her because she'd spent the night in a hotel room with a man, even if she 'hadn't done anything.' It was the goddamn prudishness, the conventionality, the phoniness, the holier-than-thou or than-the-girl part of it, the hypocrisy – because for Christ's sake, hadn't Phyl done the same thing when she was the girl's age? Had an affair with a man if she damned pleased – the man being Jeff? And then, of course, back to Mister Right, back to the respectably-married-woman act, which she so ponderously embodied now.

Was *this* what he'd been in love with all this time?

Suppose he was married to Phyl now?

Jeff felt about to die. He wasn't weak, wasn't swaying on his feet. In fact he stood like a statue, where he was. Then Phyl and Eileen moved, toward the elevators, Phyl's figure still stiff with rage, the girl's flexible and rebellious. And Jeff was reminded of what he'd thought upstairs in his hotel room: the girl, like Phyl, would go on from him, find another fellow (maybe before she married) and lead him on, and abandon him, and get married, and maybe have a daughter – very pretty, of course – who'd do the same thing, in endless progression or procession.

And there was a second terrible thought, which Jeff had now and not for the first time, that if Phyl had betrayed Guy, who'd been not yet her husband but almost, then he, Jeff, might have been betrayed also in due time, even if he had married Phyl. If promises to lovers didn't mean much, then neither would marital vows. In fact, which came first and which second? Yet it all hung together, and there was nothing lasting, for girls like Phyl, about any of it. What counted finally was 'the way things looked.' And what girls like Phyl had in common was a certain coldness at the heart.

The elevator door mercifully closed the two of them from Jeff's sight.

Jeff went and claimed his suitcase. He pulled his bill from a pocket, and paid in cash. Then he walked out of the hotel with his suitcase and attaché case, and said, 'No' to the doorman who offered to hail a taxi for him. Jeff walked on, and for no particular reason turned the first corner to the right. He was lucid enough to know that he was in a daze, that somehow nothing mattered any longer, where he went, what he did, where he was, even who he was. Or what time it was, or what country it was. For several minutes Jeff walked with his suitcase that did not weigh much.

The holier-than-thou, do-the-right-thing attitude, Jeff was thinking. It was disgusting. Not like Phyl at all! And yet it was Phyl, now. He'd been living on a dream, some crazy dream. A dream of what? Not even a dream of marrying her one day, but still a dream. If he only hadn't seen her this morning!

Well, then what?

He'd be able to live, that was what. That was clear. That was the only thing that was clear. It was something, to have something clear. And he'd succeeded with Kyrogin, and he'd be going back today to New York, to his office. And all this suddenly didn't matter a damn. All of it mattered as little as the phony home he had with Betty, the phony outward appearance of a decent marriage, a teenage son going to the right school. Money. It didn't mean anything. His life simply didn't mean anything.

Somebody jolted Jeff in the shoulders. Jeff realized he was standing at the crossing of a big four- or six-lane avenue, and he hadn't moved when the lights permitted the pedestrians to cross. But Jeff knew what he wanted to do, or rather half his mind knew, or realized. The other half didn't matter. He wasn't thinking. He knew he was past the point of thinking. Hadn't he thought enough? All this went through his head in seconds, and when a big truck came thundering toward him, going to pass him at full speed right in front of him, Jeff dropped his suitcase and attaché case and flung himself in front of it, flat down, like a football tackler tackling nothing. He felt only the impact of the cobbly street, really.

NOT ONE OF US

I t wasn't merely that Edmund Quasthoff had stopped smoking and almost stopped drinking that made him different, slightly goody-goody and therefore vaguely unlikable. It was something else. What?

That was the subject of conversation at Lucienne Gauss's apartment in the East 80s one evening at the drinks hour, seven. Julian Markus, a lawyer, was there with his wife Frieda, also Peter Tomlin, a journalist aged twenty-eight and the youngest of the circle. The circle numbered seven or eight, the ones who knew Edmund well, meaning for most of them about eight years. The others present were Tom Strathmore, a sociologist, and Charles Forbes and his wife, Charles being an editor in a publishing house, and Anita Ketchum, librarian at a New York art museum. They gathered more often at Lucienne's apartment than at anyone else's, because Lucienne liked entertaining and, as a painter working on her own, her hours were flexible.

Lucienne was thirty-three, unmarried, and quite pretty with fluffy reddish hair, a smooth pale skin, and a delicate, intelligent mouth. She liked expensive clothes, she went to a good beauty parlor, and she had style. The rest of the group called her, behind her back, a lady, shy even among themselves at using the word (Tom the sociologist had), because it was an old-fashioned or snob word, perhaps.

Edmund Quasthoff, a tax accountant in a law firm, had been divorced a year ago, because his wife had run off with another man and had therefore asked for a divorce. Edmund was forty, quite tall, with brown hair, a quiet manner, and was neither handsome nor unattractive, but lacking in that spark which can make even a rather ugly person attractive. Lucienne and her group had said after the divorce, 'No wonder. Edmund *is* sort of a bore.'

On this evening at Lucienne's, someone said out of the blue, 'Edmund didn't used to be such a bore – did he?'

'I'm afraid so. *Yes!*' Lucienne yelled from the kitchen, because at that moment she had turned on the water at the sink in order to push ice cubes out of a metal tray. She heard someone laugh. Lucienne went back to the living room with the ice bucket. They were expecting Edmund at any moment. Lucienne had suddenly realized that she wanted Edmund out of their circle, that she actively disliked him.

'Yes, what *is* it about Edmund?' asked Charles Forbes with a sly smile at Lucienne. Charles was pudgy, his shirt front strained at the buttons, a patch of leg often showed between sock and trousers cuff when he sat, but he was well loved by the group, because he was good-natured and bright, and could drink like a fish and never show it. 'Maybe we're all jealous because he stopped smoking,' Charles said, putting out his cigarette and reaching for another.

'I admit *I'm* jealous,' said Peter Tomlin with a broad grin. 'I know I should stop and I damned well can't. Tried to twice – in the last year.'

Peter's details about his efforts were not interesting. Edmund was due with his new wife, and the others were talking while they could.

'Maybe it's his wife!' Anita Ketchum whispered excitedly, knowing this would get a laugh and encourage further comments. It did.

'Worse than the first by far!' Charles avowed.

'Yes, Lillian wasn't bad at all! I agree,' said Lucienne, still on her feet and handing Peter the Vat 69 bottle, so he could top up his glass the way he liked it. 'It's true Magda's no asset. That—' Lucienne had been about to say something quite unkind about the scared yet aloof expression which often showed on Magda's face.

'Ah, marriage on the rebound,' Tom Strathmore said musingly.

'Certainly was, yes,' said Frieda Markus. 'Maybe we have to forgive that. You know they say men suffer more than women if their spouses walk out on them? Their egos suffer, they say – worse.'

'Mine would suffer with *Magda*, matter of fact,' Tom said.

Anita gave a laugh. 'And what a name, Magda! Makes me think of a lightbulb or something.'

The doorbell rang.

'Must be Edmund.' Lucienne went to press the release button. She had asked Edmund and Magda to stay for dinner, but they were going to a play tonight. Only three were staying for dinner, the Markuses and Peter Tomlin.

'But he's changed his job, don't forget,' Peter was saying as Lucienne came back into the room. 'You can't say he has to be clammed up – secretive, I mean. It's not *that*.' Like the others, Peter sought for a word, a phrase to describe the unlikability of Edmund Quasthoff.

'He's stuffy,' said Anita Ketchum with a curl of distaste at her lips.

A few seconds of silence followed. The apartment doorbell was supposed to ring.

'Do you suppose he's happy?' Charles asked in a whisper.

This was enough to raise a clap of collective laughter. The thought of Edmund radiating happiness, even with a two-month-old marriage, was risible.

'But then he's probably never been happy,' said Lucienne, just as the bell rang, and she turned to go to the door.

'Not late, I hope, Lucienne dear,' said Edmund coming in, bending to kiss Lucienne's cheek, and by inches not touching it.

'No-o. I've got the time but you haven't. How are *you*, Magda?' Lucienne asked with deliberate enthusiasm, as if she really cared how Magda was.

'Very well, thank you, and you?' Magda was in brown again, a light and dark brown cotton dress with a brown satin scarf at her neck.

Both of them looked brown and dull, Lucienne thought as she led them into the living room. Greetings sounded friendly and warm.

'No, just tonic, please . . . Oh well, a smidgin of gin,' Edmund said to Charles, who was doing the honors. 'Lemon slice, yes, thanks.' Edmund as usual gave an impression of sitting on the edge of his armchair seat.

Anita was dutifully making conversation with Magda on the sofa.

'And how're you liking your new job, Edmund?' Lucienne asked. Edmund had been with the accounting department of the United Nations for several years, but his present job was better paid and far less cloistered, Lucienne gathered, with business lunches nearly every day.

'O-oh,' Edmund began, 'different crowd, I'll say that.' He tried to smile. Smiles from Edmund looked like efforts. 'These boozy lunches . . . ' Edmund shook his head. 'I think they even resent the fact I don't smoke. They want you to be like them, you know?'

'Who's them?' asked Charles Forbes.

'Clients of the agency and a lot of the time *their* accountants,' Edmund replied. 'They all prefer to talk business at the lunch table instead of face to face in my office. 'S funny.' Edmund rubbed a forefinger along the side of his arched nose. 'I have to have one or two drinks with them – my usual restaurant knows now to make them weak – otherwise our clients might think I'm the Infernal Revenue Department itself putting – honesty before expediency or some such.' Edmund's face again cracked in a smile that did not last long.

Pity, Lucienne thought, and she almost said it. A strange word to think of, because pity she had not for Edmund. Lucienne exchanged a glance with Charles, then with Tom Strathmore, who was smirking.

'They call me up at all hours of the night too. California doesn't seem to realize the time dif—'

'Take your phone off the hook at night,' Charles's wife Ellen put in.

'Oh, can't afford to,' Edmund replied. 'Sacred cows, these worried clients. Sometimes they ask me questions a pocket calculator could answer. But Babcock and Holt have to be polite, so I go on losing sleep . . . No, thanks, Peter,' he said as Peter tried to pour more drink for him. Edmund also pushed gently aside a nearly full ashtray whose smell perhaps annoyed him.

Lucienne would ordinarily have emptied the ashtray, but now she didn't. And Magda? Magda was glancing at her watch as Lucienne looked at her, though she chatted now with Charles on her left. Twenty-eight she was, enviably young to be sure, but what a drip! A bad skin. Small wonder she hadn't been married before. She still kept her job, Edmund had said, something to do with computers. She knitted well, her parents were Mormons, though Magda wasn't. Really wasn't, Lucienne wondered?

A moment later, having declined even orange or tomato juice, Magda said gently to her husband, 'Darling . . . ' and tapped her wristwatch face.

Edmund put down his glass at once, and his old-fashioned brown shoes with wing tips rose from the floor a little before he hauled himself up. Edmund looked tired already, though it was hardly eight. 'Ah, yes, the theater – Thank you, Lucienne. It's been a pleasure as usual.'

'But such a short one!' said Lucienne.

When Edmund and Magda had left, there was a general 'Whew!' and a few chuckles, which sounded not so much indulgent as bitterly amused.

'I really wouldn't like to be married to that,' said Peter Tomlin, who was unmarried. 'Frankly,' he added. Peter had known Edmund since he, Peter, was twenty-two, having been introduced via Charles Forbes, at whose publishing house Peter had applied for a job without success. The older Charles had liked Peter, and had introduced him to a few of his friends, among them Lucienne and Edmund. Peter remembered his first good impression of Edmund Quasthoff – that of a serious and trustworthy man – but whatever virtue Peter had seen in Edmund was somehow gone now, as if that first impression had been a mistake on Peter's part. Edmund had not lived up to life, somehow. There was something cramped about him, and the crampedness seemed personified in Magda. Or was it that Edmund didn't really like *them*?

'Maybe he deserves Magda,' Anita said, and the others laughed.

'Maybe he doesn't like us either,' said Peter.

'Oh, but he does,' Lucienne said. 'Remember, Charles, how pleased he was when – we sort of accepted him – at that first dinner party I asked Edmund and Lillian to here at my place. One of my birthday dinners, I remember. Edmund and Lillian were beaming because they'd been admitted to our charmed circle.' Lucienne's laugh was disparaging of their circle and also of Edmund.

'Yes, Edmund did try,' said Charles.

'His clothes are so boring even,' Anita said.

'True. Can't some of you men give him a hint? You, Julian.' Lucienne glanced at Julian's crisp cotton suit. 'You're always so dapper.'

'Me?' Julian settled his jacket on his shoulders. 'I frankly think men pay more attention to what women say. Why should I say anything to him?'

'Magda told me Edmund wants to buy a car,' said Ellen.

'Does he drive?' Peter asked.

'May I, Lucienne?' Tom Strathmore reached for the scotch bottle which stood on a tray. 'Maybe what Edmund needs is to get thoroughly soused one night. Then Magda might even leave him.'

'Hey, we've just invited the Quasthoffs for dinner at our place Friday night,' Charles announced. 'Maybe Edmund can get soused. Who else wants to come? – Lucienne?'

Anticipating boredom, Lucienne hesitated. But it might not be boring. 'Why not? Thank you, Charles – and Ellen.'

Peter Tomlin couldn't make it because of a Friday night deadline. Anita said she would love to come. Tom Strathmore was free, but not the Markuses, because it was Julian's mother's birthday.

It was a memorable party in the Forbeses' big kitchen which served as dining room. Magda had not been to the penthouse apartment before. She politely looked at the Forbeses' rather good collection of framed drawings by contemporary artists, but seemed afraid to make a comment. Magda was on her best behavior, while the others as if by unspoken agreement were unusually informal and jolly. Part of this, Lucienne realized, was meant to shut Magda out of their happy old circle, and to mock her stiff decorum, though in fact everyone went out of his or her way to try and get Edmund and Magda to join in the fun. One form that this took, Lucienne observed, was Charles's pouring gin into Edmund's tonic glass with a rather free hand. At the table, Ellen did the same with the wine. It was especially good wine, a vintage Margaux that went superbly with the hot-oil-cooked steak morsels which they all dipped into a pot in the center of the round table. There was hot, buttery garlic bread, and paper napkins on which to wipe greasy fingers.

'Come on, you're not working tomorrow,' Tom said genially, replenishing Edmund's wine glass.

'I – yam working tomorrow,' Edmund replied, smiling. 'Always do. Have to on Saturdays.'

Magda was giving Edmund a fixed stare, which he missed, because his eyes were not straying her way.

After dinner, they adjourned to the long sun parlor which had a terrace beyond it. With the coffee those who wanted it had a choice of Drambuie, Bénédictine or brandy. Edmund had a sweet tooth, Lucienne knew, and she noticed that Charles had no difficulty in persuading Edmund to accept a snifter of Drambuie. Then they played darts.

'Darts're as far as I'll go toward exercising,' said Charles, winding up. His first shot was a bull's-eye.

The others took their turns, and Ellen kept score.

Edmund wound up awkwardly, trying to look amusing, they all knew, though still making an effort to aim right. Edmund was anything but limber and coordinated. His first shot hit the wall three feet away from the board, and since it hit sideways, it pierced nothing and fell to the floor. So did Edmund, having twisted somehow on his left foot and lost his balance.

Cries of 'Bravo!' and merry laughter.

Charles extended a hand and hauled Edmund up. 'Hurt yourself?'

Edmund looked shocked and was not laughing when he stood up. He straightened his jacket. 'I don't think – I have the definite feeling—' His eyes glanced about, but rather swimmily, while the others waited, listening. 'I have the feeling I'm not exactly well liked here – so I—'

'Oh-h, Edmund!' said Lucienne.

'What're you talking about, Edmund?' asked Ellen.

A Drambuie was pressed into Edmund's hand, despite the fact that Magda tried gently to restrain the hand that offered it. Edmund was soothed, but not much. The darts game continued. Edmund was sober enough to realize that he shouldn't make an ass of himself by walking out at once in a huff, yet he was drunk enough to reveal his gut feeling, fuzzy as it might be to him just then, that the people around him were not his true friends any more, that they really didn't like him. Magda persuaded him to drink more coffee.

The Quasthoffs took their leave some fifteen minutes later.

There was an immediate sense of relief among all.

'She is the end, let's face it,' said Anita, and flung a dart.

'Well, we got him soused,' said Tom Strathmore. 'So it's possible.'

Somehow they had all tasted blood on seeing Edmund comically sprawled on the floor.

Lucienne that night, having had more to drink than usual, mainly in the form of two good brandies after dinner, telephoned Edmund at four in the morning with an idea of asking him how he was. She knew she was calling him also in order to disturb his sleep. After five rings, when Edmund answered in a sleepy voice, Lucienne found she could not say anything.

'Hello? – Hello? Qu-Quasthoff here . . . '

When she awakened in the morning, the world looked somehow different – sharper edged and more exciting. It was not the slight nervousness that might have been caused by a hangover. In fact Lucienne felt very well after her usual breakfast of orange juice, English tea and toast, and she painted well for two hours. She realized that she was busy detesting Edmund Quasthoff. Ludicrous, but there it was. And how many of her friends were feeling the same way about Edmund today?

The telephone rang just after noon, and it was Anita Ketchum. 'I hope I'm not interrupting you in the middle of a masterstroke.'

'No, no! What's up?'

'Well – Ellen called me this morning to tell me Edmund's birthday party is off.'

'I didn't know any was on.'

Anita explained. Magda last evening had invited Charles and Ellen to a birthday dinner party for Edmund at her and Edmund's apartment nine days from now, and had told Ellen she would invite 'everybody' plus some friends of hers whom everybody might not have met yet, because it would be a stand-up buffet affair. Then this morning, without any explanation such as that Edmund or she were ill with a lingering ailment, Magda had said she had 'decided against' a party, she was sorry.

'Maybe afraid of Edmund's getting pissed again,' Lucienne said, but she knew that wasn't the whole answer.

'I'm sure she thinks we don't like her – or Edmund much – which unfortunately is true.'

'What *can* we do?' asked Lucienne, feigning chagrin.

'Social outcasts, aren't we? Hah-hah. Got to sign off now, Lucienne, because someone's waiting.'

The little contretemps of the canceled party seemed both hostile and silly to Lucienne, and the whole group got wind of it within a day or so, even though they all might not as yet have been invited.

'We can also invite and disinvite,' chuckled Julian Markus on the telephone to Lucienne. 'What a childish trick – with no excuse such as a business trip.'

'No excuse, no. Well, I'll think of something funny, Julian dear.'

'What do you mean?'

'A little smack back at them. Don't you think they deserve it?'

'Yes, my dear.'

Lucienne's first idea was simple. She and Tom Strathmore would invite Edmund out for lunch on his birthday, and get him so drunk he would be in no condition to return to his office that afternoon. Tom was agreeable. And Edmund sounded grateful when Lucienne rang him up and extended the invitation, without mentioning Magda's name.

Lucienne booked a table at a rather expensive French restaurant in the East 60s. She and Tom and three dry martinis were waiting when Edmund arrived, smiling tentatively, but plainly glad to see his old friends again at a small table. They chatted amiably. Lucienne managed to pay some compliments in regard to Magda.

'She has a certain dignity,' said Lucienne.

'I wish she weren't so *shy*,' Edmund responded at once. 'I try to pull her out of it.'

Another round. Lucienne delayed the ordering by having to make a telephone call at a moment when Tom was able to order a third round to fill the time until Lucienne got back. Then they ordered their meal, with white wine to be followed by a red. On the first glass of white, Tom and Lucienne sang a soft chorus of 'Happy Birthday to You' to Edmund as they lifted their glasses. Lucienne had rung Anita, who worked only three blocks away, and Anita joined them when the lunch ended just after three with a Drambuie for Edmund, though Lucienne and Tom abstained. Edmund kept murmuring something about a three o'clock appointment, which maybe would be all right for him to miss, because it really wasn't a top-level appointment. Anita and the others told him it would surely be excusable on his birthday.

'I've just got half an hour,' Anita said as they went out of the restaurant together, Anita having partaken of nothing, 'but I did want to see you on this special day, Edmund old thing. I insist on inviting you for a drink or a beer.'

The others kissed Edmund's cheek and left, then Anita steered Edmund across the street into a corner bar with a fancy decor that tried to be an old Irish pub. Edmund fairly fell into his chair, having nearly slipped a moment before on sawdust. It was a wonder he was served, Anita thought, but hers was a sober presence, and they were served. From this bar, Anita rang Peter Tomlin and explained the situation, which Peter found funny, and Peter agreed to come and take over for a few minutes. Peter arrived. Edmund had a second beer, and insisted upon a coffee, which was ordered, but the combination seemed to make him sick. Anita had left minutes before. Peter waited patiently, prattling nonsense to Edmund, wondering if Edmund was going to throw up or slip under the table.

'Mag's got people coming at six,' Edmund mumbled. 'Gotta be home – little before – or else.' He tried in vain to read his watch.

'Mag you call her? . . . Finish your beer, chum.' Peter lifted his first glass of beer, which was nearly drained. 'Bottoms up and many happy returns!'

They emptied their glasses.

Peter delivered Edmund to his apartment door at 6:25 and ran. A cocktail party was in swing *chez* Magda and Edmund, Peter could tell from the hum of voices behind the closed door. Edmund had been talking about his 'boss' being present, and a couple of important clients. Peter smiled to himself as he rode down in the elevator. He went home, put in a good report to Lucienne, made himself some instant coffee, and got back to his typewriter. Comical, yes! Poor old Edmund! But it was Magda who amused Peter the more. Magda was the stuffy one, their real target, Peter thought.

Peter Tomlin was to change his opinion about that in less than a fortnight. He watched with some surprise and gathering alarm as the attack, led by Lucienne and to a lesser extent Anita, focused on Edmund. Ten days after the sousing of Edmund, Peter looked in one evening at the Markuses' apartment – just to return a couple of books he had borrowed – and found both smirking over Edmund's latest mishap. Edmund had lost his job at Babcock and Holt and was now in the Payne-Whitney for drying out.

'What?' Peter said. 'I hadn't heard a word!'

'We just found out today,' said Frieda. 'Lucienne called me up. She said she tried to call Edmund at his office this morning, and they said he was absent on leave, but she insisted on finding out where he was – said it concerned an emergency in his family, you know how good she is at things like that. So they told her he was in the Payne-Whitney, and she phoned there and talked with Edmund personally. He also had an accident with his car, he said, but luckily he didn't hurt himself or anyone else.'

'Holy cow,' said Peter.

'He always had a fondness for the bottle, you know,' Julian said, 'and a thimble-belly to go with it. He really had to go on the wagon five or six years ago, wasn't it, Frieda? Maybe you didn't know Edmund then, Peter. Well, he did, but it didn't last long. Then it got worse when Lillian walked out. But now *this* job—'

Frieda Markus giggled. 'This job! – Lucienne didn't help and you know it. She invited Edmund to her place a couple of times and plied him. Made him talk about his troubles with Mag.'

Troubles. Peter felt a twinge of dislike for Edmund for talking about his 'troubles' after only three months or so of marriage. Didn't everyone have troubles? Did people have to bore their friends with them? 'Maybe he deserved it,' Peter murmured.

'In a way, *yes*,' Julian said forcefully, and reached for a cigarette. Julian's aggressive attitude implied that the anti-Edmund campaign wasn't over. 'He's weak,' Julian added.

Peter thanked Julian for the loan of the two books, and took his leave. Again he had work to do in the evening, so he couldn't linger for a drink. At home, Peter hesitated between calling Lucienne or Anita, decided on Lucienne, but she didn't answer, so he tried Anita. Anita was home and Lucienne was there. Both spoke with Peter, and both sounded merry. Peter asked Lucienne about Edmund.

'Oh, he'll be sprung in another week or so, he said. But he won't be quite the same man, I think, when he comes out.'

'How do you mean that?'

'Well, he's lost his job and this story isn't going to make it easier for him to get another one. He's probably lost Magda too, because Edmund told me she'd leave him if they didn't move out of New York.'

'So . . . maybe they will move,' said Peter. 'He told you he'd definitely lost his job?'

'Oh yes. They call it a leave of absence at his office, but Edmund admitted they're not taking him back.' Lucienne gave a short, shrill laugh. 'Just as well they do move out of New York. Magda hates *us*, you know. And frankly Edmund never was one of us – so in a way it's understandable.'

Was it understandable, Peter wondered as he got down to his own work. There was something vicious about the whole thing, and he'd been vicious plying Edmund with beers that day. The curious thing was that Peter felt no compassion for Edmund.

One might have thought that the group would leave Edmund alone, at least, even make some effort to cheer him up (without drinks) when he got out of the Payne-Whitney, but it was just the opposite, Peter observed. Anita Ketchum invited Edmund for a quiet dinner at her apartment, and asked Peter to come too. She did not ply him with drink, though Edmund had at least three on his own. Edmund was morose, and Anita did not make his mood any better by talking against Magda. She fairly said that Edmund could and should do better than Magda, and that he ought to try as soon as possible. Peter had to concur here.

'She doesn't seem to make you very happy, Ed,' Peter remarked in a man-to-man way, 'and now I hear she wants you to move out of New York.'

'That's true,' Edmund said, 'and I dunno where else I'd get a decent job.'

They talked until late, getting nowhere, really. Peter left before Edmund did. Peter found that the memory of Edmund depressed him: a tall, hunched figure in limp clothes, looking at the floor as he strolled around Anita's living room with a glass in his hand.

Lucienne was home in bed reading when the telephone rang at

one in the morning. It was Edmund, and he said he was going to get a divorce from Mag.

'She just walked out – just now,' Edmund said in a happy but a bit drunk-sounding voice. 'Said she was going to stay in a hotel tonight. I don't even know where.'

Lucienne realized that he wanted a word of praise from her, or a congratulation. 'Well, dear Edmund, it may be for the best. I hope it can all be settled smoothly. After all, you haven't been married long.'

'No. I think I'm doing – I mean she's doing – the right thing,' said Edmund heavily.

Lucienne assured him that she thought so too.

Now Edmund was going to look for another job. He didn't think Mag would make any difficulties, financial or otherwise, about the divorce. 'She's a young woman w-who likes her privacy quite a bit. She's surprisingly . . . *independent*, y'know?' Edmund hiccuped.

Lucienne smiled, thinking any woman would want independence from Edmund. 'We'll all be wishing you luck, Edmund. And let us know if you think we can pull strings anywhere.'

Charles Forbes and Julian Markus went to Edmund's apartment one evening, to discuss business, Charles later said to Lucienne, as Charles had an idea of Edmund's becoming a freelance accountant, and in fact Charles's publishing house needed such a man now. They drank hardly anything, according to Charles, but they did stay up quite late. Edmund had been down in the dumps, and around midnight had lowered the scotch bottle by several inches.

That was on a Thursday night, and by Tuesday morning, Edmund was dead. The cleaning woman had come in with her key and found him asleep in bed, she thought, at nine in the morning. She hadn't realized until nearly noon, and then she had called the police. The police hadn't been able to find Magda, and notifying anybody had been much delayed, so it was Wednesday evening before any of the group knew: Peter Tomlin saw an item in his own newspaper, and telephoned Lucienne.

'A mixture of sleeping pills and alcohol, but they don't suspect suicide,' Peter said.

Neither did Lucienne suspect suicide. 'What an end,' she said with a sigh. 'Now what?' She was not at all shocked, but vaguely thinking about the others in their circle hearing the news, or reading it now.

'Well – funeral service tomorrow in a Long Island – um – funeral home, it says.'

Peter and Lucienne agreed they should go.

The group of friends, Lucienne Gauss, Peter Tomlin, the Markuses, the Forbeses, Tom Strathmore, Anita Ketchum, were all there and formed at least a half of the small gathering. Maybe a few of Edmund's relatives had come, but the group wasn't sure: Edmund's family lived in the Chicago area, and no one had ever met any of them. Magda was there, dressed in gray with a thin black veil. She stood apart, and barely nodded to Lucienne and the others. It was a nondenominational service to which Lucienne paid no attention, and she doubted if her friends did – except to recognize the words as empty rote and close their ears to it. Afterwards, Lucienne and Charles said they didn't wish to follow the casket to the grave, and neither did the others.

Anita's mouth looked stony, though it was fixed in a pensive, very faint smile. Taxis waited, and they straggled towards them. Tom Strathmore walked with his head down. Charles Forbes looked up at the late summer sky. Charles walked between his wife, Ellen, and Lucienne, and suddenly he said to Lucienne:

'You know, I rang Edmund up a couple of times in the night – just to annoy him. I have to confess that. Ellen knows.'

'Did you,' said Lucienne calmly.

Tom, just behind them, had heard this. 'I did worse,' he said with a twitch of a smile. 'I told Edmund he might lose his job if he started taking Magda out with him on his business lunches.'

Ellen laughed. 'Oh, that's not serious, Tom. That's—' But she didn't finish.

We killed him, Lucienne thought. Everybody was thinking that, and no one had the guts to say it. Anyone of them might have said, 'We killed him, you know?' but no one did. 'We'll miss him,' Lucienne said finally, as if she meant it.

'Ye-es,' someone replied with equal gravity.

They climbed into three taxis, promising to see each other soon.

THE TERRORS OF
BASKET-WEAVING

D iane's terror began in an innocent and fortuitous way. She and
her husband, Reg, lived in Manhattan, but had a cottage on the
Massachusetts coast near Truro where they spent most weekends.
Diane was a press relations officer in an agency called Retting. Reg
was a lawyer. They were both thirty-eight, childless by choice, and
both earned good salaries.

They enjoyed walks along the beach, and usually they took walks
alone, not with each other. Diane liked to look for pretty stones,
interesting shells, bottles of various sizes and colors, bits of wood
rubbed smooth by sand and wind. These items she took back to the
unpainted gray cottage they called 'the shack,' lived with them for
a few weeks or months, then Diane threw nearly all of them out,
because she didn't want the shack to become a magpie's nest. One
Sunday morning she found a wicker basket bleached nearly white
and with its bottom stoved in, but its frame and sides quite sturdy.
This looked like an old-fashioned crib basket for a baby, because one
end of it rose higher than the other, the foot part tapered, and it was
just the size for a newborn or for a baby up to a few months. It was
the kind called a Moses basket, Diane thought.

Was the basket even American? It was amusing to think that it might have fallen overboard or been thrown away, old and broken, from a passing Italian tanker, or some foreign boat that might have had a woman and child on board. Anyway, Diane decided to take it home, and she put it for the nonce on a bench on the side porch of the shack, where colored stones and pebbles and sea glass already lay. She might try to repair it, for fun, because in its present condition it was useless. Reg was then shifting sand with a snow shovel from one side of the wooden front steps, and was going to plant more beach grass from the dunes, like a second line of troops, between them and the sea to keep the sand in place. His industry, which Diane knew would go on another hour or so until lunchtime – and cold lobster and potato salad was already in the fridge – inspired her to try her hand at the basket now.

She had realized a few minutes before that the kind of slender twigs she needed stood already in a brass cylinder beside their small fireplace. Withes or withies – the words sounded nice in her head – might be more appropriate, but on the other hand the twigs would give more strength to the bottom of a basket which she might use to hold small potted plants, for instance. One would be able to move several pots into the sun all at once in a basket – if she could mend the basket.

Diane took the pruning shears, and cut five lengths of reddish-brown twigs – results of a neighbor's apple-tree pruning, she recalled – and then snipped nine shorter lengths for the crosspieces. She estimated she would need nine. A ball of twine sat handy on a shelf, and Diane at once got to work. She plucked out what was left of the broken pieces in the basket, and picked up one of her long twigs. The slightly pointed ends, an angle made by the shears, slipped easily between the sturdy withes that formed the bottom rim. She took up a second and a third. Diane then, before she attempted to tie the long pieces, wove the shorter lengths under and over the longer, at right angles. The twigs were just flexible enough to be manageable, and stiff enough to be strong. No piece projected too far. She had cut them just the right length, measuring only with her eye or thumb before snipping. Then the twine.

Over and under, around the twig ends at the rim and through the withes already decoratively twisted there, then a good solid knot. She was able to continue with the cord to the next twig in a couple of places, so she did not have to tie a knot at each cross-piece. Suddenly to her amazement the basket was repaired, and it looked splendid.

In her first glow of pride, Diane looked at her watch. Hardly fifteen minutes had passed since she had come into the house! How had she done it? She held the top end of the basket up, and pressed the palm of her right hand against the floor of the basket. It gave out firm-sounding squeaks. It had spring in it. And strength. She stared at the neatly twisted cord, at the correct over-and-under lengths, all about the diameter of pencils, and she wondered again how she had done it.

That was when the terror began to creep up on her, at first like a faint suspicion or surmise or question. Had she some relative or ancestor not so far in the past, who had been an excellent basket-weaver? Not that she knew of, and the idea made her smile with amusement. Grandmothers and great-grandmothers who could quilt and crochet didn't count. This was more primitive.

Yes, people had been weaving baskets thousands of years before Christ, and maybe even a million years ago, hadn't they? Baskets might have come before clay pots.

The answer to her question, how had she done it, might be that the ancient craft of basket-weaving had been carried on for so long by the human race that it had surfaced in her this Sunday morn-ing in the late twentieth century. Diane found this thought rather frightening.

As she set the table for lunch, she upset a wine glass, but the glass was empty and it didn't break. Reg was still shoveling, but slowing up, nearly finished. It was still early for lunch, but Diane had wanted the table set, the salad dressing made in the wooden bowl, before she took a swat at the work she had brought with her. Finally she sat with a yellow pad and pencil, and opened the plastic-covered folder marked RETTING, plus her own name, DIANE CLARKE, in smaller letters at the bottom. She had to write three hundred words about a kitchen gadget that extracted air from plastic bags of apples, oranges, potatoes or whatever. After the air was extracted, the bags could be stored in the bottom of the fridge as usual, but the product kept much longer and took up less space because of the absence of air in the bag. She had seen the gadget work in the office, and she had a photograph of it now. It was a sixteen-inch-long tube which one fastened to the cold water tap in the kitchen. The water from the tap drained away, but its force moved a turbine in the tube, which created a vacuum after a hollow needle was stuck into the sealed bag. Diane understood the principle quite well, but she began to feel odd and disoriented.

It was odd to be sitting in a cottage built in a simple style more than a hundred years ago, to have just repaired a basket in the manner that people would have made or repaired a basket thousands of years ago, and to be trying to compose a sentence about a gadget whose existence depended upon modern plumbing, sealed packaging, transport by machinery of fruit and vegetables grown hundreds of miles (possibly thousands) from the places where they would be consumed. If this weren't so, people could simply carry fruit and vegetables home in a sack from the fields, or in baskets such as the one she had just mended.

Diane put down the pencil, picked up a ballpoint pen, lit a cigarette, and wrote the first words. 'Need more space in your fridge? Tired of having to buy more lemons at the supermarket than you can use in the next month? Here is an inexpensive gadget that might interest you.' It wasn't particularly inexpensive, but no matter. Lots of people were going to pay thousands of dollars for this gadget. She would be paid a sizable amount also, meaning a certain fraction of her salary for writing about it. As she worked on, she kept seeing a vision of her crib-shaped basket and thinking that the basket – per se, as a thing to be used – was far more important than the kitchen gadget. However, it was perfectly normal to consider a basket more important or useful, she supposed, for the simple reason that a basket was.

'Nice walk this morning?' Reg asked, relaxing with a pre-lunch glass of cold white wine. He was standing in the low-ceilinged living room, in shorts, an unbuttoned shirt, sandals. His face had browned further, and the skin was pinkish over his cheekbones.

'Yes. Found a basket. Rather nice. Want to see it?'

'Sure.'

She led the way to the side porch, and indicated the basket on the wooden table. 'The bottom was all broken – so I fixed it.'

'*You* fixed it?' Reg was leaning over it with admiration. 'Yeah, I can see. Nice job, Di.'

She felt a tremor, a little like shame. Or was it fear? She felt uncomfortable as Reg picked up the basket and looked at its underside. 'Might be nice to hold kindling – or magazines, maybe,' she said. 'We can always throw it away when we get bored with it.'

'Throw it away, no! It's sort of amusing – shaped like a baby's cradle or something.'

'That's what I thought – that it must have been made for a baby.' She drifted back into the living room, wishing now that Reg would stop examining the basket.

'Didn't know you had such talents, Di. Girl Scout lore?'

Diane gave a laugh. Reg knew she'd never joined the Girl Scouts. 'Don't forget the Gartners are coming at seven-thirty.'

'Um-m. Yes, thanks. I didn't forget. – What's for dinner? We've got everything we need?'

Diane said they had. The Gartners were bringing raspberries from their garden plus cream. Reg had meant he was willing to drive to town in case they had to buy anything else.

The Gartners arrived just before eight, and Reg made dacquiris. There was scotch for any who preferred it, and Olivia Gartner did. She was a serious drinker and held it well. An investment counselor, she was, and her husband Pete was a professor in the math department at Columbia.

Diane, after a swim around four o'clock, had collected some dry reeds from the dunes and among these had put a few long-stemmed blossoming weeds and wild flowers, blue and pink and orangy-yellow. She had laid all these in the crib-shaped basket which she had set on the floor near the fireplace.

'Isn't this pretty!' said Olivia during her second scotch, as if the drink had opened her eyes. She meant the floral arrangement, but Reg at once said:

'And look at the basket, Olivia! Diane found it on the beach today and *repaired* it.' Reg lifted the basket as high as his head, so Olivia and Pete could admire its underside.

Olivia chuckled. 'That's fantastic, Diane! Beautiful! How long did it take you? – It's a sweet basket.'

'That's the funny thing,' Diane began, eager to express herself. 'It took me about twelve minutes!'

'Look how proud she is of it!' said Reg, smiling.

Pete was running his thumb over the apple twigs at the bottom, nodding his approval.

'Yes, it was almost terrifying,' Diane went on.

'Terrifying?' Pete lifted his eyebrows.

'I'm not explaining myself very well.' Diane had a polite smile on her face, though she was serious. 'I felt as if I'd struck some hidden talent or knowledge – just suddenly. Everything I did, I felt sure of. I was amazed.'

'Looks strong too,' Pete said, and set the basket back where it had been.

Then they talked about something else. The cost of heating, if they used their cottages at all in the coming winter. Diane had hoped the basket conversation would continue a little longer. Another round of drinks, while Diane put their cold supper on the table. Bowls of jellied consommé with a slice of lemon to start with. They sat down. Diane felt unsatisfied. Or was it a sense of disturbance?

Disturbance because of what? Just because they hadn't pursued the subject of the basket? Why should they have? It was merely a basket to them, mended the way anyone could have mended it. Or could just anyone have mended it that well? Diane happened to be sitting at the end of the table, so the basket was hardly four feet from her, behind her and to her right. She felt bothered somehow even by the basket's nearness. That was very odd. She must get to the bottom of it – that was funny, in view of the basket repair – but now wasn't the time, with three other people talking, and half her mind on seeing that her guests had a good meal.

While they were drinking coffee, Diane lit three candles and the oil lamp, and they listened to a record of Mozart *divertimenti*. They didn't listen, but it served as background music for their conversation. Diane listened to the music. It sounded skillful, even modern, and extremely civilized. Diane enjoyed her brandy. The brandy too seemed the epitome of human skill, care, knowledge. Not like a basket any child could put together. Perhaps a child in years couldn't, but a child as to progress in the evolution of the human race could weave a basket.

Was she possibly feeling her drinks? Diane pulled her long cotton skirt farther down over her knees. The subject was lobbies now, the impotence of any president, even Congress against them.

Monday morning early Diane and Reg flew back to New York by helicopter. Neither had to be at work before eleven. Diane had supposed that New York and work would put the disquieting thoughts re the basket out of her head, but that was not so. New York seemed to emphasize what she had felt up at the shack, even though the origin of her feelings had stayed at the shack. What were her feelings, anyway? Diane disliked vagueness, and was used to labeling her emotions jealousy, resentment, suspicion or whatever, even if the emotion was not always to her credit. But this?

What she felt was most certainly not guilt, though it was similarly troubling and unpleasant. Not envy either, not in the sense of desiring to master basketry so she could make a truly great basket, whatever that was. She'd always thought basket-weaving an occupation for the simpleminded, and it had become in fact a symbol of what psychiatrists advised disturbed people to take up. That was not it at all.

Diane felt that she had lost herself. Since repairing that basket, she wasn't any longer Diane Clarke, not completely, anyway. Neither was she anybody else, of course. It wasn't that she felt she had assumed the identity, even partially, of some remote ancestor. How remote, anyway? No. She felt rather that she was living with a great many people from the past, that they were in her brain or mind (Diane did not believe in a soul, and found the idea of a collective unconscious too vague to be of importance), and that people from human antecedents were bound up with her, influencing her, controlling her every bit as much as, up to now, she had been controlling herself. This thought was by no means comforting, but it was at least a partial explanation, maybe, for the disquietude that she was experiencing. It was not even an explanation, she realized, but rather a description of her feelings.

She wanted to say something to Reg about it and didn't, thinking that anything she tried to say along these lines would sound either silly or fuzzy. By now five days had passed since she had repaired the basket up at Truro, and they were going up to the shack again this weekend. The five working days at the office had passed as had a lot of other weeks for Diane. She had had a set-to with Jan Heyningen, the art director, on Wednesday, and had come near telling him what she thought of his stubbornness and bad taste, but she hadn't. She had merely smoldered. It had happened before. She and Reg had gone out to dinner at the apartment of some friends on Thursday. All as usual, outwardly.

The unusual was the schizoid atmosphere in her head. Was that it? Two personalities? Diane toyed with this possibility all Friday afternoon at the office while she read through new promotion-ready material. Was she simply imagining that several hundred prehistoric ancestors were somehow dwelling within her? No, frankly, she wasn't. That idea was even less credible than Jung's collective unconscious. And suddenly she rejected the simple schizo idea or explanation also. Schizophrenia was a catch-all, she had heard, for a lot of derangements that couldn't otherwise be diagnosed. She didn't feel schizoid, anyway, didn't feel like two people, or three, or more. She felt simply scared, mysteriously terrified. But only one thing in the least awkward happened that week: she had let one side of the lettuce-swinger slip out of her hand on the terrace, and lettuce flew everywhere, hung from the potted bamboo trees, was caught on rose thorns, lay fresh and clean on the red tile paving, and on the seat of the glider. Diane had laughed, even though there was no more lettuce in the house. She was tense, perhaps, therefore clumsy. A little accident like that could happen any time.

During the flight to the Cape, Diane had a happy thought: she'd use the basket not just for floral arrangements but for collecting more *objets trouvés* from the beach, or better yet for potatoes and onions in the kitchen. She'd treat it like any old basket. That would take the mystique out of it, the terror. To have felt terror was absurd.

So Saturday morning while Reg worked on the nonelectric typewriter which they kept at the shack, Diane went for a walk on the beach with the basket. She had put a piece of newspaper in the basket, and she collected a greater number than usual of colored pebbles, a few larger smooth rocks – one orange in color, making it almost a *trompe l'oeil* for a mango – plus an interesting piece of sea-worn wood that looked like a boomerang. Wouldn't that be odd, she thought, if it really were an ancient boomerang worn shorter, thinner, until only the curve remained unchanged? As she walked back to the shack, the basket emitted faint squeaks in unison with her tread. The basket was so heavy, she had to carry it in two hands, letting its side rest against her hip, but she was not at all afraid that the twigs of the bottom would give. *Her work.*

Stop it, she told herself.

When she began to empty the basket on the porch's wooden table, she realized she had gathered too many stones, so she dropped more than half of them, quickly choosing the less interesting, over the porch rail onto the sand. Finally she shook the newspaper of its sand, and started to put it back in the basket. Sunlight fell on the glossy reddish-brown apple twigs. Over and under, not every one secured by twine, because for some twigs it hadn't been necessary. New work, and yet – Diane felt the irrational fear creeping over her again, and she pressed the newspaper quickly into the basket, pressed it at the crib-shaped edges, so that all her work was hidden. Then she tossed it carelessly on the floor, could have transferred some potatoes from a brown paper bag into it but she wanted to get away from the basket now.

An hour or so later, when she and Reg were finishing lunch, Reg laughing and about to light a cigarette, Diane felt an inner jolt as if – What? She deliberately relaxed, and gave her attention, more of it, to what Reg was saying. But it was as if the sound had been switched off a TV set. She saw him, but she wasn't listening or hearing. She blinked and forced herself to listen. Reg was talking about renting a tractor to clear some of their sand away, about terracing, and maintaining their property with growing things. They'd drawn a simple plan weeks ago, Diane remembered. But again she was feeling not like herself, as if she had lost herself in millions of people as an individual might get lost in a huge crowd. No, that was too simple, she felt. She was still trying to find solace in words. Or was she even dodging something? If so, what?

'What?' Reg asked, leaning back in his chair now, relaxed.

'Nothing. Why?'

'You were lost in thought.'

Diane might have replied that she had just had a better idea for a current project at Retting, might have replied several things, but she said suddenly, 'I'm thinking of asking for a leave of absence. Maybe just a month. I think Retting would do it, and it'd do me good.'

Reg looked puzzled. 'You're feeling tired, you mean? Just lately?'

'No. I feel somehow upset. Turned around, I don't know. I thought maybe a month of just being away from the office . . . ' But work was supposed to be good in such a situation as hers. Work kept people from dwelling on their problems. But she hadn't a problem, rather a state of mind.

'Oh ... well,' Reg said. 'Heyningen getting on your nerves maybe.'

Diane shifted. It would have been easy to say yes, that was it. She took a cigarette, and Reg lit it. 'Thanks. You're going to laugh, Reg. But that basket bothers me.' She looked at him, feeling ashamed, and curiously defensive.

'The one you found last weekend? You're worried a child might've drowned in it, lost at sea?' Reg smiled as if at a mild joke he'd just made.

'No, not at all. Nothing like that. I told you last weekend. It simply bothers me that I repaired it so easily. There. That's it. And you can say I'm cracked – I don't care.'

'I do not – quite – understand what you mean.'

'It made me feel somehow – prehistoric. And funny. Still does.'

Reg shook his head. 'I can sort of understand. Honestly. But – another way of looking at it, Di, is to realize that it's a very simple activity after all, mending or even making a basket. Not that I don't admire the neat job you did, but it's not like – sitting down and playing Beethoven's Emperor Concerto, for instance, if you've never had a piano lesson in your life.'

'No.' She'd never had a basket-making lesson in her life, she might have said. She was silent, wondering if she should put in her leave of absence request on Monday, as a gesture, a kind of appeasement to the uneasiness she felt? Emotions demanded gestures, she had read somewhere, in order to be exorcised. Did she really believe that?

'Really, Di, the leave of absence is one thing, but that basket – It's an interesting basket, sure, because it's not machine-made and you don't see that shape any more. I've seen you get excited about stones you find. I understand. They're beautiful. But to let yourself get upset about—'

'Stones are different,' she interrupted. 'I can admire them. I'm not upset about them. I told you I feel I'm not exactly myself – me – any longer. I feel lost in a strange way – *Identity*, I mean,' she broke in again, when Reg started to speak.

'Oh, Di!' He got up. 'What do you mean you told me that? You didn't.'

'Well, I have now. I feel – as if a lot of other people were inside me besides myself. And I feel lost because of that. Do you understand?'

Reg hesitated. 'I understand the words. But the feeling – no.'

Even that was something. Diane felt grateful, and relieved that she had said this much to him.

'Go ahead with the leave of absence idea, darling. I didn't mean to be so abrupt.'

Diane put her cigarette out. 'I'll think about it.' She got up to make coffee.

That afternoon, after tidying the kitchen, Diane put another newspaper in the basket, and unloaded the sack of potatoes into it, plus three or four onions – familiar and contemporary objects. Perishable too. She made herself not think about the basket or even about the leave of absence for the rest of the day. Around 7:30, she and Reg drove off to Truro, where there was a street party organized by an ecology group. Wine and beer and soft drinks, hot dogs and jukebox music. They encountered the Gartners and a few other neighbors. The wine was undrinkable, the atmosphere marvelous. Diane danced with a couple of merry strangers and was for a few hours happy.

A month's leave of absence, she thought as she stood under the shower that night, was absurd and unnecessary. Temporary aberration to have considered it. If the basket – a really simple object as Reg had said – annoyed her so much, the thing to do was to get rid of it, burn it.

Sunday morning Reg took the car and went to deliver his Black & Decker or some appliance of it to the Gartners, who lived eight miles away. As soon as he had left, Diane went to the side porch, replaced the potatoes and onions in the brown paper bag which she had saved as she saved most bags that arrived at the shack, and taking the basket with its newspaper and a book of matches, she walked out onto the sand in the direction of the ocean. She struck a match and lit the newspaper, and laid the basket over it. After a moment's hesitation, as if from shock, the basket gave a crack and began to burn. The drier sides burned more quickly than the newer apple twigs, of course. With a stick, Diane poked every last pale withe into the flames, until nothing remained except black ash and some yellow-glowing embers, and finally these went out in the bright sunshine and began to darken. Diane pushed sand with her feet over the ashes, until nothing was visible. She breathed deeply as she walked back to the shack, and realized that she had been holding her breath, or almost, the entire time of the burning.

She was not going to say anything to Reg about getting rid of the basket, and he was not apt to notice its absence, Diane knew.

Diane did mention, on Tuesday in New York, that she had changed her mind about asking for a leave of absence. The implication was that she felt better, but she didn't say that.

The basket was gone, she would never see it again, unless she deliberately tried to conjure it up in memory, and that she didn't want to do. She felt better with the thing out of the shack, destroyed. She knew that the burning had been an action on her part to get rid of a feeling within her, a primitive action, if she thought about it, because though the basket had been tangible, her thoughts were not tangible. And they proved damned hard to destroy.

Three weeks after the burning of the basket, her crazy idea of being a 'walking human race' or some such lingered. She would continue to listen to Mozart and Bartók, they'd go to the shack most weekends, and she would continue to pretend that her life counted for something, that she was part of the stream or evolution of the human race, though she felt now that she had spurned that position or small function by burning the basket. For a week, she realized, she had grasped something, and then she had deliberately thrown it away. In fact, she was no happier now than during that week when the well-mended basket had been in her possession. But she was determined not to say anything more about it to Reg. He had been on the verge of impatience that Saturday before the Sunday when she had burned it. And in fact could she even put any more into words? No. So she had to stop thinking about it. Yes.

UNDER A DARK ANGEL'S EYE

N ow he was on the last leg of his journey, the bus stretch from the airport to Arlington Hills. There would be nobody to meet him at the bus terminal, and Lee didn't mind in the least. In fact he preferred it. He could walk with his small suitcase the four or five blocks to the Capitol Hotel (he assumed it was still functioning), check in, then telephone Winston Greeves to say he had arrived. Maybe they could even wind up the business with the lawyer today, because it would be only four in the afternoon by the time Lee would be phoning Winston. It was a matter of signing a paper in regard to the house where Lee Mandeville had been born. Lee owned it, and now he had to sell it, because he needed the money. He didn't care, he wasn't sentimental about the two-story white house with the green lawn in front. Or was he? Lee honestly didn't think so. He'd had some nasty, unpleasant hours in that house, as well as a few happy ones – a barefoot boyhood, tossing a football with chums from the neighborhood on the front lawn. He had lost Louise there, too.

Lee shifted in his seat, rested his cheek against his hand which was lightly closed in a fist, and stared out the window at the Indiana landscape that drifted past. He barely recognized a small town they were going through. How long had it been, nine, no ten years since he had been to Arlington Hills. Ten years ago he had come to visit his mother in the nursing home called the Hearthside, and she had either not recognized him or pretended not to, or had really thought he was someone else. At any rate she had managed to come out with 'Don't come back!' just as he had been going out the door of her room. Winston who had accompanied Lee had chuckled and shaken his head, as if to say, 'What can you do with the old folks – except put up with them?'

Yes, they lived on forever these days. Doctors didn't let old people die, not as long as there were pills, injections, kidney machines, new drugs, all costing dearly. That was why Lee had to sell the house. For twelve years, since his mother had entered the nursing home, the house had been rented to a couple whose two children were in their teens now. Lee had never charged them much rent, because they couldn't afford a high rent, and Lee valued their reliability. But Lee's mother was now costing between five and six hundred dollars a week, her savings had run out five years ago, and Lee had borne the burden ever since, though Medicare paid some of it. His mother Edna wasn't ill, but she did need certain pills, tranquilizers alternating with pick-ups, plus checkups and special vitamins. Lee paid little attention to his mother's health, because it stayed the same year after year. She was ambulant but crochety, and never wrote to Lee, because he didn't write to her. Even before the nursing home, she had cursed Lee out by letter for imaginary faults and deeds, so Lee had washed his hands of his mother, except to pay her bills. An offspring owed that to a parent, Lee believed, just as a parent owed to a child love, care, and as much education as the parent could afford. Children were expensive and time-consuming, but the parents certainly were repaid when they became elderly and imposed the same burdens on their children.

Lee Mandeville was fifty-five, unmarried, and had a modestly successful antique shop in Chicago. He dealt in old furniture, a few good carpets, old pictures and frames, brass and silver items and silverware also. He was by no means a big wheel in the antique business, but he was known and respected in Chicago and beyond. He was trim of figure, not balding, and without much gray in his hair. His face was clean shaven, with a crease in either cheek, and he had rather heavy eyebrows above friendly, thoughtful blue-gray eyes. He liked meeting strangers in his shop, summing them up, finding out whether they wanted to buy something because it would look nice somewhere in their house or because they really fell in love with an object.

As the bus rocked and lumbered into Arlington Hills, Lee tensed himself, already uneasy, and unhappy. Well, he did not intend to see his mother this trip. He didn't want to see her, and he didn't have to. She was so far gone mentally that Lee had had power of attorney for nearly ten years. Winston had at last obtained his mother's signature for that. She had held out for months, not for any logical reason but out of stubbornness, and because she enjoyed making difficulties for other people. Twenty minutes to four, Lee saw from a glance at his wristwatch. He stood up and hauled his suitcase down from the rack before the bus had quite stopped.

'Lee! – How *are* you, Lee?'

Lee was surprised by the voice, and it took him a second to spot Win in the little crowd waiting for debarkers.'Win! *Hello!* I didn't expect to see you here!' Lee's smile was broad. They patted each other on the shoulder. 'How're things?'

'Oh – much the same,' Win replied. 'Nothing much changes around here. That's all the luggage you've got? . . . My car's over here, Lee – and Kate and I expect you to be *our guest*. All right?' Win already had Lee's suitcase in his hand. Win was in his early sixties with straight gray hair that looked always windblown. He wore navy blue trousers and a blue shirt with no tie. Win was head of an insurance company that he himself had founded, and the Mandevilles had insured their house and cars with Win for decades.

'It's kind of you, Win, but honestly, for one night – I can just as well stay at the old Capitol, you know.' Lee didn't want to say that he preferred to go to a hotel.

'Won't hear of it. Kate's got your room all ready.'

Win was walking toward his car, and Lee went with him. After all, Win had been helpful, very, with Edna, and Win seemed really pleased to have him. 'You win, Win,' Lee said, smiling, 'and thank you. How's Kate? And Mort?' Mort was their son.

'Oh – the same.' Win stuck Lee's lightweight suitcase onto the back seat of his car. 'Mort's working now in Bloomington. Car salesman.'

'Still married?' Lee recalled some awful trouble with Mort's wife – she'd run off with another man, abandoned their small child, and then, Lee thought, they had got back together again.

'No, they finally arranged a – a divorce,' Win said, and started the car.

Lee didn't know whether to say 'Good' or not, so he said nothing. Now his mother, Lee thought. That was the next question. He didn't care how his mother was. Instead, Lee said, 'I was thinking we might wind this business up this afternoon, Win. It's just a matter of signing a paper, isn't it?' The house in Barrett Avenue was sold, to a young couple named Varick – Ralph and Phyllis, Lee remembered from the real estate agent's letter.

'Ye-es,' said Win, and his heavy hands opened on the steering wheel for a couple of seconds, then closed tightly. 'I suppose we could.'

Lee gathered that Win hadn't made an appointment as yet. 'It's still old Graham, isn't it? He knows us both so well – can't we just barge in?'

'Sure – okay, Lee.'

Win Greeves steered the car into Main Street, and Lee glanced at storefronts, shop signs, seeing a lot of change since he had been here last, and for the worse aesthetically. Main Street looked more crowded, both with people and shops. Maybe Graham's old office hadn't changed. Douglas Graham was a lawyer and notary public. He had drawn up a power of attorney statement years ago, at Lee's request, so that Lee could sign checks for his mother's bills, and Winston Greeves's name had been added also in executor capacity, because Win was on the scene in Arlington Hills, and even visited his mother sometimes – though his mother didn't always recognize him, Win said – and in the last years as Edna's bank account had grown low, Lee sent five hundred dollars or a thousand to bolster it every month or so. Win sent Lee the bank statements for the account now in Lee's name, and an explanation of the bills.

'I don't need the Varicks, I suppose,' Lee said. 'To be present when I sign, I mean.'

'I know Ralph Varick's already signed,' said Win. 'Fine couple, those two. You should meet them, Lee.'

'Well – not really necessary. Give them my best wishes – if you ever see them.' Lee didn't want to go near the old house, didn't want to see it. The nice family, the Youngs, who couldn't afford to buy the house, were still there for the rest of this month, but Lee didn't want to visit them even merely to say hello. He felt sorry for them. He forced himself to ask the unavoidable. 'And I suppose my mother's just the same too?'

Win chuckled and shook his head. 'She's – yes – that's about it.'

Don't they *ever* kick the bucket, Lee thought bitterly, and nearly laughed at himself. And after he had banked the money for the house, how much longer, how many more years would his mother live, eating up five or six hundred dollars a week? Now she was eighty-six. Couldn't she go on till ninety and ninety-one? Why not? Lee remembered three grandparents out of four, plus one maternal uncle, who had all died in their nineties.

'Here we are,' said Win, pulling in at the curb.

Lee fished for a coin, and dropped it in the meter before Win could insert his. Doug Graham had no secretary, and came out of the office himself in response to the bell they had rung on entering his waiting room.

'Well, Lee – and Win. How are you, Lee? You're looking well.' Doug Graham gave Lee a warm handshake. Doug was heavier than he had been ten years ago, in his late sixties now, a big man in a baggy beige suit that showed no sign of a proper crease.

'Quite all right, Doug. And you?' Lee wished he could have said friendlier words, but they didn't come for some reason. Doug had done many a service for Lee and his mother over the years. Lee remembered with embarrassment that Doug had talked his mother out of making a will some twenty years ago, which would have cut Lee out as only offspring and nearest of kin, and bestowed all on a young black woman who cleaned the house and who had talked her way into Edna's affections.

Doug Graham quietly and calmly arranged the few papers on his desk, and pointed out where Lee was to sign. 'After you've read the agreement, of course, Lee,' said Doug with a smile.

Lee glanced through. It was a bill of sale for the Barrett Avenue house, pretty plain and simple. Lee signed. The deed was there too, with Lee's father's signature, also that of Lee's grandfather, but before that a name that was not of the family. Ralph David Varick was the last name. Lee did not have to sign this.

'Hope you're not too sentimental about it, Lee,' said Doug in his slow, deep voice. 'After all, you're not here much of late – in the last years. We've missed you.'

Lee shook his head. 'Not sentimental, no.'

The pen was handed to Winston Greeves, who got up to sign the purchase paper as witness.

'Sorry it has to be, though,' said Doug, 'somehow. And sorry about your mother.'

Again Lee felt a twinge of shame, because Doug knew, everyone knew, that his mother was not merely senile but quietly insane. 'Well – these things happen. At least she's not in pain,' Lee said awkwardly.

'That is true . . .Thank you, Win. And that about winds it up, I think . . . How long're you here for, Lee?'

Lee told him just till tomorrow, because he had to get back to his shop in Chicago. He asked what he owed Doug, and Doug said nothing at all, and again Lee felt shame, because Doug must know that he had sold the house because he couldn't otherwise meet expenses.

'We need a little drink on this,' said Doug, pulling out a whiskey bottle from a lower drawer in his desk. 'It's just about quitting time anyway, so we deserve it.'

They each had small, neat drinks, standing up. But the atmosphere remained sad and a little strained, Lee felt.

Ten minutes later, they were at the Greeveses' house – bigger than the house Lee had just signed away, with a bigger lawn and more expensive trees. Kate Greeves welcomed Lee as if he were one of the family, pressing his hand in both hers, kissing his cheek.

'Lee, I'm so glad Win persuaded you to stay! Come, I'll show you your room, then we can relax.' She took him upstairs.

There was a smell of baking and of warm cinnamon from the kitchen. His room was neat and clean, furnished with factory-made dressing table and chairs and bed, but Lee had seen worse. The Greeveses were doing their best to be nice to him.

'I'd love to take a little walk,' Lee said when he went back downstairs. 'Hardly six. Still a lot of daylight—'

'Oh, no! Stay and talk, Lee. Or I'll *drive* you around, if you'd like to see the old town.' Win seemed willing.

But that idea didn't appeal to Lee. He wanted to stretch his legs on his own, but he knew Win would protest that he'd have to walk fifteen minutes to get out of Rosedale, the residential section, and so on and so on. Lee found himself sitting in the living room with a strong scotch in his hands. Kate brought in a bowl of hot buttered popcorn.

The telephone rang, and the Greeveses exchanged a look, then Win went to get it in the hall.

Lee picked up an old glass paperweight with a spread blue butterfly in it. The paperweight was the size of a cake of soap and very pretty. He was about to ask Kate where she had got it from, when Win's voice saying *'No!'* made Lee keep his silence.

'*No*, I said,' Win said softly but in a tone of repressed wrath. 'And don't phone again tonight. I mean what I *say*.' There was a click as Win put the telephone down. When he returned to the living room, his hands were shaking slightly. He reached for his glass. 'Sorry about that,' he said to Lee with a nervous smile.

Something to do with Mort, Lee supposed. Maybe Mort himself. Lee thought it best not to ask questions. Kate also looked tense. Mort must be at least forty now, Lee thought. He was a weak type, and Lee remembered one adolescent scrape after another – a wrecked car, Mort picked up by the police for drunkenness somewhere, Mort marrying a girl because she was pregnant, the same wife Mort had just divorced, Win had said. Such troubles seemed silly to Lee, because they were so avoidable – compared to a deranged mother who lingered on and on.

'Not coming over, is he?' Kate whispered to Win as she bent to offer Win the popcorn bowl.

Win shook his head slowly and grimly.

Lee had barely heard Kate speak. They talked of other things during dinner, and only a little bit about Lee's mother. Her health was all right, she took walks in the garden there, came down to the dining room for every meal. Once a month there was a 'birthday party' for everyone whose birthday fell during that month. There was TV, not in every room, but in the communal hall downstairs.

'She still reads the Bible, I suppose,' said Lee, smiling a little.

'Oh, I suppose. There's one in every room there, I know,' Win replied, and glanced at his wife, who responded by asking Lee how his shop in Chicago was doing.

As Lee replied, he thought about his mother, grim-lipped and gruesome without her false teeth which she didn't always care to wear, reading her Bible. What did she get out of it? Certainly not the milk of human kindness, but of course that phrase was Shakespeare's. Or had Jesus said it first? The Old Testament was bloodthirsty, vengeful, even barbaric in places. His mother had always, or frequently enough, said to him, 'Read your Bible, Lee,' when he was depressed, discouraged, or when he had been 'tempted' maybe to buy a nice looking secondhand car on the installment plan, when he had been seventeen or eighteen. How innocent, buying a car on the installment plan, compared to what his mother had done when he was twenty-two! He had been engaged to Louisa Watts, madly in love with her, in love in a way, however, that could have lasted, that would have resulted in a good marriage, Lee believed. His mother had told Louisa that Lee had girls every-where, prostitute favorites too, that in his car he drove to other towns for his fun. And so on. And Louisa had been only nineteen. She had believed that, and she had been hurt. *Goddamn my mother*, Lee thought. And what had his mother gained by her lies? Keeping him at home, for herself? She hadn't. Louisa had married another man in less than a year, moved somewhere, maybe New York, and Lee had left home and gone to San Francisco for a while, worked as a longshoreman, gone to New Orleans and done the same. If Louisa only hadn't been married, he would have tried again with her, because she was the only girl in the world for him. Yes, he had met other girls, four or five. He had wanted to marry, but had never been able to convince himself (and maybe not the other girls either) that marriage would work. Then he had gone to Chicago when he had been nearly thirty.

'You don't like the pie, Lee?' asked Kate.

Lee realized that he had barely touched the hot apple pie, that he was squeezing his napkin in his left hand as if it were someone's neck. 'I do like the pie,' Lee said calmly, and proceeded to finish it.

That night, Lee slept badly. Thoughts turned in his head, yet when he tried to devote a few minutes to thinking something out, he got nowhere. It was a pleasure for him to get out of bed at dawn, dress quietly, and sneak down the stairs for a walk before anyone else was up. He hadn't bothered shaving. Lee was out of the Rosedale area in less than ten minutes. The air was sweet and clear, coolish for May. The town was awakening. There were milk trucks making deliveries, mailmen of course, and a few workmen boarding early buses.

'Lee? – It's Lee Mandeville, isn't it?'

Lee looked into the face of a young man in his twenties with brown wavy hair, in a tweed suit with shirt and tie. Vaguely Lee remembered the face, but couldn't have come up with the name if his life had depended on it.

'Charles Ritchie!' said the young man, laughing. 'Remember? I used to deliver groceries for your mother!'

'Oh, *sure*. Charlie.' Lee smiled, remembering a skinny twelve-year-old who sometimes drank a soda pop in their kitchen. 'Hey, aren't you missing your bus, Charlie?'

'Doesn't matter,' said the young man, barely glancing at the bus that was pulling away. 'What brings you here, Lee?'

'Selling the house. You remember the old house?'

'I sure do! – I'm sorry you're selling. I had the idea you might move back some time – for retirement or something.'

Lee smiled. 'I need the money, frankly. My mother's still alive, you know, and that costs a little. Not that I begrudge it, of course.' He saw Charlie's face grow suddenly earnest.

Frowning, Charlie said, 'I don't understand. Mrs Mandeville died fo— yes, about five years ago. Yes, I – *I* went to her funeral, Lee.' His eyes stared into Lee's.

Lee realized that it was true. He realized that this was why Win had insisted upon Lee's spending the night with him, so he wouldn't run into citizens of the town who might tell him the truth.

'What's the matter, sir? I'm sorry I brought it up. But *you* said—'

Lee gently took his elbow from the young man's grip, and smiled. 'Sorry. I suppose I looked about to faint! Yes.' Lee took a breath and made an effort to pull himself together. 'Yes, of course she's dead. I don't know what I was talking about, Charlie.'

'Oh, that's *okay*, Lee . . . You're really all right?'

'Sure I'm all right. And that's another bus coming, isn't it?'

Through a haze of pale yellow morning sunlight and pale green leaves, the bus approached. Lee moved away, waved good-bye, ignoring Charlie's parting words. Lee walked slowly for several minutes, not caring in what direction his steps took him.

Now Lee realized that the Hearthside people, the accountant there, or someone, must be in league with Win Greeves, because

Lee had seen real bills from the Hearthside in the last five years. Lee felt himself physically weak, as if he were walking in mud instead of on a cement pavement. And what the hell was he going to do about it? Five years. And in dollars? Twenty or twenty-four thousand dollars a year times five were – Lee smiled wryly, and stopped trying to calculate. He looked up at a street marker, and saw that he stood on a corner at which Elmhurst intersected South Billingham. He took Elmhurst, which he thought led, eastward, back to Rosedale. All he really wanted from the Greeveses' house was his suitcase.

When Lee got back to the house, he found the door unlocked, and noticed an aroma of coffee and bacon. Win came at once down the hall.

'Lee! We were a little worried! Thought maybe you'd sleep-walked right out of the house!' Win was grinning.

'No, no, just taking a walk – as I wanted to do last night.' Win was staring at him. Was he pale, Lee wondered. Probably. Lee realized that he could still be polite. That was easy. It was also safe and natural to him. 'Hope I didn't hold you up, Win?' Lee looked at his wristwatch. 'Ten of eight now.'

'Not – one – bit!' Win assured him. 'Come and have some breakfast.'

Now the food really refused to go down, but Lee kept his polite manner, sipped coffee and poked at his scrambled eggs. He saw Win and Kate exchange glances again, glances that Win tried to avoid, though his eyes kept being drawn back to his wife's as if he were hypnotized.

'Did you – uh – have a nice walk, Lee?' Win asked.

'Very nice, thanks. I ran into – Charles Ritchie,' Lee said carefully and with some respect, as if Charles had been lifted from a grocer's delivery boy to the status of one of the disciples bearing a message of truth. 'He used to deliver groceries for my mother.' Lee noticed that Win was not doing much better than he with his breakfast.

The tension grew a few degrees tighter, then Kate said:

'Win said you wanted to leave today, Lee. Can't you change your mind?'

That remark was so false, Lee suddenly blew up, inwardly. But outwardly he kept his cool, except that he tossed his napkin down. 'Sorry, but I can't. No.' His voice was hollow and hoarse. Lee stood up. 'If you'll excuse me.' He left the table and went up to his room.

Just as he was closing his suitcase, Win came in. Now Win looked white in the face, and ten years older.

Lee felt almost sorry for him. 'Yes, I heard about my mother. I think that's what's on your mind. Isn't it, Win?' Now Lee had his small suitcase in his hand, and he was ready to leave the room.

Win tiptoed to the door and closed it. His hand that he drew away from the doorknob was shaking, and he lifted it and his other hand and covered his face. 'Lee, I want you to know I'm ashamed of myself.'

Lee nodded once, impatiently, unseen by Win.

'Morton was in such trouble. That damned wife of his . . . She hasn't turned loose, there's no divorce, and it's a damned mess. The girl – I mean the wife's pregnant again and she's accusing Mort now, but I doubt if that's true, I really do. But she keeps asking for money and legally—'

'Who the hell cares?' Lee interrupted. He squeezed the suitcase handle, eager to leave, but Win blocked him like an ugly mountain. Win's eyes, wide and scared, met Lee's.

He reminded Lee of an animal, sure that it was going to be slaughtered in the next seconds, but in fact Lee had never seen an animal in such circumstances. 'I suppose,' Lee said, 'the nursing home had some kind of understanding with you. I remember the bills, anyway – recent ones.'

Win said miserably, 'Yes, yes.'

Now Lee recalled Doug Graham's words to him, when Lee had said that at least his mother wasn't in pain now, and Doug had replied that that was true. Doug knew that his mother was dead, but their conversation wouldn't have caused him to repeat that fact, and of course he had assumed Lee knew it. Lee made a start for the door.

'Lee!' Win nearly caught him by the sleeve, but he drew his hand back, as if he didn't dare touch Lee. 'What're you going to do, Lee?'

'I don't know . . . I think I'm in a state of shock.'

'I know I'm to blame. Just me. But if you only knew the straits I was in, *am* in. Blackmail – first from Mort's wife, blackmailing him, I mean, and now—'

Lee understood: Mort the son was now blackmailing his father about this business. How low could human beings sink? For some bizarre reason, Lee wanted to smile. 'How did she die?' He asked in a courteous tone. 'Stroke, I suppose?'

'Died in her sleep,' Win murmured. 'Hardly anybody came to the funeral. She'd made such enemies, y'know, with her sharp tongue . . . The man—'

'What man?' Lee asked, because Win had stopped.

'The man at the Hearthside. His name is Victor Malloway. He's – you could say he's every bit as guilty as I am. But he's the only one – else.' Again Win looked pitiably at Lee. 'What're you going to do, Lee?'

Lee took a breath. 'Well – what, for instance?' Win did not reply to that question, and Lee opened the door. 'Bye-bye, Win, and thanks.'

Downstairs, Lee said the same thanks and good-bye to Kate. The words she said did not register on Lee. Something about taking him to the bus terminal, or calling a taxi. ' . . . quite all right,' Lee heard himself saying. 'I'll make it by myself.'

He was gone, free, alone, walking with the suitcase in the direction of town, of the bus terminal. He walked all the way at an easy and regular pace, arrived at the terminal around ten, and waited patiently for the bus to the bigger town with the airport. He still felt dazed, but thoughts came anyway. They were bitter, unhappy thoughts that flowed through his mind like a polluted stream. He detested his thoughts.

And even on the moving bus, his thoughts went on, memories of his mother's odious vanity when she had been younger, her henpecking of his father (dead in his late fifties of cancer), of his mother's unremitting dislike and criticism of every girl he had ever brought to the house. Also his mother's backbiting at her own friends and neighbors, even at the ones who tried to be friendly and kind to her. His mother had always found something 'wrong' with them. And now, the truly awful thing, the terrifying fact that her life had wound up like a classic tragedy played rather behind the scenes instead of on a stage in view of lots of people. His mother had been finished off, as it were, by a few shabby crooks like Win Greeves and son, and the fellow called Victor — Mallory, was it? Indeed, they had been feeding like vultures on her rotting corpse for the past five years.

Lee did not relax until he had opened the front door of his antique shop, and surveyed the familiar interior of shining furniture, the warm glint of copper, the soft curves of polished cherrywood. He left the CLOSED sign hanging in the door, and relocked it from the inside. He must return to normal, he told himself, must carry on as usual and forget Arlington Hills, or he would become ill himself — polluted, like his river of ugly memories on the bus and on the plane. Lee bathed and shaved and by five in the afternoon removed his CLOSED sign. He had one visitor after that, a man who drifted around looking, and didn't buy anything, but that was no matter.

Only occasionally, in moments when he was tired, or disappointed about something that had gone wrong, did Lee think of the false friend Win, and wish him ill. *An eye for an eye, a tooth for a tooth*, the Bible said, the Old Testament part, anyway. But he really *didn't* want that, Lee told himself, otherwise he would be doing something now to bring Win Greeves to justice, to hit back at him. Lee could even sue him and win handily, recover expenses and then some by forcing the Greeveses to sell their handsome house in Rosedale. With that money, he could buy his own house back, his birthplace. But Lee realized that he didn't want the two-story white house where he had been born. His mother's spirit had spoiled that house, made it evil.

From Win Greeves there was silence, not a letter or a line from him of further explanation, or of an offer to repay part of what he had wrongly taken. Now and then, Lee did imagine Win worried, probably very anxious as he tried to guess what Lee might be doing about the situation. Nearly a month had passed since Lee's visit to Arlington Hills. Wouldn't Win and Kate and Mort be assuming that Lee Mandeville had taken a lawyer and that he was preparing his case against Winston Greeves and the man at the Hearthside?

Then Lee received, to his surprise, a letter from Arlington Hills addressed by typewriter and with Win's company's name, Eagle Insurance, and the spread eagle trademark in the upper left corner of the envelope. Lee turned the envelope over – no name on the back – and for a few seconds wondered what might be in it. An abject apology, maybe even a check, however small? Absurd! Or was Eagle Insurance sending him a last bill for his mother's house insurance? Lee laughed at this idea and opened the letter. It was a short typewritten note.

Dear Lee,

After all our troubles, there is one more. Mort died last Tuesday night, after running into a man and seriously injuring him (but not killing him, thank God) and then hitting a tree in his car himself. I can almost say it's a blessing, considering the trouble Mort has caused himself and us. I thought you might like to hear. We are all sad here.

Yours,

Win

Lee gave a sigh, a shrug. Well. What was he supposed to reply, or think, or care, about this? Was Win possibly expecting a letter of condolence from him? This piece of information, Lee thought, affected him not at all. Morton Greeves's life or death was simply nothing to Lee.

Later that day, when Lee was tugging off rubber boots and feeling a bit tired — he had been paint-stripping with a water hose in his back alley — he had a vision of Mort dead and bleeding, having hit a tree in his car, and thought, 'Good!' *An eye for an eye* . . . For a few seconds he relished a vengeance achieved. Morton was Win's only son, only child. Worthless all his life, and now dead! Good! Now Lee had his money for the Arlington Hills house he had sold, and he could, if he wished, buy a property he had looked at in a suburb of Chicago, a pleasant house near the lake. He could have a little boat.

An image of his mother came to Lee as he undressed for bed that night, his mother in her big wicker rocking chair in the living room, reading her Bible, peering up at him grim-mouthed (though with her teeth), and asking him why he didn't read the Bible more often. The Bible! Had it made his mother any better, kinder to her fellow men? A lot of the Bible seemed to be anti-sex, too. His mother was, certainly. If sex was so bad, Lee thought, how had his mother ever conceived him, ever got married in the first place?

'No,' Lee said aloud, and shook himself as if he were shaking something off. No, he wasn't going to entertain any thoughts of the Bible, or of vengeance, in regard to Win's family, or in regard to the man at the Hearthside whose name by now Lee had forgotten, except for the first name Victor. What kind of Victor was he, for instance? Lee smiled at the absurdity of his name, the vainglorious ring of it.

Lee had a few friends in the neighborhood, and one of them, Edward Newton, a man of Lee's age and owner of a nearby book-shop, dropped in on Lee one afternoon as he often did, to have a coffee in the back of the shop. Lee had told Edward and others of his friends that his mother had been ill when he visited Arlington Hills, and that she had died a few days after his visit. Now Edward had found a small item in the newspaper.

'Did you know him? I thought I'd show it to you, because

I remember the name Hearthside, where your mother was.'
Edward pointed to an item three inches long in the newspaper he
had brought.

SUICIDE OF NURSING HOME SUPERINTENDENT, 61

The report said that Victor C. Malloway, superintendent of
the Hearthside retirement and nursing home in Arlington Hills,
Indiana, had killed himself by closing his car and piping in the
exhaust from a running engine in his own garage at home. He left no
note of explanation. He was survived by a wife, Mary, a son Philip
and daughter Marion, and three grandchildren.

'No,' Lee said. 'No, I never met him, but I've heard his name, yes.'

'I suppose it's a depressing atmosphere – old people, you know.
And *they're* dying pretty frequently there, I'd suppose.'

Lee agreed, and changed the subject.

Win was next, Lee supposed. What would happen to him, or
what would he do to himself? Maybe nothing, after all. His own son
was dead, and how much of that death might be called suicide, Lee
wondered. Surely Mort had known from Win that the game was
up, that no more money would be coming from Lee Mandeville.
Surely too Win and Victor Malloway would have had a couple of
desperate conversations. Lee still remembered Win's defeated and
terrified face in that upstairs bedroom in Arlington Hills. Enough
was enough, Lee thought. Win was a half-destroyed man now.

With some of his money, Lee invested in ten Turkish carpets
whose quality and colors especially pleased him. He was sure he
could sell five or six at a profit, and he put a sign in his window to
the effect that an exceptional opportunity to buy quality Turkish
carpets was now offered, inquire within. The ones he did not sell
would go well in the house in the suburbs on which Lee had put a
down payment. Lee felt increasingly happy. He gave a birthday party
on his own birthday, invited ten friends out to a restaurant, then
took them back to his apartment and turned on the lights in his shop.

One of his friends played on a piano that Lee had in his shop section, and there was a lot of laughter, because the piano was slightly out of tune. Everyone sang and drank champagne and toasted Lee's health.

Lee began to furnish his new house, which was smaller than the Arlington Hills house of his family, but still had two stories and a lovely fruit garden around it. It was almost thirty miles from Lee's shop, so he did not drive there every day, but used the place mainly for weekends, though the distance was not so great that he couldn't drive in the evening to stay the night there, if he chose. Now and again he thought, with a shock, of his mother, and the fact that she had been dead nearly *six* years, not the eight or ten months that he had told all his friends. And he thought without a tweak of resentment of the hundred thousand dollars or so down the drain, money which Win had pocketed and shared with Mort and the suicide Victor. The score had been evened. A score, yes, like the score in a game that Lee was not interested in – a domino score, an anagram-game score. Best to forget it. All deaths were sad. Lee had not lifted a finger, yet Mort and Victor were dead. It had not been necessary to gouge out an eye.

Autumn came, and Lee was busy with weatherstripping in his house, when he heard a news item that caught his attention. He had heard the name Arlington Hills, but he had missed the first part. It was something about the death of a man in his own house due to a bullet wound possibly self-inflicted. Lee worked on, feeling vaguely troubled. Could Winston Greeves have been the name the announcer had said? The news would be repeated in an hour, unless something more important crowded out the Arlington Hills bit. Lee continued measuring his insulating tape, cutting, sticking down. He worked on his knees in blue jeans.

If this were Win Greeves, it was really too much, Lee thought. Enough vengeance. More than enough. Well, there were lots of people in Arlington Hills, and maybe it hadn't been Win. But Lee felt troubled, angry in a strange way, and nervous. The minutes crept as Lee worked, and when 5 p.m. came, Lee listened carefully to the news report. It was the last item before the weather: Winston Greeves, aged sixty-four, of Arlington Hills, Indiana, had died from a bullet wound that might or might not have been self-inflicted. His wife said that he had recently acquired a pistol for target practice.

Lee had listened to the news standing, and suddenly his shoulders bent and he lowered his head. He felt weak for a few seconds, then gradually his strength returned, and with it the strange anger that he had known an hour ago. It was too much. *My cup runneth over* . . . No, that wasn't it. Christ had said that. Christ wouldn't have approved of *this*. Lee was about to cover his face with his hands, when he remembered Win making the same gesture. Lee took his hands down and straightened. He went down the stairs to his living room.

To the left and right of his fireplace there were bookshelves set into the wall. He reached firmly for a black leatherbound book. This was the Bible, the same one his mother had used to read, with the top and bottom of its spine all worn and showing brown where the black had worn off the leather. Lee quickly found where the Old Testament left off and the New Testament began, and he seized the thicker Old in his left hand and tore it from the binding. He thrust it like something unclean away from him and into the fireplace where there was no fire now, and he wiped his left hand on the side of his blue jeans. The pages had all spilled apart, thin and dry. Lee struck a match.

He watched the pages burn, and become even more gossamery and quite black, and he knew he had accomplished nothing. This was not the only Old Testament in the world. He had made an angry gesture to satisfy only himself. And he felt not at all satisfied, or cleansed, or rid of anything.

A letter of condolence to Kate Greeves, Lee thought, was due. Yes, he would write it this evening. Why not now? Words came to his mind as he moved toward the table where he kept his paper and pens. A longhand letter, of course. Kate had lost her son and her husband in a span of only a few months.

Dear Kate,

By accident this afternoon I heard on my radio the sad news about Win. I can realize that it is an awful blow to receive so shortly after the death of Morton. I would like you to know that I send you my sincerest sympathies now and that I can appreciate your grief . . .

Lee wrote on smoothly and slowly. The curious thing was that he did feel sympathy for Kate. He bore her no grievance at all, though she was a partner to her husband in his deception. She was, some-how, a separate entity. This fact transcended guilt or the necessity to forgive. Lee signed his name. He meant every word of the letter.

THE STUFF OF MADNESS

When Christopher Waggoner, just out of law school, had married Penelope, he had known of her fondness for pets, and her family's fondness too. That was normal, to love a cat or dog that was part of the household. Christopher had not even thought much about the stuffed little Pixie, a white Pomeranian with shiny black artificial eyes, which stood in a corner of her father's study on a wooden base with her dates of birth and death, nor of the fluffy orange and white cat called Marmy, also preserved, which sat on the floor in another corner. A live cat and dog had lived in the Marshalls' house during his courting days, Christopher recalled, but long ago they had fallen into the taxidermist's hands, and now stood and sat respectively on an outcrop of rock in his and Penny's Suffolk garden. These were not the only animals that peopled, if the word could be used, the garden at Willow Close.

There was Smelty, a feisty little black Scotch terrier with one foot raised and an aggressive muzzle extended with bared teeth, and Jeff the Irish sheep dog, whose coat stood up the best against the elements. Some relics had been in the garden for twenty and more years. An Abyssinian cat called Riba, a name Penny had derived from some mystic experiment, stared with greenish yellow eyes from a tree branch, crouched as if to pounce on anyone walking in the path below. Christopher had seen guests catch a glimpse of the cat and recoil in alarm.

All in all, there were seventeen or eighteen preserved cats and dogs and one rabbit, Petekin, placed about the garden. The Waggoners' two children, Philip and Marjorie, long grown up and married, smiled indulgently at the garden, but Christopher could remember when they winced, when Marjorie didn't want her boyfriends to see the garden and there'd been fewer dead pets then, and when Philip at twelve had tried to burn Pixie on a bonfire, and had been caught by Penny and given the severest scolding of his life.

Now a crisis had come up, attentively listened to by their present dog and cat, Jupiter, an old red setter, and Flora, a docile black cat with white feet. These two were not used to a tense atmosphere in the calm of Willow Close. Little did they understand, Christopher thought, that he was taking a step to protect them from an eternal life after death in the form of being stuffed and made to stand outdoors in all weathers. Wouldn't any animal, if it were capable of choosing, prefer to be a few feet under the ground, dissolving like all flesh, when his time had come? Christopher had used this argument several times to no avail.

The present altercation, however, was over the possible visit of some journalists who would photograph the stuffed animals and write up Penelope's lifelong hobby.

'My old darlings in the newspaper,' Penny said in a beseeching way. 'I think it's a lovely tribute to them, Christopher, and the *Times* might reprint some of it with *one* photograph from the Ipswich paper anyway. And what's the harm in it?'

'The harm,' Christopher began calmly but trying to make every word tell, 'is that it's an invasion of privacy for me and for you too. I'm a respected solicitor – still going up to London once or twice a week. I don't want my private address to be bruited about. My clients and colleagues for the most part know my London whereabouts, only. Would you like the telephone ringing here twenty times a day?'

'Oh, Christopher! Anyone who wants your home address can get it, and you know that.'

Christopher was standing in the brick-floored kitchen with some typewritten pages of a brief in his hand, wearing house slippers, comfortable trousers and a coat sweater. He had come in from his study, because he had thought the last telephone call, which Penny had made a few moments ago, might have been to give the green light to the journalists. But Penny told him she had been ringing her hairdresser in Ipswich for an appointment on Wednesday.

Christopher tried again. 'Two days ago, you seemed to see my point of view. Quite frankly, I don't want my London associates to think I dwell in a place so – so whimsical.' He had sought for a word, abandoned the word 'macabre,' but maybe macabre would have been better. 'You see the garden a bit differently, dear. For most people, including me sometimes, it's a trifle depressing.'

He saw he had hurt her. But he felt he had to take a stand now before it was too late. 'I know you love all those memories in the garden, Penny, but to be honest Philip and Marjorie find our old pets a bit spooky. And Marjorie's two children, they giggle now, but—'

'You're saying it's only *my* pleasure.'

He took a breath. 'All I'm saying is that I don't want the garden publicized. If you think of Pixie and old Marmy,' Christopher continued with a smile, 'seeing themselves as they look now, in a newspaper, they might not like it either. It's an invasion of their privacy too.'

Penny tugged her jumper down nervously over the top of her slacks. 'I've already agreed to the journalists – just two, I think, the writer and the photographer – and they're coming Thursday morning.'

Oh, my God, Christopher thought. He looked at his wife's round, innocent blue eyes. She really didn't understand. Since she had no occupation, her collection of taxidermy had become her chief interest, apart from knitting, at which she was quite skilled and in which she gave lessons at the Women's Institute. The journalists' arrival meant a show of her own achievement, in a way, not that she did any taxidermy herself, the expert they engaged was in London. Christopher felt angry and speechless. How could he turn the journalists off without appearing to be at odds with his wife, or without both of them (if Penny acquiesced to him) seeming full-blown cranks to hold their defunct pets so sacred, they wouldn't allow photographs of them? 'It's going to damage my career – most gravely.'

'But your career is made, dear. You're not struggling. And you're in semi-retirement anyway, you often say that.' Her high, clear voice pleaded pitiably, like that of a little girl wanting something.

'I'm only sixty-one.' Christopher pulled his abdomen in. 'Hawkins's doing the same thing I am, commuting from Kent at sixty-nine.'

Christopher returned to his study, his favorite room and his bedroom for the last couple of years, as he preferred it to the upstairs bedroom and the spare room. He was aware that tears had come to his eyes, but he told himself that they were tears of frustration and rage. He loved the house, an old two-story manse of red brick, the corners of its overhanging roof softened by Virginia creeper. They had an interesting catalpa in the back garden – on one of whose limbs unfortunately Riba the Abyssinian cat sat glowering – and a lovely design of well worn paths whose every inch Christopher knew, along which he had strolled countless times, working out legal problems or relaxing from work by paying close attention to a rosebush or a hydrangea. He had acquired the habit of not noticing the macabre – yes, macabre – exteriors of pets he and Penny had known and loved in the past. Now all this was to be invaded, exposed to the public to wonder at, very likely to chuckle at too. In fact, had Penny a clue as to how the journalists intended to treat the article, which was probably going to be one of their full-page spreads, since the stuffed animals were in their way so photogenic? Who had put the idea into the heads of the *Chronicle* journalists?

One source of his anguish, Christopher knew, was that he hadn't put his foot down long ago, before Penny had turned the garden into a necropolis. Penny had always been a good wife, in the best sense of that term. She'd been a good mother to their children, she'd done nothing wrong, and she'd been quite pretty in her youth, and still took care of her appearance. It was he who had done something wrong, he had to admit. He didn't care to dwell on that period, which had been when Penny had been pregnant with Marjorie. Well, he had given Louise up, hadn't he? And Louise would have been with him now, if he had parted from Penny. How different his life would have been, how infinitely happier! Christopher imagined a more interesting, more richly fulfilled life, though he'd have gone on with his law career, of course. Louise had passion and imagination. She had been a graduate student of child psychiatry when Christopher met her. Now she had a high position in an institution for children in America, Christopher had read in a magazine, and years before that he had seen in a newspaper that she had married an American doctor.

Christopher suddenly saw Louise distinctly as she had looked when they'd had their first rendezvous at the Gare du Nord, she having been at the station to meet him, because she'd got to Paris a few hours before. He remembered her young, happy eyes of paler blue than Penny's, her soft, smiling lips, her voice, the round hat she wore with a beige crown and a black fur rim. He could recall the scent of her perfume. Penny had found out about that affair, and persuaded him to end it. How had she persuaded him? Christopher could not remember Penny's words, they certainly had not been threatening or blackmailing in any way. But he had agreed to give up Louise, and he had written as much to Louise, and then he had collapsed for two days in bed, exhausted as well as depressed, and so miserable, he had wanted to die. With the wisdom of years, Christopher realized that collapsing had been symbolic of a suicide, and that he was rather glad, after all, that he had merely spent two days in bed and not shot himself.

That evening at dinner, Penny remarked on his lack of appetite.

'Yes. Sorry,' Christopher said, toying with his lamb chop. 'I suppose old Jupiter may as well have this.'

Christopher watched the dog carry the chop to his eating place in the corner of the kitchen, and Christopher thought: another year or so and Jupiter will be standing in the garden, perhaps on three legs, in a running position for ever. Christopher firmly hoped he wouldn't be alive to see it. He set his jaw and stared at the foot of his wine glass whose stem he twisted. Not even the wine cheered him.

'Christopher, I am sorry about the journalists. They looked *me* up, and begged me. I had no idea you'd be so upset.'

Christopher had a feeling that what she said was not true. On the other hand, Penny wasn't malicious. He decided to chance it. 'You could still cancel it, couldn't you? Tell them you've changed your mind. You won't have to mention me, I trust.'

Penny hesitated, then shook her head. 'I simply don't want to cancel it. I love my garden. This is a way of sharing it – with friends and with people I don't even know.'

She probably envisaged letters from strangers saying they were going to take up the same method of preserving their pets in their houses or gardens – God forbid – and what was the name of their taxidermist? And so Christopher's will hardened. He would have to endure it, and endure it he would, like a man. He wouldn't even quit the house while the journalists were here, because that would be cowardly, but he was going to take care not to be in any photograph.

Wednesday, a pleasant and sunny day, he did not set foot in the garden. It was ruined for him. The blossoming roses, the softly bending willow, chartreuse-colored in the sunlight, seemed a stage set waiting for the accursed journalists. His work, a lot of it, making that garden so beautiful, and now the vulgarians were going to trample over the primroses, the pansies, backing up and stepping sideways for their silly photographs.

Something was building up inside Christopher, a desire to hit back at both the journalists and at Penny. He felt like bombing the garden, but that would destroy the growing things as well as part of the house, possibly. Absurd! But an insufferable wrath boiled in him. The white coat of Pixie showed left of the catalpa even from the kitchen window. A brown and white collie called Doggo was even more visible on a stone base near the garden wall. Christopher had been able to cut these out of his vision somehow — until today.

When Penny went to the hairdresser's on Wednesday afternoon, fetched by her friend Beatrice who went to the same hairdresser, Christopher took the car and drove rather aimlessly northward. He'd never done such a thing before. Waste of petrol, he'd have thought under usual circumstances, since he hadn't even a shopping list with him. His mind dwelt on Louise. *Louise* — a name he'd avoided saying to himself for years, because it pained him so. Now he relished the pain, as if it had a cleansing and clarifying power. *Louise* in the garden, that was what Penny needed to bring back to her what the past was all about. Louise, worthy of being preserved if any living creature ever had been. Penny had met her once at a cocktail party in London, while the affair was still going on, and had sensed something and later made a remark to Christopher. Months later, Penny had discovered his three photographs of Louise — though to give Penny credit, she had not been snooping, but looking for a cuff link that Christopher said he had lost in the chest of drawers. Penny had said, 'Well, Christopher — this is the girl who was at that party, is it not?' and then it had come out, that he was still seeing her. With Penny pregnant, Christopher had not been able to fight for Louise. For that he reproached himself too.

Christopher turned the car towards Bury St Edmunds, to a large department store, and found a parking place nearby. He was full of an unusual confidence that he would have his way, that everything would be easy. He looked in the windows of the store as he walked towards the entrance: summer clothing on tall mannequins with flesh-colored legs, wearing silly smiles or equally silly pouts, flamboyant with hands and arms flung out as if to say, 'Look at me!' That wasn't quite what he wanted. Then he saw her — a blonde girl seated at a little white round table, in a crisp navy blue blouse rather like a sailor's middy, navy blue skirt and black patent leather pumps. An empty stemmed glass stood on the table before her, and around her dummy men reared back barefoot in white dungarees, either topless or wearing striped blue and white jumpers.

'Where might I find the manager?' Christopher asked, but received such a vague answer from a salesgirl, he decided to push on more directly. He barged into a stockroom near the window where the girl was.

Five minutes later, he had what he wanted, and a young window dresser called Jeremy something was even carrying her to his car, the girl in the navy blue outfit, without a hat and with very dead-looking strawy straight yellow hair. Christopher had offered a deposit of a hundred pounds for an overnight rental, half to be paid back on return of the dummy and clothing in good condition, and he had added encouragement by pushing a ten-pound note into the young man's hand.

With the dummy installed in the back seat, Christopher returned to shop for a hat. He found more or less what he was looking for, a round hat trimmed with black velour instead of fur, and the crown was white and not beige, but the resemblance to Louise's hat in the photograph, which he was sure Penny remembered, was sufficient and striking enough. When he returned to the car, a small child was staring curiously at the mannequin. Christopher smiled amiably, pulled a blanket (used to keep Jupiter's paws off the back seat when he went to the vet for arthritis shots) gently over the figure, and drove off. He felt a bit pressed for time, and hoped that Penny had decided to have tea at Beatrice's house instead of theirs.

He was in luck. Penny was not home yet. Having ascertained this, Christopher carried the dummy from the car into the house via the back door. He set the figure in his chair in front of his desk and indulged in a few seconds of amusement and imagination – imagining that it *was* Louise, young and round-cheeked, that he could say something to her, and she would reply. But the girl's eyes, though large and blue, were quite blank. Only her lips smiled in a rather absent but definite curve. This reminded Christopher of something, and he went quickly up the stairs and got the brightest red lipstick he could find among several on Penny's dressing table. Then down again, and carefully, trying his best to steady his hand which was trembling as it never had before, Christopher enlarged the upper lip, and lowered the under lip exactly in the center. The upturned red corners of the lips were superb.

Just then, he heard the sound of a car motor, and seconds later a car door slamming, voices, and he could tell from the tone that Penny was saying good-bye to Beatrice. Christopher at once set the dummy in a back corner of his study, and concealed the figure completely with a coverlet from his couch. At any rate, Penny almost never looked into his study, except when she knocked on the door to call him to tea or a meal. Christopher put the bag with the hat under the coverlet also.

Penny looked especially well coifed, and was in good spirits the rest of the afternoon and evening. Christopher behaved politely, merely, but in his way, he felt in good spirits too. He debated putting the effigy of Louise out in the garden tonight versus early tomorrow morning. Tonight, Jupiter might bark, as he slept outdoors in this season in his doghouse near the back door. Christopher could take a stroll in the garden, if he happened to be sleepless at midnight, tell Jupiter to hush, and the dog would, but if he were carrying a large object and fussing around getting it placed correctly, the silly dog just might keep on barking because he was tied up at night. Christopher decided on early tomorrow morning.

Penny retired just after ten, assuring Christopher cheerfully that 'It'll all be over so quickly tomorrow,' he wouldn't know it had happened. 'I'll tell them to be very careful and not step on the flower beds.' She added that she thought he was being very patient about it all.

In his study, Christopher hardly slept. He was aware of the village clock striking faintly at quite a distance every hour until four, when the window showed signs of dawn. Christopher got up and dressed. He sat Louise again in his desk chair, and practiced setting the hat on correctly at a jaunty angle. The extended forearm, without the glass stem in the fingers of the hand, looked able to hold a cigarette, and Christopher would have put one there unlighted, except that he and Penny didn't smoke, and there were no cigarettes in the house just now. Just as well, because the hand looked also as if Louise might be beckoning to someone, having just called out someone's name. Christopher reached for a black felt pen, and outlined both her blue eyes.

There! Now her eyes really stood out and the outer corners turned up just a little, imitating the upturn of her lips.

Christopher carried the figure out the back door with the coverlet still over it. He knew where it should be, on a short stone bench on the left side of the garden which was rather hidden by laurels. Jupiter's eyes had met Christopher's for an instant, the dog had been sleeping with forepaws and muzzle on the threshold of his wooden house, but Jupiter did not bother to lift his head. Christopher flicked the bench clean with the coverlet, then seated Louise gently, and put a stone under one black pump, since the shoe did not quite touch the ground. Her legs were crossed. She looked charming – much more charming than the longhaired Pekinese called Mao-Mao who peeked from the foliage to the left of the bench, facing the little clearing as if he were guarding it. Mao-Mao's tongue, which protruded nearly two inches and had been made by the taxidermist out of God knew what, had lost all its pink and was now a sickening flesh color. For some reason, Mao-Mao had always been a favorite target of his and Penny's dogs, so his coat looked miserable.

But Louise! She was fantastically smart with her round hat on, in her crisp new navy outfit, her happy eyes directed towards the approach to the nook in which she sat. Christopher smiled with satisfaction, and went back to his study, where he fell sound asleep until Penny awakened him with tea at eight.

The journalist and the photographer were due at 9:30, and they were punctual, in a dirty gray Volkswagen. Penny went down the front steps to greet them. The two young men, Christopher observed from the sitting-room window, looked even scruffier than he had foreseen, one in a T-shirt and the other in a polo-neck sweater, and both in blue jeans. Gentlemen of the press, indeed!

Christopher had two reasons, his legal mind assured him, for joining the company in the garden: he didn't want to appear huffy or possibly physically handicapped, since the journalists knew that Penny was married and to whom, and also he wanted to witness the discovery of Louise. So Christopher stood in the garden near the house, after the men had introduced themselves to him.

'Jonathan, look!' said the man without the camera, marveling at big Jeff, the Irish sheep dog who stood on the right side of the garden. 'We must get this!' But his exclamations became more excited as he espied old Pixie, whose effigy made him laugh with delight.

The cameraman snapped here and there with a compact little machine that made a whir and a click. Stuffed animals were really everywhere, standing out more than the roses and peonies.

'Where do you have this expert work done, Mrs Waggoner? Have you any objection to telling us? Some of our readers might like to start the same hobby.'

'Oh, it's more than a hobby,' Penny began. 'It's my way of keeping my dear pets with me. I feel that with their forms around me – I don't suffer as much as other people do who bury their pets in their gardens.'

'That's the kind of comment we want,' said the journalist, writing in his tablet.

Jonathan was exploring the foot of the garden now. There was a beagle named Jonathan back to the right behind the barberry bush, Christopher recalled, but either Jonathan didn't see him or preferred the more attractive animals. The photographer drifted closer to Louise, but still did not notice her. Then, focusing on Riba, the cat in the catalpa, he stepped backward, nearly fell, and in recovering glanced behind him, and glanced again.

Penny was just then saying to the journalist, 'Mr Taylor puts a special weatherproofing on their coats with a spray . . . '

'Hey Mike! – *Mike*, look!' The second Mike had a shrill note of astonishment.

'What now?' asked Mike smiling, approaching.

'Mao-Mao,' said Penny, following them in her medium-high heels. 'I'm afraid he's not in the best—'

'No, no, the figure. Who is this?' asked the photographer with a polite smile.

Penny's gaze sought and found what the photographer was pointing at. 'Oh! – Oh, *goodness*!' Then she took a long breath and screamed, like a siren, and covered her face with her hands.

Jonathan caught her arm as she swayed. 'Mrs Waggoner! Something the matter? We didn't damage anything. – It's a friend of yours – I suppose?'

'Someone you liked very much?' asked Mike in a tactful tone.

Penny looked crushed, and for brief seconds Christopher relished it. Here was Louise in all her glory, young and pretty, sure of herself, sure of him, smack in their garden. 'Penny, a cup of tea?' asked Christopher.

They escorted Penny through the back door and into the kitchen. Christopher put the kettle on.

'It's Louise!' Penny moaned in an eerie voice, and leaned back in the bamboo chair, her face white.

'Someone she didn't want us to photograph?' asked Jonathan. 'We certainly won't.'

Before Christopher could pour the first cup of tea, Mike said, 'I think we'd better call for a doctor, don't you, Mr Waggoner?'

'Y-yes, perhaps.' Christopher could have said something comforting to Penny, he realized – that he had meant it as a joke. But he hadn't. And Penny was in a state beyond hearing anything anybody said.

'Why was she so surprised?' asked Jonathan.

Christopher didn't answer. He was on his way to the telephone, and Mike was coming with him, because Mike had the number of a doctor in Ipswich, in case the local doctor was not available. But this got interrupted by a shout from Jonathan. He wanted some help to get Penny to a sofa, or anywhere where she could lie down. The three of them carried her into the sitting room. The touch of rouge on her cheeks stood out garishly on her pale face.

'I think it's a heart attack,' said Jonathan.

The local doctor was available, because his nurse knew whom he was visiting just now, and she thought he could arrive in about five minutes. Meanwhile Christopher covered Penny with a blanket he brought from upstairs, and started the kettle again for a hot water bottle. Penny was now breathing through parted lips.

'We'll stay till the doctor gets here, unless you want us to take her directly to Ipswich Hospital,' said Jonathan.

'No – thank you. Since the doctor's on his way, it may be wisest to wait for him.'

Dr Dowes arrived soon after, took Penny's pulse, and at once gave her an injection. 'It's a heart attack, yes, and she'd best go to hospital.' He went to the telephone.

'If we possibly could, Mr Waggoner,' said Jonathan, 'we'd like to come back tomorrow morning, because today I didn't get all the pictures I need to choose from, and the rest of today is so booked up, we're due somewhere in a few minutes. – If you could let us in around nine-thirty again, we'd need just another half hour.'

Christopher thought at once of Louise. They hadn't got a picture of her as yet, and he wanted them to photograph her and was sure they would. 'Yes, certainly. Nine-thirty tomorrow. If I happen not to be here, you can use the side passage into the garden. The gate's never locked.'

As soon as they had driven off, the ambulance arrived. Dr Dowes had not asked if anything had happened to give Penny a shock, but he had gathered the journalists' purpose – he knew of the stuffed animals in the garden, of course – and he said something to the effect that the excitement of showing her old pets to the public must have been a strain on her heart.

'Shall I go with her?' Christopher asked the doctor, not wanting at all to go.

'No, no, Mr Waggoner, really no use in it. I'll ring the hospital in an hour or so, and then I'll ring you.'

'But how dangerous is her state?'

'Can't tell as yet, but I think she has a good chance of pulling through. No former attacks like this.'

The ambulance went away, and then Dr Dowes. Christopher realized that he wouldn't have minded if the shock of seeing Louise had killed Penny. He felt strangely numb about the fact that at this minute, she was hovering between life and death. Tomorrow, Penny alive or not, the journalist and the photographer would be back, and they would take a picture of Louise. How would Penny, if she lived, explain the effigy of a young woman in her garden? Christopher smiled nervously. If Penny died, or if she didn't, he could still ring up the Ipswich *Chronicle* and say that under the circumstances, because his wife had suffered such emotional strain because of the publicity, he would be grateful if they canceled the article. But Christopher didn't want that. He wanted Louise's picture in the newspaper. Would his children Philip and Marjorie suspect Louise's identity, or role? Christopher couldn't imagine how, as they had never heard Louise's name spoken, he thought, never seen that photograph which Christopher had so cherished until Penny asked him to destroy it. As for what their friends and neighbors thought, let them draw their own conclusions.

Christopher poured more tea for himself, removed Penny's unfinished cup from the living room, and carried his tea into his study. He had work to do for the London office, and was supposed to telephone them before five this afternoon.

At two o'clock, the telephone rang. It was Dr Dowes.

'Good news,' said the doctor. 'She's going to pull through nicely. An infarction, and she'll have to lie still in hospital for at least ten days, but by tomorrow you can visit . . . '

Christopher felt depressed at the news, though he said the right things. When he hung up, in an awful limbo between fantasy and reality, he told himself that he must let Marjorie know about her mother right away, and ask her to ring Philip. Christopher did this.

'You sound awfully down, Dad,' said Marjorie. 'It could have been worse after all.'

Again he said the proper things. Marjorie said she would ring her brother, and maybe both of them could come down on Sunday.

By four o'clock, Christopher was able to ring his office and speak with Hawkins about a strategy he had worked out for a company client. Hawkins gave him a word of praise for his suggestions, and didn't remark that Christopher sounded depressed, nor did Christopher mention his wife.

Christopher did not ring the hospital or Dr Dowes the rest of that evening. Penny was coming back, that was the fact and the main thing. How would he endure it? How could he return the dummy – Louise – to the department store, as he had promised? He couldn't return Louise, he simply couldn't. And Penny might tear her apart, once she regained the strength. Christopher poured a scotch, sipped it neat, and felt that it did him a power of good. It helped him pull his thoughts together. He went into his study and wrote a short letter to Jeremy Rogers, the window dresser who had given him his card in the Bury St Edmunds store, saying that due to circumstances beyond his control, he would not be able to return the borrowed mannequin personally, but it could be fetched at his address, and for the extra trouble he would forfeit his deposit. He put this letter in the post box on the front gate.

Christopher's will was in order. As for his children, they would be quite surprised, and to what could they attribute it? Not to Penny's crisis, because she was on the mend. Let Penny explain it to them, Christopher thought, and had another drink.

Drink was part of his plan, and not being used to it, Christopher quickly felt its soothing power. He went upstairs to the medicine chest in the bathroom. Penny always had little sedatives, and maybe some big ones too. Christopher found four or five little glass jars that might suit his purpose, some of them overaged, perhaps, but no matter. He swallowed six or eight pills, washed down with scotch and water, mindful to think of something else – his appearance – while he did this, lest the thought of all the pills made him throw up.

In the downstairs hall looking-glass, Christopher combed his hair, and then he put on his best jacket, a rather new tweed, and went on taking pills with more scotch. He dropped the empty jars carelessly into the garbage. The cat Flora looked at him in surprise when he lurched against a sideboard and fell to one knee. Christopher got up again, and methodically fed the cat. As for Jupiter, he could afford to miss a meal.

'M'wow,' said Flora, as she always did, as a kind of thank-you before she fell to.

Then Christopher made his way, touching doorjambs, fairly crawling down the steps, to the garden path. He fell only once, before he reached his goal, and then he smiled. Louise, though blurred at the edges, sat with the same air of dignity and confidence. She was alive! She smiled a welcome to him. 'Louise,' he said aloud, and with difficulty aimed himself and plopped on to the stone bench beside her. He touched her cool, firm hand, the one that was extended with fingers slightly parted. It was still a *hand*, he thought. Just cool from the evening air, perhaps.

The next morning the photographer and the journalist found him slumped sideways, stiff as the dummy, with his head in the navy blue lap.

THE BUTTON

Roland Markow bent over his worktable in the corner of his and his wife's bedroom, and again tried to concentrate. Schultz had neglected to report his Time Deposit gains for the end of the year. Roland was now looking at Schultz's December totals, and all Schultz's papers were here, earnings and bills paid for the twelve months of the year, but did he have to go through all those to find Schultz's Time Deposits and God knew what else – a few stocks, Roland knew – himself? Schultz was a freelance commercial artist, considered himself efficient and orderly, Roland knew, but that was far from the truth.

'Goo-*wurr*-kah!' came the mindless voice again, loudly, though two doors were shut between the voice and Roland.

'Goo-woo-*woo*,' said his wife's voice more softly, and with a smile in it.

Sickening, Roland thought. One would think Jane was encouraging the idiot! The *child*, Roland corrected himself, and bent again over Schultz's tax return.

It was a tough time of the year, late April, when Roland habitually took work home, as did his two colleagues. The Internal Revenue Service had its deadlines. *Fake it*, Roland thought in regard to Schultz's Time Deposit interest. He could estimate it in his head within a hundred dollars or so, but Roland Markow wasn't that kind of man. By nature he was meticulous and honest. He was convinced that his tax clients came out better in the long run if he turned in meticulous and honest income tax return forms for them. He couldn't phone Schultz and ask him to do it, because all Schultz's papers were here in twelve envelopes, each labeled with the name of the month. He'd have to go through them himself. And it was almost midnight.

'Goo-*wurr*-kah-*wurr-r* – kah!' screamed Bertie.

Roland could stand it no longer and leapt up, went to the door, crossed the little hall, and knocked perfunctorily before he opened the door to Bertie's room halfway.

Jane was on the floor on her knees, sitting on her heels, smiling as if she were having a glorious time. Her eyes behind the black, round-rimmed glasses looked positively merry, and her hands on her thighs were relaxed.

Bertie sat in a roundish heap before her, swimmy-eyed, thick tongue hanging out. The child had not even looked Roland's way when the door opened.

'How's the work going, dear?' Jane asked. 'Do you know it's midnight?'

'I know, can't be helped. Does he have to keep saying this "Guh-wurka" all the time? What is this?'

Jane chuckled. 'Nothing, dear. Just a game. – You're tired, I know. Sorry if we were loud.'

We. A crazy anger rose in Roland. Their child was a mongoloid, daft, hopelessly brainless. Did she have to say 'we'? Roland tried to smile, pushed his straight dark hair back from his forehead, and felt a film of sweat, to his surprise. 'Okay. Just sounded like Gurkha to me. You know, those Indian soldiers. Didn't know what he was up to.'

'G'wah-h,' said Bertie, and collapsed sideways on to the carpet. He wasn't smiling. Though his slant eyes seemed to meet Roland's for an instant, Roland knew they did not. Epicanthal folds was the term for this minor aberration.

Roland knew all the terminology for children – organisms – who had Down's syndrome. He had of course read up on it years ago, when Bertie had been born. The complicated information stuck, like some religious rote he had learned in childhood, and Roland hated all this information, because they could do nothing about Bertie, so what good was knowing the details?

'You are tired, Rollie,' said Jane. 'Mightn't it be better to go to bed now and maybe get up an hour earlier?'

Roland shook his head wearily. 'Dunno. I'll think about it.' He wanted to say, 'Make him shut *up*!' but Roland knew Jane got a pleasure out of playing with Bertie in the evenings, and God knew it didn't matter when Bertie got to sleep, because the longer he stayed up, the longer he might sleep and keep quiet the next morning. Bertie had his own room, this room, with a low bed, a couple of heavy chairs that he couldn't tip over (he was amazingly strong), a low and heavy wooden table whose corners had been rounded and sanded by Roland, soft rubber toys on the floor, so that if Bertie threw them against the window, the glass wouldn't break. Bertie had thin reddish hair, a small head that was flat on top and behind, a short flat nose, a mouth that was merely a pink hole, ever open, with his oversized tongue usually protruding. The tongue had ugly ridges down it. Bertie was always drooling, of course. The awful thing was that they were going to be stuck with him for the next ten or fifteen years, or however long he lived. Mongoloids often died of a heart condition in their teens or earlier, Roland had read, but their doctor, Dr Reuben Blatt, had detected no weakness in Bertie's heart. Oh no, Roland thought bitterly, they weren't that lucky.

Roland pressed the ballpoint pen with the fingertips of his right hand, pressed it against his palm. The worst thing was that Jane had completely changed. He watched her now, bending forward, smiling and cooing at Bertie again, as if he weren't still in the room. Jane had gained weight, she wore sloppy espadrilles around the house all the time, even to go shopping, if the weather permitted. They'd lost nearly all their friends over the past four or five years, all except the

Drummonds, Evy and Peter, who Roland felt kept on seeing them out of morbid curiosity about Bertie. They never failed to ask 'to see Bertie for a few minutes,' when they came for drinks or dinner, and they usually brought Bertie a little toy or some candy, to be sure, but their avid eyes as they looked at Bertie Roland could never forget. The Drummonds were fascinated by Bertie, as one might be fascinated by a horror film, something out of this world. And Roland always thought, out of this world, no, out of his own loins, as the Bible said, out of Jane's womb. Something had gone wrong, one chance in seven hundred, according to statistics, providing the mother wasn't over forty, which Jane had not been, she'd been twenty-seven. Well, they had hit that one in seven hundred. Roland remembered as vividly as if it had been yesterday or last week the expression on the obstetrician's face as he had come out of the labor ward. The obstetrician (whose name Roland had forgotten) had been frowning, with his lips slightly parted as if he were mustering the right words, as indeed he had been. He had known that the nurse had already given the anxiously waiting Roland a fuzzy and rather alarming announcement.

'Ah, yes – Mr Markow? – Your child – It's a boy. He's not normal, I'm sorry to say. May as well tell you now.'

Down's syndrome. Roland hadn't at once connected this with mongolism, a term he was familiar with, but seconds later, he had understood. Roland recollected his puzzlement at the news, a stronger feeling than his disappointment. And was his wife all right? Yes, and she hadn't seen the child.

Roland had seen the child an hour or so later, lying in a tiny metal box, one of thirty or so other metal boxes visible through a glass wall of the sterile and specially heated room where the newborns lay. No one had needed to point out his son to him: the miniature head with its flat top, the eyes that appeared slanted though they were closed when Roland had seen them first. Other babies stirred, clenched a little fist, opened their mouths to breathe, yawn. Bertie didn't stir. But he was alive. Oh yes, very much alive.

Roland had read up on mongoloids, and had learned that they were singularly still in the womb. 'No, he's not kicking as yet!' Roland remembered Jane saying half a dozen times to well-meaning friends who had inquired during her pregnancy. 'Maybe he's reading books already,' Jane had sometimes added. (Jane was a great reader, and had been a scholarship student at Vassar, where she had majored in political science.) And how different Jane had looked then! Roland realized that he could hardly have recognized her as the same person, Jane five years ago and Jane now. Slender and graceful, with lovely ankles, straight brown hair cut short, an intelligent and pretty face with bright and friendly eyes. She still had the lovely ankles, but even her face had grown heavier, and she no longer moved with youthful lightness. She had concentrated herself, it seemed to Roland, upon Bertie. She had become a kind of monument, something mostly static, heavy, obsessed, concentrating on Bertie and on caring for him. No, she didn't want any more children, didn't want to take a second chance, she sometimes said cheerfully, though the chances were next to nil. Both Roland and Jane had had their blood cultures photographed for chromosome count. Usually the woman was 'the carrier,' but Jane was not deficient of one chromosome, and neither was he. By no means had she a chromosome missing, which might have meant that one of the forty-five she did have carried the 'D/G translocation chromosome' which resulted in a mongoloid offspring in one in three cases. So if he and Jane did have another child, they would be back to the one-in-seven-hundred odds again.

It had more than once crossed Roland's mind to put Bertie down, as they said of dogs and cats who were hopelessly ill. Of course he'd never uttered this to Jane or to anyone, and now it was too late. He might have asked the doctor, just after Bertie's birth, with Jane's consent, of course. But now as Jane frequently reminded Roland, Bertie was a human being. Was he? Bertie's I.Q. was probably 50, Roland knew. That was the mongoloid average, though Bertie's I.Q. had never been tested.

'Rollie!' Smiling, Jane lay on her back now, propped on her

elbows. 'You do look exhausted, dear! How about a hot chocolate? Or coffee if you've really got to stay up? – Chocolate's better for you.'

Roland mumbled something. He did have to work another hour at least, as there were two more returns to wind up after Schultz's. Roland stared at his son's – yes, his *son's* – toad-like body, on its back now: stubby legs, short arms with square and clumsy hands at their ends, hands that could do nothing, with thumbs like nubbins, mistakes, capable of holding nothing. What had he, Roland, done to deserve this? Bertie was of course wearing a diaper, rather an oversized diaper. At five, he looked indeed like an oversized baby. He had no neck. Roland was aware of a pat on his arm as his wife slipped past him on the way to the kitchen.

A few minutes later, Jane set a steaming mug of hot chocolate by his elbow. Roland was back at work. He had found Schultz's Time Deposit interest payments, which Schultz had duly noted in April and in October. Roland finished Schultz and reached for his next dossier, that of James P. Overland, manager of a restaurant in Long Island. Roland sipped the hot chocolate, thinking that it was soothing, pleasant, but *not* what he needed, as Jane had informed him. What he needed was a nice wife in bed, warm and loving, even sexy as Jane had used to be. What they both needed was a healthy son in the room across the hall, reading books now, maybe even sampling Robert Louis Stevenson by now, as both Roland and Jane had done at Bertie's age, a kid who'd try to hide the light after lights-out time to sneak a few more pages of adventure. Bertie would never read a corn flakes box.

Jane had said she would sleep on the sofa tonight, so he could work at his table in the bedroom. She couldn't sleep with a light on in the bedroom. She had often slept on the sofa before – they had a duvet which was simple to put on top of the sofa – and sometimes Roland slept there too, to spell Jane on the nights when Bertie appeared restless. Bertie sometimes woke up in the night and started walking around his room, butting his head against the door or one of his walls, and one or the other of them would have to go in and talk to him for a while, and usually change his diaper. The carpet would look a mess, Roland thought, except that its very dark blue color did not show the spots that must be on it. They had sedatives for Bertie from their doctor, but neither Roland nor Jane wanted Bertie to become addicted.

'Damn the bastard!' Roland muttered, meaning James P. Overland, whose face he scarcely remembered from the two interviews he had had with Overland months ago. Overland hadn't prepared his expenses and income nearly as well as the commercial artist Schultz, and Roland's colleague Greg MacGregor had dumped the mess on him! Of course Greg had his hands full now too, Roland thought, and was no doubt burning the midnight oil in his own apartment down on 23rd Street, but still – Greg was junior to Roland and should have done the tough work first. Roland's job was to do the finishing touches, to think of every legitimate loophole and tax break that the IRS permitted, and Roland knew them all by heart. 'I'll settle Greg's hash tomorrow,' Roland swore softly, though he knew he wouldn't. The matter wasn't that serious. He was just goddamned tired, angry, bitter.

'Guh – *wurrr-rr*-kah!'

Had he heard it, or was he imagining? What time was it?

Twenty past one! Roland got up, saw that the bedroom door was closed, then nervously opened the door a little. Jane was asleep on the sofa, he could just make out the paleness of the blue duvet and the darker spot which was Jane's head, and she hadn't wakened from Bertie's cry. She was getting used to it, Roland thought. And why not, he supposed. Before 'Goo-*wurr*-kah' it had been 'Aaaaagh!' as in the horror films or the comic strips. And before that?

Roland was back at his worktable. Before that? He was staring down at the next tax return after Overland (to whom he had written a note to be read to Overland by telephone tomorrow if a secretary could reach him), and actually pondering what Bertie had used to utter before 'Aaaaagh!' Was he losing his mind? He squirmed in his chair, straightened up, then bent again over the nearly completed form, ballpoint pen poised as he moved down a list of items. It was not making any sense. He could read the words, the figures, but they had no meaning. Roland got up quickly.

Take a short walk, he told himself. Maybe give it up for tonight, as Jane had suggested, try it early tomorrow morning, but now a walk, or he wouldn't be able to sleep, he knew. He was wide awake and jumpy with nervous energy.

As he tiptoed through the dark living room towards the door, he heard a low, sleepy wail from Bertie's room. That was a mewing sort of cry that meant, usually, that Bertie needed his diaper changed. Roland couldn't face it. The mewing would eventually awaken Jane, he knew, and she could handle it. She wasn't going to a job tomorrow. Jane had given up her job with a U.N. research group when Bertie had been born, though she wouldn't have given it up, Roland found himself thinking for the hundredth time, if Bertie hadn't had Down's syndrome. She would have gone back to her job, as she had intended to do. But Jane had made an immediate decision: Bertie, her little darling, was going to be her full-time job.

It was a relief to get out into the cool air, the darkness. Roland lived on East 52nd Street, and he walked east. A pair of young lovers, arms around each other's waist, strolled slowly towards him, the girl tipped her head back and gave a soft laugh. The boy bent quickly and kissed her lips. They might have been in another world, Roland thought. They were in another world, compared to his. At least these kids were happy and healthy. Well, so had he and Jane been — just like them, Roland realized, just about six years ago! Incredible, it seemed now! What had they done to deserve this? Their fate? What? Nothing that Roland could think of. He was not religiously inclined, and he believed as little in prayer, or an afterworld, as he did in luck. A man made his own destiny. Roland Markow was the grandson of poor immigrants. Even his parents had had no university education. Roland had worked his way through CUNY, living at home.

Roland was walking downtown on First Avenue, walking quickly, hands in the pockets of his raincoat which he had grabbed out of the hall closet, though it wasn't raining. There were few people on the sidewalk, though the avenue had a stream of taxis and private cars flowing uptown in its wide, one-way artery. Now, out of a corner coffee shop, six or eight adolescents, all looking fourteen or fifteen years old, spilled on to the sidewalk, laughing and chattering, and one boy jumped twice, as if on a pogo stick, rather high in the air before a girl reached for his hand. More health, more youth! Bertie would never jump like that. Bertie would walk, could now in a way, but jump for joy to make a girl smile? Never!

Suddenly Roland burnt with anger. He stopped, pressed his lips together as if he were about to explode, looked behind him the way he had come, vaguely thinking of starting back, but really not caring how late it got. He was not in the least tired, though he was now south of 34th Street. He thought of throttling Bertie, of doing it with his own hands. Bertie wouldn't even struggle much, Roland knew, wouldn't realize what was happening, until it was too late. Roland turned and headed uptown, then crossed the avenue eastward at a red light. He didn't care if he roamed the rest of the night. It was better than lying sleepless at home, alone in that bed.

A rather plump man, shorter than Roland, was walking towards him on the sidewalk. He wore no hat, he had a moustache, and a slightly troubled air. The man gazed down at the sidewalk.

Suddenly Roland leapt for him. Roland was not even aware that he leapt with his hands outstretched for the man's throat. The suddenness of Roland's impact sent the man backwards, and Roland fell on top of him. Scrambling a little, grasping the man's throat ever harder, Roland tugged the man leftward, towards the shadow of the huge, dark apartment building on the left side of the sidewalk. Roland sank his thumbs. There was no sound from the man, whose tongue protruded, Roland could barely see, much like Bertie's. The man's thick brows rose, his eyes were wide – grayish eyes, Roland thought. With a heave, Roland moved the fallen figure three or four feet towards a patch of darkness on his left, which Roland imagined was a hole. Not that Roland was thinking, he was simply aware of a column or pit of darkness on his left, and he had a desire to push the man down it, to annihilate him. Panting finally, but with his hands still on the man's throat, Roland glanced at the darkness and saw that it was an alleyway, very narrow, between two buildings, and that part of the darkness was caused by black iron banisters, with steps of black iron that led downwards. Roland dragged the man just a little farther, until his head and shoulders hung over the steps, then Roland straightened, breathing through his mouth. The man's head was in darkness, only part of his trousered legs and black shod feet were visible. Roland bent and grabbed the lowest button of the man's gray plaid jacket and yanked it off. He pocketed this, then turned and walked back the way he had come, still breathing through parted lips. He paid no attention to two men who walked towards him, but he heard some words.

' . . . told her to go to *hell*! – Y'know?' said one.

The other man chuckled. 'No kidding!'

At First Avenue, Roland turned uptown. Roland's next thought, or rather the next thing that he was aware of, was that he stood in front of the mostly glass doors of his apartment building, for which he needed his key, but in his left side trousers pocket he had his keys, as always. He glanced behind him, vaguely thinking that the taxi that had brought him might just be pulling away. But he had walked. Of course, he had gone out for a walk. He remembered that perfectly. He felt pleasantly tired.

Roland took the elevator, then entered the apartment quietly. Jane was still asleep on the sofa, and she stirred as he crossed the living room, but did not wake up. Roland tiptoed as before. The lamp was still on, on his worktable. Roland undressed, washed quietly in the bathroom, and got into bed. He had killed a man. Roland could still feel the slight pain in his thumbs from the strain of his muscles there. That man was dead. One human being dead, in place of Bertie. That was the way he saw it, now. It was a kind of vengeance, or revenge, on his part. Wasn't it? What had he and

Jane done to deserve Bertie? What had all the healthy, normal people walking around on the earth, what had *they* done to deserve their happy state? Nothing. They'd simply been born. Roland slept.

When Jane brought him a cup of coffee in bed at half past seven, Roland felt especially well. He thanked her with a smile.

'Thought I'd let you sleep this morning no matter what,' Jane said cheerfully. 'No tax returns are worth your *health*, Rollie dear.' She was already dressed in one of her peasant skirts that concealed the bulk of her hips and thighs, a blue shirt which she had not bothered to tuck into the skirt top, her old pale blue espadrilles.'Now what for breakfast? Pancakes sound nice? Batter's all made, because Bertie likes them so much, you know. Or – bacon and eggs?'

Roland sipped his coffee. 'Pancakes sound great. With bacon too, I hope.'

'You bet, with bacon! Ten minutes.' Jane went off to the kitchen.

Roland felt in good spirits the entire day. Jane remarked on it before he left the apartment that morning, and Greg at the office said: 'Miracle man! Did you win on the horses or something? Did you see that pile of stuff on your desk?'

Roland had, and he had expected it. Greg had worked till two-thirty in the morning, he said, and he looked it. The telephones, four of them, rang all day, clients calling back after having had questions put to them by Roland or Greg by telephone or by letter. Roland did not feel so much cheerful as confident that day. He felt calm, really, and if he looked consequently cheerful, that was an accident. He could remind himself that the office had gone through last year's deadline, and the year's before that, in the same state of nerves and overwork, and they'd always made it, somehow.

Roland wore the same trousers, and the button was in the right-hand pocket. He pulled it out in a moment when he was alone in his office and looked at it in the light that came through his office window. It was grayish brown, with holes in which some gray thread remained. Roland pulled the thread out and dropped the bits into his wastebasket. Had he really throttled a man? The idea seemed impossible at ten past four that afternoon, as he stood in his pleasant office with its green carpet, pale green curtains and white walls lined with familiar books and files. The button could have come from anywhere, Roland was thinking. It could have fallen off one of his own jackets, he could have shoved it into his pocket with an idea of asking Jane to sew it on, when she found the time.

It did cross Roland's mind just after five o'clock (the office, including the two secretaries, was working till seven) to look at the *Post* tonight for the discovery of a body on – what street? A man of forty or so with moustache, named – Strangled. But Roland's mind just as quickly shied away from this idea. Why should he look in the newspapers? What had it got to do with him? There wouldn't be a clue, as they said in mystery novels. Sheer fantasy! All of it. A corpse lying on East 40th Street or 45th Street or wherever it had been? Not very likely.

In four days, the office work had greatly let up. Some clients were going to be a little late (their own fault for not having their data all together), and would have to pay small fines, but so be it. Fines weren't life or death. Roland ate better. Jane was pleased. Roland showed more patience with Bertie, and he could laugh with the child now and then. He sat on the floor and played with him for fifteen and twenty minutes at a time.

'That'll help him, you know, Rollie?' said Jane, watching them arrange a row of soft plastic blocks. Jane spoke as if Bertie couldn't understand a word, which was more or less true.

'Yep,' said Roland. The row of blocks had a space between each block and the next and Roland began setting more blocks on these gaps with the objective of building a pyramid. 'Why don't we ask the Jacksons over soon?' He looked up at Jane. 'For dinner.'

'Margie and Tom! I'd love to, Rollie!' Jane was beaming, and she brought her hands down on her thighs for emphasis. 'I'll phone them tonight. It was always you who didn't want them, you know, Rollie. They didn't mind. I mean – about Bertie. Bertie was always locked up in his room, anyway!' Jane laughed, happy at the idea of inviting the Jacksons. 'It was always you who thought Bertie bothered *them*, or they didn't like Bertie. Something like that.'

Roland remembered. The Jacksons, like most people, were disgusted by Bertie, a little afraid of him for all Bertie's smallness, as normal people were always afraid of idiots, unpredictable things that might do them harm. Now Roland felt that he wouldn't mind that. He knew he would be able to laugh, make a joke, put the Jacksons at their ease about Bertie, if they went into Bertie's room 'to visit with him' the night they came. They never asked to, but Jane usually proposed it.

The Jackson evening turned out well. Everyone was in a good mood, and Jane didn't suggest during the pre-dinner drinks time 'saying hello to Bertie,' and the Jacksons hadn't brought a toy for him, as they had a few times in the past — a small plastic beach ball, something inane, for a baby. Jane had made an excellent Hungarian goulash.

Then around ten o'clock, Jane said brightly, 'I'll bring Bertie out to join us for a few minutes. It'll do him good.'

'Do that,' said Margerie Jackson automatically, politely.

Roland saw Margerie glance at her husband who was standing with his small coffee by a bookcase. Roland had just poured brandies all round into the snifters on the coffee table. Bertie could easily sweep a couple of snifters off the low table with a swing of his hand, Roland was thinking, and he realized that he had grown stiff with apprehension or annoyance.

Bertie was carried in, in Jane's usual manner, held by the waist, face forward, and rather bumped along against her thighs as she walked. Bertie weighed a lot for a five-year-old, though he wasn't as tall as a normal child of that age.

'Aaaaagh-wah!' Bertie's small slant eyes looked the same as they might if he were in his own room, which was to say they showed no interest in or awareness of the change of scene to the living room or of the people in it.

'*There* you are!' Jane announced to Bertie, dumping him down on his diapered rump on the living-room carpet.

Bertie wore the top of his pajama suit with its cuffs turned up a couple of times because his arms were so short.

Roland found himself frowning slightly, averting his eyes in a miserable way from the unsightly – or rather, frightening – flatness of Bertie's undersized head, just as he had always done, but especially in the presence of other people, as if he wished to illustrate his sympathy with people who might be seeing Bertie for the first time. Then Margerie laughed at something Bertie had done. She had given Bertie one of the cheese stick canapés that were still on the coffee table, and he had crushed it into one ear.

Margerie glanced at Roland, still smiling, and Roland found himself smiling back, even grinning. Roland took a sip of his brandy. Bertie was a little clown, after all, and maybe he enjoyed these get-togethers in the living room. Bertie did seem to be smiling now. Occasionally he *did* smile. Little *monster*! But he'd killed a man in return, Roland thought, and stood a bit taller, feeling all his muscles tense. He, Roland, wasn't entirely helpless in the situation, wasn't just a puppet of fate to be pushed around by – *everything* – a victim of a wildly odd chance, doomed to eternal shame. Far from it.

Roland found himself joining in a great burst of laughter, not knowing what it was about, till he saw Bertie rolling on his back like a helpless beetle.

'Trying to stand on his *head*!' cried Jane. 'Ha-ha! Did you see that, Rollie, dear?'

'Yes,' said Roland. He topped up the brandies for those who wanted it.

When the Jacksons departed around eleven, Jane asked Roland if he didn't think it had been a successful evening, because she thought it had been. Jane stood proudly in the living room, and opened her arms, smiling.

'Yes, my love. It was.' Roland put his arms around her waist, held her close for a moment, without passion, without any sexual pleasure whatsoever, but with the pleasure of companionship.

His embrace was like saying, 'Thanks for cooking the dinner and making it a nice evening.'

Bertie was stowed away in his room, in his low bed, Roland was sure, though he hadn't accompanied Jane when she was trying to settle him for the night. Jane was doing things in the kitchen now. Roland went to a corner of the bedroom where he and Jane stacked old newspapers. Because of Roland's work, he kept newspapers a long while, in case he had to look for a new tax law, or bond issue, or any of a dozen such bits of news that he or his colleagues might not have cut out. What he was looking for was not old and was rather specific: an item about a man found dead on a sidewalk during the night of April 26–27. In about four minutes, Roland found an item not two inches long in a newspaper one day later than he had thought it might be. MAN FOUND STRANGLED was the little heading. Francisco Baltar, 46, said the report, had been found strangled on East 47th Street. Robbery had evidently been the motive. Mr Baltar had been a consulting engineer of Vito, a Spanish agricultural firm, and had been in New York for a short stay on business. Police were questioning suspects, the item concluded.

Robbery, Roland thought with astonishment. Not the same man, surely, unless someone had robbed the corpse. Roland realized that this was pretty likely, in New York. A robber might suppose the man was drunk or drugged, and seize the opportunity to relieve him of wallet and wristwatch and whatever. The street fitted, Roland thought, and the date. And the man's age. But Spanish, with that brownish hair? Well, Roland had heard of blond Spaniards.

But they hadn't mentioned a missing button.

On the other hand, why should they mention a missing button in an item as short as this? As clues went, a grayish brown button was infinitesimal. For the police to find the button in Roland's right-hand pocket (he kept the button in that pocket no matter which trousers he wore) would be like finding a needle in a haystack. And noticing the absence of a button on the man's jacket, why should the police assume the murderer had taken it?

Nevertheless, the finding of the corpse – or *a* corpse – gave the button a greater significance. The button became more dangerous. Roland thought of putting it in Jane's little tin box which held an assortment of buttons, but when he opened the box and saw the hundred or more innocent buttons of all sizes there, Roland simply could not.

Throw it away, Roland thought. Down the garbage chute in the hall. Better yet and easier, straight into the big plastic bag in the kitchen. Who'd ever notice or find it? Roland realized that he wanted to keep the button.

And as the weeks went by, the button took on varying meanings to Roland. Sometimes it seemed a token of guilt, proof of what he had done, and he felt frightened. Or on days when Roland happened to be in a cheery mood, the button became a joke, a prop in a story that he had told to himself: that he had strangled a stranger and snatched a button off the stranger's jacket to prove it.

'Absurd,' Roland murmured to himself one sunny day in his office as he stood by his window, turning the button over in his fingers, scrutinizing its grayish brown horn, its four empty holes. 'Just a nutty fantasy!' Well, no need ever to *tell* anyone about it, he thought, and chuckled. He dropped the button into his right-hand pocket and returned to his desk.

He and Jane were going to a resort hotel in the Adirondacks for the last two weeks of June, Roland's vacation time, and of course they were taking Bertie with them. Bertie was walking better lately, but oddly this achievement came and went: he'd been walking better at three, for instance, than he was at the moment. One never knew. Jane had bought a suit of pale blue cotton – jacket and short trousers – and had patiently let out the waist by sewing in extra material, and had shortened the sleeves, 'So he'll look nice at the dinner table at the St Marcy Lodge,' Jane said.

Roland had winced, then rapidly recovered. He had always hated taking Bertie out in public, even for walks in Central Park on Sundays, and the Lodge was going to be worse, he thought, because they'd be stuck with the same people, other guests, or under their eyes, for almost two weeks. He would have to pass through that period of curious and darting glances, unheard murmurs as people confirmed to one another, 'Mongoloid idiot,' then the period of studied eyes-averted-no-staring that such a group always progressed to.

The St Marcy Lodge was a handsomely proportioned colonial mansion set on a vast lawn, backgrounded by thick forests of pine and fir. The lobby had a homey atmosphere, the brass items were polished, the carpet thick. There was croquet on the lawn, tennis courts, horses could be rented, and there was a golf course half a mile away to which a Lodge car could take guests at any hour of the day. The dining room had about twenty tables of varying sizes, so that couples or parties could dine alone if they preferred, or join larger tables. The manager had told the Markows that the guests were never assigned tables, but had freedom of choice.

Roland and Jane preferred to take a smaller table meant for four when the dinner hour came. A pillow was brought for Bertie by a pleasant waitress, who at once changed her mind and suggested a high chair. It was easy, she said, bustling off somewhere. Roland had not protested: a high chair was safer for Bertie, because the tray part pinned him in, whereas he could topple off a cushion before anyone could right him. Bertie wore his blue suit. His ridged tongue hung out, and his eyes, though open, showed no interest in his new surroundings, which he did not even turn his head to look at.

'Isn't it nice,' Jane said, resting her chin on her folded fingers, 'that the Lodge put that crib in the room this afternoon? Just the right thing for Bertie, isn't it?'

Roland nodded, and studied the menu. He was enduring those moments he had foreseen, when the eyes of several people in the dining room had fixed on Bertie, and for a few seconds it was worse as the waitress returned with the high chair. Roland sprang up to lift Bertie into it. *Slap!* The tray part was swung over Bertie's head to rest on the arms of the chair. Roland tugged Bertie's broad hands up and plopped them on the wooden tray where his food would be set, but the hands slid back and dropped again at Bertie's sides.

Jane wiped some drool from Bertie's chin with her napkin.

The food was delicious. The eyes around them now looked at other things. Jane had edged her chair closer to Bertie's, and she patiently fed him his mashed potatoes and tiny bits of tender roast beef. The lemon meringue pie arrived hot with beautifully browned egg white on top. Bertie brought his heavy little hand down on the right side of his plate, and his half-portion of lemon pie catapulted towards Roland. Roland caught it adroitly with his left hand and laughed, dumped it back on to Bertie's plate, and soaked an end of his napkin in his glass of water to wash the stickiness off his palm and fingers.

So did Jane laugh, as if they were alone at home.

They finished a bottle of wine between them.

As they were walking towards the stairway in the lobby, with an idea of getting Bertie to bed, because it was nearly ten, Roland heard voices behind him.

' . . . a pity, you know? Young couple like that.'

' . . . could frighten other kids too. Did you notice that dog today, mom? That poodle?' This voice was young, female, with a giggle in it.

Roland remembered the dog, a black miniature poodle on a leash. The dog had stiffened and backed away from Bertie, growling, when Roland and Jane had been signing the register. Roland's hand reached into his right side pocket and squeezed the button, felt its reassuring reality, its hardness. He turned by the stairway to the two women behind him, one young and one older.

'Yes, Bertie,' he said to them. 'He's not much trouble, you know. Quite harmless. Sorry if he bothers you. He's quite a clown really. Gives us a lot of fun.' Smiling, Roland nodded for emphasis.

Jane was smiling too. 'Good evening,' she said in a friendly tone to the two women.

Both the older and younger woman nodded with awkward

politeness, plainly embarrassed that they had been overheard. '
'Evening,' said the older.

Roland and Jane held Bertie by the hands in their usual manner, hoisting him up one step at a time, sometimes two steps. They performed this chore without thinking about it. Bertie sometimes moved his blunt little feet in their blunt shoes to touch a step, but mostly he dragged them, and his legs went limp. Roland's right hand was still in his trousers pocket.

A pretty girl moved at a faster pace up the stairs on Roland's right. His eyes were drawn to her. She had soft, light brown hair, a lovely profile which instantly vanished, but she glanced back at him at the landing, and their eyes met: bluish eyes, then she disappeared. Roland had been aware of a sudden attraction towards her, like a leap within him, the first such feeling he had had in years. Funny. He was not going to approach the girl, he knew. Maybe best if he avoided looking at her if he saw her again, as he probably would. Still, it was nice to know he was capable of such an emotion, even if the emotion had completely gone in regard to Jane. He squeezed the button harder than ever as they heaved Bertie up the last step to the floor level. He had killed a man in revenge for Bertie. He had superiority, in a sense, one-upmanship. He must never forget that. He could face the years ahead with that.

WHERE THE ACTION IS

Here it was, some action finally – an armed holdup of a town bus – and Craig Rollins was in urgent need of a toilet! Nevertheless, Craig raised his camera once again and snapped, just as a scared-looking man was hopping down the steps of the halted bus. Then Craig ran, heading for Eats and Take-Away, where he knew there was a men's room by the telephones.

Craig was back in something under a minute, but by then the action seemed to be over. He hadn't heard any gunshots. A cop was blowing a whistle. An ambulance had pulled up, but Craig didn't see anybody who was wounded.

'Take it easy, folks!' yelled a cop whose face Craig knew. 'We've got everything in hand!'

'*I* haven't! They got my *handbag*!' cried a woman's voice, shrill and clear.

A June sun boiled down. It was midmorning.

'There were *three* of 'em!' yelled a man in an assertive way. 'You just got two here!'

Craig saw some shirtsleeved police hustling two young men towards a Black Maria. *Click!*

The passengers from the bus, thirty or more, milled about the street as if dazed, chatting with one another.

'Hi, Craig! Get anything good?' It was Tom Buckley, another freelance photographer a couple of years older than Craig, and friendly, though Craig considered him competition.

Craig didn't want to ask if Tom had got a shot of the guy with the gun, because Craig had missed this shot, which might have been possible at exactly the time he had had to dash to a men's room. 'Dunno till they come out!' Craig replied cheerfully. He moved closer to the police wagon, and took a picture of the two young men, who looked about twenty, as they were urged into the back of the wagon. Tom Buckley was also snapping. One or maybe even two of Tom's photos would make it in the afternoon edition of the *Evening Star*, Craig was thinking. Craig shot up the rest of his roll, aiming at any place – at a cop reassuring an elderly woman, at a girl rushing from a narrow passageway into Main Street where the bus was, and being greeted by a man and woman who might have been her parents.

Then Craig went home to develop his roll. He lived with his parents in the home where he had been born, a two-story frame house in a modest residential area. Craig had turned his bathroom – itself an adjunct to the house when he had been fifteen – into his darkroom. All his pictures looked dull as could be, worse than he had expected. No action in them, apart from a cluttered street scene of people looking bewildered. Still, Craig presented them at the office of Kyanduck's *Evening Star* about half past noon, imagining that Tom Buckley had got there a few minutes earlier and with better photos.

Ed Simmons bent his balding head over Craig's ten photographs. The big messy room held seven people at their desks, and there was the usual clatter of typewriters.

'Got there a little late,' Craig murmured apologetically, not caring if Ed heard him or not.

'Hey! You got Lizzie Davis? With her *folks*! – Hey, Craig, this one is great!' Ed Simmons looked up at Craig through horn-rimmed glasses. 'We'll use this one. Just the moment *after* – running out of that alley! Beautiful!'

'Didn't know her name,' Craig said, and wondered why Ed was so excited.

Ed showed the photo to a man at another desk. Others gathered to look at the picture, which was of a girl of twenty or younger, with long dark hair, her white blouse partly pulled out of her skirt top, looking anxious as she rushed forward towards a man and woman approaching her from Main Street.

'This is the girl who was nearly raped. Or maybe she even was,' Ed Simmons said to Craig. 'Didn't you know that?'

Craig certainly hadn't heard. Raped by whom, he wondered, then the snatches of conversation that he heard enlightened him. The third holdup boy, who was still at large, had dragged Lizzie Davis off the bus and into an alley and threatened to stick a knife in her throat, or to rape her, unless she kept her mouth shut when the police came up the alley. The police hadn't come up that alley. In the picture, Lizzie's father, in a pale business suit and straw hat, was just about to touch his daughter's shoulder, while her mother on the right in the picture rushed towards the girl with both arms spread.

Now he saw, in the upside-down photo on Ed's desk, that the girl's eyes were squeezed shut with horror or fear, and her mouth open as if she were crying or gasping for breath.

'Was she raped?' Craig asked.

The reply he got was vague, the implication being that the girl wasn't telling. So Craig's photo appeared on page two of the Kyanduck *Evening Star* that day, and one by Tom Buckley of a local cop with two of the holdup boys on the front page. Both photographs had a two-column spread.

Craig pointed out the photo to his parents that night at the supper table. Craig didn't make it every day, or even every week, a photo in the *Evening Star* or the Kyanduck *Morning News*. His father knew Ernest Davis, the girl's father, who was an old customer at Dullop's Hardware, where Craig's father was manager.

Craig received thirty dollars for his picture, which was the going rate for local photographs, no matter what they were, and Craig mentioned this, with modest pride, to his girlfriend Constance O'Leary, who was called Clancy. Craig, twenty-two and ruggedly handsome, had three or four girlfriends, but Clancy was his current favorite. She had curly reddish blonde hair, a marvelous figure, a sense of humor, and she loved to dance.

'You're the greatest,' Clancy said, at that moment diving into her first hamburger at the Plainsman Café, just outside of town, where the jukebox boomed.

Craig smiled, pleased, 'Human interest. That's what Ed Simmons said my photo had.'

And Craig didn't think any more about that picture of Lizzie Davis until ten days later, when on one of his visits to the *Evening Star* office with a batch of new photographs, Ed Simmons told Craig that the *New York Times* had telexed, wanting to use Craig's photograph in a series of articles about crime in America.

'You'd better be pleased, Craig.'

'With a credit?' Craig was nearly speechless with surprise.

'Well, natch. – Now let's see what you've got here.' Ed looked over Craig's offerings: three photos of the Kyanduck Boy Scouts' annual picnic at Kyanduck Park, and three of current weddings. Ed showed no visible interest. Tom Buckley had probably topped him on these events, Craig was thinking. 'I'll look 'em over again. Thanks, Craig.'

That was Ed's phrase when he wasn't going to buy anything.

Still, Craig's dazed smile at the news about the *New York Times* lingered on his face as he left the office. He'd never yet had a photo in the *New York Times*! What was so great about that picture?

Craig found out some five days later. His photograph was one of three in the first of a three-part series of articles in the *New York Times* called 'Crime in America's Streets.' His photograph had been cleverly cut to show it to better advantage, Craig noticed. The text beneath said:

A young woman in a small town in Wyoming rushes towards her parents, seconds after being held hostage under threat of rape by one of a three-man armed holdup team who robbed bus passengers in midmorning.

And there was his name in tiny letters at one side of the picture: Craig Rollins.

When Craig showed the article to his parents that evening, he saw real joy and surprise in their faces. Their son with his work in the *New York Times*!

'That girl Lizzie's a changed girl, you know, Mart?' Craig's father addressed his mother.

'Yes, I've heard,' said his mother. 'Edna Schwartz was talking about Lizzie just yesterday. Told me Lizzie's broken off her engagement. You know, she was supposed to get married in late June, Craig.'

Craig hadn't known. 'Was she really raped?' he asked, as if his parents might know the truth, as indeed they might, because his mother worked behind the counter of Odds and Ends, a shop that sold dry goods and buttons, and his mother chatted with nearly every woman of the town, and his father certainly saw a lot of people in the hardware store.

'She's saying so,' his mother replied in a whisper. 'At least she's hinting at it. And nobody knows if she broke off her engagement or her boyfriend did. What's his name, dear? Peter Walsh?'

'*Paul* Walsh,' corrected his father. 'You know, the Walshes up on Rockland Heights,' his father added to Craig.

Craig didn't know the Walshes, but he knew Rockland Heights, a neighborhood famous for fine houses and the well-to-do minority of the populace of Kyanduck. Snobs, he thought, to break an engagement these days because a girl's virginity might have been lost. Like prehistoric times!

Craig looked with interest at the two following articles in the *New York Times*, which he was able to see daily at the office of the *Evening*

Star. The series was about car thefts, robberies of apartments, muggings, plus the efforts of the police in big cities to control such crime, of course, but also about the danger of its increasing, now that unemployment was spreading among the under-twenty-fives. A couple of photographs Craig admired very much: one a night-shot of a teenager picking the lock of a Chinese laundry; another of a mugging in the South Bronx, in which an elderly man had been flung to the ground, his grocery bag spilled beside him, while a boy in shorts and sneakers was diving into the inside pocket of the man's jacket. Now these were damned good photographs! Why had they liked his so much, Craig wondered. Because Lizzie Davis's face was pretty? Or because she really had been raped?

'You know any more details about this Lizzie Davis thing?' Craig asked Clancy on one of their dates.

'What do you mean, details? I know she broke her engagement with the Walsh boy. And she *says* she was raped.'

'That's what I mean,' said Craig. 'Amazing.'

'What is?'

'That a guy running away from a holdup pushes a girl into an alley and rapes her – in maybe five minutes or less. I just don't believe it.'

'Oh, you don't.'

'No.'

'Well, she says so. I heard through somebody – yes, Josie MacDougal, that a journalist came to Lizzie's house to interview her about it.'

Craig frowned. 'Journalist from here? Why didn't you tell me?'

'From Chicago, I think. And anyway, I only heard about it when it was all over. Couple of weeks ago, after the *New York Times* thing. Anyway, Lizzie doesn't go out much any more, so I've heard. Stays at home. She's like a psycho.'

'Wha-at?' said Craig. 'You mean she's gone nuts – *at home*?' At the same time, Craig was thinking that another photo or two of Lizzie Davis might be a good idea, salable.

'I don't mean *nuts*,' Clancy said, her freckled face sobering with thought for a moment. 'Just that she's not interested in any kind of social life any more. She's become sort of a *reck*-loose.'

That was a bit of a puzzle to Craig Rollins, but then he didn't understand girls completely and didn't really want to. He didn't believe Lizzie Davis had been raped, though she might well have been threatened with it. Maybe she was putting on an act, breaking her engagement with the Walsh fellow because she didn't really want to marry him.

The day after that evening, part of which Clancy had spent with him in his room at home, Craig received a letter that had been forwarded to him by the *Evening Star*. His 'excellent photograph' of June 10, reprinted in the *New York Times*, had won the year's Pulitzer Prize for newspaper photography.

Craig, with lips parted in disbelief, looked at the letterhead again. It looked authentic with the committee's name, New York address and all that, but was somebody pulling his leg? The signature at the bottom was that of Jerome A. Weidmuller, Chairman of Selections Committee. The last paragraph expressed the pleasure and congratulations of the Committee, and stated that they would be in touch in regard to bestowing an award of a thousand dollars plus a citation.

Craig was afraid to mention the Pulitzer letter to his parents. It might be a joke.

But the next day, a man who said he was the secretary of Mr Weidmuller telephoned Craig at home. He said he had got Craig's telephone number from the *Evening Star*'s office. Craig was cordially invited to a dinner to be given in New York in a few days, and he would receive an invitation by post. His return air fare would be paid, plus hotel expenses in New York for one or two nights, as he preferred. 'Congratulations, Mr Rollins,' said the voice as it signed off.

If this was a joke, it was pretty convincing, Craig thought. A bit dazed, he crumpled up the wet photograph he had been developing in his darkroom, and went to the fridge for a beer to celebrate.

When an express letter arrived that same day at 6 p.m., Craig knew that the Pulitzer Prize affair was real. The air ticket was in the envelope, with the proviso that if he could not keep the date six days thence, he would notify the Committee and return the ticket. His hotel was booked, with dates, and the letter assured him that all expenses would be paid by the Committee.

'What was that?' asked his mother, who was preparing supper in the kitchen.

Craig had walked into the kitchen with the letter in his hand. 'Well, Ma – I wasn't sure it was true till now. I won the Pulitzer for my photo of Lizzie Davis.'

'The Pulitzer?' said his father. 'The Pulitzer Prize? Didn't know there was one for photography.'

Craig attended the dinner in New York. For a few seconds Craig was visible on the TV screen, his parents told him, among other Pulitzer Prize winners for the novel, journalism, drama and so on.

After that, Craig's telephone began to ring. The Kyanduck *Evening Star* passed on callers and messages to Craig. Journalists wanted to interview him. A boy of nineteen wrote to him care of the *Evening Star*, asking if he gave photography lessons. This letter made Craig smile, because he had never had any lessons himself, apart from a course in high school, a course he had dropped after a month, because the work had become too complicated. A university in California that Craig had never heard of wanted him to come and give a lecture, travel expenses paid, plus fee of three hundred dollars. A Philadelphia school of journalism invited him to make a speech of about forty-five minutes, and offered a fee of five hundred dollars. Craig intended to write both schools a polite letter of refusal, on the grounds that he had never made a speech in his life and that the idea terrified him. But after a good dinner at home, and mentioning these invitations to his parents, and his parents' saying in their old-fashioned way, 'Sure you can, Craig, if you just put your mind to it. Be friendly! People just want to see you and meet you now,' Craig decided to accept the California offer.

This affair went off amazingly well. One of the audience asked a question, after that, Craig went rolling along, talking in his own free style about hanging around the office of the Kyanduck *Evening Star* and the town police station, hoping for a good photogenic story to break, hoping even for a fire, though it wasn't maybe very nice to hope for a fire that might hurt people. And then – *this* had happened, the great day when the bus had been held up in his home town, a minor tragedy by world standards, but upsetting for some thirty or forty ordinary citizens, disastrous for the young girl called Lizzie Davis, who had intended to marry in a few days, but whose life had been shattered, maybe ruined, by *crime in the streets*. Craig hammered the crime angle, because the articles on crime in the streets had launched his photograph. Never in the speeches that followed, or in his maiden speech in California, did he say that he had given up on that famous day, that he had thought the action was over when he had taken that photograph. Never would he say, though he tried to make his speeches as amusing as possible, that he had missed the action, because he had had to run to a toilet at the crucial instant when the holdup man had been disarmed.

After four speeches, Craig had got the hang of it. And the fees were great. He began to insist on a thousand dollars plus expenses. He flew to Atlanta, Tucson, Houston and Chicago. Meanwhile, he had job offers. Would he care to join the staff of the *Philadelphia Monitor* at forty thousand dollars a year? Craig wrote a stalling, polite answer to this job offer. He sensed that the lecture circuit could dry up. A tiny town in Atlanta wanted him, but for a hundred dollars, and Craig had no intention of accepting that. He would take the highest salary offer, he thought, when he had exhausted the lecture invitations.

With the extra money from his speeches, Craig Rollins was a changed young man. He was able to buy more clothes, and discovered that he had a taste for quality in clothes and also in food. He acquired a new Japanese camera that could do more things than his old ones, which were second-hand anyway. He still had Clancy as his main girlfriend, but he had met a girl called Sue in Houston who seemed to like him a lot, and who had the money to fly to meet him sometimes in a town where he was making a speech. A pretty girl beside him enhanced his image, Craig had noticed.

Craig also went to a good barber now, his hair was not so short, and the barber fluffed it out in a style that Craig might have called sissy a few months ago, though no one could possibly have called Craig or his face sissy. He had the head and neck of a line-hitter, a tackle, which he had been on the high school football team and in his first year at Greeves College, Wyoming. Craig's grades would have got him kicked out of almost any college, he knew, but Greeves had been willing to keep him on, because of his football prowess. The coach had thought he might make All-American, but Craig had quit college after a month in sophomore year, out of sheer boredom with the scholastic part of it. Now, however, still in top physical form, Craig felt pleased with himself. He wrote to the *Monitor* saying that he had had a better offer from a California paper, but if the *Monitor* could raise their offer to fifty thousand dollars, Craig would accept, because he preferred the East Coast.

'Have you been to see Lizzie at all?' Clancy asked Craig.

'Lizzie – Davis? No, why should I?'

'Just thought it might be nice. She did bring you a lot of luck, and it seems she's so sad.'

Craig knew Lizzie was sad, because a couple of newspapers had interviewed her. Kyanduck's *Evening Star* had, of course, in a discreet little piece with a picture of Lizzie in her family's house.

So Craig telephoned the Davis residence one day around 5 p.m. A woman answered, sounding as if she might be Lizzie's mother. Craig identified himself and asked if he could speak with Lizzie.

'Well, I don't know. I'll have to ask her. She's just back from a little trip. Hold on a minute. – *Lizzie?*'

While he waited, Craig reflected that he might, with Lizzie's agreement, take a few more pictures of her.

Lizzie came on, with a sad voice. But she agreed to see him, when Craig proposed to come over in half an hour and stay just a few minutes.

Craig got into his car and picked up a bouquet of flowers at a shop on the way. He wore his camera on a strap around his neck, as if – today, anyway – his camera were as much a part of his dress as his woolen muffler.

Lizzie opened the door for him. She still had long dark hair that hung in gentle waves to below her shoulders. 'Oh, thank you. That's very sweet of you,' she said, accepting his gladioli. 'I'll get a vase for these. Sit down.'

Craig sat down in the rather swank living room. The Davises had a lot more money than his family. Lizzie came back, and set the vase in the center of the coffee table between them.

Then she proceeded to tell him about her broken engagement, five months ago now, and how quiet her life had been since.

'In a way, I've lost my self-confidence – my self-respect. No use trying to gain it back,' Lizzie said. 'That was shattering – that day.'

How had they got here so quickly, Craig wondered. Lizzie was talking to him as if he were interviewing her, though he hadn't asked her a single question.

'Just this afternoon – you won't believe it – I was being photographed in Cheyenne – for a perfume ad. I've become a photographer's model – maybe because I want to get the phobia of photographs out of my soul. Maybe I'm succeeding, I don't know.'

Craig was wordless for a moment. 'You mean – my picture embarrassed you so much? I'm sorry.'

'Not the picture so much. What *happened*,' Lizzie replied, lifting her round, dark eyes to his. 'Well, it wasn't your fault, and the picture brought you a huge success, I know. It ruined my engagement, but – Well, in a way, I'm lucky too, because there's a market for a sad-dog face like mine. I can see that. The other day I even posed for an ad for men's clothing, you won't believe it, but I was supposed to be the girl with the knowing eyes – for clothing, that is – whose face would brighten up, if the fellow I liked just wore good-looking clothes, see? Very complicated, but it really came off. If I had the photo I'd show you, but the ad isn't even out yet.'

Craig saw Lizzie's face brighten briefly, when she described the way the girl's face would brighten, if her boyfriend only wore good clothes. Then an instant later, Lizzie's glum expression was back, as if it were a garment she wore for the public. Craig moistened his lips. 'And – your fiancé? I mean – I know you broke it off a few months back. I was thinking maybe you'd both get together again.'

Lizzie's sadness deepened. 'No. No, indeed. I felt as if – I'd never want to live with a man as long as I live. Still do feel that way.'

But Lizzie was hardly nineteen as yet, Craig was thinking, though he kept silent. The funny idea came just then: he didn't believe Lizzie. What if she were faking this whole thing? Lying even about having been raped? What if she hadn't liked her boyfriend much anyway, and hadn't minded breaking off their engagement? 'I'm sure your fiancé is sad too,' Craig said solemnly.

'Oh, seems to be. That's true,' Lizzie replied. 'But I can't help that.' She sighed.

'Would you mind if I took a couple of shots of you now?'

Lizzie lifted her eyes to his again. Her eyes were alert, wary, yet interested. 'Whatever for? – Well, not while I'm in these shoes, I hope,' she added with a quick smile. She was in house shoes, but otherwise very smartly dressed in a hand-knitted beige sweater and dark blue skirt, with a gold chain around her neck.

'Don't have to take the feet,' Craig said, standing now, aiming his camera. He could sell three or four photos to New York and Philadelphia newspapers, he was sure, if he suggested that a staff writer write a few lines about her quiet life five months after the rape. *Click!* A rape that Craig was more and more sure never took place. *Click! – Click!* 'Look a bit to your left. – That's good! Hold it!' *Click!*

Five minutes later, as he was taking his leave, Craig said, 'I sure appreciate your letting me snap you again, Lizzie. And would you mind if I found a writer to do a little piece on you? N-not for the local paper,' Craig hastened to add. 'For the big papers east. Maybe west too. Might help your fashion model work, mightn't it?'

'That's true.' She was plainly reflecting on this, blinking her sad eyes. 'It's funny, you know, that *day* bringing you all that success and prizes and everything, and *me* – just ruining my life. Nearly.'

Craig nodded. 'That's a great angle for the writer.' He smiled. ''Bye, Lizzie. I'll be in touch soon.'

'Let me see the photos first, would you? I want to make the choice.'

That very evening, Craig telephoned Richard Prescott, a journalist of the *Monitor*, and gave him his ideas, which had developed a bit since he had seen Lizzie. He would be the puzzled, guilt-ridden, small town photographer who had contributed to, even caused the upset of a young woman's life.

'She really was raped?' asked Prescott. 'I remember the story and your photo, of course, but I thought she'd just been scared. The boy they caught always denied it, you know.'

Never mind, Craig started to say, but instead he replied, 'She certainly implied she was. Girls never want to say it flat out, y'know. But you get my angle, that *I'm* the one upset now, because I—' Craig squeezed his eyes shut, thinking hard. 'Because I captured in a split second that expression of a girl who's just been – assaulted. You know?'

'Assaulted. Yeah, might work fine.'

'In fact, the article should be as much about me as her.'

Prescott said he would get in touch soon, because he had another assignment on the West Coast, and might be able to squeeze Wyoming in.

Craig then rang up Tom Buckley, who agreed at once to take some pictures of Craig. Craig reminded Tom that Tom would get credit lines in some big newspapers, if he did the job. Tom was still friendly with Craig, and had never shown the least jealousy of Craig's success.

Tom Buckley came over the next morning to photograph Craig

in his modest darkroom at home, and at his worktable, brooding over a print of the now famous 'Crime in America's Streets' photo of Lizzie Davis. In this shot, Craig held the photograph at an angle at which it was recognizable, and in his other hand he held his head in the manner of a man with a terrible headache, or tortured by guilt. Tom chuckled a little as he snapped this one. 'Good angle, yeah, your feeling sorry for the girl. She's doing fine, I heard, with her modeling work.'

Craig straightened up. 'But I do feel sorry for her. Sorry about her shame and all that stuff. She sure called her marriage off.'

'She wasn't mad about that guy. And he wasn't about her. One of these things the parents were keen on, y'know? – Everybody in town knows that. You haven't been paying much attention to town gossip, Craig old boy. Too busy with your big-town newspapers lately.' Tom smiled good-naturedly.

In a curious way, Craig realized that he had to hold on to his conviction that Lizzie Davis's life had been altered, ruined – or he couldn't make a success of the article-plus-photos that he had in mind. 'You think she's a phony?' Craig asked in a soft, almost frightened voice.

'Phony?' Tom was putting away his camera. 'Sure. Little bit. Not worth much thought, is it? All the public wants is a sensational photo – someone killing themselves jumping off a building, somebody else getting shot. The hell with who's to blame for it, just give the public the action. The sex angle in your Lizzie picture gave it its kick, y'know? Who cares if she's telling the truth or not? – I don't believe for a minute she was raped.'

That conversation gave Craig something to chew on after Tom Buckley had departed. Craig was sure Tom was right. Tom was a bright fellow. The public wanted pictures of buildings bombed high in the air, a wrecked car with a body in it, or bodies lying on pavements. *Action.* Even the story wasn't terribly important, if the picture was eye-catching. Now Craig struggled like a drowning person to hang on to the Lizzie story, that she *had* been raped and had broken her engagement because of the rape. Craig knew he would have to talk to Richard Prescott as if he believed what he was saying.

Craig did. He prepared himself as if he were an actor. He emoted. He struck his forehead a couple of times, grimaced, and a genuine tear came to support him, though Prescott had a tape recorder and not a camera, unfortunately.

' . . . and then the awful moment – moments – when I realized that in my last-minute shot that day, I'd caught the nineteen-year-old girl and her anxious parents at maybe the most dramatic moment of their lives.' Craig was giving this monologue in his parents' living room, both his parents being out at their respective jobs. Prescott had a few questions jotted down in his notebook, but Craig was going along well enough on his own. 'And just after that,' Craig continued, 'the terrific, unbelievable acclaim that my photo got! Reproduced in the *New York Times*, and then winning the Pulitzer Prize! It really didn't seem fair. It made me rethink my whole life. I thought about Fate, money, fame. I even thought about God,' Craig said with earnestness, and a thrill passed over him. He believed, he knew now, that he was being sincere, and he wanted to look Prescott straight in the eyes. 'I began to ask myself—'

Prescott at that moment stuck a cigarette in his mouth, reached for his lighter, and stared at the little black machine that was recording all this.

'—what I'd done to deserve all this, when the young girl – Well, she didn't get anything from it except suffering and shame. I began to ask myself if there was a God, and if so was he a just God? Did I have to do something in return for my good luck either to him or to – I mean – maybe to the human race? I began—'

'End of tape, sorry,' Prescott interrupted. 'In fact, this might be enough. You've talked through two tapes.'

For a moment, Craig felt cut off, then glad it was over.

Prescott gave a laugh. 'That bit about religion at the end. You thinking of writing a book, maybe? Might sell.'

Craig didn't reply. He had decided in the last seconds that he didn't like Prescott. He had met Prescott only once before, in the *Monitor*'s office, knew he was highly thought of, but now Craig didn't like him.

However, the article that Prescott wrote which appeared ten days later in the *Monitor* was top-notch. Craig's words came out hardly changed, and they rang true, in Craig's opinion. In Tom Buckley's photos, Craig looked serious in one, agonized in the other. An excellent, if only one, picture of Lizzie Davis showed her seated in an armchair in her house, holding what the caption stated was a print of the photograph that had changed her life. Lizzie looked hopeful, modest and pretty, as she stared the camera straight in its eye.

The article brought Craig a few more invitations to lecture, one from a prestigious university in the east, which he accepted. He wrote to the *Monitor* saying that for the next few months he expected to be busy on his own, and so could not at once say yes to the staff photographer's job they had offered, even with the augmented salary to which they had agreed. Craig had higher aspirations: he was going to write a book about it all. When he thought of Fate's part in it, God's part, his brain seemed to expand and to take wings of fancy. He might call his book *Fate Took the Picture*, or maybe *The Lens and the Soul*. The word conscience in the title might be a bit heavy. Craig gave a few more talks, and managed easily to bring his religious thoughts and pangs of conscience into his text. 'Life is not fair sometimes – and it troubles me,' he would say to an awed or at least respectfully listening audience. 'Here I am, lauded by so many, recipient of honors – whereas the poor girl victim, Lizzie, languishes . . . '

Craig's book, *Two Battles: The Story of a Photographer and a Girl*, appeared four months later, after a rushed printing. The book was ghosted by a bright twenty-two-year-old journalist from Houston named Phil Spark, who was not given credit on the title page. *Two Battles* sold about twenty thousand copies in its first six months, thanks to aggressive publicity by its New York publisher and to a good photo of Lizzie Davis on the back of the jacket. This meant that the sales more than covered Craig's advance, so Craig was going to have more money in his pocket due to royalties. He and Clancy got married, and moved into a house with a mortgage.

He had sent half a dozen copies of *Two Battles* to Lizzie Davis, of course, and in due time she had replied with a formal note of thanks for his having told 'her story.' But she showed no sign of wanting to see Craig again, and he didn't particularly want to see her again, either. She and Craig had met briefly with the ghostwriter to get some background in regard to Lizzie's schooldays in Kyanduck.

Craig appeared on a few religious programs on TV, which did his book a world of good, and he dutifully answered almost all his fan mail – though some of it was pretty stupid, from teenagers asking how they could start out 'being a newspaper photographer.' Still, contact with the public gave Craig the feeling that he was making new friends everywhere, that America was not merely a big playground, but a friendly and receptive one, which conflicted a bit with his playing the reflective and publicity-shy cameraman. Craig eased himself over this little bump in the road by convincing himself that he had discovered another métier: exploring God and his own conscience. This seemed to Craig an endless path to greater things. Craig decided to tour America with Clancy in his new compact station wagon, and to photograph poor families in Detroit and Boston, maybe some in Texas too; and fires, of course, in case he encountered any; rape and mugging victims the same; street urchins of wherever; sad-faced animals in zoos. He would make himself famous as the photographer compelled to photograph the seamier side of life.

He envisaged a book with a few lines under each photograph which would reflect his personal conflict in regard to God and justice. Craig Rollins was convinced of his own conviction, and that was what counted. Plus the belief, of course, that such a book would sell. Hadn't he proved by *Two Battles* that such a book would sell?

THE ROMANTIC

W hen Isabel Crane's mother died after an illness that had kept
her in and out of hospitals for five years and finally at home,
Isabel had thought that her life would change dramatically. Isabel
was twenty-three, and since eighteen, when many young people
embarked on four happy years at college, Isabel had stayed at home,
with a job, of course, to help with finances. Boyfriends and parties
had been minimal, and she had been in love only once, she thought,
or maybe one and a half times, if she counted what she now considered a minor hang-up at twenty on a married man, who had been
quite willing to start an affair, but Isabel had held back, thinking it
would lead nowhere. The first young man hadn't liked her enough,
but he had lingered longer, in Isabel's affections, more than a year.

Yet six weeks after her mother's funeral, Isabel found that her life
had not changed much after all. She had imagined parties, liveliness
in the apartment, young people. Well, that could come, of course.
She had lost contact with a lot of her old high school friends, because
they had got married, moved, and now she didn't know where to
reach most of them. But the world was full of people.

Even the apartment on West 55th Street had not changed much,
though she remembered, while her mother had still been alive, imagining changing the boring Dubonnet-and-cream colored curtains,

now limp with age, and getting rid of the nutty little 'settles,' as her mother had called them, which took up space and looked like 1940 or worse. These were armless wooden seats without backs, which no one ever sat on, because they looked fragile, rather like little tables. Then there were the old books, not even classics, which filled more than half of the two bookcases (otherwise filled with better books or at least newer books), which Isabel imagined chucking, thereby leaving space for the occasional objet d'art or statuette or something, such as she had seen in magazine photographs of attractive living-room interiors. But after weeks and weeks, little of this had been done, certainly not the curtains, and Isabel found that she couldn't shed even one settle, because nobody she knew wanted one. She had given away her mother's clothes and handbags to the Salvation Army.

Isabel was a secretary-typist at Weiler and Diggs, an agency that handled office space in the Manhattan and Queens areas. She had learned typing and steno in her last year at high school. There were four other secretaries, but only Isabel and two others, Priscilla (Prissy) and Valerie, took turns as receptionist at the lobby desk for a week, because they were younger and prettier than the other two secretaries. It was Prissy, who was very outspoken, who had said this one day, and Isabel thought it was true.

Prissy Kupperman was going to be married in a few months, and she had met her fiancé one day when she had been at the front desk, and he had walked in.'Reception' was a great place to meet people, men on the way up, all the girls said. Eighty percent of Weiler and Diggs's clientele was male. A girl could put herself out a little, escort the man to the office he wanted, and when he left, ask him if his visit had been successful and say, 'My name is Prissy (or whatever) and if you need to get a message through or any special service, I'll see that it's done.' Prissy had done something along these lines the day her Jeff had walked in.

Valerie, only twenty and a more lightweight type than Prissy, had had several dates with men she had met at work, but she wasn't ready for marriage, she said, and besides had a steady boyfriend whom she preferred. Isabel had tried the same tactics, escorting young men to the office they wanted, but this so far had never led to a date. Isabel would dearly have loved 'a second encounter,' as she termed it to herself, with some of those young men, who might have phoned back and asked to speak with Isabel. She imagined being invited out to dinner, possibly at a place where they had dancing. Isabel loved to dance.

'You ought to look a little more peppy,' Valerie said one day in the women's room of the office. 'You look too serious sometimes, Isabel. Scares men off, you know?'

Prissy had been present, doing her lips in the mirror, and they had all laughed a little, even Isabel. Isabel took that remark, as she had taken others, seriously. She would try to look more lighthearted, like Valerie. Once the girls had remarked on a blouse Isabel had been wearing. This had been just after her mother's death. The blouse had been lavender and white with ruffles around the neck and down the front like a jabot. The girls had pronounced it 'too old' for her, and maybe it had been, though Isabel had thought it perky. Anyway, Isabel had never worn it again. The girls meant well, Isabel knew, because they realized that she had spent the preceding five years in a sad way, nursing her mother practically single-handed. Isabel's father had died of a heart attack when Isabel had been nineteen, and fortunately he had left some life insurance, but that hadn't been enough for Isabel and her mother to engage a private nurse to come in now and then, even part-time.

Isabel missed her father. He had been a tailor and presser at a dry cleaning shop, and when Isabel's mother's illness had begun, her father had started working overtime, knowing that her cancer was going to be a long and expensive business. Isabel was sure that this was what had led to his heart attack. Her father, a short man with brown and gray hair and a modest manner that Isabel loved, had used to come home stooped with fatigue around ten at night, but always able to swing his arms forward and give Isabel a smile and ask, 'How's my favorite girl tonight?' Sometimes he put his hands

lightly on her shoulders and kissed her cheek, sometimes not, as if he
were even too tired for that, or as if he thought she might not like it.

As for social life, Isabel realized that she hadn't progressed much
since she had been seventeen and eighteen, dating now and then
with boys she had met through her high school acquaintances, and
her high school had been an all-girls school. Isabel considered herself not a knockout, perhaps, but not bad-looking either. She was
five feet six with light brown hair that was inclined to wave, which
made a short hairdo easy and soft-looking. She had a clear skin, light
brown eyes (though she wished her eyes were larger), good teeth,
and a medium-sized nose which only slightly turned up. She had of
course, checked herself as long as she could remember for the usual
faults, body odor or bad breath, or hair on the legs. Very important,
those little matters.

Shortly after Prissy's remark about her looking too serious, Isabel
went to a party in Brooklyn given by one of her old high school
friends who was getting married, and Isabel tried deliberately to be
merry and talkative. There had been a most attractive young man
called Charles Gramm or maybe Graham, tall and fair-haired, with
a friendly smile and a rather shy manner. Isabel chatted with him
for several minutes, and would have been thrilled if he had asked
when he might see her again, but he hadn't. Later, Isabel reproached
herself for not having invited Charles to a drinks party or a Sunday
brunch at her apartment.

This she did a week or so later, inviting Harriet, her Brooklyn
hostess, and her fiancé, and asking Harriet to invite Charles, since
Harriet must know how to reach him. Harriet did, Charles promised
to come, Harriet said, and then didn't or couldn't. Isabel's brunch
went quite well with the office girls (all except one who couldn't
make it), but Isabel had no male partner in her efforts, and the
brunch did not net her a boyfriend either.

Isabel read a great deal. She liked romance novels with happy
endings. She had loved romances since she had been fourteen or
so, and since her mother's death, when she had more time, she

read three or four a week, most of them borrowed from the Public Library, a few bought in paperback. She preferred reading romance novels to watching TV dramas in the evening. Whole novels with descriptions of landscapes and details of houses put her into another world. The romances were rather like a drug, she realized as she felt herself drawn in the evenings towards the living-room sofa where lay her latest treasures, yet as drugs went, books were harmless, Isabel thought. They certainly weren't pot or cocaine, which Prissy said she indulged in at parties sometimes. Isabel loved the first meetings of girl and man in these novels, the magnetic attraction of each for each, the hurdles that had to be got over before they were united. The terrible handicaps made her tense in body and mind, yet in the end, all came out well.

One day in April, a tall and handsome young man with dark hair strode into the lobby of Weiler and Diggs, though Isabel was not at the reception desk that day. Valerie was. Isabel was just then carrying a stack of photostatted papers weighing nearly ten pounds across the lobby to Mr Diggs's office, and she saw Valerie's mascaraed lashes flutter, her smile widen as she looked up at the young man and said, 'Good morning, sir. Can I help you?'

As it happened, the young man came into Mr Diggs's office a minute later, while Isabel was putting the photostats away. Then Mr Diggs said:

' . . . in another office. Isabel? Can you get Area-six-six-A file for me? Isn't that in Current?'

'Yes, sir, and it's right here. One of these.' Isabel pulled out the folder that Mr Diggs wanted from near the bottom of the stack she had just brought in.

'Good girl, thanks,' said Mr Diggs.

Isabel started for the door, and the eyes of the young man met hers for an instant, and Isabel felt a pang go through her. Did that mean something important? Isabel carefully opened the door, and closed it behind her.

In less than five minutes, Mr Diggs summoned her back. He

wanted more photostats of two pages from the file. Isabel made the copies and brought them back. This time the young man did not glance at her, but Isabel was conscious of his broad shoulders under his neat dark blue jacket.

Isabel ate her coffee-shop lunch that day in a daze. Valerie and Linda (one of the not-so-pretty secretaries) were with her.

'Who was that Tarzan that came in this morning?' Linda asked with a mischievous smile, as if she really didn't care. She had addressed Valerie.

'Oh, wasn't he *ever*! He ought to be in movies instead of – whatever he's doing.' Valerie giggled. 'His name's Dudley Hall. *Dudley*. Imagine.'

Dudley Hall. Suddenly the tall, dark man had an identity for Isabel. His name sounded like one of the characters in the novels she read. Isabel didn't say a word.

Around four that afternoon, Dudley Hall was back. Isabel didn't see him come in, but when she was summoned to Mr Diggs's office, there he was. Mr Diggs put her on to more details about the office space on Lexington Avenue that Mr Hall was interested in. This job took nearly an hour. Mr Hall came with her into another office (used by the secretaries, empty now), and Isabel had to make four telephone calls on Mr Hall's behalf, which she did with courtesy and patience, writing down neatly the information she gleaned about conditions of floors and walls, and the time space could be seen, and who had the keys now.

As Mr Hall pocketed her notes, he said, 'That's very kind of you, Miss——'

'Isabel,' she said with a smile. 'Not kind. Just my job. Isabel Crane, my name is. If you need any extra information – quick service, just ask for Isabel.'

He smiled back. 'I'll do that. Could I phone my partner now?'

'Indeed, yes! Go ahead,' said Isabel, indicating a telephone on the desk. 'You can dial direct on this one.'

Isabel lingered, straightening papers on the desk, awaiting a possible question or a request from Mr Hall to note down something. But he was only making a date with his partner whom he called Al to meet him in half an hour at the Lexington address. Then Mr Hall left.

Had he noticed her at all? Isabel wondered. Or was she just another face among the dozen or so girl secretaries he had seen lately? Isabel could almost believe she was in love with him, but to be in love was dangerous as well as being pleasant: she might never see Dudley Hall again.

By the middle of the next week, the picture had changed. There were a few legal matters that caused Mr Hall to come to Weiler and Diggs several times. Isabel was called in each time, because by now she was familiar with the file. She typed letters, and provided Dudley Hall and Albert Frenay with clear, concise memos.

'I think I owe you a drink — or a meal,' said Dudley Hall with his handsome smile. 'Can't make it tonight, but how is tomorrow? There's The Brewery right downstairs. Good steaks there, I've tried 'em. Want to make it around six or whenever you get off? Or is that too early?'

Isabel suggested half past six, if that was all right with him.

She felt in the clouds, really in another world, yet one in which she was a principal character. She didn't mention her date to Valerie or Prissy, both of whom had commented on her 'devotion' to Dudley Hall in the last days. Isabel had made the date for 6:30 so she would have time to get home and change before appearing at The Brewery.

She did go home, and fussed so long over her make-up, that she had to take a taxi to The Brewery. She had rather expected to see Dudley Hall standing near the door inside, or maybe at the bar, but she didn't see him. At one of the tables? She looked around. No. After checking her light coat, Isabel moved towards the bar, and obtained a seat only because a man got up and gave her his, saying he didn't mind standing up. He was talking to a friend on an adjacent stool. Isabel told the barman she was waiting for someone, and would be only a minute. She kept glancing at the door whenever it opened, which was every fifteen seconds. At twenty to seven, she ordered a scotch and soda. Dudley was probably working a bit late or had had difficulty getting a taxi. He'd be full of apologies, which Isabel would say were quite unnecessary. She had tidied her apartment, and the coffeemaker was clean and ready, in case he would accept her invitation to come up for a final coffee at the end of the evening. She had brandy also, though she was not fond of it.

The music, gentle from the walls, was old Cole Porter songs. The voices and laughter around her gave her cheer, and the aroma of freshly broiled steaks began to make her hungry. The décor was old brown wood and polished brass, masculine but romantic, Isabel thought. She checked her appearance in the mirror above the row of closely set bottles. She was wearing her best 'little black frock' with a V-neck, a slender gold chain that she had inherited from her mother, earrings of jade. She had washed her hair early that morning, and she was looking her best. In a moment, she thought, glancing again at the door, Dudley would walk in hurriedly, looking around for her, spotting her and smiling when she raised her hand.

When Isabel next looked at her watch, she saw that it was a couple of minutes past 7:30. A painful shock went through her, making her almost shudder. Up to then, she had been able to believe he was just a little late, that a waiter would page her, calling out 'Miss *Crane?*' to tell her that Mr Hall would be arriving at any minute, but now Isabel realized that he might not be arriving. She was on her second scotch, which she had been sipping slowly so it would last, and she still had half of it.

'Waiting for somebody? — Buy you a drink in the meantime?' asked a heavy-set man on her left, the opposite side from the door side, whom Isabel had noticed observing her for several minutes.

'No, thanks,' Isabel said with a quick smile, and looked away from him. She knew his type, just another lone wolf looking for a pick-up and maybe an easy, unimportant roll in the hay later. Hello and good-bye. Not her dish at all.

At about five minutes to eight, Isabel paid for her drinks and

departed. She thought she had waited long enough. Either Dudley
Hall didn't want to see her, or he had had a mishap. Isabel imagined
a broken leg from a fall down some stairs, a mugging on the street
which had left him unconscious. She knew these possibilities were
most unlikely.

The next day Dudley Hall did telephone to make his excuses. He
had been stuck at a meeting with his partner plus two other colleagues from six o'clock until nearly eight, he said, and it had been
impossible to get away for two minutes to make a phone call, and
he was terribly sorry.

'Oh – not so important. I understand,' said Isabel pleasantly. She
had rehearsed her words, in case he telephoned.

'I thought by seven-thirty or so you'd surely have left, so I didn't
try to call The Brewery.'

'Yes, I had left. Don't worry about it.'

'Well – another time, maybe. Sorry about last night, Isabel.'

They hung up, leaving Isabel with a sense of shock, not knowing
how the last few seconds had passed, causing them both to hang up
so quickly.

The following Sunday morning, Isabel went to the Metropolitan
Museum to browse for an hour or so, then she took a leisurely stroll
in Central Park. It was a sunny spring morning. People were airing
their dogs, and mothers and nurses – women in uniforms, nannies
of wealthy families – pushed baby carriages or sat on benches chatting, with the carriages turned so the babies would get the most sun.
Isabel's eyes drifted often from the trees, which she loved to gaze
at, to the babies and toddlers learning to walk, their hands held by
their fathers and mothers.

It had occurred to her that Dudley Hall was not going to call her
again. She could telephone him easily, and invite him for a Sunday
brunch or simply for a drink at her apartment. But she was afraid
that might look too forward, as if she were trying too hard.

Dudley Hall did not come again to the office, because he had
no need to, Isabel realized. Nevertheless, meeting him had been

exciting, she couldn't deny that. Those few hours when she had
thought she had a date with him – well, she'd *had* one – had been
more than happy, she'd been ecstatic as she'd never been in her life
that she could remember. She had felt a little the way she did when
reading a good romance novel, but her date had been real. Dudley
had meant to keep it, she was sure. He could have done better about
phoning, but Isabel believed that he had been tied up.

In her evenings alone, doing some chore like washing drip-dry
blouses and hanging them on the rack over the tub, Isabel relived
those minutes in The Brewery, when she had been looking so well,
and had been expecting Dudley to walk through the door at any
second. That had been enchantment. Black magic. If she concentrated, or sometimes if she didn't, a thrill went over her as she
imagined his tall figure, his eyes finding her after he came through
the big brown door of The Brewery.

Eva Rosenau, a good friend of her mother's, called her up one evening and insisted on popping over, as she had just made a sauerbraten
and wanted to give Isabel some. Isabel could hardly decline, as Eva
lived nearby and could walk to Isabel's building, and besides, Eva
had been so helpful with her mother, Isabel felt rather in her debt.

Eva arrived, bearing a heavy iron casserole. 'I know you always
loved sauerbraten, Isabel. Are you eating enough, my child? You
look a little pale.'

'Really? – I don't feel pale.' Isabel smiled. The sauerbraten
was still a bit warm and gave off a delicious smell of ginger gravy
and well-cooked beef. 'This does look divine, Eva,' said Isabel,
meaning it.

They put the meat and gravy into another pot so Eva could take
her casserole home. Isabel washed the big pot at the sink. Then she
offered Eva a glass of wine, which Eva always enjoyed.

Eva was about sixty and had three grown children, none of whom
lived with her. She had never had a job, but she could do a lot of
things – fix faulty plumbing, knit, make electrical repairs, and she
even knew something about nursing and could give injections. She

was also motherly, or so Isabel had always felt. She had dark curly hair, now half gray, was a bit stocky, and dressed as if she didn't care how she looked as long as she was covered. Now she complimented Isabel on how neat the apartment looked.

'Bet you're glad to see the last of those bedpans!' Eva said, laughing.

Isabel rolled her eyes upwards and tried to smile, not wanting to think about bedpans. She had chucked the two of them long ago.

'Are you going out enough?' asked Eva, in an armchair now with her glass of wine. 'Not too lonely?'

Isabel assured her that she wasn't.

'Theo's coming for Sunday dinner, bringing a man friend from his office. Come have dinner with us, Isabel! Around one. Not sauerbraten. Something different. Do you good, dear, and it's just two steps from here.'

Theo was one of Eva's sons. 'I'll — That's nice of you, Eva.'

'Nice?' Eva frowned. 'We'll expect you,' she said firmly.

Isabel didn't go. She got up the courage to call Eva around ten on Sunday morning and to tell a small lie, which she disliked doing. She said she had extra work for the office to do at home, and though it wasn't a lot of work, she thought she should not interrupt it by going out at midday. It would have been easier to say she wasn't feeling well or had a cold, but in that case, Eva would have been over with some kind of medicine or hot soup.

Sunday afternoon Isabel tackled the apartment with a new, calmer determination. There were more of her mother's odds and ends to throw away, little things like old scarves that Isabel knew she would never wear. She moved the sofa to the other side of the room, nearer a front window, and put a settle between window and sofa to serve as an end table, a much better role for that object, and Isabel was sorry she hadn't thought of it before. 'Settle' was not even the right word for these chair-tables, Isabel had found by accident when looking into the dictionary for something else. A settle had a back to it and was longer. Another, one of many, odd usage of her mother's. The sofa rearrangement caused a change in the position of the coffee table and an armchair, transforming the living room, making it look bigger and more cheerful. Isabel realized that she was lucky with her three-room apartment. It was in an old building, and the rent had gone up only slightly in the fifteen years since her family had had it. She could hardly have found a one-room-and-kitchenette these days for the rent she was paying now. Isabel was happy also because she had a plan for that Sunday evening.

Her plan, her intention, kept her in a good mood all the afternoon, even though she deliberately did not think hard about it. *Play it cool*, she told herself. Around five, she put a favorite Sinatra cassette on, and danced by herself.

By seven, she was in a large but rather cozy bar on Sixth Avenue in the upper 50s. Again she wore her pretty black dress with the V-neck, a jade or at least green-bead necklace, and no earrings. She pretended she had a date around 7:30, not with Dudley Hall necessarily, but with somebody. Again she sat at the bar and ordered a scotch and soda, sipped it slowly while she cast, from time to time, a glance at the door. And she looked at her watch calmly every once in a while. She knew no one was going to walk in who had a date with her, but she could look around at the mostly jolly crowd with a different feeling now, quite without anxiety, as if she were one of them. She could even chat with the businessman-type on the stool next to hers (though she didn't accept his invitation to have a drink on him), saying to him that she was waiting for someone. She did not feel in the least awkward or alone, as she had finally felt at The Brewery. During her second drink, she imagined her date: a blond man this time, around thirty-four, tall and athletic with a face just slightly creased from the cold winds he had braved when skiing. He'd have large hands and be rather the Scandinavian type. She looked for such a man when she next lifted her head and sought the faces of three or four men who were coming in the door. Isabel was aware that a couple of people around her had noticed, without interest, that she was awaiting someone. This made her feel infinitely more at ease than if she had been at the bar all by herself, as it were.

At a quarter to eight, she departed cheerfully, yet with an air of slight impatience which she affected for any observer, as if she had given up hope that the person she was waiting for would arrive.

Once at home, she put on more comfortable clothes and switched on the TV for a few minutes, feeling relaxed and happy, as if she'd had a pleasant drinks-hour out somewhere. She prepared some dinner for herself, then mended a loose hook at the waist of one of her skirts, and then it was still early enough to read a few pages in her current romance novel, *A Caged Heart*, before she went to bed, taking the book with her.

Valerie remarked that she was looking happier. Isabel hadn't realized this, but she was glad to hear it. She was happier lately. Now she was going out – dressing up nicely of course – twice a week on her fantasy dates, as she liked to think of them. What was the harm? And she never ordered more than two drinks, so it was even an inexpensive way of entertaining herself, never more than six or seven dollars an evening. She had a hazy collection of men with whom she had had imaginary dates in the past weeks, as hazy as the faces of girls she had known in high school, whose faces she was beginning to have trouble identifying when she looked into her graduation book, because most of the girls had been only a part of the coming and going and dropping-out landscape of the overcrowded school. The Scandinavian type and a dark man a bit like Dudley Hall did stand out to Isabel, because she had imagined that they had gone on from drinks to dinner, and then perhaps she had asked them back to her apartment. There could be a second date with the same man, of course. Isabel never imagined them in bed with her, though the men might have proposed this.

Isabel invited Eva Rosenau one Saturday for lunch, and served cold ham and potato salad and a good chilled white wine. Eva was pleased, appreciative, and she said she was glad Isabel was perking up, by which Isabel knew she meant that she no longer looked under the shadow of her mother's death. Isabel had finally thrown out the old curtains, not even wanting to use them for rags lest she be reminded of drearier days, and she had run up new light green curtains on her mother's sewing machine.

'Good huntin'!' Valerie said to Isabel, Valerie was off on her vacation. 'Maybe you've got a secret heart interest now. Have you?'

Isabel was staying on at the office, taking her vacation last. 'Is that all you think makes the world go round?' Isabel replied, but she felt the color rise to her cheeks as if she had a secret boyfriend whose identity she would spring on the girls when she invited them to her engagement party. 'You and Roger have a ball!' Valerie was going off with her steady boyfriend with whom she was now living.

Four days before Isabel was to get her two weeks' vacation, she was called to the telephone by Prissy who was at the reception desk. Isabel took it in another office.

'Willy,' the voice said. 'Remember me? Wilbur Miller from Nebraska?' He laughed.

Isabel suddenly remembered a man of about thirty, not very tall, not very handsome, who had come to the office a few days ago and had found some office space. She remembered that he had said, when he had given his name for her to write down, 'Really Wilbur. Nobody's named Wilbur anymore and nobody comes from Nebraska, but I do.' Isabel said finally into the telephone, 'Yes.'

'Well – got any objections if I ask you out for dinner? Say Friday night? Just to say thanks, you know – Isabel.'

'N-no. That's very nice of you, Mr Miller.'

'Willy. I was thinking of a restaurant downtown. Greenwich Street. It's called the Imperial Fish. You like fish? Lobster?' Before she could answer, he went on. Should he pick her up at the office Friday, or would she prefer to meet him at the restaurant?

'I can meet you – where you said, if you give me the address.'

He had the address for her. They agreed upon seven.

Isabel looked at the address and telephone number of the Imperial Fish, which she had written down. Now she remembered Wilbur Miller very well. He had an openness and informality that was unlike most New Yorkers, she recalled, and at the same time he had looked full of self-confidence. He had wanted a two-room office, something to do with distribution of parts. Electronic parts? That didn't matter. She also remembered that she had felt an unusual awareness of him, something like friendliness and excitement at the same time. Funny. But she hadn't put herself out for him. She had smothered her feelings and even affected a little formality. Could Willy Miller of Nebraska be Mister Right? The knight on a white horse, as they said jokingly in some of the romances she read, with whom she was destined to spend the rest of her life?

Between then and Friday evening, Isabel's mind or memory shied away from what Willy Miller looked like, what his voice was like, though she well remembered. She was aware that her knees trembled, maybe her hands also, a couple of times on Friday.

Friday around six, Isabel dressed for her date with Willy Miller. She was not taking so much trouble with her appearance as she had for Dudley Hall, she thought, and it was true. A sleeveless dress of pale blue, because it was a warm evening, a raincoat of nearly transparent plastic, since rain was forecast, nice white sandals, and that was it.

She was in front of the Imperial Fish's blue-and-white striped awning at five past seven, and she glanced around for Willy among the people on the sidewalk, but he was probably in the restaurant, waiting for her. Isabel walked several paces in the uptown direction, then turned and strolled back, under the awning and past it. She wondered why she was hesitating. To make herself more interesting by being late? No. This evening with Willy could be just a nice evening, with dinner and conversation, and maybe coffee back at her apartment, maybe not.

What if she stood him up? She looked again at the awning and repressed a nervous laugh. He'd order a second drink, and keep glancing at the door, as she always did. He'd learn to know what it felt like. However, she had nothing whatsoever against Willy Miller. She simply realized that she didn't want to spend the evening with him, didn't want to make better acquaintance with him. She sensed that she could start an affair with him, which because she was older and wiser would be more important than the silly experience – She didn't know what to call that one-night affair with the second of her loves, who hadn't been even as important as the first, with whom she'd never been to bed. The second had been the married man.

She wanted to go back home. Or did she? Frowning, she stared at the door of the Imperial Fish. Should she go in and say, 'Hello, Willy. Sorry I'm late'? Or 'I'm sorry, Willy, but I don't want to keep this date.'

I prefer my own dates, she might add. That was the truth.

A passerby bumped her shoulder, because she was standing still in the middle of the sidewalk. She set her teeth. *I'm going home*, she told herself, like a command, and she began to walk uptown in the direction of where she lived, and because she was in rather good clothes, she treated herself to a taxi.

MERMAIDS ON THE
GOLF COURSE

Friday, fifteenth of June, was a big day for Kenneth W. Minderquist and family, meaning his wife, Julia, his granddaughter, Penny, aged six and the apple of his eye, and his mother-in-law, Becky Jackson, who was due to arrive with Penny.

The big house was in top-notch order, but Julia had double-checked the liquor supply and the menu – canapés, cold cuts, open-face sandwiches, celery, olives – a real buffet for the journalists and photographers who were due at eleven that morning. Last evening, a telegram had arrived from the President:

CONGRATULATIONS, KEN. HOPING TO LOOK IN
FRIDAY MORNING IF I CAN. IF NOT, BEST WISHES
ANYWAY. LOVE TO YOU AND FAMILY. TOM.

This had pleased Minderquist and made Julia, always a rather nervous hostess, check everything again. Their chauffeur-butler, Fritz, would be on hand, of course, a big help. Fritz had come with the house, as had the silverware and the heavy white napkins and the furniture and in fact the pictures on the walls.

Minderquist watched his wife with a cool and happy confidence. And he could honestly say that he felt as well now as he had three months ago, before the accident. Sometimes he thought he felt even better than before, more cheerful and lively. After all, he had had weeks of rest in the hospitals, despite all their tests for this and that and the other thing. Minderquist considered himself one of the most tested men in the world, mentally and physically.

The accident had happened on St Patrick's Day in New York. Minderquist had been one of a couple of hundred people in a grandstand with the President, and after the parade was over, and everyone in the grandstand had climbed down and were dispersing themselves in limousines and taxis, gunshots had burst out – four of them, three quick ones and one following – and quite fortuitously Minderquist had been near the President when he had seen the President wince and stoop (he had been shot in the calf), and not even thinking what he was doing, Minderquist had hurled himself on to the President like a trained bodyguard, and both of them had fallen. The last shot had caught Minderquist in the left temple, put him into a coma for ten days, and kept him in two hospitals for nearly three months. It was widely believed that if not for Minderquist's intervention, the last bullet would have hit the President in the back (newspapers had printed diagrams of what might have happened with that last shot), perhaps severing the spinal cord or penetrating his liver or whatnot, and therefore Minderquist was credited with having saved the President's life. Minderquist had also suffered a couple of cracked ribs, because bodyguards had hurled themselves on *him* after he had covered the President.

To express his gratitude, the President had presented the Minderquists with 'Sundocks,' the handsome house in which they now lived. Julia and Fritz had been here a month. Minderquist had come out of the Arlington hospital, his second, ten days ago. The house was a two-story colonial, with broad and level lawns, on one of which Fritz had set up a croquet field, and there was also a swimming pool eighteen by ten yards wide. Somehow their green

Pontiac had been exchanged for a dark blue Cadillac, which looked brand new to Minderquist. Fritz had driven Minderquist a couple of times in the Cadillac to a golf course nearby, where Minderquist had played with his old set of clubs, untouched in years. His doctors said mild sports were good for him. Minderquist thought he was in pretty good shape, but he had added a few inches to his waistline during the last weeks in the hospital.

Today, for the first time since he had emerged from the Arlington hospital, on which day there had been only a few photographers taking shots, Minderquist was to face the press. In the months before the seventeenth of March mishap, Minderquist had been in the public eye because of his closeness to the President in the capacity of economic advisor, though Minderquist held no official title. Minderquist had a Ph.D. in economics, and had been a director of a big electrical company in Kentucky, until six months ago when the President had proposed a retaining salary for him and offered him a room in the White House in which to work. One of the President's aides had heard Minderquist speak at Johns Hopkins University (Minderquist had been invited to give a lecture), and had introduced him to Tom, and things had gone on from there. *A man who talks simple and straight*, a newspaper heading had said of Minderquist earlier that year, and Minderquist was rather proud of that. He and the President didn't always see eye to eye. Minderquist presented his views calmly, with a take-it-or-leave-it attitude, because what he was saying was the truth, based on laws of economics of which the President knew not much. Minderquist had never lost his temper in Washington, DC. It wasn't worth it.

Minderquist hoped that Florence Lee of the *Washington Angle* would be coming today. Florrie was a perky little blonde, very bright, and she wrote a column called 'Personalities in Politics.' Besides being witty, she had a grasp of what a man's or woman's job was all about.

'Hon-*ey*?' Julia's voice called. 'It's after ten-thirty. How're you doing?'

'Fine! Coming!' Minderquist called back from the bedroom where he was checking his appearance in the mirror. He ran a comb through his brown and gray hair, and touched his tie. On Julia's advice, he wore black cotton slacks, a blue summer jacket, a pale blue shirt. Good colors for TV, but probably there would be none today, just journalists and a few cameras snapping. Julia was not as happy as he in Sundocks, Minderquist knew, and maybe in a few weeks they would move back to their Kentucky place, after he and Julia discussed the matter further. But now for the President's sake, for the sake of his future in Washington, which was interesting and remunerative, and for the pleasure of the media, the Minderquists had to look as if they appreciated their new mansion. Minderquist strode out of the bedroom.

'Penny and Becky aren't here yet?' he said to his wife who was in the living room. 'Ah, maybe that's them!' Minderquist had heard car tires in the driveway.

Julia glanced out of a side window. 'That's Mama's car. – Doesn't it look nice, Ken?' She gestured towards the long buffet table against a wall of the huge living room.

'Great! Beautiful! Like a wedding or something. Ha-ha!' Glasses stood in sparkling rows, bottles, silver ice buckets, plates of goodies. Minderquist was more interested in his granddaughter, and headed for the front door.

'Ken!' said his wife. 'Don't overdo it today. Keep calm – you know? And careful with your language. No four-letter words.'

'Sure, hon.' Minderquist got to the front door before Fritz, and opened it. 'Hel-lo, Penny!' He wanted to pick the little fair-haired child up and hug her, but Penny shrank back against Becky and buried her face shyly in her great-grandmother's skirt. Minderquist laughed. 'Still afraid of me? 'S matter, Penny?'

'You scared her – coming at her so fast, Ken,' said Becky, smiling. 'How are you? You're looking mighty handsome today.'

Chitchat between the women in the living room. Minderquist slowly followed the child – his only grandchild – towards the hall that led to the kitchen, but Penny darted down the hall as if running for her life, and Minderquist shook his head. His glimpse of the child's blue eyes lingered in his mind. She had used to leap into his arms, confident that he would catch her. Had he ever let her down, let her drop? No. It was since he had come out of the hospitals that Penny had decided to be 'afraid' of him.

'Kenny? Ken?' said Julia.

But Minderquist addressed his mother-in-law. 'Any news from Harriet and George, Becky?'

Harriet was the Minderquists' daughter, mother of Penny, and Harriet and her husband, George, had parked Penny at Sundocks, much to Minderquist's delight, while they took a three-week vacation in Florida. But Penny had started acting strangely towards Minderquist, crying real tears for no reason, having a hard time getting to bed or to sleep at night, so Becky, who lived twenty miles away in Virginia, had taken the child to her house a few days ago.

Minderquist never heard Becky's answer, if she made any, because the press was arriving. Two or three cars rolled up the drive. Julia summoned Fritz from the kitchen, then went to open the front door herself.

There were at least fifteen of them, maybe twenty, mostly men, but five or six were women. Minderquist's eyes sought Florrie Lee and found her! His morale rose with a leap. She brought him luck, put him at his ease. Not to mention that it was a pleasure to look at a pretty face! Minderquist looked at her until her eyes met his and she smiled.

'Hello, Ken,' she said. 'You're looking well. Glad to see you up and around again.'

Minderquist seized her slightly extended hand and pressed it. 'A pleasure to see *you*, Florrie.'

Minderquist greeted a few other people politely, recognizing some of the faces, then steered those who wanted refreshments towards the buffet table, where Fritz in his white waistcoat was already busy taking orders. A couple of cameras flashed.

'Mr Minderquist,' said an earnest, lanky young man with a

ballpoint pen and a notepad in one hand. 'Can I have a couple of minutes with you later in private? Maybe in your study? I'm with the *Baltimore Herald*.'

'Cain't promise you, son, but Ah'll try,' Minderquist replied, putting on his genial southern drawl. 'Meanwhile come over here and partake.'

Julia was pulling up chairs for those who wanted chairs, making sure that people had the drink or fruit juice that they wished. Her mother, Becky, who Minderquist thought looked very trim and well done-up today, was helping her. Becky managed a nursery in Virginia, not for children, Minderquist remembered he had said a few times to the media, when they asked him about family life, but for plants.

'Ah, tell 'em to shove it!' Minderquist said with a grin, in reply to a journalist's question, were the rumors true that he was going to retire. Minderquist was gratified by the ripple of laughter that this evoked, though he heard Julia say: 'Such language, Ken!'

Minderquist had not sat down. 'Where's Penny?' he asked his wife.

'Oh—' Julia gestured vaguely towards the kitchen.

'Going back to Washington again soon then, sir?' asked a voice from among the seated people. 'Or maybe Kentucky? Lovely place you've got here.'

'Bet yer ass – Washington!' Minderquist said firmly. 'Julia, honey, isn't there a beer for me anywhere? Where's Fritz?' Minderquist looked for Fritz, and saw him heading for the kitchen with an ice bucket.

'Yes, Ken,' Julia replied, and turned to the buffet table.

He wasn't supposed to drink anything alcoholic, because of some pills he still had to take, but he treated himself to a beer on rare occasions, such as his fifty-ninth birthday just after he had left the second hospital, and this was another rare occasion, meeting the press with his favorite female journalist, Florrie Lee, sitting just two yards away from where he stood. Minderquist ignored one boring question, as he saw Becky leading his granddaughter in from the kitchen hall, holding

Penny by the hand. Penny hung back, squirming at the sight of so many people, and Minderquist's smile grew broader.

'Here comes the sweetest little granddaughter in the world!' Minderquist said, but maybe nobody heard him, because several of the photographers started clamoring for Minderquist to pose for a shot with Penny.

'Out by the pool!' someone suggested.

They all went out, Julia too. Minderquist placed his beer glass which someone, not Julia, had put into his hand a few seconds ago, by a big flowerpot on the blue-tiled border of the pool, frowned into the bright sunlight, and kept his smile. But Penny refused to take his hand, and evaded like an eel his efforts to grasp her. Becky managed to catch Penny by the shoulders, and they grouped themselves, Minderquist, Julia, Becky and Penny, for several shots, until Penny ducked and escaped, running the length of the pool's side, and everyone laughed.

Back in the living room, the questions continued.

'Any pains now, Mr Minderquist?'

Minderquist was staring at Florrie, who he thought was giving him a special smile today. 'Na-ah,' he answered. 'If I get any pains—' He did get headaches sometimes, but he didn't want to mention that. 'Not to mention, no. I'm feeling fine, doing a little golfing—'

'When do the doctors say you can be back on the job?'

'I'm back at work now, you might say,' Minderquist replied, smiling in the direction of the question. 'Yes. I get – you know – memos from the President – make decisions.' Where was Tom? Minderquist looked over his shoulder, as if the President's car might be slipping up the driveway, or more likely a helicopter would be landing on the big lawn out there, but he had heard nothing. 'Tom said he might look in. Don't know if he can today. Does anybody know?'

Nobody answered.

'Don't you want to sit down, Ken?' Julia asked.

'No, I'm fine, thanks, hon.'

'You swim on your own out in the pool?' asked a female voice from somewhere.

'Sure, on my own,' Minderquist said, though Fritz was always in the pool with him when he swam. 'Think I've got a lifeguard out there? Or a mermaid to hold me up? Wish I had, I'd like that!' Minderquist guffawed, as did a few of the journalists. Minderquist glanced at his wife just in time to see her make a gesture which said, 'Watch it,' but Minderquist thought he was doing pretty well. A few laughs never hurt. He knew he looked full of energy, and the press always liked energy. 'Ah really would like to ride on a mermaid,' he went on. 'Now on the *golf* course—' Minderquist had been going to indulge in a little fantasy about mermaids on the golf course, but he noticed a murmur among the assembled, as if the journalists were consulting one another. Mermaids who graced the links and flipped their tails to send the balls to a more convenient position for the golfer, Minderquist had been going to say, but suddenly three people put questions to him at once.

The questioners wanted to get back to the accident, the attempted assassination of the President.

'Just how you think of it now,' a male voice said.

'Well, as I always said – it was a clear day. Peaceful, sunny. Fun. On that grandstand near the street. Till we climbed down.' Minderquist glanced at Florrie Lee who was looking straight at him, and he blinked. 'When I heard the shots—' Minderquist's mind went into a fog suddenly. Maybe he'd told the story too many times. Was that it? But the show had to go on. 'I didn't know what the shots were, you know? Could've been firecrackers or a car backfiring. Then when I saw Tom bend forward, grabbing for his leg, I somehow knew. I was standing so near the President – there was only one thing to do, so I did it,' Minderquist concluded with a chuckle, as if he had just related a funny story. He touched the dent in his left temple absently, as he watched the journalists scribbling, though some of them had tape recorders. He looked across the room at Julia, and saw her nod at him with a faint smile, meaning she thought he had said all that pretty well.

'You were talking about recreation, Mr Minderquist,' said another male voice. 'You play golf now?'

'Sure do. Fritz drives me over. Quite a few mermaids on the golf course, I must say!' Minderquist was thinking of the pretty teenaged girl golfers in their shorts and halters, flitting about like butterflies. Just kids, but they were decorative. Not so attractive as Florrie Lee though, who Minderquist realized was not only more approachable than the teenagers (one of whom had declined his offer of a soft drink at the clubhouse last week), but seemed to be inviting an approach from him this morning. Never had he seen her look at him like this, fixedly and with a subtle smile from her front-line position among the media in their chairs.

Someone laughed softly. Minderquist saw the laughter, a young man with dark-rimmed glasses, who had turned to the man beside him and was whispering something.

'*Mermaids* on the golf course?' asked a woman, smiling.

'Yes. I mean all the pretty girls.' Minderquist laughed. 'Wish there *were* mermaids, all blonde with long hair and bare bosoms. Ha-ha! By the way, I know a mermaid joke.' Minderquist tugged the sides of his jacket together, but he knew the jacket wouldn't button, and he didn't try. 'You all know the one about the Swedish mermaid who spoke only Swedish and got picked up by some English fishermen? They thought she was saying—'

'Ken, *don't!*' came Julia's voice clearly from Minderquist's left. 'Not that one.'

More laughter from the assembled.

'Let's have it, Ken!' someone said.

And grinning, Minderquist would gladly have continued, but Julia was beside him, gripping his left arm, begging him to stop, but smiling also to put a good face on it. Minderquist folded his arms with husbandly resignation. 'Okay, not that one, but it's one of my best. Anything to please the ladies.'

'You and your wife play Scrabble, sir? I noticed a Scrabble set on the table over there,' said a man.

The word 'Scrabble' was like a small bomb exploding in Minderquist's mind or memory. He and Julia didn't play any more.

The fact was, Minderquist couldn't concentrate or didn't want to. 'Oh-h, sometimes,' he said with a shrug.

Then Minderquist was aware of whispering again among a few people. He looked for Julia, and saw her taking someone's glass to replenish it. Yes, at least six heads, including even Florrie Lee's, were bent as people murmured, and Minderquist had the feeling they were picking at him, maybe saying he wasn't his old self, just trying to act as if he were. Maybe they even suspected that he was impotent now (how long would that last?), and could they know this from the doctors to whom he had spoken? But doctors weren't supposed to disclose information about their patients. *Steady improvement every day*, the newspapers had said during the coma days and after, during the days when the President had looked in to be photographed with him when he had been confined to his bed, and he was better and better up to this moment, in fact, if the newspapers took the trouble to print anything about him, and they did every couple of weeks . . . *sitting up in bed cracking jokes* . . . Sure, sometimes he felt like joking, and at other times he knew he was a changed man, made over into someone else almost, as changed as his abdomen, now bulging, or as his face, which looked bloated and sometimes a bit swimmy to him. Minderquist had heard about lobotomy, and suspected that this was what had happened to him with that bullet through his temple, but when he had asked his chief doctor, and the next doctor under him, both had emphatically denied it. 'Phonys,' Minderquist murmured with a quick frown.

'What? How's that, Mr Minderquist?'

'Nothing.' Minderquist shook his head at a plate of canapés that Fritz extended.

'Sit down for a while, Ken,' said Julia who was beside him again.

'Going okay?' he whispered.

'Just fine,' she whispered back. 'Don't worry about anything. It's nearly over.' She went away.

'Delicious liverwurst, Kenneth. Have one.' It was Florrie Lee at his side now, holding a round plate with little round liverwurst canapés on it.

'Thank you, ma'am.' Minderquist took one and shoved it into his mouth.

'You did well, Ken,' Florrie said. 'And you're looking well, too.'

He was aware of her nearness, her scent that suggested a caress, and he wanted to seize her and carry her away somewhere. Impulsively, he took her free hand. 'C'mon, let's go out in the sun,' he said, nodding towards the wide open doors on the lawn and the swimming pool.

'Could we possibly see your study, Mr Minderquist? Maybe take a picture there?'

Damn the lot of 'em, Minderquist thought, but he said, 'Sure. Got a nice one here. It's this way.' He led the way, smiling a small but real smile, because Florrie had given him a mischievous look, as if she knew he hated to turn loose of her hand. He glanced behind him and saw that Florrie was coming too, along with God knew how many others.

His study or office was book-lined, the books being all from the Kentucky house, and the square room looked orderly to say the least. His new desk had a green blotter, a letter-opener, a pen-and-pencil set, a brown leather folder (what was that for?), a heavy glass ashtray, and no papers at all on it. The wastebasket was empty. Minderquist obligingly leaned against his desk, hands gripping its edge.

Flash! Click! Click! Done!

'Thanks, Ken!'

'When do the doctors say you can go back to Washington, Ken?'

Minderquist kept his smile. 'Well – ask the doctors. Maybe next week. I dunno why not.'

Minderquist left his study as the others did, feeling relief because it was after twelve noon, the media would be thinking about lunch, and taking off. So was Minderquist thinking about lunch, and he meant to invite Florrie Lee out somewhere. Fritz could drive them anywhere. There were charming hostelries in the area, old taverns with cozy nooks and tables. And then? With Florrie, he wouldn't have any problems, he was sure.

''Bye, Mr Minderquist. Many thanks!'

'Keep well, sir!'

Cars were taking off.

Minderquist's eyes met Florrie's once more as he poured himself a scotch on the rocks at the buffet table. He deserved this one drink. He took a sip, then set the glass down. Florrie had that come-hither look again: she liked him. Minderquist moved towards her, with the intention of bowing, and proposing that he and she have lunch together somewhere.

But Florrie turned quickly away.

Minderquist grabbed her hand. She undid his grasp with a twisting movement, and walked towards the big open doors, Minderquist behind her.'Florrie?'

'Take . . . ' The rest of what Florrie said was lost.

But Florrie wasn't gone. In the sunshine, her light dress and her hair seemed all golden, like the sun itself. Minderquist followed her along the border of the pool, where Penny had run a few minutes ago.

'Ken, stop it!' Florrie called, laughing now, and she stepped behind a round table, which she plainly intended to circle if he came any closer.

Minderquist darted, choosing the left side of the table. 'Florrie – just for *lunch*! I—'

'*Ken!*'

Had that been his wife's voice? Grinning, trotting, loping, Minderquist chased Florrie down the other side of the pool, the long side, Florrie turned the corner, her little high heels flying, Minderquist leapt the corner, and fell short. His foot struck the blue-tiled edge, and suddenly he was falling sideways, towards the water.

A thud of water in Minderquist's ears blocked yelps of laughter which for a few seconds he had heard. Minderquist gulped and inhaled water, then his head poked above the surface, barely. Hands reached for him from the edge of the pool.

'You okay, Ken?'

'Good diving there! Ha-ha!'

Minderquist struggled to get up to the rim of the pool. People pulled at his arms, his belt. Someone produced a towel. Where was Florrie? Even when Minderquist had wiped his eyes, he couldn't see her anywhere, and she was all that mattered.

'Didn't hurt yourself, did you, Mr Minderquist?' asked a young man.

'No, no, Chris' sake! – What's happened to Florrie?'

'Ha-ha!'

More laughter. One man even bent double for an instant.

' 'Bye, Mr Minderquist. We're taking off.'

Minderquist strode towards the house, head high, wiping the back of his neck with the towel. He was still host in his house. He wanted to see if Florrie was all right. Minderquist looked around in the big living room, which was eerily empty. A car was pulling away down the driveway. Minderquist thought he heard his wife's voice from the direction of the hall across the living room.

'You will *not*,' Julia said.

'But this is – This can be *funny*,' said a man's voice. 'It's harmless!'

Minderquist reached the threshold of his and his wife's bedroom, whose door was open. Julia stood with a revolver in her hand, the gun that Minderquist knew lived in the top drawer of the chest of drawers to Julia's left, and Julia was pointing it at a man whose back was to Minderquist.

'Drop that thing on the floor or I'll shoot it to pieces,' Julia said in a shaking voice.

The man obediently pulled a strap over his head and let his camera sink to the carpet.

'Now get out,' Julia said.

'I wouldn't mind having that camera back. I'm with the *Baltimore*—'

'What the hell's going on here?' Minderquist asked, walking into the room.

'I want those pictures. Simple as that,' Julia said.

'Just pictures of you and Florrie by the pool, sir!' the young man said. 'Nothing wrong. A little action!'

'Of Florrie? *I* want them!' Minderquist said.

The young man smiled. 'I understand, sir. Well, y-you've sure got the pictures and the camera too. Unless you want me to get 'em developed for you.'

'No!' Julia said.

'Why not? Might be quicker,' said Minderquist.

'Empty that camera now.' Julia pointed the gun at the young man.

Two men stood in the hall, gawking.

The photographer wound up the rest of his roll, opened the camera, and laid the roll on top of the chest of drawers.

'Thanks,' Minderquist said, and put the roll into his jacket pocket, realized that the pocket was sopping wet, and pulled the roll out and held it in his hand.

''Bye, Mrs Minderquist,' said one of the men in the hall. 'And thank you both.'

''Bye, and thanks for coming,' Julia said pleasantly, both hands behind her.

The photographer put his strap around his neck again. 'Good-bye and good luck, Mr Minderquist!' He stumbled a little getting out of the doorway.

'Let me have that roll, Ken,' Julia said quietly.

'No, no, *I* want it,' Minderquist said, knowing his wife would destroy the thing if she could, just because Florrie was on it.

'I'll shoot you if you don't.' She leveled the gun at him.

Minderquist pressed his thumb against one flat end of the roll in his hand. He'd have pictures of Florrie of his own, maybe a couple of good ones that he could have blown up. 'You go ahead,' he replied.

Julia bent towards the chest of drawers, holding the gun in both hands as if it weighed a lot suddenly. She put the revolver back into the top drawer.

A SHOT FROM NOWHERE

The hotel room in which Andrew Spatz lay was yellowish and vaguely dusty, like the dry little plaza beyond his single window, like the town itself. The town was called Quetzalan. Three days ago, Andrew had taken a local bus from the city of Jalapa, not caring where the bus wandered to, and he had got off with his suitcase and box of oil paints, brushes and sketch pads in this town, because it had pleased him at his first glimpse through the bus window. It looked like a town that nobody knew of or cared about. It looked real. And on the plaza he had found the Hotel Corona, maybe the only hotel in the town.

Now, unfortunately, he was suffering from the usual intestinal cramps, and since yesterday he thought he had a fever, though in the heat it was hard to tell. In the early mornings, he set out and walked up in the hills around the town and made sketches to be used later, possibly, for paintings. He sketched everywhere, from an iron bench in the plaza, from a curb, from a table in a bar. But when noon came, and after he had had a simple meal of tacos and beans and a beer, it was time to hide from the sun for a few hours, like everyone else. Quetzalan fell silent as a ghost town from half past twelve until nearly four every afternoon. And the yellow sun bore down with unnecessary force, as if to grind into the consciousness of man and beast and plant the fact that it had conquered, that rain and coolness were far away, maybe gone forever. Andrew had strange dreams when he dozed in the afternoons.

On one afternoon he awakened from a dream of red snakes in a cave in a desert. The snakes did not notice him in the dream, he did not feel in any danger, but the dream was disturbing. Andrew threw off the sheet he had pulled over himself against the inevitable fly or two, and went to the basin in the corner of his room. He took off his drip-dry shirt, wet it again in cool water, and put it back on. His window was open about ten inches top and bottom, but no breeze came.

Andrew glanced at the window, and a movement outside caught his attention.

There was the boy again, with his milk pan for the kittens. The boy looked about thirteen, barefoot in soiled white trousers and white shirt with sleeves rolled up. He was only some six yards away from where Andrew stood in his room, so Andrew could see clearly the tin pie plate and the milk in it. Now as a skinny brindle kitten staggered from some bushes in the plaza, Andrew knew that the boy was going to draw the pan back, as he had done before.

A second kitten appeared, and as the two kittens hunched and lapped, the boy looked over his shoulder, grinning mischievously, as if to see if anyone were watching him. The plaza and the surrounding walks and streets were quite deserted. A grown cat, so thin its bones made shadows in its fur, galloped from the hotel side of the plaza towards the milk pan, and Andrew heard the boy giggle softly, and saw him scramble to his feet, spilling a little of the milk from the pan he was taking away. Why?

Andrew pulled on his jeans, shoved his feet into sneakers, and ran out of his room. Within seconds, he was outside the hotel door on the sidewalk. The boy was walking toward Andrew, but at an angle off to Andrew's right.

'Porquè—' Andrew stopped, hearing faint laughter from somewhere left of him.

The boy trotted away, dumping what remained of the milk on the street.

On his left, Andrew saw a group of three or four men, one with a hand camera of the kind that could make movies. Were they shooting a film? Was that why the boy had to repeat the cat-feeding scene? The men were middle-aged, and looked like ordinary Mexicans, though not peasants. Andrew saw one laugh, and wave a hand in a gesture that might mean 'The hell with it' or 'Muffed that one again.' At any rate, they turned away, drifted out of Andrew's sight.

Back in his room, Andrew removed sneakers and jeans and again lay on his bed on his back. What was the meaning of it? Why were three or four men, one with a camera, out in the hot sun at 2 p.m.? Was the boy an actor or was he a little sadist? Strange.

Andrew felt that the whole past month had been strange. The girl he was in love with in New York, the girl he had thought would last, had met someone else a month ago. This had so thrown him, he hadn't been able to attend classes at the Art Students League for two or three days, and he had felt a bit suicidal or at least self-destructive. He had telephoned his married sister Esther in Houston, and she had invited him to come and stay for a few days. He had not talked much to his sister, but she had been cheering. And there was Mexico which he had never seen, so near when one was already in Houston, so he had taken a slow, cheap train south. Everything he had seen was different, fascinating. But as yet Andrew didn't know what to make of his life, or of his feelings now.

His nap was ended by the jukebox of the Bar Felipe starting up in a corner of the square, which meant it was around four. The jukebox would play nonstop till nearly midnight. Andrew washed at the basin, dressed again, and gathered his sketching equipment. The hotel lobby was deserted as usual when he walked out, though there were a couple of other guests in the hotel, Mexican men, both very quiet.

At the Bar Felipe, Andrew treated himself to an iced tea, and kept an eye out for the men or any one of them whom he had seen watching the boy with the kittens. And for the boy himself. None of these came in through the open doors or walked past on the sidewalk. Other customers of Felipe, workmen with tattered sombreros, wearing tire-soled sandals, came up to the bar to drink a bottle of beer or the brightly colored orange drink that seemed very popular, and they all glanced at Andrew, but didn't stare at him as they had on his first day in town. A dog, thin as a whippet but of indeterminable breed, came up to Andrew's table hopefully, but Andrew hadn't ordered any potato chips or peanuts.

Andrew was pleased with his work of that afternoon. He had sketched two landscapes with color pencils, introducing a lot of purple in the yellow and tan hills. One drawing showed the cluster of tan and pinkish houses that formed the town.

He dined at a tiny restaurant he had discovered in a side street off the plaza, a place hardly bigger than a kitchen, with only four tables. It catered to laborers, Andrew had observed, plus a couple of men of sixty or so who were unshaven and always slightly drunk. Andrew ordered *frijoles refritos*, tortillas, and a mug of boiled milk. The smell of peppery meat in the place sickened him.

The next day repeated the day before it. Sketching in the morning, a light lunch, an orange in his room afterwards. Fruit you had to peel was free of germs, Andrew remembered, and the sweet juice was wonderfully refreshing. Beads of sweat stood on his forehead and seemed to return as soon as he had wiped them away.

Gradually, then all at once, the silence of the siesta period fell outside his window. Not a footstep sounded, not the twitter of a bird. It was the sun's time, and the time lasted nearly four hours while life cowered in little rooms like his, in shade anywhere. Andrew was lying on his back with a wet towel across his forehead, when he heard the *tink* of metal on cement. With nervous energy, and out of curiosity, he got up to see what might be moving outside.

The boy was there, in the same clothing, in the same place, and with the same pie tin of milk. And here came one kitten shakier than yesterday. And there was the boy's smile over his shoulder, quick and furtive.

Andrew's sun-bleached brows drew closer together as he stared. Now – yes, *now* the boy was sliding the pan back from the kitten who had been joined by the second kitten, and the boy set one foot under him, ready to rise with the pan.

There was a crack like a gunshot, not loud, but shocking in the silence.

The boy sagged at once, the pan made a little clatter and the milk spilled. The kittens lapped greedily. And here came the galloping older cat, the skinny brindle, as before.

A film, Andrew thought, still staring. Then he saw a red spot on the boy's shirt. It spread downward along the boy's right side. A plastic paint container that the boy had opened? Was the camera turning? The boy did not move.

Andrew got into his jeans and sneakers with crazy speed and left his room. He stopped on the sidewalk and looked left, expecting to see the camera crew again, but the corner there was deserted. No one was in sight, except the boy.

Andrew wet his lips, hesitated, then took a couple of steps in the direction of the boy, looked again to his left for the camera crew, then went on. The blood, or whatever it was, had reached the side-walk and was flowing towards the street gutter. One of the kittens was in fact interested in it.

'Hey!' Andrew said. '*Hey*, boy!' Andrew stretched a hand out, but did not touch the boy's shoulder. The boy's eyes were half open. Andrew now saw the bullet hole in the white shirt.

He trotted towards the Bar Felipe, thinking that Felipe would be more easily aroused than the hotel proprietor, who seemed to close himself behind a couple of doors at the back of the hotel during siesta time.

'Hey! – *Felipe*!' Andrew knocked on the closed wooden doors of the bar. 'Open! – *Por favor! Es importante!*' After a few seconds,

Andrew tried again. He banged with his fist. He looked around the square. Not a shutter had opened, not a head showed at any window. Crazy!

'*Qué quiere?*' asked Felipe, having opened his door a little. He wore only pajama trousers and was barefoot.

'*Un niño – herido!*' Andrew gasped, pointing.

Felipe took two cautious steps on to the hot sidewalk, so he could see along the plaza's side, and at once jumped back into the shade of his doorway, waved a hand angrily and said something which Andrew took to mean 'Don't bother me with that!'

'But – a doctor – or the police!' Andrew pushed against the doors which Felipe was trying rapidly to close, then heard a bolt being slid on the other side. Andrew trotted back to his hotel.

The hotel desk was deserted. Andrew banged his palm a couple of times on the little bell on the counter. 'Señor *Diego!*'

There was nothing to stop him from using the telephone behind the counter, but he didn't know the police number and didn't see a directory.

'Señor *Diego!*' Andrew went to the closed door to the left of the counter and knocked vigorously.

He heard a grumbling shout from behind the door, then house-slippered footsteps.

Señor Diego, a middle-sized man with gray in his hair and moustache, looked at Andrew with surprise and annoyance. 'What's the matter?' he asked, pulling his cotton bathrobe closer about him.

'A boy is dead! Out there!' Andrew pointed. 'Didn't you hear the shot? A couple of minutes ago?'

Señor Diego frowned, walked a few paces across his lobby, and peered through the open doors of the hotel. The boy was quite visible from here. The three cats, the two kittens and the older cat, were still lapping at the blood, but with less enthusiasm, as the blood was drying or not flowing any longer. 'Bad boy,' Señor Diego commented softly.

'But – we telephone the police?'

Señor Diego blinked and seemed to ponder. It was the first time Andrew had seen him without his glasses.

'The police or a doctor! – Or we carry him in?'

'No!' Señor Diego gave Andrew a scathing glance – as if he detested him, Andrew felt – and moved towards the door of his living quarters. Then he turned and looked at Andrew. 'The police will find him.'

'But maybe he's not *dead*!' Andrew felt torn between an impulse to carry the boy into the hotel, and to leave him as he was for police detectives to determine where the shot had come from. Andrew went behind the counter to the telephone, picked it up, and was looking at the disk of emergency numbers on the telephone's base, when Señor Diego yanked the telephone from his hands.

'All right, the police! *Then* you will see . . . '

Andrew could not understand the rest.

Señor Diego dialed a number. Then he mumbled several words into the telephone. '*Sí-sí*, Hotel Corona. Okay.' He hung up, and shook his head nervously. 'Do not move from this hotel!' he commanded, scowling at Andrew.

Anger flowed through Andrew, and his face felt as if it were going to explode. He went off down the hall to his room, whose door was slightly open still. *Do not move from this hotel!* Why should he? Andrew let cold water run in his basin. His face looked dark pink in the mirror. He took off his shirt again, wet it, and put it back on. At once he was too cool, even shivering. He had been listening for the sound of a car motor, and now it came. Andrew went to his window, but his eyes were drawn first to the boy in white who lay on the plaza's sidewalk, in sun and shadow. No cats now. A car door banged shut.

He heard voices in the lobby, then the creak of a couple of shutters in the plaza. A policeman in faded khaki and a visored cap bent over the boy, touched the boy's shoulder, then straightened and walked towards the hotel door.

Two policemen and Señor Diego came into Andrew's room. Suddenly all three seemed to be talking at once, but quite calmly, as in a dream, Andrew thought. The policemen questioned him calmly. Andrew kept saying, 'I *heard* the shot, yes . . . I was *here* . . . Just ten minutes ago . . . No, no. Not me, *no*! I have no gun. I saw the boy fall! . . . Ask Señor Felipe!' Andrew pointed. 'I went—'

'Señor Felipe!' said the oldest of the policemen, who now numbered three, and threw a smile at Señor Diego.

Andrew knew that he had not made his story clear. But why hadn't he? What he was saying was quite simple, even if his Spanish was primitive. He watched the policemen conferring. His ears started ringing, he wanted to sit down, but instead went to his window for some air. Three or four people now milled about the fallen boy, not touching him. Curious townspeople had at last emerged.

'You come with us,' said a moustached policeman, reaching towards Andrew as if to take him by the wrist.

Andrew was suddenly conscious of the fact that each of the policemen carried a gun at his hip and a nightstick at his other hip.

'But I can tell you everything *here*,' Andrew said. 'I *saw* it, that's all.'

'But if you shot?' said one cop.

Another policeman made a gesture as if to shut him up.

Señor Diego was smiling, murmuring something to the oldest policeman.

A handcuff snapped on one of Andrew's wrists as if by magic, and the policemen seemed to be arguing about whether to put the other wrist in the second handcuff or to attach that to a policeman's wrist, and they decided on Andrew. He was walked out between two policemen with his wrists together in front of him. The boy lay as before, and the people around him now gave their attention to Andrew and the police, who were emerging from the hotel door into the sunlight.

'My tourist card!' Andrew cried, jerking his arm away from a policeman who had hold of him. In English he said, 'I demand to have my tourist card with me!'

'Hah!' But this same policeman, after a word with a colleague, seemed to agree that they take Andrew back to his room.

Andrew took his card from the pocket in the lid of his suitcase, and a policeman took it from him, glanced at it with the air of not reading a word, then stuck it in his own back pocket.

The tan police wagon was a decrepit Black Maria with metal benches inside. Cigarette butts littered the ridged metal floor, along with stains that looked like blood and what might have been dried vomit. The car had no springs, and potholes jolted them up from the benches. The vehicle, though open to the air with its heavy wire mesh sides, seemed to hold heat like a closed oven. The policemen's shirts became darker with sweat, they took off their caps and wiped their foreheads, talking all the while merrily.

Then suddenly Andrew was on the ridged floor. He had almost fainted, had lost his balance, and now the two policemen were hauling him back on to the bench. Andrew had no strength, as in a dream in which he couldn't escape from something. It's all a dream, he thought, because of the fever he had. Wasn't he really lying on his bed in his hotel room?

The wagon stopped. They all went up a couple of steps into a yellowish stone building and into a large room with a high ceiling, maybe formerly the anteroom of a private dwelling, but which was now unmistakably a police station. An officer in uniform approached an unoccupied desk at the back of the room, beside which hung a limp and faded flag on a tall staff.

Andrew asked for the toilet. He had to ask twice, had to insist, and insist also that his handcuffs be undone. A police officer accompanied him and stood indifferently near the doorless toilet – a hole in a tiled square on the floor – while Andrew attended to his needs. There was no toilet paper, not even any newspaper scraps on the nail in the wall beside the hanging chain, which produced no water when Andrew tugged at it. It was during these unpleasant moments that Andrew became sure that he was not dreaming.

Now he was standing before the desk in the large room, with a policeman on either side of him. One policeman narrated something rapidly, and handed the man at the desk Andrew's tourist card. This was valid for a three-week stay in Mexico, and Andrew was so far well within that limit.

'Spatz – Andrew Franklin – born Orlando, Florida,' the officer murmured, and continued with his birth date.

Suddenly Andrew had a vision of his blonde sister Esther, happy and laughing, as she had looked just two weeks ago, when she had been trying to hold her two-year-old son still enough for Andrew to make a sketch. Andrew said in careful Spanish, 'Sir, there is no reason why I am here. I saw a boy – shot.'

'Hererra – Fernando,' said a policeman at Andrew's elbow, as if performing a detail of duty. The name of the boy had already been uttered a few minutes earlier.

'Sí-sí,' said the desk officer calmly, then to Andrew, 'Who shot?'

'I did not see – from where the shot came.'

'It was just outside your hotel window. Ground floor room you have. You could have shot,' said the desk officer. Or was it, 'You have shot?'

'But I have no gun!' Andrew turned to one policeman, then the other. 'You have *seen* my room.'

One policeman said something to the desk officer about the Bar Felipe.

'Ahah!' The desk officer listened to further narration.

Was the cop saying he'd got rid of a gun between his hotel room and the Bar Felipe? The shot must have come from a rifle, Andrew thought. What was 'rifle' in Spanish?

'The boy had robbed you,' said the desk officer.

'No! I did not say that, never!'

'He was a very bad boy. A criminal,' said the desk officer weightily, as if this altered the facts somehow.

'But I simply wanted to tell his death – to the Bar Felipe, to—' Andrew's hands were free, and he spread his arms to indicate a length. 'With a gun so long – surely.'

'You saw the gun?'

'*No!* I say – because of the *distance* – There was no one but the boy in the plaza when he – shot,' Andrew finished lamely, exhausted now.

The desk officer beckoned, and the two policemen came closer to the desk. All three talked softly, and all at once, and Andrew hadn't a clue as to what they were saying. Then the two policemen returned to Andrew, and each took him by an arm. They were leading him towards a hall, towards a cell, probably. Andrew turned suddenly.

'I have the right to notify the American Consulate in Mexico City!' he shouted in English to the desk officer who was on his feet now.

'We shall notify the Consulate,' he replied calmly in Spanish.

Andrew took a step towards the desk and said in Spanish, 'I want to do it, please.'

The desk officer shrugged. 'Here is the number. Shall I dial it for you?'

'All right,' said Andrew, because he didn't know the code for Mexico City. He didn't entirely trust the desk officer, but he was able to stand on the officer's left, and he saw that the number he dialed corresponded to the number in the officer's ledger beside EE UU Consulado.

'You see?' said the desk officer, after the telephone had rung at the other end eight or nine times. 'Closed until four.'

Andrew's watch showed ten past three. 'Then again at four – I try.'

The officer nodded.

The two policemen took him in charge again. Down the hall they went, and stopped at a wooden door in which a square had been cut at eye level.

The cell had one barred window, a bed, and a bucket in a corner.

'At four!' Andrew said to his escort of two, pointing to his wrist-watch. 'To telephone.'

They might not have heard him. They were chatting about something else, like old friends, and after turning of locks and sliding of a couple of bolts, Andrew heard them strolling down the hall, and their voices faded out and were replaced by a moaning and muttering much closer. Andrew looked around, half expecting to find another person in the cell with him, in a corner or under the bed, but the drunken or demented voice was coming from the other side of a brick wall that formed one side of the cell.

A crazy, boastful laugh came after a stream of angry-sounding Spanish.

The town drunk hauled in to sleep it off, Andrew supposed. Andrew sat on the bed. It felt like rock. There was one sheet on it, maybe to protect the blanket, a more valuable item, from being pressed too hard against the coarse wire that was the bed's surface. He felt thirsty.

'Ah — *waaaaah!*' said the nonstop voice in the next cell. '*Yo mi 'cuerdo — 'cuerdo — woooosh*-la! *Oof!*'

Of all strange things to happen, Andrew thought. What if it were all a show, all pretense, as in a film? Why hadn't he told the officer at the desk about the three (or four?) men he had seen yesterday, apparently photographing the boy who had been shot today, laughing even, as the boy drew the pan of milk back from the kittens? Were those men of significance? Was someone filming a 'candid' movie, and could he even be part of it? Could there be a hidden camera filming him now? Andrew glanced at the upper corners of his unlit cell, and became aware of the smell of old urine. He himself stank of nervous sweat. All he needed now was fleas or lice from the blanket. He snatched the blanket from the metal bed, and took it to the only source of light, the barred window opposite the brick wall. He didn't see any lice or fleas, but he shook the blanket anyway and a thin cockroach fell out. Andrew stepped on it, with a feeling of small triumph. The floor was of rather pretty gray stone slabs. This might have been a home once, he thought, because the floor was handsome, as was the stone floor in the big room in front. The red brick wall between him and the mumbling inmate had been recently put there. Reassured somewhat about the blanket, Andrew lay down on his back and tried to collect himself.

He could explain himself in one minute to an English-speaking person at the Consulate. If that didn't work, Mexico City was only about two hours away by car. A man from the Consulate could get here by six or so. And though Andrew had a New York address just now, his sister was next door in Houston, Texas. She could find a Spanish-speaking American lawyer. But surely things wouldn't get *that* bad!

Andrew gave a tremendous sigh and closed his eyes.

Hadn't he the right to a glass of water? Even a pitcher of it to wash with?

'Hey! – *Hey!*' he yelled, and banged on the door a couple of times. '*Agua – por favor!*'

No one came. Andrew tried the yelling and banging again, then gave it up. He had a response only from the drunk next door, who seemed to want to engage him in conversation. Andrew glanced at his watch, lay down again, and closed his eyes.

He saw the fallen boy, the spreading red on his white shirt, the dusty green of the plaza's trees. He saw it sharply, as if the scene were six yards in front of him, and he opened his eyes to rid himself of the vision.

At four, he shouted, then shouted and banged more loudly. After more than five minutes, a policeman said through the square aperture:

'*Qué pasa?*'

'I want to telephone!'

The door was opened. They walked to the desk in front, where the desk officer sat, in shirtsleeves now, with his jacket over the back of his chair. The air seemed warmer than before. Andrew repeated his request to telephone the American Consulate. The officer dialed.

This time the Consulate answered, and the officer spoke in Spanish to a woman, Andrew judged from the voice he heard faintly, then to a man.

'I must speak to someone in English!' Andrew whispered urgently.

The officer continued in Spanish for a while, then passed the telephone to Andrew.

The man at the other end did speak English. Andrew gave his

name, and said he was being held in a jail in Quetzalan for something he did not do.

'Do you have a tourist card?'

'Tourist card,' Andrew said to the desk officer, not having memorized his number, and the officer pulled a manila envelope from a desk drawer and produced the card. Andrew read the number out.

'What are you being held for?' asked the American voice.

'I witnessed a shooting outside my hotel.' Andrew described what had happened. 'I reported it and – now I'm being accused of it. Or suspected of it.' Andrew's throat was dry and hoarse. 'I need a lawyer – someone who can speak for me.'

'Your occupation, sir?' asked the cool voice.

'Painter. Well, I'm a student.'

'Your age?'

'Twenty-two. Is there someone in this area who can help me?'

'Not today, I'm afraid.'

The conversation dragged maddeningly on. The Consulate could not possibly send a representative until tomorrow noon. The slant of the man's questions gave Andrew the feeling that his interrogator was not sure whether to believe him or not. The man told Andrew that he was being held on suspicion, and that there was a limit to what the American Consulate could do at a moment's notice. Andrew was asked if he possessed a gun.

'No! – Can I give you the phone number of my sister in Houston? You can call her collect. She might be able to do something – faster.'

The man patiently took her name and telephone number, repeated that he was sorry nothing could be done today, and as Andrew stammered, wanting to make sure the man would telephone his sister, the desk officer pulled the telephone from Andrew's grasp and came out with a spate of Spanish in a good-natured, even soothing tone, added a chuckle and hung up.

'Noon tomorrow,' the desk officer said to Andrew, and turned his attention to some papers on his desk.

Had the desk officer told the Consulate that he had been drunk and disorderly? 'Can you not ask Señor Diego of the Hotel Corona to come here?'

The desk officer did not bother replying, and gestured for the policemen to take Andrew away.

Andrew asked for water, and a glass was brought quickly. 'More, please.' Andrew held his hands apart to indicate the height of a pitcher.

The pitcher arrived a few minutes after Andrew was back in his cell. He washed his face and torso with his own wet shirt, letting the water fall on the stone floor. He was angry, and at the same time too weak to be angry. Absurd! He lay on the bed half awake and half asleep, and saw a series of visions, lots of people rushing (as he had never seen them) along the sidewalks of the plaza, and the grinning mouth, the big white fangs, the bulging eyes of the Aztec god he had sketched a few days ago near Mexico City. The atmosphere was menacing in all these half-dreams.

Supper arrived around six, rice with a red pepper sauce in a metal bowl, another bowl of beans. The rice dish smelled as if the bits of meat in it were tainted, but he ate the rice and beans for the strength they would give.

Andrew spent a chilly night, curled in his blanket. He was still cold at ten in the morning. At a quarter to noon, he clamored for the door to be opened. After several minutes, a different policeman from the ones Andrew knew arrived and asked what he wanted. Andrew said he was expecting a man from the American Consulate now, and said he wanted to speak to the 'Capitano' at once, meaning the desk officer. All this was through the square in Andrew's door.

The policeman strolled away without a word, and Andrew didn't know whether he was going to be ignored or whether the policeman was going to return. The policeman returned with a second policeman, and they opened his cell door.

The desk officer had gone off to lunch, and Andrew was not allowed to use the telephone.

'I waited until twelve as I was told!' Andrew said, feeling that his Spanish was improving under his difficulties. 'I demand—'

The two men took his arms. Andrew squirmed around to look at the wide open door again, hopefully, but it was empty save for the figures of two police guards standing facing each other, or rather leaning, in the doorway.

'You wait in your cell,' said one policeman.

So Andrew was back in his cell. He had thrown up his breakfast of watery chocolate and bread hours ago, and now there was a smelly plate of something on the floor by his bed. He picked up the plate and tried to throw its contents through the barred window, but half of it fell on the floor.

'Ah — tee-eee — ta — coraz — zón . . . ' sang the idiot in the next cell. 'Adiós, mujeres . . . des al . . . '

Very likely he'd have to wait out the siesta period till four! Andrew uttered the worst curse he knew in English. The fact that he had the strength to curse cheered him. He would telephone his sister at four. He fell on his bed, not caring if he slept or not, wanting only the hours to pass until four.

Andrew was asleep when he heard the clink and scrape of various closures on his door being undone. Ten past four, he saw by his watch, and he got up from the bed, blinking.

'You come,' said a policeman.

Andrew followed the one policeman to the front room again. The desk officer was on the telephone now. Andrew had to stand for several minutes while the officer made a few calls one after the other, one a personal call: the officer was asking about somebody's baby, and spoke about a dinner next Saturday night. At last the desk officer looked at Andrew.

'Spatz Andreo — you are to leave this building, leave your hotel, leave the United States of Mexico — for your safety,' he said.

Andrew was puzzled, but leaving this building sounded pleasant. 'I am free?'

The desk officer sighed, as if Andrew were not completely

free of suspicion, or even guilt. 'You have my orders,' he murmured.

Andrew had nothing of his own in the cell, so he did not need to go back. 'The *señor* from the American Consulate—'

'No one from the Consulate is coming.'

Had the Consulate telephoned? Andrew thought it wise to ask no more questions.

'You will leave the country within twenty-four hours. Understood?' The desk officer handed Andrew his tourist card and a square of paper which he tore from a block and of which he had a carbon copy. 'Please give this paper to the Mexican border police or the passport control at the airport before eighteen hours tomorrow.'

Andrew looked at the form, which had his name, tourist card number and 18:00 written in with a pen. It was an order to leave, but in the list of 'reasons' nothing had been indicated.

'*Adíos,*' said the desk officer.

'*Adíos,*' Andrew replied.

Two policemen, one of whom drove the wagon, took Andrew to within two streets of the Hotel Corona, and asked him to get out and go straight to his hotel. Andrew started walking. He was aware that he looked filthy, and wavering from weakness he might appear drunk also, so he avoided the eyes of a couple of the townspeople – a woman with a basket of laundry on her head, an old man with a cane. They both stared at him. Had he imagined that the old man had nodded and smiled at him?

'*Señor!*' said a small boy on the sidewalk near the hotel door. This was a greeting, the boy had smiled shyly, and dashed on at a run.

Señor Diego was standing behind the counter in the hotel lobby when Andrew entered.

'*Tardes,*' Andrew said in a weary voice, and waited for his key.

'*Buenas tardes, señor,*' replied Señor Diego, laying Andrew's key on the counter. He nodded slightly, with the hint of a smile.

A contemptuous smile? Did Señor Diego know already, having been informed by a telephone call from the desk officer, that he had to leave the country in twenty-four hours? Probably. 'Can I have a bath, please?'

He could. Señor Diego went at once to the bathroom, which was down the hall from Andrew's room. Andrew had had a couple of baths there; one paid a little extra, that was all. Andrew unlocked his room door. The bed was made. Nothing seemed changed. He looked into the top of his suitcase and saw that his folder of traveler's checks was still there. His billfold was still in the inside pocket of his jacket in the closet, and he looked into it: several thousand pesos still, and maybe none at all had been removed.

Andrew took clean clothes with him into the bathroom. The humble but tidy bathroom looked luxurious. He soaped himself, washed his hair, cleaned the tub with a scrubbing brush he found in a bucket, then soaked his jeans, shirt and underpants in more hot water, soap and cleaning powder, and rinsed his hair at the basin. Life had its sweet moments! And goddamn the Consulate! A fat lot of help *they'd* been!

Or, Andrew thought a moment later as he pulled on clean Levi's, had the American Consulate rung up this morning, said or threatened something unless the police station made itself clear? Andrew decided to keep his resentment or his gratitude to himself until he learned something definite.

He hung his damp clothes on hangers at the window in his room, and put some old newspapers on the tiled floor below them. Andrew did not know what attitude to take with Señor Diego, whether to consider him friend or foe or neutral, because certainly he hadn't been helpful yesterday when the police had come and taken him away. Andrew decided to be merely polite.

'Señor Diego,' he began with a nod. 'I leave tomorrow morning. On the first bus for Mexico City. So – I should like to pay you now.'

Señor Diego reached for Andrew's note in a pigeonhole behind him, and he added the item of the bath with a ballpoint pen. '*Sí, señor.* Here you are. – You are looking better now!'

Andrew smiled despite himself, as he pulled limp pesos out of his billfold. He watched Señor Diego count his money, then get some change for him from a locked drawer under the pigeonholes. '*Gracias*. And – the boy out there—' He went on, 'He is dead?' Andrew knew he was dead, but he had to say it, in the form of half-question, half-statement.

Señor Diego's eyes grew small and sharp under his graying brows, and he nodded. 'A bad boy. *Muy malo.* Someone shot him,' he finished softly, with a shrug.

'Who?'

'*Quién sabe?* Everyone hated him. Even his family. They threw him out of the house long ago. The boy stole. Worse!' Señor Diego pointed to his temple. '*Muy loco.*'

Señor Diego's tone was friendly now, man to man. Andrew began to understand, or he thought he did. Someone with a grievance against the boy had shot him, and maybe the whole town knew who, and maybe the police had had to find someone to take the blame or at least be suspected for a while, to keep up a show of justice. Or perhaps, he thought, if he hadn't been naive enough to insist on reporting the shooting, the body would have simply lain there for hours until somebody removed it. Now Andrew understood Felipe's pushing him out of his bar, not wanting to hear what he had to say. The town had had to shut him up.

'Yes,' Andrew said, putting his pesos into his billfold. 'A bad boy – with the little cats.'

'The little *cats*! With people – shopkeepers! A thief! He was *all* bad!' Señor Diego spoke with fervor.

Andrew nodded, as if he agreed absolutely. He went back to his room, and slept for several hours.

When he woke up, it was dark. The Bar Felipe's jukebox played a mariachi song with xylophone, guitars, and an enthusiastic tenor. Andrew stretched and smiled. He smiled at his good luck. Twenty-four hours in a Mexican jail? He had read about dirtier jails, worse treatment in jails in books by Gogol, Koestler and Solzhenitsyn. He was ravenously hungry, and knew the little restaurant off the plaza would still be open, if Felipe's jukebox was playing. Andrew put on his cotton jacket against the evening cool. When he dropped his key on the counter, one of the men guests in the hotel said good evening to him, looked him in the eye, and gave him a friendly smile.

Andrew walked towards the little restaurant whose jukebox music he could hear before he reached the corner where he had to turn, the music overlapping for a few seconds with that from the Bar Felipe. There was no table free, but the young woman who served, who Andrew thought was the daughter of the woman who cooked, asked one man to move to a table with his friends, to whom he was talking anyway. Andrew was aware of more glances than on former evenings, but these glances seemed more friendly, as if the men knew him now, as if they were not merely curious about a gringo in the town.

'*Salud!*' A man of about fifty bent over Andrew's table, extending a hand. In his left hand he held a small, heavy tequila glass.

Andrew swallowed some of his first course of stuffed green peppers, put his fork down, and shook the man's thick hand.

'*Un tequila!*' said the man.

Andrew knew it would look rude to refuse. 'Okay! — *Gracias.*'

'Tequila!' the man commanded.

'Tequila!' echoed the others. '*Andre-o!*'

It was '*Andre-o!*' again when the tequila arrived. In a discreet way, the dozen men in the restaurant toasted him. The young woman waitress suggested a special dish, which she said was ready in the kitchen. It turned out to be a substantial meal. When Andrew pulled out his billfold to pay, the waitress said:

'No, *señor.*' She wagged a finger and smiled. 'You are invited tonight.'

A few of the men laughed at Andrew's surprise.

At a quarter to eight the next morning, Andrew's bus, which had been half an hour late, rolled away from the plaza on the road to Jalapa, where he would board a larger bus. The town of Quetzalan looked sweet to him now, like a place he would like to return to one day. He smiled at his recollection of a man and woman, American or English tourists he had seen getting off the bus one afternoon in the plaza: they had gazed around them, conferred, then got back on the bus. Andrew shied away from the memory of the dead boy, though the vision of his white-clad body came now and then, quick and brief as a camera flash.

In Mexico City he rang Houston. He could catch a plane and be in Houston at 6:15 that evening, he told his sister. Esther sounded delighted, but she asked why he was coming back so soon. He would tell her when he saw her, he said, but everything was fine, quite okay.

Esther's husband Bob picked Andrew up at the airport. Houston was another world: chrome and glass, Texas accents, the comforts of home at his sister and Bob's house, containers of milk and ice cream in the fridge, a two-year-old tot who was learning to call him 'Uncle Andy.'

After dinner, Andrew told them about his last couple of days in Mexico. He had to tell them, before he showed them his drawing and painting efforts, which they were eager to see. Andrew had expected to narrate it smoothly, making it a bit funny, especially his time in the old jail-formerly-palace. But he found himself groping for the right words, particularly when trying to express what he had felt when he realized that the boy was dead.

Esther's face showed that he had made his story clear, however, in spite of his stammerings.

'How awful! Before your eyes!' she said, clasping her hands in her lap. 'You should try to forget that sight, Andy. Otherwise it'll haunt you.'

Andrew looked down at the living-room carpet. Forget it? Should he? Why? Or forget the jail also, just because he hadn't realized why he was there, because the jail happened to have no toilet paper? Andrew gave a laugh. He felt older than his sister, though he was a year younger.

'Any news from – the girl you liked up in New York?' asked Bob.

Andrew's heart jumped. 'In Mexico? No,' he replied casually, and exchanged a glance with his sister. He had told his sister that he had had a bad time with a girl he liked, and of course Esther had said something to Bob. *Lorrie* was what he had to forget. Could he? Any more than he could forget the instant when he had realized that the patch of red on the white shirt was blood?

In New York, Andrew returned to his friends' apartment in SoHo, where he had a room of his own. Someone had been sleeping in his room in his absence and had paid rent, so the main owner of the apartment, Phyllis, didn't charge Andrew for the three weeks he had been gone. Andrew got his part-time job back, as the arrangements were informal and he was paid by the evening. He checked in again at the Art Students League. He made several sketches of the boy lying on the sidewalk of the plaza, and tried a gouache in green, gray and red. He did an oil of it, two oils, then paintings based on the sketches he had made of the Mexican hills. He worked afternoons at his painting, and all day on the days when he did not go to the League in the morning.

One night in the SoHo restaurant where he worked, Lorrie was sitting at a table with a big fellow with dark hair. Andrew felt as if a rifle bullet had gone through him. He spoke to another waiter, who agreed to serve Lorrie's table, which was in Andrew's assigned area. Andrew continued working, but he felt disturbed and avoided glancing at Lorrie, though he was sure that she had spotted him carrying trays, moving back and forth past her table. He loved her as much as ever.

That night Andrew could not sleep, and got out of bed and started another painting of the dead boy. Death, sudden death at thirteen. The jagged and pointed leaves of the palm trees were dusty gray-green, outlined in black, as if in mourning. A curious pigeon flew into the picture, like a disappointed dove of peace, maybe soon to be converted to a bird of prey. A ghostly and skinny kitten stood amazed on stiff legs, confronted by the milk and the blood which had just reached the cement of the walk. One of the boy's puzzled eyes was open, as was his mouth, and there was the pie pan inches from his fingers. How would the colors look by daylight? Andrew disliked painting by electric light. No matter, he had felt like painting it once more.

The dawn was coming when he fell into bed.

OPERATION BALSAM;
OR TOUCH-ME-NOT

Three Mile Island had been a catastrophe, a nearly fatal setback, no doubt about that and no use mincing words. It had alerted the American people not only to the fact that nuclear power plants could break down and release radioactive gases into the atmosphere, but also to the fact that government nuclear control authorities gave out lies to the public.

'Nothing to worry about, folks. Everything's under control,' TV and radio had said during the first anxious days, and for weeks afterward too. What American in the country at the time could forget or forgive that? Or the fact that four years later cleanup men could still not enter the chamber where the damaged core was? And that when four men, dressed as if for a moon-walk, did enter the chamber, one collapsed after a few minutes, gripped his head and said he felt awful? Only one sample of nuclear waste, not the desired four, had been snatched from the floor in this costly endeavor.

The fact was that Three Mile Island wasn't cleaned up yet. The fact was the plant owners and regulatory committees were sick of it, and wished it would disappear. But there the towers stood, one of them hopelessly out of commission and even inaccessible.

As if that weren't bad enough for the Nuclear Control Commission, the public had focused its attention on their bureau. The NCC had also lied. No longer could nuclear plants sneak huge trucks by dead of night to garbage dumps in other states, and get back home unnoticed. The trucks might bear a logo of Tidy-Baby Paper Products or Frozen Fish Straight to Your Table, the little old ladies in small towns were looking out of their windows. What were those enormous trucks doing at three in the morning creeping through *their* tiny town? The little old ladies and the Boy Scouts wrote letters to their local papers, and things went on from there to the NCC. The NCC had been caught out a few times and reproached by Washington for permitting dumping too close to inhabited areas.

For Benjamin M. Jackson, head of the NCC, existence had become a tightening vice. For the past year, he had had an ulcer which he was only half nursing, because he would not, could not give up his brace of scotches at the end of the day (if his day had an end) which he felt he had earned and merited. And he could not stop worrying about his job which was damned well-paid and which he didn't want to lose by reminding Washington too often that there simply weren't enough places that he and his staff could okay as dumps for the goddam radioactive crap.

The seas were out of the question, because departing cargoes were too well inspected in case sensitive items got to Russia. Forests had government patrols pretty thick on the ground. One man in the Environmental Watch Agency would have given Benny Jackson the nod for a dumping in Oregon State Park, but he had never been able to guarantee passage through specific patrols at the park, even though Benny had promised to see that the stuff was buried.

Benny was on paper and by oath pledged to guard against careless disposal of nuclear waste, but in fact his job had almost at once turned into one of finding by hook or by crook any place at all where waste could be got rid of. In one of his dreams, Benny had seen himself assigning each man on his Commission – and there were a hundred and thirty-seven – a container of nuclear plant waste to take home every evening and flush down the toilet, but unfortunately radioactive stuff couldn't be handled like that. The public's opinion of nuclear power plants and respect for their efficiency was low and sinking daily. New plants could not easily be built now, because of the intensity of local protests.

Then some genius in Washington, whose name Benny never learned, maybe because it was top-secret, came up with an idea: Washington would donate a football stadium with a track oval and bleachers and a roof to a certain Midwestern university, and under this stadium, below its underground carpark even, radioactive waste would be stored in lead containers, sealed in vast concrete chambers, and be forgotten. 'The area is free from earthquake . . . ' read Benny's private memo on the plan. He was to keep this quiet from even his closest colleagues for the nonce. The project was going to be rushed through with no expense spared by the Well-Bilt Construction Company of Minnesota. In a very few months, the memo said, trucks could begin rolling into the sub-basements, because the underground structure would be Well-Bilt's priority.

Benny Jackson's ulcer got a bit better at once. The Well-Bilt people were going to work round the clock and seven days a week.

It was amazing to Benny to read about the stadium-to-be in the newspapers. The university had been quite surprised by the gift from Washington, since the present administration was not known for its generosity to educational institutions. The faculty and students, learning of the size and beauty of their future stadium, sent a huge wreath of flowers to Washington with a ribbon on it saying: 'Mr President, we thank you!' Benny had tears of relief, amusement and nervousness in his eyes when he read that.

Now Benny could afford to say on the telephone, to the requests for dumping sites, that in about two months he would be able to provide space. 'Can you hold it that long?' He knew they would have to hold it longer, that was the way things always went, but it was nice to be able to write or say anything with a ring of truth in it.

Benjamin Jackson was thirty-six, with a small bald spot on his head which otherwise grew straight dark hair. Slender by nature, he was nevertheless developing a paunch. He had a civil engineer's degree from Cornell, and was married with two children. Two years ago, on his appointment as head of the NCC after a reshuffle of its top men, Benny had quit his job in New Jersey with an ecology department and moved with his family to their present home in West Virginia, two miles away from the handsome headquarters of the NCC, which was a two-story building, formerly a private prep school.

'So the touch-me-not can now be touched,' said Gerald McWhirty when Benny told him about the stadium project. 'Comforting news.'

Gerry McWhirty did not look as pleased as Benny had hoped, but then Gerry wasn't the type to get excited about anything. Gerry hated stalling and lying, and Benny often felt that Gerry didn't like his job. Gerry had a doctorate in physics, but he liked the quiet life, gardening, tinkering with something in his garage, fixing his neighbor's video or anything else that got broken. He was good at plant inspection, though a bit too fussy in Benny's opinion, and Benny had toned down Gerry's reports many a time. Coolant deficiency at a plant in Wilkes-Barre, Benny remembered, and a couple of 'night supervisors' at a plant in Sacramento who Gerry said 'didn't know straight up' about emergency procedures and ought to be replaced. Benny had concurred in regard to the supervisors, but deleted the coolant complaint, because Gerry's figures hadn't seemed to Benny impressive enough for the NCC to mention.

McWhirty often flew with a small staff on inspection tours all over the country. But Benny went alone and incognito to the Midwestern stadium project, because he was curious about its progress.

What Benny saw was gratifying indeed. A vast oval had been dynamited in the earth, earth-moving machines were busy scooping, trucks rolled away laden with soil and rock, and a couple of hundred workmen swarmed at the scene like bees around a hive. And this was a Saturday afternoon.

'Dressing rooms and showers underneath, I suppose,' said Benny to a hard-hat workman, just to get his answer.

'Air-raid shelters too,' replied the workman. 'I should say atomic fallout shelters.' He grinned as if it would never happen.

Benny nodded in a friendly manner. 'Mighty big project. It's gonna be great.'

'You one of the architects?'

'No-o. Just one of the alumni from here.' Benny cast his gaze toward the distant campus on his left as if he loved it. Then, with a good-bye wave to the workman, he went back to his taxi, and returned to the airport.

A month or so later, when Benny thought his ulcer had all but vanished, Love Canal kicked up again. The Environmental Watch Agency reported 'unexpected leakage of chemical waste' from upstream in Love Canal at the city of Niagara Falls, and Benny received a personal letter from some hothead in Washington, DC named Robert V. Clarke, who wrote like a zealot trying to climb the ladder of promotion. Benny would have been willing to bet that Clarke would be bounced off the bottom rung of the ladder very soon, but the letter had been signed also by one of the higher-ups at EWA, because the Love Canal mess contained nuclear wastes as well as 'chemical wastes,' a term often used to cover radioactive wastes if a report didn't want to admit outright to radioactivity. The higher-up's signature meant that the NCC had to do something. Some men from the NCC had gone up to examine the Love Canal air and water a year or so ago, had stayed for lunch, Benny recalled, and had okayed what they had seen and analyzed: the area was more than safe for human habitation again. Hundreds of families had been evacuated from the area in 1980, when a federal emergency had been declared due to wastes dumped during the 1940s and 1950s. Now Benny's discouraged brain produced, as its first thought: here goes a lot of money if the NCC and the EWA have to launch a new cleanup program, with more tests to justify a cleanup, and so on. Bloody, effing mess! The only thing good about the letter was the last paragraph which said the 'total review' by the EWA would not be ready before sixteen months from now. But meanwhile the NCC's co-operation and attention was requested. Love Canal, Benny knew, had been taking in thousands of dollars per month as a tourist attraction. Lots of motels, restaurants and foodshops and filling stations were there now and hadn't been there before the hoo-hah. Couldn't the EWA let well enough alone? Benny swallowed a little white pill for his ulcer, just in case. At least the owners of the motels and restaurants weren't going to complain about the latest bad news!

Benny composed and dictated a letter into a machine for his secretary. He said that the unexpected leakage at Love Canal must be due to upstream plants disobeying laws laid down by the NCC and the EWA when his committee headed by Mr So-and-so on such and such a date had visited Love Canal and pronounced the waters free of dangerous pollution. Benny omitted saying that most of the NCC information had come from the owners of a nuclear plant in the area, whose own chemists had made the tests.

Lies, lies, lies! Everyone lied. That was the way Benny justified his lies (which were often merely slantings of facts) to himself. What did trouble him was that he might not lie enough or in the right way to suit Washington, and that some eager beaver, or numbskull, or stooge might raise a stink that would cost Benny his job. Washington always thought it looked good, in case of a scandal or a balls-up somewhere, to replace the head of a regulatory committee. It cooled the public down for a while.

Meanwhile the Three Mile Island cleanup program officially continued, though in truth nothing had moved since the entry of the four men in space suits several months ago. The man who had collapsed on that occasion had been called, by the owners of the plant, a 'heat stress' victim, and they also said that the millirems he had received were about 75, or 'the equivalent of 2½ chest X-rays.' The other three men had picked up just 190 rems each. The rem (short for millirem) number bearable to the human body was 5,000 per year, a figure set by the federal government. The expensively trained cleanup men in their expensive suits had already received 3,000 each. Now with the radiation level at 200 rems per hour (reduced from 350, said the plant owners), the chief of the cleanup operations had decided that the same cleanup crew could not complete the job without incurring more than the 8,000 set as maximum for workers wearing protective suits.

'That's one of the reasons why the cleanup is so blasted expensive,' one company official had told the journalists. 'All the protection and training and rehearsal that you need to reduce dose rates add very much to the cost of the cleanup which is already past three hundred and eighty million dollars.'

In Benny's opinion, Three Mile Island never would be cleaned up, never, and now it was rather on the back burner, simmering away, no doubt releasing *something* into the surrounding air, but what the hell? It was amazing how many sightseers and curious people drove up as close as they could to the three stacks on Three Mile Island day and night, as if the closer they got, the more excited they felt. It was perhaps like being able to zoom up to a car accident when the victim still lay on the street, or to a fire still burning in a big building. One newspaper said that GPU, the owners of the plant, were 'promoting' Three Mile Island as a tourist mecca.

Thanks to Gerald McWhirty, the university stadium project received a code name, Operation Balsam. The touch-me-not plant, so called because of its explosive fruit, was also the garden balsam, Gerry explained. Operation Balsam sounded innocuous, and Benny liked it.

At the end of June a director of Well-Bilt sent Benny a letter saying that all was going very well and ahead of schedule, and that part of the basement was already in use.

'I don't know how all that concrete can be dry so soon,' Gerry McWhirty said to Benny when they met by accident at the coffee dispenser in the corridor.

Benny glanced around him. Not every person in the building knew about Operation Balsam or was meant to. 'Well-Bilt must be doing things right. They're getting all the money they need.'

'That's something, at least. That was what was the matter with Three Mile Island, you know, builders doing everything on the cheap. Those container rooms for Balsam have to be airtight, with not a millimeter allowable for subsidence.'

Benny knew. McWhirty's remarks might have worried Benny a little, but he refused to be worried. Operation Balsam was the only cheerful thing in his life now.

There was plenty uncheerful, and annoying. The same day that McWhirty had made his remark, Benny's hotline telephone rang from Washington.

'Hello, Benny. Man here. You know the cleanup crew at Three Mile Island?'

'The four men who went in, you mean?' Benny imagined the sick one worse and in some hospital, launching a lawsuit against the plant owners.

'Yeah, well, there's a lot more of them on the operation, fellows in the control room, women too. They all decided to go to California together on a junket. Whooping it up, you know? I warn you now, because you'll maybe get some flak at your office about it. It'll be on TV news tonight and I didn't want it to shock you.'

'Junket – why?' Benny asked.

'Who knows? They're all on a high, we heard. Either drunk or sniffing coke. Got to sign off now, Benny.'

Benny did watch the 6 o'clock news. The anchorman of the program tried to put a happy face on it. ' . . . tired workers on the Three Mile Island cleanup operations got together to take a well-earned break today, flying first-class from Philadelphia to San Francisco, and they look as happy as – ha-ha! – Legionnaires on a junket to Atlantic City in the old days! What is your name, please, sir?'

A swimmy-faced man uttered an unintelligible name that sounded like Joe Olsen, but it could have been George O'Brien.

'Live it down, live it up!' Olsen or O'Brien said, interrupting the anchorman merrily. '*Tha's* our motto! Yip-pee-ee!'

'We're gonna contaminate ourselves a li'l more!' a woman with smeared lipstick contributed.

'Just good clean fun!' said the laughing anchorman to his TV audience.

'My God! The goddam media trying to get at us again! Washington ought to put 'em out of business!' Benny scowled at his shocked wife for an instant before heading for the scotch bottle in the kitchen.

The rest of what the thirty or so men and women had to say about their junket was not printed in the *New York Times* or the *Washington Post*, who did mention their holiday, but it was in the *Village Voice* and *Rolling Stone*, and that was that they considered themselves 'hopelessly contaminated by radioactivity.' They had been carrying home rems in their clothing, their hair, on their skin for weeks, all for higher pay and danger money; they felt that their homes and families had been contaminated too, that they themselves might live a few more years, but who knew for how long or what might happen? So, before their hair started falling out and nausea kept them from enjoying their food, they were going to live it up. Their motto was repeated.

My God, why wouldn't it all just go away, Benny thought. His ulcer was back in full force. He couldn't tell his wife about the one bright spot, Operation Balsam, but he had to tell her about his ulcer, because he could not eat some of the dishes that she prepared.

Presumably the junketeers straggled back home after a time in quieter fashion than they had departed. But the word spread. Some of them were interviewed again, and rated a column in *Time* and *Newsweek*. They stuck to their story. The owners of the Three Mile Island plant had sacked the lot of them, but the mutinous thirty-odd to a man and woman said they were glad to have been fired. They denounced the 'filthy coverup' by the owners and the NCC and even the EWA, which ought to be concerned now with the radioactivity leaking out and damaging trees, livestock and any people dumb enough to be within twenty miles of the place.

Benny Jackson's office laboriously composed another form letter, using all the favorable facts they could find, and Benny was not even sure they were facts, but at least they had been printed in the *Post* of September 1983 in the same item that had reported less favorable information which Benny was not using. He quoted:

The spokesman for the owners of the Three Mile Island plant report that their 'dose reduction program,' designed to reduce radiation doses to cleanup workers, had cut radiation dose rates on the ground floor of the container building from 350 millirems per hour to about 200 at present.

Benny did wonder, as he dictated the statement, how the owners or anybody could reduce radiation except by letting it escape, say by just opening a window a little.

Gerald McWhirty looked over the letter at Benny's request, rubbed his reddish moustache, and nodded without comment.

'I think it's not bad,' Benny said.

'A mess,' McWhirty said. 'That's my comment on Three Mile Island. Built on the cheap, everyone knows that.'

A vague patriotism stirred shame in Benny. America doing something on the cheap! England, France and Germany seldom if ever had trouble with their nuclear power plants, certainly no cata-strophic troubles, because they did things the expensive and correct way. Benny was glad that McWhirty didn't say this now, because McWhirty had in the past.

Operation Balsam was completed in late July. The NCC received an invitation from Well-Bilt. 'Our installations are now in place. We welcome you at any time to a private and informal preview and inspection.'

Benny at first did not want to go, because his name and face were known to the media, and suppose some of them were there? Even on the ground's surface? 'This isn't an official opening of the football field too, is it?' he asked McWhirty, who had been on the telephone with Well-Bilt.

'Certainly not. I wouldn't be caught dead there at the stadium opening. It's just Operation Balsam.'

At the last moment, Benny did go, because Douglas Ferguson, an NCC director and a good friend of McWhirty's, said, 'Grab an old raincoat and come with us, Benny. Just about fifteen of us. Take-off at ten tomorrow morning, and we'll be home before midnight.'

So Benny did grab an old raincoat, because it was a bit of a disguise. He looked not the least important in it.

The NCC men were met at the Indianapolis airport by four limousines laid on by Well-Bilt.

Little pennants flew around the rim of the stadium roof, which resembled a huge half-eggshell. In the brilliant sunshine, the surrounding turf shone like emerald.

'Beautiful!' Benny exclaimed, bowled over by the changes since he had seen the place such a short time ago.

A huge truck painted plain white had turned off the road just behind them, and Benny watched it approach a clump of trees on the lawn, tilt downward, and roll out of sight. That was one of *them*, Benny knew, loaded with radioactive junk. His heart leapt with a rare sense of success. Since the sub-basement was purported to be a fallout shelter, hospital and so on, the trucks could presumably be carrying dried foodstuffs, blankets, and medical supplies.

'Service entrance,' McWhirty murmured with a smile at Benny, having seen the direction of Benny's glance.

Uniformed and armed guards met them at a gate and waved their cars through. A neatly dressed middle-aged man introduced himself as Frank Marlucci, a supervisor for Well-Bilt. They all walked into one of the broad entrances for spectators. There were ticket booths, benches, elevators.

'I suppose you'd like to see the basements first?' asked Mr Marlucci.

They would. The elevator went down and down, past CHANGING ROOMS and CARPARK, and they all got out into a concrete corridor whose ceiling was some fifteen feet high. Off this corridor led broader passages, wide enough for trucks. Arrows on the walls indicated vehicle movement direction.

'This way, please, gentlemen,' said Mr Marlucci.

Benny could hear a truck grinding in low gear somewhere. In a central room from which passageways radiated, they now saw the big lead containers being fork-lifted from the back of a white truck. Another fork-lift was depositing containers gently on to a conveyor belt. The containers disappeared in the distance like suitcases at an airport after a passenger had checked in. Benny's face spread in a smile. It all looked so wonderfully solid, so buried, so impregnable!

Even Gerry McWhirty seemed impressed. 'And the rooms? The storerooms?' he asked Mr Marlucci, shouting over the din.

Mr Marlucci beckoned, and they all began to walk. 'This one, for example.' He stopped at a steel door some ten feet square, unlocked a metal cover to the right of it, and worked a combination lock by pressing numbers. The door slid to the right into the concrete wall. 'This room's nearly full. Not quite.'

Benny couldn't judge the room's size, because the big rectangular containers lined the walls in triple or quadruple layers, and reached to the ceiling at the back. He saw McWhirty hesitate a moment, then step into the room.

McWhirty looked around at the containers, at the concrete floor and stamped on it, as if his flyweight compared to the containers' could make a difference or a shudder in the construction. 'May I see it closed again?' McWhirty asked as he walked out.

Mr Marlucci pressed a button and the door slid shut.

McWhirty ran his finger or his fingernail along the side of the door at the bottom. 'A little space here.'

Mr Marlucci shook his head emphatically. 'The door's grooved, sir, touching at the bottom – countersunk, airtight in steel housing.'

Benny wanted to ask how long the lead containers were supposed to last, but he was supposed to know. Benny knew the containers were more than a foot thick – fantastic – and that seemed made for eternity.

Farther along in the corridor, McWhirty noticed a crack in a concrete wall, and ran his finger along it.

'That's going to be fixed,' said Mr Marlucci. 'That's normal for now.'

The rooms were twenty meters square, Mr Marlucci replied to a question from one of the NCC men. He led them to the Facilities Room, another square concrete-walled room with a blue floor, a counter with stools, cooking facilities, refrigerators, tables and chairs, restrooms, a cigarette vending machine – a scene now eerily barren of a human figure.

'They're going to stick a few posters up,' said Mr Marlucci with a smile, 'so it won't look so bleak. It's really just the Balsam workers' canteen, so it doesn't have to look like a happy-hour bar.'

McWhirty wanted to see another container room. 'Maybe on the other side of the basement?'

The group began a walk equal to the breadth of the football field above them, Benny supposed, and possibly more. They had to flatten themselves against a wall to let a fork-lift roll by with six containers on it. Benny imagined that he felt the floor shake under him. Was there another basement below this? Small red tanks were fixed at intervals along these walls, and Benny thought they were fire extinguishers until on closer inspection he saw that they were labeled oxygen. A headgear like an old-fashioned gas mask topped each red tank, and the apparatus was sealed in a transparent plastic bubble. At another steel door in a row of doors, Mr Marlucci stopped, and again worked a digital lock.

'How full is the basement now?' McWhirty asked. 'A quarter? A third?'

'More than half, sir,' Mr Marlucci replied as the steel door rolled into the wall. 'Amazing how fast it's filling up. But then the trucks're coming in day and night since – oh, nearly a month.'

Now Benny's spirits sank a little. At this rate, they wouldn't be able to use Balsam for two or three urgent jobs that were on Benny's mind. 'Where's it all coming from – mainly?' Benny asked, feeling suddenly like a landlord whose apartment had been taken over by a family larger than had been agreed upon.

'Oh, you'd be surprised, sir. We have orders – top-secret, of course – from Washington to admit this and that from Texas, California, Ohio, anywhere at all they're having trouble. They're not labeled when they get here, but if they're in the right containers, we're obliged to take 'em in.'

Benny fumed in silence. Washington had higher authority, of course, but why hadn't Washington or the EWA told the NCC that they were cramming the place?

McWhirty had entered the half-full room whose door had opened, and was looking around at the walls he could see, at the corners of the lead containers. 'You've got a flashlight, haven't you, Doug? Check the back wall for cracks and moisture as far as you can.'

Douglas Ferguson pulled a flashlight from his pocket and walked in.

'At this rate,' McWhirty said to Mr Marlucci, 'this basement will be full in another month?'

'This sub-basement,' said Mr Marlucci, smiling. 'Well – I'd say another three to four weeks. We'll have it full and sealed before the football season.'

Awful, Benny thought. Washington would simply have to donate a stadium to another university somewhere, and as soon as possible.

They were drifting on toward the exit on the side of the basement they had not seen, where Mr Marlucci said they could take an elevator up to the ground level and see the stadium interior.

On the earth's surface, on the sunlit grass, Mr Marlucci shook his head as he spoke to a man in shirtsleeves and blue jeans who had asked him something. Benny was close enough to hear Mr Marlucci say:

'The fallout shelters're pretty empty now, nothing much to see yet. We're bringing in supplies, as you see.'

To Benny Mr Marlucci said, as they walked up a ramp, 'One of the professors from the university. Now here we have a view!' With widespread arms Mr Marlucci beheld the football field as if he would embrace it.

A dark gray running track framed the green of the football field. Bleachers climbed up and up, empty yet poised and focused for drama.

'Really something!' said a voice among the NCC men.

Mr Marlucci talked about the heating and ventilation systems, the First Aid room for players and for spectators if they needed it, and finally he suggested drinks and a snack at a nearby restaurant, if the gentlemen had time. The NCC men hadn't. It was after 4 now, and their plane left at 6:15. The afternoon had flown.

The limousines arrived again, congratulations, thanks and good-byes were exchanged, and the cars moved off for the airport.

Benny Jackson sat next to McWhirty on the airplane, because he wanted to hear McWhirty's impressions while they were still fresh.

'We'll look at it again in two weeks,' said McWhirty. 'Take a rem check ourselves downstairs and at all the vents. Those cracks—' McWhirty gave a laugh. 'Talk about a rush job! I want to speak with Doug.' He unfastened his seat belt and got up.

Benny heard McWhirty's voice behind him in the aisle asking, 'Where's Doug?'

'Doug?' said another voice. 'Maybe he went to the lav.'

A couple of minutes later McWhirty bent over Benny with a pained expression on his face. 'Doug's not on the plane. It just occurs to me—'

'What?' asked Benny.

McWhirty sat down stiffly. 'I didn't see him since he went into that container room. Do you suppose he got locked in there?'

'Christ, no!' Benny said at once, and thought back. 'I didn't see Marlucci close that door.'

'Neither did I, but – I just checked with the fellows and nobody remembers seeing him at the airport just now. He's back there, Benny!' With difficulty Gerry kept his voice low.

'We'll phone Well-Bilt as soon as we land.'

'We could radio now. It's a couple of hours till we land.'

'No,' said Benny, meaning the idea of radioing from the plane and asking for a container room to be opened. 'No.'

They both ordered scotches.

'Doug'll probably phone tonight from some hotel in Indianapolis,' Benny said. 'Maybe he went to a toilet in that sub-basement and got lost from us.'

It was close to 10 p.m. before they got to a telephone at the West Virginia airport. Benny was told that Frank Marlucci had left at 5:30.

'I'd like to speak to someone in charge of the sub-basement. This is Benjamin Jackson of NCC. It's urgent.'

After some delay, and much offering of more coins by the NCC men who stood outside the booth, another male voice came on, and Benny again identified himself. 'I and some colleagues were visiting the sub-basement today. I have reason to think one of our party may be locked in one of the container rooms. I'd like someone to take a look *now*.'

A pause. 'We get a lot of joke calls from the students, sir. We'll need some more identification before we – We're very busy here, sir. Good night.' The man hung up.

One of the NCC men said that maybe Doug had got out, if he had ever been in, and would phone Gerry or Benny tonight, and come back on the morning plane tomorrow. Benny and Gerry agreed that they should go home, wait for a call, but also try the two Well-Bilt-Balsam numbers again tonight.

From his own house, McWhirty telephoned Evelyn Ferguson, Doug's wife, and told her that Doug had had to stay overnight in Indianapolis to talk some details over with construction people.

Benny and Gerry McWhirty were stonewalled by the male voices that answered the telephones in the small hours of the night at the stadium. They didn't know anything about a party of visitors having inspected the stadium and 'the basements' in the afternoon, and 'Operation Balsam' produced no glimmer of recognition. The NCC, if such they were, should get in touch with the Frank Marlucci they were asking about tomorrow, and he could verify matters and take care of their requests.

'What on earth is the matter?' asked Benny's wife Beatrice, coming into the living room at two in the morning.

'Doug Ferguson – as I said – he hasn't got all the info he needs for tomorrow and I can't find what hotel he's at.'

When Benny telephoned Well-Bilt at 9:30 the same morning, he learned that Mr Marlucci was not coming to work that day. 'Mr Siegman then, please.' Benny had a short list of names of the Well-Bilt people.

'Mr Siegman's in conference now, sir. Everyone's in conference, because the press is due this afternoon to look at the stadium.'

'Who's in charge of the container rooms – *now*?' Benny asked.

Silence. 'We've only got a skeleton staff here, sir. No one person's in charge.'

'Someone like Marlucci. Look, this is urgent. I have reason to think one of our party may be locked in one of the container rooms – since yesterday and he's got to be let out!'

'Wh-which room, sir?'

'Can't tell you exactly. On the other side from where the trucks roll down. On the left side as you go along what I think is the main corridor to the other side.' Benny had the plans before him, but the passages and rooms had no numbers or letters on them. The passages radiated from the center but were crossed by circles of passages that intersected them, making the plan look rather like a spider's web, but he thought the corridor they had been in was central, so he called it the main corridor.

'There's a delivery entrance for trucks both sides, sir.'

'It's not too much trouble for you to open those rooms and have a look, is it? It's one of the half-full rooms. Do that and call me back, would you?' Benny made sure the man had his number correct.

The man did not ring back.

Doug Ferguson did not arrive on the morning plane from Indianapolis. Benny had begun chewing his minty pills, the only pain-reliever he had until he renewed his prescriptions. Gerald McWhirty was at work with a team on the NCC's 'Preliminary Report on Operation Balsam.' This was for EWA and it had to be favorable and at least sixty pages long. Marlucci had given them a sheaf of papers, which could be organized and copied. Evelyn Ferguson rang the office twice to ask if Doug were back or had communicated.

'It's not like him not to phone,' Evelyn said. 'He can phone me at any hour day or night, and he always does.'

'I know it's a heavy assignment he's got out there,' Benny said. 'He probably hasn't a minute free.'

From 2 p.m. onward that afternoon, the two Well-Bilt numbers simply didn't answer. Benny imagined the sub-basement, where the phones perhaps were, sealed off from the journalists, with no trucks rolling today, not a soul down there except Doug maybe, shouting unheard in a container room. Had the last man he had spoken to believed him about a man maybe locked in a container room?

Benny Jackson and Gerry McWhirty lingered in the NCC building after everyone else had gone home. McWhirty looked haggard, and admitted that he hadn't slept the night before. They decided to try again to reach Marlucci. Benny got busy with information on one telephone and McWhirty on another, trying to get the home number of Marlucci, who must live in the area, though it was conceivable that he had rented an apartment for the duration of the Well-Bilt job, and wouldn't be listed yet. He'd still have a telephone, Benny reasoned. Neither Indianapolis nor any town in the area had a number for Frank Marlucci. Was that really his name, Benny wondered?

It was Benny's turn to have a sleepless night. Benny had said to

McWhirty that he would go to the stadium on the plane tomorrow Thursday, and McWhirty had said no, he would go, because he was less conspicuous than the head of NCC. Benny now saw Doug's incarceration as a stupid accident, indicating inefficiency. That was how Washington would see it. It reflected upon Benny and the Nuclear Control Commission.

Nevertheless, Benny picked up his telephone the first thing Thursday morning, and rang his Washington hotline, thinking himself rather noble for putting his job at risk by doing so.

'Jackson, NCC. Is Man there?' Matt Schwartz was a man Benny often talked to, a friendly and helpful fellow, though Benny had never met him face to face. Now he was told that Man was in conference in another building and could not be reached. 'This is about Operation Balsam . . . Yes . . . Specifically we have to find a certain Frank Marlucci, one of the superintendents for Well-Bilt. We have to speak with him on the phone and we can't locate him.' Benny's tone sounded firm, but he had faltered: he had not said straightaway that an NCC man appeared to have been locked up in a container room since Tuesday afternoon.

'What do you want him for?' asked Washington.

'I need to ask him something. He wasn't at work – yesterday.' Benny had not tried this morning, he realized.

'Call you back,' said Washington, and hung up.

Washington was back in record time, the same male voice. 'Marlucci is no longer employed by Well-Bilt, sir. No use trying to reach him.'

'They must have his home number. I need to ask him—'

'We know about that. The trouble.'

Benny was surprised. 'And something's been done about it?'

'Yes, sir,' said the voice crisply.

'This has to do with Douglas Ferguson of NCC. You mean he's all right?'

'All right? What's the matter with him?'

'Wh-what did you mean by "the trouble" out there?'

'Marlucci did something wrong and got fired. We don't advise any of our people to go out there for a while. Till further notice.'

Those were orders, Benny knew. He had just time to catch Gerry McWhirty at home and tell him not to take the morning plane. McWhirty came into the office at eleven. The Well-Bilt numbers were now answering, but Benny had not been able to speak with anyone who could tell him Marlucci's personal number, or who knew if any container rooms had been opened yesterday or today to look for a man who might have been locked in one. People simply didn't know anything.

'This is Jackson of NCC,' Benny repeated to one man.

'We *understand*, sir. We can't help you.'

Once more Benny and Gerry had a faint hope that Doug might come in on the plane that arrived at 11:30. If so, he didn't telephone, and they hadn't the courage to phone his wife and ask if Doug had got home. Evelyn had rung once that morning to ask if NCC had any news, and Benny told his secretary to tell Mrs Ferguson that they hadn't heard from Doug either, but were assuming he would be back Saturday latest. Benny knew this was not going down well with Evelyn Ferguson.

The afternoon brought a further torment. Inhabitants of the Love Canal area had organized a new campaign, and starting after lunch the NCC offices were bombarded with telephone calls and telegrams from homeowners and housewives angry at having been told they had to move out again, after having been told they could move back to their once abandoned homes and apartments. The Committee for Justice at Love Canal tied up the telephones with personal calls and telegrams being read by telegraph office operators – all the messages blaming the NCC for misinformation and lies – until Benny thought he was going mad. A bomb should hit the goddam Love Canal area and their whole effing committee too!

On Friday Benny was informed by a female voice on his hotline from Washington that Frank Marlucci had been killed in a car accident yesterday afternoon in southern Indiana. Benny knew what had most likely happened: someone had deliberately run Marlucci off the road. Benny felt sickish, then reminded himself that he had heard about such things before, two or three times before. He knew why he was feeling sickish: Marlucci's death confirmed Doug's death. Benny was sick at the thought of Doug in that room half-full of containers, Doug getting weaker from thirst and hunger, from lack of air, moaning unheard, dying. Benny called McWhirty in to tell him.

'Good Christ.' McWhirty sank into a leather chair in Benny's office as if all his strength had gone.

'You think maybe Marlucci tried to get him out?' Benny asked. 'Or did get him out — dead?'

'Or loaders found him and Marlucci got the blame.' McWhirty looked drugged, but was merely exhausted. 'I figure Doug would've been dead by yesterday morning from asphyxiation.'

There was no use in trying to figure out exactly what had happened, Benny supposed. 'You think they'll just hush it up — if they found him?'

'Yes,' Gerry said.

The Well-Bilt people with their machinery would know how to get rid of a body, Benny was sure. 'What'll we tell his wife?'

McWhirty looked miserable. 'We'll have to tell her he disappeared — that he's maybe dead. I'll tell her. You know — our job has its hazards.'

'We'll make sure she gets a generous pension,' said Benny.

McWhirty went into a daze or depression which he could not shake off, but he still came to the office. He would not take a week's leave, even though his doctor ordered it.

In the following week a torrent of letters and a two-day picketing of the NCC grounds — which did much damage to the pretty lawns, what with the police trying to wrestle the more unruly protesters off the premises — disturbed the whole staff of NCC, and caused them to come to work in armored cars which they crawled into at 8:30 in the morning at appointed places. The demonstrators called themselves the New CIO or Citizens in Outrage, and the nucleus of them seemed to have come from the Three Mile Island district, but they were aiming to make Outrage a nationwide movement by teaming up with militant environmentalists. The NCC came to work and departed in a shower of stones, eggs, epithets and threats.

One day in late September, Gerald McWhirty drove his car, the older of the two he and his wife owned, over the edge of a highway into a valley and killed himself. He left no note behind. It was called an accident.

Evelyn Ferguson, who had been drinking quite a bit since her husband's disappearance (as it was called), was admitted to a reha- bilitation center in Massachusetts at government expense. Benny wrote her cheerful postcards, when he remembered to do so.

The NCC came up with an affirmative report on Operation Balsam for Washington, when the site got its official inspection in October. Benny was there, and saw even worse cracks in the con- crete than McWhirty had, but Well-Bilt promised to repair them, so the cracks were not mentioned in the report. Still worse, a rem count taken by the NCC at various vents on the exterior of the sta- dium detected 210 per hour at one, 300-odd at another, and so on, with only one of the twelve vents clean. Where was the radioactive stuff coming from? Well-Bilt promised to look into it, but mean while said it believed that the rem discharge was not high enough to cause alarm or to do perceptible damage to human, animal or plant life in the vicinity.

Benny had other problems now. A plutonium shipment, code- named the Italian Shipment because it had nothing to do with Italy, out of Houston bound for South Carolina, had disappeared, and could the NCC look into this and see if a friendly country had stolen it, or what? This made at least four lost shipments on land and sea that Benny's office was supposed to find. Benny missed Gerry McWhirty in a strange way, as if Gerry had been the voice of his conscience, which was now silenced. He missed Doug Ferguson too, but in a different way. He remembered the interesting rust-red tweed jacket that Doug had worn that last day, remembered complimenting Doug on it. Now Doug was sealed up, probably, and if so, for ever. All the container rooms had been filled and the term used by Well-Bilt was 'permanently and hermetically sealed.' Benny's ulcer was no better, but no worse either, and he had managed the inspection day at Operation Balsam quite well: he had vowed to himself not to wince, not even to think about Doug Ferguson's corpse maybe lying behind one of those square steel doors that he walked past that day, and he had succeeded.

NO END IN SIGHT

S he lies now, certainly a hundred and ninety, some say two hundred and ten, and with no end in sight. She doesn't know Sunday from Wednesday, couldn't care less, has refused to wear her hearing aid for the past ninety or more years, flushed her false teeth down the toilet at least a century ago, causing the nursing home staff to have to grind her food for her ever since. Now she's spoon-fed three times a day, four if you count 'tea,' and pees in bed in a diaper. Naomi's diapers have to be changed ten or more times in twenty-four hours, round the clock. The Old Homestead Nursing and Rest Home charges extra for their diaper-using guests.

Naomi can't or won't bother pushing a handy red-glowing electric button that hangs over the edge of her night-table, she just lets go. When it comes time to change the bed linen, which is twice a week, two nurses lift her to a nearby chair which has a hole in its seat and is called a commode. The nurses spread Naomi's gown in back, in case she is in a mood to relieve herself while they are remaking the bed.

Two nurses lift Naomi with ease, because she doesn't weigh much, into a wheelchair twice a month, and she is rolled to the 'beauty parlor' down the corridor for a shampoo and set, manicure and pedicure. This costs seventy-four dollars. Her thin white hair looks like a puff of smoke, but still her scalp has to be washed, the hair fluffed to make it look more like hair, though Naomi hasn't asked for a mirror in decades, and couldn't see into it, if she did: Naomi deliberately broke her glasses many years ago in a fit of temper, and those being the fifth pair the nursing home had had made (at Naomi's account's expense, of course), the home did not have another pair made. Or maybe the optometrist demurred, remembering how disagreeable Naomi had been the last time he had tried to fit her with glasses.

But if a pair of specs had lain by Naomi's bedside lamp, would she have put them on? No. What was she 'seeing' with her eyes half shut, as they were most of the day and night? What was she seeing in the rare moments when they were more open? What was she remembering? Were childhood memories more vivid than the events of her mature years, as everyone said? Maybe. Naomi mumbled, talked to imaginary characters sometimes, but seldom could the nurses understand what she said, and who cared? Naomi didn't say anything funny about the people around her now, as she'd done a hundred years ago when she'd used to walk, assisted by a nurse usually, into the refectory for a meal. Generations of nurses had come and gone since then, and Naomi's bizarre and snide remarks, being airy things and unwritten, had not been handed down to the memory of the current nursing staff.

Naomi's only offspring, her son Stevey, had not been wealthy when he died, but he had left his all to his mother, some seventeen thousand dollars. Stevey had never married. Of course his small fortune, which he had invested as well as possible in Time Deposits and suchlike, had long ago run out. But such is the luck of people like Naomi, that she was bequeathed another small fortune from an uncle of Stevey on Stevey's father's side, and that had lasted incredibly long, though not as long as Naomi was lasting. But more later of the odd financial situation. Stevey has been dead for about a hundred and ten years. He had a normal span of life, and died before he was eighty.

There's a TV set in Naomi's room, and she used to stare at its blank, oyster-colored screen for a few moments now and then, as if she were seeing something, would talk back to imagined personages in sitcoms, but no more. Stevey had bought the set for her when she was eighty (Naomi had been seventy-eight when she entered the Old Homestead), but as she grew more batty, the nurses had slipped the set out to other patients' rooms (charging the inmates for its use, of course), and when the set went on the blink finally, nobody had bothered fixing it, and it had been put back, kaput, in Naomi's room. In case any of her relatives turned up and remembered talk of a TV set and asked where it was, there it was. But Naomi's relatives – living, walking, visiting ones – had always been conspicuous for their absence.

The Old Homestead's administrative staff and the nurses male and female sometimes chuckled over Naomi Barton Markham. Close to two hundred, they said, if she was a day! And still going! No *reason* for her to die!

Nobody of Naomi's family had visited in a century, the story went. The uncle of Stevey had died without issue and, remembering his brother Eugene with admiration, had left what he had to Eugene's widow Naomi, whom he'd never met. Very kind of that uncle, as Naomi had married a second time to one Doug Villars, who had not been a great earner. Amazingly, Naomi's legacy had held out for sixty years or so against the marauding of the Old Homestead administration, the adding of 'special care' hours, and prescriptions for unnecessary items, the most absurd being Tums for the tummy, which Naomi did not at all need, but which the pharmacy was delighted to add to the list of items that she did need. It was a hell of a racket.

Naomi Barton Markham's room on the ground floor of the Old Homestead Nursing and Rest Home in southern Oklahoma was a small room with one window and a private bath, which Naomi had not set foot in since she had been about a hundred and twenty. The room held, besides Naomi's bed, a chair for visitors, a night-table with little bottles and a drinking glass with water in it, and on the floor near the bed a bedpan that the nurses were seldom in time to push under her, if the bedpan was needed during the times of diaper-changing.

Someone of the staff had remarked, 'Babies are a bore with wet diapers and all, and it doesn't last long, maybe just two years. But Naomi – it's been fifty years or so now.' Then later, 'It's been eighty – a *hundred* years now, hasn't it?' And a circle of nurses and maybe even a staff doctor or two would join in the laughter in the Old Homestead's round-the-clock cafeteria in the basement.

Some stories got passed on like folklore.

'When Naomi was eighty or ninety and quite lively, she used to creep at night from one room to the other, switching glasses of people's false teeth – or she'd flush 'em down the toilet! That's what I was told when I came to work here.'

This story had inspired laughter and tears of mirth in dozens of young nurses and doctors. It was true! They felt it in their bones, it was true!

And there were stories of Naomi going into the kitchen during that short period around 3 a.m., when the cooks weren't busy with something, and Naomi would pour the salt into the sugar containers and vice versa, pull the plugs on the deep-freezers, anything to be mischievous. It was a fact that Naomi had had to be confined to a big armchair for a period of several weeks, given sedatives, shortly after she had entered the Old Homestead, and any nurse could verify this, as it was on record. Some nurses had looked it up, then asked for shorter hours or more pay for caring for Naomi, because the Old Homestead was not supposed to be a loony bin.

The truth was, Naomi Barton Markham was insane, besides being senile, but insane in a way that no one could label, or define. Multiple infarcts of the brain? Why not? Good as anything, and it implied an insufficient supply of blood to the brain, a condition a couple of doctors had told Stevey that his mother had, as if that summed up and dismissed the variety of oddnesses that Naomi had displayed over the years. Whatever she had, it wasn't Alzheimer's.

Further truth was, Naomi had cursed out, since the age of

seventeen or so, nearly everyone around her, abused them in one way or another. First her boyfriends, who of course hadn't been good enough for her; then her husband Eugene Markham, said to have had the patience of Job; then her second husband Doug Villars, who had had even more patience than Eugene (Naomi knew how to pick them), and finally Stevey, who had at first worshiped the ground his mother walked on, then turned against her in an emotional and Freudian sense (he hadn't been in love with her any longer, after the age of fourteen, say), but not in a filial or legal sense, for he had always written to her if they were apart, and had continued to pay her bills as long as his rather lonely life lasted.

And now – though the word now means nothing to Naomi – it's the year 2071. Naomi's TV set sits there, looking as antique as an Atwater Kent radio might have looked in 1980. The Old Homestead is still called that, though the building has been renovated a couple of times, and expanded too, because there are more and more old folks. Naomi is lucky in still another respect: she's not in pain, doesn't need morphine or even aspirin. Incredible. Doctors from far and wide have come to study her innards, thinking, wondering: 'Can this fabulous Naomi Barton Markham have the low metabolism of the reptile?'

No. Her metabolism is pretty low, to be sure, but she does not exactly hibernate. She just keeps cool, and needs thin blankets summer and winter. But there has been a slow change. Now she talks more, talks to non-existent figures in her room, as if she has visitors. She talks often in a baby voice, and with a somewhat south-ern accent. It has begun to disturb the staff.

'Where y'all *from*?' Naomi will ask. Then she may identify an old boyfriend called Ned, whom she teases.

Or she may address her own mother, whom she lies to, and with whom Naomi exhausts herself, or pretends to – gasping as if in exasperation at not making herself understood by her mother, whom she calls Mama.

Then there is husband Eugene, whom Naomi clearly wishes to

avoid, evade, banging her bony white fist down on the bedsheets, and yelling at him to get out of her room.

All this sounds very funny, Naomi speaking without teeth. Or rather, it sounds funny for the first several weeks to the nurses, male and female, who come and go, bearing trays, taking away soiled diapers. Finally, nurses start maneuvering to get out of service in Naomi's room.

'I really can't stand it, I just can't,' said a 24-year-old female nurse from Wisconsin, plump and hardy and engaged to be married within a few weeks. 'I don't believe any of what she's saying, but it gets under my skin.'

That was it, it got under people's skin. They couldn't believe Naomi Barton Markham, yet there she was before their eyes, mumbling now and then by day and by night, talking to people of the past with such eloquence, they seemed to be standing in the room!

'Ah didn't say that an' you *know* it,' Naomi would say softly and grimly between her toothless gums, and an incoming nurse might almost drop her tray.

Despite the repetition of this and similar phrases, the nurses and doctors would glance into corners of the room to see if anyone was there, which made them feel silly and consequently a bit annoyed.

So nurses pushed the room on to new staff coming in, or neglected Naomi slightly, the diaper situation became worse for the next nurse in charge, and inevitably there was a next nurse, because the Old Homestead wasn't a charity or state institution, and they did try to keep up standards.

Journalists from newspapers, accompanied by photographers, came sometimes to visit Naomi. The photographers could always get a ghostly shot of her pale, folded little face, propped up against white pillows. Most of the time, she refused even to mumble 'Hello,' as if she sensed that by disappointing the journalists she could hurt them, show her power. Naomi was a nasty customer at heart.

Naomi had no proper birth certificate. The story went that she'd had one when she entered the Old Homestead Nursing and Rest

Home, but had got hold of it somehow and destroyed it out of vanity. She had always claimed to be younger than she really was. So was she even older than two hundred and ten?

Oddly, the coming and going of journalists and photographers and curious doctors taking X-rays and metabolism tests made Naomi less rather than more real to the Old Homestead staff.

'She's sort of like a statue now. Do you know what I mean?' asked a nurse who was drinking coffee with a colleague. 'It's like taking pictures of a monument – somehow.'

'Washington Monument lying down!' said a male nurse, smiling. 'Very pale and glowing – ha-ha! But peeing and crapping all the same!'

'She does seem to glow sometimes, when you walk into her room and it's dark,' said a middle-aged nurse in a quiet voice.

'I've noticed that too!' a younger nurse piped up. 'Pale and sort of greenish, the glow – isn't it?'

Nobody liked Naomi. She didn't show much of herself now to be liked or not, but what little she did show wasn't liked. And so it had always been, for Naomi.

In the beginning, she had been a small-town girl of slightly more than usual prettiness, with some talent for dancing. She had not lacked for boyfriends, and married at twenty-two. By that time, she was dancing with a vaudeville group which played Chicago, St Louis, New Orleans and Philadelphia.

Naomi Barton was blonde, slender, pert, not much intellectually, because she hadn't gone to school after her mediocre high school in a Tennessee town. But the man Naomi married was an ambitious and promising engineer aged thirty, Eugene Markham, madly in love with her, indeed smitten. For a time, their careers merged nicely, he doing consultant jobs in towns where Naomi had an engagement for a week or so. Naomi's career prospered. Eugene suggested to Naomi that she might aim for ballet, something more prestigious than what she was doing, which was chorus line with a few comedy acts.

'I'll get stage-fright,' said Naomi, wanting reassurance.

'Course you won't! We can afford ballet lessons! When do you want to start?'

She started lessons in Philadelphia, but just at this time, Naomi discovered that she was pregnant, and she didn't like that. It upset her.

It upset Eugene slightly, too. 'If it's only one month, or six weeks as you said – maybe you can get rid of it? Hot bath or something? I dunno.' Eugene really didn't know. It was early in the twentieth century and abortion by suction-pipe was not so well known as now, though very likely primitive peoples on faraway shores had been sucking out little unwanted embryos for hundreds if not thousands of years before the time of Naomi and Eugene.

Naomi tried hot baths plus gin, resulting in a red face for herself, much sweating, but no ensuing period. She tried a long brisk walk in Philadelphia which got her into a wrong part of town, whence she actually had to run, but still she didn't abort. At this point, Naomi became confused: she couldn't sign a new contract with her manager for the following six months, because she'd be heavy with child by then. Oddly, neither she nor Eugene thought of looking for a doctor who would perform an abortion.

'Well, let's have the child,' said Eugene, smiling. 'It's not the end of the world, darling! It just means an interruption in your career. Not even a long one. Let's cheer up. I love you, darling.' Eugene tried to kiss her, but she twisted away.

'You don't! You wanted me to get rid of our baby!' Naomi didn't weep, she wasn't loud or hysterical, she was simply determined.

Eugene could not convince her that he was not only resigned to circumstances, but even happy with them.

Naomi wanted a divorce.

Eugene was thoroughly surprised. '*Why* on earth?'

'Because you don't *want* our child and you don't *love* me!'

Naomi packed, and took a train to Memphis, where her mother then lived.

Eugene Markham followed his wife to Memphis on another train, managed to see her at her parents' house, and tried to persuade her not to seek a divorce. He failed, and spoke with her parents on the matter. Eugene spoke well and eloquently, but Naomi's parents (Eugene had been able to see them alone) took the stance that they considered 'modern and correct:' parents should not interfere in the affairs of their offspring.

Naomi got the divorce on grounds of 'incompatibility,' since there was no adultery or absence without tidings. The child, a boy, was born in the home of Naomi's parents, and Eugene's offer to pay the doctor's fee and other expenses relating to the birth was rejected by Naomi. Two or three weeks after the birth, Naomi resumed her vaudeville career (in Chicago now), and left the baby Stevey in the charge of her mother, Mrs Sarah Barton.

When Stevey was nearly four, Naomi married a man called Doug Villars, a year or so younger than herself, a simple but decent fellow with an accountant's qualification that enabled him to get a job almost anywhere. Up to now, Naomi had been able to get a job almost anywhere too, whether she worked with a troupe or not, but the picture was changing. Vaudeville was dying out, Naomi was nearing thirty, and she did not adjust to the times. As she declined in ability and fame, and consequently got fewer engagements, she fancied her reputation growing.

'It's the ordinary public that doesn't appreciate me,' she said to Doug. 'I should've stuck with my ballet lessons – as Eugene used to tell me. Eugene had *ideas*! He wasn't a bore like *you*!'

Doug Viliars could be hurt to the quick by remarks like this. But Naomi made it up to him in bed. She knew on which side her bread was buttered, and where the butter came from, Doug's modest but dependable salary. Besides, she enjoyed bed. But most of all, she enjoyed her power in bed, that was to say, her ability to say yes or no as to sex.

The boy Stevey was emotionally close to his grandmother Sarah, since she had raised him from birth to the age of four, and Stevey and his grandmother corresponded faithfully after Naomi married Doug Villars and moved out of Sarah's house. At nine and ten, Stevey was in love with his mother, as many boys are at that age, but Stevey was more in love than most boys, for the reason that his mother was seldom home. She traveled on dancing tours sometimes, while he and his stepfather stayed home, cooking and doing for themselves, and dreaming of the pretty woman who wasn't there.

Inevitably, Stevey had a difficult time adjusting to girls of an appropriate age for him, when he was fourteen and fifteen. He was supposed to be 'interested' in girls of fourteen and then sixteen and so on, he realized, but they struck him as silly children. He liked 'older women' of twenty and twenty-two, a few of whom he was able to meet, but who wouldn't have given him the time of day, he knew, he being only sixteen or so. He had no strong desire to leap into bed with them, he simply adored them, worshiped them from afar, even women aged thirty. A great reader, he was acquainted with his own syndrome by the time he was fifteen: he liked older women, and needed a mother, or a motherly type, according to Freud.

Stevey became an electrician, and did not waste much time pondering his personal hangups. He realized with faint horror that his mother was losing her mind — that was to say that by the time Stevey was twenty or so, he realized it. Stevey had left home after finishing technical school, and had lived in California, Florida and Alabama, but he kept in touch with his mother and stepfather, and visited them sometimes at Christmas. Stevey was also on good terms with his father Eugene Markham, kept in touch by an occasional letter, but Eugene had maintained a polite distance after Naomi's second marriage, which Stevey thought only natural under the circumstances. Then Doug Villars developed leukemia. Doug had some insurance, but his lingering and fatal illness ate up a lot of the couple's savings. After Doug died, Naomi 'couldn't cope,' as the textbooks put it. She'd leave something burning on the stove. She neglected her dog and cat till they were ill-nourished and flea-ridden, and her house was a mess. The neighbors complained (Naomi lived in a small bungalow in northern Oklahoma at that time), and the authorities stepped in.

Stevey was informed of this, and at once went to Oklahoma, was appalled by the state of his mother's house, and by her mental deterioration too. She didn't want to go to 'a home,' she said, but Stevey knew that he couldn't take his mother in under his own roof. She was apparently staying up half the night, prowling the house like a demented wolf, poring over old and disorderly papers which she didn't want touched. A classic case. With some difficulty, Stevey got his mother into the Old Homestead Nursing and Rest Home (she had to be confined in a padded cell for a few days there, and no other nursing home in the region had been willing even to try to take her on), paid for her house to be cleaned up, then sold it at the best price he could get. The resulting money he put on deposit to earn interest, as he foresaw a long stretch in the Old Homestead for his mother, and how right he was.

Stevey Markham wrote to his mother a couple of times, but got only one letter from her in return. She had not liked him, she wrote, for putting her into a 'silly nursing home for old people.' Why couldn't he have let her stay at home, where she had been comfortable and independent? Stevey knew his mother well enough to realize that she wanted to start an epistolary argument, back and forth. So Stevey stopped writing to his mother, and within months, she stopped too. He visited her a few times, maybe five in all, starting with Christmases, of course. But Naomi usually chose to be huffy, to reproach him for not having visited her more often. And on the fourth or maybe fifth visit, she'd feigned indifference, looking at the ceiling, as if she couldn't bear the sight of him or the presents he had brought her. She refused to speak to him, and in this Stevey recognized her old joy in hurting him, or trying to. So he gave up these visits.

Naomi's upkeep cost Stevey more than his own in the last decade of his life, as her money (really that of Doug plus the money from the sale of her house) had run out. Then as if to 'save' Stevey, the remote uncle, his father's brother, had died and bequeathed several thousand to Naomi, simply because she had been the wife of his brother Eugene. It was, Stevey thought, a minor miracle: his mother could keep going for at least another twenty years (he knew how to calculate Time Deposits and interest by now, even without a pencil), whereas Stevey couldn't say the same about himself. Broke and seventy-four, Stevey was winding down like an old clock, and he died in his sleep of a heart attack, though he had not been over-weight and had been a non-smoker. Stevey Markham had never had a proper vacation in his life. Shortly before his death, an odd thought had come to Stevey: his mother Naomi had managed to be a torture to others, a pain in the neck, even before he, Stevey, was born, by insisting on a divorce that his father had not wanted, but had agreed to, so that Stevey had been born into a fatherless home; and during his childhood his mother had picked quarrels with his stepfather Doug Villars, making their home life worse than rocky; and after Stevey's death, Naomi would continue to be a pain and an expense – to *somebody*. The State, perhaps, Oklahoma? The state with a small s, meaning the government? The Old Homestead would shunt her into something cheaper, once his uncle's money ran out. There were a lot of state-run institutions that were cheaper.

Before, during, and after, thought Stevey, as he composed himself for sleep on the last night of his life, his mother had been a trial and tribulation to all around her, had made good men weep, had made her son weep. And she lived on.

But by the time the uncle's money had run out, Naomi had become a curiosity. And people pay for curiosities. Sometimes.

Oh, yes, Naomi lives on. And she glows in the night, people say.

She mumbles, 'I'll *kill* you!' And then laughs, feebly, toothlessly. As if to say, 'I don't mean it, really.' For Naomi still senses on which side her bread is buttered, knows that without those fuzzy forms which are nurse-forms, which Naomi can barely see, she'd croak, die of thirst and hunger. So Naomi remembers to butter them up a little. But no more than necessary. In fact, she's as nasty to them as she dares be, tipping her soup over deliberately sometimes. Vaguely, she realizes that the nurses are paid slaves, that they're obliged to hang around.

She gives the nurses the creeps.

The nurses, male and female, laugh, chuckle. But they chuckle defensively. They wonder, in the back of their minds, 'Is this crazy Naomi stronger than all of us, than any of us, after all? Is she really going to live forever? – Because she's sure as hell around two hundred right now!' But they don't dare utter these questions, these ideas, even when they're alone with only one other colleague. There's something about Naomi that gives them the creeps way down deep, inside all of them. It's as if Naomi, somehow, could show them what life and death is all about. And that picture is not pretty, so they, and everybody, are, is, afraid to look at it.

They all shiver, the staff, because they know that all over the United States, all over 'the civilized world' where they don't push the old folks over cliffs anymore, that the aged outnumber the young. In fact, it's the mark of a First World and first-rate country to have cut the birthrate to zero and to take care of its elderly.

So be it. And maybe it's the right thing to do. But people like Naomi are a horror. Their children will break themselves financially to keep such people out of their own homes and in some institution, where they don't have to look at them daily. The people footing the bills know they're being ripped off by the institutions, if they're private and not state institutions, because there's so much money in keeping these elderly alive with vitamins and antibiotics all the time and an oxygen machine when necessary. Not like in the state places, where a window slightly open on a cold winter's night can carry off half a roomful of non-paying guests with pneumonia – *poof*! So much the better, there're plenty more elderly waiting to take their places, and plenty of younger people heaving a sigh of relief at getting their parents out of the house and out of sight.

'She's a horror! I can't *face* it!' said one young nurse on Naomi-duty, shoulders collapsing from tears and emotional upset.

Well, the young nurse was given a day off. She recovered after some extra sleep and returned. And, like many others, tried to avoid Naomi, tried to attend the younger inmates, those around a hundred years old. Some of them were still willing to wear their hearing aids and dentures, a blessing to the staff.

It's 2090 now, and Naomi's certainly a little over two hundred years old. She glows pale yellowish-green in the dark, eats and drinks hardly anything worth mentioning, yet pees several times and defecates usually once a day. That's a sign that Naomi Barton Markham's alive, isn't it? Those wet and nasty, stinking diapers! Naomi started life in diapers, like all of us, and she is ending it in diapers, that is if there ever is an end, but there's no end in sight, really. Her 'condition' is unchanged in the last hundred and ten years. Her bill has gone up from about $2,100 a month at the end of the twentieth century to about $6,300 now, but the Old Homestead pays it, because Naomi is such a good advertisement for them.

The newspapers can ring up and make a date for fresh photos of the old ghost and 'an interview' any time they wish, but the articles are getting so old hat, Naomi's good for a story only once a lustrum now.

However, Naomi does serve as a symbol of the remodeled Old Homestead's and other private nursing homes' competence:

LOOK WHAT A FINE NURSING HOME CAN DO — KEEP YOUR LOVED ONE ALIVE FOR EVER!

Never mind that 'for ever' might be an exaggeration. Who's going to point that out? No one dies any more, one passes away. Sounds nicer. Death is a word to be avoided. The old casket spiel goes: buy not only a satin-lined steel casket but a *double*-steel casket. It'll keep your loved one longer in a presumably lovely state, with the undertaker's cosmetic rouge visible on dead cheeks and lips for maybe three, four, five hundred years (or so it is implied, and how long would you ask for right out?), and double-steel will presumably keep the worms out longer too, though of course one mustn't use the word worms, or even think of, much less mention, the fact that worms come from those old fly eggs already within us, not from outer atmosphere or outer space, so expensive steel isn't going to help one damn against the fate that's in store for all of us.

However, back to America's private rest homes' pitch: don't you want your loved one or ones to live as long as possible? And in the greatest comfort that you can afford? Or even can't quite afford?

If other people are looking and listening, you'd better answer, 'Yes, of course.'

But if people aren't looking and listening, would you really want this? Would you want your mother or father to live 'as long as possible?' Don't you know in your bones that there's a time for each and every one of us to die?

Would you want your mom to live on and on like Naomi, glowing green-yellow in the night, peeing in a diaper, defecating at least once in two days, dependent upon someone to poke food into her mouth, dependent upon someone to change the diaper? And with no end in sight? Would you like to live on like that, unable to watch TV, unable to hear, unable to walk even with a bit of assistance, unable to read a letter that an old friend might send, indeed too far gone in the head to take in anything that someone else might read to you?

Naomi Barton Markham glows in the night, and peoples her lonely cubicle with figures from the past, people long dead, more ghostly than herself – her own parents, her ill-treated boyfriends, her neglected but faithful-to-the-last son, her kicked around spouses (two). She curses them, mocks them and laughs at them, attempts with her minimal strength to sneer and turn her face away, as in the old days, as she once did to men who loved her, even to friends who tried to be friends.

You'll finish us all, Naomi. If not you personally, then your ilk. You're a triumph of modern medicine, vitamins, antibiotics and all that. Pity you can't pay for it yourself, but we know you don't give a moment's thought to that. You're light years away from thought, reasoning and economics.

Lucky you, Naomi! That is, if you're enjoying yourself. Are you? How does this incubus feel, lying on its back with a rubber ring under the rump to avoid bedsores? What does it think about? Does it go *gubbah-gubbah-gubbah* with toothless gums, as it did in babyhood, when it was also swathed at the loins in a diaper?

Naomi Barton Markham, you'll bury us all, as long as there's an Old Homestead to rake in the shekels, as long as there's a fool or two to pay them.

NOTES ON THE STORIES

The stories in this collection are ordered chronologically by the year Patricia Highsmith wrote, rather than published, them. Where the date isn't clear, we've relied upon her diaries and notebooks. When there is no other evidence, the story appears by the date of publication.

The following publication notes are by Anna von Planta, who was Patricia Highsmith's primary editor at Diogenes Verlag in Zurich from 1985 until her death in 1995. She continues to work with the literary estate.

'Primroses are Pink': Handwritten note by PH '1936, High School'; second version written 8 September, 1937. [Although PH's diary says that PH's teacher, Mrs Jones 'took' her story, presumably for publication in the High School magazine *Bluebird*, there was no such evidence to be found.] Worldwide first publication. Copyright © Diogenes Verlag AG Zurich 2021.

'A Mighty Nice Man': Written in ca. 1940. First published in *Barnard Quarterly*, vol. XV, no. 3, Spring 1940.

'The Heroine': Written in 1941–2. An edited version was

published in *Harper's Bazaar*, August 1945. Book publication in PH *Eleven*, 1970, based on undated Typescript (TS).

'The World's Champion Ball-Bouncer': Written in 1946. First published in *Woman's Home Companion*, April 1947. Copyright © 1947 Patricia Highsmith. Copyright © 1993 Diogenes Verlag AG.

'The Still Point of the Turning World': TS, undated; written between August and November 1947. First published as 'The Envious One' in *Today's Woman*, March 1949.

'When the Fleet was in at Mobile': TS, undated, but story outline November 1948. First published in *London Life*, ed. Francis Wyndham, 3 December 1965.

'The Snail-Watcher': TS, undated. Written (initially with the title 'A Peek at Nature') between February and July 1948, reworked in 1951. First published in *Gamma 3*, ed. Charles E. Fritch, vol. 2, no. 1, 1964.

'The Great Cardhouse': TS, written August/September 1949. First published in *Story*, vol. 36, issue 3, no. 140, May–June 1963.

'One for the Islands': 2 TS, both undated, the first presumably drafted in New York, the second in Santa Fe. The author remarked in her diary on 16 June 1949: 'Wrote 7-page story this evening: One for the Islands'. First published (following the text of the second version) in PH *Slowly, Slowly in the Wind*, 1979.

'Variations on a Game': TS, undated. First story outline February 1958. First published in *Alfred Hitchcock's Mystery Magazine*, vol. 18, February 1973.

'A Dangerous Hobby': First story outline in June 1959. First published as 'The Thrill Seeker' in *Ellery Queen's Mystery Magazine*, August 1960; handwritten note by PH on magazine copy, 'A Dangerous Hobby'.

'The Terrapin': Two almost identical TS. Written (originally with the title 'A Silent Cry') ca. 1961/62. First published in *Ellery Queen's Mystery Magazine*, October 1962, vol. 40, no.4.

'Another Bridge to Cross': TS, undated. First sketch of the story

drafted in autumn 1963 (originally with the title 'The Suicide
on the Bridge'); full manuscript on 18 October 1964 in Rome.
First publication in *Ellery Queen's Mystery Magazine*, December
1964, vol. 44, no. 6.

'The Trouble with Mrs Blynn, the Trouble with the World': TS,
undated. Probably written in Aldeburgh, Suffolk, in 1963/4.
First published in *The New Yorker*, 27 May 2002.

'The Cries of Love': The first version of this story, entitled 'Quiet
Night', presumably written in New York in 1938 or 1939, first
published in *Barnard Quarterly*, Autumn 1939; twenty-seven
years later, in February 1966, PH revised and lengthened
the story, published as 'The Cries of Love' in *Woman's Home
Journal*, January 1968.

'Not in This Life, Maybe the Next': Story sketches written
between 26 April and 16 May 1967. TS carbon copy, undated,
with handwritten comment by author, 'Published Ellery
Queen c.1968'. First published with the title 'The Nature of
the Thing' in *Ellery Queen's Mystery Magazine*, April 1970.

'Woodrow Wilson's Necktie': First draft with the title 'This
Guy isn't Kidding' on 27 January 1969, based on a notebook
sketch from 17 December 1968. TS, undated, with the title
'Woodrow Wilson's Necktie'. First published in *Ellery Queen's
Mystery Magazine*, March 1972, vol. 59, no. 3.

'A Curious Suicide': No recovered TS. First published as 'Who Dies,
Who Lives?' in *Ellery Queen's Mystery Magazine*, August 1973, vol.
62, no. 2. The copy in the Swiss Literary Archives features the
author's handwritten remark on the cover: 'A Curious Suicide'.

'The Man Who Wrote Books in His Head': Story outline in
January 1972. First published in *The New Review*, ed. Ian
Hamilton, May 1974, vol. 1, no. 2.

The following stories are from *Little Tales of Misogyny*, which has
an unusual publication history. The themed short-story cycle was
first published in German as *Kleine Geschichten für Weiberfeinde* (*Little*

Tales for Misogynists) in 1975. The first English-language edition was published two years later in London. It wasn't published in America until a quarter of a century later, in 2002. Highsmith considered these stories satire, rather than actual misogyny. The collection won the Grand Prix de l'Humour Noir in 1977, and she wrote of them, 'Frankly, I laugh myself – onto the floor, or such, the kind of laughter that makes tears at the same time.' (PH, Letter to Alex Szogyi, 10–11 March 1969, Swiss Literary Archives.)

'The Breeder': First sketch in notebook on 10 February 1968.
'Oona, the Jolly Cave Woman': First handwritten version on 28 January 1969 in her notebook.
'The Artist': First plot outline with the title 'School of Arts' on 18 February 1969.
'The Fully Licensed Whore, or, the Wife': One 'Original Manuscript', one 'earliest version' as well as a middle version, with partially the same characters and the same themes, but a different plot line.
'The Perfect Little Lady': TS carbon copy, undated.

The following stories are from a further themed collection, *The Animal-Lover's Book of Beastly Murder*, also published in 1975. The first plot outlines of most of the stories were written between 1970 and 1974, parallel to the stories written for *Slowly, Slowly in the Wind* (1979). None of the animal stories is mentioned in her diary, which she kept only sporadically during these years. From correspondence between the author and her friend Barbara Ker-Seymer, it is evident that Patricia Highsmith finished a rough draft of the story 'Ming's Biggest Prey' two days after starting the manuscript for her third Ripley Novel, *Ripley's Game*. This story was the starting point for the collection: 'Every Story would be dedicated to one animal or pet – horse, monkey, goat, dog, hamster – which takes revenge on humans [. . .] The victims are hateful, and the animals act out of an instinctive sense of justice'. (PH to BKS, 15–16 March 1972)

'The Day of Reckoning': First plot outline in notebook on 2
    December 1967; seven years later, on 16 July 1974, the story
    which was first completed in October 1968 was reworked
    into a story of murder for this collection. First published with
    the title 'Day of Reckoning' in *Ellery Queen's Mystery Magazine*,
    September 1974, vol. 64, no. 3.

'Notes From a Respectable Cockroach': Plot outline in notebook
    on 10 April 1970. TS, undated. The story appears to be
    directly inspired by the author's stay in a rundown hotel on
    Washington Square in New York, as can be gathered from a
    presumably unpublished essay that refers to it: 'In their own
    manner, the cockroaches were by far more respectable than
    the hotel guests.' ('Must We Always Write for Money', 1974,
    Swiss Literary Archives)

'Chorus Girl's Absolutely Final Performance': TS, undated. First
    plot outline at the beginning of November 1970 as a possible
    idea for a novel.

'Ming's Biggest Prey': TS, undated. Plot outline with the
    title 'The Siamese Cat Murder' in notebook on 29
    February 1972.

'In the Dead of Truffle Season': TS, undated.

'Slowly, Slowly in the Wind': TS, first outline with the title 'The
    Scarecrow' on 21 March 1975. First published in *Ellery Queen's
    Mystery Magazine*, November 1976, vol. 68, no. 4.

'Something You Have to Live With': First plot outline on 15 June
    1975. First published in *Ellery Queen's Mystery Magazine*, July
    1976, vol. 68, no. 1.

'A Girl Like Phyl': TS, undated. First published (in German
    translation) as '*Ein Mädchen wie Phyl*' in (German) *Playboy*,
    vol. 8, 1980; first published in English in PH *Nothing That
    Meets the Eye*, 2002.

'Not One of Us': TS carbon copy, undated. First published in PH
    The Black House, 1981.

'The Terrors of Basket-Weaving': TS, undated. First
    published ibid.
'Under a Dark Angel's Eye': TS carbon copy, undated. First
    published ibid.
'The Stuff of Madness': TS carbon copy, undated. First
    published (in French translation) as title story of the
    collection *Le jardin des disparus,* Paris: Calmann-Lévy 1982.
    First published in English in *Harper & Queen*, London,
    September 1985.
'The Button': Manuscript and 2 TS, all undated. Handwritten note
    by Diogenes Verlag rights department on cover page, 'Written
    in 1983'. Plot outline (without title) on 11 November 1982. First
    published (in French translation) as *'Le prix de l'idiot'* in PH *Les
    sirènes du golf*, Paris: Calmann-Lévy 1984. First published in
    English in PH *Mermaids on the Golf Course*, 1985.
'Where the Action is': First story outline with title 'The Asshole'
    on 29 September 1982. First published (in French translation)
    as *'Tout pour l'action'* in *L'Express*, Paris, 14–20 January 1983.
    First published in English ibid.
'The Romantic': TS, dated by Diogenes Verlag rights department
    as '1983'. First plot outline on 25 November 1982 with
    working title 'Stand-Up'. First published in *Cosmopolitan*,
    London, September 1983.
'Mermaids on the Golf Course': TS, dated 21 November 1983. First
    plot outline in notebook on 1 November 1983 explicitly refers
    to Ronald Reagan's Press Secretary James S. Brady, who was
    injured by a bullet meant for the President on 30 March 1981,
    and left with a brain injury similar to the one suffered by the
    story's protagonist. First published (in French translation) as *'Les
    sirènes du golf'* in the eponymous short-story collection. First
    published in English in PH *Mermaids on the Golf Course*, 1985.
'A Shot From Nowhere': TS, undated. First published (in French
    translation) as *'La mort venue de nulle part'*, ibid. First published
    in English ibid.

'Operation Balsam; or Touch-Me-Not': TS, with notes from Diogenes
   Verlag editorial department, and comments by PH in response, as
   well as her note 'Corrections made 27 May '87 by me'. First story
   outline in notebook on 13 September 1983, where PH combined
   two story ideas ('Hazardous Waste' and 'Disposal Depot under
   football field in Indiana'), which were based on newspaper
   clippings glued into the notebook beneath the entry. First
   published in PH *Tales of Natural and Unnatural Catastrophes*, 1987.
'No End in Sight': TS photocopy, dated 1987. There are two
   entries in PH's notebooks that refer to the story's theme.
   The first, written on 15 March 1986 (preceded by similar
   occasions in her diary, as well as in letters to friends, and
   succeeded by many more until PH's mother's death) combines
   a report concerning the precarious state of her mother's
   health, who resided in an expensive nursing home in Texas,
   with more general reflections on old age, which she says in
   many cases means an unforeseeably long vegetative state, with
   immeasurable expenses for care. The second note, written
   on 23 April 1987, is a story sketch with the working title
   'On the Morality of Artificial Life-Preserving'. In December
   1990 Patricia Highsmith considered a continuation of this
   story with the working title 'The Tube', in which the female
   protagonist, whom the author outlines in her notebook,
   is a brain-dead old woman, whose only bodily function is
   digestion. First published ibid.

With the exception of 'Primroses are Pink' and 'The World's
Champion Ball-Bouncer', these stories have previously been published in the following collections:

'The Heroine', 'When the Fleet was in at Mobile', 'The Snail-
   Watcher', 'The Terrapin', 'The Cries of Love', 'Another
   Bridge to Cross' and 'The Cries of Love' are from *Eleven*,
   first published by William Heinemann, London, in 1970.

The stories in this volume were selected by Donna Coonan and
Christie Hickman.

ABOUT THE AUTHOR

Patricia Highsmith (1921–1995) was born in Fort Worth, Texas, but spent most of her adult life in Europe, particularly in England, France and Switzerland. She was educated at Barnard College. In her senior year she edited the college magazine, having decided at the age of sixteen to become a writer. Her first novel, *Strangers on a Train*, published in 1950, proved to be a major commercial success and was made into a classic film by Alfred Hitchcock.

Writing under the pseudonym of Clare Morgan, she then published *The Price of Salt* (now published as *Carol*) in 1953, which had been turned down by her publisher because of its frank exploration of a lesbian relationship. Her most popular literary creation was Tom Ripley, the dapper sociopath who first appeared in her 1955 novel *The Talented Mr Ripley*, which she followed with four further Ripley novels.

Graham Greene called Patricia Highsmith 'the poet of apprehension', saying that she 'created a world of her own – a world claustrophobic and irrational which we enter each time with a sense of personal danger', and *The Times* named her no.1 in their list of the greatest ever crime writers.

The author of more than twenty books, Highsmith was awarded the O. Henry Memorial award, the Edgar Allan Poe Award, Le Grand Prix de Littérature Policière and the CWA Award.